Mistresses of the Dark

★

Mistresses of the Dark

★

25 MACABRE TALES BY MASTER STORYTELLERS

Selected by Stefan Dziemianowicz, Denise Little,
and Robert Weinberg

BARNES
&NOBLE
BOOKS
NEW YORK

1998 Barnes & Noble Books

Text design by Leah Lococo

ISBN 0-7607-1002-3

Printed and bound in the United States of America

98 99 00 01 02 03 M 9 8 7 6 5 4 3 2 1

BVG

Contents

---✦---

Introduction

————— ✦ —————

What fools we are to pursue in daylight what we should leave for nighttime.

—EDNA O'BRIEN

L OOK THROUGH THE FICTION of any writer and chances are you'll find at least one tale of the macabre. For some of our most respected men and women of letters, this type of tale constitutes a subspecialty: Charles Dickens, Edith Wharton, and Henry James are just a few of the literary heavyweights who produced entire volumes of ghost stories.

Why would writers capable of distinguished work on any theme choose to explore the dark side of experience? For some, the reason is that it offers artistic or economic expedience. James dismissed *The Turn of the Screw* as a "potboiler" churned out between more worthy efforts. Louisa May Alcott wrote scores of Gothic thrillers anonymously and pseudonymously to capitalize on her era's thirst for sensational fiction. But then again, why *wouldn't* a good writer attempt fiction whose purpose is to disturb, or even to horrify? "Horror," as critic Douglas E. Winter reminds us, "is not a genre. Horror is an emotion"—and thus a vital part of the psychological geography that defines our humanity. Literature is our road map to that geography. A writer skilled at evoking sympathy or laughter from a reader would surely be capable of—and perhaps attracted to—evoking dismay or terror. To put it another way, what would a literary landscape be like that admits love and the so-called nobler emotions but excludes fear? A nice place to visit, perhaps—but does anyone really live there?

In the early part of the twentieth century, the tale of the macabre was synonymous with the ghost story. Ghosts were perfectly suited to the standards of literary decorum of the day: too intangible to provide the crude shocks of physical horror, but malleable enough to take the imprint of a wide variety of fears and obsessions. Literary ghost stories proved a popular vehicle for exploring themes ranging from the haunting power of memory to concerns with the afterlife. Their specters gave discreet shape to apprehensions that had no distinct form.

Modern literature reveals ours to be a more skeptical but no less apprehensive age. Look behind the suburban neighborhoods, the commuter jobs, and the domestic dramas that dominate contemporary fiction and you will glimpse fears and anxieties no less formidable than those that once conjured ghosts. Certainly, ghosts can still be found in contemporary fiction, but many of our best writers have devised new and provocative approaches to the dark side of the ordinary and the everyday.

Mistresses of the Dark is an anthology of tales concerned with the dark side of contemporary experience. Its selections span the past half century and its contributors represent a variety of continents and cultures: Nadine Gordimer is a resident of South Africa. Jamaica Kincaid was born on the Caribbean island of Antigua. Louise Erdrich writes from her experience as a Native American. A number of the authors began their careers before the Second World War, but most have earned their critical and popular recognition only in the past few decades. All are women.

Their stories were chosen for literary excellence and cover a broad spectrum of fiction genres. Flannery O'Connor's "The River" and Eudora Welty's "Clytie" feature settings and situations redolent of the southern Gothic tradition. Kincaid's "Ovando" and Erdrich's "Fleur" would not be out of place in discussions of magic realist fiction. Angela Carter's "The Bloody Chamber" is a modern retelling of a classic folktale, and Joyce Carol Oates's "The Virgin in the Rose-Bower or The Tragedy of Glen Mawr Manor" a pastiche of the Victorian penny dreadful. Their different styles and subjects notwithstanding, all of the stories share one common element: intense emotions that find equally intense—and discomfiting—forms of expression. In "The Parallel World," Valerie Martin writes of her heroine's "hope of finding an image that articulated her own keen sense of longing," and in so doing she seems to describe the process by which each contributor to this book fits a mood or a state of mind to its corollary in extraordinary, occasionally violent, experience.

If read in the context of the writer's other fiction, each story would no doubt strike the reader as a distillation of the complex ideas for which her work is known. Is there much difference between the bold women of Jean Rhys's novels and the heroine of her tale "A Spiritualist," save that the latter attempts to assert her will from beyond the grave? Does the uncanny climax to the graveyard adventures in Ruth Rendell's "The Dreadful Day of Judgement" set the story apart from the diabolical mysteries investigated by her series detective Chief Inspector Wexford?

Considered as a unit, however, the stories in *Mistresses of the Dark* open a window on a seldom seen literary landscape—one where the sinister and the obsessive color the view and where life's certainties are regularly subverted. In "The Ones Who Walk Away from Omelas," Ursula K. Le Guin seems to speak for all the writers in this anthology when she confesses: "This is the treason of the artist: a refusal to admit the banality of evil and the terrible boredom of pain." In the world these stories depict, the unusual and the unpredictable are inextricably interwoven with the commonplace and the routine. There is no setting so secure that it cannot reveal dangerously unstable foundations—neither the suburban shopping mall in A. M. Homes's "The Bullet Catcher" nor the peaceful rural rental property in Shirley Jackson's "The Summer People." Simple affection transforms under the burden of psychological pressure into dangerous obsession in Doris Lessing's "Plants and Girls," and maternal concern into a denial of death in Mavis Gallant's "Up North." Seemingly solid adult lives still reverberate with the aftershock of childhood trauma in Margaret Atwood's "Death by Landscape," and the natural world is home to an apparently unnatural spirit of malevolence in Patricia Highsmith's "The Pond."

In the harsh light the authors shed on their characters' lives, the most fundamental relationships reveal misshapen shadows: husband and wife in Edna O'Brien's "Number 10," child and parent in A. S. Byatt's "The July Ghost," employer and employee in Muriel Spark's "The Girl I Left Behind Me," teacher and pupil in Madeleine L'Engle's "Poor Little Saturday." The avenues by which the characters might transcend their problems turn into pathways to damnation in O'Connor's "The River," where the quest for spiritual renewal becomes an inadvertent death wish, and in Oates's "The Virgin in the Rose-Bower," where wealth and culture simply provide bigger and better closets in which to hide the skeletons.

Do these stories reflect a specifically female perspective on their themes? To the extent that any story is inextricable from the personality of its creator, perhaps.

Certainly, Erdrich's "Fleur" can be read as a myth of female empowerment in a male-dominated society, and Fay Weldon's "Spirit of the House" as an account of the *femme fatale* from the viewpoint of the *femme* un-*fatale*. Yet many of the selections are written convincingly from a male perspective, most notably Gordimer's "Letter from His Father," an explosive tale of the Freudian battle between father and son. In their preoccupation with family and romantic relationships, the stories collected here suggest that these are the areas where men and women alike feel their greatest vulnerability. Can there be any guilt more universal than that of a parent who is persuaded she has failed her child, as in Alison Lurie's "Another Halloween"?

Within these pages, the neatly ordered world we take for granted becomes the proverbial black box, and the central enigma is the individuals who inhabit it. Like the detective hero of Joyce Carol Oates's tale, the characters in these stories seek to understand the disturbing violations of their world. And often, like the protagonist of Daphne du Maurier's "Don't Look Now," they are stunned to discover what their investigations reveal about who they are and what they are capable of. The reader also will make a discovery: twenty-five leading women writers, in touch with life's nightside and anointed in this anthology as mistresses of the dark.

—The Editors
New York, 1998

Death by Landscape

★

MARGARET ATWOOD

NOW THAT THE BOYS ARE GROWN UP and Rob is dead, Lois has moved to a condominium apartment in one of the newer waterfront developments. She is relieved not to have to worry about the lawn, or about the ivy pushing its muscular little suckers into the brickwork, or the squirrels gnawing their way into the attic and eating the insulation off the wiring, or about strange noises. This building has a security system, and the only plant life is in pots in the solarium.

Lois is glad she's been able to find an apartment big enough for her pictures. They are more crowded together than they were in the house, but this arrangement gives the walls a European look: blocks of pictures, above and beside one another, rather than one over the chesterfield, one over the fireplace, one in the front hall, in the old acceptable manner of sprinkling art around so it does not get too intrusive. This way has more of an impact. You know it's not supposed to be furniture.

None of the pictures is very large, which doesn't mean they aren't valuable. They are paintings, or sketches and drawings, by artists who were not nearly as well known when Lois began to buy them as they are now. Their work later turned up on stamps, or as silk-screen reproductions hung in the principals' offices of high schools, or as jigsaw puzzles, or on beautifully printed calendars sent out by corporations as Christmas gifts, to their less important clients.

These artists painted mostly in the twenties and thirties and forties; they painted landscapes. Lois has two Tom Thomsons, three A. Y. Jacksons, a Lawren Harris. She has an Arthur Lismer, she has a J. E. H. MacDonald. She has a David Milne. They are pictures of convoluted tree trunks on an island of pink wave-smoothed stone, with more islands behind; of a lake with rough, bright, sparsely wooded cliffs; of a vivid river shore with a tangle of bush and two beached canoes, one red, one gray; of a yellow autumn woods with the ice-blue gleam of a pond half-seen through the interlaced branches.

It was Lois who'd chosen them. Rob had no interest in art, although he could see the necessity of having something on the walls. He left all the decorating decisions to her, while providing the money, of course. Because of this collection of hers, Lois's friends—especially the men—have given her the reputation of having a good nose for art investments.

But this is not why she bought the pictures, way back then. She bought them because she wanted them. She wanted something that was in them, although she could not have said at the time what it was. It was not peace: she does not find them peaceful in the least. Looking at them fills her with a wordless unease. Despite the fact that there are no people in them or even animals, it's as if there is something, or someone, looking back out.

When she was thirteen, Lois went on a canoe trip. She'd only been on overnights before. This was to be a long one, into the trackless wilderness, as Cappie put it. It was Lois's first canoe trip, and her last.

Cappie was the head of the summer camp to which Lois had been sent ever since she was nine. Camp Manitou, it was called; it was one of the better ones, for girls, though not the best. Girls of her age whose parents could afford it were routinely packed off to such camps, which bore a generic resemblance to one another. They favored Indian names and had hearty, energetic leaders, who were called Cappie or Skip or Scottie. At these camps you learned to swim well and sail, and paddle a canoe, and perhaps ride a horse or play tennis. When you weren't doing these things you could do Arts and Crafts and turn out dingy, lumpish clay ashtrays for your mother—mothers smoked more, then—or bracelets made of colored braided string.

Cheerfulness was required at all times, even at breakfast. Loud shouting and the banging of spoons on the tables were allowed, and even encouraged, at ritual intervals. Chocolate bars were rationed, to control tooth decay and pimples. At night, after supper, in the dining hall or outside around a mosquito-infested campfire ring for special treats, there were singsongs. Lois can still remember all the words to "My Darling Clementine," and to "My Bonnie Lies over the Ocean," with acting-out gestures: a rippling of the hands for "the ocean," two hands together under the cheek for "lies." She will never be able to forget them, which is a sad thought.

Lois thinks she can recognize women who went to these camps, and were good at it. They have a hardness to their handshakes, even now; a way of standing, legs planted firmly and farther apart than usual; a way of sizing you up, to see if you'd be any good in a canoe—the front, not the back. They themselves would be in the back. They would call it the stern.

She knows that such camps still exist, although Camp Manitou does not. They are one of the few things that haven't changed much. They now offer copper enameling, and functionless pieces of stained glass baked in electric ovens, though judging from the productions of her friends' grandchildren the artistic standards have not improved.

To Lois, encountering it in the first year after the war, Camp Manitou seemed ancient. Its log-sided buildings with the white cement in between the half-logs, its flagpole ringed with whitewashed stones, its weathered gray dock jutting out into Lake Prospect, with its woven rope bumpers and its rusty rings for tying up, its prim round flowerbed of petunias near the office door, must surely have been there always. In truth it dated only from the first decade of the century; it had been founded by Cappie's parents, who'd thought of camping as bracing to the character, like cold showers, and had been passed along to her as an inheritance, and an obligation.

Lois realized, later, that it must have been a struggle for Cappie to keep Camp Manitou going, during the Depression and then the war, when money did not flow freely. If it had been a camp for the very rich, instead of the merely well off, there would have been fewer problems. But there must have been enough Old Girls, ones with daughters, to keep the thing in operation, though not entirely shipshape: furniture was battered, painted trim was peeling, roofs leaked. There were dim photographs of these Old Girls dotted around the dining hall, wearing ample woolen bathing suits and showing their fat, dimpled legs, or standing, arms twined, in odd tennis outfits with baggy skirts.

In the dining hall, over the stone fireplace that was never used, there was a huge molting stuffed moose head, which looked somehow carnivorous. It was a sort of mascot; its name was Monty Manitou. The older campers spread the story that it was haunted, and came to life in the dark, when the feeble and undependable lights had been turned off or, due to yet another generator failure, had gone out. Lois was afraid of it at first, but not after she got used to it.

Cappie was the same: you had to get used to her. Possibly she was forty, or thirty-five, or fifty. She had fawn-colored hair that looked as if it was cut with a bowl. Her head jutted forward, jigging like a chicken's as she strode around the camp, clutching notebooks and checking things off in them. She was like their minister in church: both of them smiled a lot and were anxious because they wanted things to go well; they both had the same overwashed skins and stringy necks. But all this disappeared when Cappie was leading a singsong, or otherwise leading. Then she was happy, sure of herself, her plain face almost luminous. She wanted to cause joy. At these times she was loved, at others merely trusted.

There were many things Lois didn't like about Camp Manitou, at first. She hated the noisy chaos and spoon-banging of the dining hall, the rowdy singsongs at which you were expected to yell in order to show that you were enjoying yourself. Hers was not a household that encouraged yelling. She hated the necessity of having to write dutiful letters to her parents claiming she was having fun. She could not complain, because camp cost so much money.

She didn't much like having to undress in a roomful of other girls, even in the dim light, although nobody paid any attention, or sleeping in a cabin with seven other girls, some of whom snored because they had adenoids or colds, some of whom had nightmares, or wet their beds and cried about it. Bottom bunks made her feel closed in, and she was afraid of falling out of top ones; she was afraid of heights. She got homesick, and suspected her parents of having a better time when she wasn't there than when she was, although her mother wrote to her every week saying how much they missed her. All this was when she was nine. By the time she was thirteen she liked it. She was an old hand by then.

Lucy was her best friend at camp. Lois had other friends in winter, when there was school and itchy woolen clothing and darkness in the afternoons, but Lucy was her summer friend.

She turned up the second year, when Lois was ten, and a Bluejay. (Chickadees, Bluejays, Ravens, and Kingfishers—these were the names Camp Manitou assigned to the different age groups, a sort of totemic clan system. In those days, thinks Lois, it was birds for girls, animals for boys: wolves, and so forth. Though some animals and birds were suitable and some were not. Never vultures, for instance; never skunks, or rats.)

Lois helped Lucy to unpack her tin trunk and place the folded clothes on the wooden shelves, and to make up her bed. She put her in the top bunk right above her, where she could keep an eye on her. Already she knew that Lucy was an exception, to a good many rules; already she felt proprietorial.

Lucy was from the United States, where the comic books came from, and the movies. She wasn't from New York or Hollywood or Buffalo, the only American cities Lois knew the names of, but from Chicago. Her house was on the lake shore and had gates to it, and grounds. They had a maid, all of the time. Lois's family only had a cleaning lady twice a week.

The only reason Lucy was being sent to *this* camp (she cast a look of minor scorn around the cabin, diminishing it and also offending Lois, while at the same time daunting her) was that her mother had been a camper here. Her mother had been a Canadian once, but had married her father, who had a patch over one eye, like a pirate. She showed Lois the picture of him in her wallet. He got the patch in the war. "Shrapnel," said Lucy. Lois, who was unsure about shrapnel, was so impressed she could only grunt. Her own two-eyed, un-wounded father was tame by comparison.

"My father plays golf," she ventured at last.

"*Everyone* plays golf," said Lucy. "My *mother* plays golf."

Lois's mother did not. Lois took Lucy to see the outhouses and the swim-ming dock and the dining hall with Monty Manitou's baleful head, knowing in advance they would not measure up.

This was a bad beginning; but Lucy was good-natured, and accepted Camp Manitou with the same casual shrug with which she seemed to accept every-thing. She would make the best of it, without letting Lois forget that this was what she was doing.

However, there were things Lois knew that Lucy did not. Lucy scratched the tops off all her mosquito bites and had to be taken to the infirmary to be daubed with Ozonol. She took her T-shirt off while sailing, and although the counselor spotted her after a while and made her put it back on, she burnt spec-tacularly, bright red, with the X of her bathing-suit straps standing out in alarming white; she let Lois peel the sheets of whispery-thin burned skin off her shoulders. When they sang "Alouette" around the campfire, she did not know any of the French words. The difference was that Lucy did not care about the things she didn't know, whereas Lois did.

During the next winter, and subsequent winters, Lucy and Lois wrote to each other. They were both only children, at a time when this was thought to be a disadvantage, so in their letters they pretended to be sisters, or even twins. Lois had to strain a little over this, because Lucy was so blond, with translucent skin and large blue eyes like a doll's, and Lois was nothing out of the ordinary— just a tallish, thinnish, brownish person with freckles. They signed their letters LL, with the L's entwined together like the monograms on a towel. (Lois and Lucy, thinks Lois. How our names date us. Lois Lane, Superman's girlfriend, enterprising female reporter; "I Love Lucy." Now we are obsolete, and it's little Jennifers, little Emilys, little Alexandras and Carolines and Tiffanys.)

They were more effusive in their letters than they ever were in person. They bordered their pages with X's and O's, but when they met again in the summers it was always a shock. They had changed so much, or Lucy had. It was like watching someone grow up in jolts. At first it would be hard to think up things to say.

But Lucy always had a surprise or two, something to show, some marvel to reveal. The first year she had a picture of herself in a tutu, her hair in a ballerina's knot on the top of her head; she pirouetted around the swimming dock, to show Lois how it was done, and almost fell off. The next year she had given that up and was taking horseback riding. (Camp Manitou did not have horses.) The next year her mother and father had been divorced, and she had a new step-father, one with both eyes, and a new house, although the maid was the same. The next year, when they had graduated from Bluejays and entered Ravens, she got her period, right in the first week of camp. The two of them snitched some matches from their counselor, who smoked illegally, and made a small fire out behind the farthest outhouse, at dusk, using their flashlights. They could set all kinds of fires by now; they had learned how in Campcraft. On this fire they burned one of Lucy's used sanitary napkins. Lois is not sure why they did this, or whose idea it was. But she can remember the feeling of deep satisfaction it gave her as the white fluff singed and the blood sizzled, as if some wordless ritual had been fulfilled.

They did not get caught, but then they rarely got caught at any of their camp transgressions. Lucy had such large eyes, and was such an accomplished liar.

This year Lucy is different again: slower, more languorous. She is no longer interested in sneaking around after dark, purloining cigarettes from the counselor, dealing in black-market candy bars. She is pensive, and hard to wake in the mornings. She doesn't like her stepfather, but she doesn't want to live with her real father either, who has a new wife. She thinks her mother may be having a love affair with a doctor; she doesn't know for sure, but she's seen them smooching in his car, out on the driveway, when her stepfather wasn't there. It serves him right. She hates her private school. She has a boyfriend, who is sixteen and works as a gardener's assistant. This is how she met him: in the garden. She describes to Lois what it is like when he kisses her—rubbery at first, but then your knees go limp. She has been forbidden to see him, and threatened with boarding school. She wants to run away from home.

Lois has little to offer in return. Her own life is placid and satisfactory, but there is nothing much that can be said about happiness. "You're so lucky," Lucy tells her, a little smugly. She might as well say *boring* because this is how it makes Lois feel.

Lucy is apathetic about the canoe trip, so Lois has to disguise her own excitement. The evening before they are to leave, she slouches into the campfire ring as if coerced, and sits down with a sigh of endurance, just as Lucy does.

Every canoe trip that went out of camp was given a special send-off by Cappie and the section leader and counselors, with the whole section in attendance. Cappie painted three streaks of red across each of her cheeks with a lipstick. They looked like three-fingered claw marks. She put a blue circle on her forehead with fountain-pen ink, and tied a twisted bandanna around her head and stuck a row of frazzle-ended feathers around it, and wrapped herself in a red-and-black Hudson's Bay blanket. The counselors, also in blankets but with only two streaks of red, beat on tom-toms made of round wooden cheese boxes with leather stretched over the top and nailed in place. Cappie was Chief Cappeosota. They all had to say "How!" when she walked into the circle and stood there with one hand raised.

Looking back on this, Lois finds it disquieting. She knows too much about Indians: this is why. She knows, for instance, that they should not even be called Indians, and that they have enough worries without other people taking their names and dressing up as them. It has all been a form of stealing.

But she remembers, too, that she was once ignorant of this. Once she loved the campfire, the flickering of light on the ring of faces, the sound of the fake tom-toms, heavy and fast like a scared heartbeat; she loved Cappie in a red blanket and feathers, solemn, as a chief should be, raising her hand and saying, "Greetings, my Ravens." It was not funny, it was not making fun. She wanted to be an Indian. She wanted to be adventurous and pure, and aboriginal.

"You go on big water," says Cappie. This is her idea—all their ideas—of how Indians talk. "You go where no man has ever trod. You go many moons." This is not true. They are only going for a week, not many moons. The canoe route is clearly marked, they have gone over it on a map, and there are prepared camp-sites with names which are used year after year. But when Cappie says this—and despite the way Lucy rolls up her eyes—Lois can feel the water stretching out, with the shores twisting away on either side, immense and a little frightening.

"You bring back much wampum," says Cappie. "Do good in war, my braves, and capture many scalps." This is another of her pretenses: that they are boys, and bloodthirsty. But such a game cannot be played by substituting the word "squaw." It would not work at all.

Each of them has to stand up and step forward and have a red line drawn across her cheeks by Cappie. She tells them they must follow on in the paths of their ancestors (who most certainly, thinks Lois, looking out the window of her apartment and remembering the family stash of daguerreotypes and sepia-colored portraits on her mother's dressing table, the stiff-shirted, black-coated, grim-faced men and the beflounced women with their severe hair and their corseted respectability, would never have considered heading off onto an open lake, in a canoe, just for fun).

At the end of the ceremony they all stood and held hands around the cir-cle, and sang taps. This did not sound very Indian, thinks Lois. It sounded like a bugle call at a military post, in a movie. But Cappie was never one to be much concerned with consistency, or with archeology.

After breakfast the next morning they set out from the main dock, in four ca-noes, three in each. The lipstick stripes have not come off completely, and still show faintly pink, like healing burns. They wear their white denim sailing hats, because of the sun, and thin-striped T-shirts, and pale baggy shorts with the cuffs rolled up. The middle one kneels, propping her rear end against the rolled sleeping bags. The counselors going with them are Pat and Kip. Kip is no-nonsense; Pat is easier to wheedle, or fool.

There are white puffy clouds and a small breeze. Glints come from the little waves. Lois is in the bow of Kip's canoe. She still can't do a J-stroke very well, and she will have to be in the bow or the middle for the whole trip. Lucy is behind her; her own J-stroke is even worse. She splashes Lois with her paddle, quite a big splash.

"I'll get you back," says Lois.

"There was a stable fly on your shoulder," Lucy says.

Lois turns to look at her, to see if she's grinning. They're in the habit of splashing each other. Back there, the camp has vanished behind the first long point of rock and rough trees. Lois feels as if an invisible rope has broken. They're floating free, on their own, cut loose. Beneath the canoe the lake goes down, deeper and colder than it was a minute before.

"No horsing around in the canoe," says Kip. She's rolled her T-shirt sleeves up to the shoulder; her arms are brown and sinewy, her jaw determined, her stroke perfect. She looks as if she knows exactly what she is doing.

The four canoes keep close together. They sing, raucously and with defiance; they sing "The Quartermaster's Store," and "Clementine," and "Alouette." It is more like bellowing than singing.

After that the wind grows stronger, blowing slantwise against the bows, and they have to put all their energy into shoving themselves through the water.

Was there anything important, anything that would provide some sort of reason or clue to what happened next? Lois can remember everything, every detail; but it does her no good.

They stopped at noon for a swim and lunch, and went on in the afternoon. At last they reached Little Birch, which was the first campsite for overnight. Lois and Lucy made the fire, while the others pitched the heavy canvas tents. The fireplace was already there, flat stones piled into a U. A burned tin can and a beer bottle had been left in it. Their fire went out, and they had to restart it. "Hustle your bustle," said Kip. "We're starving."

The sun went down, and in the pink sunset light they brushed their teeth and spat the toothpaste froth into the lake. Kip and Pat put all the food that wasn't in cans into a packsack and slung it into a tree, in case of bears.

Lois and Lucy weren't sleeping in a tent. They'd begged to be allowed to sleep out; that way they could talk without the others hearing. If it rained, they told Kip, they promised not to crawl dripping into the tent over everyone's legs: they would get under the canoes. So they were out on the point.

Lois tried to get comfortable inside her sleeping bag, which smelled of musty storage and of earlier campers, a stale salty sweetness. She curled herself up, with her sweater rolled up under her head for a pillow and her flashlight inside her sleeping bag so it wouldn't roll away. The muscles of her sore arms were making small pings, like rubber bands breaking.

Beside her Lucy was rustling around. Lois could see the glimmering oval of her white face.

"I've got a rock poking into my back," said Lucy.

"So do I," said Lois. "You want to go into the tent?" She herself didn't, but it was right to ask.

"No," said Lucy. She subsided into her sleeping bag. After a moment she said, "It would be nice not to go back."

"To camp?" said Lois.

"To Chicago," said Lucy. "I hate it there."

"What about your boyfriend?" said Lois. Lucy didn't answer. She was either asleep or pretending to be.

There was a moon, and a movement of the trees. In the sky there were stars, layers of stars that went down and down. Kip said that when the stars were bright like that instead of hazy it meant bad weather later on. Out on the lake there were two loons, calling to each other in their insane, mournful voices. At the time it did not sound like grief. It was just background.

*　　*　　*

The lake in the morning was flat calm. They skimmed along over the glassy surface, leaving V-shaped trails behind them; it felt like flying. As the sun rose
higher it got hot, almost too hot. There were stable flies in the canoes, landing
on a bare arm or leg for a quick sting. Lois hoped for wind.

They stopped for lunch at the next of the named campsites, Lookout Point.
It was called this because, although the site itself was down near the water on a
flat shelf of rock, there was a sheer cliff nearby and a trail that led up to the top.
The top was the lookout, although what you were supposed to see from there
was not clear. Kip said it was just a view.

Lois and Lucy decided to make the climb anyway. They didn't want to
hang around waiting for lunch. It wasn't their turn to cook, though they hadn't
avoided much by not doing it, because cooking lunch was no big deal, it was just
unwrapping the cheese and getting out the bread and peanut butter, but Pat and
Kip always had to do their woodsy act and boil up a billy tin for their own tea.

They told Kip where they were going. You had to tell Kip where you were
going, even if it was only a little way into the woods to get dry twigs for kindling. You could never go anywhere without a buddy.

"Sure," said Kip, who was crouching over the fire, feeding driftwood into it.
"Fifteen minutes to lunch."

"Where are they off to?" said Pat. She was bringing their billy tin of water
from the lake.

"Lookout," said Kip.

"Be careful," said Pat. She said it as an afterthought, because it was what
she always said.

"They're old hands," Kip said.

Lois looks at her watch: it's ten to twelve. She is the watchminder; Lucy is careless of time. They walk up the path, which is dry earth and rocks, big rounded
pinky-gray boulders or split-open ones with jagged edges. Spindly balsam and
spruce trees grow to either side, the lake is blue fragments to the left. The sun is
right overhead; there are no shadows anywhere. The heat comes up at them as
well as down. The forest is dry and crackly.

It isn't far, but it's a steep climb and they're sweating when they reach the top. They wipe their faces with their bare arms, sit gingerly down on a scorching-hot rock, five feet from the edge but too close for Lois. It's a lookout all right, a sheer drop to the lake and a long view over the water, back the way they've come. It's amazing to Lois that they've traveled so far, over all that water, with nothing to propel them but their own arms. It makes her feel strong. There are all kinds of things she is capable of doing.

"It would be quite a dive off here," says Lucy.

"You'd have to be nuts," says Lois.

"Why?" says Lucy. "It's really deep. It goes straight down." She stands up and takes a step nearer the edge. Lois gets a stab in her midriff, the kind she gets when a car goes too fast over a bump. "Don't," she says.

"Don't what?" says Lucy, glancing around at her mischievously. She knows how Lois feels about heights. But she turns back. "I really have to pee," she says.

"You have toilet paper?" says Lois, who is never without it. She digs in her shorts pocket.

"Thanks," says Lucy.

They are both adept at peeing in the woods: doing it fast so the mosquitoes don't get you, the underwear pulled up between the knees, the squat with the feet apart so you don't wet your legs, facing downhill. The exposed feeling of your bum, as if someone is looking at you from behind. The etiquette when you're with someone else is not to look. Lois stands up and starts to walk back down the path, to be out of sight.

"Wait for me?" says Lucy.

Lois climbed down, over and around the boulders, until she could not see Lucy; she waited. She could hear the voices of the others, talking and laughing, down near the shore. One voice was yelling, "Ants! Ants!" Someone must have sat on an ant hill. Off to the side, in the woods, a raven was croaking, a hoarse single note.

She looked at her watch: it was noon. This is when she heard the shout. She has gone over and over it in her mind since, so many times that the first, real shout has been obliterated, like a footprint trampled by other footprints. But she is sure (she is almost positive, she is nearly certain) that it was not a shout of fear. Not a scream. More like a cry of surprise, cut off too soon. Short, like a dog's bark.

"Lucy?" Lois said. Then she called "Lucy!" By now she was clambering back up, over the stones of the path. Lucy was not up there. Or she was not in sight.

"Stop fooling around," Lois said. "It's lunchtime." But Lucy did not rise from behind a rock or step out, smiling, from behind a tree. The sunlight was all around; the rocks looked white. "This isn't funny!" Lois said, and it wasn't, panic was rising in her, the panic of a small child who does not know where the bigger ones are hidden. She could hear her own heart. She looked quickly around; she lay down on the ground and looked over the edge of the cliff. It made her feel cold. There was nothing.

She went back down the path, stumbling; she was breathing too quickly; she was too frightened to cry. She felt terrible—guilty and dismayed, as if she had done something very bad, by mistake. Something that could never be repaired. "Lucy's gone," she told Kip.

Kip looked up from her fire, annoyed. The water in the billy can was boiling. "What do you mean, gone?" she said. "Where did she go?"

"I don't know," said Lois. "She's just gone."

No one had heard the shout, but then no one had heard Lois calling, either. They had been talking among themselves, by the water.

Kip and Pat went up to the lookout and searched and called, and blew their whistles. Nothing answered.

Then they came back down, and Lois had to tell exactly what had happened. The other girls all sat in a circle and listened to her. Nobody said anything. They all looked frightened, especially Pat and Kip. They were the leaders. You did not just lose a camper like this, for no reason at all.

"Why did you leave her alone?" said Kip.

"I was just down the path," said Lois. "I told you. She had to go to the bathroom." She did not say *pee* in front of people older than herself.

Kip looked disgusted.

"Maybe she just walked off into the woods and got turned around," said one of the girls.

"Maybe she's doing it on purpose," said another.

Nobody believed either of these theories.

They took the canoes and searched around the base of the cliff, and peered down into the water. But there had been no sound of falling rock; there had been no splash. There was no clue, nothing at all. Lucy had simply vanished.

That was the end of the canoe trip. It took them the same two days to go back that it had taken coming in, even though they were short a paddler. They did not sing.

After that, the police went in a motorboat, with dogs; they were the Mounties and the dogs were German shepherds, trained to follow trails in the woods. But it had rained since, and they could find nothing.

Lois is sitting in Cappie's office. Her face is bloated with crying, she's seen that in the mirror. By now she feels numbed; she feels as if she has drowned. She can't stay here. It has been too much of a shock. Tomorrow her parents are coming to take her away. Several of the other girls who were on the canoe trip are also being collected. The others will have to stay, because their parents are in Europe, or cannot be reached.

Cappie is grim. They've tried to hush it up, but of course everyone in camp knows. Soon the papers will know too. You can't keep it quiet, but what can be said? What can be said that makes any sense? "Girl vanishes in broad daylight, without a trace." It can't be believed. Other things, worse things, will be suspected. Negligence, at the very least. But they have always taken such care. Bad luck will gather around Camp Manitou like a fog; parents will avoid it, in favor of other, luckier places. Lois can see Cappie thinking all this, even through her numbness. It's what anyone would think.

Lois sits on the hard wooden chair in Cappie's office, beside the old wooden desk, over which hangs the thumbtacked bulletin board of normal camp routine, and gazes at Cappie through her puffy eyelids. Cappie is now smiling what is supposed to be a reassuring smile. Her manner is too casual: she's after something. Lois has seen this look on Cappie's face when she's been sniffing out contraband chocolate bars, hunting down those rumored to have snuck out of their cabins at night.

"Tell me again," says Cappie, "from the beginning."

Lois has told her story so many times by now, to Pat and Kip, to Cappie, to the police, that she knows it word for word. She knows it, but she no longer believes it. It has become a story. "I told you," she said. "She wanted to go to the bathroom. I gave her my toilet paper. I went down the path, I waited for her. I heard this kind of shout . . ."

"Yes," says Cappie, smiling confidingly, "but before that. What did you say to one another?"

Lois thinks. Nobody has asked her this before. "She said you could dive off there. She said it went straight down."

"And what did you say?"

"I said you'd have to be nuts."

"Were you mad at Lucy?" says Cappie, in an encouraging voice.

"No," says Lois. "Why would I be mad at Lucy? I wasn't ever mad at Lucy." She feels like crying again. The times when she has in fact been mad at Lucy have been erased already. Lucy was always perfect.

"Sometimes we're angry when we don't know we're angry," says Cappie, as if to herself. "Sometimes we get really mad and we don't even know it. Sometimes we might do a thing without meaning to, or without knowing what will happen. We lose our tempers."

Lois is only thirteen, but it doesn't take her long to figure out that Cappie is not including herself in any of this. By we she means Lois. She is accusing Lois of pushing Lucy off the cliff. The unfairness of this hits her like a slap. "I didn't!" she says.

"Didn't what?" says Cappie softly. "Didn't what, Lois?"

Lois does the worst thing, she begins to cry. Cappie gives her a look like a pounce. She's got what she wanted.

*   *   *

Later, when she was grown up, Lois was able to understand what this interview had been about. She could see Cappie's desperation, her need for a story, a real story with a reason in it; anything but the senseless vacancy Lucy had left for her to deal with. Cappie wanted Lois to supply the reason, to be the reason. It wasn't even for the newspapers or the parents, because she could never make such an accusation without proof. It was for herself: something to explain the loss of Camp Manitou and of all she had worked for, the years of entertaining spoiled children and buttering up parents and making a fool of herself with feathers stuck in her hair. Camp Manitou was in fact lost. It did not survive.

Lois worked all this out, twenty years later. But it was far too late. It was too late even ten minutes afterwards, when she'd left Cappie's office and was walking slowly back to her cabin to pack. Lucy's clothes were still there, folded on the shelves, as if waiting. She felt the other girls in the cabin watching her with speculation in their eyes. *Could she have done it? She must have done it.* For the rest of her life, she has caught people watching her in this way.

Maybe they weren't thinking this. Maybe they were merely sorry for her. But she felt she had been tried and sentenced, and this is what has stayed with her: the knowledge that she had been singled out, condemned for something that was not her fault.

Lois sits in the living room of her apartment, drinking a cup of tea. Through the knee-to-ceiling window she has a wide view of Lake Ontario, with its skin of wrinkled blue-gray light, and of the willows of Centre Island shaken by a wind, which is silent at this distance, and on this side of the glass. When there isn't too much pollution she can see the far shore, the foreign shore; though today it is obscured.

Possibly she could go out, go downstairs, do some shopping; there isn't much in the refrigerator. The boys say she doesn't get out enough. But she isn't hungry, and moving, stirring from this space, is increasingly an effort.

She can hardly remember, now, having her two boys in the hospital, nursing them as babies; she can hardly remember getting married, or what Rob looked like. Even at the time she never felt she was paying full attention. She was tired a lot, as if she was living not one life but two: her own, and another, shadowy life that hovered around her and would not let itself be realized—the life of what would have happened if Lucy had not stepped sideways, and disappeared from time.

She would never go up north, to Rob's family cottage or to any place with wild lakes and wild trees and the calls of loons. She would never go anywhere near. Still, it was as if she was always listening for another voice, the voice of a person who should have been there but was not. An echo.

While Rob was alive, while the boys were growing up, she could pretend she didn't hear it, this empty space in sound. But now there is nothing much left to distract her.

She turns away from the window and looks at her pictures. There is the pinkish island, in the lake, with the intertwisted trees. It's the same landscape they paddled through, that distant summer. She's seen travelogues of this country, aerial photographs; it looks different from above, bigger, more hopeless: lake after lake, random blue puddles in dark green bush, the trees like bristles.

How could you ever find anything there, once it was lost? Maybe if they cut it all down, drained it all away, they might find Lucy's bones, some time, wherever they are hidden. A few bones, some buttons, the buckle from her shorts.

But a dead person is a body; a body occupies space, it exists somewhere. You can see it; you put it in a box and bury it in the ground, and then it's in a box in the ground. But Lucy is not in a box, or in the ground. Because she is nowhere definite, she could be anywhere.

And these paintings are not landscape paintings. Because there aren't any landscapes up there, not in the old, tidy European sense, with a gentle hill, a curving river, a cottage, a mountain in the background, a golden evening sky. Instead there's a tangle, a receding maze, in which you can become lost almost as soon as you step off the path. There are no backgrounds in any of these paintings, no vistas; only a great deal of foreground that goes back and back, endlessly, involving you in its twists and turns of tree and branch and rock. No matter how far back in you go, there will be more. And the trees themselves are hardly trees; they are currents of energy, charged with violent color.

Who knows how many trees there were on the cliff just before Lucy disappeared? Who counted? Maybe there was one more, afterwards.

Lois sits in her chair and does not move. Her hand with the cup is raised halfway to her mouth. She hears something, almost hears it: a shout of recognition, or of joy.

She looks at the paintings, she looks into them. Every one of them is a picture of Lucy. You can't see her exactly, but she's there, in behind the pink stone island or the one behind that. In the picture of the cliff she is hidden by the clutch of fallen rocks towards the bottom, in the one of the river shore she is crouching beneath the overturned canoe. In the yellow autumn woods she's behind the tree that cannot be seen because of the other trees, over beside the blue sliver of pond; but if you walked into the picture and found the tree, it would be the wrong one, because the right one would be further on.

Everyone has to be somewhere, and this is where Lucy is. She is in Lois's apartment, in the holes that open inwards on the wall, not like windows but like doors. She is here. She is entirely alive.

The July Ghost

★

A. S. BYATT

I THINK I MUST MOVE OUT OF WHERE I'M LIVING," he said. "I have this problem with my landlady."

He picked a long, bright hair off the back of her dress, so deftly that the act seemed simply considerate. He had been skilful at balancing glass, plate and cutlery, too. He had a look of dignified misery, like a dejected hawk. She was interested.

"What sort of problem? Amatory, financial, or domestic?"

"None of those, really. Well, not financial."

He turned the hair on his finger, examining it intently, not meeting her eye.

"Not financial. Can you tell me? I might know somewhere you could stay. I know a lot of people."

"You would." He smiled shyly. "It's not an easy problem to describe. There's just the two of us. I occupy the attics. Mostly."

He came to a stop. He was obviously reserved and secretive. But he was telling her something. This is usually attractive.

"Mostly?" Encouraging him.

"Oh, it's not like *that*. Well, not . . . Shall we sit down?"

They moved across the party, which was a big party, on a hot day. He stopped and found a bottle and filled her glass. He had not needed to ask what she was drinking. They sat side by side on a sofa: he admired the brilliant poppies bold on her emerald dress, and her pretty sandals. She had come to London for the summer to work in the British Museum. She could really have managed with microfilm in Tucson for what little manuscript research was needed, but there was a dragging love affair to end. There is an age at which, however desperately happy one is in stolen moments, days, or weekends with one's married professor, one either prises him loose or cuts and runs. She had had a stab at both, and now considered she had successfully cut and run. So it was nice to be immediately appreciated. Problems are capable of solution. She said as much to him, turning her soft face to his ravaged one, swinging the long bright hair. It had begun a year ago, he told her in a rush, at another party actually; he had met this woman, the landlady in question, and had made, not immediately, a kind of *faux pas*, he now saw, and she had been very decent, all things considered, and so . . .

He had said, "I think I must move out of where I'm living." He had been quite wild, had nearly not come to the party, but could not go on drinking alone. The woman had considered him coolly and asked, "Why?" One could not, he said, go on in a place where one had once been blissfully happy, and was now miserable, however convenient the place. Convenient, that was, for work, and friends, and things that seemed, as he mentioned them, ashy and insubstantial compared to the memory and the hope of opening the door and finding Anne outside it, laughing and breathless, waiting to be told what he had read, or thought, or eaten, or felt that day. Someone I loved left, he told the woman. Reticent on that occasion too, he bit back the flurry of sentences about the total unexpectedness of it, the arriving back and finding only an envelope on a clean table, and spaces in the bookshelves, the record stack, the kitchen cupboard. It must have been planned for weeks, she must have been thinking it out while he rolled on her, while she poured wine for him, while . . . No, no. Vituperation is undignified and in this case what he felt was lower and worse than rage: just pure, child-like loss. "One ought not to mind places," he said to the woman. "But one does," she had said. "I know."

She had suggested to him that he could come and be her lodger, then; she had, she said, a lot of spare space going to waste, and her husband wasn't there much. "We've not had a lot to say to each other, lately." He could be quite self-contained, there was a kitchen and a bathroom in the attics; she wouldn't bother him. There was a large garden. It was possibly this that decided him: it was very hot, central London, the time of year when a man feels he would give anything to live in a room opening on to grass and trees, not a high flat in a dusty street. And if Anne came back, the door would be locked and mortice-locked. He could stop thinking about Anne coming back. That was a decisive move: Anne thought he wasn't decisive. He would live without Anne.

For some weeks after he moved in he had seen very little of the woman. They met on the stairs, and once she came up, on a hot Sunday, to tell him he must feel free to use the garden. He had offered to do some weeding and mowing and she had accepted. That was the weekend her husband came back, driving furiously up to the front door, running in, and calling in the empty hall, "Imogen, Imogen!" To which she had replied, uncharacteristically, by screaming hysterically. There was nothing in her husband, Noel's, appearance to warrant this reaction; their lodger, peering over the banister at the sound, had seen their upturned faces in the stairwell and watched hers settle into its usual prim and placid expression as he did so. Seeing Noel, a balding, fluffy-templed, stooping thirty-five or so, shabby corduroy suit, cotton polo neck, he realized he was now able to guess her age, as he had not been. She was a very neat woman, faded blonde, her hair in a knot on the back of her head, her legs long and slender, her eyes downcast. Mild was not quite the right word for her, though. She explained then that she had screamed because Noel had come home unexpectedly and startled her: she was sorry. It seemed a reasonable explanation. The extraordinary vehemence of the screaming was probably an echo in the stairwell. Noel seemed wholly downcast by it, all the same.

He had kept out of the way, that weekend, taking the stairs two at a time and lightly, feeling a little aggrieved, looking out of his kitchen window into the lovely, overgrown garden, that they were lurking indoors, wasting all the summer sun. At Sunday lunch-time he had heard the husband, Noel, shouting on the stairs.

"I can't go on, if you go on like that. I've done my best, I've tried to get through. Nothing will shift you, will it, you won't *try*, will you, you just go on and on. Well, I have my life to live, you can't throw a life away . . . can you?"

He had crept out again on to the dark upper landing and seen her standing, half-way down the stairs, quite still, watching Noel wave his arms and roar, or almost roar, with a look of impassive patience, as though this nuisance must pass off. Noel swallowed and gasped; he turned his face up to her and said plaintively,

"You do see I can't stand it? I'll be in touch, shall I? You must want . . . you must need . . . you must . . ."

She didn't speak.

"If you need anything, you know where to get me."

"Yes."

"Oh, well . . ." said Noel, and went to the door. She watched him, from the stairs, until it was shut, and then came up again, step by step, as though it was an effort, a little, and went on coming, past her bedroom, to his landing, to come in and ask him, entirely naturally, please to use the garden if he wanted to, and please not to mind marital rows. She was sure he understood . . . things were difficult . . . Noel wouldn't be back for some time. He was a journalist: his work took him away a lot. Just as well. She committed herself to that "just as well." She was a very economical speaker.

So he took to sitting in the garden. It was a lovely place: a huge, hidden, walled south London garden, with old fruit trees at the end, a wildly waving disorderly buddleia, curving beds full of old roses, and a lawn of overgrown, dense rye-grass. Over the wall at the foot was the Common, with a footpath running behind all the gardens. She came out to the shed and helped him to assemble and oil the lawnmower, standing on the little path under the apple branches while he cut an experimental serpentine across her hay. Over the wall came the high sound of children's voices, and the thunk and thud of a football. He asked her how to raise the blades: he was not mechanically minded.

"The children get quite noisy," she said. "And dogs. I hope they don't bother you. There aren't many safe places for children, round here."

He replied truthfully that he never heard sounds that didn't concern him, when he was concentrating. When he'd got the lawn into shape, he was going to sit on it and do a lot of reading, try to get his mind in trim again, to write a paper on Hardy's poems, on their curiously archaic vocabulary.

"It isn't very far to the road on the other side, really," she said. "It just seems to be. The Common is an illusion of space, really. Just a spur of brambles and gorse-bushes and bits of football pitch between two fast four-laned main roads. I hate London commons."

"There's a lovely smell, though, from the gorse and the wet grass. It's a pleasant illusion."

"No illusions are pleasant," she said, decisively, and went in. He wondered what she did with her time: apart from little shopping expeditions she seemed to be always in the house. He was sure that when he'd met her she'd been introduced as having some profession: vaguely literary, vaguely academic, like everyone he knew. Perhaps she wrote poetry in her north-facing living-room. He had no idea what it would be like. Women generally wrote emotional poetry, much nicer than men, as Kingsley Amis has stated, but she seemed, despite her placid stillness, too spare and too fierce—grim?—for that. He remembered the screaming. Perhaps she wrote Plath-like chants of violence. He didn't think that quite fitted the bill, either. Perhaps she was a freelance radio journalist. He didn't bother to ask anyone who might be a common acquaintance. During the whole year, he explained to the American at the party, he hadn't actually *discussed* her with anyone. Of course he wouldn't, she agreed vaguely and warmly. She knew he wouldn't. He didn't see why he shouldn't, in fact, but went on, for the time, with his narrative.

They had got to know each other a little better over the next few weeks, at least on the level of borrowing tea, or even sharing pots of it. The weather had got hotter. He had found an old-fashioned deck-chair, with faded striped canvas, in the shed, and had brushed it over and brought it out on to his mown lawn, where he sat writing a little, reading a little, getting up and pulling up a tuft of couch grass. He had been wrong about the children not bothering him: there was a succession of incursions by all sizes of children looking for all sizes of balls, which bounced to his feet, or crashed in the shrubs, or vanished in the herbaceous border, black and white footballs, beach-balls with concentric circles of primary colours, acid yellow tennis balls. The children came over the wall: black faces, brown faces, floppy long hair, shaven heads, respectable dotted sun-hats and camouflaged cotton army hats from Milletts. They came over easily, as though they were used to it, sandals, training shoes, a few bare toes, grubby sunburned legs, cotton skirts, jeans, football shorts. Sometimes, perched on the top, they saw him and gestured at the balls; one or two asked permission. Sometimes he threw a ball back, but was apt to knock down a few knobby little unripe apples or pears. There was a gate in the wall, under the fringing trees, which he once tried to open, spending time on rusty bolts only to discover that the lock was new and secure, and the key not in it.

The boy sitting in the tree did not seem to be looking for a ball. He was in a fork of the tree nearest the gate, swinging his legs, doing something to a knot in a frayed end of rope that was attached to the branch he sat on. He wore blue jeans and training shoes, and a brilliant tee shirt, striped in the colours of the spectrum, arranged in the right order, which the man on the grass found visually pleasing. He had rather long blond hair, falling over his eyes, so that his face was obscured.

"Hey, you. Do you think you ought to be up there? It might not be safe."

The boy looked up, grinned, and vanished monkey-like over the wall. He had a nice, frank grin, friendly, not cheeky.

He was there again, the next day, leaning back in the crook of the tree, arms crossed. He had on the same shirt and jeans. The man watched him, expecting him to move again, but he sat, immobile, smiling down pleasantly, and then staring up at the sky. The man read a little, looked up, saw him still there, and said,

"Have you lost anything?"

The child did not reply: after a moment he climbed down a little, swung along the branch hand over hand, dropped to the ground, raised an arm in salute, and was up over the usual route over the wall.

Two days later he was lying on his stomach on the edge of the lawn, out of the shade, this time in a white tee shirt with a pattern of blue ships and waterlines on it, his bare feet and legs stretched in the sun. He was chewing a grass stem, and studying the earth, as though watching for insects. The man said, "Hi, there," and the boy looked up, met his look with intensely blue eyes under long lashes, smiled with the same complete warmth and openness, and returned his look to the earth.

He felt reluctant to inform on the boy, who seemed so harmless and considerate: but when he met him walking out of the kitchen door, spoke to him, and got no answer but the gentle smile before the boy ran off towards the wall, he wondered if he should speak to his landlady. So he asked her, did she mind the children coming in the garden. She said no, children must look for balls, that was part of being children. He persisted—they sat there, too, and he had met one coming out of the house. He hadn't seemed to be doing any harm, the boy, but you couldn't tell. He thought she should know.

He was probably a friend of her son's, she said. She looked at him kindly and explained. Her son had run off the Common with some other children, two years ago, in the summer, in July, and had been killed on the road. More or less instantly, she had added drily, as though calculating that just *enough* information would preclude the need for further questions. He said he was sorry, very sorry, feeling to blame, which was ridiculous, and a little injured, because he had not known about her son, and might inadvertently have made a fool of himself with some casual reference whose ignorance would be embarrassing.

What was the boy like, she said. The one in the house? "I don't—talk to his friends. I find it painful. It could be Timmy, or Martin. They might have lost something, or want . . ."

He described the boy. Blond, about ten at a guess, he was not very good at children's ages, very blue eyes, slightly built, with a rainbow-striped tee shirt and blue jeans, mostly though not always—oh, and those football practice shoes, black and green. And the other tee shirt, with the ships and wavy lines. And an extraordinarily nice smile. A really *warm* smile. A nice-looking boy.

He was used to her being silent. But this silence went on and on and on. She was just staring into the garden. After a time, she said, in her precise conversational tone,

"The only thing I want, the only thing I want at all in this world, is to see that boy."

She stared at the garden and he stared with her, until the grass began to dance with empty light, and the edges of the shrubbery wavered. For a brief moment he shared the strain of not seeing the boy. Then she gave a little sigh, sat down, neatly as always, and passed out at his feet.

After this she became, for her, voluble. He didn't move her after she fainted, but sat patiently by her, until she stirred and sat up; then he fetched her some water, and would have gone away, but she talked.

"I'm too rational to see ghosts, I'm not someone who would see anything there was to see, I don't believe in an after-life, I don't see how anyone can, I always found a kind of satisfaction for myself in the idea that one just came to an end, to a sliced-off stop. But that was myself; I didn't think *he*—not *he*—I thought ghosts were—what people *wanted* to see, or were afraid to see . . . and after he died, the best hope I had, it sounds silly, was that I would go mad enough so that instead of waiting every day for him to come home from school and rattle the letter-box I might actually have the illusion of seeing or hearing him come in. Because I can't stop my body and mind waiting, every day, every day, I can't let go. And his bedroom, sometimes at night I go in, I think I might just for a moment forget he *wasn't* in there sleeping, I think I would pay almost anything—anything at all—for a moment of seeing him like I used to. In his pyjamas, with his—his—his hair . . . ruffled, and, his . . . you said, his . . . that *smile*.

"When it happened, they got Noel, and Noel came in and shouted my name, like he did the other day, that's why I screamed, because it—seemed the same—and then they said, he is dead, and I thought coolly, *is* dead, that will go on and on and on till the end of time, it's a continuous present tense, one thinks the most ridiculous things, there I was thinking about grammar, the verb to be, when it ends to be dead . . . And then I came out into the garden, and I half saw, in my mind's eye, a kind of ghost of his face, just the eyes and hair, coming towards me—like every day waiting for him to come home, the way you think of your son, with such pleasure, when he's—not there—and I—I thought—no, I won't *see* him, because he is dead, and I won't dream about him because he is dead, I'll be rational and practical and continue to live because one must, and there was Noel . . .

"I got it wrong, you see, I was so *sensible,* and then I was so shocked because I couldn't get to want anything—I couldn't *talk* to Noel—I—I—made Noel take away, destroy, all the photos, I—didn't dream, you can will not to dream, I didn't . . . visit a grave, flowers, there isn't any point. I was so sensible. Only my body wouldn't stop waiting and all it wants is to—to see that boy. *That* boy. That boy you—saw."

He did not say that he might have seen another boy, maybe even a boy who had been given the tee shirts and jeans afterwards. He did not say, though the idea crossed his mind, that maybe what he had seen was some kind of impression from her terrible desire to see a boy where nothing was. The boy had had nothing terrible, no aura of pain about him: he had been, his memory insisted, such a pleasant, courteous, self-contained boy, with his own purposes. And in fact the woman herself almost immediately raised the possibility that what he had seen was what she desired to see, a kind of mix-up of radio waves, like when you overheard police messages on the radio, or got BBC 1 on a switch that said ITV. She was thinking fast, and went on almost immediately to say that perhaps his sense of loss, his loss of Anne, which was what had led her to feel she could bear his presence in her house, was what had brought them—dare she say—near enough, for their wavelengths to mingle, perhaps, had made him susceptible . . .

You mean, he had said, we are a kind of emotional vacuum, between us, that must be filled. Something like that, she had said, and had added, "But I don't believe in ghosts."

Anne, he thought, could not be a ghost, because she was elsewhere, with someone else, doing for someone else those little things she had done so gaily for him, tasty little suppers, bits of research, a sudden vase of unusual flowers, a new bold shirt, unlike his own cautious taste, but suiting him, suiting him. In a sense, Anne was worse lost because voluntarily absent, an absence that could not be loved because love was at an end, for Anne.

"I don't suppose you will, now," the woman was saying. "I think talking would probably stop any—mixing of messages, if that's what it is, don't you? But—if—*if* he comes again"—and here for the first time her eyes were full of tears—"if—you must promise, you will *tell* me, you must promise."

He had promised, easily enough, because he was fairly sure she was right, the boy would not be seen again. But the next day he was on the lawn, nearer than ever, sitting on the grass beside the deck-chair, his arms clasping his bent, warm brown knees, the thick, pale hair glittering in the sun. He was wearing a football shirt, this time, Chelsea's colours. Sitting down in the deck-chair, the man could have put out a hand and touched him, but did not: it was not, it seemed, a possible gesture to make. But the boy looked up and smiled, with a pleasant complicity, as though they now understood each other very well. The man tried speech: he said, "It's nice to see you again," and the boy nodded acknowledgement of this remark, without speaking himself. This was the beginning of communication between them, or what the man supposed to be communication. He did not think of fetching the woman. He became aware that he was in some strange way *enjoying the boy's company.* His pleasant stillness—and he sat there all morning, occasionally lying back on the grass, occasionally staring thoughtfully at the house—was calming and comfortable. The man did quite a lot of work—wrote about three reasonable pages on Hardy's original air-blue gown—and looked up now and then to make sure the boy was still there and happy.

*　　*　　*

He went to report to the woman—as he had after all promised to do—that evening. She had obviously been waiting and hoping—her unnatural calm had given way to agitated pacing, and her eyes were dark and deeper in. At this point in the story he found in himself a necessity to bowdlerize for the sympathetic American, as he had indeed already begun to do. He had mentioned only a child who had "seemed like" the woman's lost son, and he now ceased to mention the child at all, as an actor in the story, with the result that what the American woman heard was a tale of how he, the man, had become increasingly involved in the woman's solitary grief, how their two losses had become a kind of *folie à deux* from which he could not extricate himself. What follows is not what he told the American girl, though it may be clear at which points the bowdlerized version coincided with what he really believed to have happened. There was a sense he could not at first analyse that it was improper to talk about the boy—not because he might not be believed; that did not come into it; but because something dreadful might happen.

"He sat on the lawn all morning. In a football shirt."

"Chelsea?"

"Chelsea."

"What did he do? Does he look happy? Did he speak?" Her desire to know was terrible.

"He doesn't speak. He didn't move much. He seemed—very calm. He stayed a long time."

"This is terrible. This is ludicrous. There *is no boy*."

"No. But I saw him."

"Why you?"

"I don't know." A pause. "I do *like* him."

"He is—was—a most likeable boy."

Some days later he saw the boy running along the landing in the evening, wearing what might have been pyjamas, in peacock towelling, or might have been a track suit. Pyjamas, the woman stated confidently, when he told her: his new pyjamas. With white ribbed cuffs, weren't they? and a white polo neck? He corroborated this, watching her cry—she cried more easily now—finding her anxiety and disturbance very hard to bear. But it never occurred to him that it was possible to break his promise to tell her when he saw the boy. That was another curious imperative from some undefined authority.

They discussed clothes. If there were ghosts, how could they appear in clothes long burned, or rotted, or worn away by other people? You could imagine, they agreed, that something of a person might linger—as the Tibetans and others believe the soul lingers near the body before setting out on its long journey. But clothes? And in this case so many clothes? I must be seeing your memories, he told her, and she nodded fiercely, compressing her lips, agreeing that this was likely, adding, "I am too rational to go mad, so I seem to be putting it on you."

He tried a joke. "That isn't very kind to me, to imply that madness comes more easily to me."

"No, sensitivity. I am insensible. I was always a bit like that, and this made it worse. I am the *last* person to see any ghost that was trying to haunt me."

"We agreed it was your memories I saw."

"Yes. We agreed. That's rational. As rational as we can be, considering."

All the same, the brilliance of the boy's blue regard, his gravely smiling salutation in the garden next morning, did not seem like anyone's tortured memories of earlier happiness. The man spoke to him directly then:

"Is there anything I can *do* for you? Anything you want? Can I help you?"

The boy seemed to puzzle about this for a while, inclining his head as though hearing was difficult. Then he nodded, quickly and perhaps urgently, turned, and ran into the house, looking back to make sure he was followed. The man entered the living-room through the french windows, behind the running boy, who stopped for a moment in the centre of the room, with the man blinking behind him at the sudden transition from sunlight to comparative dark. The woman was sitting in an armchair, looking at nothing there. She often sat like that. She looked up, across the boy, at the man; and the boy, his face for the

first time anxious, met the man's eyes again, asking, before he went out into
the house.

"What is it? What is it? Have you seen him again? Why are you . . . ?"

"He came in here. He went—out through the door."

"I didn't see him."

"No."

"Did he—oh, this is so *silly*—did he see me?"

He could not remember. He told the only truth he knew.

"He brought me in here."

"Oh, what can I do, what am I going to *do?* If I killed myself—I have
thought of that—but the idea that I should be with him is an illusion I . . . this
silly situation is the nearest I shall ever get. To him. He was *in here with me?*"

"Yes."

And she was crying again. Out in the garden he could see the boy, swinging agile on the apple branch.

He was not quite sure, looking back, when he had thought he had realized what
the boy had wanted him to do. This was also, at the party, his worst piece of
what he called bowdlerization, though in some sense it was clearly the opposite
of bowdlerization. He told the American girl that he had come to the conclusion that it was the woman herself who had wanted it, though there was in fact,
throughout, no sign of her wanting anything except to see the boy, as she said.
The boy, bolder and more frequent, had appeared several nights running on the
landing, wandering in and out of bathrooms and bedrooms, restlessly, a little
agitated, questing almost, until it had "come to" the man that what he required
was to be re-engendered, for him, the man, to give to his mother another child,
into which he could peacefully vanish. The idea was so clear that it was like another imperative, though he did not have the courage to ask the child to con-
firm it. Possibly this was out of delicacy—the child was too young to be talked
to about sex. Possibly there were other reasons. Possibly he was mistaken: the
situation was making him hysterical, he felt action of some kind was required

and must be possible. He could not spend the rest of the summer, the rest of his life, describing nonexistent tee shirts and blond smiles.

He could think of no sensible way of embarking on his venture, so in the end simply walked into her bedroom one night. She was lying there, reading; when she saw him her instinctive gesture was to hide, not her bare arms and throat, but her book. She seemed, in fact, quite unsurprised to see his pyjamaed figure, and, after she had recovered her coolness, brought out the book definitely and laid it on the bedspread.

"My new taste in illegitimate literature. I keep them in a box under the bed."

Ena Twigg, Medium. The Infinite Hive. The Spirit World. Is There Life After Death?

"Pathetic," she proffered.

He sat down delicately on the bed.

"Please, don't grieve so. Please, let yourself be comforted. Please . . ."

He put an arm round her. She shuddered. He pulled her closer. He asked why she had had only the one son, and she seemed to understand the purport of his question, for she tried, angular and chilly, to lean on him a little, she became apparently compliant. "No real reason," she assured him, no material reason. Just her husband's profession and lack of inclination: that covered it.

"Perhaps," he suggested, "if she would be comforted a little, perhaps she could hope, perhaps . . ."

For comfort then, she said, dolefully, and lay back, pushing Ena Twigg off the bed with one fierce gesture, then lying placidly. He got in beside her, put his arms round her, kissed her cold cheek, thought of Anne, of what was never to be again. Come on, he said to the woman, you must live, you must try to live, let us hold each other for comfort.

She hissed at him "Don't *talk*" between clenched teeth, so he stroked her lightly, over her nightdress, breasts and buttocks and long stiff legs, composed like an effigy on an Elizabethan tomb. She allowed this, trembling slightly, and then trembling violently: he took this to be a sign of some mixture of pleasure and pain, of the return of life to stone. He put a hand between her legs and she moved them heavily apart; he heaved himself over her and pushed, unsuccessfully. She was contorted and locked tight: frigid, he thought grimly, was not the word. *Rigor mortis,* his mind said to him, before she began to scream.

He was ridiculously cross about this. He jumped away and said quite rudely, "Shut up," and then ungraciously, "I'm sorry." She stopped screaming as suddenly as she had begun and made one of her painstaking economical explanations.

"Sex and death don't go. I can't afford to let go of my grip on myself. I hoped. What you hoped. It was a bad idea. I apologize."

"Oh, never mind," he said and rushed out again on to the landing, feeling foolish and almost in tears for warm, lovely Anne.

The child was on the landing, waiting. When the man saw him, he looked questioning, and then turned his face against the wall and leant there, rigid, his shoulders hunched, his hair hiding his expression. There was a similarity between woman and child. The man felt, for the first time, almost uncharitable towards the boy, and then felt something else.

"Look, I'm sorry. I tried. I did try. Please turn round."

Uncompromising, rigid, clenched back view.

"Oh well," said the man, and went into his bedroom.

So now, he said to the American woman at the party, I feel a fool, I feel embarrassed, I feel we are hurting, not helping each other, I feel it isn't a refuge. Of course you feel that, she said, of course you're right—it was temporarily necessary, it helped both of you, but you've got to live your life. Yes, he said, I've done my best, I've tried to get through, I have my life to live. Look, she said, I want to help, I really do, I have these wonderful friends I'm renting this flat from, why don't you come, just for a few days, just for a break, why don't you? They're real sympathetic people, you'd like them, I like them, you could get your emotions kind of straightened out. She'd probably be glad to see the back of you, she must feel as bad as you do, she's got to relate to her situation in her own way in the end. We all have.

He said he would think about it. He knew he had elected to tell the sympathetic American because he had sensed she would be—would offer—a way out. He had to get out. He took her home from the party and went back to his house and landlady without seeing her into her flat. They both knew that this reticence was promising—that he hadn't come in then, because he meant to come later. Her warmth and readiness were like sunshine, she was open. He did not know what to say to the woman.

In fact, she made it easy for him: she asked, briskly, if he now found it perhaps uncomfortable to stay, and he replied that he had felt he should move on, he was of so little use . . . Very well, she had agreed, and had added crisply that it had to be better for everyone if "all this" came to an end. He remembered the firmness with which she had told him that no illusions were pleasant. She was strong: too strong for her own good. It would take years to wear away that stony, closed, simply surviving insensibility. It was not his job. He would go. All the same, he felt bad.

He got out his suitcases and put some things in them. He went down to the garden, nervously, and put away the deck-chair. The garden was empty. There were no voices over the wall. The silence was thick and deadening. He wondered, knowing he would not see the boy again, if anyone else would do so, or if, now he was gone, no one would describe a tee shirt, a sandal, a smile, seen, remembered, or desired. He went slowly up to his room again.

The boy was sitting on his suitcase, arms crossed, face frowning and serious. He held the man's look for a long moment, and then the man went and sat on his bed. The boy continued to sit. The man found himself speaking.

"You do see I have to go? I've tried to get through. I can't get through. I'm no use to you, am I?"

The boy remained immobile, his head on one side, considering. The man stood up and walked towards him.

"Please. Let me go. What are we, in this house? A man and a woman and a child, and none of us can get through. You can't want that?"

He went as close as he dared. He had, he thought, the intention of putting his hand on or through the child. But could not bring himself to feel there was no boy. So he stood, and repeated,

"I can't get through. Do you want me to stay?"

Upon which, as he stood helplessly there, the boy turned on him again the brilliant, open, confiding, beautiful desired smile.

The Bloody Chamber

⋆

ANGELA CARTER

I REMEMBER HOW, THAT NIGHT, I LAY AWAKE in the wagon-lit in a tender, delicious ecstasy of excitement, my burning cheek pressed against the impeccable linen of the pillow and the pounding of my heart mimicking that of the great pistons ceaselessly thrusting the train that bore me through the night, away from Paris, away from girlhood, away from the white, enclosed quietude of my mother's apartment, into the unguessable country of marriage.

And I remember I tenderly imagined how, at this very moment, my mother would be moving slowly about the narrow bedroom I had left behind forever, folding up and putting away all my little relics, the tumbled garments I would not need anymore, the scores for which there had been no room in my trunks, the concert programs I'd abandoned; she would linger over this torn ribbon and that faded photograph with all the half-joyous, half-sorrowful emotions of a woman on her daughter's wedding day. And, in the midst of my bridal triumph, I felt a pang of loss as if, when he put the gold band on my finger, I had, in some way, ceased to be her child in becoming his wife.

Are you sure, she'd said when they delivered the gigantic box that held the wedding dress he'd bought me, wrapped up in tissue paper and red ribbon like a Christmas gift of crystallized fruit. Are you sure you love him? There was a dress for her, too; black silk, with the dull, prismatic sheen of oil on water, finer than anything she'd worn since that adventurous girlhood in Indochina, daughter of a rich tea planter. My eagle-featured, indomitable mother; what other student at the Conservatoire could boast that her mother had outfaced a junkful of Chinese pirates, nursed a village through a visitation of the plague, shot a man-eating tiger with her own hand, and all before she was as old as I?

"Are you sure you love him?"

"I'm sure I want to marry him," I said.

And would say no more. She sighed, as if it was with reluctance that she might at last banish the specter of poverty from its habitual place at our meager table. For my mother herself had gladly, scandalously, defiantly beggared herself for love; and one fine day, her gallant soldier never returned from the wars, leaving his wife and child a legacy of tears that never quite dried, a cigar box full of medals and the antique service revolver that my mother, grown magnificently eccentric in hardship, kept always in her reticule, in case—how I teased her—she was surprised by footpads on her way home from the grocer's shop.

Now and then a starburst of lights spattered drawn blinds as if the railway company had lit up all the stations through which we passed in celebration of the bride. My satin nightdress had just been shaken from its wrappings; it had slipped over my young girl's pointed breasts and shoulders, supple as a garment of heavy water, and how teasingly caressed me, egregious, insinuating, nudging between my thighs as I shifted restlessly in my narrow berth. His kiss, his kiss with tongue and teeth in it and a rasp of beard, had hinted to me, though with the same exquisite tact as this nightdress he'd given me, of the wedding night, which would be voluptuously deferred until we lay in his great ancestral bed in the sea-girt, pinnacled domain that lay, still, beyond the grasp of my imagination . . . that magic place, the fairy castle whose walls were made of foam, that legendary habitation in which he had been born. To which, one day, I might bear an heir. Our destination, my destiny.

Above the syncopated roar of the train I could hear his even, steady breathing. Only the communicating door kept me from my husband and it stood open. If I rose up on my elbow, I could see the dark, leonine shape of his head and my nostrils caught a whiff of the opulent male scent of leather and spices that always accompanied him and sometimes, during his courtship, had been the only hint he gave me that he had come into my mother's sitting room, for though he was a big man, he moved as softly as if all his shoes had soles of velvet, as if his footfall turned the carpet into snow.

He had loved to surprise me in my abstracted solitude at the piano. He would tell them not to announce him, then soundlessly open the door and softly creep up behind me with his bouquet of hothouse flowers or his box of marrons glacés, lay his offering upon the keys and clasp his hands over my eyes as I was lost in a Debussy prelude. But that perfume of spiced leather always betrayed him; after my first shock, I was forced always to mimic surprise, so that he would not be disappointed.

He was older than I. He was much older than I; there were streaks of pure silver in his dark mane. But his strange, heavy, almost waxen face was not lined by experience. Rather, experience seemed to have washed it perfectly smooth, like a stone on a beach whose fissures have been eroded by successive tides. And sometimes that face, in stillness when he listened to me playing, with the heavy eyelids folded over eyes that always disturbed me by their absolute absence of light, seemed to me like a mask, as if his real face, the face that truly reflected all the life he had led in the world before he met me, before, even, I was born, as though that face lay underneath this mask. Or else, elsewhere. As though he had laid by the face in which he had lived for so long in order to offer my youth a face unsigned by the years.

And, elsewhere, I might see him plain. Elsewhere. But where?

In, perhaps, that castle to which the train now took us, that marvelous castle in which he had been born.

Even when he asked me to marry him, and I said "Yes," still he did not lose that heavy, fleshy composure of his. I know it must seem a curious analogy, a man with a flower, but sometimes he seemed to me like a lily. Yes. A lily. Possessed of that strange, ominous calm of a sentient vegetable, like one of those cobra-headed, funereal lilies whose white sheaths are curled out of a flesh as thick and tensely yielding to the touch as vellum. When I said that I would marry him, not one muscle in his face stirred, but he let out a long, extinguished sigh. I thought: Oh! how he must want me! And it was as though the imponderable weight of his desire was a force I might not withstand, not by virtue of its violence but because of its very gravity.

He had the ring ready in a leather box lined with crimson velvet, a fire opal the size of a pigeon's egg set in a complicated circle of dark antique gold. My old nurse, who still lived with my mother and me, squinted at the ring askance: opals are bad luck, she said. But this opal had been his own mother's ring, and his grandmother's, and her mother's before that, given to an ancestor by Catherine de Medici . . . every bride that came to the castle wore it, time out of mind. And did he give it to his other wives and have it back from them? asked the old woman rudely; yet she was a snob. She hid her incredulous joy at my marital coup—her little Marquise—behind a façade of fault-finding. But, here, she touched me. I shrugged and turned my back pettishly on her. I did not want to remember how he had loved other women before me, but the knowledge often teased me in the threadbare self-confidence of the small hours.

I was seventeen and knew nothing of the world; my Marquis had been married before, more than once, and I remained a little bemused that, after those others, he should now have chosen me. Indeed, was he not still in mourning for his last wife? Tsk, tsk, went my old nurse. And even my mother had been reluctant to see her girl whisked off by a man so recently bereaved. A Romanian countess, a lady of high fashion. Dead just three short months before I met him, a boating accident, at his home, in Brittany. They never found her body, but I rummaged through the back copies of the society magazines my old nanny kept in a trunk under her bed and tracked down her photograph. The sharp muzzle of a pretty, witty, naughty monkey; such potent and bizarre charm, of a dark, bright, wild yet worldly thing whose natural habitat must have been some luxurious interior decorator's jungle filled with potted palms and tame, squawking parakeets.

Before that? *Her* face is common property; everyone painted her but the Redon engraving I liked best, *The Evening Star Walking on the Rim of Night*. To see her skeletal, enigmatic grace, you would never think she had been a barmaid in a café in Montmartre until Puvis de Chavannes saw her and had her expose her flat breasts and elongated thighs to his brush. And yet it was the absinthe doomed her, or so they said.

The first of all his ladies? That sumptuous diva; I had heard her sing Isolde, precociously musical child that I was, taken to the opera for a birthday treat. My first opera; I had heard her sing Isolde. With what white-hot passion had she burned from the stage! So that you could tell she would die young. We sat high up, halfway to heaven in the gods, yet she half blinded me. And my father, still alive (oh, so long ago) took hold of my sticky little hand, to comfort me, in the last act, yet all I heard was the glory of her voice.

Married three times within my own brief lifetime to three different graces, now, as if to demonstrate the eclecticism of his taste, he had invited me to join this gallery of beautiful women, I, the poor widow's child with my mouse-colored hair that still bore the kinks of the plaits from which it had so recently been freed, my bony hips, my nervous, pianist's fingers.

He was rich as Croesus. The night before our wedding—a simple affair, at the Mairie, because his countess was so recently gone—he took my mother and me, curious coincidence, to see *Tristan*. And do you know, my heart swelled and ached so during the *Liebestod* that I thought I must truly love him. Yes. I did. On his arm, all eyes were upon me. The whispering crowd in the foyer parted like the Red Sea to let us through. My skin crisped at his touch.

How my circumstances had changed since the first time I heard those voluptuous chords that carry such a charge of deathly passion in them! Now we sat in a loge, in red velvet armchairs, and a braided, bewigged flunky brought us a silver bucket of iced champagne in the interval. The froth spilled over the rim of my glass and drenched my hands. I thought: My cup runneth over. And I had on a Poiret dress. He had prevailed upon my reluctant mother to let him buy my trousseau; what would I have gone to him in, otherwise? Twice-darned under-wear, faded gingham, serge skirts, hand-me-downs. So, for the opera, I wore a sinuous shift of white muslin tied with a silk string under the breasts. And everyone stared at me. And at his wedding gift.

His wedding gift, clasped round my throat. A choker of rubies, two inches wide, like an extraordinarily precious slit throat.

After the Terror, in the early days of the Directory, the aristos who'd escaped the guillotine had an ironic fad of tying a red ribbon round their necks at just the point where the blade would have sliced it through, a red ribbon like the memory of a wound. And his grandmother, taken with the notion, had her ribbon made up in rubies; such a gesture of luxurious defiance! That night at the opera comes back to me even now . . . the white dress; the frail child within it; and the flashing crimson jewels round her throat, bright as arterial blood.

I saw him watching me in the gilded mirrors with the assessing eye of a connoisseur inspecting horseflesh, or even of a housewife in the market, inspecting cuts on the slab. I'd never seen, or else had never acknowledged, that regard of his before, the sheer carnal avarice of it; and it was strangely magnified by the monocle lodged in his left eye. When I saw him look at me with lust, I dropped my eyes, but in glancing away from him, I caught sight of myself in the mirror. And I saw myself, suddenly, as he saw me, my pale face, the way the muscles in my neck stuck out like thin wire. I saw how much that cruel necklace became me. And for the first time in my innocent and confined life, I sensed in myself a potentiality for corruption that took my breath away.

The next day, we were married.

The train slowed, shuddered to a halt. Lights; clank of metal; a voice declaring the name of an unknown, never-to-be-visited station; silence of the night; the rhythm of his breathing, that I should sleep with, now, for the rest of my life. And I could not sleep. I stealthily sat up, raised the blind a little and huddled against the cold window that misted over with the warmth of my breathing, gazing out at the dark platform towards those rectangles of domestic lamplight that promised warmth, company, a supper of sausages hissing in a pan on the stove for the stationmaster, his children tucked up in bed asleep in the brick house with the painted shutters . . . all the paraphernalia of the everyday world from which I, with my stunning marriage, had exiled myself.

Into marriage, into exile; I sensed it, I knew it—that, henceforth, I would always be lonely. Yet that was part of the already familiar weight of the fire opal that glimmered like a gypsy's magic ball, so that I could not take my eyes off it when I played the piano. This ring, the bloody bandage of rubies, the wardrobe of clothes from Poiret and Worth, his scent of Russian leather—all had conspired to seduce me so utterly that I could not say I felt one single twinge of regret for the world of tartines and Maman that now receded from me as if drawn away on a string, like a child's toy, as the train began to throb again as if in delighted anticipation of the distance it would take me.

The first gray streamers of the dawn now flew in the sky and an eldritch half-light seeped into the railway carriage. I heard no change in his breathing, but my heightened, excited senses told me he was awake and gazing at me. A huge man, an enormous man, and his eyes, dark and motionless as those eyes the ancient Egyptians painted upon their sarcophagi, fixed upon me. I felt a certain tension in the pit of my stomach, to be so watched, in such silence. A match struck. He was igniting a Romeo y Julieta, fat as a baby's arm.

"Soon," he said in his resonant voice that was like the tolling of a bell and I felt, all at once, a sharp premonition of dread that lasted only as long as the match flared and I could see his white, broad face as if it were hovering, disembodied, above the sheets, illuminated from below like a grotesque carnival head. Then the flame died, the cigar glowed and filled the compartment with a remembered fragrance that made me think of my father, how he would hug me in a warm fug of Havana, when I was a little girl, before he kissed me and left me and died.

As soon as my husband handed me down from the high step of the train, I smelled the amniotic salinity of the ocean. It was November; the trees, stunted by the Atlantic gales, were bare and the lonely halt was deserted but for his leather-gaitered chauffeur waiting meekly beside the sleek black motorcar. It was cold; I drew my furs about me, a wrap of white and black, broad stripes of ermine and sable, with a collar from which my head rose like the calyx of a wildflower. (I swear to you, I had never been vain until I met him.) The bell clanged;

the straining train leapt its leash and left us at that lonely wayside halt where
only he and I had descended. Oh, the wonder of it; how all that might of iron
and steam had paused only to suit his convenience. The richest man in France.

"Madame."

The chauffeur eyed me; was he comparing me, invidiously, to the countess,
the artist's model, the opera singer? I hid behind my furs as if they were a system of soft shields. My husband liked me to wear my opal over my kid glove, a
showy, theatrical trick—but the moment the ironic chauffeur glimpsed its sim-
mering flash he smiled, as though it was proof positive I was his master's wife.
And we drove towards the widening dawn that now streaked half the sky with
a wintry bouquet of pink of roses, orange of tiger lilies, as if my husband had ordered me a sky from a florist. The day broke around me like a cool dream.

Sea; sand; a sky that melts into the sea—a landscape of misty pastels with a
look about it of being continuously on the point of melting. A landscape with
all the deliquescent harmonies of Debussy, of the études I played for him, the
reverie I'd been playing that afternoon in the salon of the princess where I'd first
met him, among the teacups and the little cakes, I, the orphan, hired out of
charity to give them their digestive of music.

And ah! his castle. The faerie solitude of the place; with its turrets of misty
blue, its courtyard, its spiked gate, his castle that lay on the very bosom of the
sea with seabirds mewing about its attics, the casements opening onto the green
and purple evanescent departures of the ocean, cut off by the tide from land for
half a day . . . that castle, at home neither on the land nor on the water, a mysterious, amphibious place, contravening the materiality of both earth and the
waves, with the melancholy of a mermaiden who perches on her rock and waits,
endlessly, for a lover who had drowned far away, long ago. That lovely, sad, sea
siren of a place!

The tide was low; at this hour, so early in the morning, the causeway rose
up out of the sea. As the car turned onto the wet cobbles between the slow mar-
gins of water, he reached out for my hand that had his sultry, witchy ring on it,
pressed my fingers, kissed my palm with extraordinary tenderness. His face was
as still as ever I'd seen it, still as a pond iced thickly over, yet his lips, that always

looked so strangely red and naked between the black fringes of his beard, now curved a little. He smiled; he welcomed his bride home.

No room, no corridor, that did not rustle with the sound of the sea, and all the ceilings, the walls on which his ancestors in the stern regalia of rank lined up with their dark eyes and white faces, were stippled with refracted light from the waves which were always in motion; that luminous, murmurous castle of which I was the chatelaine, I, the little music student whose mother had sold all her jewelry, even her wedding ring, to pay the fees at the Conservatoire.

First of all, there was the small ordeal of my initial interview with the housekeeper, who kept this extraordinary machine, this anchored, castellated ocean liner, in smooth running order no matter who stood on the bridge; how tenuous, I thought, might be my authority here! She had a bland, pale, impassive, dislikable face beneath the impeccably starched white linen headdress of the region. Her greeting, correct but lifeless, chilled me; daydreaming, I dared presume too much on my status . . . briefly wondered how I might install my old nurse, so much loved, however cozily incompetent, in her place. Ill-considered schemings! He told me this one had been his foster mother; was bound to his family in the utmost feudal complicity, "as much part of the house as I am, my dear." Now her thin lips offered me a proud little smile. She would be my ally as long as I was his. And with that I must be content.

But, here, it would be easy to be content. In the turret suite he had given me for my very own, I could gaze out over the tumultuous Atlantic and imagine myself the Queen of the Sea. There was a Bechstein for me in the music room, and on the wall, another wedding present—an early Flemish primitive of Saint Cecilia at her celestial organ. In the prim charm of this saint, with her plump, sallow cheeks and crinkled brown hair, I saw myself as I could have wished to be. I warmed to a loving sensitivity I had not hitherto suspected in him. Then he led me up a delicate spiral staircase to my bedroom; before she discreetly vanished, the housekeeper set him chuckling with some, I dare say, lewd blessing for the newlyweds in her native Breton. That I did not understand. That he, smiling, refused to interpret.

And there lay the grand, hereditary matrimonial bed, itself the size, almost, of my little room at home, with the gargoyles carved on its surfaces of ebony, vermilion lacquer, gold leaf; and its white gauze curtains, billowing in the sea breeze. Our bed. And surrounded by so many mirrors! Mirrors on all the walls, in stately frames of contorted gold, that reflected more white lilies than I'd ever seen in my life before. He'd filled the room with them, to greet the bride, the young bride. The young bride, who had become that multitude of girls I saw in the mirrors, identical in their chic navy-blue tailor-mades, for traveling, madame, or walking. A maid had dealt with the furs. Henceforth, a maid would deal with everything.

"See," he said, gesturing towards those elegant girls. "I have acquired a whole harem for myself!"

I found that I was trembling. My breath came thickly. I could not meet his eye and turned my head away, out of pride, out of shyness, and watched a dozen husbands approach me in a dozen mirrors and slowly, methodically, teasingly, unfasten the buttons of my jacket and slip it from my shoulders. Enough! No; more! Off comes the skirt; and, next, the blouse of apricot linen that cost more than the dress I had for first communion. The play of the waves outside in the cold sun glittered on his monocle; his movements seemed to me deliberately coarse, vulgar. The blood rushed to my face again, and stayed there.

And yet, you see, I guessed it might be so—that we should have a formal disrobing of the bride, a ritual from the brothel. Sheltered as my life had been, how could I have failed, even in the world of prim bohemia in which I lived, to have heard hints of *his* world?

He stripped me, gourmand that he was, as if he were stripping the leaves off an artichoke—but do not imagine much finesse about it; this artichoke was no particular treat for the diner nor was he yet in any greedy haste. He approached his familiar treat with a weary appetite. And when nothing but my scarlet, palpitating core remained, I saw, in the mirror, the living image of an etching by Rops from the collection he had shown me when our engagement permitted us to be alone together . . . the child with her sticklike limbs, naked but for her button boots, her gloves, shielding her face with her hand as though her face were the last repository of her modesty; and the old, monocled lecher who examined her, limb by limb. He in his London tailoring; she, bare as a lamb chop. Most pornographic of all confrontations. And so my purchaser unwrapped his bargain. And, as at the opera, when I had first seen my flesh in his eyes, I was aghast to feel myself stirring.

At once he closed my legs like a book and I saw again the rare movement of his lips that meant he smiled.

Not yet! Later. Anticipation is the greater part of pleasure, my little love.

And I began to shudder, like a race horse before a race, yet also with a kind of fear, for I felt both a strange, impersonal arousal at the thought of love and at the same time a repugnance I could not stifle for his white, heavy flesh that had too much in common with the armfuls of arum lilies that filled my bedroom in great glass jars, those undertakers' lilies with the heavy pollen that powders your fingers as if you had dipped them in turmeric. The lilies I always associate with him; that are white. And stain you.

This scene from a voluptuary's life was now abruptly terminated. It turns out he has business to attend to; his estates, his companies—even on your honeymoon? Even then, said the red lips that kissed me before he left me alone with my bewildered senses—a wet, silken brush from his beard; a hint of the pointed tip of the tongue. Disgruntled, I wrapped a negligee of antique lace around me to sip the little breakfast of hot chocolate the maid brought me; after that, since it was second nature to me, there was nowhere to go but the music room and soon I settled down at my piano.

Yet only a series of subtle discords flowed from beneath my fingers: out of tune . . . only a little out of tune; but I'd been blessed with perfect pitch and could not bear to play any more. Sea breezes are bad for pianos; we shall need a resident piano tuner on the premises if I'm to continue with my studies! I flung down the lid in a little fury of disappointment; what should I do now, how shall I pass the long, sea-lit hours until my husband beds me?

I shivered to think of *that*.

His library seemed the source of his habitual odor of Russian leather. Row upon row of calf-bound volumes, brown and olive, with gilt lettering on their spines, the octavo in brilliant scarlet morocco. A deep-buttoned leather sofa to recline on. A lectern, carved like a spread eagle, that held open upon it an edition of Huysmans's *Là-bas,* from some overexquisite private press; it had been bound like a missal, in brass, with gems of colored glass. The rugs on the floor, deep, pulsing blues of heaven and red of the heart's dearest blood, came from Isfahan and Bokhara; the dark paneling gleamed; there was the lulling music of the sea and a fire of apple logs. The flames flickered along the spines inside a glass-fronted case that held books still crisp and new. Eliphas Levy; the name meant nothing to me. I squinted at a title or two: *The Initiation, The Key of Mysteries, The Secret of Pandora's Box,* and yawned. Nothing, here, to detain a seventeen-year-old girl waiting for her first embrace. I should have liked, best of all, a novel in yellow paper; I wanted to curl up on the rug before the blazing fire, lose myself in a cheap novel, munch sticky liqueur chocolates. If I rang for them, a maid would bring me chocolates.

Nevertheless, I opened the doors of that bookcase idly to browse. And I think I knew, I knew by some tingling of the fingertips, even before I opened that slim volume with no title at all on the spine, what I should find inside it. When he showed me the Rops, newly bought, dearly prized, had he not hinted that he was a connoisseur of such things? Yet I had not bargained for this, the girl with tears hanging on her cheeks like stuck pearls, her cunt a split fig below the great globes of her buttocks on which the knotted tails of the cat were about to descend, while a man in a black mask fingered with his free hand his prick, that curved upwards like the scimitar he held. The picture had a caption: "Reproof of curiosity." My mother, with all the precision of her eccentricity, had told me what it was that lovers did; I was innocent but not naïve. *The Adventures of Eulalie at the Harem of the Grand Turk* had been printed, according to the flyleaf, in Amsterdam in 1748, a rare collector's piece. Had some ancestor brought it back himself from that northern city? Or had my husband bought it for himself, from one of those dusty little bookshops on the Left Bank where an old man peers at you through spectacles an inch thick, daring you to inspect his wares . . . I turned the pages in the anticipation of fear; the print was rusty. Here was another steel engraving: "Immolation of the wives of the Sultan." I knew enough for what I saw in that book to make me gasp.

There was a pungent intensification of the odor of leather that suffused his library; his shadow fell across the massacre.

"My little nun has found the prayer books, has she?" he demanded, with a curious mixture of mockery and relish; then, seeing my painful, furious bewilderment, he laughed at me aloud, snatched the book from my hands and put it down on the sofa.

"Have the nasty pictures scared Baby? Baby mustn't play with grownups' toys until she's learned how to handle them, must she?"

Then he kissed me. And with, this time, no reticence. He kissed me and laid his hand imperatively upon my breast, beneath the sheath of ancient lace. I stumbled on the winding stair that led to the bedroom, to the carved, gilded bed on which he had been conceived. I stammered foolishly: We've not taken luncheon yet; and besides, it is broad daylight . . .

All the better to see you.

He made me put on my choker, the family heirloom of one woman who had escaped the blade. With trembling fingers, I fastened the thing about my neck. It was cold as ice and chilled me. He twined my hair into a rope and lifted it off my shoulders so that he could the better kiss the downy furrows below my ears; that made me shudder. And he kissed those blazing rubies, too. He kissed them before he kissed my mouth. Rapt, he intoned: "Of her apparel she retains/Only her sonorous jewelry."

A dozen husbands impaled a dozen brides while the mewing gulls swung on invisible trapezes in the empty air outside.

I was brought to my senses by the insistent shrilling of the telephone. He lay beside me, felled like an oak, breathing stertorously, as if he had been fighting with me. In the course of that one-sided struggle, I had seen his deathly composure shatter like a porcelain vase flung against a wall; I had heard him shriek and blaspheme at the orgasm; I had bled. And perhaps I had seen his face without its mask; and perhaps I had not. Yet I had been infinitely disheveled by the loss of my virginity.

I gathered myself together, reached into the cloisonné cupboard beside the bed that concealed the telephone and addressed the mouthpiece. His agent in New York. Urgent.

I shook him awake and rolled over on my side, cradling my spent body in my arms. His voice buzzed like a hive of distant bees. My husband. My husband, who, with so much love, filled my bedroom with lilies until it looked like an embalming parlor. Those somnolent lilies, that wave their heavy heads, distributing their lush, insolent incense reminiscent of pampered flesh.

When he'd finished with the agent, he turned to me and stroked the ruby necklace that bit into my neck, but with such tenderness now that I ceased flinching and he caressed my breasts. My dear one, my little love, my child, did it hurt her? He's so sorry for it, such impetuousness, he could not help himself; you see, he loves her so . . . and this lover's recitative of his brought my tears in a flood. I clung to him as though only the one who had inflicted the pain could comfort me for suffering it. For a while, he murmured to me in a voice I'd never heard before, a voice like the soft consolations of the sea. But then he unwound the tendrils of my hair from the buttons of his smoking jacket, kissed my cheek briskly and told me the agent from New York had called with such urgent business that he must leave as soon as the tide was low enough. Leave the castle? Leave France! And would be away for at least six weeks.

"But it is our honeymoon!"

A deal, an enterprise of hazard and chance involving several millions, lay in the balance, he said. He drew away from me into that waxworks stillness of his; I was only a little girl, I did not understand. And, he said unspoken to my wounded vanity, I have had too many honeymoons to find them in the least pressing commitments. I know quite well that this child I've bought with a handful of colored stones and the pelts of dead beasts won't run away. But after he'd called his Paris agent to book a passage for the States next day—just one tiny call, my little one—we should have time for dinner together.

And I had to be content with that.

A Mexican dish of pheasant with hazelnuts and chocolate; salad; white, voluptuous cheese; a sorbet of muscat grapes and Asti spumante. A celebration of Krug exploded festively. And then acrid black coffee in precious little cups so fine it shadowed the birds with which they were painted. I had Cointreau, he had cognac in the library, with the purple velvet curtains drawn against the night, where he took me to perch on his knee in a leather armchair beside the flickering log fire. He had made me change into that chaste little Poiret shift of white muslin; he seemed especially fond of it, my breasts showed through the flimsy stuff, he said, like little soft white doves that sleep, each one, with a pink eye open. But he would not let me take off my ruby choker, although it was growing very uncomfortable, nor fasten up my descending hair, the sign of a virginity so recently ruptured that still remained a wounded presence between us. He twined his fingers in my hair until I winced; I said, I remember, very little.

"The maid will have changed our sheets already," he said. "We do not hang the bloody sheets out of the window to prove to the whole of Brittany you are a virgin, not in these civilized times. But I should tell you it would have been the first time in all my married lives I could have shown my interested tenants such a flag."

Then I realized, with a shock of surprise, how it must have been my innocence that captivated him—the silent music, he said, of my unknowingness, like *La Terrasse des audiences au clair de lune* played upon a piano with keys of ether. You must remember how ill at ease I was in that luxurious place, how unease had been my constant companion during the whole length of my courtship by this grave satyr who now gently martyrized my hair. To know that my naïveté gave him some pleasure made me take heart. Courage! I shall act the fine lady to the manner born one day, if only by virtue of default.

Then, slowly yet teasingly, as if he were giving a child a great, mysterious treat, he took out a bunch of keys from some interior hidey-hole in his jacket—key after key, a key, he said, for every lock in the house. Keys of all kinds—huge, ancient things of black iron; others slender, delicate, almost baroque; wafer-thin Yale keys for safes and boxes. And during his absence it was I who must take care of them all.

I eyed the heavy bunch with circumspection. Until that moment, I had not given a single thought to the practical aspects of marriage with a great house, great wealth, a great man, whose key ring was as crowded as that of a prison warder. Here were the clumsy and archaic keys for the dungeons, for dungeons we had in plenty although they had been converted to cellars for his wines; the dusty bottles inhabited in racks all those deep holes of pain in the rock on which the castle was built. These are the keys to the kitchens, this is the key to the picture gallery, a treasure house filled by five centuries of avid collectors—ah! he foresaw I would spend hours there.

He had amply indulged his taste for the Symbolists, he told me with a glint of greed. There was Moreau's great portrait of his first wife, the famous *Sacrificial Victim* with the imprint of the lacelike chains on her pellucid skin. Did I know the story of the painting of that picture? How, when she took off her clothes for him for the first time, she fresh from her bar in Montmartre, she had robed herself involuntarily in a blush that reddened her breasts, her shoulders, her arms, her whole body? He had thought of that story, of that dear girl, when first he had undressed me . . . Ensor, the great Ensor, his monolithic canvas *The Foolish Virgins*. Two or three late Gauguins, his special favorite the one of the tranced brown girl in the deserted house which was called *Out of the Night We Come, Into the Night We Go*. And, besides the additions he had made himself, his marvelous inheritance of Watteaus, Poussins and a pair of very special Fragonards, commissioned for a licentious ancestor who, it was said, had posed for the master's brush himself with his own two daughters . . . He broke off his catalogue of treasures abruptly.

Your thin white face, chérie; he said, as if he saw it for the first time. Your thin white face, with its promise of debauchery only a connoisseur could detect.

A log fell in the fire, instigating a shower of sparks; the opal on my finger spurted green flame. I felt as giddy as if I were on the edge of a precipice; I was afraid, not so much of him, of his monstrous presence, heavy as if he had been gifted at birth with more specific *gravity* than the rest of us, the presence that, even when I thought myself most in love with him, always subtly oppressed me. . . . No. I was not afraid of him; but of myself. I seemed reborn in his unre-flective eyes, reborn in unfamiliar shapes. I hardly recognized myself from his descriptions of me and yet—and yet, might there not be a grain of beastly truth in them? And in the red firelight, I blushed again, unnoticed, to think he might have chosen me because, in my innocence, he sensed a rare talent for corruption.

Here is the key to the china cabinet—don't laugh, my darling; there's a king's ransom in Sèvres in that closet, and a queen's ransom in Limoges. And a key to the locked, barred room where five generations of plate were kept.

Keys, keys, keys. He would trust me with the keys to his office, although I was only a baby; and the keys to his safes, where he kept the jewels I should wear, he promised me, when we returned to Paris. Such jewels! Why, I would be able to change my earrings and necklaces three times a day, just as the Empress Josephine used to change her underwear. He doubted, he said, with that hollow, knocking sound that served him for a chuckle, I would be quite so interested in his share certificates, although they, of course, were worth infinitely more.

Outside our firelit privacy, I could hear the sound of the tide drawing back from the pebbles of the foreshore; it was nearly time for him to leave me. One single key remained unaccounted for on the ring and he hesitated over it; for a moment, I thought he was going to unfasten it from its brothers, slip it back into his pocket and take it away with him.

"What is *that* key?" I demanded, for his chaffing had made me bold. "The key to your heart? Give it me!"

He dangled the key tantalizingly above my head, out of reach of my strain-ing fingers; those bare red lips of his cracked sidelong into a smile.

"Ah, no," he said. "Not the key to my heart. Rather, the key to my enfer."

He left it on the ring, fastened the ring together, shook it musically, like a carillon. Then threw the keys in a jingling heap in my lap. I could feel the cold metal chilling my thighs through my thin muslin frock. He bent over me to drop a beard-masked kiss on my forehead.

"Every man must have one secret, even if only one, from his wife," he said.

"Promise me this, my whey-faced piano player: promise me you'll use all the keys on the ring except that last little one I showed you. Play with anything you find, jewels, silver plate; make toy boats of my share certificates, if it pleases you, and send them sailing off to America after me. All is yours, everywhere is open to you—except the lock that this single key fits. Yet all it is is the key to a little room at the foot of the west tower, behind the still room, at the end of a dark little corridor full of horrid cobwebs that would get into your hair and frighten you if you ventured there. Oh, and you'd find it such a dull little room! But you must promise me, if you love me, to leave it well alone. It is only a private study, a hideaway, a 'den,' as the English say, where I can go, sometimes, on those infrequent yet inevitable occasions when the yoke of marriage seems to weigh too heavily on my shoulders. There I can go, you understand, to savor the rare pleasure of imagining myself wifeless."

There was a little thin starlight in the courtyard as, wrapped in my furs, I saw him to his car. His last words were that he had telephoned the mainland and taken a piano tuner on the staff; this man would arrive to take up his duties the next day. He pressed me to his vicuña breast, once, and then drove away.

I had drowsed away that afternoon and now I could not sleep. I lay tossing and turning in his ancestral bed until another daybreak discolored the dozen mirrors that were iridescent with the reflections of the sea. The perfume of the lilies weighed on my senses; when I thought that, henceforth, I would always share these sheets with a man whose skin, as theirs did, contained that toadlike, clammy hint of moisture, I felt a vague desolation that within me, now my female wound had healed, there had awoken a certain queasy craving like the cravings of pregnant women for the taste of coal or chalk or tainted food, for the renewal of his caresses. Had he not hinted to me, in his flesh as in his speech and looks, of the thousand thousand baroque intersections of flesh upon flesh? I lay in our wide bed accompanied by, a sleepless companion, my dark newborn curiosity.

I lay in bed alone. And I longed for him. And he disgusted me.

Were there jewels enough in all his safes to recompense me for this predicament? Did all that castle hold enough riches to recompense me for the company of the libertine with whom I must share it? And what, precisely, was the nature of my desirous dread for this mysterious being who, to show his mastery over me, had abandoned me on my wedding night?

Then I sat straight up in bed, under the sardonic masks of the gargoyles carved above me, riven by a wild surmise. Might he have left me, not for Wall Street, but for an importunate mistress tucked away God knows where who knew how to pleasure him far better than a girl whose fingers had been exercised, hitherto, only by the practice of scales and arpeggios? And slowly, soothed, I sank back onto the heaping pillows; I acknowledged that the jealous scare I'd just given myself was not unmixed with a little tincture of relief.

At last I drifted into slumber, as daylight filled the room and chased bad dreams away. But the last thing I remembered, before I slept, was the tall jar of lilies beside the bed, how the thick glass distorted their fat stems so they looked like arms, dismembered arms, drifting drowned in greenish water.

Coffee and croissants to console this bridal, solitary waking. Delicious. Honey, too, in a section of comb on a glass saucer. The maid squeezed the aromatic juice from an orange into a chilled goblet while I watched her as I lay in the lazy, midday bed of the rich. Yet nothing, this morning, gave me more than a fleeting pleasure except to hear that the piano tuner had been at work already. When the maid told me that, I sprang out of bed and pulled on my old serge skirt and flannel blouse, costume of a student, in which I felt far more at ease with myself than in any of my fine new clothes.

After my three hours of practice, I called the piano tuner in, to thank him. He was blind, of course; but young, with a gentle mouth and gray eyes that fixed upon me although they could not see me. He was a blacksmith's son from the village across the causeway; a chorister in the church whom the good priest had taught a trade so that he could make a living. All most satisfactory. Yes. He thought he would be happy here. And if, he added shyly, he might sometimes be allowed to hear me play . . . for, you see, he loved music. Yes. Of course, I said. Certainly. He seemed to know that I had smiled.

After I dismissed him, even though I'd woken so late it was still barely time for my "five o'clock." The housekeeper, who, thoughtfully forewarned by my husband, had restrained herself from interrupting my music, now made me a solemn visitation with a lengthy menu for a late luncheon. When I told her I did not need it, she looked at me obliquely, along her nose. I understood at once that one of my principal functions as chatelaine was to provide work for the staff. But all the same, I asserted myself and said I would wait until dinnertime, although I looked forward nervously to the solitary meal. Then I found I had to tell her what I would like to have prepared for me; my imagination, still that of a schoolgirl, ran riot. A fowl in cream—or should I anticipate Christmas with a varnished turkey? No; I have decided. Avocado and shrimp, lots of it, followed by no entrée at all. But surprise me for dessert with every ice cream in the icebox. She noted all down but sniffed; I'd shocked her. Such tastes! Child that I was, I giggled when she left me.

But now . . . what shall I do now?

I could have spent a happy hour unpacking the trunks that contained my trousseau, but the maid had done that already, the dresses, the tailor-mades, hung in the wardrobe in my dressing room, the hats on wooden heads to keep their shape, the shoes on wooden feet as if all these inanimate objects were imitating the appearance of life, to mock me. I did not like to linger in my overcrowded dressing room, nor in my lugubriously lily-scented bedroom. How shall I pass the time?

I shall take a bath in my own bathroom! And found the taps were little dolphins made of gold, with chips of turquoise for eyes. And there was a tank of goldfish, who swam in and out of moving fronds of weeds, as bored, I thought, as I was. How I wished he had not left me. How I wished it were possible to chat with, say, a maid; or the piano tuner . . . but I knew already my new rank forbade overtures of friendship to the staff.

I had been hoping to defer the call as long as I could, so that I should have something to look forward to in the dead waste of time I foresaw before me, after my dinner was done with, but at a quarter before seven, when darkness already surrounded the castle, I could contain myself no longer. I telephoned my mother. And astonished myself by bursting into tears when I heard her voice.

No, nothing was the matter. Mother, I have gold bath taps.

I said, gold bath taps!

No; I suppose that's nothing to cry about, Mother.

The line was bad, I could hardly make out her congratulations, her questions, her concern, but I was a little comforted when I put the receiver down.

Yet there still remained one whole hour to dinner and the whole, unimaginable desert of the rest of the evening.

The bunch of keys lay, where he had left them, on the rug before the library fire, which had warmed their metal so that they no longer felt cold to the touch but warm, almost, as my own skin. How careless I was; a maid, tending the logs, eyed me reproachfully as if I'd set a trap for her as I picked up the clinking bundle of keys, the keys to the interior doors of this lovely prison of which I was both the inmate and the mistress and had scarcely seen. When I remembered that, I felt the exhilaration of the explorer.

Lights! More lights!

At the touch of a switch, the dreaming library was brilliantly illuminated. I ran crazily about the castle, switching on every light I could find—I ordered the servants to light up all their quarters, too, so the castle would shine like a seaborne birthday cake lit with a thousand candles, one for every year of its life, and everybody on shore would wonder at it. When everything was lit as brightly as the café in the Gare du Nord, the significance of the possessions implied by that bunch of keys no longer intimidated me, for I was determined, now, to search through them all for evidence of my husband's true nature.

His office first, evidently.

A mahogany desk half a mile wide, with an impeccable blotter and a bank of telephones. I allowed myself the luxury of opening the safe that contained the jewelry and delved sufficiently among the leather boxes to find out how my marriage had given me access to a jinn's treasury—parures, bracelets, rings. . . . While I was thus surrounded by diamonds, a maid knocked on the door and entered before I spoke; a subtle discourtesy. I would speak to my husband about it. She eyed my serge skirt superciliously; did madame plan to dress for dinner?

She made a moue of disdain when I laughed to hear that; she was far more the lady than I. But imagine—to dress up in one of my Poiret extravaganzas, with the jeweled turban and aigrette on my head, roped with pearl to the navel, to sit down all alone in the baronial dining hall at the head of that massive board at which King Mark was reputed to have fed his knights . . . I grew calmer under the cold eye of her disapproval. I adopted the crisp inflections of an officer's daughter. No, I would not dress for dinner. Furthermore, I was not hungry enough for dinner itself. She must tell the housekeeper to cancel the dormitory feast I'd ordered. Could they leave me sandwiches and a flask of coffee in my music room? And would they all dismiss for the night?

Mais oui, madame.

I knew by her bereft intonation I had let them down again, but I did not care; I was armed against them by the brilliance of his hoard. But I would not find his heart amongst the glittering stones; as soon as she had gone, I began a systematic search of the drawers of his desk.

All was in order, so I found nothing. Not a random doodle on an old envelope, nor the faded photograph of a woman. Only the files of business correspondence, the bills from the home farms, the invoices from tailors, the billets-doux from international financiers. Nothing. And this absence of the evidence of his real life began to impress me strangely; there must, I thought, be a great deal to conceal if he takes such pains to hide it.

His office was a singularly impersonal room, facing inward, onto the courtyard, as though he wanted to turn his back on the siren sea in order to keep a clear head while he bankrupted a small businessman in Amsterdam or—I noticed with a thrill of distaste—engaged in some business in Laos that must, from certain cryptic references to his amateur botanist's enthusiasm for rare poppies, be to do with opium. Was he not rich enough to do without crime? Or was the crime itself his profit? And yet I saw enough to appreciate his zeal for secrecy.

Now I had ransacked his desk, I must spend a cool-headed quarter of an hour putting every last letter back where I had found it, and as I covered the traces of my visit, by some chance, as I reached inside a little drawer that had stuck fast, I must have touched a hidden spring, for a secret drawer flew open within that drawer itself; and this secret drawer contained—at last!—a file marked *Personal.*

I was alone, but for my reflection in the uncurtained window.

I had the brief notion that his heart, pressed flat as a flower, crimson and thin as tissue paper, lay in this file. It was a very thin one.

I could have wished, perhaps, I had not found that touching, ill-spelled note, on a paper napkin marked *La Coupole,* that began: "My darling, I cannot wait for the moment when you may make me yours completely." The diva had sent him a page of the score of *Tristan,* the *Liebestod,* with the single, cryptic word "Until . . ." scrawled across it. But the strangest of all these love letters was a postcard with a view of a village graveyard, among mountains, where some black-coated ghoul enthusiastically dug at a grave; this little scene, executed with the lurid exuberance of Grand Guignol, was captioned: "Typical Transylvanian Scene—Midnight, All Hallows." And on the other side, the message: "On the occasion of this marriage to the descendant of Dracula—always remember, 'the supreme and unique pleasure of love is the certainty that one is doing evil.' Toutes amitiés, C."

A joke. A joke in the worst possible taste; for had he not been married to a Romanian countess? And then I remembered her pretty, witty face, and her name—Carmilla. My most recent predecessor in this castle had been, it would seem, the most sophisticated.

I put away the file, sobered. Nothing in my life of family love and music had prepared me for these grown-up games and yet these were clues to his self that showed me, at least, how much he had been loved, even if they did not reveal any good reason for it. But I wanted to know still more; and as I closed the office door and locked it, the means to discover more fell in my way.

Fell, indeed; and with the clatter of a dropped canteen of cutlery, for as I turned the slick Yale lock, I contrived, somehow, to open up the key ring itself, so that all the keys tumbled loose on the floor. And the very first key I picked out of that pile was, as luck or ill fortune had it, the key to the room he had forbidden me, the room he would keep for his own so that he could go there when he wished to feel himself once more a bachelor.

I made my decision to explore it before I felt a faint resurgence of my ill-defined fear of his waxen stillness. Perhaps I half imagined, then, that I might find his real self in his den, waiting there to see if indeed I had obeyed him; that he had sent a moving figure of himself to New York, the enigmatic, self-sustaining carapace of his public person, while the real man, whose face I had glimpsed in the storm of orgasm, occupied himself with pressing private business in the study at the foot of the west tower, behind the stillroom. Yet if that were so, it was imperative that I should find him, should know him; and I was too deluded by his apparent taste for me to think my disobedience might truly offend him.

I took the forbidden key from the heap and left the others lying there.

It was now very late and the castle was adrift, as far as it could go from the land, in the middle of the silent ocean where, at my orders, it floated, like a garland of light. And all silent, all still, but for the murmuring of the waves.

I felt no fear, no intimation of dread. Now I walked as firmly as I had done in my mother's house.

Not a narrow, dusty little passage at all; why had he lied to me? But an ill-lit one, certainly; the electricity, for some reason, did not extend here, so I retreated to the stillroom and found a bundle of waxed tapers in a cupboard, stored there with matches to light the oak board at grand dinners. I put a match to my little taper and advanced with it in my hand, like a penitent, along the corridor hung with heavy, I think Venetian, tapestries. The flame picked out, here, the head of a man, there, the rich breast of a woman spilling through a rent in her dress—the Rape of the Sabines, perhaps? The naked swords and immolated horses suggested some grisly mythological subject. The corridor wound downward; there was an almost imperceptible ramp to the thickly carpeted floor. The heavy hangings on the wall muffled my footsteps, even my breathing. For some reason, it grew very warm; the sweat sprang out in beads on my brow. I could no longer hear the sound of the sea.

A long, a winding corridor, as if I were in the viscera of the castle; and this corridor led to a door of worm-eaten oak, low, round-topped, barred with black iron.

And still I felt no fear, no raising of the hairs on the back of the neck, no pricking of the thumbs.

The key slid into the new lock as easily as a hot knife into butter.

No fear; but a hesitation, a holding of the spiritual breath.

If I had found some traces of his heart in a file marked *Personal,* perhaps here, in his subterranean privacy, I might find a little of his soul. It was the consciousness of the possibility of such a discovery, of its possible strangeness, that kept me for a moment motionless, before, in the foolhardiness of my already subtly tainted innocence, I turned the key and the door creaked slowly back.

"There is a striking resemblance between the act of love and the ministrations of a torturer," opined my husband's favorite poet; I had learned something of the nature of that similarity on my marriage bed. And now my taper showed me the outlines of a rack. There was also a great wheel, like the ones I had seen in woodcuts of the martyrdoms of the saints, in my old nurse's little store of holy books. And—just one glimpse of it before my little flame caved in and I was left in absolute darkness—a metal figure, hinged at the side, which I knew to be spiked on the inside and to have the name: the Iron Maiden.

Absolute darkness. And about me, the instruments of mutilation.

Until that moment, this spoiled child did not know she had inherited nerves and a will from the mother who had defied the yellow outlaws of Indochina. My mother's spirit drove me on, into that dreadful place, in a cold ecstasy to know the very worst. I fumbled for the matches in my pocket; what a dim, lugubrious light they gave! And yet enough, oh, more than enough, to see a room designed for desecration and some dark night of unimaginable lovers whose embraces were annihilation.

The walls of this stark torture chamber were the naked rock; they gleamed as if they were sweating with fright. At the four corners of the room were funerary urns, of great antiquity, Etruscan, perhaps, and on three-legged ebony stands, the bowls of incense he had left burning which filled the room with a sacerdotal reek. Wheel, rack and Iron Maiden were, I saw, displayed as grandly as if they were items of statuary and I was almost consoled then, and almost persuaded myself that I might have stumbled only upon a little museum of his perversity, that he had installed these monstrous items here only for contemplation.

Yet at the center of the room lay a catafalque, a doomed, ominous bier of Renaissance workmanship, surrounded by long white candles, and at its foot, an armful of the same lilies with which he had filled my bedroom, stowed in a four-foot-high jar glazed with a somber Chinese red. I scarcely dared examine this catafalque and its occupant more closely; yet I knew I must.

Each time I struck a match to light those candles round her bed, it seemed a garment of that innocence of mine for which he had lusted fell away from me.

The opera singer lay, quite naked, under a thin sheet of very rare and precious linen, such as the princes of Italy used to shroud those whom they had poisoned. I touched her, very gently, on the white breast; she was cool, he had embalmed her. On her throat I could see the blue imprint of his strangler's fingers. The cool, sad flame of the candles flickered on her white, closed eyelids. The worst thing was, the dead lips smiled.

Beyond the catafalque, in the middle of the shadows, a white, nacreous glimmer; as my eyes accustomed themselves to the gathering darkness, I at last—oh, horrors!—made out a skull; yes, a skull, so utterly denuded, now, of flesh that it scarcely seemed possible the stark bone had once been richly upholstered with life. And this skull was strung up by a system of unseen cords, so that it appeared to hang, disembodied, in the still, heavy air, and it had been crowned with a wreath of white roses, and a veil of lace, the final image of his bride.

Yet the skull was still so beautiful, had shaped with its sheer planes so imperiously the face that had once existed above it, that I recognized her the moment I saw her: face of the evening star walking on the rim of night. One false step, oh, my poor, dear girl, next in the fated sisterhood of his wives; one false step and into the abyss of the dark you stumbled.

And where was she the latest dead, the Romanian countess who might have thought her blood would survive his depredations? I knew she must be here, in the place that had wound me through the castle towards it on a spool of inexorability. But at first, I could see no sign of her. Then, for some reason—perhaps some change of atmosphere wrought by my presence—the metal shell of the Iron Maiden emitted a ghostly twang; my feverish imagination might have guessed its occupant was trying to clamber out, though, even in the midst of my rising hysteria, I knew she must be dead to find a home there.

With trembling fingers, I prized open the front of the upright coffin, with its sculpted face caught in a rictus of pain. Then, overcome, I dropped the key I still held in my other hand. It dropped into the forming pool of her blood.

She was pierced, not by one, but by a hundred spikes, this child of the land of the vampires who seemed so newly dead, so full of blood. . . . Oh, God! How recently had he become a widower? How long had he kept her in this obscene cell? Had it been all the time he had courted me, in the clear light of Paris?

I closed the lid of her coffin very gently and burst into a tumult of sobbing that contained both pity for his other victims and also a dreadful anguish to know I, too, was one of them.

The candles flared, as if in a draft from a door to elsewhere. The light caught the fire opal on my hand so that it flashed, once, with a baleful light, as if to tell me the eye of God—his eye—was upon me. My first thought, when I saw the ring for which I had sold myself to this fate, was how to escape it.

I retained sufficient presence of mind to snuff out the candles round the bier with my fingers, to gather up my taper, to look around, although shuddering, to ensure I had left behind me no traces of my visit.

I retrieved the key from the pool of blood, wrapped it in my handkerchief to keep my hands clean, and fled the room, slamming the door behind me.

It crashed to with a juddering reverberation, like the door of hell.

I could not take refuge in my bedroom, for that retained the memory of his presence trapped in the fathomless silvering of his mirrors. My music room seemed the safest place, although I looked at the picture of Saint Cecilia with a faint dread; what had been the nature of her martyrdom? My mind was in a tumult; schemes for flight jostled with one another. . . . As soon as the tide receded from the causeway, I would make for the mainland—on foot, running, stumbling; I did not trust that leather-clad chauffeur, nor the well-behaved housekeeper, and I dared not take any of the pale, ghostly maids into my confidence, either, since they were all his creatures, all. Once at the village, I would fling myself directly on the mercy of the gendarmerie.

But—could I trust them, either? His forefathers had ruled this coast for eight centuries, from this castle whose moat was the Atlantic. Might not the police, the advocates, even the judge, all be in his service, turning a common blind eye to his vices since he was milord whose word must be obeyed? Who, on this distant coast, would believe the white-faced girl from Paris who came running to them with a shuddering tale of blood, of fear, of the ogre murmuring in the shadows? Or rather, they would immediately know it to be true. But were all honor-bound to let me carry it no further.

Assistance. My mother. I ran to the telephone; and the line, of course, was dead.

Dead as his wives.

A thick darkness, unlit by any star, still glazed the windows. Every lamp in my room burned, to keep the dark outside, yet it seemed still to encroach on me, to be present beside me but as if masked by my lights, the night like a permeable substance that could seep into my skin. I looked at the precious little clock made from hypocritically innocent flowers long ago, in Dresden; the hands had scarcely moved one single hour forward from when I first descended to that private slaughterhouse of his. Time was his servant, too; it would trap me, here, in a night that would last until he came back to me, like a black sun on a hopeless morning.

And yet the time might still be my friend; at that hour, that very hour, he set sail for New York.

To know that in a few moments, my husband would have left France calmed my agitation a little. My reason told me I had nothing to fear; the tide

that would take him away to the New World would let me out of the imprisonment of the castle. Surely I could easily evade the servants. Anybody can buy a
ticket at a railway station. Yet I was still filled with unease. I opened the lid of
the piano; perhaps I thought my own particular magic might help me now, that
I could create a pentacle out of music that would keep me from harm, for if my
music had first ensnared him, then might it not also give me the power to free
myself from him?

Mechanically, I began to play, but my fingers were stiff and shaking. At
first, I could manage nothing better than the exercises of Czerny, but simply the
act of playing soothed me and, for solace, for the sake of the harmonious ratio-
nality of its sublime mathematics, I searched among his scores until I found *The
Well-Tempered Clavier*. I set myself the therapeutic task of playing all Bach's
equations, every one, and, I told myself, if I played them all through without a
single mistake—then the morning would find me once more a virgin.

Crash of a dropped stick.

His silver-headed cane! What else? Sly, cunning, he had returned; he was
waiting for me outside the door!

I rose to my feet; fear gave me strength. I flung back my head defiantly.

"Come in!" My voice astonished me by its firmness, its clarity.

The door slowly, nervously opened and I saw, not the massive, irredeemable
bulk of my husband, but the slight, stooping figure of the piano tuner, and he
looked far more terrified of me than my mother's daughter would have been of
the Devil himself. In the torture chamber, it seemed to me that I would never
laugh again; now, helplessly, laugh I did, with relief, and after a moment's hesitation, the boy's face softened and he smiled a little, almost in shame. Though
they were blind, his eyes were singularly sweet.

"Forgive me," said Jean-Yves. "I know I've given you grounds for dismissing
me, that I should be crouching outside your door at midnight . . . but I heard
you walking about, up and down—I sleep in a room at the foot of the west
tower—and some intuition told me you could not sleep and might, perhaps,
pass the insomniac hours at your piano. And I could not resist that. Besides, I
stumbled over these—"

And he displayed the ring of keys I'd dropped outside my husband's office door, the ring from which one key was missing. I took them from him, looked round for a place to stow them, fixed on the piano stool as if to hide them would protect me. Still he stood smiling at me. How hard it was to make everyday conversation.

"It's perfect," I said. "The piano. Perfectly in tune."

But he was full of the loquacity of embarrassment, as though I would only forgive him for his impudence if he explained the cause of it thoroughly.

"When I heard you play this afternoon, I thought I'd never heard such a touch. Such technique. A treat for me, to hear a virtuoso! So I crept up to your door now, humbly as a little dog might, madame, and put my ear to the keyhole and listened, and listened—until my stick fell to the floor through a momentary clumsiness of mine, and I was discovered."

He had the most touchingly ingenuous smile.

"Perfectly in tune," I repeated. To my surprise, now I had said it, I found I could not say anything else. I could only repeat: "In tune . . . perfect . . . in tune," over and over again. I saw a dawning surprise in his face. My head throbbed. To see him, in his lovely, blind humanity, seemed to hurt me very piercingly, somewhere inside my breast; his figure blurred, the room swayed about me. After the dreadful revelation of that bloody chamber, it was his tender look that made me faint.

When I recovered consciousness, I found I was lying in the piano tuner's arms and he was tucking the satin cushion from the piano stool under my head.

"You are in some great distress," he said. "No bride should suffer so much, so early in her marriage."

His speech had the rhythms of the countryside, the rhythms of the tides.

"Any bride brought to this castle should come ready dressed in mourning, should bring a priest and a coffin with her," I said.

"What's this?"

It was too late to keep silent; and if he, too, was one of my husband's creatures, then at least he had been kind to me. So I told him everything, the keys, the interdiction, my disobedience, the room, the rack, the skull, the corpses, the blood.

"I can scarcely believe it," he said, wondering. "That man . . . so rich; so well-born."

"Here's proof," I said, and tumbled the fatal key out of my handkerchief onto the silken rug.

"Oh, God," he said. "I can smell the blood."

He took my hand; he pressed his arms about me. Although he was scarcely more than a boy, I felt a great strength flow into me from his touch.

"We whisper all manner of strange tales up and down the coast," he said. "There was a marquis, once, who used to hunt young girls on the mainland; he hunted them with dogs, as though they were foxes. My grandfather had it from his grandfather, how the marquis pulled a head out of his saddlebag and showed it to the blacksmith while the man was shoeing his horse. 'A fine specimen of the genus brunette, eh, Guillaume?' And it was the head of the blacksmith's wife."

But in these more democratic times, my husband must travel as far as Paris, to do his hunting in the salons. Jean-Yves knew the moment I shuddered.

"Oh, madame! I thought all these were old wives' tales, chattering of fools, spooks to scare bad children into good behavior! Yet how could you know, a stranger, that the old name for this place is the Castle of Murder?"

How could I know, indeed? Except that, in my heart, I'd always known its lord would be the death of me.

"Hark!" said my friend suddenly. "The sea has changed key. It must be near morning; the tide is going down."

He helped me up. I looked from the window, towards the mainland, along the causeway where the stones gleamed wetly in the thin light of the end of the night, and with an almost unimaginable horror, a horror the intensity of which I cannot transmit to you, I saw, in the distance, still far away yet drawing moment by moment inexorably nearer, the twin headlamps of his great black car, gouging tunnels through the shifting mist.

My husband had indeed returned; this time, it was no fancy.

"The key!" said Jean-Yves. "It must go back on the ring, with the others. As though nothing had happened."

But the key was still caked with wet blood and I ran to my bathroom and held it under the hot tap. Crimson water swirled down the basin, but as if the key itself were hurt, the bloody token stuck. The turquoise eyes of the dolphin taps winked at me derisively; they knew my husband had been too clever for me! I scrubbed the stain with my nailbrush but still it would not budge. I thought how the car would be rolling silently towards the closed courtyard gate; the more I scrubbed the key, the more vivid grew the stain.

The bell in the gatehouse would jangle. The porter's drowsy son would push back the patchwork quilt, yawning, pull the shirt over his head, thrust his feet into his sabots . . . slowly, slowly; open the door for your master as slowly as you can. . . .

And still the bloodstain mocked the fresh water that spilled from the mouth of the leering dolphin.

"You have no more time," said Jean-Yves. "He is here. I know it. I must stay with you."

"You shall not!" I said. "Go back to your room, now. Please."

He hesitated. I put an edge of steel in my voice, for I knew I must meet my lord alone.

"Leave me!"

As soon as he had gone, I dealt with the keys and went to my bedroom. The causeway was empty. Jean-Yves was correct; my husband had already entered the castle. I pulled the curtains close, stripped off my clothes and pulled the bedcurtains round me as a pungent aroma of Russian leather assured me my husband was once again beside me.

"Dearest!"

With the most treacherous, lascivious tenderness, he kissed my eyes, and mimicking the new bride newly wakened, I flung my arms around him, for on my seeming acquiescence depended my salvation.

"Da Silva of Rio outwitted me," he said wryly. "My New York agent telegraphed Le Havre and saved me a wasted journey. So we may resume our interrupted pleasures, my love."

I did not believe one word of it. I knew I had behaved exactly according to his desires; had he not bought me so that I should do so? I had been tricked into my own betrayal to that illimitable darkness whose source I had been compelled to seek in his absence, and now that I had met that shadowed reality of his that came to life only in the presence of its own atrocities, I must pay the price of my new knowledge. The secret of Pandora's box; but he had given me the box himself, knowing I must learn the secret. I had played a game in which every move was governed by a destiny as oppressive and omnipotent as himself, since that destiny was himself; and I had lost. Lost at that charade of innocence and vice in which he had engaged me. Lost, as the victim loses to the executioner.

His hand brushed my breast beneath the sheet. I strained my nerves yet could not help but flinch from the intimate touch, for it made me think of the piercing embrace of the Iron Maiden and of his lost lovers in the vault. When he saw my reluctance, his eyes veiled over and yet his appetite did not diminish. His tongue ran over red lips already wet. Silent, mysterious, he moved away from me to draw off his jacket. He took the gold watch from his waistcoat and laid it on the dressing table, like a good bourgeois; scooped out his rattling loose change and now—oh, God!—makes a great play of patting his pockets officiously, puzzled lips pursed, searching for something that has been mislaid. Then turns to me with a ghastly, a triumphant smile.

"But of course! I gave the keys to you!"

"Your keys? Why, of course. Here, they're under the pillow; wait a moment. What—Ah! No . . . Now, where can I have left them? I was whiling away the evening without you at the piano, I remember. Of course! The music room!"

Brusquely he flung my negligee of antique lace on the bed.

"Go and get them."

"Now? This moment? Can't it wait until morning, my darling?"

I forced myself to be seductive. I saw myself, pale, pliant as a plant that begs to be trampled underfoot, a dozen vulnerable, appealing girls reflected in as many mirrors, and I saw how he almost failed to resist me. If he had come to me in bed, I would have strangled him then.

But he half snarled: "No. It won't wait. Now."

The unearthly light of dawn filled the room; had only one previous dawn broken upon me in that vile place? And there was nothing for it but to go and fetch the keys from the music stool and pray he would not examine them too closely, pray to God his eyes would fail him, that he might be struck blind.

When I came back into the bedroom carrying the bunch of keys, that jangled at every step like a curious musical instrument, he was sitting on the bed in his immaculate shirtsleeves, his head sunk in his hands.

And it seemed to me he was in despair.

Strange. In spite of my fear of him, that made me whiter than my wrap, I felt there emanate from him, at that moment, a stench of absolute despair, rank and ghastly, as if the lilies that surrounded him had all at once begun to fester, or the Russian leather of his scent were reverting to the elements of flayed hide and excrement of which it was composed. The chthonic gravity of his presence exerted a tremendous pressure on the room, so that the blood pounded in my ears as if we had been precipitated to the bottom of the sea, beneath the waves that pounded against the shore.

I held my life in my hands amongst those keys and, in a moment, would place it between his well-manicured fingers. The evidence of that bloody chamber had showed me I could expect no mercy. Yet when he raised his head and stared at me with his blind, shuttered eyes as though he did not recognize me, I felt a terrified pity for him, for this man who lived in such strange, secret places that, if I loved him enough to follow him, I should have to die.

The atrocious loneliness of that monster!

The monocle had fallen from his face. His curling mane was disordered, as if he had run his hands through it in his distraction. I saw how he had lost his impassivity and was now filled with suppressed excitement. The hand he stretched out for those counters in his game of love and death shook a little; the face that turned towards me contained a somber delirium that seemed to me compounded of a ghastly—yes—shame but also of a terrible, guilty joy as he slowly ascertained how I had sinned.

That telltale stain had resolved itself into a mark the shape and brilliance of the heart on a playing card. He disengaged the key from the ring and looked at it for a while, solitary, brooding.

"It is the key that leads to the kingdom of the unimaginable," he said. His voice was low and had in it the timbre of certain great cathedral organs that seem, when they are played, to be conversing with God.

I could not restrain a sob.

"Oh, my love, my little love who brought me a white gift of music," he said, almost as if grieving. "My little love, you'll never know how much I hate daylight!"

Then he sharply ordered: "Kneel!"

I knelt before him and he pressed the key lightly to my forehead, held it there for a moment. I felt a faint tingling of the skin, and when I involuntarily glanced at myself in the mirror, I saw the heart-shaped stain had transferred itself to my forehead, to the space between the eyebrows, like the caste mark of a Brahman woman. Or the mark of Cain. And now the key gleamed as freshly as if it had just been cut. He clipped it back on the ring, emitting that same, heavy sigh as he had done when I said that I would marry him.

"My virgin of the arpeggios, prepare yourself for martyrdom."

"What form shall it take?" I said.

"Decapitation," he whispered, almost voluptuously. "Go and bathe yourself; put on that white dress you wore to hear *Tristan* and the necklace that prefigures your end. And I shall take myself off to the armory, my dear, to sharpen my great-grandfather's ceremonial sword."

"The servants?"

"We shall have absolute privacy for our last rites; I have already dismissed them. If you look out the window you can see them going to the mainland."

It was now the full, pale light of morning. The weather was gray, indeterminate, the sea had an oily, sinister look; a gloomy day on which to die. Along the causeway I could see trouping every maid and scullion, every potboy and panscourer, valet, laundress and vassal who worked in that great house, most on foot, a few on bicycles. The faceless housekeeper trudged along with a great basket in which, I guessed, she'd stowed as much as she could ransack from the larder. The Marquis must have given the chauffeur leave to borrow the motor for the day, for it went last of all, at a stately pace, as though the procession were a cortege and the car already bore my coffin to the mainland for burial.

But I knew no good Breton earth would cover me, like a last, faithful lover; I had another fate.

"I have given them all a day's holiday, to celebrate our wedding," he said. And smiled.

However hard I stared at the receding company, I could see no sign of Jean-Yves, our latest servant, hired but the preceding morning.

"Go, now. Bathe yourself; dress yourself. The lustratory ritual and the ceremonial robing; after that, the sacrifice. Wait in the music room until I telephone for you. No, my dear!" And he smiled as I started, recalling the line was dead. "One may call inside the castle just as much as one pleases; but outside—never."

I scrubbed my forehead with the nailbrush as I had scrubbed the key, but this red mark would not go away, either, no matter what I did, and I knew I should wear it until I died, though that would not be long. Then I went to my dressing room and put on that white muslin shift, costume of a victim of an auto-da-fé, he had bought me to listen to the *Liebestod* in. Twelve young women combed out twelve listless sheaves of brown hair in the mirrors; soon there would be none. The mass of lilies that surrounded me exhaled, now, the odor of their withering. They looked like the trumpets of the angels of death.

On the dressing table, coiled like a snake about to strike, lay the ruby choker.

Already almost lifeless, cold at heart, I descended the spiral staircase to the music room, but there I found I had not been abandoned.

"I can be of some comfort to you," the boy said. "Though not much use."

We pushed the piano stool in front of the open window so that, for as long as I could, I would be able to smell the ancient, reconciling smell of the sea that, in time, will cleanse everything, scour the old bones white, wash away all the stains. The last little chambermaid had trotted along the causeway long ago and now the tide, fated as I, came tumbling in, the crisp wavelets splashing on the old stones.

"You do not deserve this," he said.

"Who can say what I deserve or no?" I said. "I've done nothing; but that may be sufficient reason for condemning me."

"You disobeyed him," he said. "That is sufficient reason for him to punish you."

"I only did what he knew I would."

"Like Eve," he said.

The telephone rang a shrill imperative. Let it ring. But my lover lifted me up and set me on my feet; I knew I must answer it. The receiver felt heavy as earth.

"The courtyard. Immediately."

My lover kissed me; he took my hand. He would come with me if I would lead him. Courage. When I thought of courage, I thought of my mother. Then I saw a muscle in my lover's face quiver.

"Hoofbeats!" he said.

I cast one last, desperate glance from the window and, like a miracle, I saw a horse and rider galloping at a vertiginous speed along the causeway, though the waves crashed, now, high as the horse's fetlocks. A rider, her black skirts tucked up around her waist so she could ride hard and fast, a crazy, magnificent horsewoman in widow's weeds.

As the telephone rang again.

"Am I to wait all morning?"

Every moment, my mother drew nearer.

"She will be too late," Jean-Yves said, and yet he could not restrain a note of hope that, though it must be so, yet it might not be so.

The third, intransigent call.

"Shall I come up to heaven to fetch you down, Saint Cecilia? You wicked woman, do you wish me to compound my crimes by desecrating the marriage bed?"

So I must go to the courtyard, where my husband waited in his London-tailored trousers and the shirt from Turnbull and Asser, beside the mounting block, with, in his hand, the sword which his great-grandfather had presented to the little corporal, in token of surrender to the Republic, before he shot himself. The heavy sword, unsheathed, gray as that November morning, sharp as childbirth, mortal.

When my husband saw my companion, he observed: "Let the blind lead the blind, eh? But does even a youth as besotted as you are think she was truly blind to her own desires when she took my ring? Give it me back, whore."

The fires in the opal had all died down. I gladly slipped it from my finger and, even in that dolorous place, my heart was lighter for the lack of it. My husband took it lovingly and lodged it on the tip of his little finger; it would go no further.

"It will serve me for a dozen more fiancées," he said. "To the block, woman. No—leave the boy; I shall deal with him later, utilizing a less exalted instrument than the one with which I do my wife the honor of her immolation, for do not fear that in death you will be divided."

Slowly, slowly, one foot before the other, I crossed the cobbles.

The longer I dawdled over my execution, the more time it gave the avenging angel to descend. . . .

"Don't loiter, girl! Do you think I shall lose appetite for the meal if you are so long about serving it? No; I shall grow hungrier, more ravenous with each moment, more cruel. . . . Run to me, run! I have a place prepared for your exquisite corpse in my display of flesh!"

He raised the sword and cut bright segments from the air with it, but still I lingered, although my hopes, so recently raised, now began to flag. If she is not here by now, her horse must have stumbled on the causeway, have plunged into the sea. . . . One thing only made me glad; that my lover would not see me die.

My husband laid my branded forehead on the stone and, as he had done once before, twisted my hair into a rope and drew it away from my neck.

"Such a pretty neck," he said with what seemed to be a genuine, retrospective tenderness. "A neck like the stem of a young plant."

I felt the silken bristle of his beard and the wet touch of his lips as he kissed my nape. And, once again, of my apparel I must retain only my gems; the sharp blade ripped my dress in two and it fell from me. A little green moss, growing in the crevices of the mounting block, would be the last thing I should see in all the world.

The whiz of that heavy sword.

And—a great battering and pounding at the gate, the jangling of the bell, the frenzied neighing of a horse! The unholy silence of the place shattered in an instant. The blade did *not* descend, the necklace did *not* sever, my head did *not* roll. For, for an instant, the beast wavered in his stroke, a sufficient split second of astonished indecision to let me spring upright and dart to the assistance of my lover as he struggled sightlessly with the great bolts that kept her out.

The Marquis stood transfixed, utterly dazed, at a loss. It must have been as if he had been watching his beloved *Tristan* for the twelfth, the thirteenth time and Tristan stirred, then leapt from his bier in the last act, announced in a jaunty aria interposed from Verdi that bygones were bygones, crying over spilled milk did nobody any good, and as for himself, he proposed to live happily ever after. The puppetmaster, open-mouthed, wide-eyed, impotent at the last, saw his dolls break free of their strings, abandon the rituals he had ordained for them since time began and start to live for themselves; the king, aghast, witnesses the revolt of his pawns.

You never saw such a wild thing as my mother, her hat seized by the winds and blown out to sea so that her hair was her white mane, her black lisle legs exposed to the thigh, her skirts tucked round her waist, one hand on the reins of the rearing horse while the other clasped my father's service revolver, and behind her, the breakers of the savage, indifferent sea, like the witnesses of a furious justice. And my husband stood stock-still, as if she had been Medusa, the sword still raised over his head as in those clockwork tableaux of Bluebeard that you see in glass cases at fairs.

And then it was as though a curious child pushed his centime into the slot and set all in motion. The heavy, bearded figure roared out loud, braying with fury, and wielding the honorable sword as if it were a matter of death or glory, charged us, all three.

On her eighteenth birthday, my mother had disposed of a man-eating tiger that had ravaged the villages in the hills north of Hanoi. Now, without a moment's hesitation, she raised my father's gun, took aim and put a single, irreproachable bullet through my husband's head.

We lead a quiet life, the three of us. I inherited, of course, enormous wealth, but we have given most of it away to various charities. The castle is now a school for the blind, though I pray that the children who live there are not haunted by any sad ghosts looking for, crying for, the husband who will never return to the bloody chamber, the contents of which are buried or burned, the door sealed.

I felt I had a right to retain sufficient funds to start a little music school here, on the outskirts of Paris, and we do well enough. Sometimes we can even afford to go to the Opéra, though never to sit in a box, of course. We know we are the source of many whisperings and much gossip, but the three of us know the truth of it and mere chatter can never harm us. I can only bless the—what shall I call it?—the *maternal telepathy* that sent my mother running headlong from the telephone to the station after I had called her that night. I never heard you cry before, she said, by way of explanation. Not when you were happy. And who ever cried because of gold bath taps?

The night train, the one I had taken; she lay in her berth, sleepless as I had been. When she could not find a taxi at that lonely halt, she borrowed old Dobbin from a bemused farmer, for some internal urgency told her that she must reach me before the incoming tide sealed me away from her forever. My poor old nurse, left scandalized at home—what? interrupt milord on his honeymoon?—she died soon after. She had taken so much secret pleasure in the fact that her little girl had become a marquise; and now here I was, scarcely a penny the richer, widowed at seventeen in the most dubious circumstances and busily engaged in setting up house with a piano tuner. Poor thing, she passed away in a sorry state of disillusion! But I do believe my mother loves him as much as I do.

No paint nor powder, no matter how thick or white, can mask that red mark on my forehead; I am glad he cannot see it—not for fear of his revulsion, since I know he sees me clearly with his heart—but because it spares my shame.

Don't Look Now

✴

DAPHNE DU MAURIER

"DON'T LOOK NOW," JOHN SAID TO HIS WIFE, "but there are a couple of old girls two tables away who are trying to hypnotise me."

Laura, quick on cue, made an elaborate pretence of yawning, then tilted her head as though searching the skies for a non-existent aeroplane.

"Right behind you," he added. "That's why you can't turn round at once—it would be much too obvious."

Laura played the oldest trick in the world and dropped her napkin, then bent to scrabble for it under her feet, sending a shooting glance over her left shoulder as she straightened once again. She sucked in her cheeks, the first tell-tale sign of suppressed hysteria, and lowered her head.

"They're not old girls at all," she said. "They're male twins in drag."

Her voice broke ominously, the prelude to uncontrolled laughter, and John quickly poured some more chianti into her glass.

"Pretend to choke," he said, "then they won't notice. You know what it is—they're criminals doing the sights of Europe, changing sex at each stop. Twin sisters here on Torcello. Twin brothers tomorrow in Venice, or even tonight, parading arm-in-arm across the Piazza San Marco. Just a matter of switching clothes and wigs."

"Jewel thieves or murderers?" asked Laura.

"Oh, murderers, definitely. But why, I ask myself, have they picked on me?"

The waiter made a diversion by bringing coffee and bearing away the fruit, which gave Laura time to banish hysteria and regain control.

"I can't think," she said, "why we didn't notice them when we arrived. They stand out to high heaven. One couldn't fail."

"That gang of Americans masked them," said John, "and the bearded man with a monocle who looked like a spy. It wasn't until they all went just now that I saw the twins. Oh God, the one with the shock of white hair has got her eye on me again."

Laura took the powder compact from her bag and held it in front of her face, the mirror acting as a reflector.

"I think it's me they're looking at, not you," she said. "Thank heaven I left my pearls with the manager at the hotel." She paused, dabbing the sides of her nose with powder. "The thing is," she said after a moment, "we've got them wrong. They're neither murderers nor thieves. They're a couple of pathetic old retired schoolmistresses on holiday, who've saved up all their lives to visit Venice. They come from some place with a name like Walabanga in Australia. And they're called Tilly and Tiny."

Her voice, for the first time since they had come away, took on the old bubbling quality he loved, and the worried frown between her brows had vanished. At last, he thought, at last she's beginning to get over it. If I can keep this going, if we can pick up the familiar routine of jokes shared on holiday and at home, the ridiculous fantasies about people at other tables, or staying in the hotel, or wandering in art galleries and churches, then everything will fall into place, life will become as it was before, the wound will heal, she will forget.

"You know," said Laura, "that really was a very good lunch. I did enjoy it."

Thank God, he thought, thank God . . . Then he leant forward, speaking low in a conspirator's whisper. "One of them is going to the loo," he said. "Do you suppose he, or she, is going to change her wig?"

"Don't say anything," Laura murmured. "I'll follow her and find out. She may have a suitcase tucked away there, and she's going to switch clothes."

She began to hum under her breath, the signal, to her husband, of content. The ghost was temporarily laid, and all because of the familiar holiday game, abandoned too long, and now, through mere chance, blissfully recaptured.

"Is she on her way?" asked Laura.

"About to pass our table now," he told her.

Seen on her own, the woman was not so remarkable. Tall, angular, aquiline features, with the close-cropped hair which was fashionably called an Eton crop, he seemed to remember, in his mother's day, and about her person the stamp of that particular generation. She would be in her middle sixties, he supposed, the masculine shirt with collar and tie, sports jacket, grey tweed skirt coming to mid-calf. Grey stockings and laced black shoes. He had seen the type on golf-courses and at dog-shows—invariably showing not sporting breeds but pugs—and if you came across them at a party in somebody's house they were quicker on the draw with a cigarette-lighter than he was himself, a mere male, with pocket-matches. The general belief that they kept house with a more feminine, fluffy companion was not always true. Frequently they boasted, and adored, a golfing husband. No, the striking point about this particular individual was that there were two of them. Identical twins cast in the same mould. The only difference was that the other one had whiter hair.

"Supposing," murmured Laura, "when I find myself in the *toilette* beside her she starts to strip?"

"Depends on what is revealed," John answered. "If she's hermaphrodite, make a bolt for it. She might have a hypodermic syringe concealed and want to knock you out before you reached the door."

Laura sucked in her cheeks once more and began to shake. Then, squaring her shoulders, she rose to her feet. "I simply must not laugh," she said, "and whatever you do, don't look at me when I come back, especially if we come out together." She picked up her bag and strolled self-consciously away from the table in pursuit of her prey.

John poured the dregs of the chianti into his glass and lit a cigarette. The sun blazed down upon the little garden of the restaurant. The Americans had left, and the monocled man, and the family party at the far end. All was peace. The identical twin was sitting back in her chair with her eyes closed. Thank heaven, he thought, for this moment at any rate, when relaxation was possible, and Laura had been launched upon her foolish, harmless game. The holiday could yet turn into the cure she needed, blotting out, if only temporarily, the numb despair that had seized her since the child died.

"She'll get over it," the doctor said. "They all get over it, in time. And you have the boy."

"I know," John had said, "but the girl meant everything. She always did, right from the start, I don't know why. I suppose it was the difference in age. A boy of school age, and a tough one at that, is someone in his own right. Not a baby of five. Laura literally adored her. Johnnie and I were nowhere."

"Give her time," repeated the doctor, "give her time. And anyway, you're both young still. There'll be others. Another daughter."

So easy to talk . . . How replace the life of a loved lost child with a dream? He knew Laura too well. Another child, another girl, would have her own qualities, a separate identity, she might even induce hostility because of this very fact. A usurper in the cradle, in the cot, that had been Christine's. A chubby, flaxen replica of Johnnie, not the little waxen dark-haired sprite that had gone.

He looked up, over his glass of wine, and the woman was staring at him again. It was not the casual, idle glance of someone at a nearby table, waiting for her companion to return, but something deeper, more intent, the prominent, light blue eyes oddly penetrating, giving him a sudden feeling of discomfort. Damn the woman! All right, bloody stare, if you must. Two can play at that game. He blew a cloud of cigarette smoke into the air and smiled at her, he hoped offensively. She did not register. The blue eyes continued to hold his, so that he was obliged to look away himself, extinguish his cigarette, glance over his shoulder for the waiter and call for the bill. Settling for this, and fumbling with the change, with a few casual remarks about the excellence of the meal, brought composure, but a prickly feeling on his scalp remained, and an odd sensation of unease. Then it went, as abruptly as it had started, and stealing a furtive glance at the other table he saw that her eyes were closed again, and she was sleeping, or dozing, as she had done before. The waiter disappeared. All was still.

Laura, he thought, glancing at his watch, is being a hell of a time. Ten minutes at least. Something to tease her about, anyway. He began to plan the form the joke would take. How the old dolly had stripped to her smalls, suggesting that Laura should do likewise. And then the manager had burst in upon them both, exclaiming in horror, the reputation of the restaurant damaged, the hint that unpleasant consequences might follow unless . . . The whole exercise turning out to be a plant, an exercise in blackmail. He and Laura and the twins taken in a police launch back to Venice for questioning. Quarter of an hour . . . Oh, come on, come on . . .

There was a crunch of feet on the gravel. Laura's twin walked slowly past, alone. She crossed over to her table and stood there a moment, her tall, angular figure interposing itself between John and her sister. She was saying something, but he couldn't catch the words. What was the accent, though—Scottish? Then she bent, offering an arm to the seated twin, and they moved away together across the garden to the break in the little hedge beyond, the twin who had stared at John leaning on her sister's arm. Here was the difference again. She was not quite so tall, and she stooped more—perhaps she was arthritic. They disappeared out of sight, and John, becoming impatient, got up and was about to walk back into the hotel when Laura emerged.

"Well, I must say, you took your time," he began, and then stopped, because of the expression on her face.

"What's the matter, what's happened?" he asked.

He could tell at once there was something wrong. Almost as if she were in a state of shock. She blundered towards the table he had just vacated and sat down. He drew up a chair beside her, taking her hand.

"Darling, what is it? Tell me—are you ill?"

She shook her head, and then turned and looked at him. The dazed expression he had noticed at first had given way to one of dawning confidence, almost of exaltation.

"It's quite wonderful," she said slowly, "the most wonderful thing that could possibly be. You see, she isn't dead, she's still with us. That's why they kept staring at us, those two sisters. They could see Christine."

Oh God, he thought. It's what I've been dreading. She's going off her head. What do I do? How do I cope?

"Laura, sweet," he began, forcing a smile, "look, shall we go? I've paid the bill, we can go and look at the cathedral and stroll around, and then it will be time to take off in that launch again for Venice."

She wasn't listening, or at any rate the words didn't penetrate.

"John, love," she said, "I've got to tell you what happened. I followed her, as we planned, into the *toilette* place. She was combing her hair and I went into the loo, and then came out and washed my hands in the basin. She was washing hers in the next basin. Suddenly she turned and said to me, in a strong Scots accent, 'Don't be unhappy any more. My sister has seen your little girl. She was sitting between you and your husband, laughing.' Darling, I thought I was going to faint. I nearly did. Luckily, there was a chair, and I sat down, and the woman bent over me and patted my head. I'm not sure of her exact words, but she said something about the moment of truth and joy being as sharp as a sword, but not to be afraid, all was well, but the sister's vision had been so strong they knew I had to be told, and that Christine wanted it. Oh John, don't look like that. I swear I'm not making it up, this is what she told me, it's all true."

The desperate urgency in her voice made his heart sicken. He had to play along with her, agree, soothe, do anything to bring back some sense of calm.

"Laura, darling, of course I believe you," he said, "only it's a sort of shock, and I'm upset because you're upset . . ."

"But I'm not upset," she interrupted. "I'm happy, so happy that I can't put the feeling into words. You know what it's been like all these weeks, at home and everywhere we've been on holiday, though I tried to hide it from you. Now it's lifted, because I know, I just know, that the woman was right. Oh Lord, how awful of me, but I've forgotten their name—she did tell me. You see, the thing is that she's a retired doctor, they come from Edinburgh, and the one who saw Christine went blind a few years ago. Although she's studied the occult all her life and been very psychic, it's only since going blind that she has really seen things, like a medium. They've had the most wonderful experiences. But to de-scribe Christine as the blind one did to her sister, even down to the little blue-and-white dress with the puff sleeves that she wore at her birthday party, and to say she was smiling happily . . . Oh darling, it's made me so happy I think I'm going to cry."

No hysteria. Nothing wild. She took a tissue from her bag and blew her nose, smiling at him. "I'm all right, you see, you don't have to worry. Neither of us need worry about anything any more. Give me a cigarette."

He took one from his packet and lighted it for her. She sounded normal, herself again. She wasn't trembling. And if this sudden belief was going to keep her happy he couldn't possibly begrudge it. But . . . but . . . he wished, all the same, it hadn't happened. There was something uncanny about thought-reading, about telepathy. Scientists couldn't account for it, nobody could, and this is what must have happened just now between Laura and the sisters. So the one who had been staring at him was blind. That accounted for the fixed gaze. Which somehow was unpleasant in itself, creepy. Oh hell, he thought, I wish we hadn't come here for lunch. Just chance, a flick of a coin between this, Torcello, and driving to Padua, and we had to choose Torcello.

"You didn't arrange to meet them again or anything, did you?" he asked, trying to sound casual.

"No, darling, why should I?" Laura answered. "I mean, there was nothing more they could tell me. The sister had had her wonderful vision, and that was that. Anyway, they're moving on. Funnily enough, it's rather like our original game. They *are* going round the world before returning to Scotland. Only I said Australia, didn't I? The old dears . . . Anything less like murderers and jewel thieves."

She had quite recovered. She stood up and looked about her. "Come on," she said. "Having come to Torcello we must see the cathedral."

They made their way from the restaurant across the open piazza, where the stalls had been set up with scarves and trinkets and postcards, and so along the path to the cathedral. One of the ferry-boats had just decanted a crowd of sightseers, many of whom had already found their way into Santa Maria Assunta. Laura, undaunted, asked her husband for the guidebook, and, as had always been her custom in happier days, started to walk slowly through the cathedral, studying mosaics, columns, panels from left to right, while John, less interested, because of his concern at what had just happened, followed close behind, keeping a weather eye alert for the twin sisters. There was no sign of them. Perhaps they had gone into the church of Santa Fosca close by. A sudden encounter would be embarrassing, quite apart from the effect it might have upon Laura. But the anonymous, shuffling tourists, intent upon culture, could not harm her, although from his own point of view they made artistic appreciation impossible. He could not concentrate, the cold clear beauty of what he saw left him untouched, and when Laura touched his sleeve, pointing to the mosaic of the Virgin and Child standing above the frieze of the Apostles, he nodded in sympathy yet saw nothing, the long, sad face of the Virgin infinitely remote, and turning on sudden impulse stared back over the heads of the tourists towards the door, where frescoes of the blessed and the damned gave themselves to judgement.

The twins were standing there, the blind one still holding on to her sister's arm, her sightless eyes fixed firmly upon him. He felt himself held, unable to move, and an impending sense of doom, of tragedy, came upon him. His whole being sagged, as it were, in apathy, and he thought, "This is the end, there is no escape, no future." Then both sisters turned and went out of the cathedral and the sensation vanished, leaving indignation in its wake, and rising anger. How dare those two old fools practise their mediumistic trick on him? It was fraudulent, unhealthy; this was probably the way they lived, touring the world making everyone they met uncomfortable. Give them half a chance and they would have got money out of Laura—anything.

He felt her tugging at his sleeve again. "Isn't she beautiful? So happy, so serene."

"Who? What?" he asked.

"The Madonna," she answered. "She has a magic quality. It goes right through to one. Don't you feel it too?"

"I suppose so. I don't know. There are too many people around."

She looked up at him, astonished. "What's that got to do with it? How funny you are. Well, all right, let's get away from them. I want to buy some post-cards anyway."

Disappointed, she sensed his lack of interest, and began to thread her way through the crowd of tourists to the door.

"Come on," he said abruptly, once they were outside, "there's plenty of time for postcards, let's explore a bit," and he struck off from the path, which would have taken them back to the centre where the little houses were, and the stalls, and the drifting crowd of people, to a narrow way amongst uncultivated ground, beyond which he could see a sort of cutting, or canal. The sight of water, limpid, pale, was a soothing contrast to the fierce sun above their heads.

"I don't think this leads anywhere much," said Laura. "It's a bit muddy, too, one can't sit. Besides, there are more things the guidebook says we ought to see."

"Oh, forget the book," he said impatiently, and, pulling her down beside him on the bank above the cutting, put his arms round her.

"It's the wrong time of day for sight-seeing. Look, there's a rat swimming there the other side."

He picked up a stone and threw it in the water, and the animal sank, or somehow disappeared, and nothing was left but bubbles.

"Don't," said Laura. "It's cruel, poor thing," and then suddenly, putting her hand on his knee, "Do you think Christine is sitting here beside us?"

He did not answer at once. What was there to say? Would it be like this forever?

"I expect so," he said slowly, "if you feel she is."

The point was, remembering Christine before the onset of the fatal meningitis, she would have been running along the bank excitedly, throwing off her shoes, wanting to paddle, giving Laura a fit of apprehension. "Sweetheart, take care, come back . . ."

"The woman said she was looking so happy, sitting beside us, smiling," said Laura. She got up, brushing her dress, her mood changed to restlessness. "Come on, let's go back," she said.

He followed her with a sinking heart. He knew she did not really want to buy postcards or see what remained to be seen; she wanted to go in search of the women again, not necessarily to talk, just to be near them. When they came to the open place by the stalls he noticed that the crowd of tourists had thinned, there were only a few stragglers left, and the sisters were not amongst them. They must have joined the main body who had come to Torcello by the ferry-service. A wave of relief seized him.

"Look, there's a mass of postcards at the second stall," he said quickly, "and some eye-catching head scarves. Let me buy you a head scarf."

"Darling, I've so many!" she protested. "Don't waste your lire."

"It isn't a waste. I'm in a buying mood. What about a basket? You know we never have enough baskets. Or some lace. How about lace?"

She allowed herself, laughing, to be dragged to the stall. While he rumpled through the goods spread out before them, and chatted up the smiling woman who was selling her wares, his ferociously bad Italian making her smile the more, he knew it would give the body of tourists more time to walk to the landing stage and catch the ferry-service, and the twin sisters would be out of sight and out of their life.

"Never," said Laura, some twenty minutes later, "has so much junk been piled into so small a basket," her bubbling laugh reassuring him that all was well, he needn't worry any more, the evil hour had passed. The launch from the Cipriani that had brought them from Venice was waiting by the landing-stage. The passengers who had arrived with them, the Americans, the man with the monocle, were already assembled. Earlier, before setting out, he had thought the price for lunch and transport, there and back, decidedly steep. Now he grudged none of it, except that the outing to Torcello itself had been one of the major errors of this particular holiday in Venice. They stepped down into the launch, finding a place in the open, and the boat chugged away down the canal and into the lagoon. The ordinary ferry had gone before, steaming towards Murano, while their own craft headed past San Francesco del Deserto and so back direct to Venice.

He put his arm around her once more, holding her close, and this time she responded, smiling up at him, her head on his shoulder.

"It's been a lovely day," she said. "I shall never forget it, never. You know, darling, now at last I can begin to enjoy our holiday."

He wanted to shout with relief. It's going to be all right, he decided, let her believe what she likes, it doesn't matter, it makes her happy. The beauty of Venice rose before them, sharply outlined against the glowing sky, and there was still so much to see, wandering there together, that might now be perfect because of her change of mood, the shadow having lifted, and aloud he began to discuss the evening to come, where they would dine—not the restaurant they usually went to, near the Fenice theatre, but somewhere different, some-where new.

"Yes, but it must be cheap," she said, falling in with his mood, "because we've already spent so much today."

Their hotel by the Grand Canal had a welcoming, comforting air. The clerk smiled as he handed over their key. The bedroom was familiar, like home, with Laura's things arranged neatly on the dressing-table, but with it the little festive atmosphere of strangeness, of excitement, that only a holiday bedroom brings. This is ours for the moment, but no more. While we are in it we bring it life. When we have gone it no longer exists, it fades into anonymity. He turned on both taps in the bathroom, the water gushing into the bath, the steam rising. "Now," he thought afterwards, "now at last is the moment to make love," and he went back into the bedroom, and she understood, and opened her arms and smiled. Such blessed relief after all those weeks of restraint.

"The thing is," she said later, fixing her ear-rings before the looking-glass, "I'm not really terribly hungry. Shall we just be dull and eat in the dining-room here?"

"God, no!" he exclaimed. "With all those rather dreary couples at the other tables? I'm ravenous. I'm also gay. I want to get rather sloshed."

"Not bright lights and music, surely?"

"No, no . . . some small, dark, intimate cave, rather sinister, full of lovers with other people's wives."

"H'm," sniffed Laura, "we all know what *that* means. You'll spot some Italian lovely of sixteen and smirk at her through dinner, while I'm stuck high and dry with a beastly man's broad back."

They went out laughing into the warm soft night, and the magic was about them everywhere. "Let's walk," he said, "let's walk and work up an appetite for our gigantic meal," and inevitably they found themselves by the Molo and the lapping gondolas dancing upon the water, the lights everywhere blending with the darkness. There were other couples strolling for the same sake of aimless enjoyment, backwards, forwards, purposeless, and the inevitable sailors in groups, noisy, gesticulating, and dark-eyed girls whispering, clicking on high heels.

"The trouble is," said Laura, "walking in Venice becomes compulsive once you start. Just over the next bridge, you say, and then the next one beckons. I'm sure there are no restaurants down here, we're almost at those public gardens where they hold the Biennale. Let's turn back. I know there's a restaurant somewhere near the church of San Zaccaria, there's a little alley-way leading to it."

"Tell you what," said John, "if we go down here by the Arsenal, and cross that bridge at the end and head left, we'll come upon San Zaccaria from the other side. We did it the other morning."

"Yes, but it was daylight then. We may lose our way, it's not very well lit."

"Don't fuss. I have an instinct for these things."

They turned down the Fondamenta dell'Arsenale and crossed the little bridge short of the Arsenal itself, and so on past the church of San Martino. There were two canals ahead, one bearing right, the other left, with narrow streets beside them. John hesitated. Which one was it they had walked beside the day before?

"You see," protested Laura, "we shall be lost, just as I said."

"Nonsense," replied John firmly. "It's the left-hand one, I remember the little bridge."

The canal was narrow, the houses on either side seemed to close in upon it, and in the daytime, with the sun's reflection on the water and the windows of the houses open, bedding upon the balconies, a canary singing in a cage, there had been an impression of warmth, of secluded shelter. Now, ill-lit, almost in darkness, the windows of the houses shuttered, the water dank, the scene appeared altogether different, neglected, poor, and the long narrow boats moored to the slippery steps of cellar entrances looked like coffins.

"I swear I don't remember this bridge," said Laura, pausing, and holding on to the rail, "and I don't like the look of that alley-way beyond."

"There's a lamp halfway up," John told her. "I know exactly where we are, not far from the Greek quarter."

They crossed the bridge, and were about to plunge into the alley-way when they heard the cry. It came, surely, from one of the houses on the opposite side, but which one it was impossible to say. With the shutters closed each one of them seemed dead. They turned, and stared in the direction from which the sound had come.

"What was it?" whispered Laura.

"Some drunk or other," said John briefly. "Come on."

Less like a drunk than someone being strangled, and the choking cry suppressed as the grip held firm.

"We ought to call the police," said Laura.

"Oh, for heaven's sake," said John. Where did she think she was—Piccadilly?

"Well, I'm off, it's sinister," she replied, and began to hurry away up the twisting alley-way. John hesitated, his eye caught by a small figure which suddenly crept from a cellar entrance below one of the opposite houses, and then jumped into a narrow boat below. It was a child, a little girl—she couldn't have been more than five or six—wearing a short coat over her minute skirt, a pixie hood covering her head. There were four boats moored, line upon line, and she proceeded to jump from one to the other with surprising agility, intent, it would seem, upon escape. Once her foot slipped and he caught his breath, for she was within a few feet of the water, losing balance; then she recovered, and hopped on to the furthest boat. Bending, she tugged at the rope, which had the effect of swinging the boat's after-end across the canal, almost touching the opposite side and another cellar entrance, about thirty feet from the spot where John stood watching her. Then the child jumped again, landing upon the cellar steps, and vanished into the house, the boat swinging back into mid-canal behind her. The whole episode could not have taken more than four minutes. Then he heard the quick patter of feet. Laura had returned. She had seen none of it, for which he felt unspeakably thankful. The sight of a child, a little girl, in what must have been near danger, her fear that the scene he had just witnessed was in some way a sequel to the alarming cry, might have had a disastrous effect on her overwrought nerves.

"What are you doing?" she called. "I daren't go on without you. The wretched alley branches in two directions."

"Sorry," he told her. "I'm coming."

He took her arm and they walked briskly along the alley, John with an apparent confidence he did not possess.

"There were no more cries, were there?" she asked.

"No," he said, "no, nothing. I tell you, it was some drunk."

The alley led to a deserted *campo* behind a church, not a church he knew, and he led the way across, along another street and over a further bridge.

"Wait a minute," he said. "I think we take this right-hand turning. It will lead us into the Greek quarter—the church of San Giorgio is somewhere over there."

She did not answer. She was beginning to lose faith. The place was like a maze. They might circle round and round forever, and then find themselves back again, near the bridge where they had heard the cry. Doggedly he led her on, and then surprisingly, with relief, he saw people walking in the lighted street ahead, there was a spire of a church, the surroundings became familiar.

"There, I told you," he said. "That's San Zaccaria, we've found it all right. Your restaurant can't be far away."

And anyway, there would be other restaurants, somewhere to eat, at least here was the cheering glitter of lights, of movement, canals beside which people walked, the atmosphere of tourism. The letters "Ristorante," in blue lights, shone like a beacon down a left-hand alley.

"Is this your place?" he asked.

"God knows," she said. "Who cares? Let's feed there anyway."

And so into the sudden blast of heated air and hum of voices, the smell of pasta, wine, waiters, jostling customers, laughter. "For two? This way, please." Why, he thought, was one's British nationality always so obvious? A cramped little table and an enormous menu scribbled in an indecipherable mauve biro, with the waiter hovering, expecting the order forthwith.

"Two very large camparis, with soda," John said. "*Then* we'll study the menu."

He was not going to be rushed. He handed the bill of fare to Laura and looked about him. Mostly Italians—that meant the food would be good. Then he saw them. At the opposite side of the room. The twin sisters. They must have come into the restaurant hard upon Laura's and his own arrival, for they were only now sitting down, shedding their coats, the waiter hovering beside the table. John was seized with the irrational thought that this was no coincidence. The sisters had noticed them both, in the street outside, and had followed them in. Why, in the name of hell, should they have picked on this particular spot, in the whole of Venice, unless . . . unless Laura herself, at Torcello, had suggested a further encounter, or the sister had suggested it to her? A small restaurant near the church of San Zaccaria, we go there sometimes for dinner. It was Laura, before the walk, who had mentioned San Zaccaria . . .

She was still intent upon the menu, she had not seen the sisters, but any moment now she would have chosen what she wanted to eat, and then she would raise her head and look across the room. If only the drinks would come. If only the waiter would bring the drinks, it would give Laura something to do.

"You know, I was thinking," he said quickly, "we really ought to go to the garage tomorrow and get the car, and do that drive to Padua. We could lunch in Padua, see the cathedral and touch St Antony's tomb and look at the Giotto frescoes, and come back by way of those various villas along the Brenta that the guidebook cracks up."

It was no use, though. She was looking up, across the restaurant, and she gave a little gasp of surprise. It was genuine. He could swear it was genuine.

"Look," she said, "how extraordinary! How really amazing!"

"What?" he said sharply.

"Why, there they are. My wonderful old twins. They've seen us, what's more. They're staring this way." She waved her hand, radiant, delighted. The sister she had spoken to at Torcello bowed and smiled. False old bitch, he thought, I know they followed us.

"Oh, darling, I must go and speak to them," she said impulsively, "just to tell them how happy I've been all day, thanks to them."

"Oh, for heaven's sake!" he said. "Look, here are the drinks. And we haven't ordered yet. Surely you can wait until later, until we've eaten?"

"I won't be a moment," she said, "and anyway I want scampi, nothing first. I told you I wasn't hungry."

She got up, and, brushing past the waiter with the drinks, crossed the room. She might have been greeting the loved friends of years. He watched her bend over the table and shake them both by the hand, and because there was a vacant chair at their table she drew it up and sat down, talking, smiling. Nor did the sisters seem surprised, at least not the one she knew, who nodded and talked back, while the blind sister remained impassive.

"All right," thought John savagely, "then I *will* get sloshed," and he proceeded to down his campari and soda and order another, while he pointed out something quite unintelligible on the menu as his own choice, but remembered scampi for Laura. "And a bottle of Soave," he added, "with ice."

The evening was ruined anyway. What was to have been an intimate, happy celebration would now be heavy-laden with spiritualistic visions, poor little dead Christine sharing the table with them, which was so damned stupid when in earthly life she would have been tucked up hours ago in bed. The bitter taste of the campari suited his mood of sudden self-pity, and all the while he watched the group at the table in the opposite corner, Laura apparently listening while the more active sister held forth and the blind one sat silent, her formidable sightless eyes turned in his direction.

"She's phoney," he thought, "she's not blind at all. They're both of them

frauds, and they could be males in drag after all, just as we pretended at Torcello, and they're after Laura."

He began on his second campari and soda. The two drinks, taken on an
empty stomach, had an instant effect. Vision became blurred. And still Laura
went on sitting at the other table, putting in a question now and again, while
the active sister talked. The waiter appeared with the scampi, and a companion
beside him to serve John's own order, which was totally unrecognisable, heaped
with a livid sauce.

"The signora does not come?" enquired the first waiter, and John shook his
head grimly, pointing an unsteady finger across the room.

"Tell the signora," he said carefully, "her scampi will get cold."

He stared down at the offering placed before him, and prodded it delicately
with a fork. The pallid sauce dissolved, revealing two enormous slices, rounds,
of what appeared to be boiled pork, bedecked with garlic. He forked a portion
to his mouth and chewed, and yes, it was pork, steamy, rich, the spicy sauce having turned it curiously sweet. He laid down his fork, pushing the plate away, and
became aware of Laura, returning across the room and sitting beside him. She
did not say anything, which was just as well, he thought, because he was too
near nausea to answer. It wasn't just the drink, but reaction from the whole
nightmare day. She began to eat her scampi, still not uttering. She did not seem
to notice he was not eating. The waiter, hovering at his elbow, anxious, seemed
aware that John's choice was somehow an error, and discreetly removed the
plate. "Bring me a green salad," murmured John, and even then Laura did not
register surprise, or, as she might have done in more normal circumstances, accuse him of having had too much to drink. Finally, when she had finished her
scampi and was sipping her wine, which John had waved away, to nibble at his
salad in small mouthfuls like a sick rabbit, she began to speak.

"Darling," she said, "I know you won't believe it, and it's rather frightening
in a way, but after they left the restaurant in Torcello the sisters went to the
cathedral, as we did, although we didn't see them in that crowd, and the blind
one had another vision. She said Christine was trying to tell her something

about us, that we should be in danger if we stayed in Venice. Christine wanted us to go away as soon possible."

So that's it, he thought. They think they can run our lives for us. This is to be our problem from henceforth. Do we eat? Do we get up? Do we go to bed? We must get in touch with the twin sisters. They will direct us.

"Well?" she said. "Why don't you say something?"

"Because," he answered, "you are perfectly right, I don't believe it. Quite frankly, I judge your old sisters as being a couple of freaks, if nothing else. They're obviously unbalanced, and I'm sorry if this hurts you, but the fact is they've found a sucker in you."

"You're being unfair," said Laura. "They are genuine, I know it. I just know it. They were completely sincere in what they said."

"All right. Granted. They're sincere. But that doesn't make them well-balanced. Honestly darling, you meet that old girl for ten minutes in a loo, she tells you she sees Christine sitting beside us—well, anyone with a gift for telepathy could read your unconscious mind in an instant—and then, pleased with her success, as any old psychic expert would be, she flings a further mood of ecstasy and wants to boot us out of Venice. Well, I'm sorry, but to hell with it."

The room was no longer reeling. Anger had sobered him. If it would not put Laura to shame he would get up and cross to their table, and tell the old fools where they got off.

"I knew you would take it like this," said Laura unhappily. "I told them you would. They said not to worry. As long as we left Venice tomorrow everything would come all right."

"Oh, for God's sake," said John. He changed his mind, and poured himself a glass of wine."

"After all," Laura went on, "we have really seen the cream of Venice. I don't mind going on somewhere else. And if we stayed—I know it sounds silly, but I should have a nasty nagging sort of feeling inside me, and I should keep thinking of darling Christine being unhappy and trying to tell us to go."

"Right," said John with ominous calm, "that settles it. Go we will. I suggest we clear off to the hotel straight away and warn the reception we're leaving in the morning. Have you had enough to eat?"

"Oh, dear," sighed Laura, "don't take it like that. Look, why not come over and meet them, and then they can explain about the vision to you? Perhaps you would take it seriously then. Especially as you are the one it most concerns. Christine is more worried over you than me. And the extraordinary thing is that the blind sister says you're psychic and don't know it. You are somehow *en rapport* with the unknown, and I'm not."

"Well, that's final," said John. "I'm psychic, am I? Fine. My psychic intuition tells me to get out of this restaurant now, at once, and we can decide what we do about leaving Venice when we are back at the hotel."

He signalled for the waiter for the bill and they waited for it, not speaking to each other, Laura unhappy, fiddling with her bag, while John, glancing furtively at the twins' table, noticed that they were tucking into plates piled high with spaghetti, in very un-psychic fashion. The bill disposed of, John pushed back his chair.

"Right. Are you ready?" he asked.

"I'm going to say goodbye to them first," said Laura, her mouth set sulkily, reminding him instantly, with a pang, of their poor lost child.

"Just as you like," he replied, and walked ahead of her out of the restaurant, without a backward glance.

The soft humidity of the evening, so pleasant to walk about in earlier, had turned to rain. The strolling tourists had melted away. One or two people hurried by under umbrellas. This is what the inhabitants who live here see, he thought. This is the true life. Empty streets by night, and the dank stillness of a stagnant canal beneath shuttered houses. The rest is a bright façade put on for show, glittering by sunlight.

Laura joined him and they walked away together in silence, and emerging presently behind the ducal palace came out into the Piazza San Marco. The rain was heavy now, and they sought shelter with the few remaining stragglers under the colonnades. The orchestras had packed up for the evening. The tables were bare. Chairs had been turned upside down.

The experts are right, he thought. Venice is sinking. The whole city is slowly dying. One day the tourists will travel here by boat to peer down into the waters, and they will see pillars and columns and marble far, far beneath them, slime and mud uncovering for brief moments a lost underworld of stone. Their heels made a ringing sound on the pavement and the rain splashed from the gutterings above. A fine ending to an evening that had started with brave hope, with innocence.

When they came to their hotel Laura made straight for the lift, and John turned to the desk to ask the night-porter for the key. The man handed him a telegram at the same time. John stared at it a moment. Laura was already in the lift. Then he opened the envelope and read the message. It was from the head-master of Johnnie's preparatory school.

JOHNNIE UNDER OBSERVATION SUSPECTED APPENDICI-
TIS IN CITY HOSPITAL HERE. NO CAUSE FOR ALARM BUT
SURGEON THOUGHT WISE ADVISE YOU.
                                            CHARLES HILL

He read the message twice, then walked slowly towards the lift where Laura was waiting for him. He gave her the telegram. "This came when we were out," he said. "Not awfully good news." He pressed the lift button as she read the telegram. The lift stopped at the second floor, and they got out.

"Well, this decides it, doesn't it?" she said. "Here is the proof. We have to leave Venice because we're going home. It's Johnnie who's in danger, not us. This is what Christine was trying to tell the twins."

The first thing John did the following morning was to put a call through to the headmaster at the preparatory school. Then he gave notice of their departure to the reception manager, and they packed while they waited for the call. Neither of them referred to the events of the preceding day, it was not necessary. John knew the arrival of the telegram and the foreboding of danger from the sisters was coincidence, nothing more, but it was pointless to start an argument about it. Laura was convinced otherwise, but intuitively she knew it was best to keep her feelings to herself. During breakfast they discussed ways and means of getting home. It should be possible to get themselves, and the car, on to the special car train that ran from Milan through to Calais, since it was early in the season. In any event, the headmaster had said there was no urgency.

The call from England came while John was in the bathroom. Laura answered it. He came into the bedroom a few minutes later. She was still speaking, but he could tell from the expression in her eyes that she was anxious.

"It's Mrs Hill," she said. "Mr Hill is in class. She says they reported from the hospital that Johnnie had a restless night and the surgeon may have to operate, but he doesn't want to unless it's absolutely necessary. They've taken X-rays and the appendix is in a tricky position, it's not awfully straightforward."

"Here, give it to me," he said.

The soothing but slightly guarded voice of the headmaster's wife came down the receiver. "I'm so sorry this may spoil your plans," she said, "but both Charles and I felt you ought to be told, and that you might feel rather easier if you were on the spot. Johnnie is very plucky, but of course he has some fever. That isn't unusual, the surgeon says, in the circumstances. Sometimes an appendix can get displaced, it appears, and this makes it more complicated. He's going to decide about operating this evening."

"Yes, of course, we quite understand," said John.

"Please do tell your wife not to worry too much," she went on. "The hospital is excellent, a very nice staff, and we have every confidence in the surgeon."

"Yes," said John, "yes," and then broke off because Laura was making gestures beside him.

"If we can't get the car on the train, I can fly," she said. "They're sure to be able to find me a seat on a 'plane. Then at least one of us would be there this evening."

He nodded agreement. "Thank you so much, Mrs Hill," he said, "we'll manage to get back all right. Yes, I'm sure Johnnie is in good hands. Thank your husband for us. Goodbye."

He replaced the receiver and looked round him at the tumbled beds, suitcases on the floor, tissue-paper strewn. Baskets, maps, books, coats, everything they had brought with them in the car. "Oh God," he said, "what a bloody mess. All this junk." The telephone rang again. It was the hall porter to say he had succeeded in booking a sleeper for them both, and a place for the car, on the following night.

"Look," said Laura, who had seized the telephone, "could you book one seat on the midday 'plane from Venice to London today, for me? It's imperative one of us gets home this evening. My husband could follow with the car tomorrow."

"Here, hang on," interrupted John. "No need for panic stations. Surely twenty-four hours wouldn't make all that difference?"

Anxiety had drained the colour from her face. She turned to him, distraught.

"It mightn't to you, but it does to me," she said. "I've lost one child, I'm not going to lose another."

"All right, darling, all right . . ." He put his hand out to her but she brushed it off, impatiently, and continued giving directions to the porter. He turned back to his packing. No use saying anything. Better for it to be as she wished. They could, of course, both go by air, and then when all was well, and Johnnie better, he could come back and fetch the car, driving home through France as they had come. Rather a sweat, though, and the hell of an expense. Bad enough Laura going by air and himself with the car on the train from Milan.

"We could, if you like, both fly," he began tentatively, explaining the sudden idea, but she would have none of it. "That really *would* be absurd," she said impatiently. "As long as I'm there this evening, and you follow by train, it's all that matters. Besides, we shall need the car, going backwards and forwards to the hospital. And our luggage. We couldn't go off and just leave all this here."

No, he saw her point. A silly idea. It was only—well, he was as worried about Johnnie as she was, though he wasn't going to say so.

"I'm going downstairs to stand over the porter," said Laura. "They always make more effort if one is actually on the spot. Everything I want tonight is packed. I shall only need my overnight case. You can bring everything else in the car." She hadn't been out of the bedroom five minutes before the telephone rang. It was Laura. "Darling," she said, "it couldn't have worked out better. The porter has got me on a charter flight that leaves Venice in less than hour. A special motor-launch takes the party direct from San Marco in about ten minutes. Some passenger on the charter flight cancelled. I shall be at Gatwick in less than four hours."

"I'll be down right away," he told her.

He joined her by the reception desk. She no longer looked anxious and drawn, but full of purpose. She was on her way. He kept wishing they were going together. He couldn't bear to stay on in Venice after she had gone, but the thought of driving to Milan, spending a dreary night in a hotel there alone, the endless dragging day which would follow, and the long hours in the train the next night, filled him with intolerable depression, quite apart from the anxiety about Johnnie. They walked along to the San Marco landing-stage, the Molo bright and glittering after the rain, a little breeze blowing, the postcards and scarves and tourist souvenirs fluttering on the stalls, the tourists themselves out in force, strolling, contented, the happy day before them.

"I'll ring you tonight from Milan," he told her. "The Hills will give you a bed, I suppose. And if you're at the hospital they'll let me have the latest news. That must be your charter party. You're welcome to them!"

The passengers descending from the landing-stage down into the waiting launch were carrying hand-luggage with Union Jack tags upon them. They were mostly middle-aged, with what appeared to be two Methodist ministers in charge. One of them advanced towards Laura, holding out his hand, showing a gleaming row of dentures when he smiled. "You must be the lady joining us for the homeward flight," he said. "Welcome aboard, and to the Union of Fellowship. We are all delighted to make your acquaintance. Sorry we hadn't a seat for hubby too."

Laura turned swiftly and kissed John, a tremor at the corner of her mouth betraying inward laughter. "Do you think they'll break into hymns?" she whispered. "Take care of yourself hubby. Call me tonight."

The pilot sounded a curious little toot upon his horn, and in a moment Laura had climbed down the steps into the launch and was standing amongst the crowd of passengers, waving her hand, her scarlet coat a gay patch of colour amongst the more solemn suiting of her companions. The launch tooted again and moved away from the landing-stage, and he stood there watching it, a sense of immense loss filling his heart. Then he turned and walked away, back to the hotel, the bright day all about him desolate, unseen.

There was nothing, he thought, as he looked about him presently in the hotel bedroom, so melancholy as a vacated room, especially when the recent signs of occupation were still visible about him. Laura's suitcases on the bed, a second one she had left behind. Traces of powder on the dressing-table. A tissue, with a lipstick smear, thrown in the waste-paper basket. Even an old toothpaste tube squeezed dry, lying on the glass shelf above the wash-basin. Sounds of the heedless traffic on the Grand Canal came as always from the open window, but Laura wasn't there any more to listen to it, or to watch from the small balcony. The pleasure had gone. Feeling had gone.

John finished packing, and leaving all the baggage ready to be collected he went downstairs to pay the bill. The reception clerk was welcoming new arrivals. People were sitting on the terrace overlooking the Grand Canal reading newspapers, the pleasant day waiting to be planned.

John decided to have an early lunch, here on the hotel terrace, on familiar ground, and then have the porter carry the baggage to one of the ferries that steamed direct between San Marco and the Porta Roma, where the car was garaged. The fiasco meal of the night before had left him empty, and he was ready for the trolley of hors d'œuvres when they brought it to him, around midday. Even here, though, there was change. The head-waiter, their especial friend, was off-duty, and the table where they usually sat was occupied by new arrivals, a honeymoon couple, he told himself sourly, observing the gaiety, the smiles, while he had been shown to a small single table behind a tub of flowers.

"She's airborne now," John thought, "she's on her way," and he tried to picture Laura seated between the Methodist ministers, telling them, no doubt, about Johnnie ill in hospital, and heaven knows what else besides. Well, the twin sisters anyway could rest in psychic peace. Their wishes would have been fulfilled.

Lunch over, there was no point in lingering with a cup of coffee on the terrace. His desire was to get away as soon as possible, fetch the car, and be en route for Milan. He made his farewells at the reception desk, and, escorted by a porter who had piled his baggage on to a wheeled trolley, made his way once more to the landing-stage of San Marco. As he stepped on to the steam-ferry, his luggage heaped beside him, a crowd of jostling people all about him, he had one momentary pang to be leaving Venice. When, if ever, he wondered, would they come again? Next year . . . in three years . . . Glimpsed first on honeymoon, nearly ten years ago, and then a second visit, *en passant*, before a cruise, and now this last abortive ten days that had ended so abruptly.

The water glittered in the sunshine, buildings shone, tourists in dark glasses paraded up and down the rapidly receding Molo, already the terrace of their hotel was out of sight as the ferry churned its way up the Grand Canal. So many impressions to seize and hold, familiar loved façades, balconies, windows, water lapping the cellar steps of decaying palaces, the little red house where d'Annunzio lived, with its garden—our house, Laura called it, pretending it was theirs—and too soon the ferry would be turning left on the direct route to the Piazzale Roma, so missing the best of the Canal, the Rialto, the further palaces.

Another ferry was heading downstream to pass them, filled with passengers, and for a brief foolish moment he wished he could change places, be amongst the happy tourists bound for Venice and all he had left behind him. Then he saw her. Laura, in her scarlet coat, the twin sisters by her side, the active sister with her hand on Laura's arm, talking earnestly, and Laura herself, her hair blowing in the wind, gesticulating, on her face a look of distress. He stared, astounded, too astonished to shout, to wave, and anyway they would never have heard or seen him, for his own ferry had already passed and was heading in the opposite direction.

What the hell had happened? There must have been a hold-up with the charter flight and it had never taken off, but in that case why had Laura not telephoned him at the hotel? And what were those damned sisters doing? Had she run into them at the airport? Was it coincidence? And why did she look so anxious? He could think of no explanation. Perhaps the flight had been cancelled. Laura, of course, would go straight to the hotel, expecting to find him there, intending, doubtless, to drive with him after all to Milan and take the train the following night. What a blasted mix-up. The only thing to do was to telephone the hotel immediately his ferry reached the Piazzale Roma and tell her to wait—he would return and fetch her. As for the damned interfering sisters, they could get stuffed.

The usual stampede ensued when the ferry arrived at the landing-stage. He had to find a porter to collect his baggage, and then wait while he discovered a telephone. The fiddling with change, the hunt for the number, delayed him still more. He succeeded at last in getting through, and luckily the reception clerk he knew was still at the desk.

"Look, there's been some frightful muddle," he began, and explained how Laura was even now on her way back to the hotel—he had seen her with two friends on one of the ferry-services. Would the reception clerk explain and tell her to wait? He would be back by the next available service to collect her. "In any event, detain her," he said. "I'll be as quick as I can." The reception clerk understood perfectly, and John rang off.

Thank heaven Laura hadn't turned up before he had put through his call, or they would have told her he was on his way to Milan. The porter was still waiting with the baggage, and it seemed simplest to walk with him to the garage, hand everything over to the chap in charge of the office there and ask him to keep it for an hour, when he would be returning with his wife to pick up the car. Then he went back to the landing-station to await the next ferry to Venice. The minutes dragged, and he kept wondering all the time what had gone wrong at the airport and why in heaven's name Laura hadn't telephoned. No use conjecturing. She would tell him the whole story at the hotel. One thing was certain: he would not allow Laura and himself to be saddled with the sisters and become involved with their affairs. He could imagine Laura saying that they also had missed a flight, and could they have a lift to Milan?

Finally the ferry chugged alongside the landing-stage and he stepped aboard. What an anti-climax, thrashing back past the familiar sights to which he had bidden a nostalgic farewell such a short while ago! He didn't even look about him this time, he was so intent on reaching his destination. In San Marco there were more people than ever, the afternoon crowds walking shoulder to shoulder, every one of them on pleasure bent.

He came to the hotel and pushed his way through the swing door, expecting to see Laura, and possibly the sisters, waiting in the lounge to the left of the entrance. She was not there. He went to the desk. The reception clerk he had spoken to on the telephone was standing there, talking to the manager.

"Has my wife arrived?" John asked.

"No, sir, not yet."

"What an extraordinary thing. Are you sure?"

"Absolutely certain, sir. I have been here ever since you telephoned me at a quarter to two. I have not left the desk."

"I just don't understand it. She was on one of the vaporettos passing the Accademia. She would have landed at San Marco about five minutes later and come on here."

The clerk seemed nonplussed. "I don't know what to say. The signora was with friends, did you say?"

"Yes. Well, acquaintances. Two ladies we had met at Torcello yesterday. I was astonished to see her with them on the vaporetto, and of course I assumed that the flight had been cancelled, and she had somehow met up with them at the airport and decided to return here with them, to catch me before I left."

Oh hell, what was Laura doing? It was after three. A matter of moments from San Marco landing-stage to the hotel.

"Perhaps the signora went with her friends to their hotel instead. Do you know where they are staying?"

"No," said John, "I haven't the slightest idea. What's more, I don't even know the names of the two ladies. They were sisters, twins, in fact—looked exactly alike. But anyway, why go to their hotel and not here?"

The swing-door opened but it wasn't Laura. Two people staying in the hotel.

The manager broke into the conversation. "I tell you what I will do," he said. "I will telephone the airport and check about the flight. Then at least we will get somewhere." He smiled apologetically. It was not usual for arrangements to go wrong.

"Yes, do that," said John. "We may as well know what happened there."

He lit a cigarette and began to pace up and down the entrance hall. What a bloody mix-up. And how unlike Laura, who knew he would be setting off for Milan directly after lunch—indeed, for all she knew he might have gone before. But surely, in that case, she would have telephoned at once, on arrival at the airport, had the flight been cancelled? The manager was ages telephoning, he had to be put through on some other line, and his Italian was too rapid for John to follow the conversation. Finally he replaced the receiver.

"It is more mysterious than ever, sir," he said. "The charter flight was not delayed, it took off on schedule with a full complement of passengers. As far as they could tell me, there was no hitch. The signora must simply have changed her mind." His smile was more apologetic than ever.

"Changed her mind," John repeated. "But why on earth should she do that? She was so anxious to be home tonight."

The manager shrugged. "You know how ladies can be, sir," he said. "Your wife may have thought that after all she would prefer to take the train to Milan with you. I do assure you, though, that the charter party was most respectable, and it was a Caravelle aircraft, perfectly safe."

"Yes, yes," said John impatiently. "I don't blame your arrangements in the slightest. I just can't understand what induced her to change her mind, unless it was meeting with these two ladies."

The manager was silent. He could not think of anything to say. The reception clerk was equally concerned. "Is it possible," he ventured, "that you made a mistake, and it was not the signora that you saw on the vaporetto?"

"Oh no," replied John, "it was my wife, I assure you. She was wearing her red coat, she was hatless, just as she left here. I saw her plainly as I can see you. I would swear to it in a court of law."

"It is unfortunate," said the manager, "that we do not know the name of the two ladies, or the hotel where they were staying. You say you met these ladies at Torcello yesterday?"

"Yes . . . but only briefly. They weren't staying there. At least, I am certain they were not. We saw them at dinner in Venice later, as it happens."

"Excuse me . . ." Guests were arriving with luggage to check in, the clerk was obliged to attend to them. John turned in desperation to the manager. "Do you think it would be any good telephoning the hotel in Torcello in case the people there knew the name of the ladies, or where they were staying in Venice?"

"We can try," replied the manager. "It is a small hope, but we can try."

John resumed his anxious pacing, all the while watching the swing-door, hoping, praying, that he would catch sight of the red coat and Laura would enter. Once again there followed what seemed an interminable telephone conversation between the manager and someone at the hotel in Torcello.

"Tell them two sisters," said John, "two elderly ladies dressed in grey, both exactly alike. One lady was blind," he added. The manager nodded. He was obviously giving a detailed description. Yet when he hung up he shook his head. "The manager at Torcello says he remembers the two ladies well," he told John, "but they were only there for lunch. He never learnt their names."

"Well, that's that. There's nothing to do now but wait."

John lit his third cigarette and went out on to the terrace, to resume his pacing there. He stared out across the canal, searching the heads of the people on passing steamers, motor-boats, even drifting gondolas. The minutes ticked by on his watch, and there was no sign of Laura. A terrible foreboding nagged at him that somehow this was prearranged, that Laura had never intended to catch the aircraft, that last night in the restaurant she had made an assignation with the sisters. Oh God, he thought, that's impossible, I'm going paranoiac . . . Yet why, why? No, more likely the encounter at the airport was fortuitous, and for some incredible reason they had persuaded Laura not to board the aircraft, even prevented her from doing so, trotting out one of their psychic visions, that the aircraft would crash, that she must return with them to Venice. And Laura, in her sensitive state, felt they must be right, swallowed it all without question.

But granted all these possibilities, why had she not come to the hotel? What was she doing? Four o'clock, half-past four, the sun no longer dappling the water. He went back to the reception desk.

"I just can't hang around," he said. "Even if she does turn up, we shall never make Milan this evening. I might see her walking with these ladies, in the Piazza San Marco, anywhere. If she arrives while I'm out, will you explain?"

The clerk was full of concern. "Indeed, yes," he said. "It is very worrying for you, sir. Would it perhaps be prudent if we booked you in here tonight?"

John gestured, helplessly. "Perhaps, yes, I don't know. Maybe . . ."

He went out of the swing-door and began to walk towards the Piazza San Marco. He looked into every shop up and down the colonnades, crossed the piazza a dozen times, threaded his way between the tables in front of Florian's, in front of Quadri's, knowing that Laura's red coat and the distinctive appearance of the twin sisters could easily be spotted, even amongst this milling crowd, but there was no sign of them. He joined the crowd of shoppers in the Merceria, shoulder to shoulder with idlers, thrusters, window-gazers, knowing instinctively that it was useless, they wouldn't be here. Why should Laura have deliberately missed her flight to return to Venice for such a purpose? And even if she had done so, for some reason beyond his imagining, she would surely have come first to the hotel to find him.

The only thing left to him was to try to track down the sisters. Their hotel could be anywhere amongst the hundreds of hotels and pensions scattered through Venice, or even across the other side at the Zattere, or further again on the Giudecca. These last possibilities seemed remote. More likely they were staying in a small hotel or pension somewhere near San Zaccaria handy to the restaurant where they had dined last night. The blind one would surely not go far afield in the evening. He had been a fool not to have thought of this before, and he turned back and walked quickly away from the brightly lighted shopping district towards the narrower, more cramped quarter where they had dined last evening. He found the restaurant without difficulty, but they were not yet open for dinner, and the waiter preparing tables was not the one who had served them. John asked to see the *padrone*, and the waiter disappeared to the back regions, returning after a moment or two with the somewhat dishevelled-looking proprietor in shirt-sleeves, caught in a slack moment, not in full tenue.

"I had dinner here last night," John explained. "There were two ladies sitting at that table there in the corner." He pointed to it.

"You wish to book that table for this evening?" asked the proprietor.

"No," said John. "No, there were two ladies there last night, two sisters, due sorelle, twins, gemelle"—what was the right word for twins?—"Do you remember? Two ladies, sorelle vecchie . . ."

"Ah," said the man, "si, si, signore, la povera signorina." He put his hands to his eyes to feign blindness. "Yes, I remember."

"Do you know their names?" asked John. "Where they were staying? I am very anxious to trace them."

The proprietor spread out his hands in a gesture of regret. "I am ver' sorry, signore, I do not know the names of the signorine, they have been here once, twice, perhaps for dinner, they do not say where they were staying. Perhaps if you come again tonight they might be here? Would you like to book a table?"

He pointed around him, suggesting a whole choice of tables that might appeal to a prospective diner, but John shook his head.

"Thank you, no. I may be dining elsewhere. I am sorry to have troubled you. If the signorine should come . . ." he paused, "possibly I may return later," he added. "I am not sure."

The proprietor bowed, and walked with him to the entrance. "In Venice the whole world meets," he said smiling. "It is possible the signorine will find his friends tonight. Arrivederci, signore."

Friends? John walked out into the street. More likely kidnappers . . . Anxiety had turned to fear, to panic. Something had gone terribly wrong. Those women had got hold of Laura, played upon her suggestibility, induced her to go with them, either to their hotel or elsewhere. Should he find the Consulate? Where was it? What would he say when he got there? He began walking without purpose, finding himself, as they had done the night before, in streets he did not know, and suddenly came upon a tall building with the word "Questura" above it. This is it, he thought. I don't care, something has happened, I'm going inside. There were a number of police in uniform coming and going, the place at any rate was active, and, addressing himself to one of them behind a glass partition, he asked if there was anyone who spoke English. The man pointed to a flight of stairs and John went up, entering a door on the right where he saw that another couple were sitting, waiting, and with relief he recognised them as fellow-countrymen, tourists, obviously a man and his wife, in some sort of predicament.

"Come and sit down," said the man. "We've waited half-an-hour but they can't be much longer. What a country! They wouldn't leave us like this at home."

John took the proffered cigarette and found a chair beside them.

"What's your trouble?" he asked.

"My wife had her handbag pinched in one of those shops in the Merceria," said the man. "She simply put it down one moment to look at something, and you'd hardly credit it, the next moment it had gone. I say it was a sneak thief, she insists it was the girl behind the counter. But who's to say? These Ities are all alike. Anyway, I'm certain we shan't get it back. What have you lost?"

"Suitcase stolen," John lied rapidly. "Had some important papers in it."

How could he say he had lost his wife? He couldn't even begin . . .

The man nodded in sympathy. "As I said, these Ities are all alike. Old Musso knew how to deal with them. Too many Communists around these days.

The trouble is, they're not going to bother with our troubles much, not with this murderer at large. They're all out looking for him."

"Murderer? What murderer?" asked John.

"Don't tell me you've not heard about it?" The man stared at him in surprise. "Venice has talked of nothing else. It's been in all the papers, on the radio, and even in the English papers. A grizzly business. One woman found with her throat slit last week—a tourist too—and some old chap discovered with the same sort of knife wound this morning. They seem to think it must be a maniac, because there doesn't seem to be any motive. Nasty thing to happen in Venice in the tourist season."

"My wife and I never bother with the newspapers when we're on holiday," said John. "And we're neither of us much given to gossip in the hotel."

"Very wise of you," laughed the man. "It might have spoilt your holiday, especially if your wife is nervous. Oh well, we're off tomorrow anyway. Can't say we mind, do we, dear?" He turned to his wife. "Venice has gone downhill since we were here last. And now this loss of the handbag really is the limit."

The door of the inner room opened, and a senior police officer asked John's companion and his wife to pass through.

"I bet we don't get any satisfaction," murmured the tourist, winking at John, and he and his wife went into the inner room. The door closed behind them. John stubbed out his cigarette and lighted another. A strange feeling of unreality possessed him. He asked himself what he was doing here, what was the use of it? Laura was no longer in Venice but had disappeared, perhaps forever, with those diabolical sisters. She would never be traced. And just as the two of them had made up a fantastic story about the twins, when they first spotted them in Torcello, so, with nightmare logic, the fiction would have basis in fact; the women were in reality disguised crooks, men with criminal intent who lured unsuspecting persons to some appalling fate. They might even be the murderers for whom the police sought. Who would ever suspect two elderly women of respectable appearance, living quietly in some second-rate pension or hotel? He stubbed out his cigarette, unfinished.

"This," he thought, "is really the start of paranoia. This is the way people go off their heads." He glanced at his watch. It was half-past six. Better pack this in, this futile quest here in police headquarters, and keep to the single link of sanity remaining. Return to the hotel, put a call through to the prep school in England, and ask about the latest news of Johnnie. He had not thought about poor Johnnie since sighting Laura on the vaporetto.

Too late, though. The inner door opened, the couple were ushered out.

"Usual clap-trap," said the husband sotto voce to John. "They'll do what they can. Not much hope. So many foreigners in Venice, all of 'em thieves! The locals all above reproach. Wouldn't pay 'em to steal from customers. Well, I wish you better luck."

He nodded, his wife smiled and bowed, and they had gone. John followed the police officer into the inner room.

Formalities began. Name, address, passport. Length of stay in Venice, etc., etc. Then the questions, and John, the sweat beginning to appear on his forehead, launched into his interminable story. The first encounter with the sisters, the meeting at the restaurant, Laura's state of suggestibility because of the death of their child, the telegram about Johnnie, the decision to take the chartered flight, her departure, and her sudden inexplicable return. When he had finished he felt as exhausted as if he had driven three hundred miles non-stop after a severe bout of 'flu. His interrogator spoke excellent English with a strong Italian accent.

"You say," he began, "that your wife was suffering the after-effects of shock. This had been noticeable during your stay here in Venice?"

"Well, yes," John replied, "she had really been quite ill. The holiday didn't seem to be doing her much good. It was only when she met these two women at Torcello yesterday that her mood changed. The strain seemed to have gone. She was ready, I suppose, to snatch at every straw, and this belief that our little girl was watching over her had somehow restored her to what appeared normality."

"It would be natural," said the police officer, "in the circumstances. But no doubt the telegram last night was a further shock to you both?"

"Indeed, yes. That was the reason we decided to return home."

"No argument between you? No difference of opinion?"

"None. We were in complete agreement. My one regret was that I could not go with my wife on this charter flight."

The police officer nodded. "It could well be that your wife had a sudden attack of amnesia, and meeting the two ladies served as a link, she clung to them for support. You have described them with great accuracy, and I think they should not be too difficult to trace. Meanwhile, I suggest you should return to your hotel, and we will get in touch with you as soon as we have news."

At least, John thought, they believed his story. They did not consider him a crank who had made the whole thing up and was merely wasting their time.

"You appreciate," he said, "I am extremely anxious. These women may have some criminal design upon my wife. One has heard of such things . . ."

The police officer smiled for the first time. "Please don't concern yourself," he said. "I am sure there will be some satisfactory explanation."

All very well, thought John, but in heaven's name, what?

"I'm sorry," he said, "to have taken up so much of your time. Especially as I gather the police have their hands full hunting down a murderer who is still at large."

He spoke deliberately. No harm in letting the fellow know that for all any of them could tell there might be some connection between Laura's disappearance and this other hideous affair.

"Ah, that," said the police officer, rising to his feet. "We hope to have the murderer under lock and key very soon."

His tone of confidence was reassuring. Murderers, missing wives, lost handbags were all under control. They shook hands, and John was ushered out of the door and so downstairs. Perhaps, he thought, as he walked slowly back to the hotel, the fellow was right. Laura had suffered a sudden attack of amnesia, and the sisters happened to be at the airport and had brought her back to Venice, to their own hotel, because Laura couldn't remember where she and John had been staying. Perhaps they were even now trying to track down his hotel. Anyway, he could do nothing more. The police had everything in hand,

and, please God, would come up with the solution. All he wanted to do right now was to collapse upon a bed with a stiff whisky, and then put through a call to Johnnie's school.

The page took him up in the lift to a modest room on the fourth floor at the rear of the hotel. Bare, impersonal, the shutters closed, with a smell of cooking wafting up from a courtyard down below.

"Ask them to send me up a double whisky, will you?" he said to the boy. "And a ginger-ale," and when he was alone he plunged his face under the cold tap in the wash-basin, relieved to find that the minute portion of visitor's soap afforded some measure of comfort. He flung off his shoes, hung his coat over the back of a chair and threw himself down on the bed. Somebody's radio was blasting forth an old popular song, now several seasons out-of-date, that had been one of Laura's favourites a couple of years ago. "I love you, Baby . . ." He reached for the telephone, and asked the exchange to put through the call to England. Then he closed his eyes, and all the while the insistent voice persisted, "I love you, Baby . . . I can't get you out of my mind."

Presently there was a tap at the door. It was the waiter with his drink. Too little ice, such meagre comfort, but what desperate need. He gulped it down without the ginger-ale, and in a few moments the ever-nagging pain was eased, numbed, bringing, if only momentarily, a sense of calm. The telephone rang, and now, he thought, bracing himself for ultimate disaster, the final shock, Johnnie probably dying, or already dead. In which case nothing remained. Let Venice be engulfed . . .

The exchange told him that the connection had been made, and in a moment he heard the voice of Mrs Hill at the other end of the line. They must have warned her that the call came from Venice, for she knew instantly who was speaking.

"Hullo?" she said. "Oh, I am so glad you rang. All is well. Johnnie has had his operation, the surgeon decided to do it at midday rather than wait, and it was completely successful. Johnnie is going to be all right. So you don't have to worry any more, and will have a peaceful night."

"Thank God," he answered.

"I know," she said, "we are all so relieved. Now I'll get off the line and you can speak to your wife."

John sat up on the bed, stunned. What the hell did she mean? Then he heard Laura's voice, cool and clear.

"Darling? Darling, are you there?"

He could not answer. He felt the hand holding the receiver go clammy cold with sweat. "I'm here," he whispered.

"It's not a very good line," she said, "but never mind. As Mrs Hill told you, all is well. Such a nice surgeon, and a very sweet Sister on Johnnie's floor, and I really am happy about the way it's turned out. I came straight down here after landing at Gatwick—the flight O.K., by the way, but such a funny crowd, it'll make you hysterical when I tell you about them—and I went to the hospital, and Johnnie was coming round. Very dopey, of course, but so pleased to see me. And the Hills are being wonderful, I've got their spare-room, and it's only a short taxi-drive into the town and the hospital. I shall go to bed as soon as we've had dinner, because I'm a bit fagged, what with the flight and the anxiety. How was the drive to Milan? And where are you staying?"

John did not recognise the voice that answered as his own. It was the automatic response of some computer.

"I'm not in Milan," he said. "I'm still in Venice."

"Still in Venice? What on earth for? Wouldn't the car start?"

"I can't explain," he said. "There was a stupid sort of mix-up . . ."

He felt suddenly so exhausted that he nearly dropped the receiver, and, shame upon shame, he could feel tears pricking behind his eyes.

"What sort of mix-up?" Her voice was suspicious, almost hostile. "You weren't in a crash?"

"No . . . no . . . nothing like that."

A moment's silence, and then she said, "Your voice sounds very slurred. Don't tell me you went and got pissed."

Oh Christ . . . If she only knew! He was probably going to pass out any moment, but not from the whisky.

"I thought," he said slowly, "I thought I saw you, in a vaporetto, with those two sisters."

What was the point of going on? It was hopeless trying to explain.

"How could you have seen me with the sisters?" she said. "You knew I'd gone to the airport. Really, darling, you are an idiot. You seem to have got those two poor old dears on the brain. I hope you didn't say anything to Mrs Hill just now."

"No."

"Well, what are you going to do? You'll catch the train at Milan tomorrow, won't you?"

"Yes, of course," he told her.

"I still don't understand what kept you in Venice," she said. "It all sounds a bit odd to me. However . . . thank God Johnnie is going to be all right and I'm here."

"Yes," he said, "yes."

He could hear the distant boom-boom sound of a gong from the headmaster's hall.

"You had better go," he said. "My regards to the Hills, and my love to Johnnie."

"Well, take care of yourself, darling, and for goodness' sake don't miss the train tomorrow, and drive carefully."

The telephone clicked and she had gone. He poured the remaining drop of whisky into his empty glass, and sousing it with ginger-ale drank it down at a gulp. He got up, and crossing the room threw open the shutters and leant out of the window. He felt light-headed. His sense of relief, enormous, overwhelming, was somehow tempered with a curious feeling of unreality, almost as though the voice speaking from England had not been Laura's after all but a fake, and she was still in Venice, hidden in some furtive pension with the two sisters.

The point was, he *had* seen all three of them on the vaporetto. It was not another woman in a red coat. The women *had* been there, with Laura. So what was the explanation? That he was going off his head? Or something more sinister?

The sisters, possessing psychic powers of formidable strength, had seen him as their two ferries had passed, and in some inexplicable fashion had made him believe Laura was with them. But why, and to what end? No, it didn't make sense. The only explanation was that he had been mistaken, the whole episode an hallucination. In which case he needed psychoanalysis, just as Johnnie had needed a surgeon.

And what did he do now? Go downstairs and tell the management he had been at fault and had just spoken to his wife, who had arrived in England safe and sound from her charter-flight? He put on his shoes and ran his fingers through his hair. He glanced at his watch. It was ten minutes to eight. If he nipped into the bar and had a quick drink it would be easier to face the manager and admit what had happened. Then, perhaps, they would get in touch with the police. Profuse apologies all round for putting everyone to enormous trouble.

He made his way to the ground floor and went straight to the bar, feeling self-conscious, a marked man, half-imagining everyone would look at him, thinking, "There's the fellow with the missing wife." Luckily the bar was full and there wasn't a face he knew. Even the chap behind the bar was an underling who hadn't served him before. He downed his whisky and glanced over his shoulder to the reception hall. The desk was momentarily empty. He could see the manager's back framed in the doorway of an inner room, talking to someone within. On impulse, coward-like, he crossed the hall and passed through the swing-door to the street outside.

"I'll have some dinner," he decided, "and then go back and face them. I'll feel more like it once I've some food inside me."

He went to the restaurant nearby where he and Laura had dined once or twice. Nothing mattered any more, because she was safe. The nightmare lay behind him. He could enjoy his dinner, despite her absence, and think of her sitting down with the Hills to a dull, quiet evening, early to bed, and on the following morning going to the hospital to sit with Johnnie. Johnnie was safe, too. No more worries, only the awkward explanations and apologies to the manager at the hotel.

There was a pleasant anonymity sitting down at a corner table alone in the little restaurant, ordering vitello alla Marsala and half a bottle of Merlot. He took his time, enjoying his food but eating in a kind of haze, a sense of unreality still with him, while the conversation of his nearest neighbours had the same soothing effect as background music.

When they rose and left, he saw by the clock on the wall that it was nearly half-past nine. No use delaying matters any further. He drank his coffee, lighted a cigarette and paid his bill. After all, he thought, as he walked back to the hotel, the manager would be greatly relieved to know that all was well.

When he pushed through the swing-door, the first thing he noticed was a man in police uniform, standing talking to the manager at the desk. The reception clerk was there too. They turned as John approached, and the manager's face lighted up with relief.

"Eccolo!" he exclaimed. "I was certain the signore would not be far away. Things are moving, signore. The two ladies have been traced, and they very kindly agreed to accompany the police to the Questura. If you will go there at once, this agente di polizia will escort you."

John flushed. "I have given everyone a lot of trouble," he said. "I meant to tell you before going out to dinner, but you were not at the desk. The fact is that I have contacted my wife. She did make the flight to London after all, and I spoke to her on the telephone. It was all a great mistake."

The manager looked bewildered. "The signora is in London?" he repeated. He broke off, and exchanged a rapid conversation in Italian with the policeman. "It seems that the ladies maintain they did not go out for the day, except for a little shopping in the morning," he said, turning back to John. "Then who was it the signore saw on the vaporetto?"

John shook his head. "A very extraordinary mistake on my part which I still don't understand," he said. "Obviously, I did not see either my wife or the two ladies. I really am extremely sorry."

More rapid conversation in Italian. John noticed the clerk watching him with a curious expression in his eyes. The manager was obviously apologising on John's behalf to the policeman, who looked annoyed and gave tongue to this effect, his voice increasing in volume, to the manager's concern. The whole business had undoubtedly given enormous trouble to a great many people, not least the two unfortunate sisters.

"Look," said John, interrupting the flow, "will you tell the agente I will go with him to headquarters and apologise in person both to the police officer and to the ladies?"

The manager looked relieved. "If the signore would take the trouble," he said. "Naturally, the ladies were much distressed when a policeman interrogated them at their hotel, and they offered to accompany him to the Questura only because they were so distressed about the signora."

John felt more and more uncomfortable. Laura must never learn of this. She would be outraged. He wondered if there were some penalty for giving the police misleading information involving a third party. His error began, in retrospect, to take on criminal proportions.

He crossed the Piazza San Marco, now thronged with after-dinner strollers and spectators at the cafés, all three orchestras going full blast in harmonious rivalry, while his companion kept a discreet two paces to his left and never uttered a word.

They arrived at the police station and mounted the stairs to the same inner room where he had been before. He saw immediately that it was not the officer he knew but another who sat behind the desk, a sallow-faced individual with a sour expression, while the two sisters, obviously upset—the active one in particular—were seated on chairs nearby, some underling in uniform standing behind them. John's escort went at once to the police-officer, speaking in rapid Italian, while John himself, after a moment's hesitation, advanced towards the sisters.

"There has been a terrible mistake," he said. "I don't know how to apologise to you both. It's my fault, mine entirely, the police are not to blame."

The active sister made as though to rise, her mouth twitching nervously, but he restrained her.

"We don't understand," she said, the Scots inflection strong. "We said goodnight to your wife last night at dinner, and we have not seen her since. The police came to our pension more than an hour ago and told us your wife was missing and you had filed a complaint against us. My sister is not very strong. She was considerably disturbed."

"A mistake. A frightful mistake," he repeated.

He turned towards the desk. The police-officer was addressing him, his English very inferior to that of the previous interrogator. He had John's earlier statement on the desk in front of him, and tapped it with a pencil.

"So?" he queried. "This document all lies? You not speaka the truth?"

"I believed it to be true at the time," said John. "I could have sworn in a court of law that I saw my wife with these two ladies on a vaporetto in the Grand Canal this afternoon. Now I realise I was mistaken."

"We have not been near the Grand Canal all day," protested the sister, "not even on foot. We made a few purchases in the Merceria this morning, and remained indoors all afternoon. My sister was a little unwell. I have told the police-officer this a dozen times, and the people at the pension would corroborate our story. He refused to listen."

"And the signora?" rapped the police-officer angrily. "What happen to the signora?"

"The signora, my wife, is safe in England," explained John patiently. "I talked to her on the telephone just after seven. She did join the charter flight from the airport, and is now staying with friends."

"Then who you see on the vaporetto in the red coat?" asked the furious police-officer. "And if not these signorine here, then what signorine?"

"My eyes deceived me," said John, aware that his English was likewise becoming strained. "I think I see my wife and these ladies but no, it was not so. My wife in aircraft, these ladies in pension all the time."

It was like talking stage Chinese. In a moment he would be bowing and putting his hands in his sleeves.

The police-officer raised his eyes to heaven and thumped the table. "So all this work for nothing," he said. "Hotels and pensiones searched for the signorine and a missing signora inglese, when here we have plenty, plenty other things to do. You maka a mistake. You have perhaps too much vino at mezzo giorno and you see hundred signore in red coats in hundred vaporetti." He stood up, rumpling the papers on his desk. "And you, signorine," he said, "you wish to make a complaint against this person?" He was addressing the active sister.

"Oh no," she said, "no, indeed. I quite see it was all a mistake. Our only wish is to return at once to our pension."

The police-officer grunted. Then he pointed at John. "You very lucky man," he said. "These signorine could file complaint against you—very serious matter."

"I'm sure," began John, "I'll do anything in my power . . ."

"Please don't think of it," exclaimed the sister, horrified. "We would not hear of such a thing." It was her turn to apologise to the police-officer. "I hope we need not take up any more of your valuable time," she said.

He waved a hand of dismissal and spoke in Italian to the underling. "This man walk with you to the pension," he said. "Buona sera, signorine," and, ignoring John, he sat down again at his desk.

"I'll come with you," said John. "I want to explain exactly what happened."

They trooped down the stairs and out of the building, the blind sister leaning on her twin's arm, and once outside she turned her sightless eyes to John.

"You saw us," she said, "and your wife too. But not today. You saw us in the future."

Her voice was softer than her sister's, slower, she seemed to have some slight impediment in her speech.

"I don't follow," replied John, bewildered.

He turned to the active sister and she shook her head at him, frowning, and put her finger on her lips.

"Come along, dear," she said to her twin. "You know you're very tired, and I want to get you home." Then, sotto voce to John, "She's psychic. Your wife told you, I believe, but I don't want her to go into a trance here in the street."

God forbid, thought John, and the little procession began to move slowly along the street, away from police headquarters, a canal to the left of them. Progress was slow, because of the blind sister, and there were two bridges. John was completely lost after the first turning, but it couldn't have mattered less. Their police escort was with them, and anyway, the sisters knew where they were going.

"I must explain," said John softly. "My wife would never forgive me if I didn't," and as they walked he went over the whole inexplicable story once again, beginning with the telegram received on the night before and the conversation with Mrs Hill, the decision to return to England the following day, Laura by air, and John himself by car and train. It no longer sounded as dramatic as it had done when he had made his statement to the police-officer, when, possibly because of his conviction of something uncanny, the description of the two vaporettos passing one another in the middle of the Grand Canal had held a sinister quality, suggesting abduction on the part of the sisters, the pair of them holding a bewildered Laura captive. Now that neither of the women had any further menace for him he spoke more naturally, yet with great sincerity, feeling for the first time that they were somehow both in sympathy with him and would understand.

"You see," he explained, in a final endeavour to make amends for having gone to the police in the first place, "I truly believed I had seen you with Laura, and I thought . . ." he hesitated, because this had been the police-officer's suggestion and not his, "I thought that perhaps Laura had some sudden loss of memory, had met you at the airport, and you had brought her back to Venice to wherever you were staying."

They had crossed a large square and were approaching a house at the end of it, with a sign "Pensione" above the door. Their escort paused at the entrance.

"Is this it?" asked John.

"Yes," said the sister. "I know it is nothing much from the outside, but it is clean and comfortable, and was recommended by friends." She turned to the escort. "Grazie," she said to him, "grazie tanto."

The man nodded briefly, wished them "Buona notte," and disappeared across the campo.

"Will you come in?" asked the sister. "I am sure we can find some coffee, or perhaps you prefer tea?"

"No, really," John thanked her, "I must get back to the hotel. I'm making an early start in the morning. I just want to make quite sure you do understand what happened, and that you forgive me."

"There is nothing to forgive," she replied. "It is one of the many examples of second sight that my sister and I have experienced time and time again, and I should very much like to record it for our files, if you will permit it."

"Well, as to that, of course," he told her, "but I myself find it hard to understand. It has never happened to me before."

"Not consciously, perhaps," she said, "but so many things happen to us of which we are not aware. My sister felt you had psychic understanding. She told your wife. She also told your wife, last night in the restaurant, that you were to experience trouble, danger, that you should leave Venice. Well, don't you believe now that the telegram was proof of this? Your son was ill, possibly dangerously ill, and so it was necessary for you to return home immediately. Heaven be praised your wife flew home to be by his side."

"Yes, indeed," said John, "but why should I see her on the vaporetto with you and your sister when she was actually on her way to England?"

"Thought transference, perhaps," she answered. "Your wife may have been thinking about us. We gave her our address, should you wish to get in touch with us. We shall be here another ten days. And she knows that we would pass on any message that my sister might have from your little one in the spirit world."

"Yes," said John awkwardly, "yes, I see. It's very good of you." He had a sudden rather unkind picture of the two sisters putting on headphones in their bedroom, listening for a coded message from poor Christine. "Look, this is our address in London," he said. "I know Laura will be pleased to hear from you."

He scribbled their address on a sheet torn from his pocket-diary, even, as a bonus thrown in, the telephone number, and handed it to her. He could imagine the outcome. Laura springing it on him one evening that the "old dears" were passing through London on their way to Scotland, and the least they could do was to offer them hospitality, even the spare-room for the night. Then a seance in the living-room, tambourines appearing out of thin air.

"Well, I must be off," he said. "Goodnight, and apologies, once again, for all that has happened this evening." He shook hands with the first sister, then turned to her blind twin. "I hope," he said, "that you are not too tired."

The sightless eyes were disconcerting. She held his hand fast and would not let it go. "The child," she said, speaking in an odd staccato voice, "the child . . . I can see the child . . ." and then, to his dismay, a bead of froth appeared at the corner of her mouth, her head jerked back, and she half-collapsed in her sister's arms.

"We must get her inside," said the sister hurriedly. "It's all right, she's not ill, it's the beginning of a trance state."

Between them they helped the twin, who had gone rigid, into the house, and sat her down on the nearest chair, the sister supporting her. A woman came running from some inner room. There was a strong smell of spaghetti from the back regions. "Don't worry," said the sister, "the signorina and I can manage. I think you had better go. Sometimes she is sick after these turns."

"I'm most frightfully sorry . . ." John began, but the sister had already turned her back, and with the signorina was bending over her twin, from whom peculiar choking sounds were proceeding. He was obviously in the way, and after a final gesture of courtesy, "Is there anything I can do?", which received no reply, he turned on his heel and began walking across the square. He looked back once, and saw they had closed the door.

What a finale to the evening! And all his fault. Poor old girls, first dragged to police headquarters and put through an interrogation, and then a psychic fit on top of it all. More likely epilepsy. Not much of a life for the other sister, but she seemed to take it in her stride. An additional hazard, though, if it happened in a restaurant or in the street. And not particularly welcome under his and Laura's roof should the sisters ever find themselves beneath it, which he prayed would never happen.

Meanwhile, where the devil was he? The square, with the inevitable church at one end, was quite deserted. He could not remember which way they had come from police headquarters, there had seemed to be so many turnings.

Wait a minute, the church itself had a familiar appearance. He drew nearer to it, looking for the name which was sometimes on notices at the entrance. San Giovanni in Bragora, that rang a bell. He and Laura had gone inside one morning to look at a painting by Cima da Conegliano. Surely it was only a stone's throw from the Riva degli Schiavoni and the open wide waters of the San Marco lagoon, with all the bright lights of civilisation and the strolling tourists? He remembered taking a small turning from the Schiavoni and they had arrived at the church. Wasn't that the alley-way ahead? He plunged along it, but halfway down he hesitated. It didn't seem right, although it was familiar for some unknown reason.

Then he realised that it was not the alley they had taken the morning they visited the church, but the only one they had walked along the previous evening, only he was approaching it from the opposite direction. Yes, that was it, in which case it would be quicker to go on and cross the little bridge over the narrow canal, and he would find the Arsenal on his left and the street leading down to the Riva degli Schiavoni to his right. Simpler than retracing his steps and getting lost once more in the maze of back streets.

He had almost reached the end of the alley, and the bridge was in sight, when he saw the child. It was the same little girl with the pixie-hood who had leapt between the tethered boats the preceding night and vanished up the cellar steps of one of the houses. This time she was running from the direction of the church the other side, making for the bridge. She was running as if her life depended on it, and in a moment he saw why. A man was in pursuit, who, when she glanced backwards for a moment, still running, flattened himself against a wall, believing himself unobserved. The child came on, scampering across the bridge, and John, fearful of alarming her further, backed into an open doorway that led into a small court.

He remembered the drunken yell of the night before which had come from one of the houses near where the man was hiding now. This is it, he thought, the fellow's after her again, and with a flash of intuition he connected the two events, the child's terror then and now, and the murders reported in the newspapers, supposedly the work of some madman. It could be coincidence, a child running from a drunken relative, and yet, and yet . . . His heart began thumping in his chest, instinct warning him to run himself, now, at once, back along the alley the way he had come—but what about the child? What was going to happen to the child?

Then he heard her running steps. She hurtled through the open doorway into the court in which he stood, not seeing him, making for the rear of the house that flanked it, where steps led presumably to a back entrance. She was sobbing as she ran, not the ordinary cry of a frightened child, but the panic-striken intake of breath of a helpless being in despair. Were there parents in the house who would protect her, whom he could warn? He hesitated a moment, then followed her down the steps and through the door at the bottom, which had burst open at the touch of her hands as she hurled herself against it.

"It's all right," he called. "I won't let him hurt you, it's all right," cursing his lack of Italian, but possibly an English voice might reassure her. But it was no use—she ran sobbing up another flight of stairs, which were spiral, twisting, leading to the floor above, and already it was too late for him to retreat. He could hear sounds of the pursuer in the courtyard behind, someone shouting in Italian, a dog barking. This is it, he thought, we're in it together, the child and I. Unless we can bolt some inner door above he'll get us both.

He ran up the stairs after the child, who had darted into a room leading off a small landing, and followed her inside and slammed the door, and, merciful heaven, there was a bolt which he rammed into its socket. The child was crouching by the open window. If he shouted for help someone would surely hear, someone would surely come before the man in pursuit threw himself against the door and it gave, because there was no one but themselves, no parents, the room was bare except for a mattress on an old bed, and a heap of rags in one corner.

"It's all right," he panted, "it's all right," and held out his hand, trying to smile.

The child struggled to her feet and stood before him, the pixie-hood falling from her head on to the floor. He stared at her, incredulity turning to horror, to fear. It was not a child at all but a little thick-set woman dwarf, about three feet high, with a great square adult head too big for her body, grey locks hanging shoulder-length, and she wasn't sobbing any more, she was grinning at him, nodding her head up and down.

Then he heard the footsteps on the landing outside and the hammering on the door, and a barking dog, and not one voice but several voices, shouting, "Open up! Police!" The creature fumbled in her sleeve, drawing a knife, and as she threw it at him with hideous strength, piercing his throat, he stumbled and fell, the sticky mess covering his protecting hands.

And he saw the vaporetto with Laura and the two sisters steaming down the Grand Canal, not today, not tomorrow, but the day after that, and he knew why they were together and for what sad purpose they had come. The creature was gibbering in its corner. The hammering and the voices and the barking dog grew fainter, and, "Oh, God," he thought, "what a bloody silly way to die . . ."

Fleur

★

LOUISE ERDRICH

THE FIRST TIME SHE DROWNED in the cold and glassy waters of Lake Turcot, Fleur Pillager was only a girl. Two men saw the boat tip, saw her struggle in the waves. They rowed over to the place she went down, and jumped in. When they dragged her over the gunwales, she was cold to the touch and stiff, so they slapped her face, shook her by the heels, worked her arms back and forth, and pounded her back until she coughed up lake water. She shivered all over like a dog, then took a breath. But it wasn't long afterward that those two men disappeared. The first wandered off, and the other, Jean Hat, got himself run over by a cart.

It went to show, my grandma said. It figured to her, all right. By saving Fleur Pillager, those two men had lost themselves.

The next time she fell in the lake, Fleur Pillager was twenty years old and no one touched her. She washed onshore, her skin a dull dead gray, but when George Many Women bent to look closer, he saw her chest move. Then her eyes spun open, sharp black riprock, and she looked at him. "You'll take my place," she hissed. Everybody scattered and left her there, so no one knows how she dragged herself home. Soon after that we noticed Many Women changed, grew afraid, wouldn't leave his house, and would not be forced to go near water. For his caution, he lived until the day that his sons brought him a new tin bathtub. Then the first time he used the tub he slipped, got knocked out, and breathed water while his wife stood in the other room frying breakfast.

Men stayed clear of Fleur Pillager after the second drowning. Even though she was good-looking, nobody dared to court her because it was clear that Misshepeshu, the waterman, the monster, wanted her for himself. He's a devil, that one, love-hungry with desire and maddened for the touch of young girls, the strong and daring especially, the ones like Fleur.

Our mothers warn us that we'll think he's handsome, for he appears with green eyes, copper skin, a mouth tender as a child's. But if you fall into his arms, he sprouts horns, fangs, claws, fins. His feet are joined as one and his skin, brass scales, rings to the touch. You're fascinated, cannot move. He casts a shell necklace at your feet, weeps gleaming chips that harden into mica on your breasts. He holds you under. Then he takes the body of a lion or a fat brown worm. He's made of gold. He's made of beach moss. He's a thing of dry foam, a thing of death by drowning, the death a Chippewa cannot survive.

Unless you are Fleur Pillager. We all knew she couldn't swim. After the first time, we thought she'd never go back to Lake Turcot. We thought she'd keep to herself, live quiet, stop killing men off by drowning in the lake. After the first time, we thought she'd keep the good ways. But then, after the second drowning, we knew that we were dealing with something much more serious. She was haywire, out of control. She messed with evil, laughed at the old women's advice, and dressed like a man. She got herself into some half-forgotten medicine, studied ways we shouldn't talk about. Some say she kept the finger of a child in her pocket and a powder of unborn rabbits in a leather thong around her neck. She laid the heart of an owl on her tongue so she could see at night, and went out, hunting, not even in her own body. We know for sure because the next morning, in the snow or dust, we followed the tracks of her bare feet and saw where they changed, where the claws sprang out, the pad broadened and pressed into the dirt. By night we heard her chuffing cough, the bear cough. By day her silence and the wide grin she threw to bring down our guard made us frightened. Some thought that Fleur Pillager should be driven off the reservation, but not a single person who spoke like this had the nerve. And finally, when people were just about to get together and throw her out, she left on her own and didn't come back all summer. That's what this story is about.

During that summer, when she lived a few miles south in Argus, things happened. She almost destroyed that town.

When she got down to Argus in the year of 1920, it was just a small grid of six streets on either side of the railroad depot. There were two elevators, one central, the other a few miles west. Two stores competed for the trade of the three hundred citizens, and three churches quarreled with one another for their souls. There was a frame building for Lutherans, a heavy brick one for Episcopalians, and a long narrow shingled Catholic church. This last had a tall slender steeple, twice as high as any building or tree.

No doubt, across the low, flat wheat, watching from the road as she came near Argus on foot, Fleur saw that steeple rise, a shadow thin as a needle. Maybe in that raw space it drew her the way a lone tree draws lightning. Maybe, in the end, the Catholics are to blame. For if she hadn't seen that sign of pride, that slim prayer, that marker, maybe she would have kept walking.

But Fleur Pillager turned, and the first place she went once she came into town was to the back door of the priest's residence attached to the landmark church. She didn't go there for a handout, although she got that, but to ask for work. She got that too, or the town got her. It's hard to tell which came out worse, her or the men or the town, although the upshot of it all was that Fleur lived.

The four men who worked at the butcher's had carved up about a thousand carcasses between them, maybe half of that steers and the other half pigs, sheep, and game animals like deer, elk, and bear. That's not even mentioning the chickens, which were beyond counting. Pete Kozka owned the place, and employed Lily Veddar, Tor Grunewald, and my stepfather, Dutch James, who had brought my mother down from the reservation the year before she disappointed him by dying. Dutch took me out of school to take her place. I kept house half the time and worked the other in the butcher shop, sweeping floors, putting sawdust down, running a hambone across the street to a customer's bean pot or a package of sausage to the corner. I was a good one to have around because until they needed me, I was invisible. I blended into the stained brown walls, a skinny, big-nosed girl with staring eyes. Because I could fade into a corner or squeeze beneath a shelf, I knew everything, what the men said when no one was around, and what they did to Fleur.

Kozka's Meats served farmers for a fifty-mile area, both to slaughter, for it had a stock pen and chute, and to cure the meat by smoking it or spicing it in sausage. The storage locker was a marvel, made of many thicknesses of brick, earth insulation, and Minnesota timber, lined inside with sawdust and vast blocks of ice cut from Lake Turcot, hauled down from home each winter by horse and sledge.

A ramshackle board building, part slaughterhouse, part store, was fixed to the low, thick square of the lockers. That's where Fleur worked. Kozka hired her for her strength. She could lift a haunch or carry a pole of sausages without stumbling, and she soon learned cutting from Pete's wife, a string-thin blonde who chain-smoked and handled the razor-sharp knives with nerveless precision, slicing close to her stained fingers. Fleur and Fritzie Kozka worked afternoons, wrapping their cuts in paper, and Fleur hauled the packages to the lockers. The meat was left outside the heavy oak doors that were only opened at 5:00 each afternoon, before the men ate supper.

Sometimes Dutch, Tor, and Lily ate at the lockers, and when they did I stayed too, cleaned floors, restoked the fires in the front smokehouses, while the men sat around the squat cast-iron stove spearing slats of herring onto hardtack bread. They played long games of poker or cribbage on a board made from the planed end of a salt crate. They talked and I listened, although there wasn't much to hear since almost nothing ever happened in Argus. Tor was married, Dutch had lost my mother, and Lily read circulars. They mainly discussed about the auctions to come, equipment, or women.

Every so often, Pete Kozka came out front to make a whist, leaving Fritzie to smoke cigarettes and fry raised doughnuts in the back room. He sat and played a few rounds but kept his thoughts to himself. Fritzie did not tolerate him talking behind her back, and the one book he read was the New Testament. If he said something, it concerned weather or a surplus of sheep stomachs, a ham that smoked green or the markets for corn and wheat. He had a good-luck talisman, the opal-white lens of a cow's eye. Playing cards, he rubbed it between his fingers. That soft sound and the slap of cards was about the only conversation.

Fleur finally gave them a subject.

Her cheeks were wide and flat, her hands large, chapped, muscular. Fleur's shoulders were broad as beams, her hips fishlike, slippery, narrow. An old green dress clung to her waist, worn thin where she sat. Her braids were thick like the tails of animals, and swung against her when she moved, deliberately, slowly in her work, held in and half-tamed, but only half. I could tell, but the others never saw. They never looked into her sly brown eyes or noticed her teeth, strong and curved and very white. Her legs were bare, and since she padded around in beadwork moccasins they never saw that her fifth toes were missing. They never knew she'd drowned. They were blinded, they were stupid, they only saw her in the flesh.

And yet it wasn't just that she was a Chippewa, or even that she was a woman, it wasn't that she was good-looking or even that she was alone that made their brains hum. It was how she played cards.

Women didn't usually play with men, so the evening that Fleur drew a chair up to the men's table without being so much as asked, there was a shock of surprise.

"What's this," said Lily. He was fat, with a snake's cold pale eyes and precious skin, smooth and lily-white, which is how he got his name. Lily had a dog, a stumpy mean little bull of a thing with a belly drum-tight from eating pork rinds. The dog liked to play cards just like Lily, and straddled his barrel thighs through games of stud, rum poker, vingt-un. The dog snapped at Fleur's arm that first night, but cringed back, its snarl frozen, when she took her place.

"I thought," she said, her voice soft and stroking, "you might deal me in."

There was a space between the heavy bin of spiced flour and the wall where I just fit. I hunkered down there, kept my eyes open, saw her black hair swing over the chair, her feet solid on the wood floor. I couldn't see up on the table where the cards slapped down, so after they were deep in their game I raised myself up in the shadows, and crouched on a sill of wood.

I watched Fleur's hands stack and ruffle, divide the cards, spill them to each player in a blur, rake them up and shuffle again. Tor, short and scrappy, shut one eye and squinted the other at Fleur. Dutch screwed his lips around a wet cigar.

"Gotta see a man," he mumbled, getting up to go out back to the privy. The others broke, put their cards down, and Fleur sat alone in the lamplight that glowed in a sheen across the push of her breasts. I watched her closely, then she paid me a beam of notice for the first time. She turned, looked straight at me, and grinned the white wolf grin a Pillager turns on its victims, except that she wasn't after me.

"Pauline there," she said, "how much money you got?"

We'd all been paid for the week that day. Eight cents was in my pocket.

"Stake me," she said, holding out her long fingers. I put the coins in her palm and then I melted back to nothing, part of the walls and tables. It was a long time before I understood that the men would not have seen me no matter what I did, how I moved. I wasn't anything like Fleur. My dress hung loose and my back was already curved, an old woman's. Work had roughened me, reading made my eyes sore, caring for my mother before she died had hardened my face. I was not much to look at, so they never saw me.

When the men came back and sat around the table, they had drawn together. They shot each other small glances, stuck their tongues in their cheeks, burst out laughing at odd moments, to rattle Fleur. But she never minded. They played their vingt-un, staying even as Fleur slowly gained. Those pennies I had given her drew nickels and attracted dimes until there was a small pile in front of her.

Then she hooked them with five-card draw, nothing wild. She dealt, discarded, drew, and then she sighed and her cards gave a little shiver. Tor's eyes gleamed, and Dutch straightened in his seat.

"I'll pay to see that hand," said Lily Veddar.

Fleur showed, and she had nothing there, nothing at all.

Tor's thin smile cracked open, and he threw his hand in too.

"Well, we know one thing," he said, leaning back in his chair, "the squaw can't bluff."

With that I lowered myself into a mound of swept sawdust and slept. I woke up during the night, but none of them had moved yet, so I couldn't either. Still later, the men must have gone out again, or Fritzie come out to break the game, because I was lifted, soothed, cradled in a woman's arms and rocked so quiet that I kept my eyes shut while Fleur rolled me into a closet of grimy ledgers, oiled paper, balls of string, and thick files that fit beneath me like a mattress.

The game went on after work the next evening. I got my eight cents back five times over, and Fleur kept the rest of the dollar she'd won for a stake. This time they didn't play so late, but they played regular, and then kept going at it night after night. They played poker now, or variations, for one week straight, and each time Fleur won exactly one dollar, no more and no less, too consistent for luck.

By this time, Lily and the other men were so lit with suspense that they got Pete to join the game with them. They concentrated, the fat dog sitting tense in Lily Veddar's lap, Tor suspicious, Dutch stroking his huge square brow, Pete steady. It wasn't that Fleur won that hooked them in so, because she lost hands too. It was rather that she never had a freak hand or even anything above a straight. She only took on her low cards, which didn't sit right. By chance, Fleur should have gotten a full or flush by now. The irritating thing was she beat with pairs and never bluffed, because she couldn't, and still she ended up each night with exactly one dollar. Lily couldn't believe, first of all, that a woman could be smart enough to play cards, but even if she was, that she would then be stupid enough to cheat for a dollar a night. By day I watched him turn the problem over, his hard white face dull, small fingers probing at his knuckles, until he finally thought he had Fleur figured out as a bit-time player, caution her game. Raising the stakes would throw her.

More than anything now, he wanted Fleur to come away with something but a dollar. Two bits less or ten more, the sum didn't matter, just so he broke her streak.

Night after night she played, won her dollar, and left to stay in a place that just Fritzie and I knew about. Fleur bathed in the slaughtering tub, then slept in the unused brick smokehouse behind the lockers, a windowless place tarred on the inside with scorched fats. When I brushed against her skin I noticed that she smelled of the walls, rich and woody, slightly burnt. Since that night she put me in the closet I was no longer afraid of her, but followed her close, stayed with her, became her moving shadow that the men never noticed, the shadow that could have saved her.

August, the month that bears fruit, closed around the shop, and Pete and Fritzie left for Minnesota to escape the heat. Night by night, running, Fleur had won thirty dollars, but only Pete's presence had kept Lily at bay. But Pete was gone now, and one payday, with the heat so bad no one could move but Fleur, the men sat and played and waited while she finished work. The cards sweat, limp in their fingers, the table was slick with grease, and even the walls were warm to the touch. The air was motionless. Fleur was in the next room boiling heads.

Her green dress, drenched, wrapped her like a transparent sheet. A skin of lakeweed. Black snarls of veining clung to her arms. Her braids were loose, half-unraveled, tied behind her neck in a thick loop. She stood in steam, turning skulls through a vat with a wooden paddle. When scraps boiled to the surface, she bent with a round tin sieve and scooped them out. She'd filled two dishpans.

"Ain't that enough now?" called Lily. "We're waiting." The stump of a dog trembled in his lap, alive with rage. It never smelled me or noticed me above Fleur's smoky skin. The air was heavy in my corner, and pressed me down. Fleur sat with them.

"Now what do you say?" Lily asked the dog. It barked. That was the signal for the real game to start.

"Let's up the ante," said Lily, who had been stalking this night all month. He had a roll of money in his pocket. Fleur had five bills in her dress. The men had each saved their full pay.

"Ante a dollar then," said Fleur, and pitched hers in. She lost, but they let her scrape along, cent by cent. And then she won some. She played unevenly, as if chance was all she had. She reeled them in. The game went on. The dog was stiff now, poised on Lily's knees, a ball of vicious muscle with its yellow eyes slit in concentration. It gave advice, seemed to sniff the lay of Fleur's cards, twitched and nudged. Fleur was up, then down, saved by a scratch. Tor dealt seven cards, three down. The pot grew, round by round, until it held all the money. Nobody folded. Then it all rode on one last card and they went silent. Fleur picked hers up and blew a long breath. The heat lowered like a bell. Her card shook, but she stayed in.

Lily smiled and took the dog's head tenderly between his palms.

"Say, Fatso," he said, crooning the words, "you reckon that girl's bluffing?"

The dog whined and Lily laughed. "Me too," he said, "let's show." He swept his bills and coins into the pot and then they turned their cards over.

Lily looked once, looked again, then he squeezed the dog up like a fist of dough and slammed it on the table.

Fleur threw her arms out and drew the money over, grinning that same wolf grin that she'd used on me, the grin that had them. She jammed the bills in her dress, scooped the coins up in waxed white paper that she tied with string.

"Let's go another round," said Lily, his voice choked with burrs. But Fleur opened her mouth and yawned, then walked out back to gather slops for the one big hog that was waiting in the stock pen to be killed.

The men sat still as rocks, their hands spread on the oiled wood table. Dutch had chewed his cigar to damp shreds, Tor's eye was dull. Lily's gaze was the only one to follow Fleur. I didn't move. I felt them gathering, saw my stepfather's veins, the ones in his forehead that stood out in anger. The dog had rolled off the table and curled in a knot below the counter, where none of the men could touch it.

Lily rose and stepped out back to the closet of ledgers where Pete kept his private stock. He brought back a bottle, uncorked and tipped it between his fingers. The lump in his throat moved, then he passed it on. They drank, quickly felt the whiskey's fire, and planned with their eyes things they couldn't say out loud.

When they left, I followed. I hid out back in the clutter of broken boards and chicken crates beside the stock pen, where they waited. Fleur could not be seen at first, and then the moon broke and showed her, slipping cautiously along the rough board chute with a bucket in her hand. Her hair fell, wild and coarse, to her waist, and her dress was a floating patch in the dark. She made a pig-calling sound, rang the tin pail lightly against the wood, froze suspiciously. But too late. In the sound of the ring Lily moved, fat and nimble, stepped right behind Fleur and put out his creamy hands. At his first touch, she whirled and doused him with the bucket of sour slops. He pushed her against the big fence and the package of coins split, went clinking and jumping, winked against the wood. Fleur rolled over once and vanished in the yard.

The moon fell behind a curtain of ragged clouds, and Lily followed into the dark muck. But he tripped, pitched over the huge flank of the pig, who lay mired to the snout, heavily snoring. I sprang out of the weeds and climbed the side of the pen, stuck like glue. I saw the sow rise to her neat, knobby knees, gain her balance, and sway, curious, as Lily stumbled forward. Fleur had backed into the angle of rough wood just beyond, and when Lily tried to jostle past, the sow tipped up on her hind legs and struck, quick and hard as a snake. She plunged her head into Lily's thick side and snatched a mouthful of his shirt. She lunged again, caught him lower, so that he grunted in pained surprise. He seemed to ponder, breathing deep. Then he launched his huge body in a swimmer's dive.

The sow screamed as his body smacked over hers. She rolled, striking out with her knife-sharp hooves, and Lily gathered himself upon her, took her foot-long face by the ears and scraped her snout and cheeks against the trestles of the pen. He hurled the sow's tight skull against an iron post, but instead of knocking her dead, he merely woke her from her dream.

She reared, shrieked, drew him with her so that they posed standing upright. They bowed jerkily to each other, as if to begin. Then his arms swung and flailed. She sank her black fangs into his shoulder, clasping him, dancing him forward and backward through the pen. Their steps picked up pace, went wild. The two dipped as one, box-stepped, tripped each other. She ran her split foot through his hair. He grabbed her kinked tail. They went down and came up, the same shape and then the same color, until the men couldn't tell one from the other in that light and Fleur was able to launch herself over the gates, swing down, hit gravel.

The men saw, yelled, and chased her at a dead run to the smokehouse. And Lily too, once the sow gave up in disgust and freed him. That is where I should have gone to Fleur, saved her, thrown myself on Dutch. But I went stiff with fear and couldn't unlatch myself from the trestles or move at all. I closed my eyes and put my head in my arms, tried to hide, so there is nothing to describe but what I couldn't block out. Fleur's hoarse breath, so loud it filled me, her cry in the old language, and my name repeated over and over among the words.

The heat was still dense the next morning when I came back to work. Fleur was gone but the men were there, slack-faced, hung over. Lily was paler and softer than ever, as if his flesh had steamed on his bones. They smoked, took pulls off a bottle. It wasn't noon yet. I worked awhile, waiting shop and sharpening steel. But I was sick, I was smothered, I was sweating so hard that my hands slipped on the knives, and I wiped my fingers clean of the greasy touch of the customers' coins. Lily opened his mouth and roared once, not in anger. There was no meaning to the sound. His boxer dog, sprawled limp beside his foot, never lifted its head. Nor did the other men.

They didn't notice when I stepped outside, hoping for a clear breath. And then I forgot them because I knew that we were all balanced, ready to tip, to fly, to be crushed as soon as the weather broke. The sky was so low that I felt the weight of it like a yoke. Clouds hung down, witch teats, a tornado's green-brown cones, and as I watched one flicked out and became a delicate probing thumb. Even as I picked up my heels and ran back inside, the wind blew suddenly, cold, and then came rain.

Inside, the men had disappeared already and the whole place was trembling as if a huge hand was pinched at the rafters, shaking it. I ran straight through, screaming for Dutch or for any of them, and then I stopped at the heavy doors of the lockers, where they had surely taken shelter. I stood there a moment. Everything went still. Then I heard a cry building in the wind, faint at first, a whistle and then a shrill scream that tore through the walls and gathered around me, spoke plain so I understood that I should move, put my arms out, and slam down the great iron bar that fit across the hasp and lock.

Outside, the wind was stronger, like a hand held against me. I struggled forward. The bushes tossed, the awnings flapped off storefronts, the rails of porches rattled. The odd cloud became a fat snout that nosed along the earth and sniffled, jabbed, picked at things, sucked them up, blew them apart, rooted around as if it was following a certain scent, then stopped behind me at the butcher shop and bored down like a drill.

I went flying, landed somewhere in a ball. When I opened my eyes and looked, stranger things were happening.

A herd of cattle flew through the air like giant birds, dropping dung, their mouths opened in stunned bellows. A candle, still lighted, blew past, and tables, napkins, garden tools, a whole school of drifting eyeglasses, jackets on hangers, hams, a checkerboard, a lampshade, and at last the sow from behind the lockers, on the run, her hooves a blur, set free, swooping, diving, screaming as everything in Argus fell apart and got turned upside down, smashed, and thoroughly wrecked.

Days passed before the town went looking for the men. They were bachelors, after all, except for Tor, whose wife had suffered a blow to the head that made her forgetful. Everyone was occupied with digging out, in high relief because even though the Catholic steeple had been torn off like a peaked cap and sent across five fields, those huddled in the cellar were unhurt. Walls had fallen, windows were demolished, but the stores were intact and so were the bankers and shop owners who had taken refuge in their safes or beneath their cash registers. It was a fair-minded disaster, no one could be said to have suffered much more than the next, at least not until Fritzie and Pete came home.

Of all the businesses in Argus, Kozka's Meats had suffered worst. The boards of the front building had been split to kindling, piled in a huge pyramid, and the shop equipment was blasted far and wide. Pete paced off the distance the iron bathtub had been flung—a hundred feet. The glass candy case went fifty, and landed without so much as a cracked pane. There were other surprises as well, for the back rooms where Fritzie and Pete lived were undisturbed. Fritzie said the dust still coated her china figures, and upon her kitchen table, in the ashtray, perched the last cigarette she'd put out in haste. She lit it up and finished it, looking through the window. From there, she could see that the old smokehouse Fleur had slept in was crushed to a reddish sand and the stockpens were completely torn apart, the rails stacked helter-skelter. Fritzie asked for Fleur. People shrugged. Then she asked about the others and, suddenly, the town understood that three men were missing.

There was a rally of help, a gathering of shovels and volunteers. We passed boards from hand to hand, stacked them, uncovered what lay beneath the pile of jagged splinters. The lockers, full of the meat that was Pete and Fritzie's investment, slowly came into sight, still intact. When enough room was made for a man to stand on the roof, there were calls, a general urge to hack through and see what lay below. But Fritzie shouted that she wouldn't allow it because the meat would spoil. And so the work continued, board by board, until at last the heavy oak doors of the freezer were revealed and people pressed to the entry. Everyone wanted to be the first, but since it was my stepfather lost, I was let go in when Pete and Fritzie wedged through into the sudden icy air.

Pete scraped a match on his boot, lit the lamp Fritzie held, and then the three of us stood still in its circle. Light glared off the skinned and hanging carcasses, the crates of wrapped sausages, the bright and cloudy blocks of lake ice, pure as winter. The cold bit into us, pleasant at first, then numbing. We must have stood there a couple of minutes before we saw the men, or more rightly, the humps of fur, the iced and shaggy hides they wore, the bearskins they had taken down and wrapped around themselves. We stepped closer and tilted the lantern beneath the flaps of fur into their faces. The dog was there, perched among them, heavy as a doorstop. The three had hunched around a barrel where the game was still laid out, and a dead lantern and an empty bottle, too. But they had thrown down their last hands and hunkered tight, clutching one another, knuckles raw from beating at the door they had also attacked with hooks. Frost stars gleamed off their eyelashes and the stubble of their beards. Their faces were set in concentration, mouths open as if to speak some careful thought, some agreement they'd come to in each other's arms.

Power travels in the bloodlines, handed out before birth. It comes down through the hands, which in the Pillagers were strong and knotted, big, spidery, and rough, with sensitive fingertips good at dealing cards. It comes through the eyes, too, belligerent, darkest brown, the eyes of those in the bear clan, impolite as they gaze directly at a person.

In my dreams, I look straight back at Fleur, at the men. I am no longer the watcher on the dark sill, the skinny girl.

The blood draws us back, as if it runs through a vein of earth. I've come home and, except for talking to my cousins, live a quiet life. Fleur lives quiet too, down on Lake Turcot with her boat. Some say she's married to the waterman, Misshepeshu, or that she's living in shame with white men or windigos, or that she's killed them all. I'm about the only one here who ever goes to visit her. Last winter, I went to help out in her cabin when she bore the child, whose green eyes and skin the color of an old penny made more talk, as no one could decide if the child was mixed blood or what, fathered in a smokehouse, or by a man with brass scales, or by the lake. The girl is bold, smiling in her sleep, as if she knows what people wonder, as if she hears the old men talk, turning the story over. It comes up different every time and has no ending, no beginning. They get the middle wrong too. They only know that they don't know anything.

Up North

★

MAVIS GALLANT

WHEN THEY WOKE UP in the train, their bed was black with soot and there was soot in his Mum's blondie hair. They were miles north of Montreal, which had, already, sunk beneath his remembrance. "D'you know what I sor in the night?" said Dennis. He had to keep his back turned while she dressed. They were both in the same berth, to save money. He was small, and didn't take up much room, but when he woke up in that sooty autumn dawn, he found he was squashed flat against the side of the train. His Mum was afraid of falling out and into the aisle; they had a lower berth, but she didn't trust the strength of the curtain. Now she was dressing, and sobbing; really sobbing. For this was worse than anything she had ever been through, she told him. She had been right through the worst of the air raids, yet this was the worst, this waking in the cold, this dark, dirty dawn, everything dirty she touched, her clothes—oh, her clothes!—and now having to dress as she lay flat on her back. She daren't sit up. She might knock her head.

"You know what I sor?" said the child patiently. "Well, the train must of stopped, see, and some little men with bundles on their backs got on. Other men was holding lanterns. They were all little. They were all talking French."

"Shut up," said Mum. "Do you hear me?"

"Sor them," said the boy.

"You and your bloody elves."

"They was people."

"Little men with bundles," said Mum, trying to dress again. "You start your fairy tales with your Dad and I don't know what *he'll* give you."

It was this mythical, towering, half-remembered figure they were now travelling to join up north.

Roy McLaughlin, travelling on the same train, saw the pair, presently, out of his small red-lidded eyes. Den and his Mum were dressed and as clean as they could make themselves, and sitting at the end of the car. McLaughlin was the last person to get up, and he climbed down from his solitary green-curtained cubicle conspicuous and alone. He had to pad the length of the car in a trench coat and city shoes—he had never owned slippers, bathrobe, or pajamas—past the passengers, who were drawn with fatigue, pale under the lights. They were men, mostly; some soldiers. The Second World War had been finished, in Europe, a year and five months. It was a dirty, rickety train going up to Abitibi. McLaughlin was returning to a construction camp after three weeks in Montreal. He saw the girl, riding with her back to the engine, doing her nails, and his faculties absently registered "Limey bride" as he went by. The kid, looking out the window, turned and stared. McLaughlin thought "Pest," but only because children and other men's wives made him nervous and sour when they were brought around camp on a job.

After McLaughlin had dressed and had swallowed a drink in the washroom—for he was sick and trembling after his holiday—he came and sat down opposite the blond girl. He did not bother to explain that he had to sit somewhere while his berth was being dismantled. His arms were covered with coarse red hair; he had rolled up the sleeves of his khaki shirt. He spread his pale, heavy hands on his knees. The child stood between them, fingertips on the sooty window sill, looking out at the breaking day. Once, the train stopped for a long time; the engine was being changed, McLaughlin said. They had been rolling north but were now turning west. At six o'clock, in about an hour, Dennis and his mother would have to get down, and onto another train, and go north once more. Dennis could not see any station where they were now. There was a swamp with bristling black rushes, red as ink. It was the autumn sunrise; cold, red. It was so strange to him, so singular, that he could not have said an hour later which feature of the scene was in the foreground or to the left or right. Two women wearing army battle jackets over their dresses, with their hair piled up in front, like his mother's, called and giggled to someone they had put on the train. They were fat and dark—grinny. His mother looked at them with detestation, recognizing what they were; for she hated whores. She had always acted on the desire of the moment, without thought of gain, and she had taken the consequences (Dennis) without complaint. Dennis saw that she was hating the women, and so he looked elsewhere. On a wooden fence sat four or five men in open shirts and patched trousers. They had dull, dark hair, and let their mouths sag as though they were too tired or too sleepy to keep them closed. Something about them was displeasing to the child, and he thought that this was an ugly place with ugly people. It was also a dirty place; every time Dennis put his hands on the window sill they came off black.

"Come down any time to see a train go by," said McLaughlin, meaning those men. "Get up in the *night* to see a train."

The train moved. It was still dark enough outside for Dennis to see his face in the window and for the light from the windows to fall in pale squares on the upturned vanishing faces and on the little trees. Dennis heard his mother's new friend say, "Well, there's different possibilities." They passed into an unchanging landscape of swamp and bracken and stunted trees. Then the lights inside the train were put out and he saw that the sky was blue and bright. His mother and McLaughlin, seen in the window, had been remote and bodiless; through their transparent profiles he had seen the yellowed trees going by. Now he could not see their faces at all.

"He's been back in Canada since the end of the war. He was wounded. Den hardly knows him," he heard his mother say. "I couldn't come. I had to wait my turn. We were over a thousand war brides on that ship. He was with Aluminium when he first came back." She pronounced the five vowels in the word.

"You'll be all right there," said McLaughlin. "It's a big place. Schools. All company."

"Pardon me?"

"I mean it all belongs to Aluminum. Only if that's where you're going you happen to be on the wrong train."

"He isn't there now. He hates towns. He seems to move about a great deal. He drives a bulldozer, you see."

"Owns it?" said McLaughlin.

"Why, I shouldn't *think* so. Drives for another man, I think he said."

The boy's father fell into the vast pool of casual labor, drifters; there was a social hierarchy in the north, just as in Heaven. McLaughlin was an engineer. He took another look at the boy: black hair, blue eyes. The hair was coarse, straight, rather dull; Indian hair. The mother was a blonde; touched up a bit, but still blonde.

"What name?" said McLaughlin on the upward note of someone who has asked the same question twice.

"Cameron. Donald Cameron."

That meant nothing, still; McLaughlin had worked in a place on James Bay where the Indians were named MacDonald and Ogilvie and had an unconquered genetic strain of blue eyes.

"D'you know about any ghosts?" said the boy, turning to McLaughlin. McLaughlin's eyes were paler than his own, which were a deep slate blue, like the eyes of a newly born child. McLaughlin saw the way he held his footing on the rocking train, putting out a few fingers to the window sill only for the form of the thing. He looked all at once ridiculous and dishonored in his cheap English clothes—the little jacket, the Tweedledum cap on his head. He outdistanced his clothes; he was better than they were. But he was rushing on this train into an existence where his clothes would be too good for him.

"D'you know about any ghosts?" said the boy again.

"Oh, sure," said McLaughlin, and shivered, for he still felt sick, even though he was sharing a bottle with the Limey bride. He said, "Indians see them," which was as close as he could come to being crafty. But there was no reaction out of the mother; she was not English for nothing.

"You seen any?"

"*I'm* not an Indian," McLaughlin started to say; instead he said, "Well, yes. I saw the ghost, or something like the ghost, of a dog I had."

They looked at each other, and the boy's mother said, "Stop that, you two. Stop that this minute."

"I'll tell you a strange thing about Dennis," said his mother. "It's this. There's times he gives me the creeps."

Dennis was lying on the seat beside her with his head on her lap.

She said, "If I don't like it I can clear out. I was a waitress. There's always work."

"Or find another man," McLaughlin said. "Only it won't be me, girlie. I'll be far away."

"Den says that when the train stopped he saw a lot of elves," she said, complaining.

"Not elves—men," said Dennis. "Some of them had mattresses rolled up on their backs. They were little and bent over. They were talking French. They were going up north."

McLaughlin coughed and said, "He means settlers. They were sent up on this same train during the depression. But that's nine, ten years ago. It was supposed to clear the unemployed out of the towns, get them off relief. But there wasn't anything up here then. The winters were terrible. A lot of them died."

"He couldn't know that," said Mum edgily. "For that matter, how can he tell what is French? He's never heard any."

"No, he couldn't know. It was around ten years ago, when times were bad."

"Are they good now?"

"Jeez, after a *war?*" He shoved his hand in the pocket of his shirt, where he kept a roll, and he let her see the edge of it.

She made no comment, but put her hand on Den's head and said to him, "You didn't see anyone. Now shut up."

"Sor 'em," the boy said in a voice as low as he could descend without falling into a whisper.

"You'll see what your Dad'll give you when you tell lies." But she was half-hearted about the threat and did not quite believe in it. She had been attracted to the scenery, whose persistent sameness she could no longer ignore. "It's not proper country," she said. "It's bare."

"Not enough for me," said McLaughlin. "Too many people. I keep on moving north."

"I want to see some Indians," said Dennis, sitting up.

"There aren't any," his mother said. "Only in films."

"I don't like Canada." He held her arm. "Let's go home now."

"It's the train whistle. It's so sad. It gets him down."

The train slowed, jerked, flung them against each other, and came to a stop. It was quite day now; their faces were plain and clear, as if drawn without shading on white paper. McLaughlin felt responsible for them, even compassionate; the change in him made the boy afraid.

"We're getting down, Den," said his Mum, with great, wide eyes. "We take another train. See? It'll be grand. Do you hear what Mum's telling you?"

He was determined not to leave the train, and clung to the window sill, which was too smooth and narrow to provide a grip; McLaughlin had no difficulty getting him away. "I'll give you a present," he said hurriedly. But he slapped all his pockets and found nothing to give. He did not think of the money, and his watch had been stolen in Montreal. The woman and the boy struggled out with their baggage, and McLaughlin, who had descended first so as to help them down, reached up and swung the boy in his arms.

"The Indians!" the boy cried, clinging to the train, to air; to anything. His face was momentarily muffled by McLaughlin's shirt. His cap fell to the ground. He screamed, "Where's Mum? I never saw *any*thing!"

"You saw Indians," said McLaughlin. "On the rail fence, at that long stop. Look, don't worry your mother. Don't keep telling her what you haven't seen. You'll be seeing plenty of everything now."

Letter from His Father

NADINE GORDIMER

MY DEAR SON,

You wrote me a letter you never sent.

It wasn't for me—it was for the whole world to read. (You and your instructions that everything should be burned. Hah!) You were never open and frank with me—that's one of the complaints you say I was always making against you. You write it in the letter you didn't want me to read; so what does *that* sound like, eh? But I've read the letter now, I've read it anyway, I've read everything, although you said I put your books on the night-table and never touched them. You know how it is, here where I am: not something that can be explained to anyone who isn't here—they used to talk about secrets going to the grave, but the funny thing is there are no secrets here at all. If there was something you wanted to know, you should have known, if it doesn't let you lie quiet, then you can *have knowledge of it,* from here. Yes, you gave me that much credit, you said I was a true Kafka in 'strength . . . eloquence, endurance, a certain way of doing things on a grand scale' and I've not been content just to rot. In that way, I'm still the man I was, the go-getter. Restless. Restless. Taking whatever opportunity I can. There isn't anything, now, you can regard as hidden from me. Whether you say I left it unread on the night-table or whether you weren't man enough, even at the age of thirty-six, to show me a letter that was supposed to be for me.

I write to you after we are both dead. Whereas you don't stir. There won't be any response from you, I know that. You began that letter by saying you were afraid of me—and then you were afraid to let me read it. And now you've escaped altogether. Because without the Kafka will-power you can't reach out from nothing and nowhere. I was going to call it a desert, but where's the sand, where're the camels, where's the sun—I'm still *mensch* enough to crack a joke— you see? Oh excuse me, I forgot—you didn't like my jokes, my fooling around with kids. My poor boy, unfortunately you had no life in you, in all those books and diaries and letters (the ones you posted, to strangers, to women) you said it a hundred times before you put the words in my mouth, in your literary way, in that letter: you yourself were 'unfit for life'. So death comes, how would you say, quite naturally to you. It's not like that for a man of vigour like I was, I can tell you, and so here I am writing, talking . . . I don't know if there is a word for what this is. Anyway, it's *Hermann Kafka*. I've outlived you here, same as in Prague.

That is what you really accuse me of, you know, for sixty or so pages (I notice the length of that letter varies a bit from language to language, of course it's been translated into everything—I don't know what—Hottentot and Icelandic, Chinese, although you wrote it 'for me' in German). I *outlived* you, not for seven years, as an old sick man, after you died, but while you were young and alive. Clear as daylight, from the examples you give of being afraid of me, from the time you were a little boy: you were not afraid, you were envious. At first, when I took you swimming and you say you felt yourself a nothing, puny and weak beside my big, strong, naked body in the change-house—all right, you also say you were proud of such a father, a father with a fine physique . . . And may I remind you that father was taking the trouble and time, the few hours he could get away from the business, to try and make something of that *nebich*, develop his muscles, put some flesh on those poor little bones so he would grow up sturdy? But even before your barmitzvah the normal pride every boy has in his father changed to jealousy, with you. You couldn't be like me, so you decided I wasn't good enough for you: coarse, loud-mouthed, ate 'like a pig' (your very words), cut my fingernails at table, cleaned my ears with a toothpick. Oh yes, you can't hide anything from me, now, I've read it all, all the thousands and thousands of words you've used to shame your own family, your own father, before the whole world. And with your gift for words you turn everything inside-out and prove, like a circus magician, it's love, the piece of dirty paper's a beautiful silk flag, you *loved your father too much,* and so—what? *You* tell me. You couldn't be like him? You wanted to be like *him?* The *ghasa,* the shouter, the gobbler? Yes, my son, these 'insignificant details' you write down and quickly dismiss—these details hurt. Eternally. After all, you've become immortal through writing, as you insist you did, only about me, 'everything was about you, father'; a hundred years after your birth, the Czech Jew, son of Hermann and Julie Kafka, is supposed to be one of the greatest writers who ever lived. Your work will be read as long as there are people to read it. That's what they say everywhere, even the Germans who burned your sisters and my grandchildren in incinerators. Some say you were also some kind of prophet (God knows what you were thinking, shut away in your room while the rest of the family was having a game of cards in the evening); after you died, some countries built camps where the things you made up for that story *In The Penal Colony* were practised, and ever since then there have been countries in different parts of the world where the devil's work that came into your mind is still carried out—I don't want to think about it.

You were not blessed to bring any happiness to this world with your genius, my son. Not at home, either. Well, we had to accept what God gave. Do you ever stop to think whether it wasn't a sorrow for me (never mind—for once—how you felt) that your two brothers, who might have grown up to bring your mother and me joy, died as babies? And you sitting there at meals always with a pale, miserable, glum face, not a word to say for yourself, picking at your food . . . You haven't forgotten that I used to hold up the newspaper so as not to have to see that. You bear a grudge. You've told everybody. But you don't think about what there was in a father's heart. From the beginning. I had to hide it behind a newspaper—anything. For your sake.

Because you were never like any other child. You admit it: however we had tried to bring you up, you say you would have become a 'weakly, timid, hesitant person'. What small boy doesn't enjoy a bit of a rough-house with his father?

But writing at thirty-six years old, you can only remember being frightened when I chased you, in fun, round the table, and your mother, joining in, would snatch you up out of my way while you shrieked. For God's sake, what's so terrible about that? I should have such memories of my childhood! I know you never liked to hear about it, it bored you, you don't spare me the written information that it 'wore grooves in your brain', but when *I* was seven years old I had to push my father's barrow from village to village, with open sores on my legs in winter. Nobody gave me delicacies to mess about on my plate; we were glad when we got potatoes. You make a show of me, mimicking how I used to say these things. But wasn't I right when I told you and your sisters—provided for by me, living like fighting-cocks because I stood in the business twelve hours a day—what did you know of such things? What did anyone know, what I suffered as a child? And then it's a sin if I wanted to give my own son a little pleasure I never had.

And that other business you *schlepped* up out of the past—the night I'm supposed to have shut you out on the *pavlatche*. Because of you the whole world knows the Czech word for the kind of balcony we had in Prague! Yes, the whole world knows that story, too. I am famous, too. You made me famous as the father who frightened his child once and for all: for life. Thank you very much. I want to tell you that I don't even remember that incident. I'm not saying it didn't happen, although you always had an imagination such as nobody ever had before or since, eh? But it could only have been the last resort your mother and I turned to—you know that your mother spoilt you, *over-protected* they would call it, now. You couldn't possibly remember how naughty you were at night, what a little tyrant you were, how you thought of every excuse to keep us sleepless. It was all right for you, you could nap during the day, a small child. But I had my business, I had to earn the living, I needed some rest. Pieces of bread, a particular toy you fancied, make wee-wee, another blanket on, a blanket taken off, drinks of water—there was no end to your tricks and whining. I suppose I couldn't stand it any longer. I feared to do you some harm. (You admit I never beat you, only scared you a little by taking off my braces in preparation to use them on you.) So I put you out of harm's way. That night. Just for a few minutes. It couldn't have been more than a minute. As if your mother would have let you catch cold! God forbid! And you've held it against me all your life. I'm sorry, I have to say it again, that old expression of mine that irritated you so much: I wish I had your worries.

Everything that went wrong for you is my fault. You write it down for sixty pages or so and at the same time you say to me 'I believe you are entirely blameless in the matter of our estrangement.' I was a 'true Kafka', you took after your mother's, the Löwy side etc.—all you inherited from me, according to you, were your bad traits, without having the benefit of my vitality. I was 'too strong' for you. You could not help it; I could not help it. So? All you wanted was *for me to admit that*, and we could have lived in peace. You were judge, you were jury, you were accused; you sentenced yourself, first. 'At my desk, that is my place. My head in my hands—that is my attitude.' (And that's what your poor mother and I had to look at, that was our pride and joy, our only surviving son!) But I was accused, too; you were judge, you were jury in my case, too. Right? By what right? Fancy goods—you despised the family business that fed us all, that paid for your education. What concern was it of yours, the way I treated the shop assistants? You only took an interest so you could judge, judge. It was a mistake to have let you study law. You did nothing with your qualification, your expensive education that I slaved and ruined my health for. Nothing but sentence me.— Now what did I want to say? Oh yes. Look what you wanted me to admit, under the great writer's beautiful words. If something goes wrong, somebody must be to blame, eh? We were not straw dolls, pulled about from above on strings. One of *us* must be to blame. And don't tell me you think it could be you. The stronger is always to blame, isn't that so? I'm not a deep thinker like you, only a dealer in retail fancy goods, but isn't that a law of life? 'The effect you had on me was the effect you could not help having.' You think I'll believe you're paying me a compliment, forgiving me, when you hand me the worst insult any father could receive? If it's what I am that's to blame, then I'm to blame, to the last drop of my heart's blood and whatever this is that's survived my body, for what *I am*, for being alive and begetting a son! You! Is that it? Because of you *I* should never have lived at all!

You always had a fine genius (never mind your literary one) for working me up. And you knew it was bad for my heart-condition. Now, what does it matter . . . but, as God's my witness, you aggravate me . . . you make me . . . Well.

All I know is that I am to blame for ever. You've seen to that. It's written, and not alone by you. There are plenty of people writing books about Kafka, Franz Kafka. I'm even blamed for the name I handed down, our family name. *Kavka* is Czech for jackdaw, so that's maybe the reason for your animal obsession. *Dafke!* Insect, ape, dog, mouse, stag, what didn't you imagine yourself. They say the beetle story is a great masterpiece, thanks to me—I'm the one who treated you like an inferior species, gave you the inspiration . . . You wake up as a bug, you give a lecture as an ape. Do any of these wonderful scholars think what this meant to me, having a son who didn't have enough self-respect to feel himself a man?

You have such a craze for animals, but may I remind you, when you were staying with Ottla at Zürau you wouldn't even undress in front of a cat she'd brought in to get rid of the mice . . .

Yet you imagined a dragon coming into your room. It said (an educated dragon, *noch*): 'Drawn hitherto by your longing . . . I offer myself to you.' Your longing, Franz: ugh, for monsters, for perversion. You describe a person (yourself, of course) in some crazy fantasy of living with a horse. Just listen to you, '. . . for a year I lived together with a horse in such ways as, say, a man would live with a girl whom he respects, but by whom he is rejected.' You even gave the horse a girl's name, Eleanor. I ask you, is that the kind of story made up by a normal young man? Is it decent that people should read such things, long after you are gone? But it's published, everything is published.

And worst of all, what about the animal in the synagogue. Some sort of rat, weasel, a marten you call it. You tell how it ran all over during prayers, running along the lattice of the women's section and even climbing down to the curtain in front of the Ark of the Covenant. A *schande*, an animal running about during divine service. Even if it's only a story—only you would imagine it. No respect.

You go on for several pages (in that secret letter) about my use of vulgar

Yiddish expressions, about my 'insignificant scrap of Judaism', which was 'purely social' and so meant we couldn't 'find each other in Judaism' if in nothing else. This, from you! When you were a youngster and I had to drag you to the Yom Kippur services once a year you were sitting there making up stories about unclean animals approaching the Ark, the most holy object of the Jewish faith. Once you were grown up, you went exactly once to the Altneu synagogue. The people who write books about you say it must have been to please me. I'd be surprised. When you suddenly discovered you were a Jew, after all, of course your Judaism was highly intellectual, nothing in common with the Jewish customs I was taught to observe in my father's *shtetl*, pushing the barrow at the age of seven. Your Judaism was learnt at the Yiddish Theatre. That's a *nice* crowd! Those dirty-living travelling players you took up with at the Savoy Café. Your friend the actor Jizchak Löwy. No relation to your mother's family, thank God. I wouldn't let such a man even meet her. You had the disrespect to bring him into your parents' home, and I saw it was my duty to speak to him in such a way that he wouldn't ever dare to come back again. (Hah! I used to look down from the window and watch him, hanging around in the cold, outside the building, waiting for you.) And the Tschissik woman, that *nafke*, one of his actresses— I've found out you thought you were in love with her, a married woman (if you can call the way those people live a marriage). Apart from Fräulein Bauer you never fancied anything but a low type of woman. I say it again as I did then: if you lie down with dogs, you get up with fleas. You lost your temper (yes, you, this time), you flew into a rage at your father when he told you that. And when I reminded you of my heart-condition, you put yourself in the right again, as usual, you said (I remember like it was yesterday) 'I make great efforts to restrain myself.' But now I've read your diaries, the dead don't need to creep into your bedroom and read them behind your back (which you accused your mother and me of doing), I've read what you wrote afterwards, that you sensed in me, your father, 'as always at such moments of extremity, the existence of a wisdom which I can no more than scent'. So you *knew*, while you were defying me, you knew I was right!

The fact is that you were antisemitic, Franz. You were never interested in what was happening to your own people. The hooligans' attacks on Jews in the streets, on houses and shops, that took place while you were growing up—I don't see a word about them in your diaries, your notebooks. You were only *imagining* Jews. Imagining them tortured in places like your *Penal Colony*, maybe. I don't want to think about what that means.

Right, towards the end you studied Hebrew, you and your sister Ottla had some wild dream about going to Palestine. You, hardly able to breathe by then, digging potatoes on a kibbutz! The latest book about you says you were in revolt against the 'shopkeeper mentality' of your father's class of Jew; but it was the shopkeeper father, the buttons and buckles, braid, ribbons, ornamental combs, press-studs, hooks-and-eyes, boot laces, photo frames, shoe horns, novelties and notions that earned the bread for you to dream by. You were antisemitic, Franz; if such a thing is possible as for a Jew to cut himself in half. (For you, I suppose, anything is possible.) You told Ottla that to marry that goy Josef Davis was better than marrying ten Jews. When your great friend Brod wrote a book called 'The Jewesses' you wrote there were too many of them in it. You saw them like lizards. (Animals again, low animals.) 'However happy we are to watch a single lizard on a footpath in Italy, we would be horrified to see hundreds of them crawling over each other in a pickle jar.' From where did you get such ideas? Not from your home, that I know.

And look how Jewish you are, in spite of the way you despised us—Jews, your Jewish family! You answer questions with questions. I've discovered that's your style, your famous literary style: your Jewishness. Did you or did you not write the following story, playlet, wha'd'you-call-it, your friend Brod kept every scribble and you knew he wouldn't burn even a scrap. 'Once at a spiritualist seance a new spirit announced its presence, and the following conversation with it took place. The spirit: Excuse me. The spokesman: Who are you? The spirit: Excuse me. The spokesman: What do you want? The spirit: To go away. The spokesman: But you've only just come. The spirit: It's a mistake. The spokesman: No, it isn't a mistake. You've come and you'll stay. The spirit: I've just begun to feel ill. The spokesman: Badly? The spirit: Badly? The spokesman: Physically? The spirit: Physically? The spokesman: You answer with questions.

That will not do. We have ways of punishing you, so I advise you to answer, for then we shall soon dismiss you. The spirit: Soon? The spokesman: Soon. The spirit: In one minute? The spokesman: Don't go on in this miserable way . . .'

Questions without answers. Riddles. You wrote 'It is always only in contradiction that I can live. But this doubtless applies to everyone; for living, one dies, dying, one lives.' Speak for yourself! So who did you think you were when that whim took you—their prophet, Jesus Christ? What did you *want?* The *goyishe* heavenly hereafter? What did you mean when a lost man, far from his native country, says to someone he meets 'I am in your hands' and the other says, 'No. You are free and that is why you are lost'? What's the sense in writing about a woman 'I lie in wait for her in order not to meet her'? There's only one of your riddles I think I understand, and then only because for forty-two years, God help me, I had to deal with you myself. 'A cage went in search of a bird.' That's you. The cage, not the bird. I don't know why. Maybe it will come to me. As I say, if a person wants to, he can know everything, here.

All that talk about going away. You called your home (more riddles) 'My prison—my fortress'. You grumbled—in print, everything ended up in print, my son—that your room was only a passage, a thoroughfare between the living-room and your parents' bedroom. You complained you had to write in pencil because we took away your ink to stop you writing. It was for your own good, your health—already you were a grown man, a qualified lawyer, but you know you couldn't look after yourself. Scribbling away half the night, you'd have been too tired to work properly in the mornings, you'd have lost your position at the Assicurazioni Generali (or was it by then the Arbeiter-Unfall-Versicherungs-Anstalt für das Königreich Böhmen, my memory doesn't get any better, here). And I wasn't made of money. I couldn't go on supporting everybody for ever.

You've published every petty disagreement in the family. It was a terrible thing, according to you, we didn't want you to go out in bad weather, your poor mother wanted you to wrap up. You with your delicate health, always sickly—you didn't inherit my constitution, it was only a lifetime of hard work, the business, the family worries that got me, in the end! You recorded that you couldn't go for a walk without your parents making a fuss, but at twenty-eight you were

still living at home. Going away. My poor boy. You could hardly get yourself to
the next room. You shut yourself up when people came to visit. Always crawling off to bed, sleeping in the day (oh yes, you couldn't sleep at night, not like
anybody else), sleeping your life away. You invented *Amerika* instead of having
the guts to emigrate, get up off the bed, pack up and go there, make a new life!
Even that girl you jilted twice managed it. Did you know Felice is still alive
somewhere, there now, in America? She's an old, old woman with great-
grandchildren. They didn't get her into the death camps those highly-educated
people say you knew about before they happened. America you never went to,
Spain you dreamt about . . . your Uncle Alfred was going to find you jobs there,
in Madeira, the Azores . . . God knows where else. Grandson of a ritual slaugh-
terer, a *schochet,* that was why you couldn't bear to eat meat, they say, and that
made you weak and undecided. So that was my fault, too, because my poor father had to earn a living. When your mother was away from the flat, you'd have
starved yourself to death if it hadn't been for me. And what was the result? You
resented so much what I provided for you, you went and had your stomach
pumped out! Like someone who's been poisoned! And you didn't forget to write
it down, either: 'My feeling is that disgusting things will come out.'

Whatever I did for you was *dreck.* You felt 'despised, condemned, beaten
down' by me. But you despised *me;* the only difference, I wasn't so easy to beat
down, eh? How many times did you try to leave home, and you couldn't go? It's
all there in your diaries, in the books they write about you. What about that
other masterpiece of yours, *The Judgment.* A father and son quarrelling, and
then the son goes and drowns himself, saying 'Dear parents, I have always loved
you, all the same.' The wonderful discovery about that story, you might like to
hear, it proves Hermann Kafka most likely didn't want his son to grow up and
be a man, any more than his son wanted to manage without his parents' protection. The *meshuggener* who wrote that, may he get rich on it! I wouldn't wish it
on him to try living with you, that's all, the way we had to. When your hunchback friend secretly showed your mother a complaining letter of yours, to get
you out of your duty of going to the asbestos factory to help your own sister's
husband, Brod kept back one thing you wrote. But now it's all published, all, all,

all the terrible things you thought about your own flesh and blood. 'I hate them all': father, mother, sisters.

You couldn't do without us—without me. You only moved away from us when you were nearly thirty-two, a time when every *man* has a wife and children already, a home of his own.

You were always dependent on someone. Your friend Brod, poor devil. If it hadn't been for the little hunchback, who would know of your existence today? Between the incinerators that finished your sisters and the fire you wanted to burn up your manuscripts, nothing would be left. The kind of men you invented, the Gestapo, confiscated whatever papers of yours there were in Berlin, and no trace of them has ever been found, even by the great Kafka experts who stick their noses into everything. You said you loved Max Brod more than yourself. I can see that. You liked the idea he had of you, that you knew wasn't yourself (you see, sometimes I'm not so *grob,* uneducated, knowing nothing but fancy goods, maybe I got from you some 'insights'). Certainly, I wouldn't recognize my own son the way Brod described you: 'the aura Kafka gave out of extraordinary strength, something I've never encountered elsewhere, even in meetings with great and famous men . . . the infallible solidity of his insights never tolerated a single lacuna, nor did he ever speak an insignificant word . . . He was life-affirming, ironically tolerant towards the idiocies of the world, and therefore full of sad humour.'

I must say, your mother who put up with your faddiness when she came back from a day standing in the business, your sisters who acted in your plays to please you, your father who worked his heart out for his family—we never got the benefit of your tolerance. Your sisters (except Ottla, the one you admit you were a bad influence on, encouraging her to leave the shop and work on a farm like a peasant, to starve herself with you on rabbit-food, to marry that goy) were giggling idiots, so far as you were concerned. Your mother never felt the comfort of her son's strength. You never gave us anything to laugh at, sad or otherwise. And you hardly spoke to me at all, even an insignificant word. Whose fault was it you were that person you describe 'strolling about on the island in the pool, where there are neither books nor bridges, hearing the music, but not being heard.' You wouldn't cross a road, never mind a bridge, to pass the time of day, to be pleasant to other people, you shut yourself in your room and stuffed your ears with Oropax against the music of life, yes, the sounds of cooking, people coming and going (what were we supposed to do, pass through closed doors?), even the singing of the pet canaries annoyed you, laughter, the occasional family tiff, the bed squeaking where normal married people made love.

What I've just said may surprise. That last bit, I mean. But since I died in 1931 I know the world has changed a lot. People, even fathers and sons, are talking about things that shouldn't be talked about. People aren't ashamed to read anything, even private diaries, even letters. There's no shame, anywhere. With that, too, you were ahead of your time, Franz. You were not ashamed to write in your diary, which your friend Brod would publish—you must have known he would publish everything, make a living out of us—things that have led one of the famous Kafka scholars to *study* the noises in our family flat in Prague. Writing about me: 'It would have been out of character for Hermann Kafka to restrain any noises he felt like making during coupling; it would have been out of character for Kafka, who was ultra-sensitive to noise and had grown up with these noises, to mention the suffering they caused him.'

You left behind you for everyone to read that the sight of your parents' pyjamas and nightdress on the bed disgusted you. Let me also speak freely like everyone else. You were made in that bed. That disgusts me: your disgust over a place that should have been holy to you, a place to hold in the highest respect. Yet you are the one who complained about my coarseness when I suggested you ought to find yourself a woman—buy one, hire one—rather than try to prove yourself a man at last, at thirty-six, by marrying some Prague Jewish tart who shook her tits in a thin blouse. Yes, I'm speaking of that Julie Wohryzek, the shoemaker's daughter, your second fiancée. You even had the insolence to throw the remark in my face, in that letter you didn't send, but I've read it anyway, I've read everything now, although you said I put *In The Penal Colony* on the bedside table and never mentioned it again.

I have to talk about another matter we didn't discuss, father and son, while we were both alive—all right, it was my fault, maybe you're right, as I've said, times were different . . . Women. I must bring this up because—my poor boy—marriage was 'the greatest terror' of your life. You write that. You say your attempts to explain why you couldn't marry—on these depends the 'success' of the whole letter you didn't send. According to you, marrying, founding a family was 'the utmost a human being can succeed in doing at all'. Yet you couldn't marry. How is any ordinary human being to understand that? You wrote more than a quarter of a million words to Felice Bauer, but you couldn't be a husband to her. You put your parents through the farce of travelling all the way to Berlin for an engagement party (there's the photograph you had taken, the happy couple, in the books they write about you, by the way). The engagement was broken, was on again, off again. Can you wonder? Anyone who goes into a bookshop or library can read what you wrote to your fiancée when your sister Elli gave birth to our first grand-daughter. You felt nothing but nastiness, envy against your brother-in-law because 'I'll never have a child.' No, not with the Bauer girl, not in a decent marriage, like anybody else's son; but I've found out you had a child, Brod says so, by a woman, Grete Bloch, who was supposed to be the Bauer girl's best friend, who even acted as matchmaker between you! What do you say to that? Maybe it's news to you. I don't know. (That's how irresponsible you were.) They say she went away. Perhaps she never told you.

As for the next one you tried to marry, the one you make such a song and dance over because of my remark about Prague Jewesses and the blouse etc.—for once you came to your senses, and you called off the wedding only two days before it was supposed to take place. Not that I could have influenced you. Since when did you take into consideration what your parents thought? When you told me you wanted to marry the shoemaker's daughter—naturally I was upset. At least the Bauer girl came from a nice family. What I said about the blouse just came out, I'm human, after all. But I was frank with you, man to man. You weren't a youngster anymore. A man doesn't have to marry a nothing who will go with anybody.

I saw what that marriage was about, my poor son. You wanted a woman. Nobody understood that better than I did, believe me, I was normal man enough, eh! There were places in Prague where one could get a woman. (I suppose whatever's happened, there still are, always will be.) I tried to help you; I offered to go along with you myself. I said it in front of your mother, who—yes, as you write you were so shocked to see, was in agreement with me. We wanted so much to help you, even your own mother would go so far as that.

But in that letter you didn't think I'd ever see, you accuse me of humiliating you and I don't know what else. You wanted to marry a tart, but you were insulted at the idea of buying one?

Writing that letter only a few days after you yourself called off your second try at getting married, aged thirty-six, you find that your father, as a man-of-the-world, not only showed 'contempt' for you on that occasion, but that when he had spoken to you as a broad-minded father when you were a youngster, he had given you information that set off the whole ridiculous business of your never being able to marry, ever. Already, twenty years before the Julie Wohryzek row, with 'a few frank words' (as you put it) your father made you incapable of taking a wife and pushed you down 'into the filth as if it were my destiny'. You remember some walk with your mother and me on the Josefsplatz when you showed curiosity about, well, men's feelings and women, and I was open and honest with you and told you I could give you advice about where to go so that these things could be done quite safely, without bringing home any disease. You were sixteen years old, physically a man, not a child, eh? Wasn't it time to talk about such things?

Shall I tell you what *I* remember? Once you picked a quarrel with your mother and me because we hadn't educated you sexually—your words. Now you complain because I tried to guide you in these matters. I did—I didn't. Make up your mind. Have it your own way. Whatever I did, you believed it was *because of what I did* that you couldn't bring yourself to marry. When you thought you wanted the Bauer girl, didn't I give in, to please you? Although you were in no financial position to marry, although I had to give your two married sisters financial help, although I had worries enough, a sick man, you'd caused me enough trouble by persuading me to invest in a *mechulah* asbestos factory? Didn't I give in? And when the girl came to Prague to meet your parents and sisters, you wrote, 'My family likes her almost more than I'd like it to.' So it went as far as that: you couldn't like anything we liked, was that why you couldn't marry her?

A long time ago, a long way . . . ah, it all moves away, it's getting faint . . . But I haven't finished. Wait.

You say you wrote your letter because you wanted to explain why you couldn't marry. I'm writing this letter because you tried to write it for me. *You would take even that away from your father.* You answered your own letter, before I could. You made what you imagine as my reply part of the letter you wrote me. To save me the trouble . . . Brilliant, like they say. With your great gifts as a famous writer, you express it all better than I could. You are there, quickly, with an answer, before I can be. You take the words out of my mouth: while you are accusing yourself, in my name, of being 'too clever, obsequious, parasitic and insincere' in blaming your life on me, you are—yet again, one last time!—finally being too clever, obsequious, parasitic and insincere in the trick of stealing your father's chance to defend himself. A genius. What is left to say about you if—how well you know yourself, my boy, it's terrible—you call yourself the kind of vermin that doesn't only sting, but at the same time sucks blood to keep itself alive? And even that isn't the end of the twisting, the cheating. You then confess that this whole 'correction', 'rejoinder', as you, an expensively educated man, call it, 'does not originate' in your father but in you yourself, Franz Kafka. So you see, here's the proof, something *I* know you, with all your brains, can't know *for me:* you say you always wrote about me, it was all about me, your father; but it was all about you. The beetle. The bug that lay on its back waving its legs in the air and couldn't get up to go and see America or the Great Wall of China. You, you, self, self. And in your letter, after you have defended me against yourself, when you finally make the confession—right again, in the right again, always—you take the last word, in proof of your saintliness I could know nothing about, never understand, a businessman, a shopkeeper. That is your 'truth' about us you hoped might be able to 'make our living and our dying easier.'

The way you ended up, Franz. The last woman you found yourself. It wasn't our wish, God knows. Living with that Eastern Jewess, and in sin. We sent you money; that was all we could do. If we'd come to see you, if we'd swallowed our pride, meeting that woman, our presence would only have made you worse. It's there in everything you've written, everything they write about you: everything connected with us made you depressed and ill. We knew she was giving you the wrong food, cooking like a gypsy on a spirit stove. She kept you in an unheated hovel in Berlin . . . may God forgive me (Brod has told the world), I had to turn my back on her at your funeral.

Franz . . . When you received copies of your book *In The Penal Colony* from Kurt Wolff Verlag that time . . . You gave me one and I said 'Put it on the night-table.' You say I never mentioned it again. Well, don't you understand— I'm not a literary man. I'm telling you now. I read a little bit, a page or two at a time. If you had seen that book, there was a pencil mark every two, three pages, so I would know next time where I left off. It wasn't like the books I knew—I hadn't much time for reading, working like a slave since I was a small boy, I wasn't like you, I couldn't shut myself up in a room with books, when I was young. I would have starved. But you know that. Can't you understand that I was—yes—not too proud—ashamed to let you know I didn't find it easy to understand your kind of writing, it was all strange to me.

Hah! I know I'm no intellectual, but I knew how to live!

Just a moment . . . give me time . . . there's a fading . . . Yes—can you imagine how we felt when Ottla told us you had tuberculosis? Oh how could you bring it over your heart to remind me I once said, in a temper, to a useless assistant coughing all over the shop (you should have had to deal with those lazy *goyim*), he ought to die, the sick dog. Did I know you would get tuberculosis, too? It wasn't our fault your lungs rotted. I tried to expand your chest when you were little, teaching you to swim; you should never have moved out of your own home, the care of your parents, to that rat-hole in the Schönbornpalais. And the hovel in Berlin . . . We had some good times, didn't we? Franz? When we had beer and sausages after the swimming lessons? At least you remembered the beer and sausages, when you were dying.

One more thing. It chokes me, I have to say it. I know you'll never answer. You once wrote 'Speech is possible only where one wants to lie.' You were too *ultra-sensitive* to speak to us, Franz. You kept silence, with the truth: those playing a game of cards, turning in bed on the other side of the wall—it was the sound of live people you didn't like. Your revenge, that you were too cowardly to take in life, you've taken here. We can't lie peacefully in our graves; dug up, unwrapped from our shrouds by your fame. To desecrate your parents' grave as well as their bed, aren't you ashamed? Aren't you ashamed—now? Well, what's the use of quarrelling. We lie together in the same grave—you, your mother and I. We've ended up as we always should have been, united. Rest in peace, my son. I wish you had let me.

Your father,

HERMANN KAFKA

The Pond

✦

PATRICIA HIGHSMITH

ELINOR SIEVERT STOOD LOOKING DOWN at the pond. She was half thinking, half dreaming, or imagining. Was it safe? For Chris? The agent had said it was four feet deep. It was certainly full of weeds, its surface nearly covered with algae or whatever they called the little oval green things that floated. Well, four feet was enough to drown a four-year-old. She must warn Chris.

She lifted her head and walked back towards the white, two-storey house. She had just rented the house, and had been here only since yesterday. She hadn't entirely unpacked. Hadn't the agent said something about draining the pond, that it wouldn't be too difficult or expensive? Was there a spring under it? Elinor hoped not, because she'd taken the house for six months.

It was two in the afternoon, and Chris was having his nap. There were more kitchen cartons to unpack, also the record-player in its neat, taped carton. Elinor fished the record-player out, connected it, and chose an LP of New Orleans jazz to pick her up. She hoisted another load of dishes up to the long drainboard.

The doorbell rang.

Elinor was confronted by the smiling face of a woman about her own age.

'Hello I'm Jane Caldwell—one of your neighbours. I just wanted to say hello and welcome. We're friends with Jimmy Adams, the agent, and he told us you'd moved in here.'

'Yes. My name's Elinor Sievert. Won't you come in?' Elinor held the door wider. 'I'm not quite unpacked as yet—but at least we could have a cup of coffee in the kitchen.'

Within a few minutes, they were sitting on opposite sides of the wooden table, cups of instant coffee before them. Jane said she had two children, a boy and a girl, the girl just starting school, and that her husband was an architect and worked in Hartford.

'What brought you to Luddington?' Jane asked.

'I needed a change—from New York. I'm a free-lance journalist, so I thought I'd try a few months in the country. At least I call this the country, compared to New York.'

'I can understand that. I heard about your husband,' Jane said on a more serious note. 'I'm sorry. Especially since you have a small son. I want you to know we're a friendly batch around here, and at the same time we'll let you alone, if that's what you want. But consider Ed and me neighbours, and if you need something, just call on us.'

'Thank you,' Elinor said. She remembered that she'd told Adams that her husband had recently died, because Adams had asked if her husband would be living with her. Now Jane was ready to go, not having finished her coffee.

'I know you've got things to do, so I don't want to take any more of your time,' said Jane. She had rosy cheeks, chestnut hair. 'I'll give you Ed's business card, but it's got our home number on it too. If you want to ask any kind of question, just call us. We've been here six years—Where's your little boy?'

'He's—'

As if on cue, Chris called, 'Mommy!' from the top of the stairs.

Elinor jumped up. 'Come down, Chris! Meet a nice new neighbour!'

Chris came down the stairs a bit timidly, holding on to the banister.

Jane stood beside Elinor at the foot of the staircase. 'Hello, Chris. My name's Jane. How are you?'

Chris's blue eyes examined her seriously. 'Hello.'

Elinor smiled. 'I think he just woke up and doesn't know where he is. Say "How do you do," Chris.'

'How do you do,' said Chris.

'Hope you'll like it here, Chris,' Jane said. 'I want you to meet my boy Bill. He's just your age. Bye-bye, Elinor. Bye, Chris!' Jane went out the front door.

Elinor gave Chris his glass of milk and his treat—today a bowl of apple sauce. Elinor was against chocolate cupcakes every afternoon, though Chris at the moment thought they were the greatest things ever invented. 'Wasn't she nice? Jane?' Elinor said, finishing her coffee.

'Who is she?'

'One of our new neighbours.' Elinor continued her unpacking. Her article-in-progress was about self-help with legal problems. She would need to go to the Hartford library, which had a newspaper department, for more research. Hartford was only a half hour away. Elinor had bought a good second-hand car. Maybe Jane would know a girl who could baby-sit now and then. 'Isn't it nicer here than in New York?'

Chris lifted his blond head. 'I want to go outside.'

'But of course! It's so sunny, you won't need a sweater. We've got a garden, Chris! We can plant—radishes, for instance.' She remembered planting rad-ishes in her grandmother's garden when she was small, remembered the joy of pulling up the fat red and white edible roots. 'Come on, Chris.' She took his hand.

Chris's slight frown went away, and he gripped his mother's hand.

Elinor looked at the garden with different eyes, Chris's eyes. Plainly no one had tended it for months. There were big prickly weeds between the jonquils that were beginning to open, and the peonies hadn't been cut last year. But there was an apple tree big enough for Chris to climb in.

'Our garden,' Elinor said. 'Nice and sloppy. All yours to play in, Chris, and the summer's just beginning.'

'How big is this?' Chris asked. He had broken away and was stooped by the pond.

Elinor knew he meant how deep was it. 'I don't know. Not very deep. But don't go wading. It's not like the seashore with sand. It's all muddy there.' Eli-nor spoke quickly. Anxiety had struck her like a physical pain. Was she still re-living the impact of Cliff's plane against the mountainside—that mountain in

Yugoslavia that she'd never see? She'd seen two or three newspaper photographs of it, blotchy black and white chaos, indicating, so the print underneath said, the wreckage of the airliner on which there had been no survivors of one hundred and seven passengers plus eight crewmen and stewardesses. No survivors. And Cliff among them. Elinor had always thought air crashes happened to strangers, never to anyone you knew, never even to a friend of a friend. Suddenly it had been Cliff, on an ordinary flight from Ankara. He'd been to Ankara at least seven times before.

'Is that a snake? Look, Mommy!' Chris yelled, leaning forward as he spoke. One foot sank, his arms shot forward for balance, and suddenly he was in water up to his hips. 'Ugh! Ha-ha!' He rolled sideways on the muddy edge, and squirmed backward up to the level of the lawn before his mother could reach him.

Elinor set him on his feet. 'Chris, I told you not to try wading! Now you'll need a bath. You see?'

'No, I won't!' Chris yelled, laughing, and ran off across the grass, bare legs and sandals flying, as if the muddy damp on his shorts had given him a special charge.

Elinor had to smile. Such energy! She looked down at the pond. The brown and black mud swirled, stirring long tentacles of vines, making the algae undulate. It was a good seven feet in diameter, the pond. A vine had clung to Chris's ankle as she'd pulled him up. Nasty! The vines were even growing out onto the grass to a length of three feet or more.

Before 5 P.M., Elinor rang the rental agent. She asked if it would be all right with the house-owner if she had the pond drained. Price wasn't of much concern to her, but she didn't tell Mr Adams that.

'It might seep up again,' said Mr Adams. 'The land's pretty low. Especially when it rains and—'

'I really don't mind trying it. It might help,' Elinor said. 'You know how it is with a small child. I have the feeling it isn't quite safe.'

Mr Adams said he would telephone a company tomorrow morning. 'Even this afternoon, if I can reach them.'

Mr Adams telephoned back in ten minutes and told Elinor that the workmen would arrive the next morning, probably quite early.

The workmen came at 8 A.M. After speaking with the two men, Elinor took Chris with her in the car to the library in Hartford. She deposited Chris in the children's book section, and told the woman in charge there that she would be back in an hour for Chris, and in case he got restless, she would be in the newspaper archives.

When she and Chris got back home, the pond was empty but muddy. If anything, it looked worse, uglier. It was a crater of wet mud laced with green vines, some as thick as a cigarette. The depression in the garden was hardly four feet deep. But how deep was the mud?

'I'm sorry,' said Chris, gazing down.

Elinor laughed. 'Sorry?—The pond's not the only thing to play with. Look at the trees we've got! What about the seeds we bought? What do you say we clear a patch and plant some carrots and radishes—now.'

Elinor changed into blue jeans. The clearing of weeds and the planting took longer than she had thought it would, nearly two hours. She worked with a fork and a trowel, both a bit rusty, which she'd found in the toolshed behind the house. Chris drew a bucket of water from the outside faucet and lugged it over, but while she and Chris were putting the seeds carefully in, one inch deep, a roll of thunder crossed the heavens. The sun had vanished. Within seconds, rain was pelting down, big drops that made them run for the house.

'Isn't that wonderful? Look!' Elinor held Chris up so he could see out of a kitchen window. 'We don't need to water our seeds. Nature's doing it for us.'

'Who's nature?'

Elinor smiled, tired now. 'Nature rules everything. Nature knows best. The garden's going to look fresh and new tomorrow.'

The following morning, the garden did look rejuvenated, the grass greener, the scraggly rose bushes more erect. The sun was shining again. And Elinor had her first letter. It was from Cliff's mother in Evanston. It said:

Dearest Elinor,

We both hope you are feeling more cheerful in your Connecticut house. Do drop us a line or telephone us when you find the time, but we know you are busy getting settled, not to mention getting back to your own work. We send you all good wishes for success with your next articles, and you must keep us posted.

The polaroid shots of Chris in his bath are a joy to us! You mustn't say he looks more like Cliff than you. He looks like both of you . . .

The letter lifted Elinor's spirits. She went out to see if the carrot and radish seeds had been beaten to the surface by the rain—in which case she meant to push them down again if she could see them—but the first thing that caught her eye was Chris, stooped again by the pond and poking at something with a stick. And the second thing she noticed was that the pond was full again. Almost as high as ever! Well, naturally, because of the hard rain. Or was it natural? It had to be. Maybe there was a spring below. Anyway, she thought, why should she pay for the draining if it didn't stay drained? She'd have to ring the company today. Miller Brothers, it was called

'Chris? What're you up to?'

'Frog!' he yelled back. 'I *think* I saw a frog.'

'Well, don't try to catch it!' Damn the weeds! They were back in full force, as if the brief draining had done them good. Elinor went to the toolshed. She thought she remembered seeing a pair of hedge clippers on the cement floor there.

Elinor found the clippers, rusted, and though she was eager to attack the vines, she forced herself to go to the kitchen first and put a couple of drops of salad oil on the centre screw of the clippers. Then she went out and started on the long, grapevinelike stems. The clippers were dull, but better than nothing, faster than scissors.

'What're you doing that for?' Chris asked.

'They're nasty *things*,' Elinor said. 'Clogging the pond. We don't want a messy pond, do we?' *Whack-whack!* Elinor's espadrilles sank into the wet bank. What on earth did the owners, or the former tenants, use the pond for? Gold-fish? Ducks?

A carp, Elinor thought suddenly. If the pond was going to stay a pond, then a carp was the thing to clean it, nibble at some of the vegetation. She'd buy one.

'If you ever fall in, Chris—'

'What?' Chris, still stooped, on the other side of the pond now, flung his stick away.

'For goodness' sake, don't fall in, but if you do—' Elinor forced herself to go on '—grab hold of these vines. You see? They're strong and growing from the edges. Pull yourself out by them.' Actually, the vines seemed to be growing from underwater as well, and pulling at those might send Chris into the pond.

Chris grinned, sideways. 'That's not deep. Not even deep as I am.'

Elinor said nothing.

The rest of that morning she worked on her law article, then telephoned Miller Brothers.

'Well, the ground's a little low there, ma'am. Not to mention the old cesspool's nearby and it still gets the drain from the kitchen sink, even though the toilets've been put on the mains. We know that house. Pond'll get it too if you've got a washing machine in the kitchen.'

Elinor hadn't. 'You mean, draining it is hopeless.'

'That's about the size of it.'

Elinor tried to force her anger down. 'Then I don't know why you agreed to do it.'

'Because you seemed set on it, ma'am.'

They hung up a few seconds later. What was she going to do about the bill when they presented it? She'd perhaps make them knock it down a bit. But she felt the situation was inconclusive. Elinor hated that.

While Chris was taking his nap, Elinor made a quick trip to Hartford, found a fish shop, and brought back a carp in a red plastic bucket which she had taken with her in the car. The fish flopped about in a vigorous way, and Elinor drove slowly, so the bucket wouldn't tip over. She went at once to the pond, and poured the fish in.

It was a fat, silvery carp. Its tail flicked the surface as it dove, then it rose and dove again, apparently happy in wider seas. Elinor smiled. The carp would surely eat some of the vines, the algae. She'd give it bread too. Carps could eat anything. Cliff had used to say there was nothing like carp to keep a pond or a lake clean. Above all, Elinor liked the idea that there was something *alive* in the pond besides vines. She started to walk back to the house, and found that a vine had encircled her left ankle. When she tried to kick her foot free, the vine tightened. She stooped and unwound it. That was one she hadn't whacked this morning. Or had it grown ten inches since this morning? Impossible. But now as she looked down at the pond and at its border, she couldn't see that she had accomplished much, even though she'd fished out quite a heap. The heap was a few feet away on the grass, in case she doubted it. Elinor blinked. She had the feeling that if she watched the pond closely, she'd be able to see the tentacles growing. She didn't like that idea.

Should she tell Chris about the carp? Elinor didn't want him trying to find it, poking into the water. On the other hand, if she didn't mention it, maybe he'd see it and have some crazy idea of catching it. Better to tell him, she decided.

So when Chris woke up, Elinor told him about the fish.

'You can toss some bread to him,' Elinor said. 'But don't try to catch him, because he likes the pond. He's going to help us keep it clean.'

'You don't want ever to catch him?' Chris asked, with milk all over his upper lip.

He was thinking of Cliff, Elinor knew. Cliff had loved fishing. 'We don't catch this one, Chris. He's our friend.'

Elinor worked. She had set up her typewriter in a front corner room upstairs which had light from two windows. The article was coming along nicely. She had a lot of original material from newspaper clippings. The theme was alerting the public to free legal advice from small claims offices which most people didn't know existed. Lots of people let sums like $250 go by the board, because they thought it wasn't worth the trouble of a court fight. Elinor worked until 6:30. Dinner was simple tonight, macaroni and cheese with bacon, one of Chris's favourite dishes. With the dinner in the oven, Elinor took a quick bath and put on blue slacks and a fresh blouse. She paused to look at the photograph of Cliff on the dressing table—a photograph in a silver frame which had been a present from Cliff's parents one Christmas. It was an ordinary black and white enlargement, Cliff sitting on the bank of a stream, propped against a tree, an old straw hat tipped back on his head. That had been taken somewhere outside Evanston, on one of their summer trips to visit his parents. Cliff held a straw or a blade of grass lazily between his lips. His denim shirt was open at the neck. No one, looking at the hill-billy image, would imagine that Cliff had had to dress up in white tie a couple of times a month in Paris, Rome, London or Ankara. Cliff had been in the diplomatic service, assistant or deputy to American statesmen, gifted in languages, gifted in tact. He'd known how to use a pistol also, and once a month in New York he'd gone to a certain armoury for practice. What had he done exactly? Elinor knew only sketchy anecdotes that Cliff had told her. He had done enough, however, to be paid a good salary, to be paid to keep silent, even to her. It had crossed her mind that his plane was wrecked to kill him, but she was sure that was absurd. Cliff hadn't been that important. His death had been an accident, not due to the weather but to a mechanical failure in the plane.

What would Cliff think of the pond? Elinor smiled wryly. Would he have it filled in with stones, turn it into a rock garden? Would he fill it in with earth? Would he pay no attention at all to the pond? Just call it 'nature'?

Two days later, when Elinor was typing a final draft of her article, she stopped at noon and went out into the garden for some fresh air. She'd brought the kitchen scissors, and she cut two red roses and one white rose to put on the table at lunch. Then the pond caught her eye, a blaze of chartreuse in the sunlight.

'Good Lord!' she whispered.

The vines! The weeds! They were all over the surface. And they were again climbing onto the land. Well, this was one thing she could and would see about:

she'd find an exterminator. She didn't care what poison they put down in the pond, if they could clear it. And of course she'd rescue the carp first, keep him in a bucket till the pond was safe again.

An exterminator was something Jane Caldwell might know about.

Elinor telephoned Jane before she started lunch. 'This *pond*,' Elinor began and stopped, because she had so much to say about it. 'I had it drained a few days ago, and now it's filled up again . . . No, that's not really the problem. I've given up the draining, it's the unbelievable vines. The way they grow! I wonder if you know a weed-killing company? I think it'll take professional—I mean, I don't think I can just toss some liquid poison in and get anywhere. You'll have to see this pond to believe it. It's like a jungle!'

'I know just the right people,' Jane said. 'They're called "Weed-Killer," so it's easy to remember. You've got a phone book there?'

Elinor had. Jane said Weed-Killer was very obliging and wouldn't make her wait a week before they turned up.

'How about you and Chris coming over for tea this afternoon?' Jane asked. 'I just made a coconut cake.'

'Love to. Thank you.' Elinor felt cheered.

She made lunch for herself and Chris, and told him they were invited to tea at the house of their neighbour Jane, and that he'd meet a boy called Bill. After lunch, Jane looked up Weed-Killer in the telephone book and rang them.

'It's a lot of weeds in a pond,' Elinor said. 'Can you deal with that?'

The man assured her they were experts at weeds in ponds, and promised to come the following morning. Elinor wanted to work for an hour or so until it was time to go to Jane's, but she felt compelled to catch the carp now, or to try to. If she failed, she'd tell the men about it tomorrow, and probably they'd have a net on a long handle and could catch it. Elinor took her vegetable sieve which had a handle some ten inches long, and also some pieces of bread.

Not seeing the carp, Elinor tossed the bread onto the surface. Some pieces floated, others sank and were trapped among the vines. Elinor circled the pond, her sieve ready. She had half filled the plastic bucket and it sat on the bank.

Suddenly she saw the fish. It was horizontal and motionless, a couple of inches under the surface. It was dead, she realized, and kept from the surface only by the vines that held it under. Dead from what? The water didn't look dirty, in fact was rather clear. What could kill a carp? Cliff had always said—

Elinor's eyes were full of tears. Tears for the carp? Nonsense. Tears of frustration, maybe. She stooped and tried to reach the carp with the sieve. The sieve was a foot short, and she wasn't going to muddy her tennis shoes by wading in. Not now. Best to work a bit this afternoon, and let the workmen lift it out tomorrow.

'What're you doing, Mommy?' Chris came trotting towards her.

'Nothing. I'm going to work a little now. I thought you were watching TV.'

'It's no good. Where's the fish?'

Elinor took his wrist, swung him around. 'The fish is fine. Now come back and we'll try the TV again.' Elinor tried to think of something else that might amuse him. It wasn't one of his napping days, obviously. 'Tell you what, Chris, you choose one of your toys to take to Bill. Make him a present. All right?'

'One of *my* toys?'

Elinor smiled. Chris was generous enough by nature and she meant to nurture this trait. 'Yes, one of yours. Even one you like—like your paratrooper. Or one of your books. You choose it. Bill's going to be your friend, and you want to start out right, don't you?'

'Yes.' And Chris seemed to be pondering already, going over his store of goodies in his room upstairs.

Elinor locked the back door with its bolt, which was on a level with her eyes. She didn't want Chris going into the garden, maybe seeing the carp. 'I'll be in my room, and I'll see you at four. You might put on a clean pair of jeans at four—if you remember to.'

Elinor worked, and quite well. It was pleasant to have a tea date to look forward to. Soon, she thought, she'd ask Jane and her husband for drinks. She didn't want people to think she was a melancholy widow. It had been three months since Cliff's death. Elinor thought she'd got over the worst of her grief in those first two weeks, the weeks of shock. Had she really? For the past six weeks she'd been able to work. That was something. Cliff's insurance plus his pension made her financially comfortable, but she needed to work to be happy.

When she glanced at her watch, it was ten to four. 'Chrissy!' Elinor called to her half-open door. 'Changed your jeans?'

She pushed open Chris's door across the hall. He was not in his room, and there were more toys and books on the floor than usual, indicating that Chris had been trying to select something to give Bill. Elinor went downstairs where the TV was still murmuring, but Chris wasn't in the living room. Nor was he in the kitchen. She saw that the back door was still bolted. Chris wasn't on the front lawn either. Of course he could have gone to the garden via the front door. Elinor unbolted the kitchen door and went out.

'Chris?' She glanced everywhere, then focused on the pond. She had seen a light-coloured patch in its centre. *'Chris!'* She ran.

He was face down, feet out of sight, blond head nearly submerged. Elinor plunged in, up to her knees, her thighs, seized Chris's legs and pulled him out, slipped, sat down in the water and got soaked as high as her breasts. She struggled to her feet, holding Chris by the waist. Shouldn't she try to let the water run out of his mouth? Elinor was panting.

She turned Chris onto his stomach, gently lifted his small body by the waist, hoping water would run from his nose and mouth, but she was too frantic to look. He was limp, soft in a way that frightened her. She pressed his rib cage, released it, raised him a little again. One had to do artificial respiration methodically, counting, she remembered. She did this. *Fifteen . . . sixteen . . .* Someone should be telephoning for a doctor. She couldn't do two things at once.

'Help!' she yelled. 'Help me, *please!'* Could the people next door hear? The house was twenty yards away, and was anybody home?

She turned Chris over and pressed her mouth to his cool lips. She blew in, then released his ribs, trying to catch a gasp from him, a cough that would mean life again. He remained limp. She turned him on his stomach and resumed the artificial respiration. It was now or never, she knew. Senseless to waste time carrying him into the house for warmth. He could've been lying in the pond for an hour—in which case, she knew it was hopeless.

Elinor picked her son up and carried him towards the house. She went into the kitchen. There was a sagging sofa against the wall, and she put him there.

Then she telephoned Jane Caldwell, whose number was on the card by the telephone where Elinor had left it days ago. Since Elinor didn't know a doctor in the vicinity, it made as much sense to call Jane as to search for a doctor's name.

'Hello, *Jane!*' Elinor said, her voice rising wildly. 'I think Chris's drowned!— Yes! *Yes!* Can you get a doctor? Right away?' Suddenly the line was dead. Elinor hung up and went at once to Chris, started the rib-pressing again, Chris prone on the sofa with his face turned to one side. The activity soothed her a little.

The doorbell rang, and at the same time Elinor heard the latch of the door being opened. Then Jane called:

'Elinor?'

'In the kitchen!'

The doctor had dark hair and spectacles. He lifted Chris a little, felt for a pulse. 'How long—how long was he . . .'

'I don't know. I was working upstairs. It was the pond in the garden.'

The rest was confused to Elinor. She barely realized when the needle went into her own arm, though this was the most definite sensation she had for several minutes. Jane made tea. Elinor had a cup in front of her. When she looked at the sofa, Chris was not there.

'Where is he?' Elinor asked.

Jane gripped Elinor's hand. She sat opposite Elinor. 'The doctor took Chris to the hospital. Chris is in good hands, you can be sure of that. This doctor delivered Bill. He's our doctor.'

But from Jane's tone, Elinor knew it was all useless, and that Jane knew this too. Elinor's eyes drifted from Jane's face. She noticed a book lying on the cane bottom of the chair beside her. Chris had chosen his dotted numbers book to give to Bill, a book that Chris rather liked. He wasn't half through doing the drawings. Chris could count and he was doing quite well at reading too. *I wasn't doing so well at his age, I think,* Cliff had said not long ago.

Elinor began to weep.

'That's good. That's good for you,' Jane said. 'I'll stay here with you. Pretty soon we'll hear from the hospital. Maybe you want to lie down, Elinor?—I've got to make a phone call.'

The sedative was taking effect. Elinor sat in a daze on the sofa, her head back against a pillow. The telephone rang and Jane took it. The hospital, Elinor supposed. She watched Jane's face, and knew. Elinor nodded her head, trying to spare Jane any words, but Jane said:

'They tried. I'm sure they did everything possible.'

Jane said she would stay the night. She said she had arranged for Ed to pick up Bill at a house where she'd left him.

In the morning, Weed-Killer came, and Jane asked Elinor if she still wanted the job done.

'I thought you might've decided to move,' Jane said.

Had she said that? Possibly. 'But I do want it done.'

The two Weed-Killer men got to work.

Jane made another telephone call, then told Elinor that a friend of hers called Millie was coming over at noon. When Millie arrived, Jane prepared a lunch of bacon and eggs for the three of them. Millie had blonde curly hair, blue eyes, and was very cheerful and sympathetic.

'I went by the doctor's,' Millie said, 'and his nurse gave me these pills for you. They're slightly sedative. He thinks they'd be good for you. Two a day, one before lunch, one before bedtime. So have one now.'

They hadn't started lunch. Elinor took one. The workmen were just departing, and one man stuck his head in the door to say with a smile:

'All finished, ma'am. You shouldn't have any trouble any more.'

During lunch, Elinor said, 'I've got to see about the funeral.'

'We'll help you. Don't think about it now,' Jane said. 'Try to eat a little.'

Elinor ate a little, then slept on the sofa in the kitchen. She hadn't wanted to go up to her own bed. When she woke up, Millie was sitting in the wicker armchair, reading a book.

'Feeling better? Want some tea?'

'In a minute. You're awfully kind. I do thank you very much.' She stood up. 'I want to see the pond.' She saw Millie's look of uneasiness. 'They killed those vines today. I'd like to see what it looks like.'

Millie went out with her. Elinor looked down at the pond and had the satisfaction of seeing that no vines lay on the surface, that some pieces of them had sunk like drowned things. Around the edge of the pond were stubs of vines already turning yellow and brownish, wilting. Before her eyes, one cropped tentacle curled sideways and down, as if in the throes of death. A primitive joy went through her, a sense of vengeance, of a wrong righted.

'It's a nasty pond,' Elinor said to Millie. 'It killed a carp. Can you imagine? I've never heard of a carp being—'

'I know. They must've been growing like blazes! But they're certainly finished now.' Millie held out her hand for Elinor to take. 'Don't think about it now.'

Millie wanted to go back to the house. Elinor did not take her hand, but she came with Millie. 'I'm feeling better. You mustn't give up all your time to me. It's very nice of you, since you don't even know me. But I've got to face my problems alone.'

Millie made some polite reply.

Elinor really was feeling better. She'd have to go through the funeral next, Chris's funeral, but she sensed in herself a backbone, morale—whatever it was called. After the service for Chris—surely it would be simple—she'd invite her new neighbours, few as they might be, to her house for coffee or drinks or both. Food too. Elinor realized that her spirits had picked up because the pool was vanquished. She'd have it filled in with stones, with the agent's and also the owner's permission of course. Why should she retreat from the house? With stones showing just above the water, it would look every bit as pretty, maybe prettier, and it wouldn't be dangerous for the next child who came to live here.

The service for Chris was at a small local church. The preacher conducted a short, non-denominational ceremony. And afterwards, around noon, Elinor did have eight or ten people to the house for coffee, drinks and sandwiches. The strangers seemed to enjoy it. Elinor even heard a few laughs among the group which gladdened her heart. She hadn't, as yet, rung up any of her New York friends to tell them about Chris. Elinor realized that some people might think that 'strange' of her, but she felt that it would only sadden her friends to tell them, that it would look like a plea for sympathy. Better the strangers here who knew no grief, because they didn't know her or Chris.

'You must be sure and get enough rest in the next days,' said a kindly, middle-aged woman whose husband stood solemnly beside her. 'We all think you've been awfully brave . . .'

Elinor gave Jane the dotted numbers book to take to Bill.

That night Elinor did sleep more than twelve hours and awoke feeling better and calmer. Now she began to write the letters that she had to, to Cliff's parents, to her own mother and father, and to three good friends in New York. She finished typing her article. The next morning, she walked to the post office and sent off her letters, and also her article to her agent in New York. She spent the rest of the day sorting out Chris's clothing, his books and toys, and she washed some of his clothes with a view to passing them on to Jane for Bill, providing Jane wouldn't think it unlucky. Elinor didn't think Jane would think that. Jane telephoned in the afternoon to ask how she was.

'Is anyone coming to see you? From New York? A friend, I mean?'

Elinor explained that she'd written to a few people, but she wasn't expecting anyone. 'I'm really feeling all right, Jane. You mustn't worry.'

By evening, Elinor had a neat carton of clothing ready to offer Jane, two more cartons of books and one of toys. If the clothes didn't fit Bill, then Jane might know a child they would fit. Elinor felt better for that. It was a lot better than collapsing in grief, she thought. Of course it was awful, a tragedy that didn't happen every day—losing a husband and a child in hardly more than three months. But Elinor was not going to succumb to it. She'd stay out the six months in the house here, come to terms with her loss, and emerge strong, someone able to give something to other people, not merely take.

She had two ideas for future articles. Which to do first? She decided to walk out into the garden, let her thoughts ramble. Maybe the radishes had come up? She'd have a look at the pond. Maybe it would be glassy smooth and clear. She must ask the Weed-Killer people when it would be safe to put in another carp—or two carps.

When she looked at the pond, she gave a short gasp. The vines had come *back*. They looked stronger than ever—not really longer, but more dense. Even as she watched, one tentacle, then a second actually moved, curved towards the land and seemed to grow an inch. That hadn't been due to the wind. The vines were growing visibly. Another green shoot poked its head above the water's surface. Elinor watched, fascinated, as if she beheld animate things, like snakes. Every inch or so along the vines a small green leaf sprouted, and Elinor was sure she could see some of these unfurling. The water looked clean, but she knew that was deceptive. The water was somehow poisonous. It had killed a carp. It had killed Chris. And she could still detect, she thought, the rather acid smell of the stuff the Weed-Killer men had put in.

There must be such a thing as digging the roots out, Elinor thought, even if Weed-Killer's stuff had failed. Elinor got the fork from the toolshed, and she took the clippers also. She thought of getting her rubber boots from the house, but was too eager to start to bother with them. She began by hacking all round the edge with the clippers. Some fresh vine ends cruised over the pond and jammed themselves amid other growing vines. The stems now seemed tough as plastic clothes-lines, as if the herbicide had fortified them. Some had put down roots in the grass quite a distance from the pond. Elinor dropped the clippers and seized the fork. She had to dig deep to get at the roots, and when she finally pulled with her hands, the stems broke, leaving some roots still in the soil. Her right foot slipped, she went down on her left knee and struggled up again, both legs wet now. She was not going to be defeated.

As she sank the fork in, she saw Cliff's handsome, subtly smiling eyes in the photograph in the bedroom, Cliff with the blade of grass or hay between his lips, and he seemed to be nodding ever so slightly, approving. Her arms began to ache, her hands grew tired. She lost her right shoe in dragging her foot out of the water yet again, and she didn't bother trying to recover it. Then she slipped again and sat down, water up to her waist now. Tired, angry, she still worked with the fork, trying to prize roots loose, and the water churned with a muddy fury. She might even be doing the damned roots good, she thought. Aerating them or something. Were they invincible? Why should they be? The sun poured down, overheating her, bringing nourishment to the green, Elinor knew.

Nature knows. That was Cliff's voice in her ears. Cliff sounded happy and at ease.

Elinor was half blinded by tears. Or was it sweat? *Chun-nk* went her fork. In a moment, when her arms gave out, she'd cross to the other side of the pond and attack that. She'd got some out. She'd make Weed-Killer come again, maybe pour kerosene on the pond and light it.

She got up on cramped legs and stumbled around to the other side. The sun warmed her shoulders though her feet were cold. In those few seconds that she walked, her thoughts and her attitude changed, though she was not at once aware of this. It was neither victory nor defeat that she felt. She sank the fork in again, again slipped and recovered. Again roots slid between the tines of the fork, and were not removed. A tentacle thicker than most moved towards her and circled her right ankle. She kicked, and the vine tightened, and she fell forward.

She went face down into the water, but the water seemed soft. She struggled a little, turned to breathe, and a vine tickled her neck. She saw Cliff nodding again, smiling his kindly, knowing, almost imperceptible smile. It was nature. It was Cliff. It was Chris. A vine crept around her arm—loose or attached to the earth she neither knew nor cared. She breathed in, and much of what she took in was water. *All things come from water,* Cliff had said once. Little Chris smiled at her with both corners of his mouth upturned. She saw him stooped by the pond, reaching for the dead carp which floated out of range of his twig. Then Chris lifted his face again and smiled.

F RANK HOVERED NEAR THE FROST-FREE refrigerators listening to a conversation two aisles over.

"Gross, Julie, what are we getting here—pull-on pants? A washer-dryer? It's not going to fit into the bag."

"Open the other one, it's emptier."

"You know I'm not supposed to shoplift anymore."

"Don't take that, idiot! It has a sensor."

He worked his way into power tools hoping that between chain saws he'd see them. At the end of the row he poked his head around the corner. There were three girls with what he and his wife called big hair. One of them slowly turned around and dropped a blender into her shopping bag. It was Julie, his neighbors' daughter, his Saturday-evening babysitter.

"Gross, a blender. What do you need that for?"

"I can make diet drinks in my room. Besides, eventually Christmas will come and I'll need presents," Julie said.

"A blender is good. No one would ever steal a blender," the other girl said. Except for fingernails a mile long, red like they'd been dipped in fresh blood, she had no distinguishing features.

Julie put a mini-chopper in on top of the blender.

"Hurry up, I'm hungry," the third girl said. She had big breasts and wore a very short T-shirt that barely covered them, and no bra. Frank wondered if anyone had suggested that perhaps it was time she restrain herself.

"How could you be hungry? You just ate a cheeseburger and fries."

Her breasts were growing, Frank thought, they needed food.

"I threw it up."

"Are you serious?" the girl with the nails asked.

The overdeveloped girl nodded. He decided to call her Tina.

"Is this, like, a problem?" Julie asked.

"I just need a frozen yogurt or something. I have a really bad taste in my mouth," Tina said.

"I'm sure," Nails said.

Nails put a blow dryer in on top of everything and they walked out of the store.

Frank hung back as the girls got closer to the entrance. He didn't want to be right there when the security guards grabbed them. He waited by a rack of large-size flower print dresses and watched the girls walk untouched into the body of the mall. Then he hurried to catch up, wondering if it was his obligation to stop them, to drag them kicking, screaming, swearing, maybe even yelling rape, to the manager's office.

He checked his watch. He was supposed to be buying tires. He was supposed to meet his wife at the Twistie Freeze at the other end of the mall in twenty minutes.

"Oh my God, turn around, walk the other way," Nails said.

"Why?" Tina asked.

"Get with the program. It's Adam."

"So?"

"Is your bulb, like, only sixty watts?

"Oh, Adam," Nails screamed down the mall. A boy standing in front of the record store—which, Frank noticed, didn't sell records anymore, only tapes and CDs—tensed. "Adam, look who's here." Nails pointed her finger like a gun at Julie's ear. "It's Julie."

Julie slapped Nails' hand down. Nails dropped her shopping bag and slapped Julie back.

"Bitch, I was trying to help you!" she said.

In the middle of the mall Nails and Julie clawed at each other with finger-nails like switchblades.

"Come here," Nails said to Adam.

As he moved to come towards them, he stepped on his shoelaces—inten-tionally untied, as was the style—and fell forward, catching himself in a posi-tion similar to the peak of a push-up.

Frank felt the fall in his stomach, the horrible sensation of failure, the trip-ping of mankind.

Adam lay face-down on the floor as though his embarrassment was enough to kill him.

The girls laughed and walked away, their claws magically retracted by the punch line of Adam's fall.

In McDonald's, Frank stood in line next to the girls and when he and Julie accidently made eye contact, he blushed the same shade of red she did.

"Hi," he said.

"Yeah." She immediately looked down at the floor.

Frank looked at her and wondered about what she did alone in his house, with his children, on Saturday nights. He came up with nothing specific but in general the thought frightened him.

Sitting in a molded plastic booth that reminded him of his daughter's play furniture, he tried to spy on the girls. A tropical plant blocked his view. He ate a few fries and sipped the Coke. The girls were silent. Frank started to think he smelled something burning. He lifted one of the french fries to his nose and sniffed it. He extended his neck and inhaled, testing the air around him . . . plastic burning.

The three girls were kleptomaniacs, pyromaniacs, probably nymphomani-acs as well. He closed his eyes, conjuring an image of himself with a fifteen-year-old girl in a scenario that involved giggling, posing, uncoordinated and inappropriate body movements, and frustration that ultimately resulted in a spanking that was definitely pleasurable, at least for him.

A second wave of the odor overcame him. They were probably flicking their Bics against the Styrofoam containers their burgers and nuggets came in, melting them into cute little animal shapes or costume jewelry, like an arts-and-crafts project. They were burning everything. Next they'd try out the tropical plant. *Is it real, Julie? I don't know, light it. Real things don't burn.* He imagined McDonald's on fire, melting. He saw himself trying to escape, stuck in a hot pool of liquid plastic like a mouse in a glue trap. He smelled matches but no cigarettes. He smelled plastic burning and thought of toxic fumes filling the mall, working like nerve gas, killing thousands of people who would never know what hit them, the credit cards in their wallets forever fusing with their flesh.

Frank jumped up, jutting his tray out in front of him, brandishing it like a weapon. The girls were way ahead, on their way out. He glanced at their table; they'd left their trash. He went towards it; the Styrofoam containers were singed, but only slightly. There were at least twenty-five burnt matches dunked in a pool of ketchup. He sifted through the garbage—picked up a half-eaten burger and took two bites before he realized what he was doing and put it down. Under everything he found "Adam and Julie 2 Gather 4 Ever" burned into the Formica tabletop. It was still warm.

"You spelled it wrong," Frank started to shout. The word *You* came out in a loud passionate voice before he realized it was pointless. Spelling meant nothing to the girls. Frank went towards the exit, tray still very much in hand. A McDonald's security guard stopped him.

"Sorry, sir, you'll have to consume that in here."

Frank tried to peak around the guard. He shifted to one side and poked his head out. The guard shifted with him and blocked his view.

"Your fries are getting cold," the guard said.

Frank dumped his tray into a trash can, and raced into the center of the mall. Walking briskly, almost running, he went down the center of what felt like a nightmare; a brightly lit fluorescent tube filled with seating groups and planters set up like obstacles. He went after the girls asking himself, What am I chasing? What am I doing?

He went through the mall, weaving in and out of people, strollers, breathing hard, looking for Julie, Nails, and Tina, their big hair, their mini-skirts, their overloaded shopping bags. Instead of seeing them or seeing nothing at all, he saw hundreds of girls just like them, identical twins. Like in a mirror ball, a million reflections spun across the mall. High hair, skinny legs, faces caked with makeup like in a science fiction movie. They were everywhere, as though it were a dream. A strange and disturbing element came upon him like a hidden danger, causing him to panic. Boys. Suddenly, he was aware of an almost equal number of boys in dark T-shirts with bloody daggers decaled onto the front, roaming freely. They were thick in the neck, arm, and thigh, and walked slightly off balance, an overbred species. Male and female, hanging out as if this were some private party in someone's living room. The mating game. They pressed into corners, leaned back against pay phones, and exchanged phone numbers and deep kisses. They lay on the floor in front of their favorite stores, stretched out, heads propped on elbows, watching the people go by like they were watching something on MTV.

A security guard, who could have passed for a twelve-year-old dressed up for Halloween, walked by Frank. He smiled at the girls and rested his hands on the heavy leather equipment belt around his waist. The girls blushed. Frank imagined the boys took turns playing cop. When they got to the mall they flipped for it and then the winner (or was it the loser?) changed into the uniform. Frank noticed the guard had a gun, a real gun, and wondered why a twelve-year-old in a Halloween costume was carrying a real gun.

His watch beeped. He had set the alarm for the time he was supposed to meet his wife in front of the Twistie Freeze. Visually, he made another quick sweep of the area and then walked towards a clump of what looked like airport lounge chairs near the Twistie Freeze.

He sat there for a minute before he was overcome by self-consciousness and had to get up again. He went into the Twistie Freeze, bought a vanilla-and-chocolate-twist cone, and stood licking it near the door.

Across the mall, a baseball team was having a party in the Cheezy Dog. When Frank was a kid they always had barbecues after their games. They'd stay in the park playing catch and stuffing their faces until one kid threw up and then they'd all climb into someone's father's station wagon and be dropped off one by one in the sadness of dark.

Frank looked in the Cheezy Dog and saw some kid take his hot dog out of the roll, hold it in front of his crotch, and wag it at the waitress. He quickly looked away.

At the far end of the mall, a shiny jeep was parked in the middle of things. At first Frank thought it made no sense, but as he thought about it more he became convinced it was the perfect idea; he couldn't believe someone hadn't thought of it before. A car dealership in a mall. Perfecto! It was the one way to get men to come back again and again, to spend hours, lingering.

Frank stood in front of the jeep, dreaming of a different kind of life, the kind he'd read about in stories of men outdoors, fishing trips and cabins in the woods. He dripped a bit of frozen custard onto the jeep and blotted it off with his napkin, leaving a smeary place on the hood. He fantasized buying a second home somewhere by a lake.

The jeep was wrapped in plastic tape that looked like the stuff police use to rope off crime scenes. It had Z-100 printed all over it.

"What's Z-100?" he asked a kid standing next to him.

"Great metal station," the kid said.

It was as if the child had spoken in code. What the hell was a metal station, Frank wanted to know.

"What's Z-100?" he asked again.

"A radio station. They're giving it away, in about fifteen minutes," an older woman said.

He walked in circles around the jeep. He checked the sticker: fourteen thousand six hundred bucks; AM/FM radio, cassette deck, rustproof, good tires, mud flaps. He finished his cone and planned a new life. As he ran over the figures in his head and realized that any life other than the one he already lived was a complete impossibility, he became furious. Who were all the people in the mall, carrying around big shopping bags full of who knows what? They couldn't all be shoplifters. They were buying things, big, important things. Where did they get the money? They couldn't all be millionaires.

A crowd formed around Frank and the car. People started setting up folding beach chairs and plastic coolers, like what you'd put in the backyard or by the pool, in a ring around the car. The contest hadn't even started yet, and already a bottle of two hundred and fifty aspirins had been opened and was lying next to a can of Diet Coke.

The contest, I want to be in the contest, Frank thought. He imagined how proud Mary and the kids would be if he actually won something, especially something large like a car.

"Sign me up," he said to someone wearing a judge's hat.

"What's your name?"

"Frank Mann."

She looked down at her list. "Your name's not here."

"But I want to be in the contest," he whined like a child.

"Did you call in and win?"

Frank gave her a confused look.

"The first twenty people who were the one-hundredth callers when we played the Poizon Boiz 'Roll My Wheels' are in the contest. Obviously you're not one."

"There has to be some way."

"Sorry," the judge said, walking away.

Frank continued to accost anyone in a Z-100 T-shirt until another judge pulled him aside and explained in extreme detail how the entrants had qualified. There was no way to sign up late.

Frank was so upset it was all he could do to contain a tantrum. He pictured himself screaming and pointing and calling everyone names until the security force, the boy with the gun, came for him, and like a civil disobedient he went limp and had to be dragged from the mall.

"Sore loser," some girl with very big hair would say as they swept him past her.

Frank saw Julie on the other side of the car, sitting in one of the lounge chairs. He worked his way over to her.

"Are you a winner?"

"Yeah, but I had to pretend I was my mother. You have to be twenty-one to get the car. She's doing the contest."

Julie pointed at her mother, who was in a huddle with the other contestants and the judges from the radio station.

"How's it work?" Frank asked.

"You have to keep your hands on the car all the time, except five minutes an hour. No other part of your body can ever touch the car, and like, if you want, someone can stay here with you overnight."

Without thinking Frank offered to stay overnight. He imagined himself prowling the corridors at 3 A.M.

"That's okay," Julie said. "I'm staying."

A short ugly man with permanent acne began speaking into a megaphone. His voice was like chocolate mousse, deep and smooth; he was obviously a disc jockey. The contestants arranged themselves around the car, scurrying for what they thought was the best place, the hood versus the side, and so on.

"Are your hands ready?" the D.J. asked.

The contestants and Frank nodded.

"Put your paws on the car."

The contestants seemed to surge forward as the contest began, rocking the jeep slightly, perhaps raising it off the ground a half-inch or so before they settled into the poses they would have to hold for the next fifty-five minutes.

Within five minutes most of the crowd dissipated. As far as they were concerned there was nothing to look at.

By the time Mary showed up at the Twistie Freeze forty-five minutes late, Frank was morbidly depressed, filled with a second ice cream cone and a complete hatred for the American way.

"All done?" Mary asked.

"I didn't get to the tires yet," he said.

"Another time."

"Maybe tomorrow," Frank said.

She handed him her packages to carry and they walked back towards where they had originally come from.

They passed Julie's friends, standing outside the record store smoking. Mary stopped. "You shouldn't be smoking," she said.

Frank stood behind her feeling incredibly bloated: part of a large Coke, half an order of fries, a couple of bites of one of the girls' burger, and two ice cream cones. He stood in back of Mary, his stomach jutting out in front of him, not believing that he'd let himself get to this point.

Behind Mary's back, he lifted a finger to his ear and spun it in circles. Nails and Tina didn't respond. He did the bit where he took a make-believe grenade out of his pocket, pulled the pin, threw it, plugged his ears, and ducked his head to escape the explosion. Still nothing.

The two girls stood there staring, listening to Mary as though they were used to listening but never taking anything in.

Frank didn't resist when Mary reached behind her, took his hand, and led him away.

"I'll have to come back tomorrow," he told Mary, twisting his head around to see if they were laughing at him.

"I have a meeting. I won't be able to come with you," she said as though there were some rule about Frank going to the mall alone.

"So?"

"Sew buttons," she said.

It was what she always said when there was nothing left to say.

The next evening he waited until Mary left for her meeting, then said good-bye to the kids and took off for the mall. He drove fast, imagining that if he didn't get there soon, he would begin to shrivel like a helium balloon, slowly dropping down, sinking lower and lower, until he hovered six inches above the floor. By morning he'd be airless, dead, on the bucket seats.

The Pyramid Mall floated in a sea of parking spaces, laid out thirty deep so that on any given day or evening, with the exception of Saturdays, a person could find a place within ten spaces of the end and enter the mall feeling somehow lucky. The only thing pyramid-like about the place were pyramid-shaped planters filled with half-dead geraniums.

He pulled into a good space near Sears feeling what he called the guilt of necessary purpose. He had come here for a real reason. Tires. Before he could do anything, he had to go directly into Sears. He had to accomplish something so that later he could tell Mary how wonderful he was.

There were no salespeople in the tire department and Frank was too distracted to hunt one down. Frank had a certain pale nonexistence to him, like Casper the Ghost. He could fight it if he wanted to. He could summon his energy and make himself a kind of lifelike pinkish-purple that could get a fair amount of attention, but he couldn't sustain it. In Sears, he couldn't even bring himself up to a kind of light flesh tone. He just didn't have it in him. He took heart in knowing it was highly unlikely he'd ever be taken hostage in a bank robbery or hijacking.

He left Sears promising himself he'd deal with the tires later; if necessary he'd go directly to a tire store where salesmen waited day and night for guys like Frank to walk in. He went into the mall charged by the prospect of a new project—an unexpected surprise, like a bonus—finding something to buy, to bring home to Mary like show and tell.

Just outside Sears, two women from the local Red Cross sat at a folding table with a blood pressure cuff between them waiting for a victim. The atmosphere was festive. Diet experts in workout clothing mingled freely. *Stop Smoking Now.* Lungs like giant latex condoms expanded and collapsed. *Mental Illness: The Hidden Symptoms.* He reviewed the list without intending to. Bad news. According to Frank's own evaluation he had all the signs of Chronic Untreated Disturbance. According to the description he was a time bomb that could go at any minute. No warning. Health Fair '90 ended in front of Woolworth's. Two candy-striped cardboard poles marked the beginning and the end.

Frank spotted Adam—the kid who tripped over his laces the day before—in the record store. He went directly to him and slapped his hand down on the counter, stinging his palm.

"Hey, Adam," Frank said.

Adam was startled. He looked down at his shirt to see if he was wearing a name tag. He wasn't.

"Adam, talk to me."

"What?"

"Tell me about CDs—are there different kinds? Different sizes? Do they all play on the same machine?"

For the past two years, everything Frank saw or read nagged him about CDs.

Adam looked at Frank like Frank was an extraterrestrial, an undercover cop, or some new brand of idiot. He didn't say anything. The silence made Frank uncomfortable. He wanted to be friends.

"I'm serious, Adam. I'm very serious."

Adam kept staring, checking out Frank. He wanted to be sure he didn't end up on the wrong end of a joke.

"They're all the same," Adam finally said, tentatively. "You get a player and plug it into your stereo, or you can get a portable."

"What do you have?"

"Portable. I plug it into my car stereo. That's really cool."

"I bet."

Adam looked at Frank like he was still waiting for something to happen. Maybe Frank was someone's father coming to tell Adam he didn't want his daughter riding around in Adam's car with Adam blasting her eardrums anymore.

"What do you listen to?"

"I dunno," Adam said, suddenly shy.

"Well, what do your friends listen to?"

"All kinds of stuff."

"If I wanted to buy something, what would you recommend?"

"New Poizon Boiz just came in," Adam said happily.

"I'll take one. Do you sell the players here?" he asked, handing Adam his American Express card.

"You get them at Wire Wizard, upstairs, just across from King Pin."

As Adam was ringing Frank up, a big-haired girl, identical to Julie, Tina, and Nails, came up to Adam, wrapped her arms around his neck, and pushed her tongue down Adam's throat.

Every organ in Frank's body jumped. His insides rose up. He signed the charge slip, turned around, and went straight to the Wire Wizard.

"I need a CD player," he said desperately to the salesman.

"What kind?"

"A good one. A very good one. I have to be able to plug it into my stereo or my car." He felt flushed and out of breath. He thought of the freshness of a fifteen-year-old body.

"We have a few like that."

"I want the best. I have to have the best," Frank said, excitedly.

"The best is not necessarily the most expensive."

"I know that," Frank said.

What kind of guy did this kid take him for? He tapped his fingers on the counter.

"Give me what you've got," Frank said to the guy.

He felt like he had to hurry. He had to finish this soon. He had to go back and see what Adam was doing.

"This is a very good model," the guy said, taking something out of the case.

"Great," Frank said, without looking at the player. He laid his charge card on the counter, sure that this was how people did it. Credit was free, easy, there was always someone giving it away, asking you to take more.

"Do you want to hear it?"

"I trust you. I really do," Frank said, looking the guy in the eye for half a second.

When Frank got out of the Wire Wizard, Adam was gone. Lunch break, his manager said, winking.

On the down escalator Frank pulled the receipt out of the Wire Wizard bag. A hundred and eighty-nine dollars. He couldn't believe it. He'd figured it would cost fifty or sixty bucks, seventy-five at most. What had he done? What would Mary say? He quickly shifted his attitude to a more adaptive one. I'm allowed. I am absolutely allowed. I deserve it. He wouldn't tell Mary. He would find something else to bring home, something smaller, perhaps something specifically for her, like a present.

From the escalator he saw the crowd around the jeep. He counted the number of contestants left. Since yesterday eleven had walked away. According to
the woman on the escalator in front of Frank, they'd thrown up their hands and
asked to be let out. One had to be taken by ambulance when, for no apparent
reason, she started vomiting.

"How're you doing?" he asked Julie's mother.

She smiled and nodded her head.

"It's nothing yet," Julie's mother said. "Tomorrow it'll start getting good."

"I'll be here," Frank said.

"So will I."

Frank felt his presence did something to the contest. He had the idea that
the way he looked at the contestants either gave them what they needed to go
on or broke them right there on the spot. He felt powerful and necessary.

They were down to nine. They all looked willing to call it a day. An incredible assortment of junk food was scattered half-eaten among the lounge chairs
and coolers; fast food from every carry-out in the mall had been supplemented
by special-request items like Ding-Dongs and cream soda. It surprised Frank
that no one thought of the nutrition edge. No one seemed to think eating right
during the five-minute breaks might make all the difference. There were no
Tiger's Milk bars, no bowls of pasta salad, not even any goddamn Gatorade.
Who were these people? Frank wanted to know. He really wanted to know. He
imagined interviewing them during their breaks, like Geraldo Rivera, asking
what it felt like to touch the car, why they chose to spend their break standing,
talking on a pay phone, instead of lying down? He wanted to know why no one
was wearing support stockings or using heating pads on long extension cords.

As he stood trying to figure out how he could become an official consul-
tant, a girl right in front of him was disqualified. Her knee buckled and her hip
banged against the car.

"You're out," the judge called like an umpire in a baseball game.

With a completely bewildered look on her face she stepped away from the
car. Frank saw the sweaty prints her hands left on the hood. Instead of looking

at the girl he looked at the other contestants. They were taking inventory, checking each other out, placing unspoken bets on the order in which they would fall.

Frank stayed until the mall closed. Store lights blinked on and off, warning customers that the end was coming soon. Assistant managers started pulling metal security gates down and fiddling with their keys. Frank thought of people left overnight, locked in. He started walking back in the direction of Sears and then turned around and took a last look at the contestants. He imagined them all changing into their pajamas during the eleven o'clock break. Frank silently said good night to the remaining eight players and barely made it through Sears before they locked the doors. He had nothing for Mary.

On the way home he stopped at the all-night Super Pharmacy and bought Mary a Dustbuster. As he pulled into the driveway, he stuffed the bags from the Wire Wizard and the record store under the car seat.

That night, waiting to fall asleep, Frank thought of contests he'd seen on the evening news. National coverage for three people out there somewhere, sitting on a billboard scaffold. His heart swelled. The Pyramid Mall was his own, he'd been there from the start. No matter who eventually drove away with the car, part of it belonged to Frank.

The next day, he fought the urge to call the mall from his office, a cubbyhole in an overdeveloped industrial park, and ask for an update. After work, when all the accounts were reconciled, he hurried home and found his neighbor, Julie's father, sitting at his dining room table, waiting for dinner.

"My whole damn family's living out there at the mall," he said between chicken legs.

Frank didn't answer. He waited until Julie's father went home and then told Mary he was leaving.

"I have to go see about those tires," he said to Mary.

"I thought you did that last night?"

"Didn't get what I needed. I have to go back and get it over with."

On his way to the contest, he stopped by the sporting goods store. He slipped a baseball glove on and pounded his fist into the mitt a couple of times. It could heal him, he thought. It could be just the thing. With the exception of what he'd seen two days ago at the Cheezy Dog, the mitt reminded him of the better things in life. He used to have a mitt until his son had taken it to school one day and lost it.

With his free hand Frank started pulling bats out of the rack, turning them over and over, awkwardly tossing them slightly into the air, spinning and catching them, bending and flexing the glove on his left hand.

The glove was fifty-six dollars. He couldn't do it. He'd already done it last night. There was no way. He took it off and put it tenderly down on the pile, hiding it near the back, leaving room for his dreams.

In the middle of the mall, in the center of what he had come to think of as the runway, he saw Nails and Tina. Frank kept his shoulders pulled back and reminded himself that he was a grown-up and they were children. Tina stood in front of him, licking her ice cream cone in an intentionally obscene way.

"Oh, hi," she said, pretending to all of a sudden see him.

He almost died. There were men his age who had heart attacks and called it a day over less.

"Well, gotta go," Tina finally said, her cone completely gone, a ring of chocolate outlining her lips like liner.

Sixty-seven hours into the contest. Frank promised himself that when this was over everything would be better. It already was better, he told himself.

Julie's mom and a guy ten years younger were the only contestants left. The guy wore a T-shirt his girlfriend had made for him that said *Get Your Hands Off My Car.*

Julie's mother had her shoes off, her knee-high stockings rolled down to her ankles. The ankles, purple and puffy, bulged out over the hose. She kept shifting her weight from side to side, foot to foot. She seemed more like a feral raccoon than most feral raccoons ever did. Her skin was pasty, her eyes had sunk deep into her head. The black around her eyes was heavy like someone had drawn it there with a charcoal briquet.

Enough! Frank wanted to yell. Stop. Give her the car, she's earned it.

Between twenty and thirty people stood in a circle around Julie's mom and the guy, looking at them as though they were objects on view, specimens from *Night of the Living Dead*, perfect examples of the devastating side effects of spending too much time indoors.

The scene was going sour for Frank. There was a definite spin to it, a dangerous whirling that could suck a person down, like a garbage disposal. There was too much to hear, and see, and eat. Frank decided that's why the kids were lying on the floor like cancerous lumps.

It couldn't last much longer. There was no way.

Frank looked at the last two contestants and then had to look away. They were pathetic, doughy, offering themselves up for human consumption like some ritualistic sacrifice. When looking away was not enough he had to walk away. He turned around and was going home when he heard a thick popping sound, like one a plunger makes when it comes up. He turned back towards the car. The thick sucking sound was Julie's mother's hands coming up off the hood. Her hands were rising up into the air, lifting over her head, but she was still shifting her weight from foot to foot and looking down at the car as though her hands were there.

"Mom, your hands, your hands!" Julie screamed.

The other contestant froze, his hands pressed so hard on the hood they made a dent.

When the judges got to Julie's mom, they reached up and pulled her hands down to her sides. Her arms fell like levers whose springs had snapped.

She looked up and said, "What?"

Julie ran over and started shaking her. "Mom, you idiot, you lost the contest. You lost when we were so close to winning."

Frank hated Julie. She was unbelievable. A hateful child.

On the other side of the car, the guy with the T-shirt was being pounded on the back in a manner that was vaguely resuscitative, like CPR or the Heimlich maneuver.

A guy next to Frank had a radio tuned to Z-100.

"We have a winner at the Pyramid Mall," the D.J. said. "Let's go there live."

Over the radio, Frank heard the guy thanking his parents and his girlfriend. The weird thing was that Frank was looking right at the guy and the guy wasn't talking at all. He was just standing there staring. There were no microphones anywhere. Over the radio Frank heard all kinds of yelling and screaming and a round of "For He's a Jolly Good Fellow," by "all John's friends." But at the mall, with the exception of Julie yelling at her mother, it was quiet.

One of the judges handed Julie's mom an envelope.

Frank asked someone who appeared to be in charge what it was.

"Second place. Two hundred and fifty dollars," he said.

"Two hundred and fifty dollars. That's all she gets?" Frank said. "He gets a car and all she gets is a lousy two hundred and fifty bucks. Unbelievable. You guys are unbelievable. She stood on her fucking feet for sixty-seven hours and forty-eight minutes and all you're giving her is nothing."

People stared at the ground while he talked.

He felt sick. He was sick. Vomit and rage and junk food rose in him. He looked at the girl from the radio station. She shrugged. With her shoulders up near her neck, shrugging, she looked certifiably retarded. In order to keep from hitting her, from holding her personally responsible, Frank ran. He ran down the length of the mall and back again. He did it three times before he ended up at the sporting goods store.

Frank ran into the sporting goods store, grabbed the glove he'd hidden, put it on his hand, raised his arm above his head, and screamed: "It's mine. It's mine. I'm taking it. It belongs to me."

When he got no response, he ran through the store, waving his arm and the glove, still screaming. He ran through the store, out the door, and down the middle of the mall. At some point he was aware someone was chasing him, but it meant nothing. He slammed through a set of fire doors, triggered an alarm, and ended up on the edge of the parking lot, at twilight. The earth and the sky were the same deep shade of blue.

"Stop," the kid dressed as a guard yelled, his voice cracking. "Please stop where you are. Stop. Freeze."

Each time the guard shouted he was more insistent. Each time, Frank became more frenzied. He zigzagged unsteadily. He heard a shot ring through the air behind him.

"Freeze."

Frank was near the far edge of the lot, a tall hill of fill-dirt in front of him. He whirled around and crouched down, low, like a catcher. He raised the glove up in front of his face and caught the second bullet.

It struck him like a punch. He rocked back and forth, heel to toe, before falling onto his back, his knees raised in front of him like insect legs.

There was a buzzing in his ears, like a telephone constantly ringing.

Frank lay on his back in the parking lot. No shopping carts wheeled past his head. No one came near him. The glove stayed in place and the crowd over by the mall imagined him skewered, permanently sewn together like a cheap doll, his expression fixed, his hand permanently placed.

It seemed like forever before anyone heard sirens. Red and white flashing lights sucked up the twilight and made it seem much later than it was. A paramedic jumped out and pressed his fingers to Frank's jugular.

"He's alive," the medic shouted and the crowd moved forward.

"Does anybody know who it is?" the medic asked. "Anyone know his name?"

"He lives across the street from me," Julie said.

Frank fainted behind the glove. The squawking of the police radio woke him up.

"We got a bullet catcher here. Security guard hit him, when he was trying to get away with something."

I wasn't trying to get away with anything, Frank thought, and then fell back into a fuzzy kind of sleep.

They slid a board under Frank. He felt pressure, intense pressure, as though his insides were being pushed up and out. He was being squeezed to death.

Perhaps they were running him over with a steamroller, pushing him into the fresh asphalt at the edge of the lot.

He tried to remember where he'd parked the car. The CD player was still under the seat. He hoped no one would ever find it. Mary would be annoyed that he hadn't gotten the tires. Sew buttons.

The medics didn't touch his face or attempt to remove the glove. They were saving that for the doctors. By the time they tied everything in place with heavy gauze the sky had dropped deep into darkness. The mall had closed for the night. The crowd evaporated: one by one, in a great snake of a line, all the cars pulled out onto the highway. The medics dressed Frank up like a spring float and wheeled him around in a quiet parade on the empty parking lot.

The Summer People

★

SHIRLEY JACKSON

T HE ALLISONS' COUNTRY COTTAGE, seven miles from the nearest town, was set prettily on a hill; from three sides it looked down on soft trees and grass that seldom, even at midsummer, lay still and dry. On the fourth side was the lake, which touched against the wooden pier the Allisons had to keep repairing, and which looked equally well from the Allisons' front porch, their side porch or any spot on the wooden staircase leading from the porch down to the water. Although the Allisons loved their summer cottage, looked forward to arriving in the early summer and hated to leave in the fall, they had not troubled themselves to put in any improvements, regarding the cottage itself and the lake as improvement enough for the life left to them. The cottage had no heat, no running water except the precarious supply from the backyard pump and no electricity. For seventeen summers, Janet Allison had cooked on a kerosene stove, heating all their water; Robert Allison had brought buckets full of water daily from the pump and read his paper by kerosene light in the evenings and they had both, sanitary city people, become stolid and matter-of-fact about their back house. In the first two years they had gone through all the standard vaudeville and magazine jokes about backhouses and by now, when they no longer had frequent guests to impress, they had subsided to a comfortable security which made the backhouse, as well as the pump and the kerosene, an indefinable asset to their summer life.

In themselves, the Allisons were ordinary people. Mrs. Allison was fifty-eight years old and Mr. Allison sixty; they had seen their children outgrow the summer cottage and go on to families of their own and seashore resorts; their friends were either dead or settled in comfortable year-round houses, their nieces and nephews vague. In the winter they told one another they could stand their New York apartment while waiting for the summer; in the summer they told one another that the winter was well worthwhile, waiting to get to the country.

Since they were old enough not to be ashamed of regular habits, the Allisons invariably left their summer cottage the Tuesday after Labor Day, and were as invariably sorry when the months of September and early October turned out to be pleasant and almost insufferably barren in the city; each year they recognized that there was nothing to bring them back to New York, but it was not until this year that they overcame their traditional inertia enough to decide to stay at the cottage after Labor Day.

"There isn't really anything to take us back to the city," Mrs. Allison told her husband seriously, as though it were a new idea, and he told her, as though neither of them had ever considered it, "We might as well enjoy the country as long as possible."

Consequently, with much pleasure and a slight feeling of adventure, Mrs. Allison went into their village the day after Labor Day and told those natives with whom she had dealings, with a pretty air of breaking away from tradition, that she and her husband had decided to stay at least a month longer at their cottage.

"It isn't as though we had anything to take us back to the city," she said to Mr. Babcock, her grocer. "We might as well enjoy the country while we can."

"Nobody ever stayed at the lake past Labor Day before," Mr. Babcock said. He was putting Mrs. Allison's groceries into a large cardboard carton, and he stopped for a minute to look reflectively into a bag of cookies. "Nobody," he added.

"But the city!" Mrs. Allison always spoke of the city to Mr. Babcock as though it were Mr. Babcock's dream to go there. "It's so hot—you've really no idea. We're always sorry when we leave."

"Hate to leave," Mr. Babcock said. One of the most irritating native tricks Mrs. Allison had noticed was that of taking a trivial statement and rephrasing it downwards, into an even more trite statement. "I'd hate to leave myself," Mr. Babcock said, after deliberation, and both he and Mrs. Allison smiled. "But I never heard of anyone ever staying out at the lake after Labor Day before."

"Well, we're going to give it a try," Mrs. Allison said, and Mr. Babcock replied gravely, "Never know till you try."

Physically, Mrs. Allison decided, as she always did when leaving the grocery after one of her inconclusive conversations with Mr. Babcock, physically, Mr. Babcock could model for a statue of Daniel Webster, but mentally . . . it was horrible to think into what old New England Yankee stock had degenerated. She said as much to Mr. Allison when she got into the car, and he said, "It's generations of inbreeding. That and the bad land."

Since this was their big trip into town, which they made only once every two weeks to buy things they could not have delivered, they spent all day at it, stopping to have a sandwich in the newspaper and soda shop, and leaving packages heaped in the back of the car. Although Mrs. Allison was able to order groceries delivered regularly, she was never able to form any accurate idea of Mr. Babcock's current stock by telephone, and her lists of odds and ends that might be procured was always supplemented, almost beyond their need, by the new and fresh local vegetables Mr. Babcock was selling temporarily, or the packaged candy which had just come in. This trip Mrs. Allison was tempted, too, by the set of glass baking dishes that had found themselves completely by chance in the hardware and clothing and general store, and which had seemingly been waiting there for no one but Mrs. Allison, since the country people, with their instinctive distrust of anything that did not look as permanent as trees and rocks and sky, had only recently begun to experiment in aluminum baking dishes instead of ironware, and had, apparently within the memory of local inhabitants, discarded stoneware in favor of iron.

Mrs. Allison had the glass baking dishes carefully wrapped, to endure the uncomfortable ride home over the rocky road that led up to the Allisons' cottage, and while Mr. Charley Walpole, who, with his younger brother Albert, ran the hardware-clothing-general store (the store itself was called Johnson's, because it stood on the site of the old Johnson cabin, burned fifty years before Charley Walpole was born), laboriously unfolded newspapers to wrap around the dishes, Mrs. Allison said, informally, "Course, I *could* have waited and gotten those dishes in New York, but we're not going back so soon this year."

"Heard you was staying on," Mr. Charley Walpole said. His old fingers fumbled maddeningly with the thin sheets of newspaper, carefully trying to isolate only one sheet at a time, and he did not look up at Mrs. Allison as he went on, "Don't know about staying on up there to the lake. Not after Labor Day."

"Well, you know," Mrs. Allison said, quite as though he deserved an explanation, "it just seemed to us that we've been hurrying back to New York every year, and there just wasn't any need for it. You know what the city's like in the fall." And she smiled confidingly up at Mr. Charley Walpole.

Rhythmically he wound string around the package. He's giving me a piece long enough to save, Mrs. Allison thought, and she looked away quickly to avoid giving any sign of impatience. "I feel sort of like we belong here, more," she said. "Staying on after everyone else has left." To prove this, she smiled brightly across the store at a woman with a familiar face, who might have been the woman who sold berries to the Allisons one year, or the woman who occasionally helped in the grocery and was probably Mr. Babcock's aunt.

"Well," Mr. Charley Walpole said. He shoved the package a little across the counter, to show that it was finished and that for a sale well made, a package well wrapped, he was willing to accept pay. "Well," he said again. "Never been summer people before, at the lake after Labor Day."

Mrs. Allison gave him a five-dollar bill, and he made change methodically, giving great weight even to the pennies. "Never after Labor Day," he said, and nodded at Mrs. Allison, and went soberly along the store to deal with two women who were looking at cotton house dresses.

As Mrs. Allison passed on her way out she heard one of the women say acutely, "Why is one of them dresses one dollar and thirty-nine cents and this one here is only ninety-eight?"

"They're great people," Mrs. Allison told her husband as they went together down the sidewalk after meeting at the door of the hardware store. "They're so solid, and so reasonable, and so *honest*."

"Makes you feel good, knowing there are still towns like this," Mr. Allison said.

"You know, in New York," Mrs. Allison said, "I might have paid a few cents less for these dishes, but there wouldn't have been anything sort of *personal* in the transaction."

"Staying on to the lake?" Mrs. Martin, in the newspaper and sandwich shop, asked the Allisons. "Heard you was staying on."

"Thought we'd take advantage of the lovely weather this year," Mr. Allison said.

Mrs. Martin was a comparative newcomer to the town; she had married into the newspaper and sandwich shop from a neighboring farm, and had stayed on after her husband's death. She served bottled soft drinks, and fried egg and onion sandwiches on thick bread, which she made on her own stove at the back of the store. Occasionally when Mrs. Martin served a sandwich it would carry with it the rich fragrance of the stew or the pork chops cooking alongside for Mrs. Martin's dinner.

"I don't guess anyone's ever stayed out there so long before," Mrs. Martin said. "Not after Labor Day, anyway."

"I guess Labor Day is when they usually leave," Mr. Hall, the Allisons' nearest neighbor, told them later, in front of Mr. Babcock's store, where the Allisons were getting into their car to go home. "Surprised you're staying on."

"It seemed a shame to go so soon," Mrs. Allison said. Mr. Hall lived three miles away; he supplied the Allisons with butter and eggs, and occasionally, from the top of their hill, the Allisons could see the lights in his house in the early evening before the Halls went to bed.

"They usually leave Labor Day," Mr. Hall said.

The ride home was long and rough; it was beginning to get dark, and Mr.

Allison had to drive very carefully over the dirt road by the lake. Mrs. Allison lay back against the seat, pleasantly relaxed after a day of what seemed whirlwind shopping compared with their day-to-day existence; the new glass baking dishes lurked agreeably in her mind, and the half bushel of red eating apples, and the package of colored thumbtacks with which she was going to put up new shelf edging in the kitchen. "Good to get home," she said softly as they came in sight of their cottage, silhouetted above them against the sky.

"Glad we decided to stay on," Mr. Allison agreed.

Mrs. Allison spent the next morning lovingly washing her baking dishes, although in his innocence Charley Walpole had neglected to notice the chip in the edge of one; she decided, wastefully, to use some of the red eating apples in a pie for dinner, and, while the pie was in the oven and Mr. Allison was down getting the mail, she sat out on the little lawn the Allisons had made at the top of the hill, and watched the changing lights on the lake, alternating gray and blue as clouds moved quickly across the sun.

Mr. Allison came back a little out of sorts; it always irritated him to walk the mile to the mail box on the state road and come back with nothing, even though he assumed that the walk was good for his health. This morning there was nothing but a circular from a New York department store, and their New York paper, which arrived erratically by mail from one to four days later than it should, so that some days the Allisons might have three papers and frequently none. Mrs. Allison, although she shared with her husband the annoyance of not having mail when they so anticipated it, pored affectionately over the department store circular, and made a mental note to drop in at the store when she finally went back to New York, and check on the sale of wool blankets; it was hard to find good ones in pretty colors nowadays. She debated saving the circular to remind herself, but after thinking about getting up and getting into the cottage to put it away safely somewhere, she dropped it into the grass beside her chair and lay back, her eyes half closed.

"Looks like we might have some rain," Mr. Allison said, squinting at the sky.

"Good for the crops," Mrs. Allison said laconically, and they both laughed.

The kerosene man came the next morning while Mr. Allison was down getting the mail; they were getting low on kerosene and Mrs. Allison greeted the man warmly; he sold kerosene and ice, and, during the summer, hauled garbage away for the summer people. A garbage man was only necessary for improvident city folk; country people had no garbage.

"I'm glad to see you," Mrs. Allison told him. "We were getting pretty low."

The kerosene man, whose name Mrs. Allison had never learned, used a hose attachment to fill the twenty-gallon tank which supplied light and heat and cooking facilities for the Allisons; but today, instead of swinging down from his truck and unhooking the hose from where it coiled affectionately around the cab of the truck, the man stared uncomfortably at Mrs. Allison, his truck motor still going.

"Thought you folks'd be leaving," he said.

"We're staying on another month," Mrs. Allison said brightly. "The weather was so nice, and it seemed like—"

"That's what they told me," the man said. "Can't give you no oil, though."

"What do you mean?" Mrs. Allison raised her eyebrows. "We're just going to keep on with our regular—"

"After Labor Day," the man said. "I don't get so much oil myself after Labor Day."

Mrs. Allison reminded herself, as she had frequently to do when in disagreement with her neighbors, that city manners were no good with country people; you could not expect to overrule a country employee as you could a city worker, and Mrs. Allison smiled engagingly as she said, "But can't you get extra oil, at least while we stay?"

"You see," the man said. He tapped his finger exasperatingly against the car wheel as he spoke. "You see," he said slowly, "I order this oil. I order it down from maybe fifty, fifty-five miles away. I order back in June, how much I'll need for the summer. Then I order again . . . oh, about November. Round about now it's starting to get pretty short." As though the subject were closed, he stopped tapping his finger and tightened his hands on the wheel in preparation for departure.

"But can't you give us *some?*" Mrs. Allison said. "Isn't there anyone else?"

"Don't know as you could get oil anywheres else right now," the man said consideringly. "*I* can't give you none." Before Mrs. Allison could speak, the truck began to move; then it stopped for a minute and he looked at her through the back window of the cab. "Ice?" he called. "I could let you have some ice."

Mrs. Allison shook her head; they were not terribly low on ice, and she was angry. She ran a few steps to catch up with the truck, calling, "Will you try to get us some? Next week?"

"Don't see's I can," the man said. "After Labor Day, it's harder." The truck drove away, and Mrs. Allison, only comforted by the thought that she could probably get kerosene from Mr. Babcock or, at worst, the Halls, watched it go with anger. "Next summer," she told herself, "just let *him* trying coming around next summer!"

There was no mail again, only the paper, which seemed to be coming doggedly on time, and Mr. Allison was openly cross when he returned. When Mrs. Allison told him about the kerosene man he was not particularly impressed.

"Probably keeping it all for a high price during the winter," he commented. "What's happened to Anne and Jerry, do you think?"

Anne and Jerry were their son and daughter, both married, one living in Chicago, one in the far west; their dutiful weekly letters were late; so late, in fact, that Mr. Allison's annoyance at the lack of mail was able to settle on a legitimate grievance. "Ought to realize how we wait for their letters," he said. "Thoughtless, selfish children. Ought to know better."

"Well, dear," Mrs. Allison said placatingly. Anger at Anne and Jerry would not relieve her emotions toward the kerosene man. After a few minutes she said, "Wishing won't bring the mail, dear. I'm going to go call Mr. Babcock and tell him to send up some kerosene with my order."

"At least a postcard," Mr. Allison said as she left.

As with most of the cottage's inconveniences, the Allisons no longer noticed the phone particularly, but yielded to its eccentricities without conscious complaint. It was a wall phone, of a type still seen in only few communities; in order to get the operator, Mrs. Allison had first to turn the side-crank and ring once. Usually it took two or three tries to force the operator to answer, and Mrs. Allison, making any kind of telephone call, approached the phone with resignation and a sort of desperate patience. She had to crank the phone three times this morning before the operator answered, and then it was still longer before Mr. Babcock picked up the receiver at his phone in the corner of the grocery behind the meat table. He said "Store?" with the rising inflection that seemed to indicate suspicion of anyone who tried to communicate with him by means of this unreliable instrument.

"This is Mrs. Allison, Mr. Babcock. I thought I'd give you my order a day early because I wanted to be sure and get some—"

"What say, Mrs. Allison?"

Mrs. Allison raised her voice a little; she saw Mr. Allison, out on the lawn, turn in his chair and regard her sympathetically. "I said, Mr. Babcock, I thought I'd call in my order early so you could send me—"

"Mrs. Allison?" Mr. Babcock said. "You'll come and pick it up?"

"Pick it up?" In her surprise Mrs. Allison let her voice drop back to its normal tone and Mr. Babcock said loudly, "What's that, Mrs. Allison?"

"I thought I'd have you send it out as usual," Mrs. Allison said.

"Well, Mrs. Allison," Mr. Babcock said, and there was a pause while Mrs. Allison waited, staring past the phone over her husband's head out into the sky. "Mrs. Allison," Mr. Babcock went on finally, "I'll tell you, my boy's been working for me went back to school yesterday, and now I got no one to deliver. I only got a boy delivering summers, you see."

"I thought you *always* delivered," Mrs. Allison said.

"Not after Labor Day, Mrs. Allison," Mr. Babcock said firmly, "you never been here after Labor Day before, so's you wouldn't know, of course."

"Well," Mrs. Allison said helplessly. Far inside her mind she was saying, over and over, can't use city manners on country folk, no use getting mad.

"Are you *sure?*" she asked finally. "Couldn't you just send out an order today, Mr. Babcock?"

"Matter of fact," Mr. Babcock said, "I guess I couldn't, Mrs. Allison. It wouldn't hardly pay, delivering, with no one else out at the lake."

"What about Mr. Hall?" Mrs. Allison asked suddenly, "the people who live about three miles away from us out here? Mr. Hall could bring it out when he comes."

"Hall?" Mr. Babcock said. "John Hall? They've gone to visit her folks up-state, Mrs. Allison."

"But they bring all our butter and eggs," Mrs. Allison said, appalled.

"Left yesterday," Mr. Babcock said. "Probably didn't think you folks would stay on up there."

"But I told Mr. Hall . . ." Mrs. Allison started to say, and then stopped. "I'll send Mr. Allison in after some groceries tomorrow," she said.

"You got all you need till then," Mr. Babcock said, satisfied; it was not a question, but a confirmation.

After she hung up, Mrs. Allison went slowly out to sit again in her chair next to her husband. "He won't deliver," she said. "You'll have to go in tomorrow. We've got just enough kerosene to last till you get back."

"He should have told us sooner," Mr. Allison said.

It was not possible to remain troubled long in the face of the day; the country had never seemed more inviting, and the lake moved quietly below them, among the trees, with the almost incredible softness of a summer picture. Mrs. Allison sighed deeply, in the pleasure of possessing for themselves that sight of the lake, with the distant green hills beyond, the gentleness of the small wind through the trees.

The weather continued fair; the next morning Mr. Allison, duly armed with a list of groceries, with "kerosene" in large letters at the top, went down the path to the garage, and Mrs. Allison began another pie in her new baking dishes. She had mixed the crust and was starting to pare the apples when Mr.

Allison came rapidly up the path and flung open the screen door into the kitchen.

"Damn car won't start," he announced, with the end-of-the-tether voice of a man who depends on a car as he depends on his right arm.

"What's wrong with it?" Mrs. Allison demanded, stopping with the paring knife in one hand and an apple in the other. "It was all right on Tuesday."

"Well," Mr. Allison said between his teeth, "it's not all right on Friday."

"Can you fix it?" Mrs. Allison asked.

"No," Mr. Allison said, "I can not. Got to call someone, I guess."

"Who?" Mrs. Allison asked.

"Man runs the filling station, I guess." Mr. Allison moved purposefully toward the phone. "He fixed it last summer one time."

A little apprehensive, Mrs. Allison went on paring apples absentmindedly, while she listened to Mr. Allison with the phone, ringing, waiting, ringing, waiting, finally giving the number to the operator, then waiting again and giving the number again, giving the number a third time, and then slamming down the receiver.

"No one there," he announced as he came into the kitchen.

"He's probably gone out for a minute," Mrs. Allison said nervously; she was not quite sure what made her so nervous, unless it was the probability of her husband's losing his temper completely. "He's there alone, I imagine, so if he goes out there's no one to answer the phone."

"That must be it," Mr. Allison said with heavy irony. He slumped into one of the kitchen chairs and watched Mrs. Allison paring apples. After a minute, Mrs. Allison said soothingly, "Why don't you go down and get the mail and then call him again?"

Mr. Allison debated and then said, "Guess I might as well." He rose heavily and when he got to the kitchen door he turned and said, "But if there's no mail—" and leaving an awful silence behind him, he went off down the path.

Mrs. Allison hurried with her pie. Twice she went to the window to glance at the sky to see if there were clouds coming up. The room seemed unexpectedly dark, and she herself felt in the state of tension that precedes a thunderstorm, but both times when she looked the sky was clear and serene, smiling indifferently down on the Allisons' summer cottage as well as on the rest of the world. When Mrs. Allison, her pie ready for the oven, went a third time to look outside, she saw her husband coming up the path; he seemed more cheerful, and when he saw her, he waved eagerly and held a letter in the air.

"From Jerry," he called as soon as he was close enough for her to hear him, "at last—a letter!" Mrs. Allison noticed with concern that he was no longer able to get up the gentle slope of the path without breathing heavily; but then he was in the doorway, holding out the letter. "I saved it till I got here," he said.

Mrs. Allison looked with an eagerness that surprised her on the familiar handwriting of her son; she could not imagine why the letter excited her so, except that it was the first they had received in so long; it would be a pleasant, dutiful letter, full of the doings of Alice and the children, reporting progress with his job, commenting on the recent weather in Chicago, closing with love from all; both Mr. and Mrs. Allison could, if they wished, recite a pattern letter from either of their children.

Mr. Allison slit the letter open with great deliberation, and then he spread it out on the kitchen table and they leaned down and read it together.

"Dear Mother and Dad," it began, in Jerry's familiar, rather childish handwriting, *"Am glad this goes to the lake as usual, we always thought you came back too soon and ought to stay up there as long as you could. Alice says that now that you're not as young as you used to be and have no demands on your time, fewer friends, etc., in the city, you ought to get what fun you can while you can. Since you two are both happy up there, it's a good idea for you to stay."*

Uneasily Mrs. Allison glanced sideways at her husband; he was reading intently, and she reached out and picked up the empty envelope, not knowing exactly what she wanted from it. It was addressed quite as usual, in Jerry's handwriting, and was postmarked Chicago. Of course it's postmarked Chicago, she thought quickly, why would they want to postmark it anywhere else? When she looked back down at the letter, her husband had turned the page, and she read on with him: *"—and of course if they get measles, etc., now, they will be better off later. Alice is well, of course, me too. Been playing a lot of bridge lately with some people you don't know, named Carruthers. Nice young couple, about our age. Well, will close now as I guess it bores you to hear about things so far away. Tell Dad old Dickson, in our Chicago office, died. He used to ask about Dad a lot. Have a good time up at the lake, and don't bother about hurrying back. Love from all of us, Jerry."*

"Funny," Mr. Allison commented.

"It doesn't sound like Jerry," Mrs. Allison said in a small voice. "He never wrote anything like . . ." she stopped.

"Like what?" Mr. Allison demanded. "Never wrote anything like what?"

Mrs. Allison turned the letter over, frowning. It was impossible to find any sentence, any word, even, that did not sound like Jerry's regular letters. Perhaps it was only that the letter was so late, or the unusual number of dirty fingerprints on the envelope.

"I don't *know*," she said impatiently.

"Going to try that phone call again," Mr. Allison said.

Mrs. Allison read the letter twice more, trying to find a phrase that sounded wrong. Then Mr. Allison came back and said, very quietly, "Phone's dead."

"What?" Mrs. Allison said, dropping the letter.

"Phone's dead," Mr. Allison said.

The rest of the day went quickly; after a lunch of crackers and milk, the Allisons went to sit outside on the lawn, but their afternoon was cut short by the gradually increasing storm clouds that came up over the lake to the cottage, so that it was as dark as evening by four o'clock. The storm delayed, however, as though in loving anticipation of the moment it would break over the summer cottage, and there was an occasional flash of lightning, but no rain. In the evening Mr. and Mrs. Allison, sitting close together inside their cottage, turned on the battery radio they had brought with them from New York. There were no lamps lighted in the cottage, and the only light came from the lightning outside and the small square glow from the dial of the radio.

The slight framework of the cottage was not strong enough to withstand the city noises, the music and the voices, from the radio, and the Allisons could hear them far off echoing across the lake, the saxophones in the New York dance band wailing over the water, the flat voice of the girl vocalist going inexorably out into the clean country air. Even the announcer, speaking glowingly of the virtues of razor blades, was no more than an inhuman voice sounding out from the Allisons' cottage and echoing back, as though the lake and the hills and the trees were returning it unwanted.

During one pause between commercials, Mrs. Allison turned and smiled weakly at her husband. "I wonder if we're supposed to . . . *do* anything," she said.

"No," Mr. Allison said consideringly. "I don't think so. Just wait."

Mrs. Allison caught her breath quickly, and Mr. Allison said, under the trivial melody of the dance band beginning again, "The car had been tampered with, you know. Even I could see that."

Mrs. Allison hesitated a minute and then said very softly, "I suppose the phone wires were cut."

"I imagine so," Mr. Allison said.

After a while, the dance music stopped and they listened attentively to a news broadcast, the announcer's rich voice telling them breathlessly of a marriage in Hollywood, the latest baseball scores, the estimated rise in food prices during the coming week. He spoke to them, in the summer cottage, quite as though they still deserved to hear news of a world that no longer reached them except through the fallible batteries on the radio, which were already beginning to fade, almost as though they still belonged, however tenuously, to the rest of the world.

Mrs. Allison glanced out the window at the smooth surface of the lake, the black masses of the trees, and the waiting storm, and said conversationally, "I feel better about that letter of Jerry's."

"I knew when I saw the light down at the Hall place last night," Mr. Allison said.

The wind, coming up suddenly over the lake, swept around the summer cottage and slapped hard at the windows. Mr. and Mrs. Allison involuntarily moved closer together, and with the first sudden crash of thunder, Mr. Allison reached out and took his wife's hand. And then, while the lightning flashed outside, and the radio faded and sputtered, the two old people huddled together in their summer cottage and waited.

Ovando

★

JAMAICA KINCAID

A KNOCK AT THE DOOR.

It is Frey Nicolas de Ovando. I was surprised. I was not expecting him. But then on reflecting, I could see that though I was not expecting him, he was bound to come. Somebody was bound to come. On reflecting, I could see that while I sat I thought, Someone will come to me; if no one comes to me, then I will go to someone. There was that knock at the door. It was Ovando then. Immediately I was struck by his suffering. Not a shred of flesh was left on his bones; he was a complete skeleton except for his brain, which remained, and was growing smaller by the millennium. He stank. Immediately I was struck by his innocence: for he had made himself a body from plates of steel, and it was stained with shades of red, blood in various stages of decay, and he thought I would not know the difference. He carried with him the following things: bibles, cathedrals, museums (for he was already an established collector), libraries (banks, really, in which he stored the contents of his diminishing brain), the contents of a drawing room. "Ovando," I said, "Ovando," and I smiled at him and threw my arms open to embrace this stinky relic of a person. Many people have said that this was my first big mistake, and I always say, How could it be a mistake to show sympathy, to show trust, to show affection to another human being, on first meeting? How can my action, then, with its foundation fixed in love, be judged a mistake? For I loved him then, not the way I would love my mother, or my child, but with that more general and spontaneous kind of love that I feel when I see any human being. As I shall show you, my first actions should not have been rewarded as they were. But wait here a minute and I shall show you what happened next.

With a wave of my hand I threw the door open and said, "Come in." I did this with great exaggeration, for it was unnecessary. You see, he was already inside. And so too when I said, "Sit down, make yourself at home, in fact think of this as your new home," not only was he already sitting down but he said, "Yes, this is the new home I have been looking for, and I already like it so much that I have sent for my relatives in Spain, Portugal, France, England, Germany, Italy, Belgium, and The Netherlands. I know that they will like it here as much as I do, for they are just like me, we have met the same fate in the world." So many things at once seemed wrong to me that it was hard to know where to begin. I could not see his eyes; they were shut. Any number of things could explain this, I thought: perhaps he was blind, perhaps all his deeds so far had left him in a permanent state of inner bliss. And as for the relatives! Imagine whole countries populated by people with not a shred of flesh left on their bones, complete skeletons inside bodies made from plates of steel, people who had lost the ability to actually speak and could only make pronouncements, their brains growing smaller by the millennium, their bodies covered with blood in various shades of decay; whole countries of people coming to visit me even though I had not invited them, whole countries of people sitting down in my house without asking my permission!

The most confusing thing was that he had used the word *fate*. I gathered then that mere reasoning him out of his plans would not work. ("Ovando, look, let us be reasonable. All of your words and deeds toward me so far have been incredibly unjust. Already, just in the first few moments of our meeting, you have done me irreparable harm. Stop now, let me show to you the grave errors you have made." "Really, there is nothing I can do about this. A power outside and beyond me has predetermined these unalterable events. All of my actions have been made for me in eternity. All of my actions are divine.")

I could have brought a stop to what was an invasion to me, a discovery to him; after all, I too knew of divinities and eternities and unalterable events. But I looked closely at him. He was horrible on a scale I did not even know existed before. I sat at his feet and helped him take off his shoes.

For a very long time Ovando believed the world to be round. It suited him to believe that, for from his point of view he could see only horror and misery and disease and famine and poverty and nothingness. If the earth were round, thought Ovando, he could go away, far away from his immediate surroundings, far away beyond the horizon, which would prove not to be a ledge over which he would fall into a sea of blackness. For a while, then, a round earth spun on its axis in Ovando's mind's eye. At first this world was small and bare and chalk-white, like a full moon in an early evening sky; it spun around and around, growing into perfection and permanence until finally, awake or asleep, alone or in a procession, in silence or in battle, Ovando carried this round, bare, chalk-white world. Then, after a few hundred years of this, Ovando filled his earth with seas, across the seas he placed lands, the lands were covered with mountains and rivers, and the mountains and rivers hid enormous treasures. When Ovando's imagination brought forth the round earth and then the seas and then the land and then the mountains and then the rivers, he acted with great calm. But in imagining the treasures he grew agitated, and then he fainted. He took this to be a sign from his various divinities, for all visionaries take as a sign of affirmation a momentary loss of contact with the ordinariness of daily life.

"Ah, then," said Ovando, as he entered a small room. He sat at a desk and proceeded to fill countless volumes with his meditations on the spheres, divine assertions, liberation from bonds spiritual and physical, and phlebotomy. To say that his meditations were nothing more than explanations and justifications for his future actions might seem unfair, for after all is it not so that all human beings are, from moment to moment, vulnerable to overwhelming self-love? When Ovando emerged from this small room, his eyes were half-shut. The lights had burnt out many, many years earlier, but he had continued his work of filling up the volumes in the half dark, and not once did he get to sleep. In his hands now he carried a large piece of paper, a piece of paper that was as large as a front lawn, and on this piece of paper Ovando had rendered flat the imagined contents of his world. Oh what an ugly thing to see, for the lands and the seas were painted in the vile colors of precious stones just ripped from their muddy home! It looked like the effort of schoolchildren. It looked like a fragile object that had been dropped on a hard surface and its pieces first swept up in a dustpan and then gently but haphazardly placed on a tabletop. It looked like sadness itself, for it was a map. Ovando spread his map out before him. Using the forefinger of his left hand, he traced on his map a line. Months later his finger came to a stop. It was at a point not too far from where he had started. Removing his finger from his map, he let out a long, satisfying breath, and then he looked up. At that moment the world broke.

From where I sit the world looks flat. I look out to the horizon. The world ends in a sharp, flat, clear line where the seas and the sky are joined. I look out on my world. I accept it in its flatness. I am not tempted to transgress its boundaries. My world bears me no ill; on the contrary, my world bears me only goodness. I accept the goodness that my world bears me. My world with its goodness is not a burden; on the contrary, I find grace and light and comfort in my world. I find the things I need in my world. And yet—; for all hearts contain within them an eternal yearning, a yearning for a peace that is not death, a yearning for an answer to a question that cannot quite be asked. My heart is no exception and so my world is not infinite. To the stranger's eye (Ovando's) my world is a paradise. To the stranger's eye (Ovando's) everything in my world appears as if it were made anew each night as I sleep, by gods in their heavenly chambers. The climate in which I live is unchanging and kind; it does not exhaust me with extremes of hot and cold. I have by now lost interest in knowing the exact number of trees that bear me food; so, too, in the number that bear me only flowers, and in the ones that bloom only at nights and only when the moon is in its full phase.

I sit in the morning sun. I idly rub my toe against the earth beneath me, and a large vein of gold is revealed to me. I walk in the warm evening air. I stumble over the glittering stones that are scattered in my path. What can I do with all that I am surrounded by? I can fashion for myself bracelets, necklaces, crowns.

I can make kingdoms, I can make civilizations, I can lay waste. But I can see the destruction of my body, and I can see the destruction of my soul. Then in my flat world I am blessed with a certain vision. I see the end in everything around me. I see its beginnings, I see its ends. I see the way things will always be. For me then, all discovery results in contemplation. I see a thing I have never seen before, I place it in the palm of my hand; eventually I see the many purposes to which it can be put, eventually I see all its many purposes brought to an end, eventually I see it die. I replace the thing I have never seen before in the exact place in which I found it. Again let me say: I see an object, I see its myriad uses good and bad, I see it rise up to great heights. I see it hold sway, the foundations of vast enterprises are laid in it, I see it reduced again to its humble origins, a thing I can hold in my hand. In the many things I have held in my hand, from time to time I see my own humanity: I can hold religious beliefs, I can extol a moral value, I can prevent myself from entering the dungheap that is history. My world is flat. I accept this. Its borders are finite. I accept this. The flatness of my world is kind to me.

"My Sheer Might!" said Ovando loudly and then fell silent. Those three words rushed out of his mouth and vanished into the silence of things so completely that Ovando did not believe that he had said them. He had spent many years in preparation for this moment, the moment in which these words could be said. The moment in which the words could be said was the moment in which the words would be true. And so for a long time Ovando stood in front of a mirror, more in the stance of a child at play than an actor in preparation for a great part, and he tried to say the words "My Sheer Might!" At first he could only see the words glowing in the darkness inside his head. Then the words burned in a cool, soft way, an indication that they were at the beginning of their life span. In the meantime—that is, during the time Ovando stood in front of the mirror, a mirror, by the way, that reflected nothing but his own image—my own world in its flatness heaved up and down in the way of something alternately freezing and thawing out. I looked at my world: its usually serene and pleasing contours began to change before my eyes. The roots of trees were forced out of the ground. The grasses were ablaze with a fire that I did not know how to put out. The streams dried up, and the riverbeds became barren tracks. The birds all hovered overhead and blotted out the light of the sun. The unwinged creatures stood up and cried into the charged air, but their own sounds disturbed them so that they then lay down and buried their heads in their stomachs. I said, "What is it? Who is it?" and then without speech I observed this frightening wonder, waiting for the moment when my world would return to the way it had always been, waiting for the moment when I would doubt that what I saw before me had really taken place. Ovando said again, "My Sheer Might!" and this time the words did not vanish into the silence of things. This time the words became like a poisonous cloud of vapor, and they spread out, swallowing up everything in their path. In that moment the mirror into which Ovando looked, the mirror which reflected only Ovando, broke into thirteen pieces in some places, into six hundred and sixty-six pieces in other places, and in still other places into different numbers of pieces, and in all of these places the breaking of the mirror signified woe. In that moment, I, my world, and everything in it became Ovando's thralls.

One morning, Ovando arose from his bed. Assisted by people he had forcibly placed in various stages of social and spiritual degradation, he prepared a document, which, when read to me, would reveal to me my real predicament. He had by this time grown an enormous tail, which he would cause to flail about in the air whenever he was amused. What amused him was predictable: the endless suffering he could cause whenever he wished. He had also grown horns on either side of his head, and from these he hung various instruments of torture; his tongue he made forked. The document that he had prepared for me was only six inches long and six inches wide, but it was made from the pulp of one hundred and ten trees and these trees had taken ten millennia to reach the exquisite state of beauty in which Ovando found them: their trunks were smooth, and so thick that two arms wrapped around them would just meet, and they glowed ruby red in the sunlight. At the very top the leaves and branches formed globes of yellow and green that also glowed in the sun; they perfumed the air but not pervasively, not enough that one could become accustomed to it. These trees Ovando had ordered cut down so that only stumps remained, and boiled and pounded and dried, and the process repeated again and again until they were reduced to something that measured six inches by six inches. Holding it up to the light, he said, "Do you see?" and I understood him to mean not only that he could reduce these precious trees to something held between the tips of two of his fingers but that he also held in his hands the millennia in which the trees grew to maturity, their origins, their ancestry, and everything that they had ever, ever been, and so too he held me. Then on this paper Ovando wrote that he dishonored me, that he had a right to do so for I came from nothing, that since I came from nothing I could not now exist in something, and so my existence was now rooted in nothing, and though I seemed to live and needed the things necessary to the living such as food and water and air, I was dead; and so though I might seem present, in reality I was absent. This document consisted of hundreds of articles and each of them confirmed my dishonor, each of them confirmed my death, each of them confirmed my nothingness. I listened to him carefully, his voice the sound of metal rapidly corroding. At the end of this I stood up and made an extremely long and incoherent speech, so shocked I was at the brutality of tone and language of Ovando's document, so unused to such cruelty, such barbarism, such harshness. In my long and incoherent speech, which I delivered in a heartfelt and sorrowful and earnest way (for should I not be touched by my own pain, should I not be moved on seeing a picture of myself humbled by a power over which I had no desire to triumph, a power I wished would stay out of my way?), I tried to point out to Ovando that since the ideas of Honor, Death, and Nothingness were not within my view and so held no meaning for me, he could not really rob me of anything; since these ideas constituted some of his deepest beliefs it was himself then that he dishonored, it was himself then that he made dead, it was himself then that he consigned to nothingness. But Ovando could not hear me, for by that time his head had taken the shape of a groundworm, which has no ears.

Ovando has conquered the ages and placed them in medallions he wears around his neck, his waist, his wrists, and his ankles. After consulting for a long time the one he wears around his left wrist, Ovando said, "I shall raise the curtain, and my relatives shall now make their appearance." Of course, such a thing as Ovando's curtain was invisible to me. Ovando made an enormous flourish with his hands and, as if a curtain really had been parted, there suddenly, in what used to be an empty space, now stood a covered floating vessel. Ovando smiled at me, his face splitting with pleasure and conceit. Ovando's relatives arranged themselves into pairs of male and female and then began to leave their covered floating vessel. As they did so they announced in loud voices, as if it were a curse, the names of the places from which they had come: Spain, France, England, Belgium, The Netherlands, Germany, Portugal, Italy. As they entered the earth they kissed the ground, not as a sign of affection but rather as a sign of possession. They looked around and at last they saw me. In unison, like a clap of thunder, they all said, "Mine!" Ovando, seeing the danger in this, said, "Draw lots," but the people who drew my head really wanted my legs, and the people who drew my arms wanted my insides, and so on and so on until they fell on each other with a ferociousness that I could not have imagined possible. This battle now lasted for hundreds and hundreds of years, at the end of which time they should have exterminated themselves, but wherever their blood was spilt new versions of themselves grew up. It was in this way that they multiplied, by spilling blood over the earth itself.

Ovando speaks his own name. He says, "Ovando!" His name then gently leaves his lips in a long sigh, a delicious parting. Saying his name, Ovando runs his hands through his hair; saying his name, Ovando caresses his face; saying his name, Ovando gently passes his hands down his own back, through the crevices of his private parts, gently unmatting the tightly curled hair that grows in thick sworls and covers completely his child-sized penis; saying his name, Ovando gently runs his hands down one leg and up the other, across his chest, stopping to pinch sharply first one flattened breast and then the other; then raising his hands to his nostrils, he inhales deeply, and then bringing his hands to his mouth he kisses and sucks them until he feels content. His desire for his own mortal self fulfilled, he falls into a state of bliss, into a deep, deep sleep.

*　　*　　*

Ovando then lived constantly in night; but it was not a quiet night, a night that bore a soft sleep in which dreams of a long-ago-lived enchanted childhood occurred; it was not the sort of night that the day angrily interrupts, jealous of the union between the sleeper and the borderless, soft tapestry of blackness; and it was not a night of nature, which is to say the progression from the day to the opposite of day; it was not the night of just after sunset or the night of just before the sun rises. Ovando lived in the thickest part of the night, the deepest part of the night, the part of the night where all suffering dwells, including death; the part of the night in which the weight of the world is made visible and eternal terror is confirmed. In this night, Ovando's body was covered with sores (sores, not wounds, for the hand that inflicts wounds may be an unjust hand and injustice calls forth pity); he lay on a bed of broken glass bottles (not nails).

Who will judge Ovando? Who can judge Ovando? A true and just sentence would be imbued with love for Ovando. The sentence must bear within it sympathy and identification, for only if the judge resides in Ovando and Ovando resides in the judge can an everlasting judgment be passed. Ovando cannot pass judgment on himself, for, as is to be expected, he loves himself beyond measure. Such a love is a worm asleep in every heart, and must never be awakened; such a love lies like kindling in every heart, and must never be lit. A charge against Ovando, then, is that he loved himself so that all other selves and all other things became nothing to him. I became nothing to Ovando. My relatives became nothing to Ovando. Everything that could trace its lineage through me became nothing to Ovando. And so it came to be that Ovando loved nothing, lived in nothing and died in just that way. I cannot judge Ovando. I have exhausted myself laying out before him his transgressions. I am exhausted from shielding myself so that his sins do not obsess and so possess me.

THE WITCH WOMAN LIVED IN A DESERTED, boarded-up planta-tion house, and nobody knew about her but me. Nobody in the nosey little town in south Georgia where I lived when I was a boy knew that if you walked down the dusty main street to where the post office ended it, and then turned left and followed that road a piece until you got to the rusty iron gates of the drive to the plantation house, you could find goings-on would make your eyes pop out. It was just luck that I found out. Or maybe it wasn't luck at all. Maybe the witch woman wanted me to find out because of Alexandra. But now I wish I hadn't because the witch woman and Alexandra are gone forever and it's much worse than if I'd never known them.

Nobody'd lived in the plantation house since the Civil War when Colonel Londermaine was killed and Alexandra Londermaine, his beautiful young wife, hung herself on the chandelier in the ballroom. A while before I was born some northerners bought it but after a few years they stopped coming and people said it was because the house was haunted. Every few years a gang of boys or men would set out to explore the house but nobody ever found anything, and it was so well boarded up it was hard to force an entrance, so by and by the town lost interest in it. No one climbed the wall and wandered around the grounds except me.

I used to go there often during the summer because I had bad spells of malaria when sometimes I couldn't bear to lie on the iron bedstead in my room with the flies buzzing around my face, or out on the hammock on the porch with the screams and laughter of the other kids as they played torturing my ears. My aching head made it impossible for me to read, and I would drag myself down the road, scuffling my bare sunburned toes in the dust, wearing the tattered straw hat that was supposed to protect me from the heat of the sun, shivering and sweating by turns. Sometimes it would seem hours before I got to the iron gates near which the brick wall was lowest. Often I would have to lie panting on the tall prickly grass for minutes until I gathered strength to scale the wall and drop down on the other side.

But once inside the grounds it seemed cooler. One funny thing about my chills was that I didn't seem to shiver nearly as much when I could keep cool as I did at home where even the walls and the floors, if you touched them, were hot. The grounds were filled with live oaks that had grown up unchecked everywhere and afforded an almost continuous green shade. The ground was covered with ferns which were soft and cool to lie on, and when I flung myself down on my back and looked up, the roof of leaves was so thick that sometimes I couldn't see the sky at all. The sun that managed to filter through lost its bright pitiless glare and came in soft yellow shafts that didn't burn you when they touched you.

One afternoon, a scorcher early in September, which is usually our hottest month (and by then you're fagged out by the heat anyhow), I set out for the plantation. The heat lay coiled and shimmering on the road. When you looked at anything through it, it was like looking through a defective pane of glass. The dirt road was so hot that it burned even through my callused feet and as I walked clouds of dust rose in front of me and mixed with the shimmying of the heat. I thought I'd never make the plantation. Sweat was running into my eyes, but it was cold sweat, and I was shivering so that my teeth chattered as I walked. When I managed finally to fling myself down on my soft green bed of ferns inside the grounds I was seized with one of the worst chills I'd ever had in spite of the fact that my mother had given me an extra dose of quinine that morning and some 666 malaria medicine to boot. I shut my eyes tight and clutched the ferns with my hands and teeth to wait until the chill had passed, when I heard a soft voice call:

"Boy."

I thought at first I was delirious, because sometimes I got lightheaded when my bad attacks came on; only then I remembered that when I was delirious I didn't know it; all the strange things I saw and heard seemed perfectly natural. So when the voice said, "Boy," again, as soft and clear as the mockingbird at sunrise, I opened my eyes.

Kneeling near me on the ferns was a girl. She must have been about a year younger than I. I was almost sixteen so I guess she was fourteen or fifteen. She was dressed in a blue and white gingham dress; her face was very pale, but the kind of paleness that's supposed to be, not the sickly pale kind that was like mine showing even under the tan. Her eyes were big and very blue. Her hair was dark brown and she wore it parted in the middle in two heavy braids that were swinging in front of her shoulders as she peered into my face.

"You don't feel well, do you?" she asked. There was no trace of concern or worry in her voice. Just scientific interest.

I shook my head. "No," I whispered, almost afraid that if I talked she would vanish, because I had never seen anyone here before, and I thought that maybe I was dying because I felt so awful, and I thought maybe that gave me the power to see the ghost. But the girl in blue and white checked gingham seemed as I watched her to be good flesh and blood.

"You'd better come with me," she said. "She'll make you all right."

"Who's she?"

"Oh—just Her," she said.

My chill had begun to recede by now, so when she got up off her knees, I scrambled up, too. When she stood up her dress showed a white ruffled petticoat underneath it, and bits of green moss had left patterns on her knees and I didn't think that would happen to the knees of a ghost, so I followed her as she led the way towards the house. She did not go up the sagging, half-rotted steps which led to the veranda about whose white pillars wisteria vines climbed in wild profusion, but went around to the side of the house where there were slanting doors to a cellar. The sun and rain had long since blistered and washed off the paint, but the doors looked clean and were free of the bits of bark from the eucalyptus tree which leaned nearby and which had dropped its bits of dusty peel on either side; so I knew that these cellar stairs must frequently be used.

The girl opened the cellar doors. "You go down first," she said. I went down the cellar steps which were stone, and cool against my bare feet. As she followed me she closed the cellar doors after her and as I reached the bottom of the stairs we were in pitch darkness. I began to be very frightened until her soft voice came out of the black.

"Boy, where are you?"

"Right here."

"You'd better take my hand. You might stumble."

We reached out and found each other's hands in the darkness. Her fingers were long and cool and they closed firmly around mine. She moved with authority as though she knew her way with the familiarity born of custom.

"Poor Sat's all in the dark," she said, "but he likes it that way. He likes to sleep for weeks at a time. Sometimes he snores awfully. Sat, darling!" she called gently. A soft, bubbly, blowing sound came in answer, and she laughed happily. "Oh, Sat, you are sweet!" she said, and the bubbly sound came again. Then the girl pulled at my hand and we came out into a huge and dusty kitchen. Iron skillets, pots and pans, were still hanging on either side of the huge stove, and there was a rolling pin and a bowl of flour on the marble topped table in the middle of the room. The girl took a lighted candle off the shelf.

"I'm going to make cookies," she said as she saw me looking at the flour and the rolling pin. She slipped her hand out of mine. "Come along." She began to walk more rapidly. We left the kitchen, crossed the hall, went through the dining room, its old mahogany table thick with dust although sheets covered the pictures on the walls. Then we went into the ballroom. The mirrors lining the walls were spotted and discolored; against one wall was a single delicate gold chair, its seat cushioned with pale rose and silver woven silk; it seemed extraordinarily well preserved. From the ceiling hung the huge chandelier from which

Alexandra Londermaine had hung herself, its prisms catching and breaking up into a hundred colors the flickering of the candle and the few shafts of light that managed to slide in through the boarded-up windows. As we crossed the ballroom the girl began to dance by herself, gracefully, lightly, so that her full blue and white checked gingham skirts flew out around her. She looked at herself with pleasure in the old mirrors as she danced, the candle flaring and guttering in her right hand.

"You've stopped shaking. Now what will I tell Her?" she said as we started to climb the broad mahogany staircase. It was very dark so she took my hand again, and before we had reached the top of the stairs I obliged her by being seized by another chill. She felt my trembling fingers with satisfaction. "Oh, you've started again. That's good." She slid open one of the huge double doors at the head of the stairs.

As I looked in to what once must have been Colonel Londermaine's study I thought that surely what I saw was a scene in a dream or a vision in delirium. Seated at the huge table in the center of the room was the most extraordinary woman I had ever seen. I felt that she must be very beautiful, although she would never have fulfilled any of the standards of beauty set by our town. Even though she was seated I felt that she must be immensely tall. Piled up on the table in front of her were several huge volumes, and her finger was marking the place in the open one in front of her, but she was not reading. She was leaning back in the carved chair, her head resting against a piece of blue and gold embroidered silk that was flung across the chair back, one hand gently stroking a fawn that lay sleeping in her lap. Her eyes were closed and somehow I couldn't imagine what color they would be. It wouldn't have surprised me if they had been shining amber or the deep purple of her velvet robe. She had a great quantity of hair, the color of mahogany in firelight, which was cut quite short and seemed to be blown wildly about her head like flame. Under her closed eyes were deep shadows, and lines of pain about her mouth. Otherwise there were no marks of age on her face but I would not have been surprised to learn that she was any age in the world—a hundred, or twenty-five. Her mouth was large and mobile and she was singing something in a deep, rich voice. Two cats, one black, one white, were coiled up, each on a book, and as we opened the doors a leopard stood up quietly beside her, but did not snarl or move. It simply stood there and waited, watching us.

The girl nudged me and held her finger to her lips to warn me to be quiet, but I would not have spoken—could not, anyhow, my teeth were chattering so from my chill which I had completely forgotten, so fascinated was I by this woman sitting back with her head against the embroidered silk, soft deep sounds coming out of her throat. At last these sounds resolved themselves into words, and we listened to her as she sang. The cats slept indifferently, but the leopard listened, too:

> *I sit high in my ivory tower,*
> *The heavy curtains drawn.*
> *I've many a strange and lustrous flower,*
> *A leopard and a fawn*
>
> *Together sleeping by my chair*
> *And strange birds softly winging,*
> *And ever pleasant to my ear*
> *Twelve maidens' voices singing.*
>
> *Here is my magic maps' array,*
> *My mystic circle's flame.*
> *With symbol's art He lets me play,*
> *The unknown my domain,*
>
> *And as I sit here in my dream*
> *I see myself awake,*
> *Hearing a torn and bloody scream,*
> *Feeling my castle shake . . .*

Her song wasn't finished but she opened her eyes and looked at us. Now that his mistress knew we were here the leopard seemed ready to spring and devour me at one gulp, but she put her hand on his sapphire-studded collar to restrain him.

"Well, Alexandra," she said, "who have we here?"

The girl, who still held my hand in her long, cool fingers, answered, "It's a boy."

"So I see. Where did you find him?"

The voice sent shivers up and down my spine.

"In the fern bed. He was shaking. See? He's shaking now. Is he having a fit?" Alexandra's voice was filled with pleased interest.

"Come here, boy," the woman said.

As I didn't move, Alexandra gave me a push, and I advanced slowly. As I came near, the woman pulled one of the leopard's ears gently, saying, "Lie down, Thammuz." The beast obeyed, flinging itself at her feet. She held her hand out to me as I approached the table. If Alexandra's fingers felt firm and cool, hers had the strength of the ocean and the coolness of jade. She looked at me for a long time and I saw that her eyes were deep blue, much bluer than Alexandra's, so dark as to be almost black. When she spoke again her voice was warm and tender: "You're burning up with fever. One of the malaria bugs?" I nodded. "Well, we'll fix that for you."

When she stood and put the sleeping fawn down by the leopard, she was not as tall as I had expected her to be; nevertheless she gave an impression of great height. Several of the bookshelves in one corner were emptied of books and filled with various shaped bottles and retorts. Nearby was a large skeleton. There was an acid stained washbasin, too; that whole section of the room looked like part of a chemist's or physicist's laboratory. She selected from among the bottles a small amber-colored one, and poured a drop of the liquid it contained into a glass of water. As the drop hit the water there was a loud hiss and clouds of dense smoke arose. When it had drifted away she handed the glass to me and said, "Drink. Drink, my boy!"

My hand was trembling so that I could scarcely hold the glass. Seeing this, she took it from me and held it to my lips.

"What is it?" I asked.

"Drink it," she said, pressing the rim of the glass against my teeth. On the first swallow I started to choke and would have pushed the stuff away, but she forced the rest of the burning liquid down my throat. My whole body felt on fire. I felt flame flickering in every vein and the room and everything in it swirled around. When I had regained my equilibrium to a certain extent I managed to gasp out again, "What is it?"

She smiled and answered,

"Nine peacocks' hearts, four
bats' tongues,
A pinch of moondust and a
hummingbird's lungs."

Then I asked a question I would never have dared ask if it hadn't been that I was still half drunk from the potion I had swallowed, "Are you a witch?"

She smiled again, and answered, "I make it my profession."

Since she hadn't struck me down with a flash of lightning, I went on. "Do you ride a broomstick?"

This time she laughed. "I can when I like."

"Is it—is it very hard?"

"Rather like a bucking bronco at first, but I've always been a good horse-woman, and now I can manage very nicely. I've finally progressed to sidesaddle, though I still feel safer astride. I always rode my horse astride. Still, the best witches ride sidesaddle, so . . . Now run along home. Alexandra has lessons to study and I must work. Can you hold your tongue or must I make you forget?"

"I can hold my tongue."

She looked at me and her eyes burnt into me like the potion she had given me to drink. "Yes, I think you can," she said. "Come back tomorrow if you like. Thammuz will show you out."

The leopard rose and led the way to the door. As I hesitated, unwilling to tear myself away, it came back and pulled gently but firmly on my trouser leg.

"Good-bye, boy," the witch woman said. "And you won't have any more chills and fever."

"Good-bye," I answered. I didn't say thank you. I didn't say good-bye to Alexandra. I followed the leopard out.

She let me come every day. I think she must have been lonely. After all I was the only thing there with a life apart from hers. And in the long run the only reason I have had a life of my own is because of her. I am as much a creation of the witch woman's as Thammuz the leopard was, or the two cats, Ashtaroth and Orus (it wasn't until many years after the last day I saw the witch woman that I learned that those were the names of the fallen angels).

She did cure my malaria, too. My parents and the townspeople thought that I had outgrown it. I grew angry when they talked about it so lightly and wanted to tell them that it was the witch woman, but I knew that if ever I breathed a word about her I would be eternally damned. Mama thought we should write a testimonial letter to the 666 Malaria Medicine people, and maybe they'd send us a couple of dollars.

Alexandra and I became very good friends. She was a strange, aloof creature. She liked me to watch her while she danced alone in the ballroom or played on an imaginary harp—though sometimes I fancied I could hear the music. One day she took me into the drawing room and uncovered a portrait that was hung between two of the long boarded-up windows. Then she stepped back and held her candle high so as to throw the best light on the picture. It might have been a picture of Alexandra herself, or Alexandra as she might be in five years.

"That's my mother," she said. "Alexandra Londermaine."

As far as I knew from the tales that went about town, Alexandra Londermaine had given birth to only one child, and that stillborn, before she had hung herself on the chandelier in the ballroom—and anyhow, any child of hers would have been Alexandra's mother or grandmother. But I didn't say anything because when Alexandra got angry she became ferocious like one of the cats, and was given to leaping on me, scratching and biting. I looked at the portrait long and silently.

"You see, she has on a ring like mine," Alexandra said, holding out her left hand, on the fourth finger of which was the most beautiful sapphire and diamond ring I had ever seen, or rather, that I could ever have imagined, for it was a ring apart from any owned by even the most wealthy of the townsfolk. Then I realized that Alexandra had brought me in here and unveiled the portrait simply that she might show me the ring to better advantage, for she had never worn a ring before.

"Where did you get it?"

"Oh, she got it for me last night."

"Alexandra," I asked suddenly, "how long have you been here?"

"Oh, a while."

"But how long?"

"Oh, I don't remember."

"But you must remember."

"I don't. I just came—like Poor Sat."

"Who's Poor Sat?" I asked, thinking for the first time of whoever it was that had made the gentle bubbly noises at Alexandra the day she found me in the fern bed.

"Why, we've never shown you Sat, have we!" she exclaimed. "I'm sure it's all right, but we'd better ask Her first."

So we went to the witch woman's room and knocked. Thammuz pulled the door open with his strong teeth and the witch woman looked up from some sort of experiment she was making with test tubes and retorts. The fawn, as usual, lay sleeping near her feet. "Well?" she said.

"Is it all right if I take him to see Poor Little Saturday?" Alexandra asked her.

"Yes, I suppose so," she answered. "But no teasing," and turned her back to us and bent again over her test tubes as Thammuz nosed us out of the room.

We went down to the cellar. Alexandra lit a lamp and took me back to the corner furthest from the doors, where there was a stall. In the stall was a two-humped camel. I couldn't help laughing as I looked at him because he grinned at Alexandra so foolishly, displaying all his huge buck teeth and blowing bubbles through them.

"She said we weren't to tease him," Alexandra said severely, rubbing her cheek against the preposterous splotchy hair that seemed to be coming out, leaving bald pink spots of skin on his long nose.

"But what—" I started.

"She rides him sometimes." Alexandra held out her hand while he nuzzled against it, scratching his rubbery lips against the diamond and sapphire of her ring. "Mostly She talks to him. She says he is very wise. He goes up to Her room sometimes and they talk and talk. I can't understand a word they say. She says it's Hindustani and Arabic. Sometimes I can remember little bits of it, like *iderow, sorcabatcha*, and *anna bihed bech*. She says I can learn to speak with them when I finish learning French and Greek."

Poor Little Saturday was rolling his eyes in delight as Alexandra scratched behind his ears. "Why is he called Poor Little Saturday?" I asked.

Alexandra spoke with a ring of pride in her voice. "I named him. She let me."

"But why did you name him that?"

"Because he came last winter on the Saturday that was the shortest day of the year, and it rained all day so it got light later and dark earlier than it would have if it had been nice, so it really didn't have as much of itself as it should, and I felt so sorry for it I thought maybe it would feel better if we named him after it . . . She thought it was a nice name!" she turned on me suddenly.

"Oh, it is! It's a fine name!" I said quickly, smiling to myself as I realized how much greater was this compassion of Alexandra's for a day than any she might have for a human being. "How did She get him?" I asked.

"Oh, he just came."

"What do you mean?"

"She wanted him so he came. From the desert."

"He *walked!*"

"Yes. And swam part of the way. She met him at the beach and flew him here on the broomstick. You should have seen him. He was still all wet and looked so funny. She gave him hot coffee with things in it."

"What things?"

"Oh, just things."

Then the witch woman's voice came from behind us. "Well, children?"

It was the first time I had seen her out of her room. Thammuz was at her right heel, the fawn at her left. The cats, Ashtaroth and Orus, had evidently stayed upstairs. "Would you like to ride Saturday?" she asked me.

Speechless, I nodded. She put her hand against the wall and a portion of it slid down into the earth so that Poor Little Saturday was free to go out. "She's sweet, isn't she?" the witch woman asked me, looking affectionately at the strange, bumpy-kneed, splay-footed creature. "Her grandmother was very good to me in Egypt once. Besides, I love camel's milk."

"But Alexandra said she was a he!" I exclaimed.

"Alexandra's the kind of woman to whom all animals are he except cats, and all cats are she. As a matter of fact, Ashtaroth and Orus are she, but it wouldn't make any difference to Alexandra if they weren't. Go on out, Saturday. Come on!"

Saturday backed out, bumping her bulging knees and ankles against her stall, and stood under a live oak tree. "Down," the witch woman said. Saturday leered at me and didn't move. "Down, sorcabatcha!" the witch woman commanded, and Saturday obediently got down on her knees. I clambered up onto her, and before I had managed to get at all settled she rose with such a jerky motion that I knocked my chin against her front hump and nearly bit my tongue off. Round and round Saturday danced while I clung wildly to her front hump and the witch woman and Alexandra rolled on the ground with laughter. I felt as though I were on a very unseaworthy vessel on the high seas, and it wasn't long before I felt violently seasick as Saturday pranced among the live oak trees, sneezing delicately.

At last the witch woman called out, "Enough!" and Saturday stopped in her traces, nearly throwing me, and kneeling laboriously. "It was mean to tease you," the witch woman said, pulling my nose gently. "You may come sit in my room with me for a while if you like."

There was nothing I liked better than to sit in the witch woman's room and to watch her while she studied from her books, worked out strange looking mathematical problems, argued with the zodiac, or conducted complicated experiments with her test tubes and retorts, sometimes filling the room with sulphurous odors or flooding it with red or blue light. Only once was I afraid of her, and that was when she danced with the skeleton in the corner. She had the room flooded with a strange red glow and I almost thought I could see the flesh covering the bones of the skeleton as they danced together like lovers. I think she had forgotten that I was sitting there, half hidden in the wing chair, because when they had finished dancing and the skeleton stood in the corner again, his bones shining and polished, devoid of any living trappings, she stood with her forehead against one of the deep red velvet curtains that covered the boarded-up windows and tears streamed down her cheeks. Then she went back to her test tubes and worked feverishly. She never alluded to the incident and neither did I.

As winter drew on she let me spend more and more time in the room. Once I gathered up courage enough to ask her about herself, but I got precious little satisfaction.

"Well, then, are you maybe one of the northerners who bought the place?"

"Let's leave it at that, boy. We'll say that's who I am. Did you know that my skeleton was old Colonel Londermaine? Not so old, as a matter of fact; he was only thirty-seven when he was killed at the battle of Bunker Hill—or am I getting him confused with his great-grandfather, Rudolph Londermaine? Anyhow he was only thirty-seven, and a fine figure of a man, and Alexandra only thirty when she hung herself for love of him on the chandelier in the ballroom. Did you know that the fat man with the red mustaches has been trying to cheat your father? His cow will give sour milk for seven days. Run along now and talk to Alexandra. She's lonely."

When the winter had turned to spring and the camellias and azaleas and

Cape Jessamine had given way to the more lush blooms of early May, I kissed Alexandra for the first time, very clumsily. The next evening when I managed to get away from the chores at home and hurried out to the plantation, she gave me her sapphire and diamond ring which she had swung for me on a narrow bit of turquoise satin. "It will keep us both safe," she said, "if you wear it always. And then when we're older we can get married and you can give it back to me. Only you mustn't let anyone see it, ever, ever, or She'd be very angry."

I was afraid to take the ring but when I demurred Alexandra grew furious and started kicking and biting and I had to give in.

Summer was almost over before my father discovered the ring hanging about my neck. I fought like a witch boy to keep him from pulling out the narrow ribbon and seeing the ring, and indeed the ring seemed to give me added strength and I had grown, in any case, much stronger during the winter than I had ever been in my life. But my father was still stronger than I, and he pulled it out. He looked at it in dead silence for a moment and then the storm broke. That was the famous Londermaine ring that had disappeared the night Alexandra Londermaine hung herself. That ring was worth a fortune. Where had I got it?

No one believed me when I said I had found it in the grounds near the house—I chose the grounds because I didn't want anybody to think I had been in the house or indeed that I was able to get in. I don't know why they didn't believe me; it still seems quite logical to me that I might have found it buried among the ferns.

It had been a long, dull year, and the men of the town were all bored. They took me and forced me to swallow quantities of corn liquor until I didn't know what I was saying or doing. When they had finished with me I didn't even manage to reach home before I was violently sick and then I was in my mother's arms and she was weeping over me. It was morning before I was able to slip away to the plantation house. I ran pounding up the mahogany stairs to the witch woman's room and opened the heavy sliding doors without knocking. She stood in the center of the room in her purple robe, her arms around Alexandra who was weeping bitterly. Overnight the room had completely changed. The skeleton of Colonel Londermaine was gone, and books filled the shelves in the corner of the room that had been her laboratory. Cobwebs were everywhere, and broken glass lay on the floor; dust was inches thick on her worktable. There was no sign of Thammuz, Ashtaroth or Orus, or the fawn, but four birds were flying about her, beating their wings against her hair.

She did not look at me or in any way acknowledge my presence. Her arm about Alexandra, she led her out of the room and to the drawing room where the portrait hung. The birds followed, flying around and around them. Alexandra had stopped weeping now. Her face was very proud and pale and if she saw me miserably trailing behind them she gave no notice. When the witch woman stood in front of the portrait the sheet fell from it. She raised her arm; there was a great cloud of smoke; the smell of sulphur filled my nostrils, and when the smoke was gone, Alexandra was gone, too. Only the portrait was there, the fourth finger of the left hand now bearing no ring. The witch woman raised her hand again and the sheet lifted itself up and covered the portrait. Then she went, with the birds, slowly back to what had once been her room, and still I tailed after, frightened as I had never been before in my life, or have been since.

She stood without moving in the center of the room for a long time. At last she turned and spoke to me.

"Well, boy, where is the ring?"

"They have it."

"They made you drunk, didn't they?"

"Yes."

"I was afraid something like this would happen when I gave Alexandra the ring. But it doesn't matter . . . I'm tired . . ." She drew her hand wearily across her forehead.

"Did I—did I tell them everything?"

"You did."

"I—I didn't know."

"I know you didn't know, boy."

"Do you hate me now?"

"No, boy, I don't hate you."

"Do you have to go away?"

"Yes."

I bowed my head. "I'm so sorry . . ."

She smiled slightly. "The sands of time . . . Cities crumble and rise and will crumble again and breath dies down and blows once more . . ."

The birds flew madly about her head, pulling at her hair, calling into her ears. Downstairs we could hear a loud pounding, and then the crack of boards being pulled away from a window.

"Go, boy," she said to me. I stood rooted, motionless, unable to move. "GO!" she commanded, giving me a mighty push so that I stumbled out of the room. They were waiting for me by the cellar doors and caught me as I climbed out. I had to stand there and watch when they came out with her. But it wasn't the witch woman, my witch woman. It was *their* idea of a witch woman, someone thousands of years old, a disheveled old creature in rusty black, with long wisps of gray hair, a hooked nose, and four wiry black hairs springing out of the mole on her chin. Behind her flew the four birds and suddenly they went up, up, into the sky, directly in the path of the sun until they were lost in its burning glare.

Two of the men stood holding her tightly, although she wasn't struggling, but standing there, very quiet, while the others searched the house, searched it in vain. Then as a group of them went down into the cellar I remembered, and by a flicker of the old light in the witch woman's eyes I could see that she remembered, too. Poor Little Saturday had been forgotten. Out she came, prancing absurdly up the cellar steps, her rubbery lips stretched back over her gigantic teeth, her eyes bulging with terror. When she saw the witch woman, her lord and master, held captive by two dirty, insensitive men, she let out a shriek and began to kick and lunge wildly, biting, screaming with the bloodcurdling, heartrending screams that only a camel can make. One of the men fell to the ground, holding a leg in which the bone had snapped from one of Saturday's kicks. The others scattered in terror, leaving the witch woman standing on the veranda supporting herself by clinging to one of the huge wisteria vines that curled around the columns. Saturday clambered up onto the veranda, and knelt while she flung herself between the two humps. Then off they ran, Saturday still screaming, her knees knocking together, the ground shaking as she pounded along. Down from the sun plummeted the four birds and flew after them.

Up and down I danced, waving my arms, shouting wildly until Saturday and the witch woman and the birds were lost in a cloud of dust, while the man with the broken leg lay moaning on the ground beside me.

The Ones Who Walk Away from Omelas

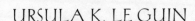

URSULA K. LE GUIN

(Variations on a theme by William James)

WITH A CLAMOR OF BELLS that set the swallows soaring, the Festival of Summer came to the city Omelas, bright-towered by the sea. The rigging of the boats in harbor sparkled with flags. In the streets between houses with red roofs and painted walls, between old moss-grown gardens and under avenues of trees, past great parks and public buildings, processions moved. Some were decorous: old people in long stiff robes of mauve and grey, grave master workmen, quiet, merry women carrying their babies and chatting as they walked. In other streets the music beat faster, a shimmering of gong and tambourine, and the people went dancing, the procession was a dance. Children dodged in and out, their high calls rising like the swallows' crossing flights over the music and the singing. All the processions wound towards the north side of the city, where on the great water-meadow called the Green Fields boys and girls, naked in the bright air, with mud-stained feet and ankles and long, lithe arms, exercised their restive horses before the race. The horses wore no gear at all but a halter without bit. Their manes were braided with streamers of silver, gold, and green. They flared their nostrils and pranced and boasted to one another; they were vastly excited, the horse being the only animal who has adopted our ceremonies as his own. Far off to the north and west the mountains stood up half encircling Omelas on her bay. The air of morning was so clear that the snow still crowning the Eighteen Peaks burned with white-gold fire across the miles of sunlit air, under the dark blue of the sky. There was just enough wind to make the banners that marked the race-course snap and flutter now and then. In the silence of the broad green meadows one could hear the music winding through the city streets, farther and nearer and ever approaching, a cheerful faint sweetness of the air that from time to time trembled and gathered together and broke out into the great joyous clanging of the bells.

Joyous! How is one to tell about joy? How describe the citizens of Omelas?

They were not simple folk, you see, though they were happy. But we do not say the words of cheer much any more. All smiles have become archaic. Given a description such as this one tends to make certain assumptions. Given a description such as this one tends to look next for the King, mounted on a splendid stallion and surrounded by his noble knights, or perhaps in a golden litter borne by great-muscled slaves. But there was no king. They did not use swords, or keep slaves. They were not barbarians. I do not know the rules and laws of their society, but I suspect that they were singularly few. As they did without monarchy and slavery, so they also got on without the stock exchange, the advertisement, the secret police, and the bomb. Yet I repeat that these were not simple folk, not dulcent shepherds, noble savages, bland utopians. They were not less complex than us. The trouble is that we have a bad habit, encouraged by pedants and sophisticates, of considering happiness as something rather stupid. Only pain is intellectual, only evil interesting. This is the treason of the artist: a refusal to admit the banality of evil and the terrible boredom of pain. If you can't lick 'em, join 'em. If it hurts, repeat it. But to praise despair is to condemn delight, to embrace violence is to lose hold of everything else. We have almost lost hold; we can no longer describe a happy man, nor make any celebration of joy. How can I tell you about the people of Omelas? They were not naïve and happy children—though their children were, in fact, happy. They were mature, intelligent, passionate adults whose lives were not wretched. O miracle! but I wish I could describe it better. I wish I could convince you. Omelas sounds in my words like a city in a fairy tale, long ago and far away, once upon a time. Perhaps it would be best if you imagined it as your own fancy bids, assuming it will rise to the occasion, for certainly I cannot suit you all. For instance, how about technology? I think that there would be no cars or helicopters in and above the streets; this follows from the fact that the people of Omelas are happy people. Happiness is based on a just discrimination of what is necessary, what is neither necessary nor destructive, and what is destructive. In the middle category, however—that of the unnecessary but undestructive, that of comfort, luxury, exuberance, etc.—they could perfectly well have central heating, subway trains, washing machines, and all kinds of marvelous devices not yet invented here, floating light-sources, fuelless power, a cure for the common cold. Or they could have none of that: it doesn't matter. As you like it. I incline to think that people from towns up and down the coast have been coming in to Omelas during the last days before the Festival on very fast little trains and double-decked trams, and that the train station of Omelas is actually the handsomest building in town, though plainer than the magnificent Farmers' Market. But even granted trains, I fear that Omelas so far strikes some of you as goody-goody. Smiles, bells, parades, horses, bleh. If so, please add an orgy. If an orgy would help, don't hesitate. Let us not, however, have temples from which issue beautiful nude priests and priestesses already half in ecstasy and ready to copulate with any man or woman, lover or stranger, who desires union with the deep godhead of the blood, although that was my first idea. But really it would be better not to have any temples in Omelas—at least, not manned temples. Religion yes, clergy no. Surely the beautiful nudes can just wander about, offering themselves like divine soufflés to the hunger of the needy and the rapture of the flesh. Let them join the processions. Let tambourines be struck above the copulations, and the glory of desire be proclaimed upon the gongs, and (a not unimportant point) let the offspring of these delightful rituals be beloved and looked after by all. One thing I know there is none of in Omelas is guilt. But what else should there be? I thought at first there were no drugs, but that is puritanical. For those who like it, the faint insistent sweetness of *drooz* may perfume the ways of the city, *drooz* which first brings a great lightness and brilliance to the mind and limbs, and then after some hours a dreamy languor, and wonderful visions at last of the very arcana and inmost secrets of the Universe, as well as exciting the pleasure of sex beyond all belief; and it is not habit-forming. For more modest tastes I think there ought to be beer. What else, what else belongs in the joyous city? The sense of victory, surely, the celebration of courage. But as we did without clergy, let us do without soldiers. The joy built upon successful slaughter is not the right kind of joy; it will not do; it is fearful and it is trivial. A boundless and generous contentment, a magnanimous triumph felt not against some outer enemy but in communion with the finest and fairest in the souls of all men everywhere and the splendor of the world's summer: this is what swells the hearts of the people of Omelas, and the victory they celebrate is that of life. I really don't think many of them need to take *drooz*.

Most of the processions have reached the Green Fields by now. A marvelous smell of cooking goes forth from the red and blue tents of the provisioners. The faces of small children are amiably sticky; in the benign grey beard of a man a couple of crumbs of rich pastry are entangled. The youths and girls have mounted their horses and are beginning to group around the starting line of the course. An old woman, small, fat, and laughing, is passing out flowers from a basket, and tall young men wear her flowers in their shining hair. A child of nine or ten sits at the edge of the crowd, alone, playing on a wooden flute. People pause to listen, and they smile, but they do not speak to him, for he never ceases playing and never sees them, his dark eyes wholly rapt in the sweet, thin magic of the tune.

He finishes, and slowly lowers his hands holding the wooden flute.

As if that little private silence were the signal, all at once a trumpet sounds from the pavilion near the starting line: imperious, melancholy, piercing. The horses rear on their slender legs, and some of them neigh in answer. Soberfaced, the young riders stroke the horses' necks and soothe them, whispering, "Quiet, quiet, there my beauty, my hope. . . ." They begin to form in rank along the starting line. The crowds along the racecourse are like a field of grass and flowers in the wind. The Festival of Summer has begun.

Do you believe? Do you accept the festival, the city, the joy? No? Then let me describe one more thing.

In a basement under one of the beautiful public buildings of Omelas, or perhaps in the cellar of one of its spacious private homes, there is a room. It has one locked door, and no window. A little light seeps in dustily between cracks in the boards, secondhand from a cobwebbed window somewhere across the cellar. In one corner of the little room a couple of mops, with stiff, clotted, foul-smelling heads, stand near a rusty bucket. The floor is dirt, a little damp to the touch, as cellar dirt usually is. The room is about three paces long and two wide: a mere broom closet or disused tool room. In the room a child is sitting. It could be a boy or a girl. It looks about six, but actually is nearly ten. It is feeble-minded. Perhaps it was born defective, or perhaps it has become imbecile through fear, malnutrition, and neglect. It picks its nose and occasionally fumbles vaguely with its toes or genitals, as it sits hunched in the corner farthest from the bucket and the two mops. It is afraid of the mops. It finds them horrible. It shuts its eyes, but it knows the mops are still standing there; and the door is locked; and nobody will come. The door is always locked; and nobody ever comes, except that sometimes—the child has no understanding of time or interval—sometimes the door rattles terribly and opens, and a person, or several people, are there. One of them may come in and kick the child to make it stand up. The others never come close, but peer in at it with frightened, disgusted eyes. The food bowl and the water jug are hastily filled, the door is locked, the eyes disappear. The people at the door never say anything, but the child, who has not always lived in the tool room, and can remember sunlight and its mother's voice, sometimes speaks. "I will be good," it says. "Please let me out. I will be good!" They never answer. The child used to scream for help at night, and cry a good deal, but now it only makes a kind of whining, "eh-haa, eh-haa," and it speaks less and less often. It is so thin there are no calves to its legs; its belly protrudes; it lives on a half-bowl of corn meal and grease a day. It is naked. Its buttocks and thighs are a mass of festered sores, as it sits in its own excrement continually.

They all know it is there, all the people of Omelas. Some of them have come to see it, others are content merely to know it is there. They all know that it has to be there. Some of them understand why, and some do not, but they all understand that their happiness, the beauty of their city, the tenderness of their friendships, the health of their children, the wisdom of their scholars, the skill of their makers, even the abundance of their harvest and the kindly weathers of their skies, depend wholly on this child's abominable misery.

This is usually explained to children when they are between eight and twelve, whenever they seem capable of understanding; and most of those who come to see the child are young people, though often enough an adult comes, or comes back, to see the child. No matter how well the matter has been explained to them, these young spectators are always shocked and sickened at the sight. They feel disgust, which they had thought themselves superior to. They feel anger, outrage, impotence, despite all the explanations. They would like to do something for the child. But there is nothing they can do. If the child were brought up into the sunlight out of that vile place, if it were cleaned and fed and comforted, that would be a good thing, indeed; but if it were done, in that day and hour all the prosperity and beauty and delight of Omelas would wither and be destroyed. Those are the terms. To exchange all the goodness and grace of every life in Omelas for that single, small improvement: to throw away the happiness of thousands for the chance of the happiness of one: that would be to let guilt within the walls indeed.

The terms are strict and absolute; there may not even be a kind word spoken to the child.

Often the young people go home in tears, or in a tearless rage, when they have seen the child and faced this terrible paradox. They may brood over it for weeks or years. But as time goes on they begin to realize that even if the child could be released, it would not get much good of its freedom: a little vague pleasure of warmth and food, no doubt, but little more. It is too degraded and imbecile to know any real joy. It has been afraid too long ever to be free of fear. Its habits are too uncouth for it to respond to humane treatment. Indeed, after so long it would probably be wretched without walls about it to protect it, and darkness for its eyes, and its own excrement to sit in. Their tears at the bitter injustice dry when they begin to perceive the terrible justice of reality, and to accept it. Yet it is their tears and anger, the trying of their generosity and the acceptance of their helplessness, which are perhaps the true source of the splendor of their lives. Theirs is no vapid, irresponsible happiness. They know that they, like the child, are not free. They know compassion. It is the existence of the child, and their knowledge of its existence, that makes possible the nobility of their architecture, the poignancy of their music, the profundity of their science. It is because of the child that they are so gentle with children. They know that if the wretched one were not here snivelling in the dark, the other one, the flute-player, could make no joyful music as the young riders line up in their beauty for the race in the sunlight of the first morning of summer.

Now do you believe them? Are they not more credible? But there is one more thing to tell, and this is quite incredible.

At times one of the adolescent girls or boys who go to see the child does not go home to weep or rage, does not, in fact, go home at all. Sometimes also a man or a woman much older falls silent for a day or two, and then leaves home. These people go out into the street, and walk down the street alone. They keep walking, and walk straight out of the city of Omelas, through the beautiful gates. They keep walking across the farmlands of Omelas. Each one goes alone, youth or girl, man or woman. Night falls; the traveler must pass down village streets, between the houses with yellow-lit windows, and on out into the darkness of the fields. Each alone, they go west or north, towards the mountains. They go on. They leave Omelas, they walk ahead into the darkness, and they do not come back. The place they go towards is a place even less imaginable to most of us than the city of happiness. I cannot describe it at all. It is possible that it does not exist. But they seem to know where they are going, the ones who walk away from Omelas.

THERE WAS A BOY WHO LIVED IN A SMALL HOUSE in a small town in the center of Africa.

Until he was about twelve, this house had been the last in the street, so that he walked straight from the garden, across a railway line, and into the veld. He spent most of his time wandering by himself through the *vleis* and the *kopjes*. Then the town began to grow, so that in the space of a year a new suburb of smart little houses lay between him and the grass and trees. He watched this happening with a feeling of surprised anger. But he did not go through the raw new streets to the *vlei* where the river ran and the little animals moved. He was a lethargic boy, and it seemed to him as if some spell had been put on him, imprisoning him forever in the town. Now he would walk through the new streets, looking down at the hard glittering tarmac, thinking of the living earth imprisoned beneath it. Where the veld trees had been allowed to stay, he stood gazing, thinking how they drew their strength through the layers of rubble and broken brick, direct from the breathing soil and from the invisibly running underground rivers. He would stand there, staring; and it would seem to him that he could see those fresh, subtly running streams of water moving this way and that beneath the tarmac; and he stretched out his fingers like roots toward the earth. People passing looked away uncomfortably. Children called out: "Moony, moony, mooning again!" Particularly the children from the house opposite laughed and teased him. They were a large, noisy family, solid in the healthy strength of their numbers. He could hardly distinguish one from another; he felt that the house opposite was filled like a box with plump, joyous, brown-eyed people whose noisy, cheerful voices frightened him.

He was a lanky, thin-boned youth whose face was long and unfinished-looking; and his eyes were enormous, blue, wide, staring, with the brilliance of distance in them.

His mother, when he returned to the house, would say tartly: "Why don't you go over and play with the children? Why don't you go into the bush like you used to? Why don't you. . . . "

He was devoted to his mother. He would say vaguely, "Oh, I don't know," and kick stones about in the dust, staring away over the house at the sky, knowing that she was watching him through the window as she sewed, and that she was pleased to have him there, in spite of her tart, complaining voice. Or he would go into the room where she sat sewing, and sit near her, in silence, for hours. If his father came into the room he began to fidget and soon went away. His father spoke angrily about his laziness and his unnatural behavior.

He made the mother fetch a doctor to examine the boy. It was from this time that Frederick took the words "not normal" as his inheritance. He was not normal; well, he accepted it. They made a fact of something he had always known because of the way people looked at him and spoke to him. He was neither surprised nor dismayed at what he was. And when his mother wept over him, after the doctor left, he scarcely heard the noise of her tears; he smiled at her with the warm childish grin that no one else had ever seen, for he knew he could always depend on her.

His father's presence was a fact he accepted. On the surface they made an easy trio, like an ordinary family. At meals they talked like ordinary people. In the evenings his father sometimes read to him, for Frederick found it hard to read, although he was now halfway through his teens; but there were moments when the old man fell silent, staring in unconcealable revulsion at this son he had made; and Frederick would let his eyes slide uncomfortably away, but in the manner of a person who is embarrassed at someone else's shortcomings. His mother accepted him; he accepted himself; that was enough.

When his father died he was sorry and cried with his fists in his eyes like a baby. At the graveside the neighbors looked at this great shambling child, with his colorless locks of hair and the big red fists rubbing at his eyes, and felt relieved at the normal outburst of grief. But afterward it was he and his mother alone in the small suburban house; and they never spoke of the dead father who had vanished entirely from their lives, leaving nothing behind him. She lived for her son, waiting for his return from school, or from his rambles around the streets; and she never spoke of the fact that he was in a class with children five years his junior or that he was always alone at weekends and holidays, never with other children.

He was a good son. He took her tea in the mornings at the time the sun rose and watched her crinkled old face light up from the pillow as he set down the tray by her knees. But he did not stay with her then. He went out again quickly, shutting the door, his eyes turned from the soft, elderly white shoulders, which were not, for him, his mother. This is how he saw her: in her dumpy flowered apron, her brown sinewy arms setting food before him, her round spectacles shining, her warm face smiling. Yet he did not think of her as an old lady. Perhaps he did not see her at all. He would sometimes put out his great lank hand and stroke her apron. Once he went secretly into her bedroom and took her hairbrush off the dressing table and brushed the apron, which was lying on the bed; and he put the apron on and laughed out loud at the sight of himself in the mirror.

Later, when he was seventeen, a very tall, awkward youth with the strange-lighted blue eyes, too old to be put to bed with a story after supper, he wandered about by himself through that area of ugly new houses that seemed to change under the soft brightness of the moon into a shadowy beauty. He walked for hours, or stood still gazing dimly about him at the deep starry sky or at the soft shapes of trees.

There was a big veld tree that stood a short way from their gate in a space between two street lamps, so that there was a well of shadow beneath it which attracted him very much. He stood beneath the tree, listening to the wind moving gently in the leaves and feeling it stir his hair like fingers. He would move slowly in to the tree until his long fingers met the rough bark; and he stroked the tree curiously, learning it, thinking: under this roughness and hardness moves the sap, like rivers under the earth. He came to spend his evenings there, instead of walking among the houses and looking in with puzzled, unenvious eyes through the windows at the other kind of people. One evening an extraordinarily violent spasm shook him, so that he found himself locked about that harsh strong trunk, embracing it violently, his arms and thighs knotted about it, sobbing and muttering angry words. Afterward he slowly went home, entering the small, brightly lighted room shamedly; and his great blue eyes sought his mother's, and he was surprised that she did not say anything, but smiled at him as usual. Always there was this assurance from her; and as time went past, and each night he returned to the tree, caressing and stroking it, murmuring words of love, he would come home simply, smiling his wide childish smile, waiting for her to smile back, pleased with him.

But opposite was still that other house full of people; the children were growing up; and one evening when he was leaning against the tree in deep shadow, his arm loosely about it, as if around a tender friend, someone stopped outside the space of shadow and peered in saying: "Why, Moony, what are you doing here by yourself?" It was one of the girls from that house, and when he did not reply she came toward him, finally putting out her hand to touch his arm. The touch struck cruelly through him, and he moved away; and she said with a jolly laugh: "What's the matter? I won't eat you." She pulled him out into the yellowy light from the street lamp and examined him. She was a fattish, untidy, bright girl, one of the middle children, full of affection for everything in the world; and this odd, silent youth standing there quite still between her hands affected her with amused astonishment, so that she said, "Well, you are a funny boy, aren't you?" She did not know what to do with him, so at last she took him home over the street. He had never been inside her house before, and it was like a foreign country. There were so many people, so much noise and laughter, and the wireless was shouting out words and music. He was silent and smiling in this world which had nothing to do with himself.

His passive smile piqued the girl, and later when he got up saying: "My mother's waiting for me," she replied, "Well, at any rate you can take me to the movies tomorrow."

He had never taken a girl out; had never been to the movies save with his parents, as a child is taken; and he smiled as at a ridiculous idea. But next evening she came and made him go with her.

"What's the matter, Moony?" she asked, taking his arm. "Don't you like me? Why don't you take girls out? Why do you always stay around your mother? You aren't a baby any longer."

These words he listened to smiling; they did not make him angry, because she could not understand that they had nothing to do with him.

He sat in the theater beside the girl and waited for the picture to be over. He would not have been in the least surprised if the building and the screen and the girl had vanished, leaving him lying under a tree with not a house in sight, nothing but the veld—the long grasses, the trees, the birds and the little animals. Afterward they walked home, and he listened to her chattering, scolding voice without replying. He did not mind being with her; but he forgot her as soon as she had gone in at her gate. He wandered back across the street to his own gate and looked at the tree standing in its gulf of shadow with the moonlight on its branches. He took two steps toward it and stopped; another step, and stopped again; and finally turned with a bolting movement, as if in fear, and shambled quickly in to his mother. She glanced up at him with a tight, suspicious face; and he knew she was angry, though she did not speak. Soon he went to bed, unable to bear this unspoken anger. He slept badly and dreamed of the tree. And next night he went to it as soon as it was dark, and stood holding the heavy dark trunk in his arms.

The girl from opposite was persistent. Soon he knew, because of the opposition of his mother, that he had a girl, as ordinary young men have girls.

Why did she want him? Perhaps it was just curiosity. She had been brought up in all that noise and warm quarreling and laughter; and so Frederick, who neither wanted her nor did not want her, attracted her. She scolded him and pleaded with him: "Don't you love me? Don't you want to marry me?"

At this he gave her his rambling, confused grin. The word marriage made him want to laugh. It was ridiculous. But to her there was nothing ridiculous in it. In her home, marriages took place between boys and girls, and there were always festivals and lovemaking and new babies.

Now he would take her in his arms beside the tree outside the gate, embracing her as he had embraced the tree, forgetting her entirely, murmuring strangely over her head among the shadows. She hated it and she loved it; for her, it was like being hypnotized. She scolded him, stayed away, returned; and yet he would not say he would marry her.

This went on for some time; though for Frederick it was not a question of time. He did not mind having her in his arms under the tree, but he could not marry her. He was driven, night after night, to the silent lovemaking, with the branches of the tree between him and the moon; and afterward he went straight to his room, so as not to face his mother.

Then she got ill. Instead of going with the girl at night, he stayed at home, making his mother drinks, silently sitting beside her, putting wet handkerchiefs on her forehead. In the mornings the girl looked at him over the hedge and said, "Baby! Baby!"

"But my mother's sick," he said, finding these words with difficulty from the dullness of his mind. At this she only laughed. Finally she left him. It was like a tight string snapping from him, so that he reeled back into his own house with his mother. He watched the girl going in and out of her house with her sisters, her brothers, her friends, her young men; at nights he watched her dancing on the veranda to the gramophone. But she never looked back at him. His mother was still an invalid and kept to her chair; and he understood she was now getting old, but it did not come into his head that she might die. He looked after her. Before going off to the office at the railways, where he arranged luggage under the supervision of another clerk, he would lift his mother from her bed, turn away from her while she painfully dressed herself, support her into a chair by the window, fetch her food, and leave her for the day. At night he returned directly to her from work and sat beside her until it was time to sleep. Sometimes, when the desire for the shadowy street outside became too strong, he would go out for a little time and stand beside his tree. He listened to the wind moving in the branches and thought: It's an old tree, it's too old. If a leaf fell in the darkness he thought: The leaves are falling—it's dying; it's too old to live.

When his mother at last died, he could not understand that she was dead. He stood at her graveside in the efficient, cared-for cemetery of this new town, with its antiseptic look because of the neatness of the rows of graves and the fresh clean sunlight, and gazed down at the oblong hole in the red earth, where the spades had smoothed the steep sides into shares of glistening hardness, and saw the precisely fitting black box at the bottom of the hole, and lifted his head to stare painfully at the neighbors, among whom was the girl from opposite, although he did not see her.

He went home to the empty house that was full of his mother. He left everything as it was. He did not expand his life to fill the space she had used. He was still a child in the house, while her chair stood empty, and her bed had pillows stacked on it, and her clothes hanging over the foot.

There was very little money. His affairs were managed by a man at the bank in whose custody he had been left, and he was told how much he could spend. That margin was like a safety line around his life; and he liked taking his small notebook where he wrote down every penny he spent at each month's end to the man at the bank.

He lived on, knowing that his mother was dead, but only because people had said she was. After a time he was driven by his pain down to the cemetery. The grave was a mound of red earth. The flowers of the funeral had died long ago. There was a small headstone of granite. A bougainvillea creeper had been planted on the grave; it spread its glossy green branches over the stone in layers of dark shining green and clusters of bleeding purple flowers. The first time he visited the cemetery he stood staring for a long time. Later he would sit by the headstone, fingering the leaves of the plant. Slowly he came to understand that his mother lay underneath where he sat. He saw her folded in the earth, her rough brown forearms crossed comfortably on her breast, her flowered apron pulled down to her fat knees, her spectacles glinting, her wrinkled old face closed in sleep. And he fingered the smooth hard leaves, noting the tiny working veins, thinking: They feed on her. The thought filled him with panic and drove him from the grave. Yet he returned again and again, to sit under the pressure of the heavy yellow sunlight, on the rough warm stone, looking at the red and purple flowers, feeling the leaves between his fingers.

One day, at the grave, he broke off a branch of the bougainvillea plant and returned with it to the house, where he set it in a vase by his bed. He sat beside it, touching and smoothing the leaves. Slowly the branch lost its color and the clusters of flowers grew limp. A spray of stiff, dead, pale leaves stood up out of the vase; and his eyes rested on it, brilliant, vague, spectral, while his face contracted with pain and with wonder.

During the long solitary evenings he began again to stand at his gate, under the stars, looking about him in the darkness. The big tree had been cut down; all the wild trees in that street were gone, because of the danger from the strong old roots to the bricks of the foundations of the houses. The authorities had planted new saplings, domestic and educated trees like bauhinea and jacaranda. Immediately outside his gate, where the old tree had been, was one of these saplings. It grew quickly: one season it was a tiny plant in a little leaning shed of grass; the next it was as high as his head. There was an evening that he went to it, leaning his forehead against it, not thinking, his hands sliding gently and unsurely up and down the long slim trunk. This taut supple thing was nothing he had known; it was strange to him; it was too slight and weak and there was no shadow around it. And yet he stood there night after night, unconscious of the windows about him where people might be looking out, unconscious of passers-by, feeling and fumbling at the tree, letting his eyes stray past to the sky or to the lines of bushy little saplings along the road or to the dusty crowding hedges.

One evening he heard a bright, scornful voice say: "What do you think you're doing?" and he knew it was the girl from opposite. But the girl from opposite had married long ago and was now an untidy, handsome matron with children of her own; she had left him so far behind that she could now nod at him with careless kindness, as if to say: Well, well, so you're still there, are you?

He peered and gawked at the girl in his intense ugly way that was yet at-

tractive because of his enormous lighted eyes. Then, for him, the young and vigorous creature who was staring at him with such painful curiosity became the
girl from opposite. She was in fact the other girl's sister, perhaps ten years her
junior. She was the youngest of that large, pulsing family, who were all married
and gone, and she was the only one who had known loneliness. When people
said, with the troubled callousness, the necessary callousness that protects society against its rotten wood: "He's never been the same since the death of his
mother; he's quite crazy now," she felt, not merely an embarrassed and funda-
mentally indifferent pity, but a sudden throb of sympathy. She had been watching Frederick for a long time. She was ready to defend him against people who
said, troubled by this attraction of the sick for the healthy, "For God's sake what
do you see in him, can't you do better than that?"

As before, he did as she wanted. He would accompany her to the movies.
He would come out of his house at her call. He went walking with her through
the dark streets at night. And before parting from her he took her into his arms
against the sapling that swayed and slipped under their weight and kissed her
with a cold persistence that filled her with horror and with desire, so that she
ran away from him, sobbing, saying she would never see him again, and returned inevitably the next evening. She never entered his house; she was afraid
of the invisibly present old woman. He seemed not to mind what she did. She
was driven wild because she knew that if she did not seek him out, the knowledge of loss would never enter him; he would merely return to the lithe young
tree, mumbling fierce, thick, reproachful words to it in the darkness.

As he grew to understand that she would always return no matter how she
strove and protested, he would fold her against him, not hearing her cries, and
as she grew still with chilled fear, she would hear through the darkness a dark
sibilant whispering: "Your hair, your hair, your teeth, your bones." His fingers
pressed and probed into her flesh. "Here is the bone, under is nothing only
bone," and the long urgent fingers fought to defeat the soft envelope of flesh,
fought to make it disappear, so that he could grasp the bones of her arm, the
joint of her shoulder; and when he had pressed and probed and always found
the flesh elastic against his hands, pain flooded along her as the teeth closed in

on her neck, or while his fist suddenly drove inward, under her ribs, as if the tension of flesh were not there. In the morning she would be bruised. She avoided the eyes of her family and covered up the bruises. She was learning, through this black and savage initiation, a curious strength. She could feel the bones standing erect through her body, a branching undefeatable tree of strength; and when the hands closed in on her, stopping the blood, half-choking her, the stubborn half-conscious thought remained: You can't do it; you can't do it, I'm too strong.

Because of the way people looked in at them, through the darkness, as they leaned and struggled against the tree, she made him go inside the hedge of the small neglected garden, and there they lay together on the lawn, for hour after hour, with the cold high moon standing over them, sucking the warmth from their flesh, so they embraced in a cold, lethal ecstasy of pain, knowing only the cold, greenish light, feeling the bones of their bodies cleave and knock together while he grasped her so close that she could scarcely draw each breath. One night she fainted, and she came to herself to find him still clasping her, in a cold strong clasp, his teeth bared against her throat, so that a suffocating black pressure came over her brain in wave after wave; and she fought against him, making him tighten his grip and press her into the soil, and she felt the rough grasses driving up into her flesh.

A flame of self-preservation burned up into her brain, and she fought until he came to himself and his grip loosened. She said, "I won't. I won't let you. I won't come back again." He lay still, breathing like a deep sleeper. She did not know if he had heard her. She repeated hurriedly, already uncertain, "I won't let you." He got up and staggered away from her, and she was afraid because of the destructive light in the great eyes that glinted at her in the moonlight.

She ran away and locked herself in her bedroom. For several days she did not return. She watched him from her window as he strode huntedly up and down the street, lurking around the young tree, sometimes shaking it so that the leaves came spinning down around him. She knew she must return; and one evening she drifted across the street and came on him standing under the lithe young tree that held its fine glinting leaves like a spray of tinted water upward in the moonlight over the fine slender trunk.

This time he reached out and grasped her and carried her inside to the lawn. She murmured helplessly, in a dim panic, "You mustn't. I won't."

She saw the hazy brilliant stars surge up behind his black head, saw the greenish moonlight pour down the thin hollows of his cheeks, saw the great crazy eyes immediately above hers. The cages of their ribs ground together; and she heard: "Your hair, dead hair, bones, bones, bones."

The bared desperate teeth came down on her throat, and she arched back as the stars swam and went out.

When people glanced over the hedge in the strong early sunlight of next morning they saw him half-lying over the girl, whose body was marked by blood and by soil; and he was murmuring: "Your hair, your leaves, your branches, your rivers."

Another Halloween

★

ALISON LURIE

Y OU'VE GOT TO ADMIT THERE'S SOMETHING uncomfortable about Halloween as a holiday. I mean, what are we celebrating? Not the American Revolution, or the family, or God, or the New Year, nothing like that. Nothing respectable. Instead of flags or holly or colored lights, the streets are full of weird-looking dwarfish creatures, monsters and witches and animals running on their hind legs. You might say, Oh, they're only our kids, and other people's kids. But how do you know for sure?

In ancient Rome, where the whole thing started according to what I've read, they called it the Day of the Dead. That was who came back every year and they didn't come back in good shape or in a good mood. The dead were disoriented and destructive, like people in a late stage of Alzheimer's. They slid out of their tombs at sunset and drifted through town in their trailing, rotted grave clothes, gabbling unintelligibly in Latin. It's in Shakespeare: "the sheeted dead/Did squeak and gibber in the Roman streets." People left out saucers of food and drink, and barricaded themselves in their houses, which was probably the smart thing to do.

I don't care much for Halloween, not since what happened to a woman I knew called Marguerite Robbins. She lived next door to us in Corinth when our children were small, in one of a block of clunky frame houses, too close together. They were roomy inside though, with big old kitchens and deep front porches. I was really close to a couple of the other young mothers on the block; they were like family, maybe better than family.

It wasn't that way with Marguerite. But her Jamie was our Joel's age, and they were best friends, so we met practically every day. We got on well enough; but I always felt kind of overgrown and clumsy around her; she was so daintily pretty: pale blonde, with a round baby face and short-fingered hands like an expensive doll. Her nails were a matched set of tiny perfect polished shells. She wore rubber gloves for housework, and makeup even at breakfast: powder-pink lipstick and powder-blue eye shadow.

Also she made me feel noisy. She had the sort of cool manners that always make me think of words like *pleasant* and *cordial*. She never had much to say, or raised her voice, and she didn't like it when somebody else did. If I blew my top because Joel'd wet the bed again, or the washer wouldn't drain, she would murmur, "Oh, that's too bad," and literally move back, as if a wave full of dirty seaweed had slopped too close to her on a beach.

Anyhow. The weird stuff started the Robbinses' first Halloween, a month or so after they moved in. All the older kids on the block had gone out trick-and-treating, but Jamie and Joel were still too small. Marguerite's husband had a meeting and she asked if I'd like to keep her company. From the sound of her voice I knew she was imagining teenage hooligans who would smash her windows or squirt red paint over her when she opened the door. I told her nothing like that ever happened in our neighborhood, but she didn't sound convinced.

So I asked Fred to hold the fort and went over to Marguerite's maple-and-chintz Early American sitting room, which always reminded me of our dentist's office. She had a big basket of polished Golden Delicious apples and little boxes of raisins on the table by the door. Not what I would have chosen; let's face it, kids want candy.

At first there were so many trick-and-treaters we hardly had time to drink our coffee, but then things slowed down and I began to consider going home.

Then the bell rang again. I heaved myself up in case it might be someone I knew, though I was eight months pregnant and felt like a bathtub on wheels. There were four or five kids: a cute lady pirate, a Mickey Mouse, and a couple of tramps with burnt-cork mustaches and eyebrows, but nobody I recognized.

Marguerite handed out the health food and shut the door, and then she turned and asked in a wound-up voice, "Ruthie, who was that child in the rabbit costume?"

I hadn't noticed any, I said.

"In back of the others. She was wearing one of those bunny sleepers with feet, and a white mask."

I shook my head.

"You must have seen her," Marguerite insisted. "About five years old, and she had an old wrinkled white pillowcase for a bag."

"Nope; I'm sorry."

Marguerite gave me a look that said I was stupid and unobservant. Then she went back to the sitting room and poured herself more coffee without offering me any, which was really unusual for her.

"It's just—" she said, holding her cup in both doll's hands, not looking at me but out the window at the light from her jack-o'-lantern wavering on the porch railings. "You see, when I was a child—The little sister of a girl I knew was hit by a car on Halloween, and she was wearing a costume like that. So it rather upset me."

"Well, hell, of course," I agreed. "What an awful thing to happen!"

"I wasn't involved, actually," said Marguerite. "I knew her by sight, that was all. But it *was* rather awful. More coffee?"

"No thanks." I was glowing with sympathy like an electric heater. "It's always so damn scary when a child gets hurt, even if you hardly know them. Last summer this little boy was visiting across the street, and he fell off his tricycle and cut his head open. While I was running toward him I felt this absolute panic—I should have known it couldn't be that bad, because he'd got right up again, but he was screaming so loud, and his face was covered in blood, though in the end he only had to have two stitches. I could hardly breathe, I was sort of—"

"Yes, I remember you telling me," Marguerite interrupted.

"Oh, did I? Sorry." I shut up.

"Glen should be home soon," she added, and then she politely swallowed a yawn: she didn't open her pretty rose-pink mouth, but her whole face got longer in that unmistakable way. So I took the hint and left.

Well, time passed, and I almost forgot the whole business. I saw Marguerite often because of the kids, but I hadn't got to like her much better. Maybe it was her nicey-nice manners, or her attitude toward local projects. You know how it is, somebody's always trying to organize sales of Girl Scout cookies or soliciting for the Heart Fund, or asking you to go door-to-door with a petition to save wildlife. Most of us usually went along, but not Marguerite.

What really put me off was the cool, composed way she always refused. For instance, one time Joel and Jamie's daycare center was holding a raffle to fund a new climbing frame, and I asked Marguerite to take a couple of tickets. They were only a dollar each, and you could win a weekend in New York or a heap of other prizes. If it had been me who couldn't come up with two bucks I would have fallen all over myself apologizing. Marguerite just said politely, "Oh, no thank you, Ruthie," as if I'd offered her a stale doughnut.

When Halloween came round again Joel and Jamie were four, old enough for trick-and-treating, and I volunteered to take them. Jamie was a clown, and Joel had got it into his head to be Little Bear; I had to go to three stores to find the fake fur, but I have to say he looked pretty damn cute. Marguerite didn't come with us: her husband was home, but he had a report to write and couldn't be disturbed, or so she said.

Well, next morning just after Joel and Jamie had left for day care there was a knock at the back door, and it was Marguerite. Which was odd to start with, because she always phoned first to see if it was a "good time" to come over.

She looked terrible. Her pink lipstick was on crooked, and her flowered blouse was buttoned wrong, so that one side of its Peter Pan collar seemed about to take off.

"Well, hi. Come on in," I said.

Marguerite took half a step forward; then she just stood in a sort of huddle by the door. "I wanted to thank you again," she said. "For taking Jamie out last night. He really," she started again, and stopped dead.

"That's okay, it was fun. He's a good kid," I said, which was true. "Here, have some coffee." I pulled out a chair and she sat down kind of uneven, on one edge of it.

Then the kettle began boiling and whistling, and Fred walked into the room behind her and called out "Rabbit!" for good luck because it was the first day of the month. That's a family tradition, dating back to when we met. I hadn't heard of the custom then, and when I woke up in Fred's bedroom for the first time I saw him standing by the open window in his bathrobe and he called, "Rabbit!" and I said, "Oh, where?" and I jumped up naked and ran to look out, and I was practically face-to-face and chest to chest with two guys playing Frisbee. I hadn't noticed the night before that his apartment building was on a slope, the way most everything is in Corinth.

Anyhow. My startle reaction that day in Fred's room wasn't a patch on Marguerite's. She looked as if she were going to throw up, and her mug slipped and splashed the table with coffee.

"I'm terribly sorry," she squeaked, and then she didn't utter a word until Fred had chugged down his orange juice and gone out for his run.

Then she leaned forward and said in a kind of loud whisper, "I saw her again, Ruthie. That same little girl who came to the house last year."

"Little girl?" I said. Then I remembered. "You mean the one in the bunny costume, that reminded you of some kid you once knew."

"Yes, did you see her?"

"No, sorry. But of course we weren't out long."

"She came again." Marguerite announced this as if it were some really bad world news.

"Oh yeah?" I was skeptical. "Are you sure it was the same one? I mean, hell, there must have been lots of little kids out last night in those bunny sleepers. Besides, you know most children won't wear the same costume two years running. You remember that fairy getup with the gauze wings Josie made for Mary

Lou last year, a size too large so she could use it again, only now Mary Lou doesn't believe in fairies, she had to be a space pilot—" Then I happened to look at Marguerite's face and shut up.

"It was the same little girl," she said. She was tormenting the paper napkin I'd given her, twisting it round and round. "With that same old pillowcase. And the left ear of the rabbit mask bent sideways, and her eyes looking at me through the holes."

"Maybe you just thought it was her," I suggested. It had occurred to me that when Marguerite had seen that accident she had got a childhood trauma, and since then anybody in a bunny sleeper was a reminder. "Because of that kid you knew who got hit by a car."

"Killed," Marguerite said. "She was killed." She wrung the neck of the paper napkin. "I was there."

That wasn't what you told me last year, I started to say, but I made an effort and swallowed it.

"I wasn't really involved, of course. I was simply out trick-or-treating with her older sister," Marguerite went on finally. "My friend's mother made her take Kelly with us. Only round the block, and then she was supposed to go home, but she wouldn't. Annie gave her a push up the front walk, but she just stood there, whining that it wasn't fair, because we were going to get more candy.

"We ignored her, but Kelly started following us down the street. She kept calling, 'Wait for me, wait for me!' and we shouted back, 'Go on home, you stupid baby!'

"Finally we started running to get away from her. We got to the corner and ran across North Avenue, and Kelly ran after us. Only she couldn't run very fast, or see very well through the rabbit mask, and an old lady in a Buick came around the corner and hit her."

"Oh, God," I said. "And you saw it happen? That's terrible."

"I didn't actually see the car hit her. But I heard it: first this high shriek, that was the brakes, and then somebody screaming. Only it wasn't Kelly screaming, it was the old lady driver. Kelly was just lying by the curb under the streetlight, with her rabbit face turned sideways, not moving. Except her pillowcase was open, and Tootsie Rolls and candy corn were rolling all over the pavement."

"God," I said. "Well, no wonder you freak out when somebody shouts 'Rabbit!' After my aunt left the space heater on and her summer cottage practically burned down with her in it, she said that whenever she smelled wood smoke, for the next twenty years—" I stopped myself. "Hey, I'm sorry. I mean, of course it upset you."

"It didn't really upset me," Marguerite said. "After all, I wasn't responsible. Naturally I was disturbed at the time, but I got over it." She took a breath and smiled as if her teeth hurt.

"Mm," I said, making a big effort not to contradict her. "Well, I guess it was worse for the family."

"Oh, yes. It more or less ruined their lives, as a matter of fact."

"Really."

"And the driver's, too. She was cleared in court, but she sold the Buick and gave up her license, because she still felt guilty, even though it wasn't anybody's fault. Then she tried to give Kelly's family quite a lot of money, but they were too angry to accept it."

"Really?" I said, though afterward when I thought about it I wasn't so surprised.

"Yes; that was odd. But about ten years later she died and left it to them anyway. Only by that time Kelly's parents were divorced and her sister was in a drug treatment center. And naturally the old lady's own relatives didn't care for it at all. They tried to break the will." Marguerite smiled again; it was her normal little sweet smile now.

"What a depressing story," I said.

"Yes, it is, rather," agreed Marguerite. She seemed quite recovered except for her blouse, which was still buttoned wrong. "Well, I'd better get back. Thank you for the coffee."

After she left I sat there for a while. It had finally dawned on me that what she thought she kept seeing on Halloween was the ghost of the little girl who'd been killed. Then I had an idea. I thought that if I could find the actual kid who'd been wearing that bunny costume the night before, Marguerite would get over her delusion.

During the next few days I asked almost everyone on the block, only it turned out nobody had seen any bunny rabbits. I finally decided the kid must have come in a car, the way you heard people from the projects do sometimes. They get their children dressed up and take them to some part of town where they can collect expensive candy, and maybe even money. Of course the right part of Corinth for that was on the other side of the campus, but maybe whoever was driving the car didn't realize it till their kids had been to Marguerite's house on the corner and collected her depressing apples and raisins.

After that I forgot the whole thing for a while. I had a one-year-old and a four-year-old and I was trying to hold down a part-time job and half-asleep on my feet most of the time. Marguerite seemed to be okay again, only I was getting kind of tired of her. We'd been living next door for over two years, but after that once she would never talk about anything personal. If you asked who she liked in the local elections, or if she'd been happy in kindergarten, she'd just give you that cool polite little smile and say, "I haven't thought about it," or "I really can't remember." And I'd begun to notice that she always did a little bit less than her share of driving and watching the kids, something Fred and other people had mentioned a while back.

Most of the other mothers on the block were seriously fed up with Marguerite by this time, especially Josie, my best pal across the street, who had never forgiven her for refusing to help campaign against the waste-disposal plant. Marguerite had remarked that after all, by the time the plant was built most of us would probably have moved away. If you knew Josie, you'd know that was about the worst excuse anybody could have thought of.

What I didn't like most of all was that Josie and the rest of them kind of acted as if I was responsible for Marguerite. "Do you want to know what your friend has done now?" somebody would say, for instance. "She's not my friend," I'd want to answer, but instead I'd start making up excuses for Marguerite, blaming her husband, or the migraine headaches she used to have.

Anyhow, it got to be another Halloween—our last one in Corinth, but we didn't know that then. Joel and Jamie were five, still too young to go out on their own. It was Marguerite's turn to take them, and for once her husband had agreed to give away the treats. She asked if I wanted to come along, and I said okay. I knew Joel would like it, and besides I thought maybe Marguerite was nervous about being out on her own because of her delusion about the rabbit.

It was an unpleasant night: cold and wet, with rain leaking down through the bare trees, and drifts of greenish-grey fog rising from the pavement. Joel was got up as a red dinosaur—what a job that had been—and Jamie was some kind of space monster. They both thought they were pretty fierce; they kept growling at everyone we met, and they'd refused to wear their slickers. Also they didn't want us to come to the door with them—we had to wait on the path out of the light, under our umbrellas.

When we were halfway around the block and on our way home I happened to look down the street and saw a bunch of kids crossing the road, maybe thirty feet away. The smallest one, trailing behind the rest, was wearing a bunny sleeper.

That was when I made my first bad mistake. I said to Marguerite, "Hey, look, there's a kid in a rabbit costume, like the one you saw last year."

She went all white and funny. "Where?" she squeaked, and stared round like someone who hears an explosion and doesn't know what direction it came from.

I pointed down the street. The little kid had stopped at the far corner and was looking back at us. She gave a kind of wave, or maybe she was just trying to get a better grip on the pillowcase she was dragging, and then she went on, running to catch up to the others.

"I've got to see— Would you mind? I'll be right back," Marguerite said.

"Sure, that's okay," I agreed. I figured Marguerite would find out who the kid was, and get over being knocked sideways every time she saw a rabbit.

Marguerite didn't even say thanks. She was already hurrying down the wet sidewalk: running a few steps in the high heels she always wore, then walking a few, then running again.

"Wait for me!" she called. But the rabbit was only a white blob now down at the end of the next block, and it didn't stop; maybe it hadn't even heard.

For a moment I just stood there, even though Joel and Jamie were already pulling at me, wanting to go on to the next house. I could see Marguerite's pale raincoat and paler hair shine and dim as she moved through the cones of misty brightness under the street lamps, getting smaller and farther away. Unloading your job on me again, was what I thought. Then she turned a corner, and that was the last I saw of her.

We finished the block, and Marguerite still wasn't back. I took Jamie home and told Glen his wife had gone to speak to some child she thought she knew, and he said, "Oh, okay."

But later at our house, when Joel was dumping his candy onto the kitchen table, I had the idea that maybe I should go out again and look for Marguerite. I even started to put on my raincoat.

If it had been one of my real friends I would've gone without thinking. But instead I paused and said to myself, What's the point? Whether or not she's caught up with the kid in the bunny costume, she has to be back soon. And if you do find her she'll give you that polite look that is her specialty. What are you doing here, why are you sticking your nose into my business? that look will say, the way it so often has.

I don't think that way anymore. Now I believe women have to take responsibility for other women, even ones they don't much like. And I think that if I'd gone after Marguerite maybe I would have been in time.

None of us heard the crash. It was four long blocks off anyhow, on the main road. The guy who hit her claimed Marguerite just rushed out in front of his old Buick convertible, but nobody believed him because he already had two convictions for DWI, so he got six months and lost his license. I felt a little sorry for him, but I didn't say anything.

I think about it sometimes. I tell myself that Corinth was probably full of bunny sleepers that night, and that lots of people give their kids old pillowcases to collect candy in. I try to believe I just imagined that the rabbit's mask had one ear bent down; or that even if it did, it wouldn't be anything to get into a state about.

But that's not the worst. The worst is that sometimes I'm convinced she's still out there, and I'll see her again. Not the little girl in the bunny costume: Marguerite. I can't get rid of the idea that some Halloween night when I look out past the little witches and clowns and spacemen on our porch, she'll be there too: standing halfway down the path in her pale raincoat under a bat-black umbrella, waiting for me.

The Parallel World

VALERIE MARTIN

I MAGINE THAT A WOMAN IS ALLOWED TO GO AWAY to perfect solitude. She stays in a little house. The grass around it is high and the footpath that leads to it twists and even disappears in places so that no one is tempted to follow it. The woman stays alone in the house; she sleeps alone at night. Her room is alive with mice that come out when it is dark and cavort, amusing themselves at the expense of her sleep. Soon she will be used to them, will sleep without hearing them, or when she does hear them, she will no longer care to notice them. But at first she can't rest, and in the daytime she lies in the grass outside, for the cabin is among the trees and she likes the sun. Down among the grasses, thinking to find sleep, she finds a new world, what she calls the parallel world. It lies between the ground and the tips of the long grasses.

For a time she is aware of the parallel world only at certain moments. Gazing at the small area of ground between her knees brings it sharply into focus. She hears a dull buzzing of insect life, but she cannot determine, sometimes, if the sound comes from inside or outside her own skull. Then she presses her fingers against the thin flesh that covers her forehead, pressing and pressing while the buzzing sound grows louder and more insistent. She can detect a pattern, like a wispy hair net, stretched over the grass before her, and it seems to shimmer in the morning light as if it were touched with water. She senses activity both in the microscopic world, where strange unicellular animals carry on their affairs in deep silence, and in the macroscopic world of planets and stars, whirling in the blackness of space. The earth, she thinks, has begun to brood upon her fate, and some of us are beginning to hear her sad thoughts.

She fails to find any meaningful activity in the level of consciousness she is herself, thanks to centuries of evolution, constrained to inhabit. She cannot know the earth nor can she care for her fellows who are not, it seems, any longer of the earth. An escape into a world of aliens could not result in deeper loneliness than she feels among beings of her own kind. When she lies among the grasses all alone, it is true that she runs the gamut of emotions, from an ecstasy of unnatural intensity to a brooding despair, mixed with fear, which causes her to suspect her own sanity. But none of these emotions is thrust upon her. She is not confronted, when contemplating the parallel world, with her fellow in suffering. In fact it is the absence of anything resembling human emotion that renders this world cause for joy and, paradoxically, despair.

One night, after a week of such solitude, she wakes up thinking of a time when she was in an audience at a poetry reading. The poet was a Nigerian, a man who was thin, charming, and as dark as the polished wood podium on which he had set his white sheaf of verses. He read a poem about a train trip. He was a prince, she knew this; his father had been the equivalent of a king; and he had ridden the train from the deep heart of the jungle, his father's village, to the city where he was to go to school. He described, in his poem, how he stood at the open window, breathing in the still heat of the jungle, when he saw the angry flock of birds, how they surrounded the train as it broke free from the line of dark foliage into the flat plain beyond, how they dipped and dived about the hurtling cars, shouting to the half-civilized travelers, of whom the poet was one, "Come back to the animal kingdom. Come back to the animal kingdom."

She remembers his voice as she comes out of sleep, precisely the sound of it, the slightly foreign, prep school accent of his speech, and she can see again the way he stood, leaning over the podium as if it were the train window, looking aghast at the air beating about his face as he repeats what he heard the birds cry: "Come back to the animal kingdom. Come back to the animal kingdom."

It had touched her, that poem; it was the kind of poem she sat through reading after dull reading in the hope of finding an image that articulated her own keen sense of longing. When the poem was over, she applauded with the rest, careful not to show how his words had touched her, and after that, when she walked out into the clear, cold night air, she had held those words tight to her chest and, warmed by them, walked the two blocks to her car in a state of extraordinary calm.

Now she sits up in bed and she can hear his voice again, so clearly, as if it is in the room with her, as if the mice scurrying in the eaves call out to her, "Come back. Come back to the animal kingdom." She confronts a new possibility. This solitude may in fact bring her into a new and unexpected place, and because she is frightened of this place, she begins to talk to herself. As she exists only inside the life of someone else, her communication with herself is overheard, though hardly understood, like the continual conversations that pass in all of us between what we call the heart and the mind, which we hear but do not credit, mistaking them for daydreams or for idle thoughts.

She asks herself questions. What sorts of worlds can we contain? How can we avoid wasting precious time before death? Are we animals, or are we something else?

In the morning, when she finds a milkweed pod, she splits open the thick green skin and peels it away, exposing a layer of cross-hatched, spongy material, like a honeycomb. Inside this layer is another of flat seeds that lie packed together, so like fish scales, layered evenly from one end to the other. Then, when these are brushed aside, she finds the silken threads at the center, which, when exposed, give off an odor of inviolate purity. This silken interior is always a surprise. Children gasp to discover it and will hoard the threads or hide them in special places, as if they were uncommon treasure. She imagines, as she opens the silken cache to the light, how it has been long protected inside its many-layered sheath, and it is, for a moment, as if she has turned her own soul out of its hard case and found that innocent pure center where pain is not felt as pain; that white garden where divinity walks and waits, quietly, patiently.

Her hearing has become acute. The only sounds are the dull persistent buzz of insect life and the constant rustling of air among leaves and grasses. Each day she detects new sounds, minute sounds: a leaf disconnecting from a branch and fluttering downward, the dull roar that comes from the earth when she presses her ear against it, and always the steady beating of her own heart, which she hears from the inside of her ears, like an obsessive thought. To take her mind off the hopelessness of this sound she stretches out in the grass. For the creatures who live there the grasses are as big as trees, and the shifting and twitching of these trees, their perpetual vibration as they follow the sun in its course, make it difficult to find today a roadway or even a path that will be there tomorrow. The creatures who live there move about aimlessly in a colorless void of constant danger, and they live their brief lives without being able to think. They are many-eyed. When they see one another they meet in such a multiplicity of dimensions that they exchange first glances in a hall of mirrors. Every image is repeated and repeated on the eye into infinity. This is one of the many difficulties that plague the spinners.

For there is always the spinning of countless webs, which cannot be heard and hardly seen. The inspection and maintenance of these millions of sticky threads occupy every instant of the spinners' lives. They live to spin and spin to live, without artistry but without impatience. In the grasses the webs glisten in the morning light at so many different levels that the view from below is a myriad of sparkling meshwork, like the high carved vaults of Gothic churches. Here and there among the vaulting, wrapped like mummies, some half devoured, hang the corpses of the captured.

This is the sky in the parallel world. The busy citizens who live below it look up from time to time, but they cannot know their nature or their fate. They can scarcely find their way to one another. And because they must die within a day or two of being born, the urge to life is all there is to life. Finding food, mating quickly and often, knowing time as the incidence of seconds, what can they contain but an hysterical, busy, buzzing force to life?

She learns that even in their furious brief lives there is time for fear. She hears their fear before she sees what they fear. The buzzing ceases for one instant and the silence that consumes its place is the sound of terror. She cannot move, though she hears him now, long before she sees him, tearing through the grasses, flattening everything that comes in his path, a snake, as black as the death he leaves behind him, barreling toward her like an express train. He passes within inches of her face. His flat black eye is cunning, his lifted head almost comical as he veers away from her; but she sees in his eyes that his consciousness is deep, his life is long. He can take his time. He may even bask in the sun, as she does, for the pleasure of it. And he is capable of rage, of coldblooded stinging fury. A moment after he is seen, he is thoroughly gone, and the reconstruction of the parallel world begins.

It takes some time before she can allow insects to crawl upon her without brushing them away. At first she distinguishes between those she will tolerate and those she won't. Crickets, ladybugs, and a small green beetle who resembles a tiny frog are allowed; ants and flies are not. She is also particular about where they are allowed: on her legs, feet, back, and arms, but never on her face or under her clothing. Gradually these distinctions become less important. An ant is allowed the freedom of her leg. She wearies of rejecting a particularly insistent fly. A beetle enters the sleeve of her blouse and she does not bother to refuse him. A mosquito lands on her forearm and she only watches, sun-dazed, amused by the fussy grandmotherly way she chooses her spot, inserts the long proboscis, and relaxes her thin legs so that her body tilts back to allow for maximum intake. She draws in the blood. A single drop will glut her, the woman thinks; why not let her have it. It seems an inoffensive enough violation, not worth slapping.

She remains now motionless for hours. What began as observation has become an occupation, so that she never feels busier than when she is among the grasses. The parallel world makes a havoc of her body. Her skin is burned from the sun and swollen from the accumulated poisons of those insects who come upon her. When it rains, the water collects in the small of her back and she becomes, momentarily, a watering hole for weary travelers. She witnesses the destruction of a monstrous beetle, set upon by a band of murderous ants. Another day there is a battle between two crickets, who fight on even after one has decapitated his opponent so that his head dangles from a fiber, the fierce mandibles still grinding in outrage. When this struggle is over the victor joins the ants in consuming the spoils, unaware of her gaze, which is fixed upon him. She watches but does nothing, and the cricket for a little time is the lord of all he surveys.

She will not interfere, for she has seen that in this world there is no real hope of another world, though there is certainly evidence that it exists. But the inhabitants are blind to it. They will not see it. There is so little time, hardly any rest, so much to do to stay alive for the next moment. Sleep is snatched in minute intervals, too dangerous to enjoy. The inside curve of her knee, which has been so thoroughly explored by an ant only moments ago, might already have appeared as landscape in his dreams. In the mornings, when she lowers her enormous body down into the grasses, whole cities are demolished, but by the time she rises again she has been absorbed into the parallel world. Roads have been built over and around her, tents pitched in her shadow, information has been exchanged about her true dimensions, her remotest provinces.

She is still all day long until the evening surprises her, for there is no standing and gazing at the sunset in the parallel world, nor does night fall upon it; rather, the darkness rises from the warm dirt like a chill through fever. And she rises with the darkness to find the moon afloat over the grasses, sailing in her black sea, which is not like any sea we know but as flat as paper. The blackness surrounds the moon, is before, behind, above, below her, yet she seems to float upon it.

The woman goes in to her bed alone and there she lies, her sensibilities inflamed from the prolonged observation of the insect world in all its fury; the buzzing, stinging center of it is the center of her dreams. She has two dreams. In the first the image of the parallel world is etched upon her face. She accepts this transformation as passively as certain mountainsides have allowed the hewing of enormous and grotesque human faces. But though she cannot object, her whole consciousness is possessed of a fearful protest, and she wakes in a rage. She is awake, she composes herself, then waits for sleep again, and as she waits the blankets are snatched away, drawn down greedily from the end of the bed as if by angry hands, clawed away from her so that she sits up in terror. Oh, this is the unexpected visceral reality that we know in dreams, yet she is certain that it is no dream. She is propelled from the bed, lifted high above it by a force like an engine, steady and relentless; then she is dashed to the floor, face down, so speedily that she hasn't time to raise her hands to protect her face, and when she strikes the floor, though there is no pain, she can hear the bones in her face cracking, and the blood wells thickly over her tongue. But it is not over yet. She is lifted again, hurled downward again, and she tries only to keep from screaming, for nothing else is in her power.

She wakes; her feet are on the floor before she has time to will herself awake. She stumbles to the bathroom, slams her palm against the light switch, and startles herself into a cry of pain, for in the mirror she finds, beneath her eyelids, two wide, cold, black discs where her eyes should be, two insect eyes, many-faceted and terrifying. She turns her head this way and that; her reflection is everywhere, thousands of images and each one an identical horror. Terrible to see and difficult to see out of, these new eyes throb hatefully in her eye sockets like twin hearts. She covers them with her hands and turns away.

Though she is a horror, she is not afraid, for this is her secret: she exists inside another woman, a very ordinary woman with an ordinary face. Both women know that these new eyes, these terrifying eyes, can be seen only by looking long and deeply into the eyes of the outer woman.

And no one would be likely to look in this way at anyone else.

Later, when she wakes in the empty stillness of her room, her first thought is "I'm still alive."

This thought is repeated, not with any sense of wonder or relief, but as a cold observation. The loneliness of being, at last, fully conscious is intolerable, and the thought of it, again and again, is as futile as firing bullets into a wilderness.

Outside, the grasses hum with activity and the cycles of life and death consume one another, closer and closer.

Number 10

✶

EDNA O'BRIEN

EVERYTHING BEGAN TO BE BETTER for Mrs. Reinhardt from the moment she started to sleepwalk. Every night her journey yielded a fresh surprise. First it was that she saw sheep—not sheep as one sees them in life, a bit sooty and bleating away, but sheep as one sees them in a dream. She saw myriads of white fleece on a hilltop, surrounded by little lambs frisking and suckling to their hearts' content.

Then she saw pictures such as she had not seen in life. Her husband owned an art gallery and Mrs. Reinhardt had the opportunity to see many pictures, yet the ones she saw at night were much more satisfying. For one thing, she was inside them. She was not an outsider looking in, making idiotic remarks, she was part of the picture: an arm or a lily or the gray mane of a horse. She did not have to compete, did not have to say anything. All her movements were preordained. She was simply aware of her own breath, a soft, steady, sustaining breath.

In the mornings her husband would say she looked a bit frayed or a bit intense, and she would say, "Nonsense," because in twenty years of marriage she had never felt better. Her sleeping life suited her, and of course, she never knew what to expect. Her daily life had a pattern to it. Weekday mornings she spent at home, helping or supervising Fatima, the Spanish maid. She gave two afternoons a week to teaching autistic children, two afternoons were devoted to an exercise class, and on Fridays she shopped in Harrods and got all the groceries for the weekend. Mr. Reinhardt had bought a farm two years before, and weekends they spent in the country, in their newly renovated cottage. In the country she did not sleepwalk, and Mrs. Reinhardt wondered if it might be that she was inhibited by the barbed-wire fence that skirted their garden. But there are gates, she thought, and I should open them. She was a little vexed with herself for not being more venturesome.

Then one May night, back in her house in London, she had an incredible dream. She walked over a field with her son—in real life he was at university—and all of a sudden, and in unison, the two of them knelt down and began scraping the earth up with their bare hands. It was a rich red earth and easy to crumble. They were so eager because they knew that treasure was about to be theirs. Sure enough, they found bits of gold, tiny specks of it which they put in a handkerchief, and then, to crown her happiness, Mrs. Reinhardt found the loveliest little gold key and held it up to the light while her son laughed and in a baby voice said, "Mama."

Soon after this dream Mrs. Reinhardt embarked on a bit of spring cleaning. Curtains and carpets for the dry cleaner's, drawers depleted of all the old useless odds and ends that had been piling up. Her husband's clothing, too, she must put in order. A little rift had sprung up between them and was widening day by day. He was moody. He got home later than usual, and though he did not say so, she knew that he had stopped at the corner and had a few drinks. Once that spring he had pulled her down beside him on the living-room sofa and stroked her thighs and started to undress her within hearing distance of Fatima, who was in the kitchen chopping and singing. Always chopping and singing or humming. For the most part, though, Mr. Reinhardt went straight to the liquor cabinet and gave them both a gin, pouring himself a bigger one because, as he said, all her bloody fasting made Mrs. Reinhardt lightheaded.

She was sorting Mr. Reinhardt's shirts—T-shirts, summer sweaters, thick crew-neck sweaters—and putting them each in a neat pile, when out of his seersucker jacket there tumbled a little gold key that caused her to let out a cry. The first thing she felt was a jet of fear. Then she bent down and picked it up. It was exactly like the one in her sleepwalk. She held it in her hand, promising herself never to let it go. What fools we are to pursue in daylight what we should leave for nighttime.

Her next sleepwalking brought Mrs. Reinhardt out of her house into a waiting taxi and, some distance away, to a mews house. Outside the mews house was a black-and-white tub filled with pretty flowers. She simply put her hand under a bit of foliage and there was the latchkey. Inside was a little nest. The wallpaper in the hall was the very one she had always wanted for their house, a pale gold with the tiniest white flowers—mere suggestions of flowers, like those of the wild strawberry. The kitchen was immaculate. On the landing upstairs was a little fretwork bench. The cushions in the sitting room were stiff and stately, and so was the upholstery, but the bedroom—ah, the bedroom.

It was everything she had ever wanted their own to be. In fact, the bedroom was the very room she had envisaged over and over again and had described to her husband down to the last detail. Here it was—a brass bed with a little lace canopy above it, the entire opposite wall a dark metallic mirror in which dark shadows seemed to swim around, a light-blue velvet chaise longue, a hanging plant with shining leaves, and a floor lamp with an amber shade that gave off the softest of light.

She sat on the edge of the bed, marveling, and saw the other things that she had always wanted. She saw, for instance, the photo of a little girl in First Communion attire; she saw the paperweight that when shaken yielded a miniature snowstorm; she saw the mother-of-pearl tray with the two champagne glasses—and all of a sudden she began to cry, because her happiness was so immense. Perhaps, she thought, he will come to me here, he will visit, and it will be like the old days and he won't be irritable and he won't be tapping with his fingers or fiddling with the lever of his fountain pen. He will smother me with hugs and kisses and we will tumble about on the big bed.

She sat there in the bedroom and she touched nothing, not even the two white irises in the tall glass vase. The little key was in her hand and she knew it was for the wardrobe and that she had only to open it to find there a nightdress with a pleated top, a voile dance dress, a silver-fox cape, and a pair of sling-back shoes. But she did not open it. She wanted to leave something a secret. She crept away and was home in her own bed without her husband being aware of her absence. He had complained on other occasions about her cold feet as she got back into bed, and asked in Christ's name what was she doing—making tea or what? That morning her happiness was so great that she leaned over, unknotted his pajamas, and made love to him very sweetly, very slowly, and to his apparent delight. Yet when he wakened he was angry, as if a wrong had been done him.

Naturally, Mrs. Reinhardt now went to the mews house night after night, and her heart would light up as she saw the pillar of the house with its number, 10, lettered in gold edged with black. Sometimes she slipped into the brass bed, knowing it was only a question of time before Mr. Reinhardt followed her there.

One night as she lay in the bed, a little breathless, he came in very softly, closed the door, removed his dressing gown, and took possession of her with such force that afterward she suspected she had a broken rib. They used words that they had not used for years. She was young and wild. A lovely fever took hold of her. She was saucy while he kept imploring her to please marry him, to please give up her independence, to please be his—adding that even if she said no, he was going to whisk her off. Then to prove his point he took possession of her again. She almost died, so deep and so thorough was her pleasure, and each time, as she came back to her senses, she saw some little object or trinket that was intended to add to her pleasure—once it was a mobile in which silver horses chased one another around, once it was a sound as of a running stream. He gave her some champagne and they drank in utter silence.

But when she wakened from this idyll she was in fact in her own bed and so was he. She felt mortified. Had she cried out in her sleep? Had she moaned? There was no rib broken. She reached for the hand mirror and saw no sign of wantonness on her face, no tossed hair, and the buttons of her nightdress were neatly done up to the throat.

He was a solid mass of sleep. He opened his eyes. She said something to him, something anxious, but he did not reply. She got out of bed and went down to the sitting room to think. Where would it all lead to? Should she tell him? She thought not. All morning she tried the key in different locks, but it was too small. In fact, once she nearly lost it because it slipped into a lock and she had to tease it out with the prong of a fork. Of course, she did not let Fatima, the maid, see what she was doing.

It was Friday, their day to go to the country, and she was feeling reluctant about it. She knew that when they arrived they would rush around their garden and look at their plants to see if they'd thrived, and look at the rose leaves to make sure there was no green fly. Then, staring out across the fields to where the cows were, they would tell each other how lucky they were to have such a nice place, and how clever. The magnolia flowers would be fully out, and she would stand and stare at the tree as if by staring at it she could imbue her body with something of its whiteness.

The magnolias were out when they arrived—like little white china egg-cups, each bloom lifted to the heavens. Two of the elms definitely had the blight, Mr. Reinhardt said, as the leaves were withering away. The elms would have to be chopped, and Mr. Reinhardt estimated that there would be enough firewood for two winters. He would speak to the farm manager, who lived down the road, about this. They carried in the shopping, raised the blinds, and switched on the central heating. The little kitchen was just as they had left it, except that the primroses in the jar had faded and were like bits of yellow skin. She unpacked the food they had brought, put some things in the fridge, and began to peel the carrots and potatoes for the evening meal. Mr. Reinhardt hammered four picture hangers into the wall for the new prints that he had brought down. From time to time he would call her to ask what order he should put them in, and she would go in, her hands covered with flour, and rather absently suggest a grouping.

She had the little key with her in her purse and would open the purse from time to time to make sure that it was there. Then she would blush.

At dusk she went out to get a branch of apple wood for the fire, in order to engender a lovely smell. A bird chirped from a tree. It was more sound than song. She could not tell what bird it was. The magnolia tree was a mass of white in the surrounding darkness. The dew was falling and she bent for a moment to touch the wet grass. She wished it were Sunday, so that they could be going home. In London the evenings seemed to pass more quickly and they each had more chores to do. She felt in some way she was deceiving him.

They drank some red wine as they sat by the fire. Mr. Reinhardt was fidgety but at the very same time accused her of being fidgety. He was being adamant about the Common Market. Why did he expound on the logistics of it when she was not even contradicting him? He got carried away, made gestures, said he loved England, loved it passionately, that England was going to the dogs. When she got up to push in a log that had fallen from the grate, he asked her for God's sake to pay attention.

She sat down at once, and hoped that there was not going to be one of those terrible, unexpected, meaningless rows. But blessedly they were distracted. She heard him say "Crikey!" and then she looked up and saw what he had just seen. There was a herd of cattle staring in at them. She jumped up. Mr. Reinhardt rushed to the phone to call the farm manager, since he himself knew nothing about country life, certainly not how to drive away cattle.

She grabbed a walking stick and went outside to prevent the cows from falling in the swimming pool. It was cold outdoors and the wind rustled in all the trees. The cows looked at her, suspicious. Their ears pricked. She made tentative movements with the stick, and at that moment four of them leaped over the barbed wire and back into the adjoining field. The remaining cow began to race around. From the field the four cows began to bawl. The fifth cow was butting against the paling. Mrs. Reinhardt thought, I know what you are feeling—you are feeling lost and muddled, and you have gone astray.

Her husband came out in a frenzy, because when he had rung the farm manager no one was there. "Bloody never there!" he said. His loud voice so frightened the poor cow that she made a leap for it and got stuck in the barbed wire. Mrs. Reinhardt could see the barb in her huge udder and thought, What a place for it to have landed. They must rescue her. Very cautiously they both approached the animal; the intention was that Mr. Reinhardt would hold the cow while Mrs. Reinhardt freed the flesh. She tried to be gentle. The cow's smell was milky and soft compared with her roar, which was beseeching. Mr.

Reinhardt caught hold of the hindquarters and told his wife to hurry up. The cow was bucking. As Mrs. Reinhardt lifted the bleeding flesh away, the cow took a high jump and was over the fence and down the field, where she hurried to the river to drink.

The others followed her, and suddenly the whole meadow was the scene of bawling and mad commotion. Mr. Reinhardt rubbed his hands and let out a sigh of relief. He suggested that they open a bottle of champagne. Mrs. Reinhardt was delighted. Of late he had become very thrifty and did not permit her any extravagances. In fact, he had been saying that they would soon have to give up wine because of the state of the country. As they went indoors he put an arm around her. And back in the room she sat and felt like a mistress as she drank the champagne, smiled at him, and felt the stuff coursing through her body. The champagne put them in a nice mood and they linked as they went up the narrow stairs to bed. Nevertheless, Mrs. Reinhardt did not feel like any intimacy; she wanted it reserved for the hidden room.

They returned to London on Sunday evening, and that night Mrs. Reinhardt did not sleep. Consequently she walked nowhere in her dreams. In the morning she felt fidgety. She looked in the mirror. She was getting old. After breakfast, as Mr. Reinhardt was hurrying out of the house, she held up the little key.

"What is it?" she said.

"How would I know?" he said. He looked livid.

She called and made an appointment at the hairdresser's. She addressed herself. She must not get old. Later when her hair was set she would surprise him—she would drop in at his gallery and ask him to take her to a nice pub. On the way she would buy a new scarf and knot it at the neck and she would be youthful.

When she got to the gallery, Mr. Reinhardt was not there. Hans, his assistant, was busy with a client from the Middle East. She said she would wait. The new secretary went off to make some tea. Mrs. Reinhardt sat at her husband's desk, brooding, and then idly she began to flick through his desk diary, just to pass the time. Lunch with this one and that one. A reminder to buy her a present for their anniversary—which he had done. He had bought her a beautiful ring with a sphinx on it.

Then she saw it—the address that she went to night after night. Number 10. The digits danced before her eyes as they had danced when she drove up in the taxi the very first time. All her movements became hurried and mechanical. She gulped her tea, she gave a distracted handshake to the Arab gentleman, she ate the ginger biscuit and gnashed her teeth, so violently did she chew. She paced the floor, she went back to the diary. The same address—three, four, or five times a week. She flicked back to see how long it had been going on. It was no use. She simply had to go there.

At the mews, she found the key in the flower tub. In the kitchen were eggshells and a pan in which an omelet had been cooked. There were two brown eggshells and one white. She dipped her finger in the fat; it was still warm. Her heart went ahead of her up the stairs. It was like a pellet in her body. She had her hand on the bedroom doorknob, when all of a sudden she stopped in her tracks and became motionless. She crept away from the door and went back to the landing seat.

She would not intrude, no. It was perfectly clear why Mr. Reinhardt went there. He went by day to keep his tryst with her, be unfaithful with her, just as she went by night. One day or one night, if they were very lucky, they might meet and share their secret, but until then Mrs. Reinhardt was content to leave everything just as it was. She tiptoed down the stairs and was pleased that she had not acted rashly, that she had not broken the spell.

The River

★

FLANNERY O'CONNOR

T HE CHILD STOOD GLUM AND LIMP in the middle of the dark living room while his father pulled him into a plaid coat. His right arm was hung in the sleeve but the father buttoned the coat anyway and pushed him forward toward a pale spotted hand that stuck through the half-open door.

"He ain't fixed right," a loud voice said from the hall.

"Well then for Christ's sake fix him," the father muttered. "It's six o'clock in the morning." He was in his bathrobe and barefooted. When he got the child to the door and tried to shut it, he found her looming in it, a speckled skeleton in a long pea-green coat and felt helmet.

"And his and my carfare," she said. "It'll be twice we have to ride the car."

He went in the bedroom again to get the money and when he came back, she and the boy were both standing in the middle of the room. She was taking stock. "I couldn't smell those dead cigarette butts long if I was ever to come sit with you," she said, shaking him down in his coat.

"Here's the change," the father said. He went to the door and opened it wide and waited.

After she had counted the money she slipped it somewhere inside her coat and walked over to a watercolor hanging near the phonograph. "I know what time it is," she said, peering closely at the black lines crossing into broken planes of violent color. "I ought to. My shift goes on at 10 P.M. and don't get off till 5 and it takes me one hour to ride the Vine Street car."

"Oh, I see," he said. "Well, we'll expect him back tonight, about eight or nine?"

"Maybe later," she said. "We're going to the river to a healing. This particular preacher don't get around this way often. I wouldn't have paid for that," she said, nodding at the painting, "I would have drew it myself."

"All right, Mrs. Connin, we'll see you then," he said drumming on the door.

A toneless voice called from the bedroom, "Bring me an ice-pack."

"Too bad his mamma's sick," Mrs. Connin said. "What's her trouble?"

"We don't know," he muttered.

"We'll ask the preacher to pray for her. He's healed a lot of folks. The Reverend Bevel Summers. Maybe she ought to see him sometime."

"Maybe so," he said. "We'll see you tonight," and he disappeared into the bedroom and left them to go.

The little boy stared at her silently, his nose and eyes running. He was four or five. He had a long face and bulging chin and half-shut eyes set far apart. He seemed mute and patient, like an old sheep waiting to be let out.

"You'll like this preacher," she said. "The Reverend Bevel Summers. You ought to hear him sing."

The bedroom door opened suddenly and the father stuck his head out and said, "Good-by, old man. Have a good time."

"Good-by," the little boy said and jumped as if he had been shot.

Mrs. Connin gave the watercolor another look. Then they went out into the hall and rang for the elevator. "I wouldn't have drew it," she said.

Outside the gray morning was blocked off on either side by the unlit empty buildings. "It's going to fair up later," she said, "but this is the last time we'll be able to have any preaching at the river this year. Wipe your nose, Sugar Boy."

He began rubbing his sleeve across it but she stopped him. "That ain't nice," she said. "Where's your handkerchief?"

He put his hands in his pockets and pretended to look for it while she waited. "Some people don't care how they send one off," she murmured to her reflection in the coffee shop window. "You pervide." She took a red and blue flowered handkerchief out of her pocket and stooped down and began to work on his nose. "Now blow," she said and he blew. "You can borry it. Put it in your pocket."

He folded it up and put it in his pocket carefully and they walked on to the corner and leaned against the side of a closed drugstore to wait for the car. Mrs. Connin turned up her coat collar so that it met her hat in the back. Her eyelids began to droop and she looked as if she might go to sleep against the wall. The little boy put a slight pressure on her hand.

"What's your name?" she asked in a drowsy voice. "I don't know but only your last name. I should have found out your first name."

His name was Harry Ashfield and he had never thought at any time before of changing it. "Bevel," he said.

Mrs. Connin raised herself from the wall. "Why ain't that a coincident!" she said. "I told you that's the name of this preacher!"

"Bevel," he repeated.

She stood looking down at him as if he had become a marvel to her. "I'll have to see you meet him today," she said. "He's no ordinary preacher. He's a healer. He couldn't do nothing for Mr. Connin though. Mr. Connin didn't have the faith but he said he would try anything once. He had this griping in his gut."

The trolley appeared as a yellow spot at the end of the deserted street.

"He's gone to the government hospital now," she said, "and they taken one-third of his stomach. I tell him he better thank Jesus for what he's got left but he says he ain't thanking nobody. Well I declare," she murmured, "Bevel!"

They walked out to the tracks to wait. "Will he heal me?" Bevel asked.

"What you got?"

"I'm hungry," he decided finally.

"Didn't you have your breakfast?"

"I didn't have time to be hungry yet then," he said.

"Well when we get home we'll both have us something," she said. "I'm ready myself."

They got in the car and sat down a few seats behind the driver and Mrs.

Connin took Bevel on her knees. "Now you be a good boy," she said, "and let me get some sleep. Just don't get off my lap." She lay her head back and as he watched, gradually her eyes closed and her mouth fell open to show a few long scattered teeth, some gold and some darker than her face; she began to whistle and blow like a musical skeleton. There was no one in the car but themselves and the driver and when he saw she was asleep, he took out the flowered hand-kerchief and unfolded it and examined it carefully. Then he folded it up again and unzipped a place in the innerlining of his coat and hid it in there and shortly he went to sleep himself.

Her house was a half-mile from the end of the car line, set back a little from the road. It was tan paper brick with a porch across the front of it and a tin top. On the porch there were three little boys of different sizes with identical speck-led faces and one tall girl who had her hair up in so many aluminum curlers that it glared like the roof. The three boys followed them inside and closed in on Bevel. They looked at him silently, not smiling.

"That's Bevel," Mrs. Connin said, taking off her coat. "It's a coincident he's named the same as the preacher. These boys are J. C., Spivey, and Sinclair, and that's Sarah Mildred on the porch. Take off that coat and hang it on the bed post, Bevel."

The three boys watched him while he unbuttoned the coat and took it off. Then they watched him hang it on the bed post and then they stood, watch-ing the coat. They turned abruptly and went out the door and had a conference on the porch.

Bevel stood looking around him at the room. It was part kitchen and part bedroom. The entire house was two rooms and two porches. Close to his foot the tail of a light-colored dog moved up and down between two floor boards as he scratched his back on the underside of the house. Bevel jumped on it but the hound was experienced and had already withdrawn when his feet hit the spot.

The walls were filled with pictures and calendars. There were two round photographs of an old man and woman with collapsed mouths and another pic-ture of a man whose eyebrows dashed out of two bushes of hair and clashed in a heap on the bridge of his nose; the rest of his face stuck out like a bare cliff to fall from. "That's Mr. Connin," Mrs. Connin said, standing back from the stove for a second to admire the face with him, "but it don't favor him any more." Bevel turned from Mr. Connin to a colored picture over the bed of a man wearing a white sheet. He had long hair and a gold circle around his head and he was sawing on a board while some children stood watching him. He was going to ask who that was when the three boys came in again and motioned for him to follow them. He thought of crawling under the bed and hanging onto one of the legs but the three boys only stood there, speckled and silent, waiting, and after a second he followed them at a little distance out on the porch and around the corner of the house. They started off through a field of rough yellow weeds to the hog pen, a five-foot boarded square full of shoats, which they intended to ease him over into. When they reached it, they turned and waited silently, leaning against the side.

He was coming very slowly, deliberately bumping his feet together as if he had trouble walking. Once he had been beaten up in the park by some strange boys when his sitter forgot him, but he hadn't known anything was going to happen that time until it was over. He began to smell a strong odor of garbage and to hear the noises of a wild animal. He stopped a few feet from the pen and waited, pale but dogged.

The three boys didn't move. Something seemed to have happened to them. They stared over his head as if they saw something coming behind him but he was afraid to turn his own head and look. Their speckles were pale and their eyes were still and gray as glass. Only their ears twitched slightly. Nothing happened. Finally, the one in the middle said, "She'd kill us," and turned, dejected and hacked, and climbed up on the pen and hung over, staring in.

Bevel sat down on the ground, dazed with relief, and grinned up at them.

The one sitting on the pen glanced at him severely. "Hey you," he said after a second, "if you can't climb up and see these pigs you can lift that bottom board off and look in thataway." He appeared to offer this as a kindness.

Bevel had never seen a real pig but he had seen a pig in a book and knew they were small fat pink animals with curly tails and round grinning faces and bow ties. He leaned forward and pulled eagerly at the board.

"Pull harder," the littlest boy said. "It's nice and rotten. Just lift out thet nail."

He eased a long reddish nail out of the soft wood.

"Now you can lift up the board and put your face to the . . ." a quiet voice began.

He had already done it and another face, gray, wet and sour, was pushing into his, knocking him down and back as it scraped out under the plank. Something snorted over him and charged back again, rolling him over and pushing him up from behind and then sending him forward, screaming through the yellow field, while it bounded behind.

The three Connins watched from where they were. The one sitting on the pen held the loose board back with his gangling foot. Their stern faces didn't brighten any but they seemed to become less taut, as if some great need had been partly satisfied. "Maw ain't going to like him lettin' out thet hawg," the smallest one said.

Mrs. Connin was on the back porch and caught Bevel up as he reached the steps. The hog ran under the house and subsided, panting, but the child screamed for five minutes. When she had finally calmed him down, she gave him his breakfast and let him sit on her lap while he ate it. The shoat climbed the two steps onto the back porch and stood outside the screen door, looking in with his head lowered sullenly. He was long-legged and humpbacked and part of one of his ears had been bitten off.

"Git away!" Mrs. Connin shouted. "That one yonder favors Mr. Paradise that has the gas station," she said. "You'll see him today at the healing. He's got the cancer over his ear. He always comes to show he ain't been healed."

The shoat stood squinting a few seconds longer and then moved off slowly. "I don't want to see him," Bevel said.

They walked to the river, Mrs. Connin in front with him and the three boys strung out behind and Sarah Mildred, the tall girl, at the end to holler if one of them ran out on the road. They looked like the skeleton of an old boat with two pointed ends, sailing slowly on the edge of the highway. The white Sunday sun followed at a little distance, climbing fast through a scum of gray cloud as if it meant to overtake them. Bevel walked on the outside edge, holding Mrs. Connin's hand and looking down into the orange and purple gulley that dropped off from the concrete.

It occurred to him that he was lucky this time that they had found Mrs. Connin who would take you away for the day instead of an ordinary sitter who only sat where you lived or went to the park. You found out more when you left where you lived. He had found out already this morning that he had been made by a carpenter named Jesus Christ. Before he had thought it had been a doctor named Sladewall, a fat man with a yellow mustache who gave him shots and thought his name was Herbert, but this must have been a joke. They joked a lot where he lived. If he had thought about it before, he would have thought Jesus Christ was a word like "oh" or "damn" or "God," or maybe somebody who had cheated them out of something sometime. When he had asked Mrs. Connin who the man in the sheet in the picture over her bed was, she had looked at him a while with her mouth open. Then she had said, "That's Jesus," and she had kept on looking at him.

In a few minutes she had got up and got a book out of the other room. "See here," she said, turning over the cover, "this belonged to my great grandmamma. I wouldn't part with it for nothing on earth." She ran her finger under some brown writing on a spotted page. "Emma Stevens Oakley, 1832," she said. "Ain't that something to have? And every word of it the gospel truth." She turned the next page and read him the name: "The Life of Jesus Christ for Readers Under Twelve." Then she read him the book.

It was a small book, pale brown on the outside with gold edges and a smell like old putty. It was full of pictures, one of the carpenter driving a crowd of pigs out of a man. They were real pigs, gray and sour-looking, and Mrs. Connin said Jesus had driven them all out of this one man. When she finished reading, she let him sit on the floor and look at the pictures again.

Just before they left for the healing, he had managed to get the book inside his innerlining without her seeing him. Now it made his coat hang down a little farther on one side than the other. His mind was dreamy and serene as they walked along and when they turned off the highway onto a long red clay road winding between banks of honeysuckle, he began to make wild leaps and pull forward on her hand as if he wanted to dash off and snatch the sun which was rolling away ahead of them now.

They walked on the dirt road for a while and then they crossed a field stippled with purple weeds and entered the shadows of a wood where the ground was covered with thick pine needles. He had never been in woods before and he walked carefully, looking from side to side as if he were entering a strange country. They moved along a bridle path that twisted downhill through crackling red leaves, and once, catching at a branch to keep himself from slipping, he looked into two frozen green-gold eyes enclosed in the darkness of a tree hole. At the bottom of the hill, the woods opened suddenly onto a pasture dotted here and there with black and white cows and sloping down, tier after tier, to a broad orange stream where the reflection of the sun was set like a diamond.

There were people standing on the near bank in a group, singing. Long tables were set up behind them and a few cars and trucks were parked in a road that came up by the river. They crossed the pasture, hurrying, because Mrs. Connin, using her hand for a shed over her eyes, saw the preacher already standing out in the water. She dropped her basket on one of the tables and pushed the three boys in front of her into the knot of people so that they wouldn't linger by the food. She kept Bevel by the hand and eased her way up to the front.

The preacher was standing about ten feet out in the stream where the water came up to his knees. He was a tall youth in khaki trousers that he had rolled up higher than the water. He had on a blue shirt and a red scarf around his neck but no hat and his light-colored hair was cut in sideburns that curved into the hollows of his cheeks. His face was all bone and red light reflected from the river. He looked as if he might have been nineteen years old. He was singing in a high twangy voice, above the singing on the bank, and he kept his hands behind him and his head tilted back.

He ended the hymn on a high note and stood silent, looking down at the water and shifting his feet in it. Then he looked up at the people on the bank.

They stood close together, waiting; their faces were solemn but expectant and every eye was on him. He shifted his feet again.

"Maybe I know why you come," he said in the twangy voice, "maybe I don't.

"If you ain't come for Jesus, you ain't come for me. If you just come to see can you leave your pain in the river, you ain't come for Jesus. You can't leave your pain in the river," he said. "I never told nobody that." He stopped and looked down at his knees.

"I seen you cure a woman oncet!" a sudden high voice shouted from the hump of people. "Seen that woman git up and walk out straight where she had limped in!"

The preacher lifted one foot and then the other. He seemed almost but not quite to smile. "You might as well go home if that's what you come for," he said.

Then he lifted his head and arms and shouted, "Listen to what I got to say, you people! There ain't but one river and that's the River of Life, made out of Jesus' Blood. That's the river you have to lay your pain in, in the River of Faith, in the River of Life, in the River of Love, in the rich red river of Jesus' Blood, you people!"

His voice grew soft and musical. "All the rivers come from that one River and go back to it like it was the ocean sea and if you believe, you can lay your pain in that River and get rid of it because that's the River that was made to carry sin. It's a River full of pain itself, pain itself, moving toward the Kingdom of Christ, to be washed away, slow, you people, slow as this here old red water river round my feet.

"Listen," he sang, "I read in Mark about an unclean man, I read in Luke about a blind man, I read in John about a dead man! Oh you people hear! The same blood that makes this River red, made that leper clean, made that blind man stare, made that dead man leap! You people with trouble," he cried, "lay it in that River of Blood, lay it in that River of Pain, and watch it move away toward the Kingdom of Christ."

While he preached, Bevel's eyes followed drowsily the slow circles of two silent birds revolving high in the air. Across the river there was a low red and gold grove of sassafras with hills of dark blue trees behind it and an occasional pine jutting over the skyline. Behind, in the distance, the city rose like a cluster of warts on the side of the mountain. The birds revolved downward and dropped lightly in the top of the highest pine and sat hunch-shouldered as if they were supporting the sky.

"If it's this River of Life you want to lay your pain in, then come up," the preacher said, "and lay your sorrow here. But don't be thinking this is the last of it because this old red river don't end here. This old red suffering stream goes on, you people, slow to the Kingdom of Christ. This old red river is good to Baptize in, good to lay your faith in, good to lay your pain in, but it ain't this muddy water here that saves you. I been all up and down this river this week," he said. "Tuesday I was in Fortune Lake, next day in Ideal, Friday me and my wife drove to Lulawillow to see a sick man there. Them people didn't see no healing," he said and his face burned redder for a second. "I never said they would."

While he was talking a fluttering figure had begun to move forward with a kind of butterfly movement—an old woman with flapping arms whose head wobbled as if it might fall off any second. She managed to lower herself at the edge of the bank and let her arms churn in the water. Then she bent farther and pushed her face down in it and raised herself up finally, streaming wet; and still flapping, she turned a time or two in a blind circle until someone reached out and pulled her back into the group.

"She's been that way for thirteen years," a rough voice shouted. "Pass the hat and give this kid his money. That's what he's here for." The shout, directed out to the boy in the river, came from a huge old man who sat like a humped stone on the bumper of a long ancient gray automobile. He had on a gray hat that was turned down over one ear and up over the other to expose a purple bulge on his left temple. He sat bent forward with his hands hanging between his knees and his small eyes half closed.

Bevel stared at him once and then moved into the folds of Mrs. Connin's coat and hid himself.

The boy in the river glanced at the old man quickly and raised his fist. "Believe Jesus or the devil!" he cried. "Testify to one or the other!"

"I know from my own self-experience," a woman's mysterious voice called from the knot of people, "I know from it that this preacher can heal. My eyes have been opened! I testify to Jesus!"

The preacher lifted his arms quickly and began to repeat all that he had said before about the River and the Kingdom of Christ and the old man sat on the bumper, fixing him with a narrow squint. From time to time Bevel stared at him again from around Mrs. Connin.

A man in overalls and a brown coat leaned forward and dipped his hand in the water quickly and shook it and leaned back, and a woman held a baby over the edge of the bank and splashed its feet with water. One man moved a little distance away and sat down on the bank and took off his shoes and waded out into the stream; he stood there for a few minutes with his face tilted as far back as it would go, then he waded back and put on his shoes. All this time, the preacher sang and did not appear to watch what went on.

As soon as he stopped singing, Mrs. Connin lifted Bevel up and said, "Listen here, preacher, I got a boy from town today that I'm keeping. His mamma's sick and he wants you to pray for her. And this is a coincident—his name is Bevel! Bevel," she said, turning to look at the people behind her, "same as his. Ain't that a coincident, though?"

There were some murmurs and Bevel turned and grinned over her shoulder at the faces looking at him. "Bevel," he said in a loud jaunty voice.

"Listen," Mrs. Connin said, "have you ever been Baptized, Bevel?"

He only grinned.

"I suspect he ain't ever been Baptized," Mrs. Connin said, raising her eyebrows at the preacher.

"Swang him over here," the preacher said and took a stride forward and caught him.

He held him in the crook of his arm and looked at the grinning face. Bevel rolled his eyes in a comical way and thrust his face forward, close to the preacher's. "My name is Bevvvuuuuul," he said in a loud deep voice and let the tip of his tongue slide across his mouth.

The preacher didn't smile. His bony face was rigid and his narrow gray eyes reflected the almost colorless sky. There was a loud laugh from the old man sitting on the car bumper and Bevel grasped the back of the preacher's collar and held it tightly. The grin had already disappeared from his face. He had the sudden feeling that this was not a joke. Where he lived everything was a joke. From the preacher's face, he knew immediately that nothing the preacher said or did was a joke. "My mother named me that," he said quickly.

"Have you ever been Baptized?" the preacher asked.

"What's that?" he murmured.

"If I Baptize you," the preacher said, "you'll be able to go to the Kingdom of Christ. You'll be washed in the river of suffering, son, and you'll go by the deep river of life. Do you want that?"

"Yes," the child said, and thought, I won't go back to the apartment then, I'll go under the river.

"You won't be the same again," the preacher said. "You'll count." Then he turned his face to the people and began to preach and Bevel looked over his shoulder at the pieces of the white sun scattered in the river. Suddenly the preacher said, "All right, I'm going to Baptize you now," and without more warning, he tightened his hold and swung him upside down and plunged his head into the water. He held him under while he said the words of Baptism and then he jerked him up again and looked sternly at the gasping child. Bevel's eyes were dark and dilated. "You count now," the preacher said. "You didn't even count before."

The little boy was too shocked to cry. He spit out the muddy water and rubbed his wet sleeve into his eyes and over his face.

"Don't forget his mamma," Mrs. Connin called. "He wants you to pray for his mamma. She's sick."

"Lord," the preacher said, "we pray for somebody in affliction who isn't here to testify. Is your mother sick in the hospital?" he asked. "Is she in pain?"

The child stared at him. "She hasn't got up yet," he said in a high dazed voice. "She has a hangover." The air was so quiet he could hear the broken pieces of the sun knocking the water.

The preacher looked angry and startled. The red drained out of his face and the sky appeared to darken in his eyes. There was a loud guffaw from the bank and Mr. Paradise shouted, "Haw! Cure the afflicted woman with the hangover!" and began to beat his knee with his fist.

"He's had a long day," Mrs. Connin said, standing with him in the door of the apartment and looking sharply into the room where the party was going on. "I reckon it's past his regular bedtime." One of Bevel's eyes was closed and the other half closed; his nose was running and he kept his mouth open and breathed through it. The damp plain coat dragged down on one side.

That would be her, Mrs. Connin decided, in the black britches—long black satin britches and barefoot sandals and red toenails. She was lying on half the sofa, with her knees crossed in the air and her head propped on the arm. She didn't get up.

"Hello Harry," she said. "Did you have a big day?" She had a long pale face, smooth and blank, and straight sweet-potato-colored hair, pulled back.

The father went off to get the money. There were two other couples. One of the men, blond with little violet-blue eyes, leaned out of his chair and said, "Well Harry, old man, have a big day?"

"His name ain't Harry. It's Bevel," Mrs. Connin said.

"His name is Harry," *she* said from the sofa. "Whoever heard of anybody named Bevel?"

The little boy had seemed to be going to sleep on his feet, his head drooping farther and farther forward; he pulled it back suddenly and opened one eye; the other was stuck.

"He told me this morning his name was Bevel," Mrs. Connin said in a shocked voice. "The same as our preacher. We been all day at a preaching and healing at the river. He said his name was Bevel, the same as the preacher's. That's what he told me."

"Bevel!" his mother said. "My God! what a name."

"This preacher is name Bevel and there's no better preacher around," Mrs. Connin said. "And furthermore," she added in a defiant tone, "he Baptized this child this morning!"

His mother sat straight up. "Well the nerve!" she muttered.

"Furthermore," Mrs. Connin said, "he's a healer and he prayed for you to be healed."

"Healed!" she almost shouted. "Healed of what for Christ's sake?"

"Of your affliction," Mrs. Connin said icily.

The father had returned with the money and was standing near Mrs. Connin waiting to give it to her. His eyes were lined with red threads. "Go on, go on," he said, "I want to hear more about her affliction. The exact nature of it has escaped . . ." He waved the bill and his voice trailed off. "Healing by prayer is mighty inexpensive," he murmured.

Mrs. Connin stood a second, staring into the room, with a skeleton's appearance of seeing everything. Then, without taking the money, she turned and shut the door behind her. The father swung around, smiling vaguely, and shrugged. The rest of them were looking at Harry. The little boy began to shamble toward the bedroom.

"Come here, Harry," his mother said. He automatically shifted his direction toward her without opening his eyes any farther. "Tell me what happened today," she said when he reached her. She began to pull off his coat.

"I don't know," he muttered.

"Yes you do know," she said, feeling the coat heavier on one side. She unzipped the innerlining and caught the book and a dirty handkerchief as they fell out. "Where did you get these?"

"I don't know," he said and grabbed for them. "They're mine. She gave them to me."

She threw the handkerchief down and held the book too high for him to reach and began to read it, her face after a second assuming an exaggerated comical expression. The others moved around and looked at it over her shoulder. "My God," somebody said.

One of the men peered at it sharply from behind a thick pair of glasses. "That's valuable," he said. "That's a collector's item," and he took it away from the rest of them and retired to another chair.

"Don't let George go off with that," his girl said.

"I tell you it's valuable," George said. "1832."

Bevel shifted his direction again toward the room where he slept. He shut the door behind him and moved slowly in the darkness to the bed and sat down and took off his shoes and got under the cover. After a minute a shaft of light let in the tall silhouette of his mother. She tiptoed lightly cross the room and sat down on the edge of his bed. "What did that dolt of a preacher say about me?" she whispered. "What lies have you been telling today, honey?"

He shut his eye and heard her voice from a long way away, as if he were under the river and she on top of it. She shook his shoulder. "Harry," she said, leaning down and putting her mouth to his ear, "tell me what he said." She pulled him into a sitting position and he felt as if he had been drawn up from under the river. "Tell me," she whispered and her bitter breath covered his face.

He saw the pale oval close to him in the dark. "He said I'm not the same now," he muttered. "I count."

After a second, she lowered him by his shirt front onto the pillow. She hung over him an instant and brushed her lips against his forehead. Then she got up and moved away, swaying her hips lightly through the shaft of light.

He didn't wake up early but the apartment was still dark and close when he did. For a while he lay there, picking his nose and eyes. Then he sat up in bed and looked out the window. The sun came in palely, stained gray by the glass. Across the street at the Empire Hotel, a colored cleaning woman was looking down from an upper window, resting her face on her folded arms. He got up and put on his shoes and went to the bathroom and then into the front room. He ate two crackers spread with anchovy paste, that he found on the coffee table, and drank some ginger ale left in a bottle and looked around for his book but it was not there.

The apartment was silent except for the faint humming of the refrigerator. He went into the kitchen and found some raisin bread heels and spread a half jar of peanut butter between them and climbed up on the tall kitchen stool and sat chewing the sandwich slowly, wiping his nose every now and then on his shoulder. When he finished he found some chocolate milk and drank that. He would rather have had the ginger ale he saw but they left the bottle openers where he couldn't reach them. He studied what was left in the refrigerator for a while—some shriveled vegetables that she had forgot were there and a lot of brown oranges that she bought and didn't squeeze; there were three or four kinds of cheese and something fishy in a paper bag; the rest was a pork bone. He left the refrigerator door open and wandered back into the dark living room and sat down on the sofa.

He decided they would be out cold until one o'clock and that they would all have to go to a restaurant for lunch. He wasn't high enough for the table yet and the waiter would bring a highchair and he was too big for a highchair. He sat in the middle of the sofa, kicking it with his heels. Then he got up and wandered around the room, looking into the ashtrays at the butts as if this might be a habit. In his own room he had picture books and blocks but they were for the most part torn up; he found the way to get new ones was to tear up the ones he had. There was very little to do at any time but eat; however, he was not a fat boy.

He decided he would empty a few of the ashtrays on the floor. If he only emptied a few, she would think they had fallen. He emptied two, rubbing the ashes carefully into the rug with his finger. Then he lay on the floor for a while, studying his feet which he held up in the air. His shoes were still damp and he began to think about the river.

Very slowly, his expression changed as if he were gradually seeing appear what he didn't know he'd been looking for. Then all of a sudden he knew what he wanted to do.

He got up and tiptoed into their bedroom and stood in the dim light there, looking for her pocketbook. His glance passed her long pale arm hanging off the edge of the bed down to the floor, and across the white mound his father made, and past the crowded bureau, until it rested on the pocketbook hung on the back of a chair. He took a car-token out of it and half a package of Life Savers. Then he left the apartment and caught the car at the corner. He hadn't taken a suitcase because there was nothing from there he wanted to keep.

He got off the car at the end of the line and started down the road he and

Mrs. Connin had taken the day before. He knew there wouldn't be anybody at her house because the three boys and the girl went to school and Mrs. Connin had told him she went out to clean. He passed her yard and walked on the way they had gone to the river. The paper brick houses were far apart and after a while the dirt place to walk on ended and he had to walk on the edge of the highway. The sun was pale yellow and high and hot.

He passed a shack with an orange gas pump in front of it but he didn't see the old man looking out at nothing in particular from the doorway. Mr. Paradise was having an orange drink. He finished it slowly, squinting over the bottle at the small plaid-coated figure disappearing down the road. Then he set the empty bottle on a bench and, still squinting, wiped his sleeve over his mouth. He went in the shack and picked out a peppermint stick, a foot long and two inches thick, from the candy shelf, and stuck it in his hip pocket. Then he got in his car and drove slowly down the highway after the boy.

By the time Bevel came to the field speckled with purple weeds, he was dusty and sweating and he crossed it at a trot to get into the woods as fast as he could. Once inside, he wandered from tree to tree, trying to find the path they had taken yesterday. Finally he found a line worn in the pine needles and followed it until he saw the steep trail twisting down through the trees.

Mr. Paradise had left his automobile back some way on the road and had walked to the place where he was accustomed to sit almost every day, holding an unbaited fishline in the water while he stared at the river passing in front of him. Anyone looking at him from a distance would have seen an old boulder half hidden in the bushes.

Bevel didn't see him at all. He only saw the river, shimmering reddish yellow, and bounded into it with his shoes and his coat on and took a gulp. He swallowed some and spit the rest out and then he stood there in water up to his chest and looked around him. The sky was a clear pale blue, all in one piece—except for the hole the sun made—and fringed around the bottom with treetops. His coat floated to the surface and surrounded him like a strange gay lily pad and he stood grinning in the sun. He intended not to fool with preachers any more but to Baptize himself and to keep on going this time until he found the Kingdom of Christ in the river. He didn't mean to waste any more time. He put his head under the water at once and pushed forward.

In a second he began to gasp and sputter and his head reappeared on the surface; he started under again and the same thing happened. The river wouldn't have him. He tried again and came up, choking. This was the way it had been when the preacher held him under—he had had to fight with something that pushed him back in the face. He stopped and thought suddenly: it's another joke, it's just another joke! He thought how far he had come for nothing and he began to hit and splash and kick the filthy river. His feet were already treading on nothing. He gave one low cry of pain and indignation. Then he heard a shout and turned his head and saw something like a giant pig bounding after him, shaking a red and white club and shouting. He plunged under once and this time, the waiting current caught him like a long gentle hand and pulled him swiftly forward and down. For an instant he was overcome with surprise: then since he was moving quickly and knew that he was getting somewhere, all his fury and fear left him.

Mr. Paradise's head appeared from time to time on the surface of the water. Finally, far downstream, the old man rose like some ancient water monster and stood empty-handed, staring with his dull eyes as far down the river line as he could see.

The Virgin in the Rose-Bower
or The Tragedy of Glen Mawr Manor
✶
JOYCE CAROL OATES

> *If I—am You—*
> *Shall You—be me?*
> *If You—scorn I—*
> *Where then—We—*
> *Be—?*
> "IPHIGENIA"

Editor's Note

IT IS FREQUENTLY OBSERVED BY OUR self-righteous critics that we amateur "collectors" of Murder are antiquarians at heart: unapologetically to the right in matters political, moral, and religious: possessed of a near-insatiable passion for authenticity, down to the most minute, revealing, and lurid detail: impatient with the *new* (whether it be new and untried modes of murder, or new and untried modes of mystery), and enamored of the *old*. Studying the history of crime, as, indeed, history more generally, with the hope of comprehending human nature,—or, failing that lofty ambition, comprehending the present era—cannot interest the purist. For, as the outspoken De Quincey has argued,— Is not Murder an art-form? And does any art-form require justification?

Herewith, I am happy to present that perennial favorite of *aficionados* of American mystery, *The Virgin in the Rose-Bower;* or, *The Tragedy of Glen Mawr*

Manor, which, albeit most informally, introduces young Xavier Kilgarvan to his destiny as a detective *sui generis.* (In Winterthurn City itself the case has long enjoyed a variety of appellations, amongst them, most bluntly, "The Glen Mawr Murders" and "The Glen Mawr 'Angel' Murders," etc. Not one person— including even that exploitive scribbler of murder mysteries, Mr. Mountjoy Price—has had the wish, or the audacity, to refer to this controversial episode of Xavier Kilgarvan's life as "Xavier Kilgarvan's First Case": nor is it this editor's intention to do so.)

How to best describe this old, much-analyzed, yet still tantalizing mystery of more than a century ago! Though it would seem at first blush to declare itself a classic of the *locked-room* variety, and though, doubtless, numberless collectors prize it for that reason, I have always believed that its fame (or notoriety) resides in the fact that, despite heroic effort, *it was never satisfactorily solved.* Or, at any rate, the solution to the mystery was never made public; and the murderer, or murderers, never brought to justice.

And for very good reasons,—as the reader will doubtless agree.

The unexplained murders at Glen Mawr Manor, and in its vicinity, aroused great terror in the inhabitants of Winterthurn, somewhat out of proportion (it seems to us today) to the actual number of violent deaths involved. For a liberal count of corpses, so to speak, yields but four outright murders; and one self-inflicted death. (The deaths, mutilations, victimizations, etc., of a miscellany of animals in the vicinity being of less significance, though, doubtless, still a potent factor in the arousal of fear.) Yet it might be considered that there is such a phenomenon as *soul-murder,* of as great a moral harm as murder of the body: in which case, one, or perhaps two, or even three, additional "deaths" might be acknowledged. (For instance, it happened that as a consequence of their horrific experiences, Mrs. Abigail Whimbrel and Mrs. Roxana Murphy were plunged into the abyss of *hopeless insanity,* from which no physician could rescue them. Though it falls somewhat beyond the scope of this history, I should like to record that Mrs. Whimbrel lived to a sickly old age,—well into her ninety-seventh year, it is said—at the Mt. Moriah Hospital for Nervous Invalids, where her grieving family had seen fit to place her; while the fortune hunter Mrs. Murphy,—or Mrs. Kilgarvan, as she might legally be called—suffered an extreme abreaction to a sedative dose of belladonna, administered by Dr. Colney Hatch, and died within twelve days of her husband.)

Superstitious the inhabitants of Winterthurn doubtless were, to have feared, for decades, "angels," or "angel-figures," loosed in the night and frequently in the day: and naïve in their stubborn belief that a preternatural force emanated from the Manor. Yet it were well for the contemporary reader to withhold judgment; and to reflect that our ancestors, though oft appearing less informed than ourselves, were perhaps far more sensitive,—nay, altogether more astute, in comprehending Evil.

Quicklime

SCARCELY WAS IT DAWN OF A REMARKABLY chill morning in May,— indeed, large damp clumps of snow were being blown about like blossoms— when, seemingly out of nowhere, Miss Georgina Kilgarvan, the eldest daughter of the late Judge, appeared, accompanied by her Negro servant Pride, to ring the bell of a tradesman named Phineas Cutter (of Cutter Brothers Mills, on the Temperance Vale Road), and to make a most unusual request. Poor Phineas!— awakened harshly from sleep, afflicted with deafness in his right ear, he must have bethought himself whether this veiled and dark-clad vision was indeed the Judge's spinster daughter, or a specter out of troubled dreams: for how could it be,—nay, how *should* it be—that Miss Georgina of Glen Mawr Manor, heavily clothed in her mourning costume, and as always discreetly veiled, had come on foot to his store to make a purchase of,—*fifty pounds of quicklime?*

Little wonder, then, that Phineas Cutter cupped his hand to his ear, and stammeringly requested of the lady that she repeat her words.

While the diminutive Negro servant stood some yards distant, his crabbed expression giving no sign that he heard, or cared to hear, what his mistress said, Georgina Kilgarvan, speaking in a low, rapid, forceful voice, in which no evident agitation could be discerned, apologized for having disturbed Phineas at

an unnatural hour; in truth, she did not know the precise time, as clocks at Glen
Mawr vied with one another, in telling the time,—for they had been tampered
with, it seems, since her father's death,—but that unhappy fact had no bearing
here, and she did not wish to pursue it. The situation was: she found herself in
immediate need of a certain gardening substance, a compound of some sort,—
lye, lime, quicklime? she could not recall precisely—only that it was a most potent material, employed commonly by gardeners,—a whitish substance with
disinfectant and purgative powers: lye, or lime, or quicklime,—spread on or-
ganic materials, she believed, to hasten their decomposition; to effect a general
cleansing, a purifying of that which was rotting and foul,—and evil,—and a
source of contagion: *quicklime,* she thought it. As she was a gardener, albeit on
a modest scale, she required this substance for her garden, and wished to
purchase fifty pounds of it, without delay, which her servant would carry home
for her: for it was her firm intention to begin work on her rose-garden that
very morning.

Speaking now in a more peremptory tone, and still without raising her veil,
Miss Georgina Kilgarvan explained that she had not cash on her person, but,
"as her father had done business with Mr. Cutter for many years, and his father
before him, with Mr. Cutter's father, she was confident that he would trust her
to pay in the usual manner; and would simply bill Glen Mawr,"—this being information of a totally needless sort, as business with Glen Mawr was always
transacted in that manner.

Phineas Cutter is to be forgiven for his somewhat dazed response to the
lady's request, for the situation possessed that exquisite air of the utterly *rational* conjoined with the *irrational* that is a characteristic of dreams: the vision of
a tall, dark-clad, veiled lady, her seal-skin cape falling majestically to her feet,
her manner courteous, yet edged with a faint air of impatience, or contempt: the
which was wondrously heightened by the very early hour, and the soundless, yet
wildly melodic, disportment of soft, wet, giant clumps of snow that swirled
about and clung melting to her black bonnet and cape. Ah, it might have been
that one of the "life statues" from the nearby cemetery had roused itself, to make
a teasing visit,—these statues being uncannily realistic in their proportions and

stances, though executed in chill stone; or might it be a prank of some sort, played upon him to test his credulousness,—someone who had got himself up in disguise, as the "Blue Nun" of Glen Mawr Manor? (For it had happened more than once in the past several years that Cutter Mills, like many another establishment in the area, had been visited by pranksters,—or outright vandals: and though the wily culprits always eluded capture, it was generally believed, and charged, that they were young men of "good family,"—spoiled youths whose notion of amusement it might well be to overturn Phineas's outhouse, or tie his billy goat atop his roof, or, indeed, trick him into thinking that Erasmus Kilgarvan's eldest daughter was paying him a visit.)

As Miss Georgina was altogether herself, in flesh and blood, Phineas quickly bestirred himself to comply with her strange request: for, like any tradesman, he feared provoking displeasure in his customers, and particularly in a member of the Kilgarvan family. Miss Georgina had acquired a reputation for eccentricity over the years, and for dealing somewhat punitively with shop-keepers, tradesmen, servants, and the like, who failed to meet with her exacting standards,—to the extent to which it had begun to be said, before her father's death, that one would as readily deal with Erasmus Kilgarvan as with the "Blue Nun." (Behind her back Miss Georgina was thus called, in reference to her per-petual costume, of long, full, oft shapeless dresses and skirts, of no shades other than navy or midnight blue, or black itself; and silk-lined capes of varying de-grees of antiquity; and dark, austere bonnets, and hats, in the styles of bygone seasons. She was invariably veiled, not only in public but, it was said, frequently in private as well: though, in truth, so few persons encountered her in recent years, since her resignation from the faculty of the Parthian Academy for Girls and her gradual withdrawal from society, that such observations must have been the fruit of mere rumor. The veils consisted of the sheerest gossamer; or were smartly dotted in black velvet; or were made of a somewhat disfiguring species of netting; or, more frequently of late, they were of so darkly opaque a gauze, the observer was hard put to imagine a human face within, and a pair of secretive watchful eyes—! Little wonder, then, that when Miss Georgina Kilgarvan ap-peared in public, whether in the relative seclusion of church services at the Grace

Episcopal Church on Berwick Avenue or on the street, small children openly gaped at her, and the unmannered amongst the adults covertly stared,—for the remarkable woman did very much resemble a *nun;* or, it might be said, a handsome and self-possessed species of *witch.*)

Phineas made the offer of delivering the sack of quicklime to the Manor somewhat later in the day: but Miss Georgina irritably interrupted him, and stressed again her need for the "gardening substance" straightaway. So Phineas brought Pride with him, into the storeroom, that he might hand over the unwieldy sack; and, perhaps, discreetly inquire of the old Negro what on earth was bedeviling his mistress, to make her behave so queerly—! For he had heard,—or, rather, his wife and daughter had made mention of the fact—that, since the abrupt death of Chief Justice Erasmus Kilgarvan of the Winterthurn County Court, some weeks previous, things were in great upset at Glen Mawr Manor; and one or two servants had already given notice. There were rumors too of Miss Georgina's cruel treatment of her two young half-sisters . . . And was not Simon Esdras Kilgarvan, the Judge's brother, lapsed into a very odd state of mourning, or grief . . .

Old Pride, however, gave evidence of disdaining Mr. Cutter's friendly chatter, no less emphatically than his mistress; and did not deign to cast a rheumy eye in his direction, or allow his very black, and very wrinkled, face to relax into a smile, though poor Phineas did his best to "draw him out." Thus the transaction was completed, in a most businesslike fashion: and Phineas Cutter stood in his doorway, wiping his hands on his overalls, to watch mistress and servant glide away into the swirl of snowflurries, with no backward glance. *Lye, lime, quicklime,—ah yes quicklime!—fifty pounds, please,—for my roses, Mr. Cutter, please,—at once,—with no delay: and charge it to the Kilgarvan account.*

In speaking of the incident afterward, particularly as the months and years passed, Phineas Cutter could not resist embellishing it somewhat,—noting that the "Blue Nun's" gloved hands visibly trembled; or that the stark pallor of her skin was discernible through her veil; or that her voice betrayed agitation, and guilt. In later years he was to insist, without, it seems, being conscious of the falsehood, that mistress and servant exchanged many a "significant" glance in his presence; and that Miss Georgina found it necessary to lean on Pride's arm, as they walked away. Ah, and had not the woman's *black, piercing, uncanny eyes* fixed themselves most disturbingly on his face—!

Withal, there was something appealing, and even romantic, about the scene: an air of the poignant and the melancholy: and the haunting. For was not Miss Georgina a most enigmatic figure, in her mourning costume, with a mantle of soft melting snowflakes on her head and shoulders, delicate as the finest lace? And was it not an act of thoughtless desperation, *never to be explained,* that a lady of her social station should come on foot, upward of three miles, along a rough country road, before the sun had well risen,—thereby exposing herself to all manner of gossip and speculation?

This, on the morning of May 3, some hours before the discovery of the death of Miss Georgina's infant cousin, up at the Manor.

Yet Phineas Cutter remained standing in his doorway for some minutes, gazing into the distance, though Miss Georgina and her servant had long since disappeared; and the snow began soundlessly to melt. Was there not something pitiable, and half tragic, about Erasmus Kilgarvan's eldest daughter, Phineas thought; had it not been her fate to be sorely disappointed,—nay, humiliated— many years ago, in an affair of the heart?

Trompe L'Oeil

Impatient with waiting. With longing. So lonely. Hungry. These many years. Impatient to love. To nurse. Our time fast approaches . . .

It was near midnight of May 2, not more than six hours before Phineas Cutter was to be roused so discourteously from his sleep, that Mrs. Abigail Whimbrel (Miss Georgina's cousin by way of her mother's family, the Battenbergs of Contracoeur) started from her sleep, for the second or third time since retiring: and suffered so foreign a sensation through her being,—part nervous excitation, part languor of a heavy sensuous sort—she halfway feared *some un-natural presence had slipped into her bed-chamber.*

"Who is here?—who dares disturb us? I shall ring for a servant—!"

With trembling fingers Mrs. Whimbrel lit the oil lamp by her bedside table: and saw nothing that might be deemed out of the ordinary, save, perhaps, the wildly distended shadows caused by the lamp's flame, and her own most uncommonly pale reflection in a bronze-frosted mirror on the facing wall. Though possessed of an enviably placid, and even quiescent, nature, and very rarely, for her sex, prone to outbursts of emotion or hysteria,—save at those inevitable times when female vicissitudes make war, as it were, upon mental equilibrium— Mrs. Whimbrel bethought herself that she must rise from her bed to examine the room and check once more the slumber of her infant son, who, having been fretful earlier, had been placed by his nurse, at Mrs. Whimbrel's adamant request, in a wicker crib close by her bed.

But all seemed well in the bed-chamber, though Abigail continued to feel some uneasiness at the lushly decorated room into which Cousin Georgina had put her: and at a queer undefined agitation of the air, which may have been the consequence of ill-fitting windows, or mismatched floorboards underfoot, belied by the gaily elegant French carpets, and, indeed, by the lavish furnishings on all sides. Yet her mother's heart was consoled by the depth and peaceableness of her baby's slumber, and by the perfection,—ah, would it never fail to pierce her heart, as if taking her unawares?—of his tiny being. "Why, then, sweet Charleton, if *you* are undisturbed, I am quite the fool to stir up a fuss," Abigail whispered. For some fond moments she stood gazing into the crib, taking note of the infant's tiny rosebud of a mouth (which looked to her as if, damply pursed, it awaited a stealthy kiss); and the near-imperceptible quivering of his eyelids (did he dream?—did he, perhaps, dream of *her*,—and of his happiness at her breast?); and the ravishingly charming way in which his hands, loosely shaped into "fists," rested on the white eiderdown coverlet. Though knowing herself foolishly indulgent, she could not resist brushing a fair silky curl from the baby's forehead; and leaning as gently as possible over the crib, to impart a ghostly kiss upon that same brow. That Mrs. Abigail Whimbrel doted over-much upon Charleton Hendrick Whimbrel II (named for his paternal grandfa-ther, the distinguished General Whimbrel of the Patriots' War of 1837) was a consequence of the fact that this youngest of the Whimbrels' several children would be the last child God would entrust to her care: for so her family physi-cian had told her, and she knew it must be so. Ah, would it not be afterward ad-judged an act of singular imprudence, to have brought the baby to troubled Glen Mawr Manor—where, it took no very prescient imagination to perceive, neither mother nor baby was *entirely* wished-for at the present time.

"We shall not be here long, and Cousin Georgina shall be rid of us,—poor unhappy creature!" Abigail murmured aloud, with more forcefulness than she had intended: for, of a sudden, little Charleton opened wide his liquid-blue eyes, and appeared, for an instant, to stare up at her. Did he truly wake?—or was he yet safely asleep? Ah, God's most exquisite little angel, entrusted to a mere mortal's care—! With relief Abigail determined that he had not actually awak-ened, which was, of course, altogether to the good: for, when he had cried and "carried on" earlier in the day, shortly after their arrival at the Manor, Cousin Georgina had not been charmed: informing Abigail somewhat needlessly that Glen Mawr was ordinarily peaceful,—nay, perfectly silent—and that the clamor of a baby's angry wailing was distinctly out of place. Startled, yet laugh-ingly, Abigail had protested that little Charleton's crying was scarcely an ex-pression of anger, but only of colicky discomfort, and upset at unfamiliar surroundings,—quite natural, in fact, in a baby of his tender months. Georgina seemingly attended to her words with courtesy; yet, a minute later, she reiter-ated her own observation, in a grave voice, adding that *the men should dislike it in particular,* as any sort of noise interfered with concentration. Seeing Abigail's startled look, perhaps, Georgina at once bethought herself, and amended that Uncle Simon Esdras should not like it,—"being very sensitive of late to undue distractions and interruptions that threaten progress on his *Treatise.*" A faint rubescent flush to the elder woman's cheeks, at her innocent, yet piteous, "slip of the tongue," and a stiffening of her mouth, warned Abigail against attempting commiseration at this awkward moment.

"It is altogether natural that poor Georgina 'feels' her father's presence, as if he were still alive," Abigail observed, with a small *frisson*, "—for, indeed, at Glen Mawr, it does seem the case that the 'great man' has but stepped out of the room, and will shortly be back!"

Little Charleton again stirred, and made a whimpering, mewing sound; and, in some agitation, Abigail stroked his warm brow yet again, and adjusted the coverlet, and his tiny pillow; and essayed to comfort him with a familiar lullaby of the nursery, for, alas, he must not begin to cry so quickly!—

> *Little Baby Bunting*
> *Father's gone ahunting*
> *Gone to get a new fur skin*
> *To wrap the Baby Bunting in!*

> *Little Baby Bunting*
> *Father's gone ahunting . . .*

For some precarious seconds it seemed he might wake, and throw himself into a spasm of wailing: for was Abigail not, despite her maternal solicitude and boundless love, a most fearsome *giantess* in his vision?

Fortunately, however, he did lapse into sleep: and the relieved mother returned to her bed, with the intention of reading, as sleep, for her, now seemed cruelly distant: and perhaps not desirable. Thus it was, she took up her Bible, and essayed to read, that her soul might be calmed; and the disagreeable confusion of her thoughts, of but a few minutes previous, quelled. Yet she halfway wondered whether, in truth, those thoughts had been hers at all; or some queer product of her sojourn here, in this intimidating guest room,—the "General's Room," it was known as, or the "Honeymoon Room"—where Cousin Georgina had insisted she must stay, as it was the "only decent room kept in readiness for visitors." She had, she feared, insulted her cousin by her initial response to it, in protesting that it was far too grand, and too formal, and, she knew not why, too *chill* a space, for her to inhabit alone. Might she and Georgina not share a bed,—or, at the very least, a bed-chamber for the night—as they had done upon several occasions in their girlhood? But this wistful query was seemingly *not heard.*

All incongruously, and, it seemed, with not the faintest trace of mockery or sarcasm, Georgina said of a sudden: "Dear Cousin, I cannot wonder that you are disappointed in us,—that you find our way of life at the Manor much reduced from what it was. While Father lived this house too lived: his step, his voice,—nay, his very breath—reverberated throughout. But, ah!—no more of that; for I see by your frown that I am being morbid. And poor Georgina, poor spinster, *is forbidden to be morbid,* by Dr. Hatch himself. Yet it seems naught but 'plain dealing,' to observe that we are, since that catastrophe of late March, an etiolated sort of household, at best: three sisters in stunned mourning, and a bachelor uncle so bemazed, I fear, by his brother's death, he has yet to comprehend its import. No, no, dear Abigail," Georgina said, turning stiffly aside, as if she feared a precipitous embrace, and again speaking with puzzling incongruity,—her thoughts, it seemed, hopping hither and yon: "we are obliged to be frugal now at Glen Mawr, as, I am told, Father's finances were left in a confused state; and it will be many a month, or year, before we are on an 'even keel' once again. We must be humble. Thérèse and Perdita quite understand, for they are not,—praise God, they have never been—*spoiled girls;* and Uncle Simon shall be made to understand. It is not our lot, you see, to dissipate our income in idle pleasures,—to throw the Manor open to visitors, and relatives up and down the pike,—though of course, being hospitable, we should like very much to do so. Ah, would I were a writer of romances, and a heroine of the lending library, and not, as Fate would have it, a mere *poetess!*—though, it seems," Georgina said, with a bemused twist of her lips, "I am scarcely that, any longer."

It is not to be wondered at that Abigail found herself quite nonplussed at this trailing, yet lugubrious speech: in truth silenced, with as much dispatch, as if her elder cousin had rudely bade her be still. ("Why, I had sought only to share her bedroom for the night," poor Abigail, stung, inwardly murmured, "and have been served a stern admonition not to expect *luxury!*")

*   *   *

As it was the custom for most of the members of Abigail's family, excepting of course the very youngest children, to read the Bible twice daily, either in the company of others or alone, it is perhaps comprehensible that her mind sometimes drifted from Holy Writ to attach itself to matters of a profane nature: yet this proclivity seemed the more emphatic, and the more irresistible, as Mrs. Whimbrel lay stiffly propped up with pillows, in her lonely bed,—alas, many miles from her home in Contracoeur and her belovèd Mr. Whimbrel—and essayed to read, with a silent shaping of her lips, from the Epistles of John. Ah, how vexing!—how nettlesome! For, though the spacious bed-chamber was silent save for the mournful ticking of a pendulum clock on the mantel and the low persistent murmurousness of the wind against the several windows, she could not, it seems, attend to the Word of God: but felt her thoughts urge themselves in another direction, very like a willful horse straining at the bit.

Her attention was drawn to the facing mirror, which, though lightly frosted in bronze, displayed with some clarity both herself and her bed, and the extraordinary *trompe l'oeil* mural by Fairfax Eakins that had been commissioned by Phillips Goode Kilgarvan some decades previous and painted directly on the wall and a portion of the ceiling. A small golden plaque announced the title "The Virgin in the Rose-Bower," and Abigail Whimbrel was capable of discerning certain religious elements and motifs in it,—the Virgin, for instance, held the Christ Child somewhat awkwardly on her knee; yet, withal, she thought it a decidedly queer painting, and marred by a pagan,—or might it be Popish?—extravagance of flesh.

Of a sudden, answering to a whim she would have been hard pressed to explain, Abigail rose from her bed, and went to the door, and laid her ear against it; and, hearing nothing, *firmly bolted it.* She then went to each of the tall windows, in turn, and locked them as best she could, saying to herself the while: "Albeit I am at Glen Mawr, and not in a strange inn or hotel, I know myself and Charleton unquestionably safe,—yet shall sleep the more soundly, for knowing too that the room is *secured from within.*"

She then returned to her bed, and bethought herself that now, at last, she might darken the room; for nothing could possibly harm her, save the childish phantasms of sleep. As Cousin Georgina would be gravely insulted to discover the precautions she had taken, Abigail resolved to rise long before dawn and to undo all the locks and bolts,—there being little risk of her oversleeping, as Baby should stir, and fret, and cry for his first repast of the day, not long past five o'clock.

Scarcely had Abigail settled into an ancient mohair chair in Georgina's drawing room, and carefully arranged her skirts and petticoats, and taken up her cup of tea,—scarcely had she exchanged greetings, and subdued smiles, with her young cousins Thérèse and Perdita (who had come downstairs to tea, it appeared, with timid reluctance, clad in unflattering dresses of black mousseline, with drooping collars, loose sashes, and distinctly tattered hems),—when Georgina essayed to apologize for the fact that Abigail and her baby had been met at the train station by one of the Manor servants only, and not by Georgina herself, or Simon Esdras: the excuse coolly offered, *that they were otherwise employed.* To this "apology" that had very much the air of an affront, poor Abigail could but murmur an assent; and busied herself with her tea, and inquiries after the health of the Kilgarvans, while her eye moved about the room to take in what it could,—a portrait in oils of the late Chief Justice in his judicial robes, above the mantel, most imposing in its muscular harmonies of shadow and light; a somewhat untidy stack of books, set beside Georgina's chair; the inert though wheezing form of a large mastiff,—Jupiter his name—lying sprawled on the carpet near Abigail's feet, with as much agèd aplomb, as if he slept in some secluded place. Her own keen eye following Abigail's, Georgina observed, in a low, dry, uninflected voice, that she hoped Abigail would not report back to Contracoeur "on the doubtful state of our household: for it is a fact I cannot disguise, that the servants have been fickle of late, and will get themselves dismissed. Alas as Father has said, it is the times—!"

Abigail Whimbrel essayed some suitable reply, though feeling most perplexed: for how was it possible, Cousin Georgina seemed not to *like* her; or even in a way to *know* her? Nor did the younger sisters contribute any element of smiling freshness, or vivacity: lapsing into silence after making their dutiful,—

nay, forced—replies; and gazing with brooding and melancholy eyes at the carpet. When Abigail's sociable voice subsided, naught was heard save the ticking of a mantel clock, which struck the ear as not fully rhythmic; and the sighing, laborious breath of the old mastiff; and, distantly, from upstairs, the renewed crying of little Charleton. (Ah, how he had fretted on the train!—giving both Abigail and his nursemaid a great deal of pleasurable trouble. But now that he had nursed and had been put to bed for his afternoon nap, Abigail resolved that she would not run away upstairs at his bidding.)

The subject was revived, of the abruptness of Erasmus Kilgarvan's death,— the distinguished jurist having died in the courtroom, in full session, some six weeks previous: the which animated Georgina for a while, so that her narrow eyes shone, and a faint blush shadowed her cheeks. Yet this too ran its course; and it was with an ironical voice that Georgina concluded: "Thus you find us, his daughters. *His* heiresses. Left quite behind. As you see. Ah, dear Abigail, you *must* not judge us harshly, and frown upon us so prettily!—for we are not at all *morbid;* but only,—*his.*"

Abigail stammeringly protested that she did not judge at all: but had come to Glen Mawr solely out of friendship, as she could imagine how heavily grief lay upon the household.

"Grief lies upon our household,—I hope I speak for my sisters as well?—no more heavily," Georgina flatly announced, "than might be required."

As no servant appeared to pass about the tea things, Thérèse lay aside her grayish tangle of crocheting, and, with an appealing sort of awkwardness, elected to do so: proffering Abigail a second cup of tea and handing about a plate of crustless sandwiches thickly smeared with butter, and salmon paste,— which, Abigail's keen eye determined, was *not* overly fresh. This half-sister of Georgina's, nearly three decades her junior, was now fourteen years of age, yet childlike in both manner and appearance: her pinched face being neither pretty nor actually plain,—her slender nose with its subtle Kilgarvan crook, and her small sweet mouth, being features of decided promise,—while her dark eyes, it almost seemed, were hooded, and sunk too deeply in their sockets. Abigail had heard that Thérèse was passionately religious, and an outstanding scholar: yet how forlorn her expression, how dim and melancholy her smile—! Nor did it contribute to her charm that her right eyelid quivered, as if she feared a harsh word, or a blow from an invisible hand: a singularly unfortunate trait in a young lady of good family.

As to Perdita, the youngest of the sisters, and by far the most comely,—this child made so little effort to please, with scarcely a smile for her Contracoeur cousin, or more than a mumbled reply, Abigail knew not what to think. She was decidedly pretty, or more than pretty: with a heart-shaped face, and delicately curving brows, and the Kilgarvan nose, and thick-lashed eyes which, even when narrowed, gave a hint of spirited intelligence, or willfulness. Yet her air was aggrieved and sullen; her skin so pale as to suggest anemia, or green-sickness; and her lower lip swollen with pouting. (Though perhaps it was actually swollen: Abigail noted a bruise of a flavid purple, singularly unflattering, along her jaw: and scratches on the backs of both her hands. A clumsy child, along with being sullen,—prone to mishaps and falls.) Though Abigail made every effort to provoke a smile in her, and to draw her out in conversation, she stubbornly held her ground, as it were; and sat in her chair with a comical sort of formality, her backbone resolutely straight, and her head held rigid, in imitation,—Abigail supposed it must be unconscious—of her late father, who had, as all the family knew, a mania for correct posture; and much contempt for those who did not observe it.

Abigail was startled, however, to note that, while Georgina was preoccupied in extracting from a pile of condolence cards one of especial significance she wished to show Abigail, the twelve-year-old Perdita secured two or three of the salmon sandwiches from off the tray, in a deft, covert, and, as it were, rapacious motion,—and devoured them with a greedy avidity more appropriate in a starving animal than in a charming young lady! Detected, she flashed unrepentant eyes at Abigail: yet remained stonily unsmiling: and would not warm to her cousin.

As Georgina spoke of the gratifying number of condolence cards and letters she had received since Erasmus's funeral, Abigail took pained note of the spinster's waxen pallor, which might have been becoming, in the fashion of the

times, in a woman some years younger, or possessed of more agreeable features:
but was decidedly unflattering in Georgina. Though but three years older than
Abigail, Georgina gave every appearance of being a dozen years older: for her
high, narrow, finely wrinkled brow was the more deeply creased when, it
seemed, she was struck by a vexatious thought,—which, to judge from her manner at tea, was fairly often. At the Judge's funeral, Abigail recalled with what
stiff, numbed, yet unfailingly efficient propriety Georgina had behaved: having
made most of the funeral arrangements herself, and seeing, however cursorily,
to the comfort of the many visitors who had journeyed to Winterthurn to pay
their final respects to Erasmus Kilgarvan. Brisk, and forthright, and coolly
gracious, her eye not reddened from crying, nor her slender hand given to trembling, the "Blue Nun" had not failed at her duty, no more than she had failed,—
as everyone whispered—to manage Erasmus's household for most of her adult
life: and to take on the responsibilities of mistress of Glen Mawr, after the
somewhat clouded death of her father's second wife, when Thérèse and Perdita
were very young children. (Of the actual manner of death of the sickly and, it
was said, *unnatural* Hortense Spies,—who had married the middle-aged Erasmus when scarcely more than a girl herself—Abigail knew very little: and
deemed it best, as all the family counseled, not to inquire.)

A most enigmatic portrait Miss Georgina Kilgarvan now presented to her
cousin's kindly, yet anxious, eye: her cheeks distinctly hollowed, yet her eyes
possessing a mica-like glint, or glitter, that bespoke some suppressed excitation:
and did she not retain, for all her air of a spinster's stiff posture, a girlishness,—
a most appealing artlessness—of old? Abigail had gone away to boarding school
at the Canandaigua Episcopal Female Seminary some miles to the west, where
her cousin Georgina was already a student,—nay, one of the "leaders"—and she
could see, in the Georgina of the present, certain remnants of that schoolgirl, in
whom high spirits, willfulness, and a penchant for sarcasm contended. She
would have liked to inquire, discreetly, after Georgina's poetry: as to whether
she had in truth abandoned it,—as, it was said, her father wished; but knew not
how to introduce the subject. (Georgina had published a few poems, under the
nom de plume of "Iphigenia," which Abigail had had pointed out to her, in one

or another of the magazines: difficult, obscure, riddle-some, and, it seemed to Abigail's untrained eye, needlessly disagreeable verse!—which baffled the intellect with its clotted syntax, and the ear, with its failure to rhyme. As a schoolgirl at Canandaigua she had quite intimidated her teachers, as well as her fellow students, with her *promise* as a poetess; yet her development afterward, so far as Abigail and others in the family could determine, was most disappointing.)

At Canandaigua, Georgina had been the editor of *Canandaigua Bluets,* the young ladies' annual anthology of *belles lettres;* she had been the leader of expeditions "into the field," to observe birds, trees, wildflowers, and the like; she had walked away, as it were, with many of the honors,—in such divers subjects as Latin, and French, and Elocution, and the Classics, and English Literature; she had blossomed, to the amazement of all the Kilgarvans, from a taciturn, withdrawn, sickly miss, given to inordinate brooding, to a forthright and handsome young lady,—which must have pleased her father, as he had feared, with great justification, an unwholesome sort of influence from Georgina's mother, who had died when the girl was but ten.

She had then gone away to New York City, to the continued amazement of the family, there to matriculate at Barnard College: and insisting upon taking her residence, not with anyone she knew (for several distant cousins, of an older generation, lived there), but in a boarding house for young single ladies in Morningside Heights. Precisely how long Georgina stayed there, Abigail could not recall: but remembered dimly that she had returned home to nurse her ailing father, once or twice, and then had been pressed into returning home permanently, without taking her degree. Erasmus had suffered an ulcerous condition, it was said; or heart pains; or gout; or,—but Abigail could not recall. (It was a massive stroke that had finally killed him, striking him down dead: yet all remarked how unexpected such a blow was, as, for a gentleman of his years and industry, he had enjoyed uncommonly good health—!) Settling back into her home at Glen Mawr, Georgina had acquired an excellent position as an instructress at the Parthian Academy for Girls, some nine or ten miles away, in Winterthurn City; and had adjusted herself with little complaint, it was said, to having her "wings clipped,"—though not ceasing, evidently, to write her curious little verses.

All unexpectedly, she had been courted, in her thirty-second year, by a gentleman of poetical and musical inclinations, by the name of Guillemot,—whether Maurice, or Malcolm, Abigail could not recall; but, as this somewhat mysterious personage was exposed as a craven *fortune hunter* (or so family legend would have it), the courtship had been most unceremoniously terminated, with no official engagement; and so much distress on poor Georgina's part, it was said she never fully recovered: quitting her position at the Academy soon after, and "taking the veil,"—which is to say, turning by degrees into a spinster of eccentric habits and dress. Ah, unhappy Georgina!—Abigail recalled with pain a visit she and Mr. Whimbrel had made to Glen Mawr, some eight or ten years ago, when, shown into this very drawing room by the butler, they had surprised Georgina at her desk, in the act of poetical creation,—and so discountenanced her, she clasped her writing materials to her bosom and ran out of the room like a frightened rabbit; and refused to come downstairs again, no matter how sternly Judge Kilgarvan commanded her. "My daughter is shamed, it seems, to be discovered at her scribbling," Erasmus had said, with every attempt to make light of a most unsettling incident, "yet she persists in the folly: and will not even shrink from publishing the results! Perhaps, dear little Abigail, *you* might whisper some sense into her ear—?"

But Abigail had no more dared approach her elder cousin at that time than she did now, on any terms intimate, or at all direct.

Thus it was, Georgina had passed through her girlhood, and her young womanhood, with, it seemed, a dismaying swiftness: known now through the city as the "Blue Nun"—a figure of pity, curiosity, and not a little trepidation. When they had come to the Manor to inform her of Erasmus Kilgarvan's untimely death, it was reported that she leapt from her chair like a doe pierced through the heart, by the hunter's bullet; that for long minutes she stared frozen into space, her blanched lips shaped to an eerie smile; and that, finally, as the enormity of the shock made its impress upon her, her face drained of all blood, and, gasping and choking, her fingers tearing at her bodice, she sank heavily to the floor. "O dear Father! O God! Where is Thy pity—!" she exclaimed, before descending into blessèd unconsciousness.

Thus, Abigail's melancholy reverie, the while Georgina spoke of those acquaintances, public officials, associates of the Judge's, and certain relatives who had,—or was it that they had *not?*—expressed the proper degree of sympathy upon the tragic occasion. Thérèse and Perdita sat stiffly motionless, as if daring neither to concur nor to object,—though Abigail gathered, from a slight tremor of Thérèse's lip, and a more emphatic sullenness on the part of Perdita, that the sisters had heard these complaints many times in the past; and found them tiresome. With especial ire Georgina took up the subject of the "other Kilgarvans" of Winterthurn City: this being a family of very limited means, dwelling near Wycombe Place, and headed by Erasmus's young half-brother, Lucas, who had been struck from their father's will some years before,—for what particular reason, Abigail did not know. All atumble came Georgina's words now, as if she had been awakened from an oversolemn trance, and might at last vent her spleen. "Just barely, dear Abigail, could they restrain themselves, at Father's gravesite," she said severely, "the *pack* of them: Mr. and Mrs. and great hulking boys, with little pretense of displaying even a hypocrite's sorrow; and many a hint of the savage triumph they felt at viewing poor Father's casket. Mr. Lucas Kilgarvan, the *half-breed,*—nay, do not wince, dear Cousin, for I shall call him that, as Father did: the profligate,—the ruffian,—the ingrate,—the *toymaker,*— whom I shall never call Uncle: nor any of those brutes, cousins of *mine.* No, Cousin Abigail," Georgina said, though Abigail had made no motion to interrupt, "we can never forgive Lucas for the despicable publicity he sought, in contesting Grandfather's will: nay, and pursuing the case to the highest court in the state. How mortified poor Father was!—and Simon Esdras as well, for all his reserve. Never,—never—can we forgive: we *dare* not."

Abigail said, with tentative boldness: "Cousin Georgina, I fear you exaggerate the situation, for I was present at the funeral, and at your father's gravesite, and it did not strike *me* that Lucas and his family behaved—"

"Nay, you are not very perceptive," Georgina said, "or, it may be, you are too *good:* for Goodness, as Father has said, stumbles and gropes in the dark, possessing but a single eye; and depending upon the rest of us for,—for guidance."

So rudely silenced, Abigail bethought herself how best to reply, and sipped nervously at her tea, which she could not taste: the while her infant son's crying sounded faintly from upstairs and agèd Jupiter stirred, and fretted, and sighed in his slumber, with a most human species of resignation. As if following the course of her thoughts, Georgina continued the assault, saying that it was scarcely a secret that the "pack" of Wycombe Street Kilgarvans rejoiced in Erasmus Kilgarvan's death; that it was highly likely they had engaged an attorney, to seek again a reversal of the will; that it was altogether obvious at the funeral that the sons,—the youngest in particular—were restless, and insolent, and clearly *bored:* being, after all, mere animals,—loutish boys.

Abigail gently protested that she could see no basis for alluding to Lucas Kilgarvan and his family as a *pack:* for was not Lucas in truth a Kilgarvan, despite the unfortunate falling-out between himself and his elder brothers; and was not his wife a De Forrest,—the De Forrests being old Winterthurn stock indeed; and were not the sons more properly designated *young gentlemen* than either *louts,* or *boys?* For the eldest, Bradford, must be at least twenty-five years of age; and the youngest, Xavier,—for was not Xavier the one with the curly black hair?—must surely be sixteen years old, and quite grown up. Moreover—

At this, however, Georgina appeared inordinately distressed; and drew a grayish lace handkerchief out of her sleeve, with which she dabbed at her upper lip and brow; and murmured in an agitated voice that it quite baffled her why Abigail should wish to take *their* side, since she evidently preferred Erasmus Kilgarvan's family, to visit. Nor was it comprehensible to Georgina why Abigail should make it a point to designate Lucas's sons by *name:* there being a particular anathema in the household regarding *Xavier,*—the which word Georgina pronounced as if it were a foreign term, and vile. Abigail could not resist displaying surprise at this revelation: and Georgina continued hurriedly to explain that the boy in question, "Xavier," had behaved most atrociously in the cemetery, paying but a perfunctory attention to the minister's words, and casting his eyes,—indeed, his *bold and smoldering gaze*—where he would: upward to the clouds, downward to the earth, to one side, to another, upon Georgina herself, and, most invidiously, upon Perdita. "Why, the insolent creature stared at me as if desirous of penetrating my innermost thoughts," Georgina said, breathing now somewhat shallowly, "and as to his motives for contemplating my sister, I dare not speculate. Yet I should not have minded the insult to us, and to Father's memory, if my shameless little wench of a sister had not, all coyly, and with but a clumsy attempt at secrecy, *gazed upon him in return*."

An involuntary twitch in Perdita stimulated Georgina to press onward, and to declare, with an ironic smile for Abigail's benefit, that Perdita naturally denied the charges: "For she is most adroit in feigning both innocence and tears. Yet it would require a far more clever child than she to fool 'Miss Georgina': for *I saw what I saw, and what I cannot see, I can surmise*."

This perplexing outburst was met by silence: for poor Perdita sat stiffly immobile in her chair, with no more spirit than a wooden doll,—albeit her lower lip trembled, and the tight clasping of her hands indicated significant distress. Abigail glanced from one sister to the other, feeling most awkward indeed, and wondering if the subject had grown too urgent to be deflected by a lightsome remark, or a query on some neutral matter. How very pale Georgina had grown, and how queerly her dark eyes glittered! "Might it be that some innocent question regarding the late Judge's personal papers, and whether Georgina had plans to edit them, would 'save the day'—?" Abigail inwardly murmured. Yet she felt very much the schoolgirl, beneath Georgina Kilgarvan's unflagging gaze, and dared not speak.

Then, all boldly, though in a palpitant voice, Thérèse sought to defend her sister: saying that Georgina was surely mistaken, as *she* had noticed nothing amiss in Perdita's behavior, whether during the funeral service, or in the cemetery. "Albeit we were all distracted by the occasion, Perdita no less than you and me," Thérèse said hurriedly, as if she feared being interrupted, "—yet I would swear to it, that she did not misbehave, in such a way. We have covered this ground in the past, Georgina, and I must reiterate, though risking your anger, that both Perdita and I were totally taken by surprise when, upon our return home, on that most harrowing of days, you so violently excoriated our cousin Xavier—"

"Ah, you delight in his name!" Georgina said. "Doubtless you luxuriate in the mere sound of it,—the purulent syllables—the *melody!*"

"Why, Georgina, Xavier *is* our cousin, and he *is* a Kilgarvan," Thérèse falteringly said. "How should I *not* know his name?"

Georgina commanded her to be still, and to hold her tongue for the remainder of the hour: else Cousin Abigail should carry back to Contracoeur the remarkable news that the Kilgarvan sisters, though in mourning for their father, enjoyed nothing more than discussing young boys over tea. Perdita, it seems, was a "past mistress" of deception, though plying the world with an angelic face calculated to wring the hearts of fools. Of divers morbid, unclean, secret, and thoroughly perverse practices, indulged in (she had no doubt) by the "pious" Thérèse no less than Perdita, Georgina would not speak; nor did she allow herself even to think; and she recommended a like attitude for Abigail, in regard to her young children.

For some painful seconds it appeared that Perdita might succumb to angry tears, which, Abigail feared, would the more antagonize Georgina; but the child held herself in commendable control; until, of a sudden, another spasmodic twitch overcame her body, and she raised her eyes,—ah, how darkly brilliant, how wondrously insolent, those eyes!—and said in a voice eerily matched to Georgina's, in tone and rhythm: "You lie. It is not true. I have no friend in him. This 'Xavier.' I have no friend. I know no one,—and no one knows me. I love no one,—and no one loves—"

"Quite enough," Georgina said. "You will go upstairs at once: your tea is concluded."

Abigail sought to intercede, but none of the principals paid her heed: and it struck her as significant that Georgina should speak these words with an air of gratified triumph; and that Perdita, though visibly trembling with rage, should rise with such dutiful alacrity, and make an old-fashioned half-curtsy in Abigail's direction, and straightaway leave the room. "Such impudence," Georgina said softly, "fairly begs for the whip: but must content itself by going without dinner."

Briefly, when the tea things were about to be cleared away, and Abigail was quite fatigued, Simon Esdras made his belated appearance,—with such mumbled apologies, it was impossible to know what he said.

Though the white-haired gentleman was unfailingly amiable, with a low bow and a gracious smile for Abigail, that lady suffered the distinct impression that her uncle *did not recognize her:* and it seemed most impolitic for her to introduce herself. All clearly, Simon Esdras's attention was elsewhere, doubtless back in his study: and the tea he vaguely sipped, and the several sandwiches he ate, failed to make any tangible impression on him. Inquiring after the ladies' health,—making idle and witty commentary upon the weather,—stirring three or four sugar cubes in his tea, with inexpert turns of his spoon: thus Simon Esdras, the "private thinker," navigated the shoals of the drawing room, with little expenditure of his spirit. "Ah, yes?—hmmm!—*yes,—* so it has invariably struck me, indeed!" he murmured, with a kindly crinkling of his eyes and a thin, though benign, smile.

Simon Esdras, now in his mid- or late sixties, had been a youthful prodigy who had published, at the age of nineteen, a monograph addressing itself to the epistemological foundations of mankind's perception of existence,—its precise title being *A Treatise on the Probable "Existence" of the World.* (Neither Abigail nor any other member of her family, alas, had had much success in penetrating the elaborate coils and clots of Simon Esdras's prose: though harboring no doubt that their brilliant relative was correct in his reasoning.) So far as Abigail knew, subsequent works from Simon Esdras's pen had failed to make a like impression upon the philosophical world, doubtless as a result of their unusual difficulty, and challenge to "the complacency of American and European thought": but Simon Esdras was not in the slightest deterred, and was said to be in pursuit of his vision with yet more vigor than before. "Had I been of a temper to 'suffer fools gladly' in the academic world," Simon Esdras once observed, in a rare moment of self-commentary, "I should by now be unquestioned in my position, at the very pinnacle of that tiny, and most devilishly slippery, pyramid of professorial rank: but lacking such latitudinarianism, in social no less than philosophical coinage, I must content myself with the triumphs of solitude,—and of Posterity."

In his person, the philosopher struck an altogether amiable, and even unassuming, figure, being rather more "roly-poly" than not: of conspicuously less than medium height: with a small, high, adamantly round belly: a moon-shaped face in which hazel eyes were widely and innocently set, and the Kilgarvan nose decidedly snubbed, to exude a boyish air. Thus it seemed to Abigail a wondrous thing, and entirely to her uncle's credit, that, being a gentleman, and well aware of the disparity between his intelligence and that of his companions, he behaved with an utter lack of pretension; and turned upon the world an expression of guileless and acute *interest*, in conjunction with an air of the *unfocused*, and the *unjudging*. So it seemed that, while his outer eye moved about normally, his inner eye fixed itself upon other matters entirely, of a private nature. He beamed upon Abigail; he engaged Abigail in lightsome parlor chatter; he took no notice of Perdita's absence, nor, indeed, of the tense "atmosphere" into which he had so artlessly stepped; the while the fine mechanism of his brain pursued its arcane interests.

When Thérèse proffered him the plate of sandwiches, he smilingly helped himself, observing generally that it mattered not a whit to him *what* he ate, or even *that* he ate, so long as he should be freed of vexatious metaphysical questions as to the *actual substance* of what he ate; or, indeed, *why* he ate.

Abigail then inquired after Simon Esdras's health: for which polite query he thanked her: but said that, as he was no hypochondriac, he rarely troubled to analyze his interior state, or even to take notice as to whether his heart beat, or no: this too being a topic largely given over to females. "Inner or outer weather," the white-haired philosopher declared smilingly, "it is all the same, to me!"

Again, the ladies laughed, though not with an excess of exuberance; and, as she saw Simon Esdras was about to take his leave, Abigail proffered her condolences once again to him, hoping that he would soon recover from the shock of the Judge's untimely death. These words gave Simon Esdras pause, it seemed, for he frowned fleetingly; and set down his cup at so crooked an angle, tea slopped into his saucer. Yet it was in a charmingly placid voice that he said: "Madame, it is doubtful that any event, in *time,* can be proven *untimely:* for does not the very statement fly in the face of Logic? If one dies, moreover, it follows that one has died neither before nor after 'his' time, but precisely *at* 'his' time: the simple proof of the matter being, *that he has died.* Why, dear lady, do you think it logical, or even possible, that we might die *before,* or *after,* 'our' proper times—?"

Poor Abigail could not determine whether this question was merely rhetorical or serious: thus she fumblingly essayed to answer it, while Simon Esdras smiled in her direction, but gave little sign of attending to her words: and, of a sudden, laying his napkin down, declared that he must be off, for his work beckoned, and he had not "*time* to deal with such knotty subjects, even with persons of demonstrated brilliance like herself."

After he had made his gracious exit, the ladies sat in subdued silence; then Abigail ventured the opinion that Simon Esdras *was* a most original genius, of which the family had good reason to be proud: yet it must give him pain to be pressed into drawing-room conversation of the usual sort.

"No, dear Abigail," Georgina said, "such trivial matters cannot give Uncle pain; for I have reason to believe, he has rarely experienced so vulgar a thing in all his sixty-odd years. Pain, as you must know, is too common altogether: it is but a female prerogative."

. . . *How inappropriate for Baby & me to be placed in this opulent bedchamber,* Abigail took note in her diary, to which she had restlessly turned when, it seemed, Holy Writ failed her, *a room for a General & his bride, surely,—a room for a queen—yet one's soul is dwarfed in such chill splendor: & Baby & me much the better served to be housed in more humble quarters.*

The General's Room, or, to give it its more notorious appellation, the Honeymoon Room, was executed in conspicuously ornate French style: which is to say, more precisely, in the "Americanized" manner of the Louis Seize revival style of the France of Napoleon. Its original decor must have been eighteenth-century, as it had been prepared for General Pettit Kilgarvan and his beauteous young second wife, a daughter of Thomas Pinckney's, a full century before; in the 1870s it was redone by Georgina's grandfather, the somewhat eccentric Phillips Goode, whose stated aim it was to see all three of his sons,—Erasmus, Simon Esdras, and young Lucas—firmly ensconced at the very pinnacle, as he phrased it, of their chosen professions: and to see Glen Mawr Manor established as one of the premier "jewels" of the Winterthurn Valley: money being no problem, for a gentleman of Revolutionary blood who had increased his fortune tenfold in those unparalleled years following the War Between the States.

Thus it was, Phillips Goode heard word of the fashionable architect Richardson, and his controversial "monumental" style, and hired him, at great expense, to redo several rooms at Glen Mawr, the most resplendent being the room in which Abigail now found herself: which boasted not one but two exquisite French fireplaces, decorated in filigree, mosaics, and mirrored surfaces; and numberless graceful niches, for the display of costly *objets d'art;* and an entire wall magnificently covered in morocco, or a most cunning imitation; and gilt-framed mirrors with etched glass, in designs of gay floating cherubs, ivy, roses, and the like,—the which reflected, to Abigail's way of thinking, singularly disagreeable ghost-images of herself. The room's furnishings, in a bold composite of Louis Seize, Italian Renaissance, and something approaching the medieval, had all been provided by the famed Herter Brothers of New York City, and were most impressive indeed: yet the outstanding feature of the Honeymoon Room was its several Fairfax Eakins paintings, in ingenious *trompe l'oeil* style,—the which Phillips Goode had hoped would call wide cultural attention to Glen Mawr, and to his role as a patron of the arts.

The most ambitious of these paintings was a mural that covered much of a wall, and part of the ceiling, freely copied from a fifteenth-century German painting known as "The Virgin in the Rose-Bower" (artist unknown). While speaking with Abigail earlier that day, Georgina had said in a somewhat uncharacteristic moment of frankness that her late father bitterly regretted the fact that his sire had been so extravagant as to have Eakins paint his masterpiece directly on the wall. "So it is, and always shall be, that Glen Mawr's splendid 'Virgin in the Rose-Bower' blooms unseen," Georgina said, her voice low with passion, "—a great loss to all lovers of our native American art."

Doubtless it was a principle of aesthetic harmony, Abigail thought, that the artist had executed the mural with so resolute an eye for balance and symmetry: for all the figures, despite their floating, and careening, and lurching about, had been placed upon a sort of grid,—this being the central trellis of the rose-bower, which looked, to the superficial glance, rather like a spider's web. Abigail made a show of admiring the Virgin, though, in her surly medieval, or Teutonic, guise, she seemed little desirous of awakening admiration in the viewer; and wondered aloud, to Georgina, whether it *might* result in some such predicament,—being *divine,* that is, while at the same time being *human.* "Indeed," Abigail observed, with a slight shudder, "*I* should find it a distinctly uncomfortable position to have given birth under such circumstances: and to take up the mantle, as it were, of maternal responsibility, at the request of Our Lord Himself. And, also, oh dear!—how it should disturb Mr. Whimbrel as well!— the role of St. Joseph being somewhat ambiguous, as I recall."

It was not the figures of the Virgin and Child, however, but those of the angelic host, executed in flamboyant *trompe l'oeil* style, that gave the mural its disconcerting effect. One or two angels were painted in a conventional flat manner; but all the rest appeared in motion; and alive; and in three dimensions. Several of the more developed angels, executed with their heads, shoulders, and torsos out of proportion to the rest of their bodies, gave the uncanny impression of leaning out of the wall,—so much so that Abigail had to resist the childlike impulse to raise an arm, that she might ward them off. There were upward of a dozen of these remarkable cherubs: some recognizably,—and altogether shamelessly—male; some daintily feminine; some more sensuously and unapologetically female; and one or two of indeterminate gender. Ah, what a cornucopia of wings!—large, and absurdly small; straight, curved, bent, and hooked; feathered in silky black, or silver, or white; or feathered not at all, it seemed, so much as *scaled.* As if the artist had been lazily indifferent to his craft, the quality of the angels' faces differed widely, some being most skillfully rendered, and others but hurriedly. One or two possessed the rubicund heartiness of the Germanic or

Dutch nationality; some clearly derived from a more delicate Latinate heritage; some, with pronounced cheekbones, and sly, slanted, almond-shaped eyes, betrayed Mongol blood. There were complexions of so stark an alabaster white, the wan Georgina seemed healthy set beside them; while the more portly angels exhibited a florid puffiness, of the kind associated with sybaritic overindulgence—! And how puzzling, too, the contrasting facial expressions: rapt adoration in one; indifference in another; and *hauteur;* and faint repugnance; and bemusement; and childlike wonder; and,—but did Abigail's affrighted eye mislead her?—*frank lascivious interest,* directed toward the chaste Virgin herself.

So entranced was Georgina, she seemed to have forgotten Abigail altogether in her frowning admiration of the figures: and only roused herself to observe, finally, that she never entered the Honeymoon Room without being reminded of those mysterious words of St. Theresa's,—"An angel with a flaming golden arrow pierced my heart repeatedly. The pain was so great that I screamed aloud, but simultaneously felt such infinite sweetness that I wished the pain to last eternally . . . It was the sweetest caressing of the soul by God."

Uttering these words in a reverent tone, Georgina was, of a sudden, overcome by a fit of coughing and breathlessness; and shrank from Abigail's solicitousness, as if wishing not to be touched. Abigail was reminded of a scene of many years previous,—why, at her own wedding-day banquet, in her parents' Contracoeur home:—when Georgina, in the midst of the fish course, began to cough and choke with such violence that it was feared she might have swallowed a bone: and Judge Kilgarvan suggested, in a brusque but not unkindly voice, that she betake herself upstairs until she was recovered from her fit, and less flushed, and "fit again for decent eyes." Poor Georgina!—she who was so proud, and so fastidious in her bearing, and so self-conscious! With her napkin hiding half her flaming face, she had had to suffer not only the discomfort of the coughing spell (caused by nothing more substantial than a mouthful of Burgundy wine) but the humiliation of feeling all eyes in the dining room upon her: and knowing that her artful pompadour had been shaken loose, and certain swaths of false hair, designed to disguise the thinness of her own, revealed to the keen eyes of the ladies.

Now, as then, Georgina had steadfastly resisted aid; and Abigail, feeling re-buffed, took note of the ghost-reflections of herself and her cousin in one of the large mirrors: the one tall, pale, alarmingly thin, with a skin that seemed to ra-diate white heat; the other much shorter, and plumper, and healthier in her skin tone and general bearing,—yet, it seemed, far less *intriguing*. Though they stood near each other, the two women gave every impression of being absolute strangers; figures in a coolly executed mural, that hinted of no tender ties of blood and kinship. "Nay, do not fuss, Abigail," Georgina managed to say, when her breath was shakily restored, *"I am quite all right."*

Impatient with waiting. With longing. So lonely. So hungry. These many years. O cruel belovèd Mother: our time now approaches.

She had nodded off to sleep, it seems, her diary sliding from her lap and her stubbed quill pen quite lost in the languorous folds of the bed. Yet she was able to bestow another kiss on Baby's warm brow; and to give the wicker cradle a fi-nal rocking caress; and to extinguish the lamp's flame, that voluptuous shadows might rush forward, from the bed-chamber's niches and mirrors, to embrace her. *O Mother. O belovèd. O cruel. These many years . . .*

Why did the sight so disturb?—angels with the cruel-hooked wings of bats or vultures, all apulse with their secret life, the painted flesh they inhabited, which did not satisfy them. An angel most lewdly stroked the strings of his mandolin while a companion angel, female, with peacock's feathers of an oily slickness, strummed at her harp, squinting and dimpling. Abigail's head had grown heavy in the space of a few seconds. Her calfskin diary had been spirited away: ah, and the pen!—would not ink despoil the bed linens?

A baby or midget angel no larger than a rat, with comical wings that were but wisps of down sprouting from his shoulders, crouched at the Virgin's chaste foot, piccolo in hand, and carmine lips pursed in an attitude of kissing, or suck-ing: such boldness!—but then he was naught but a babe, and knew no better. Surprised by pain, Abigail whimpered aloud, pushing the small head from her breast. Why, how was it possible, Charleton had slipped into her bed, and burrowed beneath the covers, and opened her nightgown? He had never done such a thing before: and now his lips were greedy, and pulled with an amazing violence at poor Abigail's nipple—! *Impatient. Impatient. O cruel belovèd* . . .

Close about her were fluttering wings, and high-pitched anxious cries, and a tumult of flesh,—ruddy, and creamy-pale, and starkly white; on all sides mouths, sucking lips, bared teeth; eyes that winked and glittered. *O Mother: cruel Mother! We have waited so long!* Abigail drew breath to scream but could not utter a sound, for, of a sudden, the babe's gums grew teeth, of a remarkable sharpness, which fastened in her flesh and could not be shaken away. Flushed cheeks,—dimpled bellies,—mouths, and lips, and tongues: so many: and Infant Jesus's ravenous mouth at her breast, wildly sucking her life from her. *It is our time. It is our time. You cannot resist.* "Monsters," Abigail cried, "—and devils: how dare you touch me thus? *I am not your mother.*"

Yet it seemed she could not resist: and the lapping and sucking noises grew louder: for if, in a frenzy, she pushed one heated face aside, did not another, equally greedy, nudge forward to take its place? All desperately she tugged at the forelock of a great shambling boy-angel, a creature but flimsily clad, with protuberant blue eyes, and garish flushed cheeks, and lardy thighs and buttocks so disfigured by dimples, they appeared pocked: but tears of angry despair ran hotly down his cheeks,—how then could she deny him? "But spare Charleton! Spare my Charleton!" Abigail pleaded. Both her breasts, though already streaming blood, were taken up, in ravenous mouths, and sorely abused: no angel being willing to give way until, sated, sighing, he sank beside her, burrowing and clutching close. "I am sinful,—yet blameless," Abigail murmured. "O dear God have mercy—." The very wall beside her head echoed in uncouth laughter, amidst the drunken sound of pipes, and horns, and mandolins, and tambourines. Slippery as an eel, an infant cherub crawled exhilarant to the foot of the bed, beneath the covers, to suck, with unparalleled audacity, at Abigail's toes—! Whereupon a swoon of such incalculable sweetness overtook her, she had no breath with which to protest: and no words: for it seemed the very Devil clutched her fast in his grip, and would not release her.

The Keening

OUR TIME IS SIX WEEKS PREVIOUS; our setting, the gravesite of Chief Justice Erasmus Kilgarvan, in the Temperance Vale Cemetery. For it is here that a most puzzling event occurred, even as Reverend De Forrest led a small contingent of mourners in a final prayer for the repose of Mr. Kilgarvan's soul.

Of a sudden, it seemed that a peculiar alteration of the air defined itself: the wintry sun, though hidden all morning behind cruel-ribbed banks of cloud, now glared forth, and harshly illuminated certain granite and marble surfaces in the cemetery; and, with especial malevolence, the high-polished surface of Erasmus Kilgarvan's ebony casket. Why, it seemed for a disconcerting instant that the very stones might speak! Then, to the amazement of all, an uncanny sound lifted: faint, musical, aggrieved, yet subtly angry; of so eerily poignant a quality, it could scarcely be attributed to the cry of a mere bird or animal. Yet it did not seem to be human: nor was it issuing from any of the mourners assembled close about the Kilgarvan tomb.

Numerous persons glanced up in surprise, and some alarm. But none of the deceased's daughters was weeping; Miss Georgina in particular, standing stiff beside her uncle Simon Esdras, her face nearly hidden behind a black muslin veil, gave no outward sign of distress. The sound retreated; then lifted yet again, and defined itself as a high-pitched tremulous wail, or *keening*, of such inexpressible grief, it was all but unbearable to hear.

Ah, what a temptation it was, for the youngest of the mourners, to investigate the source of the sound: but of course no one wished to interrupt Reverend De Forrest's concluding prayer. Even young Xavier Kilgarvan stood his ground, his head bowed in an attitude of prayer, though his sensitive nerves were roused at once; and he knew himself in the presence of *mystery*.

I hope it is not to young Xavier's discredit that he felt some small disappointment that the funeral ceremony at Grace Episcopal Church had proceeded with no remarkable interruptions: for there had been a most alarming rumor, spread promiscuously through town, that divers lowlife persons would rush into the church to disrupt the prayers,—these being enemies of the deceased. But all had proceeded with a tedious sort of solemnity; and the lengthy funeral procession, snaking its slow way through town, had rather more evoked awe and frowning apprehension than any visible expression of malcontent. Then, too, the late Chief Justice had been provided with a substantial police escort,—the which assuredly discouraged acts of mischief.

"Can it be," young Xavier inwardly wondered, "that my hateful uncle will be laid in his grave in *peace?*"

A curious sort of impiety, one might think: but it must be recalled that the boy had been fed, since earliest childhood, all sorts of confused tales of the way in which his father, Lucas, had been disinherited by Phillips Goode Kilgarvan, on that gentleman's very deathbed: to the great advantage of Erasmus and Simon Esdras. And, too, at the time of the Glen Mawr murders, Xavier was but a fresh-cheeked lad of sixteen, who liked to imagine opposition, and actual enmity, where perhaps there was naught but indifference.

Though it was often charged against Xavier Kilgarvan, in later years, that he had been a Free Thinker, or an Anarchist, or a traitor to his class,—indeed, a born troublemaker—from boyhood onward, the facts are otherwise: for our young man, though bristling with every sort of adolescent impulse, and nursing, as it were, a smoldering species of resentment, was very much a child of his time. It would have greatly incensed him to hear reasoned arguments against the Episcopal Church; or against his conception of the Divine Power of the Universe. (Fortunately, the youth had been but slightly exposed to such atheistical notions as Darwinism, Communism, and Anarchism, though he had found Mr. Reade's curious *Martyrdom of Man* in a secondhand bookstore, and intended to peruse it soon.) While kneeling at his daily prayers Xavier oft pondered over certain principles of faith which vexed him, as they were so slippery to grasp; but he had not the sensibility of the doubter. Already, though hardly more than a child in years, he had essayed to bring together the fundamental principles of his religious faith and his "detective's" faith,—for he had long fancied, in secret, a career of crime detection. "The Universe is so constructed, I believe, that *balance* and *justice* are inherent in it," he thought, knitting his smooth brow,"—God the Father being the highest manifestation of Truth, and Jesus Christ our sole means of apprehending that Truth. Yet," he sighed, running impatient fingers through his curly hair,"—I must confess that these are but words to me; and I am bound to put my faith in,—faith."

As it was Lucas Kilgarvan's stubborn dream that, of his several sons, one or two at least might become gentlemen, despite the family's loss of fortune, he had enrolled Xavier in the prestigious Winterthurn Academy for Boys: albeit the tuition was extremely high, and Mr. Kilgarvan might well have used the money to settle some of his debts. At school, however, Xavier managed to excel in most of his studies; and evinced a quick, inquisitive mind, to the delight of his teachers. He was discovered to have a natural if undisciplined flair for drawing; an energetic sort of talent for music; and, in his spare hours, he liked to construct experimental models for his father's toymaker's workshop (albeit his successes quickly bored him, and his failures roused him to fits of ill temper). Unknown to his parents, he had acquired, since the age of thirteen, an alarming appetite for nickel-and-dime novels of the trashiest,—nay, the most lurid— species: and surreptitiously exchanged with his classmates every manner of adventure tale, of the Wild West, the Seven Seas, and "crime detection," which the majority of the Academy boys read with shameless avidity when they ought rather to be studying their Caesar.

He was proud rather than vain, despite his angelic good looks, the main source of his irritation being the fact that his family had "come down" so visibly in the world: for he knew how the Kilgarvans of Wycombe Street were oft designated, with chilling dispatch, as the "poor" Kilgarvans,—to distinguish them from their wealthy relatives who lived at Glen Mawr. And, ah!—how deep the insult cut into the sensitive youth!

Likenesses of Xavier Kilgarvan as a boy betray such classic masculine beauty, it is not to be wondered at that Miss Georgina should suspect her young cousin and her young half-sister of "romantic" mischief: for, with his Grecian profile, and his dreamy opal-gray eyes, and his olive-pale complexion so readily suffused with warmth, and, framing all, his abundant, lustrous, ebony-black curls,—

how should Xavier fail to suggest a type of precocity that is both innocent and childlike, yet gravely unsettling,—and, withal, especially disturbing to those who have had some experience with romance of the more delirious sort, and its attendant tragedies? (For it was well known through Winterthurn that poor Georgina had suffered a broken heart in her youth.)

So it came about that Georgina imagined that her handsome young cousin Xavier,—whom, in truth, she scarcely knew!—was boldly staring at her, with the intention of "penetrating" her brain; and that he cast improper eyes upon Perdita,—even as the party of some thirty mourners stood assembled on one of the loftiest ridges of the cemetery, before the noble granite mausoleum of the Kilgarvans.

Indeed, in his restlessness, Xavier had allowed his gaze to settle upon the twelve-year-old Perdita: and it began to perplex him, that this mere child, whom he had hardly noticed in the past, now radiated so somber, yet so potent, a girlish beauty, he found himself quite strangely absorbed. "Girls" as such interested him not at all; "romance" was but a word,—and an unappealing word at that. And he quite naturally felt some animosity toward all the Kilgarvans of Glen Mawr,—whom it pleased him to consider his and his father's enemies.

It was while Xavier stood staring in his cousin's direction that the air so radically altered, and the sun seemed to burst forth from a dozen blinding angles, reflected from tombstones on all sides; and the unearthly keening sound materialized, to the distress of the mourners. Alas, what was it?—from whence did it issue? Rising as if from the grasses underfoot, or falling with exquisite lightness from the boughs of the agèd beech trees,—an expression of sorrow lightly tinted, it seemed, with anger,—now joined by another, and that by yet another: a chorus of grief never before heard in Winterthurn.

Then, of a sudden, before it could be distinctly *heard*, the sound dropped away.

Xavier Kilgarvan's senses were roused at once, but he knew not how to behave: and bethought himself that perhaps he had imagined it, and must not cause any disruption while Reverend De Forrest continued with his prayer.

Scarcely five yards away stood Miss Georgina herself, who betrayed not the slightest awareness of having heard anything out of the usual: a commanding presence, even on this morning of grief, in a black silk-and-wool mourning costume only spartanly adorned with ribands, and a very plain black hat, and a fur-lined woolen traveling cape (from out her mother's trousseau of forty-odd years previous, it was whispered, and, alas, somewhat moth-eaten): her head only slightly bowed, as if pride in the midst of her unparalleled sorrow, and in her station, kept her thus erect,—and, indeed, scornful of weakness. *Does all of Winterthurn watch?* the stiff-backed spinster seemed to muse. *Very well, then: I shall deprive them of any spectacle.*

All covertly, though, I suppose, somewhat rudely, Xavier observed his elder cousin: noted the splashes of damp on her traveling cape; noted her mismatched gloves—though each was black, their subtly warring textures proclaimed them unmated; noted the way in which her black muslin veil was sucked arrhythmically against her nose and mouth, and then released, and again sucked back, by the action of her hoarse breathing, leaving a patch of damp . . . Studying the "Blue Nun" thusly, Xavier felt a small pang of pity for her, rather than sympathy, for she *had* been entirely devoted to her father; and, though she had always turned a chill eye upon his entire family, rebuffing even Mrs. Kilgarvan's overtures of friendship, he could quite see that her life was "tragic" in the loose sense of the word. "*Cousins* we are said to be, by blood," Xavier thought, "yet *strangers* we are in fact: though more irrevocably divided than most strangers, in that we can never become *friends*."

Close beside Miss Georgina stood Simon Esdras, in whom Xavier had a more than ordinary interest: for he had closely perused his father's agèd copy of *A Treatise on the Probable "Existence" of the World*, which was said to have been published on the philosopher's nineteenth birthday: and found it a most tantalizing and knotty document, quite incomprehensible as to its meaning! Xavier had inquired of his father what the argument of the *Treatise* was—in brief: Did the world exist, or no; or was there merely the *probability* of its existing? But Lucas Kilgarvan had said he didn't know; and was of the opinion that the *Treatise* was proclaimed an act of youthful genius, and its author touted as another Spinoza, or Aristotle, by philosophers on both sides of the Atlantic, precisely because one could discern no "argument" in the book at all. The first *Treatise* was followed by a second, after a space of more than a decade, and though this monograph—*A Treatise on the "Probable" Existence of the World*—was said to thoroughly refute the claims of the first, Xavier could make very little sense of it; and tossed it irritably aside after a few hours' examination. (Which, indeed, was the general response, for the second *Treatise,* according to Xavier's father, "fell upon deaf ears," and received no reviews or notices, save one indignant dismissal in the English journal *Mind.*) At the age of forty-seven Simon Esdras published a third *Treatise,* by way of a private press located at Nautauga Falls, but this, *A Treatise on the Probable Existence of the "World,"* Lucas Kilgarvan did not own; and Xavier had not yet taken the time to locate it, in the public library, or to borrow it from the headmaster at the Academy: for he had begun to mistrust his ability to reason philosophically. The third *Treatise* was said to have met with slightly more enthusiasm than the second, though not proclaimed a work of genius: which disappointing response so outraged Simon Esdras, he declared he would henceforth boycott the world of philosophy, and never publish again. Yet a slim pamphlet of thirty-odd pages did appear, on his sixty-second birthday, with the formidable title *A Prolegomenon Concerning a Treatise on the "Probable Existence" of the World,*—this privately printed document exciting interest in only one fellow thinker, of whom no one in Winterthurn had ever heard: Charles Sanders Peirce, at this time residing in lonely exile in a small Pennsylvania town three hundred miles away. (It was believed that Peirce's lengthy letter to Simon Esdras proved gratifying, and somewhat restored his faith in the ability of the philosophical world to recognize his gifts: yet, such was Simon Esdras's indifference to social occasions, and his scorn for the "folly of seeking out persons in the flesh," that he and Peirce were never to meet; nor did their correspondence continue.)

Nonetheless, Xavier harbored some interest in his uncle: and might well have tried to befriend him had not the older gentleman behaved ambiguously in the matter of the contested will (announcing himself as indifferent to its outcome, yet profiting, nevertheless, from the judgment against Xavier's father); and had not the Manor been declared "off limits" to him and his brothers, by all adult parties involved in the dispute. "For he is, at the very least," Xavier reasoned, "an unusual relative; and might very well have something to teach me." But if Simon Esdras had any awareness of his four nephews, let alone any special interest in the youngest, he had certainly never given any sign: and when the curious wailing sound began, and, for an accidental moment, Xavier and Simon Esdras locked eyes, there appeared to be no recognition in the older man's silvery-gray gaze,—nor did his affable countenance betray any agitation beyond a fluttering of pale eyelashes. An enigmatic personage, indeed!—for Xavier thought him, in his lifelong willful seclusion in pursuit of Truth, more remarkable even than his renowned brother Erasmus; and decidedly more "colorful" than Xavier's own father.

The queer luminous-gray tone of Simon Esdras's eyes, enhanced by the lenses of his pince-nez, reminded Xavier of cats' or owls' eyes,—reflecting rather than absorbing light. Yet, in his somewhat shiny black suit that fitted him so indifferently, a narrow swath of stubble unshaven on his chin, he had so unstudied and *human* an air, it was impossible not to feel a measure of affection for him: and Xavier fancied he saw a distant smile playing about his thin lips . . .

Clothed in identical black capes of a heavy cotton-woolen fabric that possessed an unflattering sheen, wearing kindred black hats that might well, by the look of them, have been handed down by Georgina, the sisters Thérèse and Perdita maintained their wooden posture, at Simon Esdras's left elbow; and stood with heads meekly bowed, and cheeks agleam with tears, even as the eerie keening sound arose—though Xavier believed he could discern a nervous tic in the elder's eye; and sweet little Perdita, startled into glancing upward, revealed, through the gossamer veil that chastely covered her eyes, a gaze of extraordinary intensity. (And was not the reddened tip of her nose uniquely charming, Xavier thought; and the tremulous air of her pale parted lips; and her tiny foot, tightly encased in a black kidskin shoe, which peeped out, as it were, beneath the hem of her heavy dress?) But in the next instant, as the sourceless noise dropped away, the sisters the more resolutely bowed their heads, and clasped their dark-gloved hands against their bosoms. Did they hear? Xavier wondered. Or did they not? Yet he forbade himself to stare; for he knew that, at the very least, rude behavior on his part, at his uncle's gravesite, would only distress his mother.

Xavier listened closely but heard no further sound, save Miss Georgina's hoarse rapid breathing; and the random and forlorn calls of birds. The irreverent notion struck him that the dead man had awakened of a sudden, to discover himself imprisoned in his satin-lined coffin,—as, indeed, he had imprisoned so many criminals in the course of his career: and those faint wailing cries of sorrow and anger,—might they not be his, sounding distantly from out the coffin? A most disagreeable fancy!

But Xavier deemed himself too much a rationalist to believe in such things. "That the dead are thoroughly dead, to this life at least, no matter how they are transmogrified in Heaven (or in Hell)," Xavier thought, "I take to be self-evident, and shall never question. Such superstitions are for the untutored, and certain members of the female sex." Yet he could not resist the judgment that, if any gentleman in Winterthurn deserved so hideous a fate as to awake imprisoned in his own coffin, it was Chief Justice Erasmus Kilgarvan.

When news of Erasmus Kilgarvan's death spread through Winterthurn, it was greeted with some measure of incredulity, for so vigorous had the elderly jurist been, so very much in the public eye, that one might have thought him indestructible: with his ruddy flushed skin, piercing silver-gray eyes, sturdy, compact, and rather bullish body, and, withal, his air of ceaseless energy: the very *power* residing in his soul. That he was felled by a stroke while addressing the courtroom seemed in a way apt, for, as the outspoken Miss Imogene Westergaard observed, upon hearing the news of her neighbor's demise, it was the only way in which old Erasmus might be cut down,—by a lightning-bolt, so to speak, issued with no warning.

Though Erasmus Kilgarvan was a familiar and much-admired presence about town, dining out four or five evenings a week, in private homes, or in one or another of his clubs,—amongst them, the Winterthurn Yacht Club and the prestigious Corinthian Club—he was one of the more temperamental of the several well-to-do "bachelor-widowers" in Winterthurn society: and could not always be trusted to suffer fools gladly in his hosts' drawing rooms. Gregarious and even somewhat sybaritic as he was; loving rich foods, alcoholic spirits, good-natured ripostes, and anecdotes of a colorful or even slightly risqué nature; a "jolly fellow"; a "man among men"; a gallant amongst the ladies; an indefatigable charmer when he wished to be so—nevertheless he held the Law in such high regard, he might fly into a rage if certain ideals, judgments, or sentences were questioned; and had acquired, over a period of forty years, a reputation as a jurist of stern and unparalleled *purity*. (Which is to say that, unlike the majority of his associates, and even his "cronies" in town, Erasmus Kilgarvan could not be bribed: nay, not even swayed by sentiments of a personal or pragmatic nature.)

It was a matter of debate amongst the ladies as to whether the Judge's porcine features inclined toward the handsome, or toward the disagreeably smug; or whether the striking effect of his bald, blunt, bulletlike head was felicitous, or otherwise; nor was there widespread consensus as to whether he had "treated" his two wives well, or had behaved admirably in summoning his daughter Georgina back from New York City, where she had been attending college, that she might nurse him back to health,—and remain with him as his companion, forever afterward. (As to the matter of the suitor, Mr. Guillemot: a number of the ladies frankly believed that Erasmus had driven the feckless young man away—but this is idle conjecture, and not to be credited.) Debatable too was the Judge's procedure, in scrupulously following the *letter of the Law,* and complying with his senile father's wish to disinherit his half-brother Lucas *completely:* and the continued wisdom of his severity, in regard to his three daughters. (Georgina, it seems, soon ceased to give him any difficulty, and settled in, as it were, to a life of domestic seclusion, in her early thirties; at the time of Erasmus's death, Thérèse and Perdita were driven each schoolday morning to the Parthian Academy for Girls, by the Negro servant Pride, and picked up again each afternoon, promptly at three o'clock: rarely allowed to visit their classmates' homes, and only once or twice yearly given the privilege of staying late for tea, at the headmistress's residence.) Such systematical severity, some observers thought, inclined to excess, for the girls *were* young and attractive, and might have enjoyed harmless schoolgirl friendships; but others, perhaps more reasonably, believed Erasmus eminently practical in wishing to shield his daughters, at their impressionable age, from certain unpleasant facts of life. Had not the world grown disagreeably motley and fast-paced, in the past several decades?—and had not poor Georgina herself been cruelly wounded, by her headstrong ventures into it?

"It is only out of love that Erasmus acts with so adamant a paternal solicitude," Reverend De Forrest frowningly said, "and I think we would all be grievously in error to offer criticism where we are only ignorant."

Though controversial in these divers ways, Erasmus Kilgarvan was assuredly *not* controversial in his fierce devotion to the Law, and in his unbending efforts to render justice where it was due. As his associates of many years argued, the Judge was, in truth, loath to condemn and punish; but, as he dwelt in a fallen, sinful world, where innocence might well be defined as the *unfulfilled potential for evil*, and guilt itself was but *a matter of degree*, he was obliged to take his responsibilities seriously: and is to be forgiven, I hope, for his steadfast belief that he was ordained by God, as well as by the State, in his judicial role. "Mercy is a luxury," he frequently said, in defending a prison sentence of especial harshness, or, indeed, a death sentence, "while Justice is notoriously frugal. The one is very easy to scatter about, and will draw friends, as honey draws flies; the other wins precious few friends, and numberless enemies. But when God shows us our duty, *we must follow it.*" Nor would he consent to surrender his onerous burden, when advancing years brought with them certain vexing infirmities,—gout, dyspepsia, shortness of breath and temper, and a growing deafness in one, or both, ears.

(As to whispered slanderous charges that Erasmus Kilgarvan naturally inclined toward the prosecution in any case, and was apt to express sardonic views over the strategies,—whether bumbling or expert—of those defense attorneys unfortunate enough to argue before him, these are, I think, quite groundless; and enjoy coinage only in a slacker, more lenient era, when life and property are so cheaply held even by jurists, that negligible sentences are handed down daily, and criminals are soon freed, to commit further crimes against the innocent.)

Heavy fines, incarcerations of many years, death by hanging: these sentences Erasmus Kilgarvan delivered with an air of solemn vigor that contrasted wondrously with his puckish private manner, revealed at the Corinthian Club, where he could unbutton, as it were, and relax, and speak frankly. Rarely did he jest at the expense of the poor wretches he had sent to the gallows; but he was not so intolerably pious a judge as to forbid his drinking companions to do so. Dr. Colney Hatch, in reminiscing over the grand old days of Erasmus Kilgarvan's reign in Winterthurn, expressed the view commonly held, that it was an inexplicable oversight that the Judge was never named to the Supreme Court of the United States: a miscarriage of justice that must have deeply wounded the principal, though, being a gentleman to his fingertips, of course he never breathed a word about it. As Reverend De Forrest said of Judge Kilgarvan in his heartfelt funeral oration, he labored "not for earthly glory, but in the service of his God." And this judgment, I think, remains uncontested.

The most luridly publicized of the numberless cases tried before Erasmus Kilgarvan was, as the reader might recall, that of Miss (or Mrs., as she titled herself) Hester Vaugh, a good many years before the time of our present narrative. This painful, and, indeed, still controversial case, studied in law schools until the present day, brought Erasmus Kilgarvan to the attention of the populace; and subjected him to numerous charges and insults delivered by a particularly noisome gaggle of "Suffragettes," led by Miss Elizabeth Cady Stanton. (Indeed, the Hester Vaugh case, and Judge Kilgarvan's refusal to alter his stand on it, was very likely the initial cause of the rift betwixt him and his young half-brother, Lucas.) The young woman, Vaugh, seventeen years of age at the time of her arrest for infanticide, had been a common housemaid in the domestic establishment of a family named Poindexter, in South Winterthurn; evidently of loose and unformed morals, she allowed herself to be seduced by her employer, and was impregnated; and, after being evicted from the household by her gravely offended mistress, she possessed no more presence of mind than to *illegally trespass* on property owned by the Empire State–Chesapeake Railroad,—giving birth to her bastard offspring in an unheated tenement building, in such crude and filthy conditions that it was not to be wondered at, that the infant survived a scant hour or two.

All of Winterthurn was outraged, though the more proper sort of lady did not wish to acknowledge her awareness of the scandal; several gentlemen of the cloth made Hester Vaugh the subject of their sermons, on the tragic fruits of sin and the ever-growing immoralism of the times. After a much-publicized trial of some ten days, attended by hundreds of persons and presided over by Associate Justice Erasmus Kilgarvan (at that time but a youthful figure of thirty-eight), a jury of twelve Winterthurn citizens found the defendant *guilty of murder in the first degree:* guilty, indeed, of an "unnatural dereliction of maternal duty, in bringing about, by failing to prevent, the death of a helpless infant."

The Vaugh person was duly sentenced to death by hanging, in compliance with the statute: but, before the execution could be carried out, one or another muckraking journalist from downriver seized upon the lurid tale, and inflated its significance (with such emboldened headlines as A WINTERTHURN TRAGEDY: FALLEN MAIDEN & DOOMED BABE), bringing it to the attention of the idle and captious throughout the Northeast,—including, as it turned out, the rabble-rousing Suffragette group headed by the Stanton woman. What a misfortune for Winterthurn City, and for the earnest young Judge Kilgarvan—! Where the twelve gentlemen of the jury had seen a *murderess* of the most loathsome sort, compounding brutality with immorality, the free-thinking women saw a hapless *victim;* where Associate Justice Erasmus Kilgarvan had seen an unrepentant criminal who must be hanged by the neck until dead, certain overliberal persons saw a heroine who deserved freedom and the opportunity to "remake her young life,"—if not, indeed, sentimental pity and acclaim in the gutter press.

Was there ever such a perturbation in all the annals of Justice of Winterthurn!—with aroused and oft-uninformed passions on both sides; and families divided in sentiment; and meddlesome editorials and articles not only splashed across the Northeast but featured in England and on the Continent,—where, it is to be assumed, native-born criminals were in short supply.

The State Supreme Court, however, was not to be intimidated by the picketing of its stately halls, by free-thinking women and their hangers-on; or by a particularly meretricious series of articles entitled MALE JUSTICE & FEMALE SUFFERING, which appeared under the by-line of "Nellie Bly" (one Elizabeth Cochrane) for the *New York Tribune*. After due consideration of the original conviction and sentencing, and a close examination of the trial's proceedings under Erasmus Kilgarvan, the Supreme Court unanimously ruled to uphold the conviction; and issued a solemn statement, in which all the Justices concurred, that as death on the gallows commonly followed a conviction of murder in the first degree, Hester Vaugh's sentence was altogether just: and the Supreme Court saw no reason to interfere in the transactions of the lower court in this instance.

So it was, upon a pleasantly sunny day in June, by happenstance on Erasmus Kilgarvan's thirty-ninth birthday, the Vaugh murderess went to the gallows at the state prison in Powhatassie: so emaciated and broken she had to be carried to the platform in a chair (for, to compound her sin of infanticide, the unrepentant woman had attempted, in clumsy wise, to commit suicide by refusing to eat): so lost to all sense of decorum and Christian honor, she screamed at the chaplain who attended her, and vowed that she would return,—"in what guise I know not"—to take her revenge. Despite her weakened condition she was said to have put up a considerable struggle, and did not expire for some minutes, though her neck was snapped at once.

Thus, the notorious Hester Vaugh case, or scandal,—which had the unlooked-to effect of enhancing Erasmus Kilgarvan in the eyes of certain citizens: though that gentleman never ceased to explain that he had but followed the recommendation of the jury, and harbored no especial rancor for the defendant, any more than he harbored a stealthy sympathy. "Justice is duty," the youthful judge often said, "and the precise calibration of justice is a most exacting duty. But no man of the Law shrinks from such a task."

The reader may be interested to learn that, despite her coarse threats of revenge, Hester Vaugh assuredly did *not* return to Winterthurn in any guise: nor did the Poindexter family, or the twelve jurors, or, indeed, Erasmus Kilgarvan himself, suffer any unusual consequences as a result of the trial and its sordid publicity,—beyond, that is, the ordeal of embarrassment itself, which, many of the principals said, was punishment enough. For the better sort of Winterthurn citizen, then as now, rightly shuns the vulgar glare of *publicity*.)

As for the more recent case of the contested will of Phillips Goode Kilgarvan, which had taken place some three years before Xavier's birth: evidently it happened that, on his deathbed, the eighty-seven-year-old gentleman had taken it into his head to *disinherit* his youngest son, for what specific reason or reasons was never altogether clear (though Lucas had angered and disappointed him numberless times, by failing to establish a career for himself, and by marrying with precipitate haste, and by neglecting to show proper filial regard): this decision being made of a sudden, with, it seems, his very dying breath, in the company of four upstanding witnesses,—Erasmus, Simon Esdras, Dr. Colney Hatch, and the Kilgarvans' attorney, Mr. Henry Peregrine. That the dictated will which was to negate all preexisting wills possessed an air of the febrile, the disordered, and the rash; that Phillips Goode's signature was decidedly shaky, and granted to be his only by the sworn insistence of the witnesses; that certain abusive remarks pertaining to "tainted blood" and "half-bred blood" were not excised,—these troubling factors should not, I hope, sway our thinking on the matter, for, though the litigious young Lucas Kilgarvan fought the will up to the highest court in the State, and went about town sorely abusing both his brothers, and swore that his father had been coerced, or that the entire will was a fabrication, the final judgment was *against* him and *for* his brothers: the Justices of the Supreme Court ruling unanimously that a father has the privilege of disinheriting an unruly son, up to the very moment of death, provided he is, as the witnesses swore Phillips Goode assuredly *was*, "of sound mind and body."

A most disagreeable case, which caused many a tongue to wag in Winterthurn and elsewhere: but, in truth, an altogether simple one, in which fairly clear principles of law were evoked. (As to the whispered innuendos regarding Lucas Kilgarvan's "tainted blood,"—and the reader will recall that Georgina spoke of Lucas as a "half-breed" as well—this relates to the fact that Phillips

Goode's second wife, Miriam D'Ivers of Mt. Moriah, was said to have been
very distantly related to a French settler by the name of Camille D'Ivers, who
had, in the early 1700s, taken for a mistress, or actually wed, an Oneida Indian
squaw, which unfortunate union evidently resulted in issue. So many generations later, after the passage of so many turbulent decades, one might well
conclude that the "taint" of mixed blood had been entirely dissolved, in
Anglo-Saxon solution: but this supposition Phillips Goode did not make, it
seems, once the fiery passions of romantic love had ebbed, and the flaws in the
woman he had wed became distinct. Whether the old tale of tainted blood, or,
indeed, the "blood" itself, had any actual influence on Lucas Kilgarvan's behavior, one cannot presume to judge: but it was a matter that Xavier, of all the Kilgarvan sons, took most to heart, and rarely allowed himself to speak of, for his
adolescent pride was sorely wounded; and he could not abide it, that any of his
schoolmates might pity him for so ambiguous a connection . . .)

Of Winterthurn mysteries of a minor and domestic sort, none excited sympathetic comment more frequently amongst persons of society,—not excluding
even Erasmus Kilgarvan's most intimate male companions, who had known
him all their lives—or aroused more speculation, than *why*, and *how*, a man of
such superior intelligence and proven canniness (at forty-three the youngest
Chief Justice, at the county level, in the State's judicial history) chanced to
marry not one, but two, women of *inferior mettle*,—leaving the luckless man a
widower twice over, with three daughters on his hands.

The first wife, Miss Vivian Battenberg, who died when Georgina was but
ten years of age, had been so self-absorbed, neurasthenic, and negligent in her
household duties as to have failed to appear downstairs at the Manor, fully
clothed, for the last several years of her life; the second, Miss Hortense Spies,
was a yet more pathetic presence at the Manor, dying under clouded circumstances (the consequence, it was said, of a spiritual malaise of an hereditary sort)
when Thérèse was not yet three years of age, and Perdita a sickly babe of
ten months.

Indeed, even Erasmus Kilgarvan's detractors could not fail to feel some pity for him, tinged with a measure of impatience, that he should twice err in choosing a mate: and, withal, prove incapable of siring a male heir to propagate his name. (Doubtless it angered him greatly that his half-brother, Lucas, should prove so very manly as to have fathered *four sons:* and these lads, by way of a young woman no more physically robust, it would seem, than either of Erasmus's wives.)

That a young man in his twenties might succumb to the blandishments of a beguiling face and figure (Miss Battenberg of Contracoeur being as pretty a débutante, in her season, as the Valley boasted), or the yet more subtle temptations of a considerable fortune (for the Battenbergs had invested, like the Kilgarvans, in munitions manufacturing and related enterprises, at that most fortuitous of times in our history,—the late 1850s),—that, in short, he might precipitously *fall in love,* to repent at leisure, was not, in itself, puzzling: for, certainly, a number of Winterthurn marriages, embarked upon with touching idealism, soon ran aground upon the hardscrabble realities of daily life; and the riddlesome failure of charming young ladies to mature into worthy wives and mothers. (As an aside, I should mention here that Dr. Colney Hatch, the physician most frequently employed by the leading families of Winterthurn,—the Kilgarvans, the Westergaards, the Von Goelers, the De Forrests, the Peregrines, etc.—had oft expressed the intention of publishing a scientific study on this troublesome subject, closely investigating female incapacities as they are exposed in divers stages: childhood, puberty, early marriage and motherhood, menopause, and senility. He had hoped to establish an actual correlation betwixt the *anatomy* of the sex and its social, moral, and intellectual *destiny:* but, so overworked was this zealous gentleman, so frequently was he called, ofttimes in the middle of the night, to the boudoirs of hypochondriacal ladies who feared they were dying, and who *must* have him, that, I am afraid, he dissipated his energies; and, like many another dedicated physician of the older type, he surrendered all hope of fame, in the service of an indefatigable round of patients—!)

The melancholy love match betwixt Erasmus Kilgarvan and Vivian Battenberg, ending in the virtual disappearance, or "fading away," of the once-lively beauty, was, as I say, scarcely remarkable in itself. What puzzled Erasmus's relatives and small circle of intimate acquaintances was the poor man's misfortune, after an interval of seventeen sobering years, to marry *yet another* weak-minded, childish, and chronically neurasthenic woman in Hortense Spies: as prone to idiopathic disorders, household mishaps, and day- and night-time chimeras of the most morbid sort as the first Mrs. Kilgarvan. Phillips Goode threw up his hands in despair, as it were, over his eldest son's perplexing taste in women. "To sire sons who will survive for more than a few days," he said, "it is necessary to marry more than a pretty face, or a bewitching instep." The old gentleman was said to have been more broken in spirit than his son, after the premature birth, and death within a week, of a baby boy baptized Phillips Goode Kilgarvan II,— this piteous infant born after a labor of some twenty-odd hours, of the second wife Hortense. (At this time Thérèse was not twelve months old; and Perdita, of course, had not yet been born.)

Dr. Colney Hatch, whose experience with the Kilgarvan household was authoritative, thought it a tragedy for Erasmus that both wives, in their differing ways, were poorly suited for childbearing, and, indeed, for conjugal relations of the most conservative sort: the one being of a meager, bony frame, and inclining toward anemia and light-headedness; the other, of a spongy sort of plumpness, and inclining toward hemophobia. In addition to the common admixture of female complaints, originating in the uterus, each young woman suffered from a propensity for respiratory and digestive upsets; unforeseen allergies to those medications Dr. Hatch most frequently prescribed; fits of hysteria brought on by needless speculation upon the nature of salvation, damnation, Heaven, Hell, etc., which their brains were ill-equipped to ponder; insomnia; neuralgia; hypesthesia; bouts of hyperpnea; postpartum depression, the more exacerbated by sore, inflamed, easily bruised breasts, whose maternal milk was tainted by watery blood; and, most enigmatic of all, a veritable cornucopia of minor injuries, brought about, it seems, by sheer clumsiness of comportment—for there was never anyone in all of Winterthurn City like the mistresses of Glen Mawr Manor for toppling downstairs, colliding with doors, shelves, partitions, headboards, and the like!

Alas, that such gentle, pretty, sweet-natured creatures should prove so awkward, and so prone to accident, as to be forever bruising and banging their heads, torsos, pelvic regions, and thighs; cracking their ribs and blacking their eyes, in nocturnal tumbles from bed (caused, it was thought, by paroxysms of night-time terror); scratching, cutting, and even stabbing themselves, with letter-openers, hat-pins, carving knives, and the like; loosening their teeth; dislocating their fingers; spraining their wrists and ankles; even rupturing their spleens, in falls into the cellar that would have been comical had they been less pathetic. The first Mrs. Kilgarvan had accidentally set fire to her lovely brown hair, by leaning too near a candle; the second Mrs. Kilgarvan had so roughly shut her smallest finger in a closet door, the nail had turned black and fallen off. The one lost all appetite, and would have starved herself had not her husband and her physician forcibly intervened; the other acquired wild, exotic, ungovernable tastes, and would have gobbled down glue, starch, raw beans, berries, pen nibs, etc., had not the same gentlemen kept watch. Shortly after Georgina's birth, the first Mrs. Kilgarvan expressed so deranged a horror of nursing (for, she claimed, her infant girl was insatiable in her hunger, and wanted not merely mother's *milk*, but mother's very *blood*), and of cohabiting with her lawfully wed spouse, that she took to hiding in remote corners of the Manor, not excepting the "dungeon" in the oldest section of the cellar, which, in Colonial days, had been used as a sort of informal prison for misbehaving slaves, tenant farmers, and the like—! (Upon one shameful occasion, when a number of the Judge's associates were gathering in the drawing room, for an evening of whiskey, cigars, and forthright political discussion, the distraught Vivian Kilgarvan, at first nowhere to be found, was finally tracked down, so to speak, by the incensed husband himself, in a fetid corner of the cellar, where, naked inside her fur-lined traveling cloak, she sang to herself, and rocked to and fro, holding against her bosom not her own flesh-and-blood babe Georgina but a mere porcelain doll—!)

After the death of the first Mrs. Kilgarvan, the household quieted considerably: there being, apart from the numerous domestic staff, only Erasmus and his brother Simon Esdras (who, deeply absorbed in the writing of his *Treatise*,

rarely troubled to come downstairs to dine), and the motherless waif
Georgina,—a diminished family, assuredly, yet not, it seems, an entirely unhappy one. Sober, subdued, retiring, but contented: a halcyon period that came
to a rude end when a meddlesome Battenberg dowager, visiting the Manor
unannounced, declared that it was "unwholesome" for a thirteen-year-old girl
to live alone with her father and her eccentric uncle, in a household bereft of
feminine influence. Far from being insulted or enraged at this intrusion into his
domestic affairs, Erasmus Kilgarvan seems to have conceded the Battenberg
lady's point, and to have agreed to send his daughter away to school,—to the
Canandaigua Episcopal Female Seminary, in a bucolic region some two hundred miles to the west; and though the widower must have suffered pangs of
inordinate loneliness in the great house, he did not seek remarriage for nearly
two decades.

As for Miss Hortense Spies, the second Mrs. Kilgarvan,—the marriage
seems to have been ill-advised from the start, for Erasmus was some twenty-five
years older than his comely young spouse; and his ever-increasing judicial responsibilities, as well as a certain crankiness and irascibility of manner, militated
against an idyllic household. (All of Winterthurn speculated, too, as to the nervous hostility betwixt wife and stepdaughter—for were they not, Hortense and
Georgina, *very nearly the same age?*) An early pregnancy; the birth of Thérèse; a
second pregnancy, resulting in the death of the infant Phillips Goode II; yet another pregnancy, perhaps following too closely upon the others, resulting in the
birth of the undersized Perdita,—and soon afterward a lapse into such wayward
and unpredictable behavior, her distraught husband could no longer allow her
to appear in public.

How, and why, answering to what cruel logic, did this perverse change
come about?—that the second Mrs. Kilgarvan should, after a space of nearly
two decades, strive to emulate the first, *as if by unnatural sisterly rapport:* Miss
Hortense Spies, of one of Winterthurn's oldest families, so sweetly docile, so
unfailingly devout a young Christian woman, who in her virgin artlessness had
rejected, it was said, any number of gentlemen her own age, as they seemed in-
sufficiently "fired by idealism,"—she of the full soft bosom and hips, the wavy

chestnut-red hair, the childlike addiction to comfits, chocolate, and honey: shading, alas, by degrees into a slovenly attired harridan with bruised eyes, her fair skin raked by her own nails, her manner oscillating betwixt a leaden despondency and a shrill shrieking hysteria—? Dr. Hatch, finding evidence of fresh bruises, scratches, and cuts on those parts of his patient's body it was his professional duty to examine, confessed himself perplexed by the situation, for, it seems, the young Mrs. Kilgarvan had taken to *punishing herself,* even to the point of whipping her soft body with a riding crop!—which morbid practice, she had dully explained, "was nothing more than she deserved: being foul, sinful, and of no more worth than a piece of barnyard filth." Dr. Hatch firmly demurred; pointing out to the wretched woman that so mistreating her body, and thereby rendering herself ill-suited for the solemn duties of wifehood and motherhood, was in itself a sin, and must displease God greatly: whereupon the patient began to sob with all the abandon of a spoiled, sickly child, and her husband, who had been pacing nearby (the examination having taken place behind a screen, in the master bedroom at Glen Mawr Manor), fell of a sudden into such despondency, he began to shout and curse at her; and so forgot his friendship of long standing with Dr. Hatch, he ordered him from the room, as if the respected physician were a common servant—!

(Dr. Hatch afterward confided in an acquaintance, at the Corinthian Club,—which palatial retreat on Berwick Place the Judge frequented less regularly, as his marital situation presumably worsened—that he could not comprehend the sinister metamorphosis, save in terms of *an hereditary malaise,* in virulent union with *female pathology of an undefined sort.* Nor did his customary methods of treating such disorders, involving vinegar douches, vigorous daily purges,—by way of Epsom salts, laxatives, and cold-water enemas—and bloodletting,—by way of a rare subspecies of leech affixed to the female genitalia— appear to be having much salutary effect. "So mysterious is the alteration in young Mrs. Kilgarvan," the good doctor said pensively, "that, were one not a rationalist, and fervently on the side of progress, an hypothesis of 'demonic possession' might well be entertained.")

More and more frequently, the willful young woman absented herself from society; refused to heed her weeping baby girls; refused to admit Dr. Hatch into her presence; grew feverish over the reading of meretricious female romances,—among them *Villette,* found beneath a cushion in her boudoir after her death; and hid away, for long hours at a time, in the cavernous unheated attic, or in the chill Honeymoon Room (where, in a happier season, she and her bridegroom had spent their wedding night), or, most perversely, in the farthest reaches of the cellar with its low-beamed ceiling, and its numberless cobwebs, and its damp earthen floor. The alarmed housekeeper, subsequently dismissed by Judge Kilgarvan, told him she had distinctly heard her mistress *conversing with someone in the cellar:* a woman, it seemed, who had answered her in low, languid, drawling, somewhat mocking tones! (Though, of course, there was no one in the cellar—apart from the unhappy Mrs. Kilgarvan herself.)

As a consequence of the irresponsible tattling of servants, all of Winterthurn was to learn the tragic circumstances of Mrs. Kilgarvan's death, but a few days before the third birthday of her elder daughter: discovered, in an airless and foul-smelling corner of the cellar, dying in retching agony of a self-administered potion (diagnosed by the county coroner as *rat-poison paste, made of arsenic*), with a note scrawled in a miniature childish hand pinned to her bosom: *'Tis my own doing & no other—my belovèd Husband Erasmus is blameless— O pray for him & all who remain behind in the Vale of Tears: do not pray for Hortense, as she is DAMN'D & THE DEVIL'S OWN.*

(It was poor Georgina, returned at the end of a day of teaching at the Parthian Academy, who found the wretched woman only minutes before her death,— seeming to know by panicked intuition, as the servants afterward said, as soon as she set foot in the house, that *something frightful had happened.* And how she did cry and carry on, surrendering to helpless spasms of tears!—the stiff and rarely yielding stepdaughter now grieving for her father's young wife with as much selfless abandon as if it were her own mother, or sister, whom she had lost.)

Though it was widely claimed that Judge Kilgarvan had died most unexpectedly, seized by a massive stroke that paralyzed him in midbreath, and sent him crashing to the floor before the affrighted eyes of the entire courtroom, not a few persons had quietly noted, over a twelve-month or more, the elderly gentleman's increasing impatience with servants, and with his daughter Georgina, and a general acerbity of manner that might have betokened ill-health.

The Kilgarvans of Wycombe Street had themselves witnessed one of the Judge's more flamboyant outbursts, approximately three weeks before his death, when, leaving Grace Episcopal Church after the Sunday service, he had, it seems, lost his footing on a patch of icy sidewalk, and flailed out in a sudden rage against Miss Georgina, raining blows upon the abashed woman's head and shoulders with his walking stick, and shouting epithets of such vulgarity as one would have supposed a gentleman of his breeding and character would not know: the while the "Blue Nun," veiled as always, and encumbered by her heavy black skirts, meekly withstood the assault, until such time as Erasmus's arm wearied, and servants hastened to their aid.

Witnesses to this display of temper were deeply troubled, and many did their best to erase it from memory, for, in truth, this flush-faced old man with the clouded bulging eyes, and the head sleek and bald as a bullet, was *not* Chief Justice Erasmus Kilgarvan, in his essence: and they were hard put to interpret his spittle-flecked words,—"You are invincible! You shall conquer, in the end! *You*—and *you*— and *you!*"—uttered in rhythm with his blows, as tears sprang from his eyes, with as much despairing vehemence as if Miss Georgina were not one woman, but many.

Young Xavier Kilgarvan carried away with him this shocking spectacle of his "uncle"—or, to be precise, his "half-uncle"—behaving with such brutish anger, on the very steps of Grace Church; and is to be forgiven, I think, for the satisfaction with which he pondered it. Yet even Xavier, so prescient in certain things, was quite astonished at the news of the Judge's death—for, it seems, he had gloomily imagined the old man to be *immortal*.)

As to the circumstances of Erasmus Kilgarvan's death, which even his enemies could not fail to think unbefitting a person of his stature and dignity: these were especially ironic, in that, by sheer coincidence, he was handing down a sentence of some severity (upward of fifty years in the State Correctional Facility for Men at Powhatassie), when the convicted felon rose to his feet, and wildly waved his fist, and began to shout incoherent words to the effect that "God has claimed vengeance as His alone,"—whereupon Judge Kilgarvan was so stupefied at this rare act of impudence, in the hallowed marble-and-stucco interior of the domed Winterthurn County Courthouse, in *his* courtroom of so many years, that a weakened blood vessel in his brain snapped: and the poor man went mute in the midst of his speech: and, of a sudden bizarrely mottled (in lurid patches of crimson, pink, and white), in the face, fell to the floor clawing and tearing at his high starched collar, and at the neck of his judge's black gown. *And was never to rise again from where Fate had pitched him.*

So public a death, in so defiled a context; so cruelly timed; so ignominious as to its particulars—these factors rendered Erasmus Kilgarvan's death especially ironic; and could not fail to provoke the more superstitious amongst the populace into claiming that the convicted man *had called forth Divine wrath upon Judge Kilgarvan.* Alas, so hoary, and reasoned, and dispassionate a jurist, who had passed judgment on wrongdoers of every stripe, not excepting criminals of good and sometimes superior intelligence (which, as all practitioners of the Law will attest, adds a special challenge to the task): struck down, as it were, by the maniacal ravings of one Horace Godwit, of that tribe of poor whites who dwelt in the scrubby foothills south of Mt. Provenance, in the most wretched sort of squalor and moral debasement: how should the humiliation of it not outlive him, and taint his honor? It was the more unfortunate, that Godwit was a creature of the lowest sort, possessing, or feigning to possess, a sub-normal intelligence; that his trial had involved testimony so frequently lewd, the courtroom had had to be cleared of all spectators, including men; that a most poisonous and snarled congeries of tales had emerged, involving forced prostitution in the notorious lumbermen's brothels at Rivière-du-Loup, some ten miles northwest of Winterthurn City . . . Throughout the fifteen days of the trial, Judge Kilgarvan had exhibited an admirable formality that quite masked his abhorrence for the defendant, and for certain of the prosecution's witnesses (one of them being a Dr. Holyrod Wilts, a physician and, it was rumored, abortionist, in the hire of the brothel owners): he had displayed very little of the sickened revulsion he must have felt, as, by degrees, it came to light that Horace Godwit, though self-defined as a farmer, was actively involved in the brothel trade, and had sold several of his daughters (both legitimate and illegitimate) into white slavery: and, beyond this, most unspeakably of all, he had committed certain gross and unnatural crimes with his very own daughters,—*the youngest being but eleven years of age.*

Scarcely is it to be wondered at, then, that Erasmus Kilgarvan, interrupted in midspeech by this wretch's vainglorious outburst,— *"Vengeance is mine, sayeth the Lord! Vengeance is mine!"*—suffered so extreme a shock to his sensibility that his strained nerves broke; and, one side of his mouth twisting upward in a grimace of commingled rage, incredulity, and grief, he fell crashing to the floor, with as much stunning weight, it almost seemed, as the bronze bust of his own likeness, in Roman style, which had, but the previous autumn, been ensconced in the high-vaulted foyer of the Courthouse, alongside likenesses of George Washington, Abraham Lincoln, Julius Caesar, and, not least, Moses and Solomon, in their stern-browed manly glory.

As Reverend De Forrest concluded his remarks, stressing, a second time, the unsurpassed moral integrity of the deceased, and his devotion to the commonweal ("whereby public justice was ever favored above private interest"), the keening sounds lifted yet again, light, rarefied, melodic, sweetly elusive: and this time Xavier felt so inexpressibly yearning a sensation,—ah, how potent! how heart-swelling!—he could barely force himself to remain stationary, in reverent silence.

From whence did the haunting cries derive?—and what was their airy substance? Xavier sensed a kindred restiveness in the younger people present: his brothers Bradford, Roland (or Wolf, as he was often called), Colin—poor Colin, at nineteen as much a feckless *boy* as Xavier himself, and infinitely better-natured!—and, some yards away (but did he dare to look?—he must!) those altogether *strange* and *forbidden* cousins of his: Thérèse with eyes resolutely downcast, her prayerbook clasped to her meager bosom; Perdita betraying some agitation,—for surely she *did* hear the cries—and forgetting herself so completely, she chanced to raise her eyes, and to send darting glances about,—the which were scarcely diminished in their intensity by her veil, but, oddly, wondrously, enhanced!—or so it seemed to the lovestruck Xavier, who stared, and stared, as the sounds of an indefinable sweetness pulsed through his veins, and finely, lightly, tantalizingly, vibrated along his spinal column. And would she glance at him? And would he suffer the shock of *seeing*, and of *knowing*, as their eyes locked—?

So it was, the young cousins seemed to discover each other *for the first time:* and Xavier Kilgarvan, his adolescent blood in a tumult, his heart perceptibly accelerating its beat, experienced one of those lightning-strokes of yearning,—in which desire, passion, and love of the highest degree of purity are commingled—that not only illuminate our lives with ferocious intensity, but pierce them in two, and alter them forever.

The Spectacle in the Honeymoon Room

BY ELEVEN O'CLOCK IN THE MORNING of May 3, news of some "unknown and hideous catastrophe" at Glen Mawr Manor,—whether involving Simon Esdras, or the "Blue Nun," or the young sisters (who had not arrived for classes at the Parthian Academy), or another, unnamed party—had begun to spread through Winterthurn City with such uncanny swiftness that the boys in Mr. Pitt-Davies' mathematics class learned of it: and Xavier, being informed by a scrawled note from young Ringgold Peregrine, crudely tossed onto his desk, that MURDER had been committed at his relatives' grand house, was so astonished, and so gripped with a sudden panic (for, it must be confessed, the phantasmal image of Perdita was rarely distant from his imagination, and, in thinking of the Manor, he thought solely of her and her well-being), that, rather more with trancelike compulsion than brash defiance, he rose at once from his seat, and paid no heed to his startled schoolmaster,—not even to mumble a word of apology or excuse—and ran from the room.

So distressed was young Xavier, he left the Winterthurn Academy for Boys by way of the front entrance on Berwick Place, caring not a whit if he should be espied: and ran along the street, stopping passersby to inquire of them, if they knew what had happened at the Manor: with so little of his customary concern for his appearance, and for the decorum of his public behavior, that he minded not if one or two persons smiled at the spectacle of a youth dressed in the smart green blazer of the Academy, hurrying along, with his tie blown back over his shoulder, and his mop of curls all disheveled.

Along crowded Berwick Avenue he ran, pausing breathless to inquire at the tobacconist's, if anyone there had heard the news; bursting into the near-deserted offices of the *Gazette,* where the female employees stared; intruding in a private conversation betwixt a couple alighting from a carriage; threading his way through traffic along Union Avenue to make his impatient inquiry to several clerks, two Negro bootblacks, and a number of startled and offended gentlemen, in the high-domed gilded lobby of the Winterthurn Arms. But no one knew how to reply to him: and many persons quite amazed him by not knowing to which "Manor" he referred.

Down narrow Charity Street, where he paused to make a futile inquiry at the Sweet Shoppe; down Pinckney; down Hazelwit; again crossing Union Avenue; inquiring of pedestrians, news vendors, policemen, drivers of hackney cabs, the German proprietor of a butcher's shop on Water Street who thought him crazed,—until, panting, he flung himself through the doors of the brown-stone police headquarters at Water and Railroad: where, to his near-sobbing disappointment, he was turned brusquely away, and ordered to take his leave with more restraint than he had entered.

"But surely you can give me some information," Xavier protested, "for I am a relative of the Kilgarvans—I *am* a Kilgarvan—and must know whether a murder has been committed at the Manor: and whether a young girl has been injured."

But the police lieutenant behind the desk reiterated his command that Xavier leave the station; for not even high-and-mighty Academy boys could burst into headquarters, and cause a commotion.

Xavier then ran, in greater distress than before, westward along Railroad,—

now approaching Wycombe Street, which, for divers reasons, he wished to avoid—in order that he might confront his brother Colin, who worked at a livery stable close by: the plan quickly formed in his fevered brain that he would borrow cash from his brother, to hire a hackney cab to take him out to the Manor, a considerable distance away. "For it may be," the breathless youth murmured, "that *she* is in particular need of solace; and may even be awaiting my arrival."

Colin, alas, would prove incapable of lending Xavier so generous a sum,—less out of guarded frugality than as a consequence of his own indigence; so it happened that Xavier had to humble himself, and take the clattering Union Avenue trolley to the very end of the line; and, after that, to hike afoot nearly three miles along the Old River Road, until he came to the great arched gate of Glen Mawr Manor—which, as he might have foreseen, was locked fast, and guarded by sheriff's deputies.

Though a more enterprising adventurer or "detective" might have slipped stealthily away, to scale the twelve-foot limestone wall surrounding the Manor at a sequestered place, or, even, to approach it from the river (a challenge Xavier, Colin, and numerous schoolboy acquaintances had, in fact, taken on a half-dozen times in the past),—though Xavier knew from his habitual gorging of pulp novelettes (celebrating such ambiguous heroes as Eugène François Vidocq of the Parisian Sûreté, and the Bow Street Runners, and Inspector Bucket of Scotland Yard, and America's own George B. Jashber) that he might do better to investigate the "scene of the crime" himself, no matter the consequences,— he seems to have been sufficiently discouraged by the deputies' remarks as to give up, for the afternoon, such hopes: and to content himself with learning, from a deputy named Clegg (an acquaintance of his brother Wolf's), the following imperfect account of the "catastrophe" that had befallen the Glen Mawr Kilgarvans, sometime during the preceding night . . .

By eight-thirty o'clock the household was nervously undecided; by nine o'clock, in a tremor of alarm and apprehension, for no one, including Mrs. Whimbrel's devoted Irish nursemaid, knew quite what to do,—whether to continue knocking, ever more forcibly, at the bolted door of the Honeymoon Room; or whether to discreetly withdraw, under the assumption that Mrs. Whimbrel simply wished to slumber the morning through, and would appear downstairs, with little Charleton, when she wished.

(Yet, as the Irish girl half-tearfully repeated, it was *very* unlike her mistress to lie abed so late, for, back home, she rose each morning at seven o'clock, punctually; and the baby had never yet slept past dawn. Thus it seemed to her incontestable,—though she surely did not wish to cause any upset—that something had gone amiss; and why, indeed, *should the door be locked?*)

So the minutes passed, in whispered agitation; and none of the domestic staff knew what strategy to take.

Miss Georgina had arisen even earlier than was customary, it seemed, and had gone out, accompanied by old Pride, no one knew where: whether she had gone on an errand, afoot; or whether she had perambulated along the mist-shrouded bank of the river, in prayerful meditation, as, even in inhospitable weathers, she oft-times did,—no one was to know until, some hours afterward, the proprietor of Cutter Mills, on the Temperance Vale Road, would report his mystifying transaction with her: which only served to aggrandize, rather than diminish, the mystery. (Nor would the elderly Pride condescend to explain, to either the authorities or his fellow servants,—for he was of a sour and taciturn disposition, and generally disliked, even by the Negroes.)

As midmorning waxed, however, and the damp flurried snow began to melt, and the overcast sky gave way, by degrees, to a sunny expanse of blue more suitable to the season, it did become evident that something had happened to Mrs. Whimbrel: and that Miss Georgina must be summoned: for Simon Esdras rarely rose before eleven o'clock, and, even then, could not be relied upon to offer any advice concerning the household,—such matters being too trivial, and too vulgar, for his attention. (Both Thérèse and Perdita stood about confused, in their school uniforms, yet little inclined to leave the Manor: nor did the old Negro ready the carriage to take them into the city: for, it seemed, this was a weekday morning quite out of the ordinary,—though what was amiss no one knew, or dared to contemplate.)

Called forth, Miss Georgina responded with some irritation, as, to her way of thinking, her cousin might sleep until noon, should she so wish: nor did it seem entirely infelicitous that the Whimbrel infant had not yet begun to wail. But she rapped at the door soundly enough; called out Abigail's name; rattled the knob; and even pressed her ear against the oaken panels, yet could hear nothing. (The Irish nursemaid, and one or two of the Manor staff, had similarly applied their ears to the door, earlier,—and heard, or seemed to hear, noises within, of an indefinable nature.) "It seems Mrs. Whimbrel sleeps," Miss Georgina said, with knitted brow, and downcast shadowed eyes, "—and very soundly. Yet, I suppose, she cannot be allowed to sleep forever."

At this, Thérèse hurried forward, and asked if she might be of assistance: but Georgina, scarcely glancing at her, told her to return to her bed-chamber,— for what help might *she* be, unless she could reduce herself to a vapor, and wriggle through the keyhole? Some yards away, at the head of the stairs, little Perdita stood, sucking at a forefinger; but had more discretion than to approach Georgina. "The Honeymoon Room is locked,—decidedly locked—occupied— sequestered—taken over, indeed," Georgina murmured, again rattling the door-knob, and drawing back her lips in a joyless smile that revealed pale gums, "but, I suppose, it cannot be allowed to remain so, forever." And yet again she rapped on the door, with such sudden violence that one of her knuckles began to bleed.

So the morning of May 3 passed, with wretched slowness: and several of the servants took note of the curious fact that Jupiter, far from sniffing and nosing about the upstairs hall, as one might have expected of him, betook himself, shivering, and whimpering like a cowardly pup, to hide beneath the kitchen stairs—!

At last Simon Esdras was summoned, and came to join the others, at first vexed at being called away from his work (for he but dimly recalled that a houseguest had come to stay at the Manor, and had forgotten altogether that it was a niece from Contracoeur, with a babe in arms): then, realizing the gravity of the situation, he too rapped upon the door, and turned the knob, and called out, to inquire if something was amiss—but was greeted, like the others, with silence. By now, Miss Georgina's composure had begun to erode; like Thérèse she paced aimlessly about, and wrung her hands, and returned to knock on the door, with ever-increasing agitation. Simon Esdras commanded Mrs. Whimbrel to unlock the door, as everyone was gravely upset; he expressed his great disappointment in her that she should be so thoughtless as to throw a household of womenfolk into disarray; raising his voice, and betraying a faint tremor of alarm, he warned that her parents and her husband would be notified of her behavior, and that she should *never again be welcome at Glen Mawr.*

Alas, not even these threats could bestir her!—and now clocks throughout the house were chiming ten-thirty; and it became obvious that drastic measures must be taken.

Simon Esdras removed his pince-nez, and absently polished them on his sleeve, the while, in a voice of methodical and uninflected calm, he stated the logical alternatives: whether to smash the door in or remove it from its brass hinges; or to order one of the menservants to scale the outer wall of the house, and break a window. As Miss Georgina seemed not to hear, or to comprehend, he repeated himself: and again repeated himself,—"The one; or the other? The door; or the window?"—while a dozen servants milled uselessly about, and Thérèse sobbingly prayed aloud that no one was harmed.

How long the household might have remained at this snarled impasse, had not the child Perdita so precociously acted, one cannot speculate: but, of a sudden, she appeared running from the back stairs (where she had disappeared unnoticed), an ax from the woodshed in her slender arms, and an expression of affrighted resolution on her face—! It may have been that she proffered the unwieldy instrument to her uncle, or to her eldest sister, who shrank from touching it: or to one of the servants: but, as no one accepted it from her, she made the decision to use it herself; and, demonstrating a remarkable strength for one so tender in years, and so delicate of frame, she simply began to batter at the door,—once, twice, thrice, and yet a fourth time, and a fifth!—as the heavy oaken panels cracked and gave way, with sickening shrieks, beneath the ax's mortal blows!

Thus it was, little Perdita, gasping for breath, her wavy hair all atangle about her heated face, broke in the door of the Honeymoon Room: and exposed the hellish spectacle inside: which was of a species that defies description, even as, being viewed, it stuns and repulses the eye,—and threatens the observer with faintness.

For there, reclining gracelessly on the antique canopied bed, amidst blood-stained sheets, and torn silken spread, one plump white breast bared as if for nursing, lay the vacant-faced Abigail Whimbrel, scarcely recognizable as the robust woman of the previous day: humming tunelessly beneath her breath the old nursery rhyme of "Baby Bunting"; and, with piteous maternal solicitude, pressing against her bosom the limp, lifeless form of her belovèd baby: the which tiny figure could be seen even from a distance of some yards, to have suffered a savage assault,—part of the throat and torso, and much of the back of the tender head, having been, it seemed, *eaten away*.

"*Iphigenia*"

IN LATER YEARS IT WAS THOUGHT that Miss Georgina Kilgarvan began to publish her queer, crotchety, unmelodic poesy only after the disappearance of her suitor, and the death by "misadventure" of her young stepmother: but in truth this was not the case, for even as a schoolgirl at the Canandaigua Female Seminary she had placed, as it were, stealthily, certain riddlesome poems in the very literary magazine it was her responsibility to edit, under divers coy pseudonyms—one of them being "Iphigenia."

As to what purpose lay behind this subterfuge, and why, indeed, the name "Iphigenia" had been expressly chosen: why a young miss still in her teens should lock herself away in her room, or prowl about the woods like Crazy Eliza of old—a madwoman of Colonial years still celebrated in ballads, oft-times of a bawdy nature, in the hill country—brooding, and shunning company, and scrawling lines in a school notebook that might have been put to better use; and what, in fact, her obscure versifying meant: no one, not even Georgina's childhood acquaintance (for it would be to inflate the significance of their relationship, to call her *friend*) Miss Clarice Von Goeler, could have said.

Certain early verses, published under her own name, did not displease her family, and even gave promise of some native talent: for, consider the solemnity, the precocious wisdom, and the near-perfection of the rime, in these lines penned by Georgina in memory of her deceased mother:

> *All that, poor mortal, to thee blinds, to God is day,*
> *And all our fates, He knoweth:*
> *Thus rest assured, 'tis no confus'd way*
> *The spirit eternal goeth.*

(Owing to an unfortunate falling-out between the two families,—the Kilgarvans of Winterthurn City and the Battenbergs of Contracoeur—following close upon the untimely death of Georgina's mother, it happened that Georgina was not able to visit her mother's grave for many years, and then in secret defiance of her father's wishes: for the Battenbergs had been quite bellicose in their insistence that their daughter be buried at home, in the Battenberg family plot in Contracoeur; and Erasmus Kilgarvan had been so despondent, and, it may be, had harbored so potent a silent fury against his departed wife, that he had not protested. Nor had Georgina been allowed, owing to the Judge's extreme sensitivity on the subject, to speak of her mother in his presence, let alone betray effusive tears and sentiment. Yet, when with childish hope she presented him with this little poem, it was said that he knit his brow, and brushed tears from his eyes, and gripped his daughter's arm with sudden passion, murmuring: "Ah, yes, 'this so; 'tis ever so!—*All our fates, He knoweth*—")

With the passage of time, however, as Georgina grew into a tall, willowy, headstrong young miss, a queer admixture of the outspoken and the taciturn, the gregarious and the reclusive (for while she thrived, as it were, upon the rougher sort of schoolgirl athletic activities, and had an insatiable appetite for chairing meetings, she nonetheless rejoiced in solitude, and could vanish for hours at a time),—as she encountered new and alien influences, in New York City primarily (and precisely what those influences were, with whom she was intimate while attending Barnard, no one in Winterthurn, not even Miss Von Goeler, was to know),—as, in short, she left behind the simplicities of child-hood, and took on the knotty complexities of adulthood, her poetical talent was by degrees corrupted, and a new and ever more strident voice asserted itself, to the despair of all. Now there were rude jarring images, and dashed-off lines; a penchant for the sickly, the morbid, the willfully unfeminine; an air not of Christian calm, but of pagan febricity. It was scarcely a secret in Winterthurn that those poems by the poetess "Iphigenia," appearing irregularly in journals of such varying prestige as the local *Gazette,* and *Hudson Valley Leaves,* and *Vanderpoel Review,* and *Atlantic Monthly,* were by Miss Georgina Kilgarvan of Winterthurn: scarcely a secret, too, that her family very much objected to them, and were responsible for the eventual curtailment of the poetess's "career,"—though, as it would turn out, upward of five hundred of these incoherent scrib-blings were to be found, in packets of creamy-rose stationery, held together by yarn looped through them in the spine, amidst the spinster's personal effects af-ter her death.

That "Iphigenia" was a foreign-sounding name, arcane, enigmatic, sugges-tive of the exotic and the forbidden, no one could doubt: that it had been cho-sen for reasons of subterfuge and coyness, seemed altogether plain. A Greek goddess?—a mortal woman?—a personage from Attic tragedy, whose fate might be as repulsive to consider, as it was distant from the self-evident truths of Christian doctrine? Such speculations freely aired themselves, amidst ac-quaintances of the Kilgarvans, and, indeed, those who scarcely knew them at all,—for Winterthurn City was, in those times, so modestly populated (con-taining some twenty thousand persons, if South Winterthurn were included) as to allow everyone to know everyone else, and to gossip, whether idly or mali-ciously, with unstinting zest.

And who should not think it a matter for speculation that Miss Georgina Kilgarvan, the Judge's daughter, should so forget her station in society, and her obligations to her father's rank, as to wish to publish, for the smiling perusal of all, such overexuberant lines as these,—

> *Blow,—winds! Toss,—sea!*
> *'Tis but my Soul*
> *In shameless hunger—*
> *Of Thee!*

and,

> *In my skull the mourners tramp'd—*
> *& church bells sounded, to & fro—*
> *The very air turned—Inky—*
> *'Til Your love drew me thru—*

and,

> *Father of All—*
> *Sin do—appall—*
> *Thy Love so near—*
> *E'en terror, endear—*

Meritorious Christian sentiment, yet was the tone of such verse not somehow improper?—were the rhythms not too forced, too sprightly, indeed, too suggestive of female excitation? It was suspected that the *Winterthurn Gazette* published a dozen of Miss Georgina's poems, over a period of years, solely because the elderly proprietress of the "Poetry Page" had long been a champion of Georgina's, harking back to Georgina's schoolgirl days; it was known that *Hudson Valley Leaves,* a ladies' venture exclusively, required of its contributors that they help defray printing costs, and agree to buy up a number of copies of each issue in which their work appeared. As to what possessed the poetry editors of the more distinguished journals to publish, even sparingly as they did, "Iphigenia's" awkward effusions,—no one in Winterthurn could have said. Even Miss Clarice Von Goeler professed surprise: for *her* religious odes, though strictly metered and unfailingly rimed, were consistently rejected by both the *Vander-poel Review* and the *Atlantic Monthly*.

As Xavier Kilgarvan was balked in his earliest effort to gain access to the *scene of the crime*, or, by firsthand detection, to attempt to *penetrate, pierce, unravel, illuminate*, or in any wise *solve*, the mystery of the infant Whimbrel's death, he directed his boyish energies to poking about, as it were, in agèd back issues of the *Gazette*, kindly provided for him by a librarian: and, in his confused hope that he might, all by accident, hit upon some stray *clue* regarding the catastrophe, he stumbled upon a number of "Iphigenia's" poems, dating back to many years before his own birth. The most memorable of the verses he copied out, he knew not altogether why, in a school notebook,—

> *Know, Sweet Babe—*
> *Thy Father's hand—*
> *Rudders—all thou fearest—*
> *'Tis of Him—of HIM—*
> *(& not of ME—)*
> *These Seraphim sing—*
> *Thou hearest—!*

Slaughtered Lambs

IT WAS AT THE VERY END OF MAY, on a humid, overcast, hazily warm morning,—now some twenty-six days since the tragedy at Glen Mawr Manor—that Xavier recklessly played truant from school, and inveigled his brother Colin into accompanying him, that they might investigate a report of "mysteriously slaughtered lambs" belonging to a farmer named Upchurch, whose property bordered that of Glen Mawr Manor: a boyish excursion that not only would result in no clear *evidence, clues*, or *leads*, so far as Xavier was concerned, but would cause, for reasons ever to remain obscure, an actual rift between the brothers.

In brooding over the incident afterward, Xavier would not know whether to blame himself,—for, indeed, Mr. Kilgarvan, sensing his son's unwholesome interest in the "mystery" at the Manor, had expressly forbidden him to pursue it ("You are not to go anywhere near Glen Mawr," he said, so forgetting himself that he gripped Xavier's shoulder hard, and made the slender boy wince, "not because the place is accursed, not because your relatives would, in any case, turn you away, but because *I,* your *father,* forbid it")—or whether to blame the queer hurtful malaise of that spring morning, which, quite apart from the piteous and sickening spectacle of the mutilated lambs themselves, suggested some cause-less rift in the human soul: the heavy, settled, hazy air of a premature summer subject to random incursions of chill, from a capricious northeast wind that blew across the mountains. What most disturbed the youthful "detective" (for so, in truth, the sixteen-year-old schoolboy secretly thought himself) was that events from this date onward seemed to proceed not only with a logic of their own but with a logic *antithetical to his wishes:* which was never the case, so far as he could determine, in the adventures of Sherlock Holmes, C. Auguste Dupin, George B. Jashber, or the canny Pudd'nhead Wilson.

Xavier is to be forgiven a certain canniness of his own, verging, I suppose, upon actual improbity, when, while sulkily acceding to his father's unusually harsh admonition, in his innermost heart he thought, *Xavier Kilgarvan does what he wishes,—what Mystery requires of him, to be solved.*

So it was, he enjoined Colin to absent himself from a morning's work at the livery stable on Railroad Street, and to bicycle some ten miles out into the country, that they might investigate this most recent in a series of unexplained incidents involving livestock, in the general vicinity of Glen Mawr Manor. (Over a period of several weeks there had been isolated reports of slaughtered and part-devoured kids, piglets, calves, and spring lambs; a yearling pony and a fully mature sheep had died from a loss of blood.) As to what predators were re-sponsible for these assaults,—the sheriff's office could offer only the theory that they had been committed by a pack of wild dogs, unusually vicious coyotes, or actual wolves (for, in these years long past, timber wolves still inhabited the mountainous terrain surrounding Mt. Provenance). It goes without saying that the more ignorantly superstitious amongst the country folk murmured of certain fabulous creatures about whom mountain legends had long accrued,—the giant snowy-white "King of the Wolves," batlike flying reptiles with hooked beaks, great bloodsucking vampire bats, et al.; and since whispered rumors had spread of Mrs. Whimbrel's incoherent mutterings, before her collapse, of "angels" and "angel-demons," it naturally followed that such shadowy creatures were sighted as well,—though in no case could witnesses agree upon a description. (Nor did anyone really know what Abigail Whimbrel had raved of, in her dazed and delirious state, on the morning of May 3: for so far as the authorities were concerned, her near-unconscious condition precluded anything approaching testimony, or a reliable account.)

When the Kilgarvan boys arrived at the Upchurch farm, the sheriff and his deputies had already departed, and Upchurch, discovered in the act of burying the dead lambs, did not seem overly pleased to see them approach: for there had been a great many "gawkers and gapers," as he expressed it, milling about his property through the morning, and he was sick of busybodies tramping in his pasture. Xavier swallowed his pride, and asked only if he and Colin might "examine" the corpses: whereupon the shrewd Mr. Upchurch, handing over his shovel to Xavier, told him they were welcome to examine all they wished, if their stomachs could bear it; provided they completed the job of burial,—making certain that the lambs were buried at least *four feet deep,* so that scavengers should not unearth them.

Xavier readily assented to this proposition, and Colin, less readily: for the elder boy, being rather more acquainted with manual labor than his brother, looked upon it with less favor.

Before Mr. Upchurch excused himself, Xavier dared to ask him a few questions regarding the lambs: and was informed that the three corpses had been discovered very early that morning, in the lower pasture; that the bleating of the ewes (which continued still,—an uncanny, stirring sound not unlike a human keening) first aroused the farmer's attention; that nothing *quite* like it had happened in the past, though, in Upchurch's grandfather's time, white-furred wolves some ten feet in length made forays into barnyards when their natural prey was scarce in the mountains,—albeit no one had ever trapped or shot one of these creatures, nor had they been sighted in the past thirty years. Frank Shearwater, the sheriff of Winterthurn County, was of the opinion that wild dogs were responsible for the slaughter, and so Upchurch intended to set out steel-jawed traps to protect his livestock; but, as he told the boys with some bitterness, he halfway wondered if he should retain a Berwick Square attorney ("Berwick Square" having reference to professional gentlemen—lawyers, physicians, stockbrokers—of a reputedly élite, or in any case costly, stature) to inquire into bringing a lawsuit against the Kilgarvans of Glen Mawr Manor, since, in the opinions of many country people, it was from the Manor these "predators" came. Seeing the boys' startled expressions, Upchurch went on to say that the entire clan of Kilgarvans,—harking back to Colonial times—were a bloodthirsty lot, as apt to turn upon their own kin as upon outsiders: and it was not so very surprising, to those who knew of their ways, that an infant should be killed up there, since numberless queer things had transpired in the Manor, over the years,—though he was not one to speak idly and irresponsibly. His neighbor Phineas Cutter, however, told a most suspicious tale indeed, of the "Blue Nun," who had awakened him before dawn on the very morning the killing was discovered . . .

The farmer spoke with such cold vehemence, and with so furrowed a brow, that neither Xavier nor Colin was inclined, as the reader might well imagine, to reveal his identity; or to choose to interrogate the older man much further. Xavier said, in a faltering voice, that he did not quite see *how* any predators, as such, might come from the Manor: for he had heard that the Kilgarvans' mastiff, though toothless with age, and surely innocent, had been summarily shot by one of the sheriff's deputies, at the sheriff's command, when, at the very first, it was imagined that the dog had somehow killed the baby—and the Kilgarvans kept no other beasts at the present time. This reasonable objection Upchurch negligently brushed aside, and reiterated his notion of bringing a lawsuit against the "high and mighty" Kilgarvans: for whether the predators be *natural* or *unnatural* creatures, whether, like dogs, they *crept along the earth* or, like "demon birds," they *flew*, there was growing suspicion in the neighborhood that the Kilgarvans, and only they, were responsible for the slaughtered livestock. In turning abruptly away, Upchurch wagged a forefinger at Xavier, and instructed him to bury the lambs deep, and carefully, before he left.

As exhilarating a prospect as it had seemed, earlier that morning, to *investigate with their own eyes* the several slaughtered lambs of which they had just heard (news of any kind spreading swiftly through the city, well in anticipation of the *Gazette*), the actual experience was altogether different: for neither boy was truly prepared for the stark, pitiful, *palpable* reality of the small corpses. Xavier, being easily sickened, and inclining toward the squeamish, had to resist with all his strength the impulse to gag; and the sudden childlike desire to weep, or to run away. For the *physicality* of the dead lambs (involving, as it did, the presence of buzzing bottle-green flies, and swarms of red ants) was nearly too much for him, and struck him, he knew not why, as a kind of betrayal . . . When the great Vidocq came upon murdered men and women, or, indeed, had a hand in murdering them himself; when Jonathan Whicher of the original "Scotland Yard" examined a corpse; when such amateur detectives as Dupin and Holmes arrived at the scene of a crime—why, it had never seemed to greatly distress them that an actual physical presence lay before them: nor did it strike the reader, by way of the language employed, that *something had truly occurred* of an *irreversible* and *irremediable* sort. For now, blinking and staring at the dead lambs, Xavier saw not only *victims, corpses,* and *evidence,* but fellow sentient beings who had, not long previously, been alive; and were now dead. And he felt a sickened paralysis, as the unwanted thought entered his brain that, even should he solve the mystery, even should there be a "mystery" to be "solved," the lambs would not live again: for their time on earth was over.

Such niceties of thought did not suggest themselves to Colin, who merely grunted in disgust: observing that the lambs were, indeed, "dead and done for,—wounded in the necks": that there was nothing else to be seen, or learned: that Upchurch had played them for fools, and they well deserved their ill-luck, in being required to dig a grave four feet deep in such resistant, clayey soil. For emphasis, Colin gave Xavier a sharp little blow on the upper arm; and muttered that he had half a mind not even to assist him, since this wild-goose chase was primarily Xavier's doing.

Xavier coolly replied that he would be pleased to dig the grave himself; and that he hoped to gain more from the investigation than Colin's cursory discoveries.

So it was, Xavier swallowed hard, and forced himself to examine the pitiful creatures more closely, while Colin, contented with turning them over with his foot, stood with arms akimbo, whistling thinly under his breath. Xavier blinked tears of helpless sympathy from his eyes: for, ah! were the baby animals not sweet, and innocent, and comely, even in their stiffened postures?—was not the odor of their spilt blood and violated flesh poignant?—did they not seem to gaze at him, through fine-lashed eyes, with expressions of such soulful intelligence, he could well frighten himself with thinking he stared into a mirror? *If these be but animal corpses,* the youth uneasily pondered, *how shall I feel, confronted with a human corpse?* He would, he resolved, beg of the county coroner, Hans Deck, that he might one day be allowed admittance into the morgue,— thereby to see an actual corpse, and to steel himself against cowardly responses.

Gradually, his strength, his calm, and his reason returned; and he took out of his jacket his artist's sketchbook and a piece of charcoal, that he might quickly limn the spectacle before him; telling the disgruntled Colin that he had lately made inquiries into the techniques of killing employed by certain canines, and believed that these lambs must have been killed by another sort of creature after all. A dog plunges to the kill by hamstringing an animal, and ripping out its stomach; a coyote, by crushing the larynx, thereby inducing strangulation; a wolf . . . "One can readily see that these lambs have been attacked from above," Xavier said, "for note the deep puncture marks along the spines, and on the necks: and is it likely that these marks have been made by *canine teeth?* Rather more likely by claws, or talons. It is said that dogs and coyotes will eat their way through their prey by way of the hindquarters, and into the stomach, whereas these victims have been assaulted at the neck, and the rear of the head,—as, it seems, Abigail Whimbrel's baby was assaulted—and, too, not one rib has been cracked in all three: and canines rejoice in cracking ribs as they feed. Ah, what a pity, that the pasture is all grass, and there are no prints, for then we should assuredly *know*—*!* Do you not think it suspicious, too, Colin, that so little of the carcasses has been devoured—?"

As Colin's interest in the slaughtered lambs had rapidly diminished, and was not to be pricked even by his brother's surprising recitation of facts, still less by "suspicion," his reply was but a murmur of bland assent; and he detached himself from the scene, to drift off in the direction of a most idyllic pond, or waterhole, a short distance away at the foot of a grassy slope. If Xavier was somewhat disappointed in his brother's response, he gave no sign, but continued with his rapid sketches, making one after the other with such dexterity (though, it should be said, not always with scrupulous accuracy), it almost seemed his fingers moved of their own volition: and allowed him that curious, and somehow *elating*, sensation he invariably had while drawing, or composing tunes at the piano,—of the more enhancing his senses by their simple employment. For did it not seem to him, as he sketched the dead lambs, and the contours of the pasture about them, and the irregular outline of a hedgerow beyond, even as he attempted, with deft rough strokes of his charcoal stick, to suggest the texture, and the hazy glowering oppression, of the sky overhead,— did it not seem that, by these efforts, he could suddenly *see more?*—that it might be his privilege, in the next minute or two, to *see beyond?*

As, in the first confused minutes when Mr. Shearwater, the county sheriff, and several of his deputies arrived at Glen Mawr Manor, late in the morning of May 3, it seemed to be the consensus,—most vociferously, though disjointedly, expressed by Miss Georgina Kilgarvan—that a pet dog, grown unaccountably vicious, had attacked the baby during the night, it seemed only reasonable that the deputies seek out the cowering, quivering, clearly terrified creature, in his burrow beneath a stairway: and, with very little hesitation or compunction, execute him at once. Thus, the summary end of the agèd, near-toothless, arthritic Jupiter, a mastiff of yet-noble proportions, who had, in his prime, been Judge Kilgarvan's especial favorite: subject to this cruel dismissal, for being suspected of an act not in his character, and performed *in a locked room*.

That Jupiter was responsible for the infant Whimbrel's death is plainly absurd; yet there were to be a number of persons, among them the stubborn Simon Esdras, who insisted that this was so: though not, for one reason or another, the "Blue Nun," who afterward changed her opinion, to concur with the coroner's report,—that the specific cause of death was unknown, but rats (of the gigantic Norway species) were most likely to blame. As for the bereft mother's ravings of *angels,* and *angel-demons,* and *Baby Jesus,*—these were so clearly the consequence of a disordered imagination, drawn in part from a remarkably lifelike mural painted on the wall and ceiling, that they were dismissed as worthless: albeit Mr. Shearwater and his men treated Mrs. Whimbrel,—as, indeed, they treated the entire Kilgarvan household—with unfailing if guarded courtesy.

Initially distracted, and speaking with a frightened stammer, Simon Esdras rallied by degrees: and seemed finally to take solace in the "tragical syllogism," as he expressed it, that, *as Jupiter had been responsible for the outrage, and Jupiter had been removed from the scene with such dispatch, the task of the authorities would seem to be completed:* and they might now take their leave. For naught remained for the principals save the usual exigencies of grief, yet another visit to the churchyard,—this time, he supposed, far away in Contracoeur: and he very much doubted he would be able to attend.

So far as Thérèse and Perdita were concerned, their stunned and bewildered air, their youth, and what gave every impression of their genuine ignorance, quite precluded them from giving testimony: nor were the servants helpful, beyond a few much-repeated statements, and some contradictory information, of minimal worth. When, later in the day, Phineas Cutter reported the visit of Miss Georgina to his establishment, and the nature of her purchase, Mr. Shearwater returned to speak with her; but satisfied himself as to her innocence, as it were, regarding any especial information. (Miss Georgina, though visibly shaken, and drained of that palely radiant energy which oft-times suffused her, answered the sheriff's several questions in a small, still, yet never inaudible voice; and made an excellent impression on him,—for had he not heard idle tales of the "Blue Nun" for many years?—in her somber but freshly ironed black muslin housedress, with stand-up collar in Belgian lace, and impeccably starched cuffs. *Why* she had gone out so unusually early in the day,—*why* she had made her purchase of fifty pounds of quicklime not seven hours, it was estimated, after the tragedy,—was explained very simply: she realized that her need for the gardening aid was pressing, as it had been her intention to work *that morning,* indeed, through the morning, in the rose-garden at the rear of the house, which had been shamefully neglected of late; and which her belovèd father had particularly prized . . .)

Meeting young Harmon Bunting, the assistant pastor of Grace Episcopal Church, who was, it seems, on his way to the Manor to offer the solace of their common faith to the Kilgarvans, Sheriff Frank Shearwater shook his hand, and spoke with him for several minutes, happening to mention, in an abashed aside, that he had long been curious as to Miss Georgina's *true self,*—for tongues did wag in Winterthurn City, and his own womenfolk were not guiltless!—but found their interview, though brief and formal, highly gratifying, and rewarding in its own way. This attempt at a species of camaraderie between Mr. Shearwater (who was well regarded in the county, but scarcely well born), and Mr. Bunting (the descendant of the Joshua Bunting who had, some *two hundred thirty years previous,* led an entirely successful attack against a bastion on the Winterthurn River, manned by the settlers of New Sweden), came to very little, as the youthful pastor would never stoop to common gossip about one of his parishioners, let alone a personage of such distinction as Erasmus Kilgarvan's eldest daughter. In a courteous, but unmistakably prim, reply, Mr. Bunting said that an interview with a lady must invariably be highly gratifying, and doubtless rewarding as well: but he could not imagine why, in this hour of fresh grief, poor Miss Kilgarvan had been harassed.

Despite the findings of the authorities, and a lengthy article on the front page of the *Gazette,* calculated to have a calming effect upon the inhabitants of the area (for Mr. Osmyn Goshawk, the editor and publisher of the paper, had always had the highest regard for Erasmus Kilgarvan), it *was* the case that tongues wagged and wagged, with an ever-increasing fervor, in the days and weeks to follow. The coroner's suspicion of *Norway rats*, made public, was scandalous and titillating, indeed: all of Winterthurn City, from the most affluent households descending to the most impoverished, reasoned that it should never be outlived that *rats* of any sort might be acknowledged at Glen Mawr Manor,—the "Showplace of the Valley," as Phillips Goode had boastfully named it. Yet the verdict came too quickly, and perhaps even too plausibly, to satisfy: and was brushed aside by many, with as much elated contempt as the notion that the Judge's agèd mastiff had been guilty. A brutal deed it had been, but had it necessarily been the work of a mere *brute*—? Might not a human agent (whether mortal or demonic) have been involved—?

So disagreeable were most of the rumors and speculations that spread through the town in May, so improbable the reports of "eyewitnesses," that I hesitate to include here more than a brief sampling, drawn from R. S. Gilder's copious study, *The Kilgarvans of Glen Mawr Manor: An History and an Interpretation* (1899); but such an approach is required, if the reader is to grasp the mentality of the times, and the fulsome barrage of fables, fancies, tales, and outright lies that the youthful detective confronted, in his unflagging, if oft-times directionless, search for the Truth.

The Westergaards, whose seventy-acre estate was contiguous with Glen Mawr on the east, claimed to see, at dusk, "undulating figures of an unearthly luminosity" playing in the pine and beech woods belonging to the Kilgarvans: but had no success in identifying them, let alone capturing them (as young Valentine Westergaard wished to do). Miss Imogene Westergaard, the outspoken and somewhat free-thinking heiress daughter of the Colonel, twenty-seven years old but fired with the verve of a self-proclaimed spinster twice her age, insisted that these "undulating figures" approached her, with an air of actual enticement, while she walked her twin Irish terriers along the river path: but that the dogs' frenzied yapping drove them away. (Level-headed as Miss Westergaard was in most respects, observers believed that her testimony could not be taken seriously, in this case, as her clumsy descriptions of *angels, cherubs,* or *vaporous human infants* resembled too closely the ravings of Abigail Whimbrel, and had doubtless been influenced by them. And Miss Westergaard's ire was the more fueled, when, attempting to visit Georgina a fortnight after the tragedy, she was told by a most discourteous black butler that his mistress was not in: and cared not to receive visitors when she was.)

As for Miss Georgina,—of a sudden everyone whispered of her, and knew fresh news of the "Blue Nun," oft of a highly contradictory and implausible nature! For instance, it was said that she had locked herself in her bed-chamber, and refused most foods; that she disciplined herself harshly,—taking purges of a violent nature, administering enemas and douches of the most pitiless sort, injuring herself with hat-pins, candle-flames, riding crops, etc.; that she would communicate only with old Pride, and then through a locked door. Ringgold Peregrine, Henry's son, a corpulent, sweet-natured, idle youth, swore that he had seen Miss Georgina walking in the woods, at the edge of Juniper Park: that she was dressed in her habitual mourning clothes, which must have been uncomfortably warm in the sunshine; that she was heavily veiled, with a dark velvet hood, instead of a hat, completely covering her head; that she carried what Ringgold supposed to be a walking stick at first, but which was, in fact, a riding crop . . . What was surprising was Miss Georgina's behavior: for, as she walked along, hurrying, in a swaying erratic stride, of a kind young Ringgold had never observed in a lady, she paused frequently to swipe at the ground with the riding crop, *as if something invisible were creeping along beside her and nipping at her ankles.* Despite the congenital slothfulness for which Ringgold was known amongst his schoolmates, he was, it seems, well mannered enough when the situation arose: and knew that, as a Peregrine, it might well be deemed his responsibility to "protect" Miss Georgina Kilgarvan if she required protection,—for it was most unusual, indeed, to glimpse a lady of Miss Georgina's stature strolling without an escort in Juniper Park. Ringgold therefore called out to her, to ask if she needed assistance: whereupon Miss Georgina behaved yet more oddly, in glancing over her shoulder at him for the briefest of instants (with what expression—whether surprise, alarm, chagrin, ire—he could not discern through her thick veil), then turning away, and walking hurriedly deeper into the woods, *with no word or sign of recognition.* Poor Ringgold, already somewhat short of breath, stood on the path staring after her, in utter perplexity, and watched as her somber figure disappeared into the woods, with very little sound,—for, indeed, it seemed to him that even the birds had ceased their chattering, and the squirrels their raucous scolding, as the "Blue Nun" passed rapidly beneath.

(When this tale was told to Xavier, however, by the excitable young Ringgold, it was most skeptically received: for, as Xavier pointed out, Ringgold had not so much as glimpsed the lady's face, nor had he the slightest shred of evidence that she was swiping at something invisible,—for, if it were *invisible,* how might it then be seen? Such "eyewitness" accounts could scarcely be taken seriously, Xavier scornfully said, as if, for the moment, he were Monsieur Dupin, or Sherlock Holmes himself, confronted with a particularly obtuse individual,—and, indeed, the reliability of amateur witnesses is notorious throughout the history of crime.)

Equally unreliable, and colored with a surprising cruelty, were the divers tales told of poor Thérèse and Perdita, who had bravely returned to classes at the Parthian Academy, that they might not fall behind their classmates: for now, it seems, it was openly observed, by even those girls who had been amiable enough in the past, that the Kilgarvan sisters were most odd; had been odd from the start; sighed too frequently in the classroom, and wept too frequently in the cloakroom; aroused scorn by working so very diligently at her studies, in the case of Thérèse, and impatience, by an excess of brooding, in the case of Perdita; kept to themselves, or, conversely, failed to keep sufficiently to themselves,—for if Perdita approached a group of girls they coolly turned aside, and Thérèse's deskmate of many months now shrank from her, and requested of the headmistress that she be moved elsewhere. For, it seems, the sisters offended not only by their presence but by an odor that emanated from them, of something most rank, chill, unclean, and sickly. (Like singed feathers, one girl claimed. Like wet fur, claimed another. Like milk just beginning to turn; or agèd soiled clothes; mildew; mold; rot; waste; dark brackish unspeakable blood.)

Felicity Peregrine widened her periwinkle-blue eyes and lowered her voice to a whisper, as she swore she had seen *Thérèse's shadow detach itself from her and drift away,* on one of the school's graveled walks; Mary-Louise Von Goeler evoked frightened giggles by swearing that she had, entirely by accident, touched Perdita's wrist, *to discover that the girl's skin was clammy and cold,* as that of,—why, she would not wish to say. And how fierce was the expression Perdita turned upon her: darkly bright eyes ablaze like a cat's, with ill-suppressed fury!

And all the Parthian girls agreed that the Kilgarvan sisters knew more than they acknowledged regarding the death of the Whimbrel baby,—more, certainly, than the fools in the sheriff's office suspected.

(When these reckless accusations were repeated in Xavier's presence, he had all he could do to keep from bursting out in rage; and felt the insult against sweet Perdita as keenly as if a razor-sharp blade had been drawn against his unprotected skin.)

The headmistress of the school, Clarice Von Goeler (a maiden aunt of the cruel talebearer Mary-Louise), had long made it her mission to befriend Thérèse and Perdita, both because she pitied the girls, being motherless; and because she yet cherished her girlhood friendship with Georgina, who was, in her steadfastly loyal view, "one of the very few outstanding *individuals* of her acquaintance,—of either sex." Though the relationship between Clarice and Georgina had long since atrophied, for no reason Clarice could discover, she continued to write little notes to Georgina from time to time, inviting her to accompany her sisters to tea at the headmistress's residence, or to dinner, or on a Sunday excursion along the river to one of the majestic old inns: most of which invitations, despite their gracious tone, and unforced offer of sympathy and affection, went unanswered. (For in this, and in a host of related issues, the Judge's daughter quite betrayed her heritage, in her shocking *rudeness.*) Miss Von Goeler was a tall, flaxen-haired woman of young middle age, healthily colored, forthright, yet, upon occasion, given to periods of introspection: reserved, one might say, out of stubbornness rather than timidity: with very little patience for gossip, scandal, and the like. So it was, when thoughtless persons asked of her what the "Blue Nun" was truly like, or how matters truly stood at Glen Mawr (as if, indeed, Clarice had set foot in the house for some ten or twelve years), she was likely to flare up in a temper, and reply that "it was no one's concern, and a vulgar sort of diversion, to make such queries." A tale making the rounds, which was repeated to Xavier's mother by a lady friend, had it that the headmistress had called both Kilgarvan girls to her office to speak in private with them, and to ask if she might be of assistance: with the startling consequence that Thérèse burst into speechless sobs, and little Perdita grew very white in the face, saying, in a voice of quivering pride, "Thank you for your pity, Miss Von Goeler, but we do not *require* it, and we do not *wish* it,"—or words to that effect (for the story, as one might suspect, underwent numerous alterations and embellishments as it spread through town).

As he had so long led a life of willful seclusion, and could scarcely be said to thrust himself upon the attentions even of the enlightened public, Simon Esdras Kilgarvan escaped general notice, and was the subject of few tales. So it was, the Kilgarvans of Wycombe Street were astonished one evening at the dinner table when, in his usual blithe and unthinking manner, Wolf told them that his circle of friends,—by which he meant the Rock Barrens racetrack circle, which included young Valentine Westergaard and Calvin Shaw—had quite solved the mystery of Glen Mawr: it was Simon Esdras who had murdered the baby, for he would have had a key to the bed-chamber, and only Simon Esdras, of all the household, was *unquestionably mad.* So bluntly, yet so casually uttered, these words did not evoke the response Wolf had anticipated, even from his brothers; Mrs. Kilgarvan pressed her hand to her bosom, in mute consternation; and Mr. Kilgarvan, after a moment's shocked silence, told his son that he was no gentleman, but a lowlife ruffian, to speak in so coarse a way at the dinner table,—and of his own uncle. "You will excuse yourself at once, and leave us," Mr. Kilgarvan said. "But, sir," Wolf protested, attempting a smile, "surely you must understand that our theory is not *altogether* serious." "The more scurrilous, then, the lot of you," Mr. Kilgarvan said, with trembling lips, "and you *will* take your leave at once."

It was not long after that evening, however, when reports spread of Simon Esdras,—or a white-haired gentleman who closely resembled him—in any number of unlikely places, including the rougher areas of South Winterthurn, and the unlicensed establishments of Rivière-du-Loup. Whether he drank to dazed excess, or tried his inexpert hand at gambling and cards, or consorted with women of a certain unspecified category,—none of the talebearers was prepared to say. It *was* the case, however, that Simon Esdras now attended church more faithfully, including even Wednesday evening services (to which he escorted Thérèse and Perdita,—Miss Georgina being temporarily invalided); and he caused a stir by showing up, unannounced, at a meeting of the Thursday Afternoon Society, having mistaken the day's program of verse recitation by Miss Iris Kathleen Hume for a symposium of some sort on a Scottish philosopher, of whom no one in the Society had ever heard. On the more somber side, he had taken to dropping in at the Corinthian Club, which he had not visited for forty years, and wandering about both downstairs and upstairs, *as if in search* (so observers believed) *of his dead brother:* with a most mournful, distracted, childlike expression on his pink-flushed face, and a wistful smile for all who came forward to shake his hand. Only a night or two prior to the Kilgarvan boys' adventure at the Upchurch farm, Valentine Westergaard chanced to encounter the philosopher on the granite steps between the Club's stately gryphon figures, and, seeing that Simon Esdras smiled toward him in a somewhat stupefied manner, put himself at his aid, and offered to escort him home. According to young Westergaard, the old gentleman breathed a sweet liquorish breath, yet behaved, in a sense, in no more tipsy a way than usual: plucking at his sleeve, and inquiring of him whether Heraclitus was correct in asserting that one cannot plunge into the same river twice; or whether, to reason more adroitly, Simon Esdras Kilgarvan was correct in asserting that one can either not plunge into the river (sic) once, which is to say, at all, as the "river" is but a figure of speech, or not not plunge (sic) into the "river," as the river is ubiquitous, and carries all mortals along, to we know not where. When Valentine did no more than chuckle uneasily, not grasping that an actual proposition had been put to him, Simon Esdras repeated it, in a high petulant voice that betrayed an uncommon anxiety. "So it is, young man, you must choose," the philosopher said, "—Heraclitus, or Kilgarvan: which is it?" Canny though young Westergaard was, and a very devil at cards and horses, he had no mind for the knottier issues of philosophy, and answered in a vague cheery tone that he "would put his money on *Plato*,"—the only philosopher of whom he had heard, and by whom his grandfather the Colonel swore: which answer was, as it turned out, most brilliant, as it not only impressed Mr. Kilgarvan but silenced him for the remainder of the drive home. Then, at the Manor, he shook Valentine's hand and offered him formal thanks, for having "pricked him in his sophist slumber": for Plato, though mad, doubtless contained a yet more ubiquitous Truth, that "river" and "he-who-plunges" are similarly unreal, or, conversely, "real" to the same degree. "In any case," Simon Esdras said, with a sudden sunny smile, "I shall think hard upon it: and it may be, after all, that Erasmus *yet lives*,—and none of us must die."

Upon returning from a business trip to Vanderpoel and the western reaches of the Valley, Bradford Kilgarvan reported the alarming news that the family's very name, once so distinguished, had become, of late, shrouded in mystery and confused scandal: that Erasmus's entirely natural death was being whispered of as "unnatural" and "unexplained": that not one, but several infants, had died at the Manor: that the "Blue Nun" was most irresponsibly linked with a woman, not even an ancestress, of the late 1790s,—harking back beyond Phillips Goode's time—who had, it seems, poisoned several husbands in Winterthurn. Alas, many an old shameful tale, attached as much to the Kilgarvans' neighbors as to them, was being resuscitated, and passed off as new—!

Protest as Bradford assuredly did, with as much gentlemanly tact, forbearance, and good humor as he could summon forth, that these stories were greatly exaggerated, and that, in any case, the Kilgarvans of Glen Mawr Manor were very different persons from the Kilgarvans of Wycombe Street,—yet he failed, in his own estimation, to greatly alter those notions. Still more worrisome was the puzzling development that those store owners or managers (among them the overseer of the Children's Floor of the great Brant Brothers Cast Iron Palace, in downtown Vanderpoel) who had, in the past, unhesitatingly ordered Mr. Kilgarvan's toys in considerable quantities, because of the very name *Kilgarvan*, now professed less enthusiasm; and agreed to order, it almost seemed with reluctance, certain specialties of the Winterthurn workshop (the wooden Noah's Ark, the fretwork humblybeg, the ever-popular "crying" doll, above all the splendid rocking horse) that were belovèd of the children of the well-to-do, and not available elsewhere, from other toymakers or suppliers. Bradford was deeply insulted when one shopkeeper, while placing his order, expressed the hope that the toys should not prove "dangerous": for he had heard—why, he knew not precisely *what* he had heard!

Informed of such perfidious matters, Lucas Kilgarvan at first flared up in manly anger: then, within an hour, lapsed into that listless melancholia to which he was, it seems, prone. Never did he utter aloud a word of complaint or self-pity, not to his belovèd wife, not even to his most trusted son Bradford: yet it was evident that he suffered: and that, after so many years of unflagging industry and deserved praise for the masterly craftsmanship of his custom-made toys, he still could not rest in the assumption of *financial stability.* So it was, year upon year, the effect, it seemed, of the virulent animosity his elder brother had conceived for him, for clouded reasons . . .

Young Xavier, sensing these things, did not violate his father's pride by speaking of them: but vowed with the more heated fervor that he should one day restore his father's fortune to him, and his reputation; that he should exorcise for all times even the rumor of his father's (and his own) "tainted blood,"— baseless though it was, and trivial. But, ah!—was the very name of *Kilgarvan* now accursed?—might he be forced to leave Winterthurn to realize his destiny?

While gazing at the slaughtered lambs, and covering page after page of his sketchbook with deft, feathery strokes in charcoal, Xavier slipped, by degrees, into a pleasurable light trance: and, his restless brother being otherwise absorbed in wandering about the lower pasture, Xavier felt his spirit expand, and grow ever more airy and insubstantial, the while thoughts of a most exotic species seemed to lift from the trampled grasses underfoot, and fold him in their warm embrace . . .

Of a sudden, Xavier was forcibly reminded of a dream he had had the previous night, bearing upon little Perdita, in which the lovely child had appeared,—in what attire, for what purpose, whether with hair loosed or no, the youth was shamed to recall—in his bed-chamber, by luminous moonlight: a vision of such fleeting sweetness, he had felt it imprinted upon his very being; and awoke with strangulated breath (alas, to naught but his too-familiar room, in which, close beside him, Colin slumbered with deep rasping breaths,—the blameless sleep of any healthsome lad).

Now, not a yard distant from Upchurch's lambs, this dream-image reappeared: and in the next instant vanished: nor could Xavier, though his heart strained, and desire leapt in his wrists, summon it back. Instead, other shapes appeared, of a graceful tantalizing nature: winged, it seemed: floating: gentle: transparent. A tiny hand, the palm heated, the fingers surprisingly strong, insinuated itself into his, to force the stick of charcoal away.

Not clearly audible, yet unmistakably near, a voice murmured his name, and called him *Cousin:* being joined by another, and yet a third: high-pitched, melodic, sweet, yearning, familiar yet unutterably strange. *Xavier! Dear Xavier! Dear Cousin!* He felt a warm breath on his cheek and throat; felt his curls saucily tousled; his tense shoulders stroked; his sides, his torso, and, ah! the more saucily yet, *his very nipples,*—the while hairs stirred on the back of his neck, and his flesh lifted in goosebumps. *Cousin, sweet cousin! O most comely of boys! O, are you ours?* Enthralled, Xavier stood without moving, scarcely daring to breathe, as a pair of damp lips brushed boldly against his, in the first kiss of a *forbidden kind* the innocent youth had ever experienced. Soft-caressing voices sounded close about his head, fine as the humming of honeybees; and, with motions both timid and brazen, the tiny invisible hands stroked, and pinched, and plucked, and essayed to tickle, through his clothes. *Dear Xavier! Dear Cousin! Can it be, you are ours? O sweetest of boys!* The dream was so fraught with slow-pulsed pleasure, the voices so irresistible in their pleading, Xavier feared he might be on the brink of sin: and made an attempt to rouse himself, and to wake, as he oft-times did in the early morning, by jerking his head suddenly upon his pillow to shake off the languorous shackles of sleep.

So it seemed, for a moment, he *was* awake: and naught before him,—the piteous small bodies of the lambs, the farmer's coarse-handled shovel propped against a fence, the very slant and contours of the grassy slope—had been altered a whit. Yet, in the next pulsebeat, he heard again the heated, urgent voices, and felt again the numberless impatient fingers, and wondered if he should die of such suffocating sweetness!—for the incantatory *Cousin, dear Cousin, O Xavier, O beautiful boy!* rose to near-rapture, washing and lapping about him.

From whatever source the necessary strength derived,—whether some hastily recalled passage of the Book of Common Prayer, or an imagined admonitory phrase of one of his detective-heroes, or, indeed, the healthful impulses of his own virgin soul—Xavier managed to rouse himself a second time, and to wrench his hand free of the steely little fingers. His lips of their own volition shaped a silent prayer,—*O release me!*—and in that instant the youth fully awakened: to discover himself crouched on trembling legs above the dead lambs, his body both uncomfortably heated yet chill, and his clothes dampened with perspiration.

The voices, of that haunting mellifluousness, had abruptly fled *as if they had never been:* and Xavier blinked dumbly, to see his precious sketchpad and charcoal stick had fallen at his feet.

"How strange!—how disagreeably strange!" the lad bethought himself, stooping to retrieve his things. "And yet, why should I suffer any upset, for a mere dream?"

As Colin had, it seems, thoughtlessly wandered off, Xavier made the decision to dig the mass grave by himself: which laborious and unromantic task had at least the salutary effect of waking him yet more fully, and driving from him all dream-phantasms, pleasurable or otherwise—! In other circumstances he might have contented himself with doing his task as quickly, and as offhandedly, as possible,—for, of the Kilgarvan boys, he ranked with Wolf, as frequently unreliable in household matters: but, as Upchurch had so sternly charged him to dig the grave four feet deep, and to cover the lambs well, Xavier toiled to fulfill these requirements, oft pausing to catch his breath, or wipe at his damp brow, or, indeed, turn hurriedly aside that he might overcome a sudden spasm of nausea.

When, at last, he finished his laborious chore, his back ached most cruelly, and blisters had already formed on his hands: but the pitiful creatures were at least hidden from sight, beneath a mound of fresh dirt: and Xavier did not think that Upchurch could criticize him, or complain of him, or rank him with the mere gawkers and busybodies who had tramped about earlier. "So it is, Xavier Kilgarvan must acquire a reputation for being altogether *dedicated*, and, indeed, *professional*," Xavier declared inwardly, propping the shovel up against the fence with care.

His mood was somewhat dampened, however, when, having found his brother napping just beyond the pond, in a cozy sort of bed or burrow he had fashioned in the tall grasses, Colin turned upon him a most uncharacteristic expression: both groggy and startled, and distinctly peevish: his broad, high-colored, handsome face reddening, it seemed, with irritation or obscure embarrassment. While asleep he had evidently been bitten by flies or mosquitoes, as upward of a dozen red, puffy, ugly miniature wounds now appeared on his face and throat; he had scratched at these with such unconscious violence that several were bleeding; and his fingernails were edged with his own blood. Seeing his belovèd brother thus, and being greeted with a surliness he had not expected (for, in the mornings, it was always Colin who woke easily, with a fresh, sunny smile, and an immediate appetite for breakfast, and Xavier who lashed out with childish ire), Xavier felt a pinprick of alarm: might something have happened to Colin in his sleep?—and why, indeed, had he chosen to sleep at so unpropitious a time?—for the boy was husky and broad-shouldered and possessed, it seemed, of twice Xavier's energy, and generally scornful of those who required daytime naps.

It took Colin but a few seconds to overcome his grogginess, and to rise to his feet, assuring Xavier, with a negligent wave of his hand, that he was *quite* all right,—though stupefied with boredom, and resentful as well, of having been "dragged along" on one of Xavier's foolhardy adventures.

Xavier halted in his path, for he had, it seems, anticipated some brotherly gratitude, if not actual surprise and admiration, for his labor in burying the lambs unassisted: but, as this was not forthcoming, and Colin continued in his ungracious temper,—averring, with a curl of his lip, that he was heartily sick of "detection," and halfway thought he should report the morning's excursion to their father—Xavier too lapsed into a sullen silence; in which mood the boys bicycled home.

Alas, Colin exacted a subtle sort of revenge, in pedaling with such consistent swiftness, and no ostensible effort, that he soon left his panting brother behind; for the younger boy had not the strength in his leg muscles, or the lung capacity, to keep pace with him. That this was performed, as it were, unintentionally,—that Colin seemed merely not to notice Xavier's absence beside him—made the insult all the more cutting. Too proud to call after his brother, Xavier doggedly pedaled in his wake, watching Colin's broad, bent shoulders, and the muscles that rippled across them, and the unflagging motions of his legs, until, by degrees, as the country road dipped, and rose, and twisted, and dipped yet again, the older boy passed out of sight.

"If I—Am You—"

IT WAS ON A SUN-DRENCHED AFTERNOON in early May, some thirteen years before, when the air of Parthian Square shimmered greenly in the wake of a brief shower, and all the world, it seems, was giddy with the scent of lilac, that Miss Clarice Von Goeler of the Parthian Academy for Girls (at this time but the headmistress's assistant, and a popular instructress in Music, Elocution, and Deportment) had so curious an adventure while accompanying her friend Georgina Kilgarvan to Dr. Hatch's office on Berwick Square that she brooded over it for months,—for years: and only after Miss Georgina's shocking death, not two weeks before her forty-third birthday, did she speak of it to several of her female relatives: the studied consensus being, they could make no more sense of the incident than of "Iphigenia's" clotted poesy of old . . . !

In brief, the event came about in this way: Clarice was in the midst of conducting her third-form girls in a spirited recitation of an ode to spring by John Greenleaf Whittier when, of a sudden, the door was flung open, and two distraught girls burst into the room to say that their teacher, Miss Kilgarvan, had been overcome by an attack of breathlessness,—that she had gone red in the face, and staggered from her desk,—that she had fallen to the classroom floor in a faint,—*and gave every impression of ceasing to breathe.* Whereupon, without a second's hesitation, Clarice hurried down the corridor to her friend's classroom, to discover, with infinite relief, that Georgina had partway revived, and was being assisted to her feet by several girls. Indeed, the dazed woman was feebly protesting that she was quite all right now,—she was quite restored to herself,—and they had no need of milling about, and coming so close: for she could not recall having given anyone permission to leap from her desk . . .

How luridly colored was Georgina's handsome face, blotched with hectic red, yet waxen-pale beneath!—how stupefied with fear, her rapidly blinking eyes!—though she made a show of attempting to stand erect, and refusing further assistance, declaring, in a voice so weakened it scarcely sounded like her own, that she did not wish to be touched, as she was now fully recovered,—*and must complete the day's lesson.*

Clarice, however, could not be so easily dissuaded. It was self-evident, in her opinion, that Georgina was distinctly unwell,—for was she not, even now, short of breath, and swaying on her feet?—no matter her protests, the class must be dismissed, and she must allow Clarice to take her at once, by hackney cab, to Dr. Hatch,—the physician's office being but a few blocks distant, near the city hospital. Georgina essayed to stand her ground, reiterating, with enfeebled breath, that she had quite recovered, that it had been a trifling attack of light-headedness and that, under no circumstances, was the headmistress,—or, indeed, anyone—to be informed—for she must, she *must,* remain with her class, she *must* complete the day's lesson, else—

"Georgina, you are not yourself,—you *are* ill," Clarice interrupted, in a voice both alarmed and chiding, "and if you possess a whit of the common sense we expect of our students, you will acknowledge that fact."

At this, Georgina drew breath to contend, but was, it seemed, overtaken by a fresh wave of dizziness; and, to the startled concern of all, did a most uncharacteristic thing, *in bursting into girlish tears.*

✶   ✶   ✶

(That Miss Kilgarvan, the most exacting disciplinarian at the Parthian Academy, the instructress most feared, most admired, and, alas, most frequently imitated behind her back, should succumb to a fainting spell in her classroom, let alone copious tears,—why, was this not wondrous?—was this not delicious?—in truth, was it not remarkable? For so sternly fixèd was Georgina Kilgarvan's character, in the minds of Parthian students, that those who had not witnessed the outburst could not believe it: and were queerly resistant to being convinced. "Why, I might more readily believe, as the Spanish peasants do, that a statue of the Virgin Mary has shed tears," one of the bolder young ladies asserted, "than I might believe, or wish to believe, that Miss Kilgarvan has shed tears.")

As Winterthurn City girls of a near-identical age and social background, Miss Clarice Von Goeler and Miss Georgina Kilgarvan had been drawn together, at the Canandaigua Seminary: though Georgina's homesickness was decidedly less pronounced than Clarice's, and her penchant for solitude, and the studying of inhospitable texts (works of Aeschylus and Sophocles read in the original), and the scribbling of idiosyncratic rhymes had a dampening effect upon their friendship. Clarice had no less a "personality" at the school than Georgina, and was not the sort to pursue an acquaintanceship where but a modicum of encouragement was offered: so it came about, it must be said to Clarice's secret sorrow, that though she was in truth Georgina's "closest" friend at Canandaigua, she was not, in truth, a "close" friend—!

Yet ties between them, of a sort, did exist: for each sensed herself the *unmarriageable*, if not the *unlovable*, type: and so busied herself with activities of a rich diversity, and a generally unflagging air of intellectual vivacity, that no observer, of either sex, might have known whether it was indifference, or timidity, or private fear, that most potently governed her soul. Physically, too, they were alike, in being taller by several inches than the average girl, and less naturally given to gracious motion; the one possessed of fine dark hair and eyes, and the long, aquiline, slightly hooked Kilgarvan nose; the other blond, with frank hazel eyes, and a snubbed nose, and a somewhat stolid jaw. Both loved poetry, and aspired to composing it: but though Georgina, as editor of *Canandaigua Bluets*, consented to publish several of Clarice's poems, she refrained from uttering a word of praise,—which tacit disapproval, or dislike, wounded Clarice's feelings.

Ties there were, however, of whatever intangible kind, for, after graduation, when Georgina went bravely away to study at Barnard, and Clarice remained closer to home, at the Nautauga Falls College for Women, an unexpected correspondence ensued: this being one of those odd relationships that bloom, as it were, through the mails, with surprising vigor, and even a modicum of affection. How flattered,—indeed, how warmed—how *delighted* Clarice was! Whether Georgina truly cared for Clarice's lush impressions of her college, and of her professors, or whether she derived greater pleasure from her own writing,— lengthy, acerbic, "dashed off" letters chock-a-block with vivid descriptions of such features of New York life as elevated trains, A. T. Stewart's gigantic dry goods store, Fifth Avenue and Park Avenue on Sunday mornings, the "demonically inspired" sermons of Henry Ward Beecher, which, it seems, Georgina had ventured to Brooklyn several times to hear,—it would be difficult to say: but when Judge Kilgarvan fell ill, and summoned his daughter home, the epistolary friendship was abruptly terminated; and, to Clarice's bewilderment and hurt, no "real" friendship took its place. They visited each other, and had tea in town, and attended meetings together of the Thespian Society, and the Junior Ladies' Auxiliary of the Corinthian Club, and the Thursday Afternoon Society; yet Clarice had the distinct feeling that Georgina sometimes looked upon her with actual fear,—that she should suddenly presume upon their girlish "postal" intimacy, and deeply embarrass them both.

After both young women joined the faculty of the Parthian Academy, however, and became, in a manner of speaking, "professionals," their relations were somewhat easier. Clarice might freely complain of the headmistress's crotchets, or of the board of trustees (a gathering of elderly females to whom the tumult of the 1850s had marked "the beginning of the end"); Georgina might complain of the frivolity of their young charges, and their inability to master the rudiments of English grammar, albeit they knew the latest slang. If Clarice complained, from time to time, of her family (for Mrs. Von Goeler had greeted

Clarice's thirtieth birthday not as an anticipation of the disgrace of spinster-
dom, but as an acknowledgment of it), Georgina demurred from offering complaints of her own,—though Erasmus Kilgarvan had taken a simple-minded
sort of young lady for his second wife, not three years before, and rumor had it,
through Winterthurn, that stepmother and stepdaughter were *not* the very best
of friends. Nor did Clarice and Georgina make reference to those awkward little "poems" that appeared from time to time, in the *Gazette* and elsewhere, under a conspicuous nom de plume.

Yet, through the years, it was Clarice's hidden sentiment, not only that
Georgina was in truth her closest and dearest and most *sisterly* friend, but that,
in some ill-comprehended way, she possessed the like value in Georgina's
heart . . . !

"But I suppose we shall never speak of such things," Clarice sighingly observed, "for they are so very vaporous, where is the vocabulary to engird them?
And I should be, no doubt, as tongue-tied as Georgina!"

The fainting spell in the classroom occurred approximately eighteen months
before the arrival in Winterthurn of young Malcolm Guillemot, and initiated a
period of such capricious ill-health that Georgina thought it best to take tem-
porary leave from her teaching responsibilities: the chronology of which was to
be twisted about, in later accounts, so that it would seem, more romantically,
that Mr. Guillemot,—or his abrupt withdrawal from the scene—had precipitated Georgina's illness. (In truth, as many persons knew, Georgina Kilgarvan
had always suffered intermittent and inexplicable "lapses of health": being robust one day, and weakly pale the next; possessed of a normal appetite upon one
occasion, and sickened by food upon the next. Though never before given to actual tears, she was susceptible to dark, raging moods, and sometimes forgot herself in the classroom, raising her voice against her abashed, frightened students,
out of proportion to their sins. She scorned certain excesses of the "weaker
sex,"—thought the perennial invalids about town were self-pitying babies, un-
deserving of sympathy,—yet was often invalided herself, for three or four weeks
at a time. A tale was told of her, that when Miss Verity Peregrine pressed upon

her a packet of iron tablets, that she might build up her strength and make her coloring more attractive, Georgina archly replied, "Attractive to *whom?*"—and refused the offer. There were periods when she seemed to affect a deliberate carelessness in her toilet, and in her apparel, wearing dresses that hung on her like sacks, as if to disguise her inordinate thinness; and to refute the very notion of feminine responsibility.)

As Dr. Colney Hatch was the Kilgarvans' family physician, he must have been familiar with Georgina's vicissitudes of health; yet, when Clarice brought her into his office, patient and doctor behaved with a most puzzling formality,—Dr. Hatch being as distant, and as stubborn, as Georgina. For just as Georgina adamantly claimed that she was *not unwell,* and *did not wish to be touched,* so the frowning physician declared that he would not examine any patient of his, or, indeed, any person at all, who did not wish to be examined. Clarice impatiently interrupted to say that Georgina assuredly *was* unwell; and that any fool, simply by glancing at her, could discern it: but neither patient nor physician would budge, there being a distance of some five or six feet between them. "I cannot understand this," Clarice cried, looking from one to the other, "and wonder if I am in the presence of madmen!"

Dr. Hatch was a middle-aged gentleman of moderate height, inclining toward the stout, with a grave, dour expression, and heavy jowls, given a "sparkle" of sorts by the flash of a gold tooth, and the gold-rimmed bifocals that fitted his face so compactly. His reputation in Winterthurn City was impeccable; he had never married, and was a deacon at Grace Episcopal Church; he mingled with the very best families, and had memberships in the very best clubs; he inspired in his patients respect if not affection; his word was law in medical matters; one can scarcely imagine that he suffered insults lightly. Yet, when Clarice spoke as she did, the good doctor refrained from losing his temper: and, though coloring markedly, contented himself with repeating in a quiet voice that he would not "subject to any examination, any person who did not freely wish to be examined: excepting of course children, who had no jurisdiction over themselves."

Clarice appealed again to Georgina, without success; and yet again to Dr.

Hatch, without success. For, though Georgina looked altogether sickly, her complexion mottled and her eyes ringed in shadow, though her breathing was audibly quickened, and she had need to support herself, however unobtrusively, by resting against a table,—Dr. Hatch kept his distance from her, his gaze now affixed to a point somewhere in space, beyond his visitors' heads, and went on to speak of the importance of unfailing morning regularity: which was, he believed, the cornerstone of all forms of regularity, and of good health. "Congestion in the head is most likely a consequence of congestion in the bowels," Dr. Hatch said, "—both being symptoms of an overwrought nature, in the female sex in particular, when the strain of unaccustomed *ratiocination* takes its toll. Thinking, reading, writing, etc.,—these place an inordinate strain on the system, and bring about any number of disorders. Purges are a necessity; douches with vinegar or salt solution; enemas, of the cold-water variety; and the like. A week of enforced rest might be prescribed,—or two weeks, or three: but, as I say, I do not press my services upon any person who has not come willingly to my office, and who has not freely requested my opinion." The physician fell silent, wiping his hands on a handkerchief, his manner no more forceful than previously, but no less firm. As he seemed about to bow and take his leave,—Clarice and Georgina being in his waiting room, and not in an interior office—it seemed to Clarice that she must protest yet again: but what might she say? Georgina had turned away, to adjust her hat, and to more firmly secure a strand of hair that had worked itself loose at the nape of her neck; her expression was both drained and gratified, apprehensive, yet relieved; how like a frightened child, Clarice observed, who has escaped some punishment or duty—!

"Thank you, Dr. Hatch," Georgina said, with a wild sort of good humor, as, her long fingers working blindly, she adjusted a hat-pin skillfully through the crown of her hat. "I shall take your advice to heart, as it were: and trust that, if a bill is forthcoming from your office, it will be mailed to *me,* at the Parthian Academy, and not to my father at home."

With a slight bow, Dr. Hatch murmured that he should not of course think of billing her: for no examination, and no consultation, had in truth taken place.

*   *   *

Some days later, as she was leaving for school, Clarice discovered, to her delight, a small wicker basket hanging from her doorknob, filled with sprays of lilac,—of lavender, deep purple, and white hues: most beautiful, indeed most captivating, to both the sense of sight and the sense of smell. She brought it inside, to discover, beneath the lilacs, a poem written in Georgina's blunt though meticulous hand, inscribed "to C.—," and signed "Iphigenia."

"RIDDLE-WISDOM"

If I—am You—

Shall You—be me?

If You—scorn I—

Where then—We—

Be—?

Quickly Clarice reread these enigmatic lines, and again reread them,—with the unlooked-to result that, of a sudden, she burst into tears: for she did not,—ah, she could not!—make any sense of them, or of her unhappy friend: and she knew beforehand that if she were to confront Georgina, to inquire of her what the "Riddle-Wisdom" was, and what mystery appeared to govern Georgina's life, she would be greeted by a chill, stony demeanor: and not a word of explanation, or affection.

The Corpse

As YOUNG XAVIER KILGARVAN privately thought himself a pitiful sort of detective, having failed to investigate the *scene of the crime* at Glen Mawr Manor, and having, moreover, yet to examine an *actual corpse* (or even to gaze upon one not formally attired, and meticulously groomed, by the undertaker's skillful hand), he resolved to make amends: one day soon, he knew not precisely when, to make a bold sortie against the Manor: and one day *very* soon, to view a dead body at the county morgue,—for he had several times appealed to Mr. Deck that, when a likely corpse was in his keeping, Xavier might be summoned.

All too quickly, it seemed, in the first week of June, word came to Xavier that he might drop by the morgue, at his convenience: the message brought to him by a mystified neighborhood boy while Xavier was in the midst of his morning chores. (He had been prevailed upon by his father to aid Mr. Kilgarvan's Negro assistant Tobias in packing several dozen boxes of toys for railway shipment, a task he particularly disliked: for was it not tedious, and menial, and mechanical?—was it not dismayingly brainless? Xavier especially resented packing dolls, for, being breakable, they required a great deal of attention, and he was sure to be blamed if any accidents occurred en route. Also, though he had seen it for years, Mr. Kilgarvan's famed "Bonnie" doll, with its faint kittenish cry that emanated from its midriff, and its hinged eyelids that snapped open so starkly, never failed to startle him: for the glassy eyes, whether brown, or green, or the blue of the clearest sky, always stared, it seemed, directly at *him*.)

So it was, he made his decision to slip quietly away, though but a quarter of the toys had been packed, and Mr. Kilgarvan was certain to be angry with him: for he could not, he reasoned, allow such humble exigencies of his *personal life* to interfere with his *profession*. (As for Tobias, being fond of Xavier, and, in any case, possessed of a charitable disposition, he assured the lad that he did not mind in the slightest being left to pack the crates single-handed: for, by so doing, he could satisfy himself that they were done properly.)

As Xavier ran by way of alleys, lanes, and footpaths the short distance to Courthouse Green, where, at the rear of the stately domed courthouse building, certain county functions were housed,—the sheriff's headquarters, the jail, the morgue—he felt buoyed along by a wondrous sort of elation: and all the sights, sounds, and odors that presented themselves to his confused delectation seemed but the expression of a single grand *substance,* and overarching *purpose.* Indeed, since having taken on the secret mantle of the Detective, Xavier often felt that *anything* and *everything* was significant: and bore, he knew not immediately how, upon the mystery at Glen Mawr Manor, *if only he possessed the wit to interpret it.*

This certainty began to ebb somewhat, as, now breathless, the boy entered the drab and near-windowless stucco building that housed the morgue, and was greeted with little hospitality by an elderly filing clerk, who seemed not to know his name, or why he had come. If he did not wish to identify the body that had just come in, if he was not a relative, then what was his business at the morgue?—a question put to him with such chill indifference, Xavier would not have known how to reply; and was saved by Hans Deck's intervention.

"The lad has come not to identify our 'John Doe' of the moment," Mr. Deck bemusedly said, allowing a companionable arm to fall upon Xavier's shoulder, "but, I believe, to identify Death."

So it was, Xavier was led along a narrow and near-lightless corridor, to a refrigerated chamber at the rear of the building, which gave the uneasy impression of being subterranean: and presented, with no propaedeutic courtesy, with an actual corpse,—the dead body of a youth "freshly killed" in a brawl out the Old Winterthurn Pike, in the region of Rivière-du-Loup. With a gesture somehow lacking in finesse, Mr. Deck whipped off the soiled white sheet that covered the man, to reveal, to Xavier's affrighted eye, a naked masculine body,— a body badly abused—a body so demeaned by divers imperfections (pimples, warts, moles, boils; misshapen and filth-encrusted toes; slack fatty tissue at the waist, belly, and thighs; an Adam's apple painfully prominent; discolorations or bruises virtually everywhere; eyes open in glassy idiocy; bloodied lips agape, to reveal irregular and yellowed teeth)—that Xavier could but blink, and stare, and swallow, and blink the more: for he had expected to see something quite different, *though he knew not precisely what.*

Though Hans Deck's reputation in the city was that of an upstanding but somewhat chill and disagreeable personality, a consequence, doubtless, of the somber trappings of his trade, he spoke most congenially,—indeed, almost warmly—to poor Xavier, who stood staring down at the corpse on its slanted porcelain table, with no more boyish vivacity than that of an actual relative of the victim, and no more conversation than a mute. "'Tis Death you gaze upon," Mr. Deck said, in a near-tender voice, "—the poor fool that was, the 'John Doe' who had lately inhabited that flesh, having fled forevermore."

Xavier made an enfeebled attempt to respond to this, and to ease himself away from the elder gentleman's comradely arm, which lay, still, upon his shoulder; but Mr. Deck gave no sign of hearing, and continued, in a grave, low, caressing voice, to explain that the dead man was most likely about twenty-eight years of age; that, under the cognomen of "Buck" he had been employed upriver, at one of the lumber camps; that, in a drunken state, he had been so badly beaten about the stomach, torso, and head (the back of the skull being broken,—would Xavier care to see?), he had died of internal injuries, of a multifarious nature. As to *who* had killed him, or *why*,—it was doubtful that Shearwater could make any arrests, or would even trouble to attempt them, for no witnesses might ever be found to the slaying: and, indeed, it had probably not been a "slaying" as such, since the brutish young man would doubtless have beaten his opponent or opponents to death, in similar wise, if circumstances had been but slightly altered. "Such legalistic niceties do not concern us," Mr. Deck said,—now giving "Buck" a playful rap on the shin bone with his knuckles,—"who deal primarily with the flesh; and limit our musings to it."

At this, Xavier faintly essayed another response, for it had struck him,—with the force of both the wildly comical and the horrific—that the luckless young man possessed a coarse sort of family resemblance to the male Kilgarvans: there being something about the hard slant of the brow, and the husky set of the chin, and even about the dark guileless eyes that reminded him of his brothers, Bradford and Colin. But this observation was too weakly asserted for Mr. Deck to hear; and the gentleman was in any case expostulating on several pathological conditions (exclusive of the violent hemorrhages that had caused death) of uncommon interest to be found in the corpse. For instance, the divers sores,—*pustules, tubercles, blebs, scales, crusts, fissures,* and *papules;* liberally scattered across the body, with the innocence of mere freckles—were, as Xavier might know, the unmistakable symptoms of venereal disease, in its secondary stage: a scourge and a warning of God that young men must behave with propriety at all times, and resist the wiles of the female sex,—apart, that is, from the blessèd marital bed. "For it is very much as Reverend De Forrest would have it," Mr. Deck said, "that so repulsive a disease is, in a sense, an actual boon of God, for its efficacy in warning us against the snares of the flesh. Why, last month, I had on this selfsame slab an old codger so rotted with his sins, you could see his actual brain through a hole the size of a silver dollar in the roof of his mouth!— a hellish sight, I assure you, yet most powerfully instructive. Though *he* had been too far gone, for years, to profit from it. But I trust," Mr. Deck said, in a more kindly tone, "your father has well acquainted you with such wisdom."

In truth, Lucas Kilgarvan had somewhat abrogated his paternal duty, in postponing a discussion of this nature with his youngest, and most sensitive, son: for even the unperturbable Bradford, and the raffish Wolf, and the stolid Colin, had evinced considerable upset at being exposed to the harrowing daguerreotypes in Dr. Horace Motley's *A Recent History of Disease and Pathology,* and Dr. Findley Litz's famed *Scourges of God,*—these being the two most frequently employed texts in Winterthurn City, in these years, for enlightening young men to the *facts of life.* Yet such was Xavier's caution that he did not wish to question Mr. Deck more closely, as to the nature of this "wisdom."

Of interest as well, the coroner said, seizing a particularly bruised flap of skin in the lower region of the deceased's belly, was this evidence of advanced abdominal hernia: which must have given the young man a great deal of discomfort. And, too, had Xavier's keen eye taken in the malformation of several toes; the oversized and apish nature of the genitals; the concentration of pustules at the navel; the sickly rotted teeth; and the general *unwholesomeness* of the corpse,—apart, that is, from the actual markings of death? "Dr. Hatch, who dropped by late last night, on his way home from the hospital, paused to see what our 'catch' of the day was: and informally diagnosed one of his ailments as a kidney disorder, which would have resulted in a particularly odious death, by way of uremic poisoning," Mr. Deck said, in a voice both sympathetic and chiding, as he lifted the corpse's battered lips to show his gums; and,—as Xavier involuntarily winced—lifted up his eyelids to show his yellowed and bloodshot eyeballs. "Colney works very hard, as you know; yet he told me he is eager to acquire our 'John Doe' for his dissection laboratory at the hospital,—many of the corpses sent him being, it seems, badly deteriorated, as a consequence of extreme old age and indigence," Mr. Deck said. He pinched the corpse's cheek, and chuckled, saying that "Buck" was fortunate to be finding his way to Dr. Hatch's professional hands: for *bodysnatchers* of the most shameless sort were operating throughout the state, digging up the dead in paupers' cemeteries, and elsewhere, and peddling them,—why, God knew where!—this "business" having become quite a scandal in recent years.

Xavier could not even bring himself to murmur an assent to this speech, as, by degrees, the warmth of his skin had yielded to the metallic chill of the morgue; and his earlier ebullience had long since ebbed, to be replaced by a sensation of light-headedness and nausea. Ah, his hopes!—his schoolboy intentions! He had wished to query Hans Deck *closely* on the matter of the Whimbrel infant's death, and whether the coroner's office, or the sheriff's office, had ascertained that rats' teeth would make the sort of wounds and marks to be found on the baby; he had hoped, after a sort of camaraderie had been forged, here in the morgue, that he might prevail upon Mr. Deck to show him divers reports, records, even photographic evidence (if such existed), pertaining to the death. But all this was swept away on a rising tide of nausea that terrified as it sickened: and Xavier recalled with especial horror the breakfast of boiled eggs, sausage, kidneys, and buttermilk pancakes liberally soaked in maple syrup that he had devoured with so innocent an appetite not four hours previous.

"Unlike Alexander the Great," Hans Deck said cheerily, "I require no slave beside me, to whisper in my ear that I am *mortal:* so long as I stay close to my sanctuary here, hidden away behind the Courthouse so very cozily—!"

It then happened that Mr. Deck lifted one of the corpse's limp, hairy, badly bruised arms, to let it fall back heavily upon the table; and, it seemed, poor "Buck" responded with a flicker of startled displeasure about the eyes; with the consequence that Xavier felt his vision spin, and his very soul go cold, and his knees lose all their strength: and saw the floor rear up to strike him with an amazing suddenness—!

In short, the hapless youth *fainted*,—as his elder companion gazed upon him with a bemused and pitying eye.

"'Tis only Death," he murmured, "—Death, and not Life: and how might mere *Death* injure you, my boy?"

At Glen Mawr Manor:
The Dungeon

I

A FORTNIGHT AFTER HIS VISIT TO the Winterthurn county morgue, Xavier made a decision to brave Glen Mawr Manor itself,—no matter who forbade it, or warned against it; or what fears he himself harbored. For he had suffered so potent a dream the previous night, he knew himself *fated.* "And if I am in danger," he thought with somber childlike resolve, "God will protect me, for my purpose, surely, is good."

It may have been a source of further encouragement to him to learn, by overhearing a fragment of a conversation between his mother and a lady friend, that Miss Georgina Kilgarvan was said to be confined to her bed at the Manor: and that so goodly a percentage of the Manor's domestic staff,—both whites and Negroes—had departed, since early May, that most of the rooms were shut off; and Henry Peregrine, the family's attorney for several decades, was strongly advising the Kilgarvans to decamp, and live elsewhere in Winterthurn for the time being. (Not only was the great old house falling into disrepair, but, as certain servants and tradesmen whispered, it seemed to be haunted by the faint, pitiable, yet unfailingly horrific wails of a baby, which emanated from the walls and ceilings at any hour of the day.)

As to any further official developments of the case: there were none. Nor did Mr. Shearwater, or his deputies, or any of the city police, take it kindly when they were questioned of their "progress" in the matter: for while they could not consider the case closed, they scarcely wished to consider it open, for divers reasons. (It was rumored that a lowlife secret society, whether the Knights of the White Camelia, or the Brethren of Jericho, or an unknown third, had taken it upon themselves to make an unofficial investigation of the case, to see whether the foul deed might have been committed by one of the Kilgarvans' Negro servants: their prime suspect being the elderly Pride, who had long displeased whites in the area with his truculence, and his failure to ingratiate himself with them. No persons of good society would have anything to do with such riff-raff "vigilante" groups, which had, it seems, sprung into being spontaneously, in the troubled year 1865, though doubtless drawing upon old Copperhead sentiment, which had been strong in the Valley: Mr. Kilgarvan in particular denounced them as "un-American," "un-Christian," and "un-human," and worried that Mr. Goshawk's *Gazette* did not take a firmer stand against them. So it was, Xavier knew very little about them; and the rumors, in any case, may well have been groundless.)

A firsthand particle of information pertaining to Mr. Simon Esdras Kilgarvan was gleaned, as it were, accidentally, while Xavier was in the cobbler's shop on Charity Street, on an errand for his mother, and happened to overhear a conversation between Mrs. Harrier Von Goeler and old Miss Verity Peregrine. The philosopher had been overindulging in alcoholic spirits of late, with a childlike innocence, and unfortunate results, in numerous places about town,—not only the staid Corinthian Club, where he might be watched over, but in less decorous establishments along Water Street, and even in South Winterthurn, where only the name *Kilgarvan* might be known. It was said that he had startled Reverend De Forrest by speaking of Erasmus as if, in some way, he were yet alive, but behaving "reprehensibly"; and by musing at awkward length upon the need,—now fallen to him—to propagate a male heir, to carry on Glen Mawr's tradition. "For Erasmus, despite his tiresome pride in his manhood, and the disagreeable *heatedness* of his blood, did fail most shamefully along these lines," Simon Esdras averred, with a melancholy shake of his head, yet, it was reported, a queer sort of smile.

Xavier knew himself summoned to the Manor, and fated for,—he dared not guess: when, very late of a Sabbath eve, past two o'clock by the solemn tolling of divers church bells, he woke startled from a dreamless slumber to see, gliding across the floorboards of his room, in a long white nightgown of some filmy material, barefoot, with her wavy hair atumble down her back, *none other than the diminutive figure of his cousin Perdita.* As in life, whether "spied upon" in church by Xavier, or glimpsed somewhat more by accident, leaving the Parthian

Academy in the company of her sister, the young girl did not deign to notice him, or to acknowledge his existence by more than a *frisson* of her head and shoulders, so too in this most intimate of contexts she did not glance in his direction: nor did she seem to take cognizance of the fact that Colin slept beside him, faintly snoring, in his customary heavy slumber.

Xavier was so astonished, he rose on one elbow to stare, and quite risked losing her, for all his clumsy boldness: but, it seemed, the lovely girl was possessed of too much pride, and too deeply imbued a sense of propriety, to be thus routed. Making no sound, gliding on her small, white, exquisite feet, Perdita passed through an effulgence of moonlight, the silken ribands at her breast lightly fluttering, and her slender arm upraised: for she was holding a sprig of lilac to her lips, the heady fragrance of which was, in that very instant, released most powerfully into the air. "How is it possible! How,—and why!" Xavier inwardly whispered, the while, all agape, he rudely stared; and felt his besotted heart knocking against his ribs.

Since that harrowing day in the cemetery, now many weeks past, when Xavier had heard that melodic, teasing, never-explained sound sift out of the very air,—and had seen, for the first time, truly, his youngest cousin (who, until that extraordinary moment, had impressed him as being but a sallow-faced peevish child, of no interest to a youth his age)—why, he had behaved most strangely, in wandering out of his way in the city that he might, by chance, catch a glimpse of her: lounging about the base of the bronze memorial to Nathan Hale in Parthian Square, for instance; or strolling with hearty nonchalance along that stretch of Berwick Avenue where the ladies' millinery and glove shops were located,—for someone had mentioned seeing Thérèse and Perdita, in the company of the dowager Mrs. Bunting (young Harwood Bunting's mother), entering one of these little stores. None of these actions need have been deemed "spying"; but Xavier uneasily supposed that that was his intention, for his heart leapt a dozen or more times when, mistakenly, he believed he had caught sight of Perdita: or,—such was the youth's infatuation—when he believed he had caught sight of Thérèse! Once, while moodily walking along the lower end of Water Street, in a rough sort of neighborhood, Xavier had found himself staring at a freight train that rattled past: the locomotive with its fan-ning white smoke, that, in its chugging and wheezing power, suggested to him some urgency (and, alas, some futility) residing in his own breast; the noisy clat-tering cars, thirty or more, that appeared to be empty; the caboose with its pair of unlit red lamps, and a hollow-cheeked porter lounging at the rail, gazing blankly toward Xavier. And how abrupt it was, the sudden cessation of noise, when the last of the cars had passed!—like a restoration of sweet calm to his own troubled soul. He had been brooding overmuch, of late, of Perdita; and Mrs. Whimbrel (now confined, it was said, to a hospital, that she might not do harm to herself or her remaining children); and of certain problems within his own household; and of his secret failure as a "detective,"—the which glamorous enterprise was scarcely what he had expected, being, it began to seem, virtually impossible to undertake.

Now Perdita, in pale diaphanous attire, her wavy tresses loosed upon her shoulders, and her delicate heart-shaped face turned just slightly aside, had, it seemed, come to *him:* tiptoeing noiselessly past his moonlit window, a spray of lilac raised to her face, that she might inhale its rich sensuous aroma, with dark nostrils just perceptibly widened, and thick-lashed eyes nearly closed. Her awareness of him,—for it was a certainty, his beating heart informed him, that she *was* aware—made the long wondrous moment all the more enchanting: for she would soon glance at him over her shoulder,—would she not?—ah, would she *not?* Xavier stared, and stared; his parched lips moved to utter her name; but no sound issued forth; nor could he, as he realized of a sudden, move any of his limbs or his head, *being paralyzed.*

"She has died, up at the Manor," Xavier thought, going cold with fright, "and this form is but her spirit, her departing ghost! And I am too late to save her!"

Taking no notice of him, or of the sleeping Colin beside him, the graceful figure advanced to the whitewashed brick fireplace in the inner wall, and, as Xavier stared, in a veritable paroxysm of amazement, her slender fingers groped for, and deftly found, the loose brick that had long been Xavier's secret; and eased it soundlessly out; and took, or seemed to take (for the fireplace was partly in shadow, and Xavier could not be certain what he saw), a ruby ring he had hidden there long ago—!

Silent, and resolutely unhurried,—though, surely, she must know how passionately he watched—Perdita slipped the ring on her finger: and seemed about to glance back over her shoulder at Xavier when, of a sudden, a clattering on the cobblestones outside caused her to vanish: for it was the milkman's horse and wagon, and no longer two o'clock, but four-thirty!—and Xavier woke dazed and agitated with the name Perdita on his lips.

He knew it was naught but a dream, and he would not succumb to the temptation of rising from his bed, to check his hiding place in the wall: for long ago he had found a ruby ring in the street, covered in filth, and thought he might present it to his mother,—and hid it away,—and afterward wondered guiltily if he had done wrong, in not reporting it—and, alas, it *was* too late,—and the ring *was* beautiful,—and so he had most irresponsibly procrastinated, and dared not reveal his find. Now, it seemed, the dream-spirit of Perdita had come to make her claim: though assuredly Xavier had but imagined her presence—?

Yet, in the morning, when, unobserved, he went to the fireplace to grope behind the brick,—he discovered to his astonishment that the ring was missing after all.

It *was* missing, and in its place had been left a dried and shrunken sprig of lilac,—its tiny blossoms scarcely more than dust, and its sweet fragrance long since vanished.

II

AFTER SO UNEASY AND PROTRACTED an anticipation, Xavier found his approach to Glen Mawr,—by way of the handsome half-mile avenue of pink-toned gravel only slightly overgrown with weeds, and edged in sumptuous bridal wreath, with a double row of gracious old plane trees on either side—surprisingly unimpeded: and it was only as he ascended the great stone steps of the mansion, which were semicircular, and of the size and weight of ancient millstones, that he grew somewhat nervous, imagining himself observed. And yet, what harm might come to him? And on so splendid a June morning? It had been the youth's strategy to approach Glen Mawr in no craven, stealthy way,—by the rear, for instance, ascending from the river—as one or another of his detective heroes, of doubtful integrity, might have attempted: he was a Kilgarvan, after all, and thought it wisest to make his approach as openly, and as innocently, as if he *had* been summoned, and could not possibly be denied entrance. (For the occasion he had dressed in a somber cotton-and-woolen suit, with a stiff-starched white shirt, like any young gentleman making a formal visit to so noble a house, having explained to his mother that he was embarked upon an adventure of sorts,—but hinting to her, not altogether honestly, that it had to do with summer employment. "And will you be applying to Osmyn Goshawk, as your father has suggested?" Mrs. Kilgarvan anxiously asked. How Xavier replied to her, with a courteous murmur that succeeded in conveying both a negative and a positive response, and an embarrassed disdain for the very question,—I do not know: but it should not be held against him that, at the onset of his "career," he must needs now and then tell fibs to his mother.)

Yet, forthright though he was, and unhesitatingly as he had rung, and then rapped, for entrance, no one came to the door: and for some painful minutes, *knowing* himself observed, he paced about, hands in his pockets and head bowed, as if brooding whether to depart. His face colored slightly; he grew uncomfortably warm; and thought it an impractical decision, after all, to have dressed so formally, as if for church,—for if the Kilgarvans denied him entrance, why, then, it might well be, Xavier should have to force his way in by surreptitious means. Was not Glen Mawr partly his father's and, through his father, his own?—by all *moral*, if not precisely *legal*, necessity?

Thus he paced about beneath the great-columned portico, and cast his eye upon the tall stone urns, with their Egyptian cast, on either side of the door; and upon the numerous tall, narrow, English-style windows of the façade, which cloudily reflected light, and gave the illusion of a ghostly human presence beyond. (Imposing though Glen Mawr assuredly was, with its steep slate roofs, and massive stone-and-stucco chimneys, and ornamental trim in Italianate style, the fact that nearly half of the windows had been shuttered, both upstairs and down, very much detracted from its aesthetic harmony: and gave, so Xavier thought, an appearance of shabbiness and neglect.)

In the company of other boys, Xavier had frequently trespassed upon the forbidden territory of Glen Mawr, approaching it from the rear, which is to say from the river: for Juniper Park at its easternmost extreme was naught but a great woods, shading into the Glen Mawr forest, and one might unknowingly leave the one and penetrate the other, if warnings against trespassing were infrequent; or had been torn down. But, from the river, one soon came to a high stone wall, cruelly spiked at its top, and littered with glass: which, while whetting schoolboy appetites for adventure, did a great deal to thwart them. Xavier had never seen the terraced "Japanese" garden his grandfather had insisted upon building, at inordinate expense, into the hill beyond the wall; nor had he seen the various subordinate buildings attached to the house,—the washhouse, the bakehouse, the meathouse, the gardeners' sheds, the old slaves' quarters (which, his father bitterly declared, was more sturdy a structure, being built of brick and stucco, than the ramshackle wood-frame house,—formerly an inn—where the Kilgarvans of Wycombe Street were forced to live): but of course he had been told of them: and had long imagined a haughty sort of grandeur where, now, in the morning's hazy warmth, with the sweet scent of bridal wreath and rambling rose undercut by a deeper, harsher, yet not unpleasant odor of lichen, toadstools, and rotting leaves, he was forced to revise his estimation: for the Manor, which had been intended to be so conspicuous a showplace in the Winterthurn Valley, a testament to Phillips Goode's lavish good taste, as well as to his fortune, had indeed fallen into decline,—and why his eldest son had allowed this, with *his* fortune, was legitimately to be wondered at.

("Perhaps, Father, he feels guilt for his crime against you," Xavier once suggested, when the subject had come up, as it frequently did, "and is ashamed to hire workmen to do repairs, or even to hire new servants as the old die off, for that reason." But, though the well-phrased statement had doubtless pleased Mr. Kilgarvan, he could not bring himself to concur, saying, with a wry shake of his head, that so reptilian a criminal as Erasmus Kilgarvan would never identify himself as a criminal, let alone suffer so human an emotion as simple shame: "For all that he does, my boy, is perpetrated, in his eyes, as an expression of rectitude,—and not personal wish." Xavier had thought for a moment; then said, with flashing eyes, and a spirit of angry bitterness not unlike his father's own: "Why, then, he *is* invulnerable!—and can even God discover a way to punish a sinner *who does not sin?*")

As these troubled thoughts sifted through his mind, and caused a pulse to beat behind his eyes with such sullen forcefulness, he frowned in pain, Xavier heard a faint tapping, and his murmured name: and saw, at a casement window nearby, leaning out, the figure of a slender young girl in black,—*lovely Perdita herself.*

With hurried, cautious gestures, as if she feared being detected, Perdita motioned to him to come beneath the window, that she might help him climb inside: and was, for that purpose, lowering a mourning shawl, in black brocade richly fringed, for him to grasp. "The front entrance to our house is always kept bolted," the girl told Xavier beneath her breath, in a low, melodic, rippling voice that seemed, in its murmurous beauty, to vibrate along his very nerves.

So it came about that Xavier recklessly ran to the window, and, with protestations of extreme gratitude, climbed into the house long forbidden to him, as readily as any of his adventurer heroes might have done; and, one might surmise, with considerably more childlike abandon. What felicity, her presence at the window!—and what rare courage, in a girl of her age, to invite an intruder into her very home: nay, to lend him her own small white hand, in so doing!

Scarcely able to catch his breath, Xavier managed to utter only her name,— "Perdita"—in a choked, and somewhat incredulous, voice.

"Yes," she whispered, "but quick, quick—come inside: and take care that the window is bolted behind you."

Perdita looked very much as she had looked at her father's melancholy gravesite, in March, and less as she had looked in Xavier's bed-chamber the previous night: though beauteous enough, with a perfect petal-smooth skin and fine, fierce, dark-lashed eyes, she was inordinately pale, even to appearing sickly; and was possessed of a precocious air of bereavement which, about the eyes in particular, expressed itself in subtle, fleeting modulations of irony. Alas, only twelve years of age, and so irreversibly mature! With a gesture as much of impatience as solicitude, she urged Xavier forward, that she might draw the brocaded shawl safely in, and fasten the casement windows.

For a long awkward minute, then, the cousins stared at each other, with unabashed exultation; but dared not touch. Xavier could not yet altogether believe his good fortune, but stood panting, and blinking, and essaying feebly to smile, as if fearful that some sudden rude motion of his, or unguarded gesture, might cause Perdita to "vanish" on the spot: and only by degrees, as the vertiginous hammering of his heart slowed, did he see that this was no faery child, but a very real young girl: *his* Perdita.

"You are very brave to allow me in," he said in a rapid, lowered voice, glancing over his shoulder, "for I know how your sister,—I mean your eldest sister— despises all of my family. And I *know* I cannot be welcome here."

So softly and shyly did Perdita speak, Xavier had to bend to her, to hear: "Well,—*you* are very brave to come here," she said.

The large, deep-set, liquid-bright eyes were as Xavier hungrily remembered them, or nearly; the chestnut-brown hair was less lustrous, it seemed, but wonderfully thick and wavy, despite the spartan style into which it had been twisted; the small mouth,—now smiling, or straining to smile—was as lovely as any besotted youth might wish. Had Xavier not, in his fevered dreams, often envisioned those lips,—had he not, in truth, pressed his own desperately against them? So strange as they were, were they not also familiar?—as known to him as his own mirrored countenance?

Perdita, though several inches shorter than Xavier, was not so diminutive as he recalled from the day of the funeral; nor would the casual eye have dismissed her as a mere child. A palely blooming *womanliness* lay within the timidity of *girlhood,* evidenced by a graceful and innocent coquetry of her wrist, shoulder, and chin; and the graceful white curve of her throat. (Xavier saw that her slender fingers were *ringless.*) As for her ill-laundered mousseline dress, in a gray so harshly dark it might have been black,—Xavier noted only that its tight standup collar and narrow-ribbed bodice were executed in fine bobbin lace, and

that its layered skirt was too long, and tattered about the hem. Yet even this attire, with its air of the cast-off and scorned, was, in his eyes, as becoming as a
silken gown of the gayest hue—!

Surely this *was*, yet *could not be*, the enchanting specter-girl who had trespassed Xavier's bed-chamber the night before, and stolen away his prized ring,
to leave a sprig of desiccated blossoms (which he carried now in his vest pocket,
close to his heart) in its place—?

Thus, like any gently bold young lover, Xavier dared to grasp Perdita's hand
in his: finding it chill, and fragile-boned as the smallest song sparrow, and
slightly resistant, with a natural maidenly restraint. Speaking softly, with as
much trembling formality as he could summon forth in the presence of his
belovèd (for so dramatic, extreme, and *adult* an expression is not inappropriate
in this remarkable context), Xavier stated his mission at Glen Mawr: his simple
and straightforward request to examine the room in which the tragedy had
lately occurred, that he might see, with his amateur's eye, if any *clues* remained;
and his proffering of any assistance lying within his power, to both Perdita and
Thérèse, if they required it.

Perdita abruptly withdrew her hand from his, and turned shyly away;
seemed about to speak; then, after a blushing hesitation, said that she could not
quite comprehend his meaning, in offering her and Thérèse "assistance": but
hoped, certainly, that he did not mean to insult. ("For Glen Mawr is our home,"
she said. "We were born here: we know no other place.") So far as an exploration of the Honeymoon Room, or even much of the house was concerned, she
saw no pressing reason for the examination, but no reason to impede it: as
Xavier was her cousin, and must mean well. She doubted, however, that he
would discover much of value, as the sheriff and his men, and a noisome troupe
of police, detectives, and "experts" of divers kinds, from as far away as Vanderpoel, had poked about for days and found nothing. "Save evidence of rats?"
Xavier asked.

But Perdita had already turned away, to lead him on his search, a forefinger
to her pretty lips, and her manner both stealthy and playful, as if this were, to
her, but a child's game: and she and her cousin both children.

They passed through the Judge's library, a long, narrow room paneled in black walnut, with a faded carpet underfoot, and, above the mantel, a somewhat dark portrait, in oils, of their famed ancestor General Pettit Kilgarvan, whose likeness Xavier had frequently studied, with boyish curiosity, shading into anxiety, whether that great man's blood might yet flow, in some wise, in his own veins. Upon the mantel was a cast-iron bull, in belligerent stance; and, lying atop a table, as if it had just been set down, Erasmus's gnarled *Don't-tread-on-me* walking stick. Xavier paused, to take note of the great mahogany desk, which must have measured six feet along its width; and the several leather chairs; and, upon the bookshelves, rising to the shadowy ceiling, leather-bound tomes stamped in gilt, of the multivolum'd works of such giants of the law as Nathan Dane, and James Kent, and Ephraim Kirby, and Joseph Story, and Theophilus Parsons, and the great Lemuel Shaw himself,—these names being dimly known to him from his father's remarks, and Mr. Kilgarvan's embittered pursuit of Law. Xavier was about to take up one of the books, but Perdita dissuaded him, saying that they must hurry; and must not touch anything. "For Georgina, when she is well again, will discover it at once. Every object in this room, Cousin, has its particular placing, and cannot be disturbed even by the maids,—else Georgina flies into a rage."

Xavier followed his companion into the foyer, which opened for two stories, and pleased the eye rather more than did the Judge's library, as it was less shrouded in shadow. The painted and gilded ceiling was supported by tall, somewhat thick Grecian columns, with much ornamentation at their base; the floor was of a pallid milky-red marble, badly discolored, and beginning generally to crack; opening off the foyer were several stone archways of a medieval character, executed in red sandstone. How potently Xavier's heart flooded with a sensation of *resentment,*—for such palatial pretensions, and such ill-used wealth, denied to him and his family!

"Yet," the heated youth inwardly murmured, "I would scorn to live here, if the Manor *were* open to me: for some insults are past forgiving."

"Cousin, come! Why are you lingering?" Perdita whispered; and, with girlish solicitude, pulled at his wrist.

They ascended a broad, curving, majestic staircase (as splendid, Xavier was forced to admit, as any he had ever seen in Winterthurn,—in the homes of the De Forrests and the Peregrines, for instance); and to the carpeted landing, where, overhead, an enormous crimson-and-gold fanlight was ablaze with sun. Here Xavier's sharp eye lit upon what he perceived to be a *clue* of some sort,— for was it not peculiar, indeed, that the fine-carved mahogany banister should be so crudely scarred, as if by the strokes of an ax, for a space of several yards? He stopped Perdita, and inquired of her, in a whisper, whether Judge Kilgarvan was responsible for these angry markings: but Perdita, scarcely glancing at the banister, told him that it was but an "historical conversation piece," going back for generations,—to when the British General Gadwell and his officers had occupied Glen Mawr, in '77; and the General had shouted for his men to hurry downstairs; and, losing his temper, had ridden his horse to the landing, raging and hacking at the banister with his sword, when they did not quickly enough obey.

Chastened by this explanation, Xavier allowed himself to be led the rest of the way upstairs, in silence; and along a dim-lit corridor, hung with numerous portraits in oils of faces too blurred to be recognized, though he did not doubt they were kin of his; and to the very doorway of the Honeymoon Room,—the oaken door itself being partly smashed, and hanging as if drunken upon its hinges. "Here,—it is very much as it was,—excepting of course for what the in-truders have done," Perdita said. Xavier followed slowly in her wake, blinking, and looking from side to side, with the air of a frightened child: for was this the *scene of the crime,* to be entered so readily?—with so little ceremony? "I wonder you are not terrified to go inside," Xavier said awkwardly, "or even that you have not mended the door with some sturdy wood, and nailed it shut." Perdita glanced at him, in genuine surprise; and frowned; and asked, with a wan, droll smile: "But *why* should we be terrified of a mere room? Unlike Cousin Abigail Whimbrel, we live here by rights: and have lived here all our lives."

Xavier entered the room guardedly nonetheless, his eyes rapidly darting from side to side: yet, apart from the opulence of the furnishings and the exces-sive ornamentation of the walls and ceiling, which he adjudged as comically vulgar, though doubtless costly, he could see nothing immediately remiss, or "suspicious": save perhaps the wider of the two fireplaces, and its spacious chimney, which looked as if it might accommodate an adult figure (might an assailant have climbed down into the room from the roof?); and the several *trompe l'oeil* paintings, which fascinated, yet finally repelled, with their deliberate air of the *artificially lifelike*. As for the place of death,—the carved antique bed with its silken canopy, and its look of inappropriate splendor—Xavier had only to approach it, and to draw his hand along the brocaded cover, to sense that all that had been remarkable about it had fled. Yet here it stood, before him: and here he was, at the *scene of the crime* at last. "So it has happened that my good luck has prevailed," Xavier said, as much to himself as to Perdita,—"for I now stand in the very place in which the Whimbrel infant died, and the unhappy Abigail Whimbrel went mad."

"Yes, it is a pity: she should not have pressed herself, and her hapless babe, upon us," Perdita softly said.

Xavier but half attended to her words, moving about the room, staring, and stooping, and sniffing, and blinking; noting uneasily how his mirrored reflection aped him, from a dozen glassy surfaces, commingled with overelaborate etchings of ivy, roses, grapevines, etc., and designs in bronze and white, painted directly on the mirrors: his image, and that of the pale-browed Perdita who watched him, brought together in a sort of minuet, in utter silence. That an unspeakable incident of an unknown species had transpired in this bed-chamber, not many weeks previous; that it might very well have been an actual, though senseless, murder; that its cause, or its agent, *might* be sought out one day soon, and exposed, and explained, and "solved"; that what lay in the beclouded realm of the *mysterious* could be transposed, by the rigorous logic of detection, into the *comprehensible,*—was this not remarkable? For, after all, Xavier reasoned with mounting excitement, God Himself is a presence underlying, and giving unity to, all ostensibly discrete phenomena: what appears to the untutored eye as Chaos may be read, by the proper intelligence, and by the proper faith, as Order. He had not yet worked it out, to his own satisfaction, nor did his detective-heroes pause to brood over such matters,—being, of necessity, caught up in *action;* but he was certain, he knew not altogether why, that his Christian faith, and the upbringing which his belovèd parents had provided, would have much to do with his prowess as a detective. "Ah, if only one could remember *forward*," the youth inwardly murmured,—as the multifariousness of the room before him, and, indeed, the room diffracted into numberless rooms by mirrors, so threatened to overwhelm him that the pain between his eyebrows, in the hard-boned region of the glabella, grew for a moment more severe,—"and all that is now baffling, vexing, and mysterious, could be read as History!" Yet, though he paused to draw breath, the euphoria of his heartbeat continued.

With reverent fingers he examined the great canopied bed,—the heavy goose-feather pillows, encased in fine, spotless white linen; the various quilts, comforters, coverlets, linens, etc.; the horsehair mattress, which gave evidence of having been recently and very vigorously cleaned, yet yielded, still, numerous faint stains and discolorations; and then the silken tapestries draped about the bed; and the minutely carved posts. True, there was nothing helpful here: and Perdita's bemused attention made him self-conscious: but he was confident that, in any case, he *was* following a correct procedure. How more directly might George B. Jashber have approached the situation; or Sherlock Holmes; or, indeed, the shrewdly bumptious Pudd'nhead Wilson, who had, as it were, pioneered in the science of *fingerprinting*,—at this time virtually unknown in the States, and sneered at in both Paris and London? And there was the imperturbable C. Auguste Dupin, whose words now echoed, for some reason, in Xavier's brain, as if the great man were personally directing him: *"Perhaps it is the very simplicity of the thing that puts you at fault."*

But Xavier, now standing with his hands on his hips, and surveying the room more generally, could not see how so lavishly glittering a surface, replete with so many differing textures, colors, and dimensions,—the very paradigm, it nightmarishly seemed, of the great world itself—might be reduced to any sort of *simplicity.* Or did he merely lack eyes to see that which stared him in the face—?

Perdita said, in a lowered voice, that the agents of the baby's death were evidently rats,—a giant species—a species hitherto unknown at the Manor—that made their way by some undetermined method into the room, on that tragic night, and had not been glimpsed again since: the which should have rendered poor Jupiter blameless, in her Uncle Simon's judgment, yet did not: and did not Xavier think Uncle most cruel to persist in blaming Jupiter? As Xavier did not know how best to reply to this artless query, he murmured an assent, taking care not to allow his gaze to fix upon his cousin with an inordinate boldness: for the danger was, it seemed, his impassioned blood might too strongly beat, and cause Perdita to become frightened: to "vanish," as it were, from out his rapt vision—! In a gentle voice he inquired of her whether she did not think it somewhat peculiar that giant rats of an "unknown species" might attack a sleeping baby, and so disappear,—into the walls, or the ceiling, or the very air—as to leave no trace behind: whether some other agent, not, perhaps, an animal at all, might be sought? Perdita bit at her plump lower lip, and appeared to be thinking deeply; then averred that no other agent might be sought, as there *was* no other agent: for, after all, the bed-chamber had been locked and bolted before Mrs. Whimbrel retired. Xavier asked if no one had heard the baby's cries during the night, or any sound from the mother: and again Perdita looked puzzled, and stared half-smiling at the carpet; and said, with a childish want of guile: "Ah, but babies often cry,—do they not?—and wail, and fuss, and soil themselves, and cause a great commotion. It is thought by some to be their attraction, I suppose, that they are so *uncalculating in their effects;* by others, a disadvantage that, when aroused, they always sound as if they are being killed. So, though I cannot recall having heard the sound of a baby's crying, on that night, I do not believe I would have supposed it remarkable,—there being, after all, an actual baby under our roof at that time."

Xavier was so fascinated by his young cousin's low, soft, somewhat husky voice; and her lovely eyes; and the sweet simplicity of her manner,—that he found her words rather more logical than otherwise; and decided he must not ask whether the house yet echoed the baby's cries, and was, in vulgar terms, "haunted," for so foolish a question, hinting of rank superstition, would surely strike the wrong note. Nor did he wish to ask whether Perdita,—or, indeed, anyone at the Manor—knew how avidly it seemed to be wished, in town, that the old house *be* haunted.

Next, he busied himself in examining the fireplaces, and the chimneys,— with no conspicuous results; and the several tall windows, and their faded draperies; and the closets with their showy mirrored doors; and various items of costly furniture,—couches upholstered in silks and satins, chairs of rococo design, bureaus of mahogany deeply carved in plumes, fruits, scrolls, et al., and a massive black walnut armoire in Oriental design, cunningly mirrored, with no less than two dozen drawers, each empty save for tissue paper, and the dried bodies of dead insects. Alas, and he felt the compulsion to examine each drawer thoroughly!—the while the pulse in his forehead dully throbbed, and his starched collar pricked against his throat. Doubtless like Sheriff Shearwater and the rest, he diligently searched for a *secret passageway,* but found nothing save dustballs, and mouse droppings, and cobwebs, and the husklike corpses of yet more insects. His head throbbed the more when, by accident, he saw in a mirror-maze of countless angles and diffractions the lovely face of his cousin in an expression,—ah, how sweet! how subtly ironic! and, it seemed, how *fond!*— of patient amusement at his industry.

He then turned his attention to the heavy gilt-framed mirrors; and the *trompe l'oeil* paintings, which, all along, had been a source of distraction to him: a pulsatile movement, shading into actual writhing, in the corner of his eye: colors that were too strident, human or cherubic figures that were too insistent,—about, it seemed, to rouse themselves from the wall and lean into the room,—amidst a tangle of grasses, vines, grapes, and rose bushes in which roses luridly bloomed, like damp, pouting, crimson-pink mouths. As a very young boy Xavier had been fascinated by such blatant virtuoso demonstrations of the artist's skill in "tricking the eye": he had often stared at a small oil in his Grandmother De Forrest's drawing room, of a pet monkey with a jeweled collar caught in the act, by his mistress, of making off with a massive bunch of purple grapes,—the "trick" of the painting being its illusion of possessing three dimensions, as the guiltily affrighted monkey leapt (or so it eerily seemed!)

toward the viewer. For some years, Xavier had imagined such japery to be syn-onymous with "art," and had essayed to imitate it, with disappointing results; then, with the passage of time, he had lost interest, and now gazed upon such things with ill-concealed scorn, no matter how others continued to admire them. This mural of Fairfax Eakins, for instance, ranging across much of a wall, and a goodly portion of the ceiling, was intended, it would seem, to express a *holy sentiment*, as the Virgin Mary and the Christ Child were nominally at its center: yet, as the most superficial glance suggested, the purpose of the painting was simply to amuse and to titillate, with angels' heads, shoulders, torsos, el-bows, limbs, wings of divers sizes and shapes, leaning, or falling, or plunging out of the wall, upon the viewer's head. Indeed, the more Xavier stared, the more distaste, shading into actual revulsion, he felt: for were the angels not ungainly, in their overly "realistic" flesh?—and their dazed, or vacuous, or smug, or leer-ing, or contemptuous, expressions not highly offensive? How queer, their wings!—hooked like a bat's in caricature; or tall and befeathered; or scaled; or possessed of a peacock's brilliance.

As he stared, Xavier was gripped by a childish sense that the angelic host was, in turn, observing him, with expressions of withheld mirth: a comely an-drogynous figure seemed about to wink at him, holding a flute to its lips; a puffy-faced adolescent angel, of about Xavier's age, seemed to have arched his eyebrow a bit higher, tilting in Xavier's direction; a more sinister creature, with talons instead of feet, and the drooping black-feathered wings of a bird of prey, was regarding him with scarce-concealed hunger,—and derision. How queerly unsettling, this "religious" subject!—and with what virtuoso flippancy it was ex-ecuted!—as if, in a sense, the painter had secretly regarded his work as pro-found, even while he mocked the viewer, and his wealthy patron, with every stroke of his brush.

Xavier observed to his cousin, who stood a discreet distance away, her hands clasped before her, that he had not, within memory, encountered so *bizarre* a painting: for one could not interpret it as reverent, nor could one dis-miss it as willfully sacrilegious; one could not mock it, as it *was* a mockery; and one could certainly not ignore it.

Perdita murmured that she could not follow her cousin's abstruse logic, and had so little training in aesthetics, she wished to make no judgment on the matter: save to observe that, as she quietly phrased it, "angels *may* turn demon, with the passage of time,—if starved of the love that is their sustenance."

At this moment, a drop of water, or some more viscous liquid substance, which had been forming by degrees in the narrowed eye of an angel overhead, grew suddenly heavy enough to fall: and Xavier instinctively put out his hand to catch it: a *teardrop,* one might almost fancy, or, judging by its faint crimson stain, a *blooddrop,*—which the bemazed youth, scarcely thinking what he did, brought to his lips to taste.

"It's blood," he murmured,—and his heart lurched.

But in the next instant he had sufficiently recovered himself to observe, in a more composed tone, that the ceiling must be leaking; that rainwater must have accumulated in the attic overhead, to make its way through intermittently, under pressure,—for this was one of the countless vexations the Kilgarvans of Wycombe Street had with *their* house; roofs being evidently very costly to repair. Perdita startled him by taking his hand to examine it: but by now the drop had vanished, and only a faint crimson discoloration remained in the palm—the consequence, no doubt, of rainwater dyed by paint.

"Blood, you say,—blood?" Perdita said, her eyes darkening, and her voice urgent. "Yet how might it be *blood,* dripping merely from the ceiling?"

"No, it was not blood," Xavier said. "I am certain, Cousin, it was not blood,—only a raindrop."

"And yet,—you tasted it: I saw you bring it to your lips."

"Yet it was not blood, for how could it be blood, as you say?" Xavier asked, disguising the uneasiness he felt. "As to why I tasted it,—I do not know: an infantile sort of impulse, perhaps, for which I cannot account."

As no further drops fell from the ceiling,—the pale angel's eye being, evidently, now dry—Xavier moved away, to make a final cursory examination of the room: and to tax himself with Monsieur Dupin's admonition as to the *simplicity* of the situation. "Yet," he thought, "is it not invariably, and smugly, the case that any human situation can be defined as *simple* by those who dwell, as it

were, above it; and refined out of temporal existence by one or another author-
ial stratagem? For if one dwells here below, in the very midst of the puzzle, the
navigation of the next hour,—nay, the next *minute*—is a challenge."

Perdita docilely agreed to lead him upstairs, into the attic, that he might examine the space directly above the room; though, as he told himself sternly, he
must not expect to find anything so remarkable as a pool of blood. While the
young people were making their cautious way along the corridor, to a back
stairs, Xavier was startled to hear a voice or voices nearby: but was assured by
Perdita that they were in no danger of being detected,—it was doubtless Uncle
Simon reading aloud a passage from his *Treatise,* in the solitude of his spartan
room, that he might, as he said, test the resiliency of his prose to see whether it
possessed that *steely thinness* which all metaphysical pondering required, to save
it from muddle. ("It is said in town," Xavier whispered, "that Uncle has been behaving strangely of late: being, first of all, far more often *seen;* and several times
in the company of an unknown woman, many years his junior." Blushing prettily, Perdita seemed at first loath to reply; then leaned to Xavier, and murmured
in his ear with childish ire: "It is not so. It cannot be. They lie: it is as Georgina
says, they always lie. Uncle works on his *Treatise* upward of twelve hours daily;
Father's death has very much impressed upon him the nature of,—as he says
in *his* words—the 'intractability of the phenomenal world,' and the fact of his
own impending mortality. So it is, he works near-constantly,—and rarely
leaves home.")

As Xavier might have foreseen, the cavernous low-ceilinged attic of Glen
Mawr, airless, stifling hot, disagreeably abuzz with flies, proved no less "in-
tractable" than the Honeymoon Room: being a veritable graveyard of stored
and cast-off things, draped with sheets, and awash in such a profusion of odors
(of dust, mildew, rot, moth-crystals; the droppings and decayed corpses of mice,
birds, bats, etc.; the desiccated shellac coating the taped surfaces of dressmak-
ers' dummies; etc.), the luckless youth felt sickened within the first minute of
his entry. But Perdita bravely led him forward, through a maze of steamer
trunks, upright cartons, paintings, furniture, ladies' hat-boxes mounting to the
ceiling, mirrors in whose grime-coated glasses twin images, scarcely of "boy"

and "girl," eerily floated, and all the melancholy useless paraphernalia of a household: bringing him, by instinct it seemed, to the approximate area he desired, directly above the Honeymoon Room. But, ah!—was he not disappointed to see that, indeed, no *pool of blood* lay underfoot, but only a coating of dust,—or, rather, numberless coatings of dust, through which the footprints of various years might be dimly discerned, amidst the tinier pawprints of mice.

Gamely, Xavier made an effort to investigate, he knew not precisely what: and felt the more self-conscious, and a bit of a dandy and a fool, under the close scrutiny of his cousin. With a gingerly motion he drew a dust-heavy sheet from off an ottoman, in itself discolored by dust, to discover naught but a little gathering of dead moths, their wings turned to paper, and their bodies but dried husks. Elsewhere, in opening with fumbling fingers a lady's hat-box tightly bound with twine, he frightened up a mouse, whose panicked scuttling quite startled both himself and Perdita, and made the pulse behind his eyes throb the more sullenly.

So malodorous was the air, and so inhospitable the general terrain, he could not bring himself to stay for very many minutes; and busied himself poking, and prying, and sniffing, about a massive sideboard of Chippendale design, rather more because its numerous drawers were *locked* than because it aroused his suspicions. This ungainly piece of furniture, not unlike one belonging to his De Forrest grandparents, was perhaps eight feet in length, with excessive Oriental ornamentation in mock-bamboo trim, and bird "claws" for feet, and raised sections at either end, housing a series of drawers with bamboo knobs. The high-gloss French finish had long since faded; the lavish cornucopia carvings on either side of the splashboard were all but obscured in dust; so layered with grime was the oval mirror, Xavier would have been hard put to recognize his own image there, afloat in a cloudy sea. Two of the drawers opened easily, and were empty; the others were locked; as was the large central panel,—a fact Xavier's boyish self told him must be *suspicious,* but his more mature self supposed meant very little. Yet he poked and pried about, under his cousin's sweet gaze, as methodically as possible, for, even so prematurely in his "career," he knew that he must not surrender to the tide of *doubt, hopelessness,* and *near-*

sickened self-contempt, it seemed to him altogether reasonable to feel at this juncture.

Alas, how opportunely it always happened, at precisely such "calm" moments in the adventures of Xavier's detective-heroes, that a *clue* of some sort thrust itself forward; or even a sudden eructation of danger. But, sadly, this was not to be Xavier's experience in the attic; and it was with an air of somewhat shamed disappointment that he gave up, and followed Perdita back to the stairs. All fleetingly it crossed his mind that, even here, in this unprepossessing region, he *was* being observed: and could not help himself from glancing uneasily about. But of course there was nothing to be seen; and, apart from the idle buzzing of the flies, nothing to be heard.

"And now, perhaps, dear Xavier, you might take your leave," Perdita said, with a worried glance to both sides, as the young people stealthily descended the stairs, "—for while Georgina is confined to her sickbed, and not likely to discover us, I cannot answer to poor Thérèse's wanderings,—or to old Pride, who might turn up anywhere, in 'guarding,' as he imagines it, our household; and I am certain the tyrant carries tales back to his mistress, about all of us."

Xavier felt the wisdom, and the reasonableness, of his companion's words; and surely his own instinct urged him to escape, with great relief, to the freshness of the June sunshine,—indeed, to all the vast, unfettered, healthsome world beyond Glen Mawr Manor! But some measure of detectively stubbornness resided in his breast; and, it may have been, a romantic disinclination to leave little Perdita: for when again might he hope to see her?—when again, to stand so close beside her, to gaze upon her enchanting face, to exchange such intimate confidences? More than once, during the course of the past hour, occupied as he was with *investigation,* the cunning youth had stolen a glance at his cousin; and felt the forbidden knowledge that he might, *if he wished to press hard enough,* dare to brush his lips against her cheek,—nay, against her very lips! Now it came over him again, with the force of delirium, that it was within his power, *if he so wished,* to take Perdita's small hand, and fondle it; to caress her shoulders, and her lovely neck; to bring his warm lips close,—ah, very close— to her ear, her throat, her mouth; to confess to her, in a low, tremulous, yet altogether sincere voice, that he believed he was in love with her: if *love* was not an offense, or an outrage to her tender ear.

But he dared not risk such boldness: and contented himself with drawing very close to her, and stooping to murmur in her ear, whether he might explore, however briefly, the *cellar:* and then, he promised, he would be off,—and never trouble her again on such a fool's errand.

Perdita's cheeks faintly colored, as if taking heat from Xavier's warm breath; and a childish frown appeared between her delicate brows. She reiterated her suggestion that he leave, and quickly,—for a considerable space of time had passed since his arrival. (To his uneasy surprise, Xavier saw by means of a grandfather's clock nearby that *more than two hours had elapsed!*—with the brevity and fluidity of less than one.) Still he persisted: touching as if by accident the girl's arm, and her slender shoulder: and promising that he would remain below-stairs only ten minutes, or less: and then he *would* be gone.

After a prolonged hesitation Perdita sighed, and essayed to smile, with a droll and innocently coquettish upward turn of her eyes, saying that she might as well acquiesce; that she was after all accustomed to such: and only hoped that Georgina would not find out and, when the strength in her arm returned, subject her to a sound whipping. When Xavier evinced surprise at hearing this, Perdita somewhat irritably drew away, saying that neither she nor Thérèse had ever been punished, by Georgina or by their dear father, without having brought it on themselves: and she, Perdita, was by far the worse offender. "But surely you are not actually *whipped?*" Xavier said, staring at her. "For it was altogether rare that my father ever laid a hand to *us,* over the years: and Wolf was particularly deserving as a boy." Perdita shrugged her shoulders, and made a charming little grimace, saying that "Justice was a more precious matter than mere Mercy,"— that, in any case, she had only used a figure of speech: *whipping* to signify *scolding.*

Being led down a narrow stairs to the cellar, Xavier had prescience enough to take, from a shelf, a waxen stub of candle, and to light it, that they might see some six or eight feet before them—but, alas, not very clearly. He was reminded as they descended, Perdita just before him, of an old fairy tale or legend his mother used to read to him, oft-times as he drifted off to sleep, of children entering a dark wood: a boy and a girl, alone and lost, or soon to be lost: clutching at each other in fearful desperation. Yet it seemed to him, even in the face of the murky and ill-smelling cellar, with its earthen floor, that to be *lost* in such a space, in lovely Perdita's company, would prove a delight indeed—!

So they descended; and walked stumblingly about; assailed by divers odors of mustiness, and rot, and drainage, and rich dark earth, and food gone rancid; and Xavier's sensitive nostrils picked up a faint smell of something decaying, or feculent,—which so disgusted him, he halfway wished to turn back. Perdita whispered that she knew very little of the cellar, save that it did not extend beneath the entire house, but only the central area; that it frequently flooded in the spring; and that there *were* rats, surely, throughout,—for which reason, she said, shivering, she wished not to stay there very long.

Still, Xavier wished to poke about, so long as his candle lasted. He followed the sound of trickling water until he came to a stone wall embedded in the earth; he followed the scent of decayed fruit until he came to a storage room; he groped about until his hand brushed against an iron grating, and sizable iron hinges, on a heavy oaken door,—a dungeonlike chamber, it seemed, not very distant from the stairway, but recessed beneath it.

He asked Perdita what this was, but she seemed not to know: a part of the fruit cellar, perhaps: though why a mere storage room should have a door with an iron bolt, and a grated opening, *very* like a dungeon cell, she could not say. Xavier tugged at the door, which, though difficult to move, and creaking on its hinges, was unlocked; and went boldly inside, his candle aloft, to reveal, amidst somber cobwebbed shadows, a windowless space of some ten feet in diameter, of an irregular circular shape. Divers odors assailed him, of a kind he did not care to identify: and he felt for a moment he might be ill. Though, upstairs, he had been uncomfortably perspiring for some time, he now began to shiver, so that his teeth came near to chattering; and the sensitive hairs at the nape of his neck stirred. What place was this? What human presence even now emanated from it? Though altogether empty, and starkly devoid of any "evidence," it seemed to him a place of unmistakable damnation.

Perdita whimpered that they *must* leave, but Xavier paid her no mind, stooping to examine the hard-packed earthen floor, in which a multitude of footprints might be discerned, most with compact little heels, as of a lady's tiny shoe; and squatting to examine some scratchings, or actual writing, in one area of the stone wall. "It is nothing," Perdita said in a frightened voice, in which an air of impatience might have been discerned. "It is very old, and worthless, going back to ancient times: I beg of you, Cousin, do come out." But Xavier squatted now on his heels, holding the tremulous candle-flame aloft, that he might, with painstaking difficulty, decipher the letters so crudely carved in the rock: for, it seemed, there was a message of sorts here, and a most remarkable one, in the form of *verse*. Ignoring Perdita's entreaties, and even her shy pokings against his shoulder, and the brush of her knuckles against his hair,—which would, doubtless, at another time, have greatly aroused him—Xavier haltingly read out these words:

> *Herein, a broken Sinner—*
> *Ah, engorged in Shame!—*
> *Godly Husband & Father—*
> *Blessèd be* Thy *name!*
> *If—You will forgive—*
> *& I rise to Your bosom—again—*

"But the verse breaks off," Xavier said aloud, "and the rhyme is not completed." Nor could he, by groping about, and peering along the stretch of the damp chill rock, locate any further markings.

So absorbed was the impetuous youth in his search, he was but dimly aware of Perdita's distress, or ire; and of the strain upon his back and thighs; and the sickly throbbing of his head. How strange was this discovery, and what exultation flooded him—! Now he knew that he had not been mistaken to believe that *anything* and *everything* possessed meaning: and that, with luck and persistence, *he* should decipher it. He inquired of his companion who might have scratched that verse into the rock, and when, and why: if the language did not suggest to her that of her own sister Georgina;—assuming that Perdita was familiar with her sister's odd poetry, as he was. Irritably, in a voice of uncharacteristic harshness, Perdita said that the "doggerel" he had quoted dated back, as she had explained, to "ancient times": that, many generations ago, before anyone who now lived was born, certain "criminal" Indians, slaves, and servants had been sequestered in the cellar of Glen Mawr, for safekeeping, *she* knew not altogether why: but so her father had chanced to mention, and so it must be true.

As he was examining with his fingertips the abrasive, marred surface of the stone, to see if he might discover any further markings, Xavier failed to fully attend to her words, or her reiterated plea that he at last come *out:* for, she declared, she could not breathe in so foul a place, and felt sickened to her very soul. Xavier murmured an assent; but was inwardly cursing himself that he had not the wherewithal to make a rubbing of the verse,—tissue paper and charcoal being all that he would need. "Next time," the perspiring youth bethought himself, "I shall come better prepared."

Not a minute afterward, while he was still vainly groping along the wall, he felt an emanation of sharply cold air: and only chanced to look over his shoulder, at the very moment the oaken door swung shut, and locked!—with a remarkable force, as if it had been blown by a violent wind, or angrily pushed. And, ah!—with what horror he saw that Perdita was no longer close behind him, but had, it seems, "vanished": nor did she answer to his strangulated cry, as he sprang to the door, to discover that it was bolted from without.

In this precipitant motion, the unhappy boy dropped his candle-stub, and *the airless space was engirded in darkness.*

So numbed was Xavier by this remarkable development, he could scarcely grasp the sequence of events, still less what he might do: and such was his pitiful gallantry that, for the first several minutes, he could not comprehend that sweet Perdita had slammed the door upon him; and imagined that she might be in danger, and requiring of his aid. Thus it was, he murmured only her name, repeatedly, beseechingly, as if it were a summons,—or a plea,—or a prayer.

"*Perdita—!*"

But no sound responded,—save the tranquil trickling of water across rock.

The Lost Suitor

As to Miss Georgina Kilgarvan's aloof, faunlike, yet, it was claimed, unfailingly courteous young man, Mr. Malcolm Guillemot,—believed, in truth, to be two or three years her junior—there had seemed to Winterthurn a substantial gathering of facts regarding him, in the twelve-month space of time during which he "courted" Georgina: yet, as these shards, ellipses, impressions, and mere innuendos (frequently contradictory) failed, it seemed perversely, to add up to a uniform portrait, general mystification and disappointment were felt on all sides. Of the actual likelihood of Miss Georgina Kilgarvan becoming a bride, there was an informal consensus amongst the Kilgarvans' set that this would never transpire: but a contentious division as to whether the match must fail because Chief Justice Erasmus Kilgarvan would never give up his cherished daughter (and to a young man, it was whispered, of exceedingly modest resources,—both his father and grandfather being Presbyterian ministers in a neighboring state); or as a consequence,—so the men jocosely predicted—of Mr. Guillemot's *delayed good sense.*

Indeed, it was a perennial debate as to Miss Georgina's virtues in the comparative light of those of other Winterthurn heiresses of her generation. A goodly contingent of ladies, the older matrons in particular, held that Erasmus's eldest daughter was a decidedly handsome young woman, with fine sharp "snapping" eyes, and a smile that charmed when it would, and an excellent carriage,—albeit there was sometimes a haughtiness in even her warmer manner that unsettled where it wished to please. Yet numerous other persons, amongst them detractors of the Judge, or those who had actually felt the deadly whiplash of his scorn, deemed her *sour,* and *petulant,* and *frankly plain:* as if the defiant *unprettiness* of her verse were matched by her public manner. Miss Kilgarvan was a *lady,* it was granted,—but only by virtue of her station, and not her character.

For was "Iphigenia" not, like her poetry, a vexing sort of puzzle: intransigent, offensive, with an air of concealing far more than she yielded—?

* * *

Of the thirty-odd ladies present at that meeting of the Thursday Afternoon Society, at which the visiting lecturer Mr. Guillemot recited in a high, impassioned, slightly quavering voice his "renderings into English" of certain lyric
poems of Heine, some declared themselves most struck by his large, wide-set,
sensitive brown eyes, their gaze affixed, it seemed, in space; and by the marble-
like smoothness of his narrow brow; and by the charming way in which, as if
windblown, his silky fair hair fell in two distinct "wings" about his delicate face.
Others, no less equally impressed, took note of the stylish cut of his frock coat
and trousers, in a subtle hue of heather beige; and the propriety of his ascot tie,
in russet satin; and the subdued richness of his vest, embroidered in scarlet,
beige, and creamy silk. It was afterward debated as to whether the young visitor
had recited his translations with a lisp, or no; and whether he had, at the
podium, rocked gently to and fro, with the mesmerizing rhythms of the verse.
And the ladies were in amiable disagreement concerning the effect of his performance: the most controversial of the pieces being Heine's "Die Götter
Griechenlands," which, some averred, was almost *too* powerful in certain of
its lines,—

> *And you also I recognize,—you too, Aphrodite:*
> *Golden once, and now, alas, silver!*
> *Though the charm of the bridal gown adorns you,*
> *Secretly I dread your beauty;*
> *And if your chaste body should delight me*
> *Like other heroes, I would die of terror.*
> *As a Death Goddess you reveal yourself:*
> VENUS LIBITINA!

—these final words being uttered by Mr. Guillemot in so impassioned a tone,
his very voice seemed to shudder.

Afterward it was asserted, altogether erroneously, that Malcolm Guillemot
had been gazing upon Miss Georgina Kilgarvan throughout his performance,
and that he had, from the first, directed his recitation toward *her.* Clarice Von

Goeler, who had accompanied Georgina to the meeting, knew that this was hardly the case, and was to recall, for years afterward, with a pang of jealousy, how avidly Georgina had hung upon Guillemot's every syllable,—how, indeed, the young woman had leaned forward in her seat, her neck and shoulders near-quivering with strain. During the question period, when tea and sandwiches were being served, Georgina had somewhat recovered herself, and asked the handsome visitor whether it was a valid supposition, or a mere whimsy of her own, that "all poetry was, in a sense, *translation*, or *artful rendering*, of the Un-known depths of passion, into the Known strictures of language."

Precisely how Mr. Guillemot essayed to answer this riddlesome question of "Iphigenia's,"—whether in truth the startled gentleman *had* answered it—very few witnesses could afterward agree. But that he had, for the remainder of the hour, fixed his attention pointedly upon Miss Georgina Kilgarvan, all concurred.

Thereafter, in the weeks and months following, Georgina and Mr. Guillemot were frequently seen together, alone, or in the company of Georgina's father,—riding in the Judge's handsome brougham, along Berwick Avenue, or the River Road, or through Juniper Park; in the sumptuous tearoom of the Winterthurn Arms, or amidst the quaint wrought-iron tables and chairs of the Charity Street Sweet Shoppe; at an open-air watercolor exhibit on Courthouse Green; at an acclaimed production of *Lohengrin* at the Grand Opera House in Vanderpoel. Less frequently, doubtless out of reserve, they were seen together as a couple at one or another of the season's social events: the lavish Peregrine-Shaw nuptials, the Annual Strawberry Fête of the Ladies' Auxiliary of the Corinthian Club, Colonel Westergaard's fox-hunting weekend (at which, it should be hastily re-ported, very few of the guests actually rode horseback, let alone beheld foxes torn to pieces by impassioned dogs); Mr. Guillemot slender, pale, affable enough, yet distinctly reserved; and Miss Kilgarvan flushed with girlish plea-sure, yet shy, it seemed, of being observed, by the parents of her students in par-ticular,—as if she feared being criticized, or held up to contempt, or jeered at behind her back.

Very odd it was, that, during even those halcyon months of Romance,—deemed to be Georgina's first—the clotted and indecorous verse of "Iphigenia" continued to appear, in such divers publications as *Hudson Valley Leaves,* and *Godey's Lady's Book:* as the sport of editors, it was whispered by Georgina's detractors; or as a consequence of actual bribery.

Though Georgina never spoke of Malcolm Guillemot to Clarice Von Goeler, or to any of her female acquaintances, in any terms less than resolutely impersonal (as "Mr. Guillemot, the poet and translator"), it would have required no inordinately acute eye to discern that the Judge's daughter was at last in love; and artlessly so. For was her complexion not touched with a rosy sort of warmth, and less sallow than anyone had ever observed?—was her gaze not bright, and direct, and less overshadowed by irony? Though held to be slightly stiff in Mr. Guillemot's actual presence, or given to nervously fluttering her fan, like a very young girl, Georgina was, it seemed, blessed with new energy, in other contexts: for she taught her classes at the Parthian Academy with inspiration and zeal (as even those girls who hated her were forced to admit), and did her charity work with less ill-concealed impatience; and was one of the Winterthurn organizers in a course for ladies in "first aid," offered by the local hospital. (It had struck Georgina with the air of a revelation that, by the adroit use of one's fingers, *one might actually do something to affect the well-being of another.* Though professing, like all the ladies, an extreme horror of the very sight of blood, and a "weakness about the chest" aroused by any thought of physical distress, Georgina applied herself diligently to the instruction: learning emergency procedures to be followed in case of divers accidents and crises,—woundings, drownings, strokes, heart attacks, chokings, the breaking of arms, legs, etc., and childbirth. How deftly her long fingers worked, applying tourniquets, and gauze bandages, and splints; with what utter absorption she practiced cleansing wounds, and making injections; giving artificial respiration; learning even to induce vomiting; even how to give enemas, in theory at least. Long after the course was over, and the majority of the ladies had forgotten all they had learned, Georgina carried about with her, in her handbag, a compact kit filled with the paraphernalia of the trenches, so to speak: gauze strips, ammonia in vials, compresses of numerous sizes, bandages and bandage scissors, inoculation needles, etc. Sadly, she had no occasion to practice her new-acquired skill, so far as anyone knew,—save when pretty young Mrs. Shaw, pregnant with her first child, sank into a swoon in the midsummer airlessness of Grace Church; and was revived within minutes, by Miss Georgina Kilgarvan's alacrity in breaking open a vial of spirits of ammonia beneath her nostrils. And even in so doing, poor Georgina risked censure, for the public nature of her "performance," as certain persons—including her own father—called it: and for her conspicuous intrusion upon territory that might be said to have been reserved for Dr. Colney Hatch, or another gentleman physician.)

Georgina Kilgarvan's *spinsterish irony,*—held in abeyance, as it were, for the duration of Malcolm Guillemot's courtship—was to return with some grim ferocity after that gentleman vanished from her side: and the zealousness of her teaching at the Parthian Academy was to drain away, like water from out a cracked vase: and, not least to disappear was her handiness at proffering "first aid" in public,—though no one was to know whether she continued to carry her medical kit about with her, over the years, hidden away in her alligator handbag.

A decade later Lucas Kilgarvan was to recall, with some poignancy, two enigmatical experiences of his, pertaining to his niece and her erstwhile "suitor" (this term requiring quotation marks, as no engagement, official or unofficial, was ever mentioned): each of which he was prevailed upon to recount to his youngest son, who begged him to tell all he knew of Georgina's past, in the weeks and months following the initial tragedy at Glen Mawr.

The earliest incident was of fairly little significance, involving, as it did, Lucas's failure to draw Malcolm Guillemot out in commonplace conversation, and to establish some sort of congenial masculine rapport between them, on the late-morning train to Nautauga Falls, one winter's day. After having introduced himself as the younger brother of Erasmus Kilgarvan, and the somewhat youthful uncle of Miss Georgina (there being but seven years' difference in their ages), Lucas inquired warmly of Mr. Guillemot whether he would like to join him in the club car for a cigar; or, somewhat later, for lunch in the dining car. Would he, at the very least, like to share a hackney cab at the Falls—?

But the watchful young gentleman was too shy for such abrupt camaraderie; or too shrewdly valued his privacy to allow Lucas to intrude (he made it a point, it seemed, to keep his place in his book of Longfellow's verse, while Lucas spoke with him); or,—so Lucas reasoned afterward, with a flush of humiliation—he knew very well the strained relations between himself and Erasmus, arising primarily as a consequence of Lucas's opposition, in his late teens, to the "justice" of the notorious Hester Vaugh case. (Ah, the brashness of youth!—for not only had Lucas quarreled with Chief Justice Erasmus Kilgarvan over the finer points of Miss Vaugh's *guilt*, and the law's definition of *infanticide:* he had also gone about town denouncing his brother: and had even penned an intemperate letter to the *Gazette,* which the Goshawks had, all surprisingly, published. Erasmus was never to forgive him, and never to forget,— and, it seemed, Malcolm Guillemot was privy to this knowledge.)

"To be snubbed by 'Malcolm,'" Lucas hotly murmured, "—why, it is like being thrown off course, mounted upon a stallion, by a mere *butterfly.*"

As to the second, and more complex, episode: this transpired one Sunday evening in June of the following year, near the end of Mr. Guillemot's friendship with Georgina, as it turned out (though no one knew at the time,—indeed, an "official announcement" was generally expected, amongst the Kilgarvans' social set). The setting was Juniper Park, near the splendid old band pavilion: the time, not long past dusk, when fireflies had made their first tremulous appearance of the night; and many a child had at last fallen asleep in his mother's lap; and the Winterthurn Marching Band,—some thirty-odd gentlemen, livened as much by jovial high spirits as by musical skill—had temporarily laid aside their instruments, to allow for a half-hour's intermission in their concert. Lucas Kilgarvan, a new straw hat rakishly set atop his head, had been sent by his wife to fetch ices for herself and the boys,—Xavier being but five and a half years old at this time—and had, all by accident, been detained by the milling crowd: with the unforeseen, and, indeed, sincerely unwished, result that he chanced to over-hear snatches of a decidedly queer conversation, between a husky-voiced young woman and her male companion: the very voices, Lucas gradually realized, *of Georgina and Mr. Guillemot.*

As their words were sporadic rather than even, and seemed at times to drop away altogether into silence, Lucas could not have vouchsafed that he heard what it seemed he heard; nor could he have sworn whose voice, amidst the general merriment of the crowd, was *whose,*—for Georgina's oft-times inclined toward the low, the dry, and the sardonic; and Mr. Guillemot's, toward the thin and high-pitched.

Fired by a melancholic urgency as they were, were these words not, at the very same time, touched,—ah, so cruelly!—by the comical?

". . . soon, then. For it is my . . ."

". . . cannot. You *know* I cannot."

"Indeed, please!"

"Nay, I beg of *you:* please."

". . . a matter of . . ."

"You are cruel."

". . . stubborn."

". . . a matter of expediency."

"You *know* it cannot be."

"Until such time as . . ."

"But you *know* he will not."

"Yet it is my . . ."

". . . beg of you, please!"

"And of *you* . . . !"

After a pause of some awkwardness, during which time Lucas felt his face heat with the guilty ambiguity of his position,—for was he not, in truth, *eaves-dropping?*—at last Georgina said, in a tone of resignation: "How much more merciful if one were a brass instrument, all noise and confidence, and no contemptible creature of mere *flesh* . . ."

By the time Lucas could make his escape undetected, to return to his youthful family on the far side of the pavilion, his ices were badly melted; and his mood grown sober, with pity for his unhappy niece.

It must have been in early autumn that it was belatedly discovered that Miss Georgina's "gentleman" had not been glimpsed for some weeks; and, of a sudden, tongues began to wag; and female relatives made discreet inquiries at the Manor, as to Mr. Guillemot's availability for one or another social occasion. Georgina was confined to her room with an illness, declared to be *minor,* and requiring no solicitude: then again, it was said that she planned an ambitious journey abroad, to Paris, Florence, and Rome; and would be leaving presently. Crueler still, and quite without foundation, were rumors that the Judge's daughter had been precipitately *jilted;* and that Erasmus's chagrin was such, he would seek revenge through the courts, directing a "breach of promise" suit on behalf of his wronged daughter—! So ubiquitous, and so slanderous, was this persistent rumor that Henry Peregrine, the Kilgarvans' chief attorney, saw fit to refute it upon several occasions in Winterthurn drawing rooms: yet did poor Georgina no especial favor by angrily declaring that "the abused young lady had suffered heartbreak and humiliation enough, without such nonsense being noised about."

A yet more pitiless rumor, and equally without foundation, was that, like the specter of Crazy Eliza of old, the Kilgarvan heiress wandered about her ancestral home in a shamefully disheveled state, barefoot, unwashed, her hair loosed to her hips, and tangled with leaves and burrs. Singing such mournful and near-tuneless little songs, it was said, as "My Love's A-roaming," and "The Ghostly Swain," and "Shall You Come Home Again, Michael O'Meara?" she braided her hair with willow straw, and affixed, to her meager bosom, such wildflowers,—bluets, anemones, tiny asters—as, it seemed, most enhanced her waxen pallor. In this, she was closely watched at all times by both a nurse and a manservant, sworn by the Judge to absolute secrecy: for, ah! would it not have been scandalous indeed, if such things were generally known—?

The "Little Nun"

POOR THÉRÈSE KILGARVAN—!

It could not have failed to escape the sensitive young girl that, of late, careless persons had begun to distinguish between her and Perdita by speaking of the "Plain One," and the "Pretty One"; nor that she was sometimes called the "Little Nun," in contradistinction to the "Blue Nun,"—both terms being inexcusably cruel. It was natural that Thérèse, motherless as a child, should have turned gratefully to God for solace; natural too that, like many another Winterthurn girl of her age and station, she should have been drawn to *goodness*. Thus, how unfair, to be spoken of so slightingly behind her back—!

"Can you guess what they call us when they imagine we cannot hear?" Perdita once asked Thérèse, with a sly creasing of her brows; but the elder wisely turned away, with a prim admonishment that, as such things were not for their ears, why should they condescend to hear? "For, dear sister," Thérèse said, with a trembling lip, "I do not wish to think evil of others, any more than I wish to hear evil of myself."

Thérèse was not yet four years of age when her mother died; and it was her and her sister's lot to be reared, in the main, by her half-sister Georgina, their elder by some twenty-eight years. ("What a pity it is," Mrs. Lucas Kilgarvan frequently observed, "that relations between the two houses are so blighted! For Thérèse and Perdita are good, sweet girls, clearly lonely, if not starved for female companionship,—other than that of Miss Georgina's, I mean. And I, who have sons but no daughters, should have dearly loved to 'mother' them!")

Though a "little nun" in a sense, in her Christian behavior, Thérèse was hardly immune to ordinary schoolgirl sentiments. So far as Georgina allowed, she participated in divers harmless activities at the Parthian Academy; and, though not overly popular with her classmates, she was, in general, not disliked by them,—until very recent times. Now, though the proud young girl never acknowledged whisperings and innuendos, and the rude stares of certain of her classmates, it did not escape her that she and Perdita were singled out for censure: sometimes pitied, and sometimes contemned, for being Kilgarvans and dwelling at Glen Mawr.

"Let them mock us, and say what they will!" Perdita said fiercely. "They will pay for it all, one day—!"

"Nay, nay, dear sister," Thérèse replied at once, "you must not speak in such desperation!—surely it is a sin!"

Being a maiden of tender years, and yet more tender passions, Thérèse was quite ashamed to discover herself, *at her father's very funeral,* staring for long unwavering minutes at her cousin Xavier,—the youngest son of the detested Wycombe Street Kilgarvans, of whom, all her young life, she had heard such disagreeable things.

Yet, ah!—was Xavier not handsome?—and fresh-cheeked?—and innocent in his bearing?—and quite oblivious, it seemed, of the ignominy borne by his father?

Xavier was not truly a cousin of Thérèse's, but a sort of half- or quarter-cousin; for his father, Lucas, was but a half-uncle of hers, and descended from the D'Ivers side of the family. (Which is to say, by way of Phillips Goode's second wife, Miriam D'Ivers,—who, as family legend had it, was the distant descendant of an unsanctioned liaison between a French settler of wayward inclinations and an Indian woman.) In his youth, Lucas had been interested in breeding and racing horses; then he had studied law,—until, it was rumored, Erasmus's great success discouraged him; for a year or so he had attended the Episcopal Theological Seminary in Hartford, Connecticut; he had married too young, against his father's wishes; he had borrowed recklessly on the strength of his future inheritance, to set up a foolish sort of business,—a *toymaking workshop!*—scarcely a profession for one of his social stature. "A contemptible failure," Erasmus Kilgarvan oft murmured, "and a traitor to his heritage beside."

(Yet Thérèse and Perdita soon learned that toys from the Wycombe Street carpentry shop were greatly prized by children, and remembered with especial fondness by those on the brink of growing up: the lovingly crafted dollhouses with their miniature furnishings, and tiny inhabitants; the custom-made rocking horses, designed for individual children; the ingenious jigsaw puzzles limning familiar Winterthurn scenes; the Noah's Ark with its procession of charming animals, all in pairs, save the phoenix; the trains, boats, wagons, galleons, turtle-seats, and sleighs for dolls; most famously, the "Bonnie" doll that blinked, and stared, and slept, and woke, to issue a most human mewing cry, very like an infant.)

At Glen Mawr, Lucas Kilgarvan was known as a *common perjurer* as well: for, it seems, he had done that most unforgivable of things,—he had lied in court, under oath. Neither Thérèse nor Perdita knew a great deal about the case, as such matters were kept private amongst the adults; yet it was no secret that their grandfather had, on his very deathbed, repented of his leniency toward the ne'er-do-well amongst his sons, and struck him from his will: with the consequence that Erasmus and Simon Esdras were then the sole heirs; and Lucas, acting out of both greed and desperation, and, no doubt, a craven desire for revenge, contested the revised will up to the State Supreme Court, with no success. Georgina, who rarely condescended to comment upon such activities, as she called them, of the *Lilliputian "Big" World,* once said of their despised young uncle that he quite deserved his fate for going his own way so wantonly. "One knows not whether to pity him as a fool, or abhor him as a monster," Georgina said, "for marrying, and setting up shop, and whelping four,—or is it five?—sons, on the gossamer strength of a *future inheritance.*"

Yet, during the funeral obsequies, Thérèse had been struck, quite against her inclination, by Lucas's somber, stricken, kindly visage: and the hint of a tear gleaming in his eye: and the grief that seemed to announce itself in his very posture. And how intently he had stared at the handsome ebony casket, as the pall-bearers bore it to the mausoleum: a look of such appalled bewilderment, and childlike loss, it might have been that he mourned his brother after all.

Briefly, Thérèse considered Mrs. Kilgarvan, whose semblance of warmth and maternal solicitude, Georgina had warned, might not be trusted; and the several husky sons,—Bradford, Roland, Colin,—great hulking louts, as Georgina called them; until her eye fell upon the youngest, Xavier,—and quite hooked, and snagged, in sudden girlish sentiment.

"But I must wrench my gaze from him," she thought, "for, surely, my feelings verge on sin; and Father will never forgive me, if he but suspects."

So it happened that the "little nun," hidden behind her dark tulle veil, and dressed in discreet mourning attire, succumbed to Fate: one of those haphazard ecstasies, or fancies, which we of superior age and experience must not too readily dismiss. For was not this child's very namesake St. Theresa herself, transformed by a similar passion,—the *virginal bride*, one might say, of a parallel ecstasy?

Nay, it is wrong for us to too swiftly brush aside adolescent passions; particularly as, in this case, they are to have such significant consequences.

From that day onward, Thérèse uttered many a prayer that God might absolve her of her unwholesome "love" for Xavier Kilgarvan. Yet, perversely, she prized the tender image of her cousin's angelic, yet decidedly masculine, beauty; she dreamt of his dark curly tresses, and his olive-pale skin, and the artless grace of his being. And though he never gazed upon her, she imagined, with a shudder that ran through her slender frame, how powerful it would be, how exquisite a shock, if he ever did.

By degrees, poor Thérèse lapsed into imagining, in her most distraught hours, that Xavier, though scarcely more than a boy, might prove an actual source of aid to Perdita and herself,—that he might be a savior of sorts,—albeit the notion was confused and blasphemous. (Yet certainly it was not Thérèse's fancy that she now saw Xavier so often, in Parthian Square, or along the shady streets near school, strolling with customary schoolboy swagger and never glancing in her direction?)

So it was with both amazement and chagrin that, one mild June morning, she chanced to look out the window of her bed-chamber, to see Xavier himself approaching the house, in plain view: meeting with her sister Perdita as if by prearrangement: and climbing, with boyish insouciance, *into the very house—!*

"What business have they together? How have they managed to communicate with each other? Ah, dear God, if Georgina learns of this—!" So Thérèse muttered aloud, near-overcome with jealousy; and for a long time she could not move from her casement window, as if all her limbs had grown leaden.

"Can it be," she wondered aloud, "that they are sweethearts?—that Georgina's suspicions are true?"

Thérèse stood at attention behind her closed door, and listened intently; but heard nothing. Where was Perdita taking Xavier? And how had it come about that Xavier dared to approach Glen Mawr? Alas, it was a wicked sort of game, Thérèse thought,—and Xavier had best be aware that he was not really welcome in this house.

Many a time Georgina had stormed that Perdita, for all her prettiness, was "of the Devil's party,—stamped with His look about the eyes": and, in truth, Thérèse sometimes halfway fancied there was truth in the charge. For only a wicked, wicked girl would aid a young man in entering a house by stealth, where he was not wanted, and where in fact he was forbidden . . . .

The agitated girl went to her bed, to kneel beside it, and pray to Jesus Christ that all might be well: that no evil be perpetrated beneath her father's roof. So fervently did she pray, so extreme was her distress, that she grew suddenly exhausted; and lapsed into a light fitful sleep; from which she roused herself some time later, confused and shaken.

"Heavenly Father, let it be but a dream, and *he* in no danger—!" she murmured aloud.

But some disquietude of the air, some subtle, yet unmistakable, alteration of the household, warned her that all was not well. Thus she left her room, trembling, to seek out Perdita,—in vain; and to hurry along the many corridors of the house, looking for,—why, she knew not *what:* Xavier himself, or a phantasmagoric figure out of her own dream-fancy?

Her womanly instinct led her at last downstairs, to the gloomy depths of the Manor: where, at once, she heard piteous sounds,—appeals for help muffled through a wall's thickness,—and, ah!—the enfeebled pounding of fists! In that instant she knew what naughty game Perdita had played: for, some years previous, when they were both mere children, Perdita had enticed Thérèse into the cellar, under the pretense of an innocent prank, and had locked her, for one terrifying hour, in the fruit cellar, or "dungeon," as it was sometimes called, beneath the stairs,—a mere child's game, doubtless, yet most frightening to Thérèse.

"Why, did you think I would never let you out?—did you think I would throw away the key, and let you starve to death?" Perdita had asked, her eyes grave with insult. "Why, then,—*you* are very wicked!"

So it was, caring not at all for her appearance, or for the condition of her smock, or collar, or morning-cap, or stockings,—whether her cheeks be rosy, or stricken with pallor—Thérèse hurried down the cellar stairs, and made her groping way to the chamber in which Xavier was confined: and, with but a minute's fumbling effort, managed to force open the rusted sliding bolt,—and free the stricken youth from his prison.

Poor Xavier, to be glimpsed at such a moment!—covered in dust and cobwebs and grime,—badly soaked in perspiration, so that every particle of his clothing was damp, and his person gave off a rank barnyard odor,—his "gentleman's" fingers torn and bleeding,—his voice hoarse from shouting, and from great wracking sobs that scarce befitted a man: how could he display the proper manly gratitude to the young girl who had rescued him?—how could he even restrain himself, to gaze into her face, and murmur words of civil thanks?

Well, it must be ingloriously recorded here that Xavier simply fled: giving but the most distracted of nods to his benefactress,—indeed, did he not push roughly past her?—and, with never a backward glance, sobbing still and panting, he ran from the house, and along the pink-pebbled drive, to the stony portals at the road, and beyond,—ah, as far as his panicked legs would take him: not a remnant,—nay, not a shred—of his former confidence remaining. Poor boy! Not a coward, perhaps, yet surely not the hero he had wished to be!

Thérèse had whispered after him, "Farewell, dear Cousin, and for your soul's sake, never return again!"—but of course he did not hear.

"The Accursèd Kilgarvans"

IT WERE BEST TO SKIM LIGHTLY over the next several months in this history, both in the interests of editorial brevity and that we might allow poor Xavier to recover, as it were, some diminished sense of his Kilgarvan pride, and some small hope of his "professional" future: there being, in any case, no events of especial significance until the fatalities of the autumn,—save perhaps a curious incident reported to have occurred at Phineas Cutter's home, very early one July morning. (This negligible happenstance—much embellished, I am sure, by repeated narrations, and by the eagerness of common folk to participate in the tragedies of their betters, was: when Jabez Dovekie, the burly red-haired iceman employed by Hazelwit's Ice, arrived to make his delivery at the Cutters', he found Mrs. Cutter and her daughter Ariela in a state of dizzied alarm: for, when they had come into the kitchen that morning, it was to discover a "winged creature thumping and fluttering against the window,"—at first glance a small bird, or bat—but *very* desirous of entry, and *very* malevolent of aspect. The somewhat too impetuous Ariela had gone to the window, to tap at it, and frighten the creature away, but had recoiled in screaming consternation: for the thing was neither bird nor bat, it seemed, but possessed a *tiny wizened human face,*— that of an infant greatly aged, and most hideous to gaze upon! When the iceman arrived, Ariela had but partly recovered, and her mother was close to swooning as well: but so bold was Dovekie, and so little disposed to believe women's nonsense, that, with but a moment's hesitation, he strode outside to investigate: finding no demonic creature, nor any evidence of one, save a gigantic moth of unusual iridescent beauty, beating its powdery wings in a cobwebbed corner below the rain-gutter,—which he seized in his great ham of a fist, and destroyed in an instant. Despite the moth's uncommon size, it offered no resistance to its human assailant, but very nearly dissolved to dust in his hand, which did not wash off, or wear off, for over a week: giving Dovekie a most peculiar aura, one hand bronzed and darkened by the sun, and the other covered in a faint margaric powdery sheen, said to glimmer in the dark. As to whether the winged creature possessed a human face, wizened or no,—Dovekie said laughingly that he had not noticed, having no time for such women's giddiness; but knowing only what must be *done*.)

This apparition of sorts was hurriedly attributed by many to an influence of Glen Mawr Manor, not many miles distant; as were two untimely deaths,—that of old Pride, the Kilgarvans' Negro servant; and Miss Imogene Westergaard, one of Winterthurn's most renowned heiresses—which occurred in mid-September, each in the vicinity of the Kilgarvan estate.

It was, in fact, against the rear wall of the Manor garden, part-hidden in a clump of wild rambler rose, that Pride was found, by one of the few servants remaining in the Kilgarvan employ: the luckless old man having been hanged by his neck, and somewhat mutilated, and even "branded" about the chest and back, with the letter *B*—these countless *B*'s being of about three inches in height, and made to overlap, with the impression of a manic exuberance in the seared flesh:

This unsightly death was attributed by some to a supernatural agency emanating from the Manor,—the abode, as certain observers began to openly say, of "the accursèd Kilgarvans"—and, by others, to obscure rites of voodoo vengeance, peculiar to the more primitive races: but no satisfactory explanation was ever arrived at: and, in the light of matters deemed more pressing, as they involved white citizens of a certain elevated rank, the "mystery" of Pride's demise was soon forgotten; or spoken of only in whispers, by local Negroes. (It seemed, however, that the old man was as stubborn in death as he had been in life, and oft returned to disturb persons in divers settings in Winterthurn: the fresh produce markets on Water Street, the dry goods stores, the feed supply mills, etc., which, in life, he had patronized with a lordly air, in the name of the Manor; and the near-deserted servants' wing at the house, where, it was said, he liked to tramp heavily about, groaning and cursing "all the long wretched line of the Kilgarvans, back to Adam, and beyond." Upon several occasions he was sighted on Berwick Avenue, driving a clattering ghost-carriage, drawn by a matched team of ghost-horses; and once, in the most extraordinary visitation, he was seen by the Von Goelers' cook, grinding a pungent mixture of mocha and java coffee beans, in an iron coffee mill nailed to the kitchen wall—! No explanation could be offered for any of these appearances, the last-named being, of course, the most suspect,—for was not the Von Goeler cook a black herself, and notoriously given to spooks and suchlike fancies? Thus it was, young Xavier Kilgarvan was quite surprised to hear his own father *defend* the likelihood of ghosts: for where rank injustice has been perpetrated, and the Law is of no avail, shall not a man's spirit seek some manner of balance, or restitution?—or the meager solace of revenge, in committing mischief? Given to moods of marked sobriety since the death of his elder brother, Mr. Kilgarvan chided Xavier for his shallow,—nay, adolescent—skepticism: and quoted Dr. Johnson on the subject of the supernatural: "A total disbelief of ghosts is adverse to the opinion of the existence of the soul between death and the Last Day." To this, the dismayed youth replied that a belief in "ghosts" might countenance a belief in virtually anything else: for what might *not* be explained by the supernatural, or the Unknown? He thought it plausible that all human events had human causes, or causes to be rationally examined: in the instance of the lynched Pride, surely a *human agent,* close to home, was—

"But since you not only lack proof of your charge," Mr. Kilgarvan testily interrupted, "but lack the means to acquire that proof, you might be better served by believing in the Unknown, or what you will; or, at the very most, holding your tongue." Which so disconcerted the lad, he offered no further commentary on the subject.)

As for the death of Miss Imogene Westergaard, which so badly shook Winterthurn, and usurped attention from all else,—until the fatality involving Simon Esdras later in the autumn: when it happened that the headstrong young heiress failed to return from her morning walk with her dogs, nearing seven-thirty, her brother Valentine, breakfasting somewhat earlier than usual, rubbed his eyes of a sudden, and murmured in a queer stricken voice that "something had gone amiss,"—he knew not what: and, with no hesitation, rose from the table to run out in search of his sister, who had long provoked disapproval and worry amongst her family by insisting upon making her way *unescorted;* and continuing to exercise her Irish terriers by walking along the river within a scant quarter-mile of Glen Mawr Manor. Indeed, in recent months, when even able-bodied workingmen and tradesmen could be prevailed upon to approach the Manor only with difficulty, it seemed that Miss Westergaard was more adamant than before in *her* refusal to be cowed, as she phrased it, by "superstitious idiocies." So impetuous had the young lady been, and so certain of the beneficent force of her personality, she had several times attempted to visit with the reclusive Georgina, to no avail: and, refusing to be discouraged by the "Blue Nun's" signal lack of interest, never neglected to include her, and her young sisters, on invitations to tea at Ravensworth Park—this being the historic name of the large sandstone-and-granite house in which Colonel Westergaard and his family lived. As to her motives for so persistently forcing herself where clearly she was not wanted, Miss Westergaard was said to have laughed in delight, and made the claim that it was in *that* the challenge lay: "For where we are *wanted,* why, then, our victories are sorry trifles indeed! It is only where we are *not wanted* that imagination waxes rich." In spurning several eligible suitors, since the night of her débutante ball some eight years previous, Imogene Westergaard had, of necessity, angered and even alarmed certain persons, who had made no secret of the fact that her bluestocking-spinster stance was most nettlesome: the more so in that, unlike, for instance, poor Georgina Kilgarvan, Imogene *was* uncommonly attractive; and in the full flush of womanly health.

It was in a charming grove of beech and dogwood, not many yards from the Kilgarvan property, and about thirty feet from the river, that Imogene's body was discovered, not long past eight o'clock, by her distraught brother Valentine: who, so overcome at first by the sight of the poor, bloody, abused body, could not comprehend that his sister was no longer living; but knelt by her side, and tried to revive her, with many a protestation of chiding grief. His upset was such, he had not noticed the bludgeoned bodies of the twin Irish terriers, lying but a short distance away, where it seemed they had been negligently tossed, into a tangled patch of briars.

Poor Imogene Westergaard was discovered to have died of multiple wounds, inflicted by an unknown weapon, most likely a knife: Hans Deck estimated these wounds,—which were of a crude, gaping, barbaric nature, wildly distributed about the neck, bosom, forearms, and legs—to be "beyond one hundred; indeed, countless." In all likelihood the young lady had been overtaken on the river path, and attacked from behind; and thrown to the ground; and murdered; and, as the piteous flattened and bloody grasses would indicate, dragged on her back to the little grove of trees. Yet her attacker had not seriously hoped to hide her body, as the grove was very near the path; nor had he attempted to disguise it, by covering it with branches, leaves, dirt, etc.

The mystery was the more compounded, and attributed, not least by the more credulous, to the *supernatural influences* of the area, in that no footprints were to be found in the softened earth surrounding the body, save of course Valentine Westergaard's: and no marks, no evidence, no *clues*, were ever to be located,—though Mr. Shearwater and his deputies claimed to have busied themselves for days, in examining the scene of the crime; and questioning certain lowlife persons, residing in South Winterthurn, who were known to have a distinct motive for seeking revenge against the Westergaards. (But a scant six years previous, Colonel Westergaard had aroused much interest, and not a little wrath in some quarters, by, of a sudden, firing unionized workers in his several factories along the river, and importing some one hundred Chinese laborers from the Pacific Coast, who, far from wishing unionization, were willing to work for contracts offering a modest $25 per month: and very diligently and uncomplainingly, it was said. A certain smoldering resentment yet continued in the area, however, so far as the discharged workers and their families were concerned; and it was generally known that threatening remarks, of a drunken nature, had been directed against the Colonel from time to time.)

Despite the efforts of the law enforcement officers, however, and one or two initially promising leads, the person or persons who so brutally killed Miss Imogene Westergaard were not apprehended: which naturally stirred superstitious imaginings all the more. "Yet it cannot possibly serve the community, or Justice," the beleaguered Mr. Shearwater said, with some exasperation, "to arrest anyone at all, and urge him to confess: though it begins to seem that such a move would be greeted with approval on all sides—!"

So disheartened was Xavier Kilgarvan by his humiliating, and altogether terrifying, experience at Glen Mawr,—of which, it should be here recorded, the abashed youth tried hard not to think—that he yielded for some days to his father's stern admonition that he keep his distance from the scene of the "new" crime; and not go poking about, or even making discreet inquiries. It was notoriously easy to offend the old Colonel: and Valentine himself, though a most charming young gentleman, and a bosom friend of Wolf's, was known to possess a mercurial temper.

After a week's stoic resistance, however, Xavier felt that he could keep away no longer: and stealthily proceeded to the scene of the crime: only to find every square inch of the area tramped over, by hundreds of footprints; and many of the lower branches of trees torn off, and small rocks dislodged, making any investigation useless. It had been a brainstorm of his to search the river for the murder weapon, which, thus far, the sheriff's office had not done: but this muddy and exhausting enterprise, taking the better part of a steamy September afternoon, yielded no fruit apart from tangled fishing lines and hooks, agèd rusted strips of wire, shards of glass, waterlogged dolls, parts of baby buggies, and parts of rowboats. Having cut his foot somewhat severely on a sharp piece of metal, the luckless Xavier limped to shore, to sit disconsolate on the bank, and watch the blood emerge, drop by pitiless drop, from his flesh, and fall into the slow-churning water. "At such 'uneventful' times in a detective's experience," he sullenly bethought himself, "it is more or less the rule that *something urgent will happen:* yet I have no fear that, today, anything at all will occur,"— the which humble prophecy turned out to be true.

The Fatal Wedding Night

AS THE TESTIMONY OF MRS. ROXANA MURPHY,—or, I should say, Mrs. Simon Esdras Kilgarvan—was to prove no less incoherent than that of

Mrs. Abigail Whimbrel some five months previous, it was never to be known
with any degree of accuracy, or chronological fidelity, all that transpired in the
accursèd Honeymoon Room, on the night of Simon Esdras's ill-advised wedding
to his "fancy woman": or, indeed, what wild and altogether uncharacteristic
species of masculine bravado,—provoked, it may have been, by an excess of alcoholic spirits, including the costliest of French champagnes!—had encouraged
the philosopher to bring his bride to Glen Mawr, on that wind-tossed October night; in cruel defiance, as Winterthurn afterward whispered, of Miss
Georgina's express wishes. (As it happened, the "Blue Nun" was so discountenanced, and so deeply abhorred the prospect of spending even a single night beneath the same roof with the "newlyweds," that, forcing herself up from her
invalid's couch, she fled the Manor altogether, her two half-sisters in tow, and
secured the entire top floor of a boarding house for gentlewomen, on an elegant
tree-lined street off Berwick Square: this being the place, and, assuredly,
nowhere else, the distraught spinster spent the night of October 9, when her
uncle met his hideous death.)

After the discovery, in the morning, of this fresh, and, some would say,
needless tragedy,—poor Simon Esdras having been assailed and mutilated,
much like the Whimbrel infant, and Mr. Upchurch's spring lambs; and the unfortunate Roxana, a bride of less than twenty-four hours, propelled into hopeless madness—it came to be reported, through town, that Simon Esdras had
quite deliberately chosen to spend his wedding night in the very room imagined
to be *haunted:* and that he had done so out of willfulness, and contempt for superstitious fears, in full confidence that, *as the "rabid" Jupiter had long ago been removed,* the room was totally free of danger,—indeed, was it not the most
luxurious and desirable of honeymoon settings in all of the Valley? And it would
cost him not a single penny—!

In boasting of this plan a fortnight earlier, Simon Esdras had told Osmyn
Goshawk, all smilingly, and with a childlike enthusiasm, that the more he considered the unusual circumstances of his betrothal, the more *obliged* did he feel,
as a rationalist no less than a Kilgarvan, to refute the sickly nonsense accruing
to his ancestral home: for did not common sense, no less than the discipline of

Logic, suggest that, as there can be no Evil per se, apart from evil persons, evil creatures, evil actions, etc.,—the nod being given here to Aristotle, and not Plato—there can be *no Evil residing in (mere) (extended) Space;* which is to say, *in a mere room?* One might consider, too, whether Hume's astringent notions of *causality* and *acausality* might not apply; whether Leibniz's *monad-vision* might not be relevant; whether certain elementary propositions in Simon Esdras's own *Treatise on the "Probable" Existence of the World,* penned some thirty-two years before—viz., "A spatial object must be situated in nonspatial, or Infinite, space"; "What possesses the property of *being,* cannot *be* expressed"; "Only propositions may express Logical Form (but) cannot contain it,"—might not prove helpful as well. With a most charming faint blush, and a lowering of his eyes, the philosopher confided to Osmyn that, at the present time, his own fiancée was not yet fully convinced of this argument; but he had every reason to hope that she was "coming round" to his position. Indeed, this robust young widow, formerly the wife of a Railroad Street tavernkeeper, had naught about her of false decorum, or simpering female coyness; and possessed, in his proud opinion, more common sense in her *littlest finger or toe* than all of the Winterthurn ladies combined. "She has said, it would give *her* infinite pleasure to spend our wedding night at Glen Mawr: indeed, to spend all the remaining days of our lives there, as 'lord' and 'lady' of the Manor, so to speak," Simon Esdras said, with a deepening blush, and a slight wavering of his affable smile: for, as Osmyn later reported, it was so remarkable a thing for Simon Esdras Kilgarvan, of all persons, to be *affianced,* he seemed to contemplate it with a faint air of incredulity himself; and uttered his words as if they might be those of another.

As to whether so simple an emotion as *fear* might not dictate one's actions,—Simon Esdras replied to this hesitant query of Osmyn's in a somewhat loftier tone, saying that the amorphous state of mind to which the term "fear" attached could not exist, apart from the term itself: and, as there was no language *ab initio,* it was a logical impossibility; and one to be dismissed from all serious consideration. "As every 'grammar' secretly communicates its own *picture-proposition* of the Cosmos, what is illusory may be for some functional,— as, I believe, my compatriot Charles Sanders Pierce has argued, in somewhat more clumsy terms," Simon Esdras stated, raising his forefinger, as if to discourage his companion from interrupting, "—the paradox then being, is the functional illusory *in fact*, or merely *in theory?*" Poor Osmyn Goshawk felt quite lost by this abstruse reasoning, though, as he afterward said, he had not in the slightest *doubted* the logic of Simon Esdras's argument; and was certainly nodding as the elder gentleman so amicably spoke. Indeed, the original question relating to fear was soon forgotten, as the philosopher proceeded vigorously to investigate, point by point, divers concepts that refuted, or even annihilated, opposing theories. Somehow, too, the matter of *syllogistic necessity* arose ("All X are Y,—E is X,— ∴ E *is* or *is not* Y"), having to do with the deceased Erasmus: about whom Simon Esdras spoke in a most peculiar manner,—part chiding, part gloating, yet, withal, in a tone of puzzled sobriety. "Thus I know it my duty,—and in this dear Roxana concurs," Simon Esdras murmured, "—to succeed where, it seems, my brother so ingloriously failed: *and thereby to invent a revolutionary Logic,* imbued with the fresher air of the New World, and free of all Old World and Attic muddle."

To this, Osmyn Goshawk nervously acquiesced; as, it seems, he could scarcely quarrel.

The ladies were less patient, and far more scandalized, in reference to the "wayward Kilgarvan bachelor," as certain observers called him: for they considered that, at his advanced age, when he might better have been thinking of Last Things, he was very much remiss in falling in love (as Mrs. Harrier Von Goeler put it) with a "pair of gypsy eyes,"—and eyes scarcely innocent of a veritable battery of tricks of crude cosmetry. "Roxana Murphy," whether *Miss* or *Mrs.*, was a woman by no means young, yet given to brash youthful ways; and decked out (as the witty Mrs. Von Goeler again observed) like a steamboat of old,—all frippery, all noise, part gambling casino, part floating brothel. Her tavernkeeper husband had died, it was said, under circumstances never satisfactorily explained; while perhaps not totally atheistical, she inclined toward the indifferent, in matters of religion,— claiming to be upon one occasion, Methodist; upon another, Baptist; upon yet another, "lapsed Catholic"! Most outrageous was the woman's studied *haughti-*

ness when, by accident, she and her gentleman escort encountered members of the Kilgarvans' social set, of old; for, it seems, "Mrs. Murphy" coolly declined to ingratiate herself with the Winterthurn ladies: and stared stonily past their flower-bedecked hats, while harmless amenities were exchanged. The hussy!— the trollop! Any fool, save Simon Esdras himself, could see how shamelessly she plotted to marry him for his money; and to overleap the lowliness of her station by becoming mistress of Glen Mawr Manor,—whose portals, in the days of Erasmus Kilgarvan, a creature of her ilk could not have hoped to enter. Alas, if only Simon Esdras were not a mere babe in matters of the corporeal life—!

Since the subject bordered upon the indelicate, if not the frankly indecent, the ladies could speak but obliquely of it: and oft-times surrendered to stammering blushes, at what was almost, though not quite, voiced. Yet how could it be that the aging philosopher, for so many decades scornful of the material, not to say the biological, world, was now yielding to an impulse most gross, and most enigmatical—? How could it be that Simon Esdras was capable of noting a female figure, of any sort, let alone responding to it?—he who had, as it was whispered, so vaguely attended to the melancholy fates of his pretty sisters-in-law, *with whom he shared a household,* as to have perennially confused the two women, up to the very morning of Hortense's funeral. His belated sentiments regarding the tradition of primogeniture they could, perhaps, more readily comprehend; but even these, as Simon Esdras elaborated upon them, and upon his *Kilgarvan duty,* soon struck a note of unworldliness, and frank absurdity. "It may have been that Simon Esdras too thoughtlessly dismissed the world of *existence,* in favor of that of *essence,*" one of the bolder of the ladies speculated. "Yet, at his age,—for I believe he is nearing seventy?—he may find it somewhat arduous in making his way back."

This witty if slightly suggestive remark provoked both blushes and restrained mirth: and the yet wittier observation, by a still bolder lady, that, judging by Mrs. Murphy's air of expediency, as well as her proven cunning, no very great problem should present itself in "getting" her with child,—and providing the elderly bridegroom with an heir.

*   *   *

It was at the very end of June that Simon Esdras began behaving in a conspicuous manner, affecting a dandy's costume,—consisting of white duck trousers
strapped under kid boots, and immaculate white linen coat, and snowy vest,
and flowing coppery-silk ascot—and appearing about town, alone or with the
brazen Mrs. Murphy, at social occasions to which, it seems, he had not invariably been invited. A lawn tennis fête at Shadow-Wood House, the ancestral
abode of the Peregrines; a recital given by the piano students of Madame Char-
pentier, in the old Buonaparte Mansion; the Culpp-Flaxen nuptials, in the First
Presbyterian Church; divers baptisms, weddings, confirmations, and funerals,—including of course that of poor Imogene Westergaard, which the
philosopher attended by himself, eyeglasses sparkling with boyish wonder, and
mouth fixed in a queer half-smile, both censorious and grieving. To the
Colonel, and other stricken Westergaards, Simon Esdras explicitly declined to
offer his condolences; but was heard to murmur repeatedly, with many a quirky
shake of his head, that "it was all a bungle,—an error, a muddle,—a *vulgar mistake:* and they were best served by transcending it, or dismissing it forthwith."

One brisk Saturday afternoon in late September, as Xavier was slipping unobtrusively from the dusty recesses of the Pinckney Street Book Shop,—where,
unknown to his parents, he had placed an extravagant order for several books on
Continental criminology, as well as a monograph on Sir Francis Galton's controversial theory of *fingerprinting*—he chanced to encounter his Uncle Simon
Esdras, with the redoubtable Mrs. Murphy on his arm: the smiling gentleman
attired in snowy white, with a vest of some knit material, in magenta, and a
blood-red carnation in his lapel; the lady dressed with a matching boldness, in
many layers of shimmering apricot-colored silks, and a slope-brimmed organdy
hat, and an excess of Venetian lace. Xavier could not prevent himself from
blushing as Simon Esdras not only deigned to recognize him as a nephew, and
to hit, after several jocular tries, upon his actual name: but insisted that Xavier
join him and his lady for a spot of tea, in Charity Street.

(Which remarkable invitation Xavier certainly could not decline,—nor did he
regret it afterward, as this would prove the last time he saw Simon Esdras alive.)

Yet, dazzled as he was by his uncle's circumlocutory manner of speech, and by Mrs. Murphy's blooming and perfumed presence,—for, indeed, Simon Esdras's fiancée did possess snapping "gypsy eyes," which she fixed upon young Xavier with especial interest—he could not concentrate with any degree of success on what was being presented, or argued, or implied, or insinuated; nor did he derive much satisfaction from his tea, or the several mocha tarts and almond puff pastries urged upon him, by the silent, but smiling, Mrs. Murphy. Within a fortnight, Simon Esdras informed him, he and his charming companion would be *man and wife*,—the offices to be performed by a county justice of the peace, with as much brevity as possible; but this action should not mean, as certain gossipers would have it, any disrespect for his late brother,—on the contrary, in fact. "If one posits a belief in the *immortality of the soul*, which is the foundation stone, I believe, of the Christian way of thinking," Simon Esdras said slowly, "one must acknowledge it as self-evident that the soul, being immortal, and bodiless, and no longer taken up with the vagaries of the flesh, cannot concern itself with the pettinesses of this world: thus, our actions *here* are not relevant. If, however," he said, now laying a warm hand on Xavier's wrist, and gazing solemnly at, or toward, him, "one posits a belief in the *mortality of the soul*, one must acknowledge it as equally self-evident that the soul, being mortal, perishes with the body: thus, the actions of the living cannot possibly be relevant,—as any fool might conclude." To this carefully modulated speech, both Xavier and Mrs. Murphy assented: though Xavier had begun to feel the strain of the situation, and suffered a boyish wish to be elsewhere. Why did it strike him with such queer potency that his elderly uncle, though no less self-possessed than he had ever been, and fairly glowing with health, and a touching sort of pride in his female companion, was yet shadowed by,—by Xavier knew not what: an invisible fluttering or rustling, as of wings: an air of the *fateful*, and even the *doomed*, quite at odds with the cheery white wrought-iron tables of the Sweet Shoppe, and the conspicuous finery of the majority of the customers, and, indeed, the tarts and puffs and ices being daintily consumed. "Nay, it is only my irresponsible imagination," Xavier sternly chided himself, "which has never yet served me well, or proved itself reliable."

The awkward session concluded with a surprising alteration of tone on the part of Simon Esdras: who lifted his glasses to rub roughly at his eyes, and to reiterate his position that no disrespect for his late brother could possibly be intended, or inferred, regardless of what his niece,—that "most irrational and unhappy Georgina"—chose to believe: for did they not live in an enlightened era, in the closing decades of the nineteenth century, with fresh advances in science and invention and Logic being made on all sides?—and were the pristine motives of a *gentleman in love* to be questioned, by a morality couched in the prejudices of the Dark Ages? Testily, as if his silent companions had challenged him, Simon Esdras said that he so despised the vagrant muddle of superstition, he would no more condescend to question it than he would, for instance, inquire of the Sweet Shoppe manageress the recipe involved in making one of these pastries. Through the decades of his life he had never succumbed to any sort of failure of reasoning: and he had always evinced a fastidious impatience with such, whether it manifested itself in the coarsest species of peasant religion or in the infinitely more refined, though scarcely less nonsensical, species embodied by the proud Christian Church, in its numerous factions!—this impassioned speech being uttered in a voice of sufficient volume, as to enable all the patrons in the shop to absorb it if they wished.

"And, in addition," the now somewhat flushed philosopher said, "whether the world be 'real,' or but 'illusion': whether its existence be 'probable,' or only 'possible,' *or a mere airy bubble residing in a mad person's brain:* I, Simon Esdras Kilgarvan, refute it thus!"—all brashly, and unexpectedly, seizing his fiancée's plump hand, and raising it to his lips, with a ferocious disregard, it seemed to the blushing Xavier, for all who might overhear, or frankly stare.

At Glen Mawr Manor: The Attic

THAT *THE MYSTERY OF GLEN MAWR MANOR;* or, *The Virgin in the Rose-Bower,* was solved by the youthful Xavier Kilgarvan only in a manner of speaking, and that, I am afraid, *unofficially,* is to be explained by the peculiar circumstances surrounding his secret visit to Glen Mawr, some ten days after Simon Esdras's funeral: and by the sudden onslaught of illness,—diagnosed by Dr. Hatch as a particularly virulent strain of *brain fever*—that laid him low for nearly two months, bringing with it not only such inevitable symptoms as a high temperature alternating with convulsive chills, and frequent terror of unseen things, and raving and incoherent speech, and loss of appetite, but *partial amnesia*,—so that, though the bold young detective may be said to have successfully plumbed the depths of the "mystery," he was unable afterward to recall its crucial details, save in broken, jumbled, and hallucinatory guise. As this circumstance was coupled with the tragic death of Miss Georgina Kilgarvan,—who, though she lingered for eleven weeks as a consequence of an ingestion of *arsenic paste,* never regained consciousness—it came about that the cause of the divers atrocities, and the source of an incalculable terror amongst the citizenry, was both discovered,—and lost forever!

In contemplating this state of affairs some years afterward, and his own descent into illness in particular, Xavier Kilgarvan yet brooded over whether he had been inordinately luckless or, indeed, blessed by his Maker. "For if God had wished me to remember, in unfailing detail, why, then, I should certainly remember," Xavier considered, "and, as that is not the case, and what I recall is most *horrific,* and *repellent,* and, indeed, *unspeakable,*—surely it is all to the good?"

It was on the mild, moonlit, yet capriciously gusty, night of October 21, not long after church bells had sounded the hour of eleven, that Xavier satisfied himself that his brother Colin was deep in slumber; and slipped stealthily from their bed-chamber, and down the back stairs; and out into the lightless lane, or alley, directly behind,—where the clever lad had placed his bicycle, in readiness for the adventure at hand; and his schoolboy's satchel, in which he had jammed such gear as he reasoned a detective might find useful: matches, and tallow candles; and ropes of varying lengths and textures; and a handsome double-bladed steel knife borrowed, with no precise acknowledgment, from his brother Wolf; and divers tools from Mr. Kilgarvan's workshop, similarly borrowed. As Xavier had no doubt that he would return home well before dawn,—before, even, the hooves of the iceman's horse sounded against the cobblestone of Wycombe Street—he did not greatly concern himself that any of these items might be missed; or that he himself might be missed. "I shall pedal out to Glen Mawr as quickly as possible, and examine the Honeymoon Room once again, and see what there is to be seen, with no witnesses," he inwardly resolved, "and return at once, with no wasteful lingering; or childish diversions of a foolhardy kind."

(As to what Xavier meant by the slurred reference to "childish diversions,"—this had to do with his shameful imprisonment in the fruit cellar, and the circumstances of his rescue, some months before. Unable to grasp the motive, or the meaning, or even the nature, of Perdita's prank, Xavier sometimes questioned whether, in truth, it had actually been deliberate,—or an accident resulting from a sudden fright, experienced by the delicate girl; or even a sudden gust of wind, snaking its way down the stairs, to strike the heavy door with exceptional force. Withal, the abashed youth, who still prized his cousin in his innermost heart, found it most felicitous, in general, not to dwell upon the puzzling incident; nor even to recall Thérèse's kindness.)

While we envision Xavier zealously bicycling along the near-deserted streets of Winterthurn City,—southward, and eastward, along Wycombe, and Pinckney, and Hazelwit; past Parthian Square with its great plane trees; past Courthouse Green, where the sturdy columns of the Courthouse glimmered pale in the half-light; to the darkened expanse of the picturesque River Road, which will carry him, in less than ninety minutes, to Glen Mawr—it were well to record certain elements of the scene that doubtless made very little impression upon Xavier himself: the ceaseless rippling play of the river's shadowed waves on his right hand; the patches and wisps of cloud blown across the moon,—itself an etiolated presence in the autumn sky; and the unnatural dreamlike silence that engirded all, beyond the mournful sound of the wind high in the trees.

And, too, as Xavier so fearlessly pedals along, it were well for me to record, that the youth would have made this second investigation of the scene of the crime some days earlier, but had been prevented by the unreliable behavior of his brother Colin: who, since the excursion in late May to the Upchurch farm, seemed to have suffered some minute, though distinct, alteration in character, so that Xavier could not foresee when he would retire for the night, or, once abed, when he would sink into his customary sensual abandonment, of deep slumber; nor could the perplexed Xavier predict whether Colin would *remain* abed,—for every fifth or sixth night, it seemed, he gave the impression of waiting, with cunning, until Xavier slept, so that, with uncharacteristic stealth, *he might slip from his bed, and from the room.* (Brooding over the puzzling metamorphosis in his brother, who was, of late, given to frowning and twitching silences, and outbursts of irascibility, and sudden displays of temper,—which manifested themselves in jabs, pokes, and actual blows, directed against Bradford and Wolf, as well as Xavier, and Colin's own friends—Xavier could not decide whether, of late, Colin had taken to running with a set of "young bloods," as Wolf did; or whether he had succumbed to a romance of some unknown sort, with a girl of questionable upbringing. It was Xavier's conclusion, after many hours of *ratiocinative detective work,* that Colin,—and no spectral apparition— had stolen the ruby ring Xavier had secreted in the fireplace; but of course he could not prove his suspicion, and hardly dared raise the issue with Colin, save in oblique and sly asides, which, to his way of thinking, provoked guilty flushes in his brother's face and a decided evasiveness of manner.)

Despite the daring, if not the actual recklessness, of this night's undertaking, Xavier felt very little trepidation as he approached the front gate of the Manor, which was chained and bolted shut: for it was scarcely a secret through town that the great old house was now completely empty of human inhabitants, and that the authorities had counted it a superfluous task to close off the entrances, and board up the doors and windows, and post signs warning against unauthorized visitors,—for who in his right mind, as Norland Clegg had remarked to Xavier, would choose to trespass in that ghoulish place; or even to venture onto the property itself—? "He would have to be a consummate fool, indeed," the sheriff's deputy had said, with a bemused shake of his head.

* * *

To this, Xavier had of course murmured a politic assent; but privately shivered, with an indefinable, yearning anticipation,—a sense, it almost seemed, of being on the verge of deliciously, ecstatically, *finally* awakening; of being roused from a slumberous trance, to the purity of uncontaminated oxygen; and to some remarkable vision, which, though thrust upon him from *without,* yet corresponded to something uniquely his own, from *within* . . .

Of late, the activities of home and school that had long absorbed his energies seemed both tedious and futile, the preoccupations of mere boys: he disappointed his teachers by daydreaming in school, he disappointed his father by daydreaming in the workshop, he quite worried his mother by unaccountable silences and sulks and absences, and, ah!—his shrinking from her touch. (Mrs. Kilgarvan supposed it normal that a youth of sixteen years should no longer wish to be caressed and petted by his mother; but she *did* miss the special attachment, for she considered him her baby still.) The family took note that Xavier's moody countenance brightened only when the subject of the "mystery" at Glen Mawr was raised; and then he was likely to say the most disagreeable things,—for instance, that any fool could see that Imogene Westergaard had not been murdered by the same agent that had murdered Mrs. Whimbrel's baby, as "the modes of death were radically different."

Indeed, as Xavier once said at the breakfast table, the "mystery" of the situation was, in a manner of speaking, why all of Winterthurn wanted to link the disparate deaths—!

With but a little difficulty, Xavier managed to gain entry to the forbidden house by way of a pair of French doors, opening onto a side terrace, that had been boarded shut in a most slovenly and desultory manner: and, not yet needing to light a candle, as a consequence of the moon's diffuse glow, made his way, neither hastily nor with an excess of caution, through a shadowed drawing room that smelled of dust, to the high-domed foyer, with its Grecian columns, and wide curved stairway, and air of arrogant ostentation that had so stung the youth's pride and envy some months before: ah! and roused him to a yearning for justice, or for revenge, that had thrummed along his fevered nerves—! Not wishing to pause, and to risk the incursion of a melancholy thought, in sudden recollection of Perdita, Xavier ascended the staircase as swiftly as discretion would allow: and, with a dreamlike alacrity, found himself in the upstairs corridor: scarcely daring to breathe as he approached the doorway of the dread Honeymoon Room, in which his uncle had lately died, and his bride had been so affrighted, it was said the unhappy woman would never regain her sanity . . .

Here, overcome by a sudden spasm of shivering that, to his shame, caused his teeth to rattle, Xavier did pause, but only for a minute: and, fumbling to light a candle, proceeded to enter the room,—which impressed him, beyond the sickening beat of his own heart, as wondrously tranquil. Steeled against attack, the very hairs on the nape of his neck astir, Xavier came forward with his candle aloft, that he might glance swiftly on all sides, and breathe in the air of this forbidden place,—a singular, yet not entirely repulsive, admixture of dust, and damp, and age, and melancholy splendor, faintly tinged with the odor of blood. He paused, listening: but no sound ensued: and, it seemed, even the night's capricious wind had ebbed. His eye gleaned, from the divers contours, shapes, shadows, and glassy surfaces, no evidence of any presence save his own: and that, a pale ghost-figure, hesitant of step, and indeterminate of age, gender, and identity, ensconced in utter silence, within the gilt frames of the numberless mirrors. Only the enormous *trompe l'oeil* mural,—the grim-visaged Virgin with Child, surrounded by a host of floating angels—drew his attention, and this but momentarily. "A mere room,—four walls, and a ceiling, and a carpeted floor," he murmured aloud, "—yet what secrets does it contain?"

Here, sprawled across the blood-soaked bed linens, one hand, it was said, trailing against the floor, and his ravaged head tipped back at a most grotesque angle, Xavier's Uncle Simon Esdras had been found by his manservant, on the morning of October 10, *stone dead:* his bride half-hidden, in a far corner of the room, crouched on her haunches and swaying slightly from side to side, blood liberally splashed upon her beribboned white nightgown, and her expression,— so the terrified servant told the authorities—more frightful in its *vacuity* than his master's had been in its anguished horror. Untouched, evidently, by the agent that had so barbarously killed her bridegroom, Mrs. Murphy,—which is to say, *Mrs. Kilgarvan*—proved so bereft of her senses, she took no notice of the servant as he approached, or, later, of Mr. Shearwater and his deputies: but strenuously resisted their efforts to aid her, and, in the end, had to be borne bodily out of the chamber of death, writhing, and squirming, and twisting mad as an eel, her scream, as it was afterward reported, the more horrific,—for being silent.

That this hideous scene had transpired less than a fortnight previous, in this very space, struck Xavier as remarkable, for now all was peaceful indeed; and, as he busied himself lighting candles at strategic positions in the room,— including the twelve candles, part-melted, of a many-branched candelabrum set upon the bedside table—Xavier wondered at a sudden infusion of his own strength, returning to him in waves; and a sense of mingled excitement, and boyish belligerence. Was it not within his grasp, conceivably, to resolve this mystery before the night was over?—and to bring his findings homeward, in triumph? How amazed all would be who knew him, and had too readily dismissed him as a mere schoolboy—! With a delicious rapidity his fears now transformed themselves into certitude, and muscular excitation: for Xavier could not help but feel, even in this place of slaughter, that God watched over him,—nor even that God's especial love for *him* might be, in certain spaces, suspended.

Thus it was, he prepared himself for his vigil: taking a seat in a chair equidistant from the bed and the door, but pushed back prudently against the wall; and drawing his legs cautiously up, to sit "Indian style"; with his satchel close beside him, opened, in case he had sudden need of Wolf's knife, or any other handy implement for self-defense. (As for the great canopied bed itself, which had witnessed such inexplicable suffering,—though the offensive bed linens had been taken away, and replaced by a spotless white eiderdown coverlet,—Xavier had no more the stomach to too closely investigate the condition of the mattress than he had the temerity to stretch out on the bed. He much envied the casualness with which certain detectives and police investigators examined such blood-soaked evidence, but had begun to doubt whether he would ever acquire it.)

Doubtless it was the influence of the host of candles burning in divers areas of the bed-chamber, their commingled glow being most gentle, and soothing, and harmonious, and suffused with a romantic sort of beauty: for it was not many minutes before, falling into a light drowse, Xavier began to think of his cousin Perdita; and remembered with a pang that irradiated pleasure through his being, even as it stung, the perfection of her heart-shaped face,—the petal-smooth pallor of her skin,—the haunting conjunction in her of the *childish*, and the *woefully mature*. Ah, if only she were with him now, how exhilarated he should be, despite the loneliness of his watch—! He recalled a church service of some Sundays previous, before Simon Esdras's death, when his eye had moved upon his cousin's bent profile, in a pew not far distant: lingering sadly, yet, as it were, hungrily, upon it: taking no note (I am sorry to say) of Thérèse, who sat beside her, in no less girlishly devout a posture. Far overhead, as if in Heaven itself, the organ sounded its thunderous chords, and the congregation reverently sang,—

Praise God from Whom all blessings flow!
Praise Him all creatures here below!

—and Xavier felt the breath of an angel close beside him, feathered wings in such rapid motion, it were as if a hummingbird had drifted near, warm, and perfumed, and delightful to the eye!—yet startling him into waking, so that his head jerked upright, and his eyelids fluttered, and, for a moment, he scarcely knew where he was: languorously embraced in a dream, in his own boyhood bed; or many miles distant, in a forbidden chamber of his "ancestral" home. There was some confusion, too, as to whether Perdita had been his guide to this place, or whether he had made his way alone . . .

He stirred in his cushioned chair; and looked uneasily about; seeing nothing that hinted of life, or motility, save his own dim and vaporous reflection in a mirrored door nearby that caught other like reflections, to toss them, it

seemed, back and forth, most vertiginously, from one side of the room to another, and one corner to another, to Infinity. He rubbed his eyes, to goad himself to greater wakefulness; and saw that the French furnishings of the room,
and the glittering chandelier, and the bronzed, gilded, and glassed surfaces, and,
not least, the remarkable painting by Eakins, were indeed impressive; and wondered that he could have been so unfeeling as to have missed their uncommon
value earlier,—in truth, to have judged them as ostentatious and vulgar. "Or is
it," the perplexed youth inquired of himself, "a consequence of the recent
tragedy, and the spillage of Kilgarvan blood *in this very space,* that accounts for
an air of the solemn, and the exalted?"

At some distance there sounded the faint tinkling laughter of children, pre-
dominant among them a girl's high-pitched breathless titter: yet was she to be
chastised for being merely restless, and silly?—and not at all naughty! Xavier's
eyelids drooped; his head began to nod on his shoulders; all evenly, and deeply,
his breath came and went. "Yet I am not asleep," he declared boastfully, "for that
would be a most tragical error, in this *damned place.*"

A tall, willowy, slope-shouldered angel, burdened with the most comical
wings,—narrow, and oily-black, the feathers densely curled—drew near the boy
in the chair, and murmured something sly, and puckered his lips as if to kiss:
but, in the next instant, vanished utterly—!

Whereupon more laughter sounded. And the exhalation of breaths was such,
every candle-flame in the room cowered: and one or two actually went out.

The released fragrances of jasmine, rosewater, lilac. A closer, more intimate
odor, which Xavier could not identify. Ah, if he might burrow, burrow, burrow!—to the very foot of the bed, beneath the heavy quilt! *But that is forbidden.
As certain scents are forbidden.*

So rapidly did the paired hummingbirds draw near, they revealed themselves as bats, with cruel hooked wings, and tiny red-glaring eyes. Xavier
reached out smilingly to stroke them,—for he was but a baby, and could not
know wickedness—but recoiled at the chill leathery touch of their skin. Very
white, very wet, their small needlelike teeth! *O do not hurt me,* Xavier begged.
Where is Momma, that she would allow them so near—?

Mrs. Kilgarvan closed the book of nursery tales, the one with the Cat and the Fiddle and the Cow and the Moon embossed in red and gilt on the cover. All silently she laid the book aside; and rose to her feet; and blew out the candle, *though Xavier was fully awake and pleaded with her not to leave him alone in the dark.* Stooping to kiss him, she smelled of eau de cologne: Xavier stared helplessly at her through his sleep-locked eyelids. If she loved him, how could she leave him alone in the dark—?

Now the Virgin Mary in her somber blue robes deigned to glance in his direction; and, on her lap, the Christ Child cast a peevish jealous gaze: for was not Xavier as comely, and far more manly?—thus two cherubs whispered, their breaths close upon Xavier's face, and their plump fingers running lightly over his body. He stirred; he shivered; he groaned aloud,—yet in exquisite silence; he watched them with apprehension through his closed eyes; while still the Virgin Mary regarded him with an air of intense concentration, her eyes like burning agates, her skin so whitely hot, no mortal would dare draw near.

Caressing,—tickling,—pinching,—most brazenly *stroking:* thus the pretty cherubs hovering over Xavier; while in the near distance a hornpipe sounded, high and lewd; and a mandolin, strummed with yearning fingers; and something very like a child's tambourine. Xavier would have squirmed free of the cherubs' fingers, but, alas, was he not paralyzed, in his every muscle?—in even his neck, and his head? Nor could he truly open his eyes, to gain freedom, and to recall his soul.

"Unclothe yourself! O beautiful boy! You are not ashamed, surely? For you are one of us,—oh surely!"

"*Is* he ashamed? Then he must be chastised!"

"He must be set right!"

"Sweet Cousin, most handsome of brothers—"

"Sweet Xavier, do not resist: ah, yes: like *this*—"

"But he is ashamed!—he does not love us!"

"He dares not love us!"

"He is cruel!—he is wicked!"

"Unclothe him at once!"

"O beautiful boy, *our own*—"

Blushing, Xavier cowered, and squirmed, and protested in a child's affrighted voice,—but in silence; all passionately he would have pushed away the hot, shameless, pinching, poking fingers,—had he been able: but, alas, was he not trapped in the lurid comfort of sleep, paralyzed through his being?—was he not so amazed, at the sly pinches of his earlobes and nipples, the rough strokes against his thighs, a cherub's fleet kiss, a ghost-bite, a sucking sensation beneath the downy curve of his jaw,—so amazed, and, indeed, so overwhelmed, *that anyone should touch him in such secret wise,* he dared not draw breath?

And, ah! what an intoxication astir in the air!—angels with eyes that glared with love, and skin white-hot, and wings giddily beating!—now a breath perfumed, it seemed, with the most fragrant of dried flowers, from out Mrs. Kilgarvan's potpourri jar; now a breath bespeaking the shadowed interior of the milkman's empty cans, a most disagreeable, yet alluring, blend of the metallic and the rancid! The tender notes of a flute grew ever more high-pitched, and higher still: and now the random kisses turned to bites: teeth, lips, tongues; the most greedy of mouths, the most emboldened of caresses; the fluttering of dark-feathered wings, the eructation of harsh laughter; a commotion in the air, a frantic beating, *beating*—

"You are devils," Xavier murmured aloud, "and you dare not touch *me.*"

Whereupon, of a sudden, he was catapulted to wakefulness,—and saw that he was alone in the near-darkened room: that most of the candles had gone out: and that, beating close about the many-branched candelabrum, was naught but a cloud of harmless insects, primarily gnats and moths—!

Yet the perspicacious youth was not so disarmed by relief, nor so enfeebled by the terror of his dream, that it did not occur to him that the cherubs might be both *phantasms,* yet *real:* for were not his exposed hands bitten, and lightly bleeding; and was it not the case, which the felicity of a nearby mirror at once resolved, that his forehead, and cheeks, and jaw, and throat,—nay, and even the upper region of his torso, where the shirt had been surreptitiously drawn away—showed distinct evidence of biting?—and of bites *too carnivorous in intent* to be explained away by the happy coincidence of a cloud of insects, drawn to the candles' flame?

His Kilgarvan blood pulsing hotly through his veins, fueled as much by a manly sort of outrage, at this offense against his body, as by the delectation of fear, Xavier withdrew his brother's knife from his satchel, and opened the longer and more wicked of the blades; and, atremble with caution, slipped from his chair, to investigate yet again the area of the canopied bed, and the mural of lunging and pouting angels overhead,—the which, it now seemed to his eye, quivered with a most inexplicable species of emotion, subdued, withheld, yet potent with rage: nay, did not the tallest, and most husky, and most rubicund of the angelic host frankly stare at Xavier, with silver protuberant eyes? And did not the pale angel who had, long ago, wept a blood-dimmed tear, to fall upon Xavier's astonished palm, now gaze upon him with eyes of exquisite yearning?—the poignant hunger of Desire, but hunger nonetheless!

"You *are* devils," Xavier said aloud, "though you be hidden inside mere paint, and that fading, and cracking, and flaking away into airy nothingness! Yet is it not altogether *preposterous*, and *contrary to reason*—." Thus he drew nearer to the painting, which yielded, for all its conjurer's bag of tricks, but two sober dimensions, the which, surely, hid no mystery; and had not the power to bite human flesh, still less to devour it. At this instant, however, his keen eye may have picked up some small scuttling or scurrying noise overhead, caused by a mouse's passage; or the muffled crackle of silver tissue paper,—of the sort commonly used to line bureau drawers, for purposes of tidiness; or, indeed, the agitated confluence of divers elements, not least the roused tumult of his own heart, which stirred yet a second wakefulness,—*that of memory.* Thus it was the youth murmured aloud, scarcely before he knew the import of his words: "Why, they are in the attic overhead: *that* is their hiding place!"

So it was, Xavier made his swift, and doubtless reckless, way, to the gloom-embowered attic of Glen Mawr, which he had so fruitlessly investigated under

Perdita's guidance, many months before; and which, it seems, he had totally forgotten, as his investigation had proved not only sterile, but most humbling. Ah,
how courageous!—how unhesitating!—to penetrate that place of shadows, with
naught but a candle-stub to light his way, and his brother's knife to protect him!
"If only Perdita were here once again," Xavier inwardly murmured, "how
blessed should my passage be!"

Lacking that sweet presence, however, Xavier did not at all poorly, in re-
constructing his footsteps, as it were, amidst the dizzying assault of scents,—
and smells,—and stenches: and in defiance of an atmosphere of panicked
desperation, the more enigmatic for its being *silent as the grave.* Making but one
or two blundering turns through the maze of furniture, cartons, and boxes, and
bumping his head against an unseen beam but a single time, Xavier arrived,
panting, at the item he sought,—the massive Chippendale sideboard with the
bamboo trim, and the ebony finish near-obscured by dust, and the numerous
locked drawers, which, on his earlier venture, he had failed to open. "Here,—
dear God, it is *here,*—*here* and nowhere else—that the devils reside!"

—Thus the jubilant words torn from the boy's throat, to ring most oddly in
that place of desolation, with their tone of exuberance and gloating triumph.

Not hesitating so much as a minute, yet, withal, not without a measure of
calm, and deliberation, and exactitude, Xavier made dextrous if unfamiliar use
of the steel-bladed knife to pry, and chip at, and finally loosen one of the center
drawers open: and bravely yanked it out: to see, therein ensconced, a sight that
quite *froze his blood*—for, alas, there is no fresh expression in our native tongue
that will here serve, with as much linguistic appositeness, or candor. In brief,
Xavier's stunned eyes were fixed upon what gave every impression of being not
one, but an ill-matched pair, of *infant corpses:* so badly mummified with the passage of time, their skins had darkened, and turned leathery; and their part-
opened eyes, fringed by the most minute of lashes, had hardened to a substance
akin to milky glass. Two human babes, or, more precisely, their mummy remains: tidily, and, it may have been, lovingly, wrapped in strips of torn wool,
that had dried and hardened with the pitiable flesh to leather: the wire twisted

about their throats so deeply embedded, and so rusted, Xavier's eye could scarcely perceive it at first, by the candle's flickering light.

Yet still unhesitating, and acting with the same dispatch, Xavier pried open the second drawer, and then the third,—discovering in one a similar pair of infant corpses, and in the other but a single corpse, though of a somewhat older child, very like two or three months of age. These, like the others, had suffered the cruel entwining of wire about their throats; and had been wrapped in similar "swaddling clothes"; and placed with care in the drawers, amidst silver paper lining. How small, how perfect, the infant faces, surprised in their napping repose!—eyes, and eyebrows, and noses, and mouths, wondrously perfect, in *Kilgarvan miniature;* and perfect too the tender heads, and wisps of fair hair, and all the flexed and frozen fingers—!

Having exposed such horrific treasure, Xavier swayed above it, and felt his senses begin to reel, for could it be, he was actually *seeing* what his gaze absorbed?—and no dream-caprice, or idle schoolboy fancy, sullied his imagination?

"*How,*—and *whose*—"

—These being the only words, chokingly uttered, of which the affrighted youth was capable, before all breath left him, and all strength ran from his legs; and a corner of the sideboard careened upward most sickeningly, to deal him a sharp crack on the head: and to blot out his senses, in merciful oblivion.

Felo-de-Se

THOUGH WINTERTHURN TALKED OF little else for months, and speculations of the most inventive sort ran rampant, it was never to be grasped what connection, if any, lay between Miss Georgina Kilgarvan's criminal act of self-destruction (performed sometime in the midmorning of October 22, in the gardener's supply shed at Glen Mawr) and the abrupt cessation of killings, atrocities, and divers "hauntings" in the area: for indeed it was the case, as both official documents and local legend attest, that, with the incapacitation and eventual death of the Judge's spinster daughter, *all preternatural incidents stopped.*

Thus no one doubted,—though no one, excepting not even the most irresponsible of observers, could explain why,—that the "mystery" out at Glen Mawr was at last exorcised.

As the unhappy woman sank into a coma from which she never awakened,—save, from time to time, to writhe, and twitch, and fight with unseen figures, and moan out such enigmatic phrases as "O why . . ." and "It *cannot* be . . ." and "Where have you gone . . . !"—it was impossible for the authorities to question her: still less was it possible for them to issue formal charges against her for the crime of "attempted suicide," or *felo-de-se,*—as serious an offense against the statute, as the crime of murder itself. Dr. Colney Hatch, who was in close attendance upon the dying woman, insisted that she revealed nothing to him, in all the long weeks of her decline: nor did various hospital assistants, report anything out of the ordinary: nor Reverend De Forrest: nor, indeed, poor Georgina's own grief-stricken relatives, including her half-sisters Thérèse and Perdita.

Thus it was, the secret lay interred with the "Blue Nun," in the Kilgarvan mausoleum in the old Temperance Vale Cemetery,—whence it cannot be retrieved.

(As for the luckless Xavier, who felt such horror, incredulity, and sickened repugnance for all that, however broken and fragmented, he was able to recall of his experience in the attic,—it should not be held against the youthful detective that, after his illness of many weeks, he shrank from contemplating the "mystery": for did this fruitless exercise not invariably bring with it a quivering of his delicate nerves, and a heaviness in his heart, and a piercing staccato pain through his head? Most specifically, Xavier dreaded recalling the febrific vision he had had, while lying in a state between consciousness and unconsciousness on the unswept attic floor,—an unlooked-to vision of his cousin Georgina gliding on silent feet, austere as always, and veiled in her mourning attire: making her way to the Chippendale sideboard, and, stooping, gathering the small corpses from it, with many an ejaculation,—of ire, of sorrow, of weeping despair. One by one she lifted the mummified figures, with scarcely a glance at her helpless cousin at her feet,—who visibly suffered a cruel bleeding wound to the head, and might well, for all she knew, have required emergency medical attention. Poor Xavier!—knowing not whether he woke, or slept; or had been catapulted to some dim-lit anteroom of Hell itself.

Indeed, Xavier Kilgarvan was never to know, *with any degree of certainty*, whether this figure of the "Blue Nun" was naught but a hallucination; or Miss Georgina in incomminute flesh and blood. All resolutely, and, as it were, proudly, she ignored him while gathering her pitiable brood to her bosom, that she might secret them away, and bury them for all time: doubtless with the aid of that quicklime she had bought in such indiscreet haste, many months before. *Where* she buried them Xavier was never to know, nor did he seek to know: but when he came partway to his senses in the morning, and pulled himself, with great difficulty, to his feet, his fevered eye took in the fact that *the drawers of the sideboard were now empty,*—empty of everything save tattered and stained silver tissue, and a host of dead insects, dried and insubstantial as flakes of leaf!)

Epilogue: Mr. Guillemot's Testimony

IT WAS PRECISELY EIGHTEEN YEARS following that event-filled autumn,—long after he himself had suffered expulsion, in a manner of speaking, from Winterthurn—that Xavier Kilgarvan, while registering for a bachelor's suite in a small hotel near Gramercy Park, in New York City, chanced to note the shaky signature of *Malcolm Guillemot* several lines above his own: and gasped aloud with certainty that this must be the very same gentleman who had been Miss Georgina's "suitor" of a season long past.

Thus, though Xavier was embarked, at this time, on a most obdurate and teasing case (in consultation with a prominent toxicologist in the employ of the District Solicitor of the County of Manhattan), he took steps to seek out Mr. Guillemot, that he might tactfully,—in truth, very indirectly—question him regarding the tragical Georgina: though it must be said that, through the years, the "mystery" of Glen Mawr was not one Xavier Kilgarvan cared to contemplate with any pleasure.

And his investigation *did* yield fruit, of however an ambiguous sort: causing him to reiterate inwardly those familiar words of Monsieur Dupin's: *Perhaps it is the very simplicity of the thing that puts you at fault.*

Though unusually frail of build, and so pale his skin possessed a bluish translucence, Mr. Malcolm Guillemot not only was willing to speak with Xavier (who presented himself as an "interested party") of his Winterthurn adventure of thirty years before; but roused himself to speak with some passion, in an unfaltering high-pitched voice. Had Xavier not known the gentleman's approximate age, which could not be much beyond sixty, he would have supposed him far older: belonging, indeed, to a distant generation. As some of his monologue in the hotel's dining room, amidst the genial hubbub of voices and the tinkling of tea things, was indecipherable to Xavier's ear, and a great deal, I am afraid, was rambling and superfluous, it is a severely edited version I shall offer here.—

"... thus, young man, as was our wont in those days, I repeated my hopeful proposal to said lady ... and was yet again rejected! ... this being (so I was kindly advised) naught but a maiden's stratagem ... indeed, a necessity of sorts. Being but a foolish sort of youth then ... in truth, two or three years younger than the lady ... I felt the prick of stung vanity, no less than that of wounded sentiment! ... yet bethought myself, that the lady *was* enamored of me, if looks, smiles, allusions, and innuendos of divers sorts might be trusted. (Though I hope I am not being ungallant in so saying, it oft-times struck me that the lady was more enamored of *me,* than I of *her.*) In any case, my pride (if not my masculine fervor for possession) would not allow me to withdraw from the field ... for I *was* quite fond of her ... her high qualities of intelligence and sensitivity ... her frequent displays of wit ... her lapse, so to speak, to girlish *sweetness* ... being most admirable qualities: albeit conversation did not invariably sparkle between us, and sometimes we fell each into a blushing silence ...

from which it was the very Devil to wriggle free! . . . and one did not always regret an interruption from the father at that juncture.

"Thus, yet again I girded my loins, to propose a most heroic *third time*, while strolling with the lady in the English garden at Glen Mawr . . . for that was, I believe, the name of the estate; and while we were strolling, the lady's arm crooked lightly through mine, I nervously repeated my plea, *that she consent to be my belovèd wife.* To my surprise, then, she behaved most amazingly: by choking with laughter, and drawing away: and wiping tears from her flushed face, with the sleeve of her crêpe dress—! Then again, before I could make any response whatsoever, she gripped my arm most forcibly . . . indeed, in an excitable and playful manner (which, I must confess, I ill knew how to interpret) . . . and drew me to a side terrace of the house . . . where her father (who was, as perhaps you know, a high-ranking judge in the state), and several gentlemen of his age and approximate rank, were seated at cards. So baffled was I, and so stricken with surprise, I allowed myself to be 'dragged forward,' with a numb and stiffened gait, and presented, as it were, to the company! . . . as the lady gave way to her unseemly mirth, and, with her fingers still closed hard about my arm, cried out in a strident voice: 'Father! O do excuse me! Father dear! *Do* excuse me! For but a minute! 'Tis but a minute!—nay, a half-minute! Gentlemen, *do* excuse us! Father, my friend Mr. Guillemot has given notice *for the third time* that he seeks your eldest daughter's hand in marriage: and that he should like to speak in private with you, at your convenience. Do you hear, Father?—at your convenience! *Do* excuse—!' And so on, and so forth, in this remarkable vein, all the while laughing soundlessly, and gasping for air! Precisely how long this wretched scene continued I cannot say . . . though, poor fool, I stood transfixed with horror, where a shrewder gentleman would have fled . . . my regard for the lady (I scarcely need note) having vanished at once, as if 'twere mere smoke blown by the wind.

"The Judge skillfully hid his shock and disgust at this outburst (for I have no doubt that is what he felt), and uttered but a few well-chosen words, in a voice of restraint, to the effect that his daughter should betake herself at once into the house . . . as she must be suffering from heat stroke . . . and was in danger of collapse. Whereupon . . . ah, how painful! . . . how piercing the memory! . . . the lady released her terrible grip on my arm, and lapsed into silence at once, and turned away, in immediate obeisance to her father's command . . . hurrying in a most graceless fashion . . . her skirts catching about her legs, and her hat askew . . . indeed, all but *running* into the house, before the eyes of the staring gentlemen!

"And so, young man, I left Glen Mawr Manor.

"And I never set eyes upon the lady again.

"And, as the 'feeling' I had cherished for her vanished with such alacrity, upon that summer's day, I felt no inclination to communicate with her ever again . . . or, ever again, to return to Winterthurn."

In the privacy of his suite Xavier Kilgarvan recorded his notes for the case, in his customary code, though his hand trembled, and every fiber of his being quivered with repugnance. At last he threw down his pen, and murmured aloud, "No,—it is too loathsome: and two of his daughters yet live," and, after but a moment's hesitation, committed the offensive notes to the fire,—with which impulsive gesture *The Virgin in the Rose-Bower* must, alas, be finally laid to rest.

The Dreadful Day of Judgement

★

RUTH RENDELL

T HERE WERE FOUR OF THEM working in the cemetery. They were
employed by the city corporation—to do what? Even the foreman was
vague about their duties which had not been very precisely specified.
Not to clear the central part, certainly, for that would have been a task not for
four but for four hundred. And a wildlife sanctuary, for which purpose it was
designated, must be wild. To tidy it, then, to remove the worst signs of vandal-
ism, to carry away such gravestones as had fallen, to denude certain of the many
winding paths of the intrusive bramble and ivy and nettle. When they asked the
foreman whether this should be done or that, he would say to use their own
judgement, he couldn't be sure, he would find out. But he never did. Sometimes
an official from the corporation came and viewed the work and nodded and disappeared into the hut with the foreman to drink tea. As the winter came on the
official appeared less often, and the foreman said it was a hopeless task, they
needed more men, but the corporation could no longer afford to spend the
money, they must just do the best they could.

The hut was just inside the main gates. The foreman had a plan of the
cemetery pinned to the wall next to Gilly's calendar of the girl in the transparent nightdress. He had a kettle and a spirit stove, but the cups and the teapot
had been brought by Marlon who got them from his mother. The hut was always hot and smelly and smoky. The foreman chain-smoked and so did Marlon, although he was so young, and everywhere in the hut were saucers full of

ash and cigarette stubs. One day Gilly, who didn't smoke, brought into the hut a tin can he had found in an open vault. The foreman and Marlon seemed pleased to have a new, clean ashtray, for they never considered emptying the others but let them fill up and spill about the floor.

'Marlon'd be scared stiff if he knew where that came from,' said John. 'He'd die of fright.'

But Gilly only laughed. He found everything about the cemetery funny, even the soldiers' graves, the only well-tended ones, that the Imperial War Graves Commission still looked after. In the beginning he had amused himself by jumping out on Marlon from behind a monument or a pillared tomb, but the foreman, lethargic as he was, had stopped that because Marlon was not quite as they were, being backward and not able to read or write much.

The main gates hung between what the foreman called stone posts but which John alone knew were Corinthian columns. A high wall surrounded the cemetery, which was of many acres, and the periphery of it, a wide space just inside the wall, had been cleared long before and turfed and planted with trees that were still tiny. This was to be a public park for the townsfolk. It was the centre, the deep heart of the place, once the necropolis for this mercantile city, that was to be left for the birds and such small animals who would venture in and stay.

Many species of bird already nested in the ilexes and the laurels, the elms and the thin, silver-trunked birch trees. Crows with wings like black fans, woodpeckers whose tap-tap-tapping could be heard from the almost impenetrable depths, little birds which even John couldn't name and which crept rather than hopped over the lichen on the fallen stones. It was silent in there but for the rare rustle of wings or the soft crack of a decayed twig dropping. The city lay below, all round, but in winter it was often masked by fog, and it was hard to believe that thousands lived down there and worked and scurried in glare and noise. Their forbears' tombs stood in rows or gathered in clusters or jostled each other haphazardly: domed follies, marble slabs, granite crosses, broken columns, draped urns, simple stones, all overgrown and shrouded and half-obscured. Not a famous name among them, not a memorable title, only the obscure dead, forgotten, abandoned, capable now of nothing more than to decree a hush.

The silence was violated only by Gilly's talk. He had one topic of conversation, but that one was inexhaustible and everything recalled him to it. A name on a tomb, a scrap of verse on a gravestone, a pair of sparrows, the decorously robed statue of an angel. 'Bit of all right, that one,' he would say, stroking the stone flesh of a weeping muse, his hands so coarse and calloused that John wondered how any real woman could bear them to touch her. Or, lifting the ivy from a grave where lay a matron who had married three times, 'Couldn't get enough of it, could she?' And these reflections led him into endless reminiscences of the women he had had, those he now possessed, and anticipations of those awaiting him in the future.

Nothing stayed him. Not the engraved sorrow of parents mourning a daughter dead at seventeen, not the stone evocations of the sufferings of those dead in childbirth. Some of the vaults had been despoiled and left open, and he would penetrate them, descending subterranean stairs, shouting up to John and Marlon from the depths that here was a good place to bring a girl. 'Be OK in the summer. There's shelves here, make a good bed, they would. Proper little boudoir.'

John often regretted the thing he had done which made Gilly admire him. It had been on his first day there. He knew, even before he had done it, that this was to show them he was different from them, to make it clear from the start that he was a labourer only because there was no other work obtainable for such as he. He wanted them to know he had been to a university and was a qualified teacher. The shame and humiliation of being forced to take this unskilled work ate into his soul. They must understand his education had fitted him for something higher. But it had been a foolish vanity.

There had been nothing in the deep cavity any more but stones and dead leaves. But he had jumped in and held up a big pitted stone and cried ringingly: 'That skull had a tongue in it and could sing once. How the knave jowls it to the ground, as if 'twere Cain's jawbone that did the first murder!'

Gilly stared. 'You make that up yourself?'

'Shakespeare,' he said. 'Hamlet,' and the awe on Gilly's unformed pug-nosed face made him go on, excited with success, a braggart in a squalid pit. 'Prithee, Horatio, tell me one thing. Dost thou think Alexander looked o' this fashion i' the earth? And smelt so? pah!'

Marlon had gone white, his face peaked between the falls of thin yellow hair. He wore a heavy blue garment, a kind of anorak, but it gave him a medieval look standing there against the chapel wall, an El Greco sky flowing above its tower, purple and black and rushing in scuds above this northern Toledo. But Gilly was laughing, begging John to go on, and John went on, playing to the groundlings, holding the stone aloft. 'Alas, poor Yorick . . .' until at last he flung it from him with the ham actor's flourish, and up on the path again was being clapped on the back by Gilly and told what a brain he'd got. And Gilly was showing what he was and what all that had meant to him by demanding to have that bit again, the bit about the lips that I have kissed I know not how oft.

Marlon hadn't laughed or congratulated him. Bewildered, frightened by the daring of it and the incomprehensibility, he fumbled to light a fresh ciga-rette, another of the sixty he would smoke that day. Cigarettes were all he had, a tenuous hold on that real world in which his mother, sixteen years before, had named him after a famous actor. The smoke flowed from his loose lips. In a way, but for that cigarette, he might have been an actor in a miracle play perhaps or in a chorus of madmen. On that day as on all the others that followed, he walked behind them as they made their way back through the shaded aisles, un-der the leather-leaved ilexes, between the little houses of the dead.

In the hut there was tea to be drunk, and then home, the foreman off to his semidetached and his comfortable wife, Marlon to his mother and stuffy rooms and television commercials, John to his bedsit, Gilly (as John, the favoured, was now privileged to be told) to the arms of a casino owner's wife whose husband lacked a gravedigger's virility.

The chapel was built of yellowish-grey stones. It had an octagonal nave, and on its floor thin, hair-like grass grew up between the flags. To one of its sides was attached a square tower, surmounted at each angle by a thin ornamented spire. The four spires, weather-worn, corroded, stained, were like four needles encrusted with rust. The workmen used the chapel as a repository for pieces of broken stone and iron rails. Even Gilly's bullying could not make Marlon go inside. He was afraid of Gilly and the foreman, but not so afraid as he was of the echoing chapel and of the dust beneath his feet.

Gilly said, 'What'd you do, Marl, if you turned round now and it wasn't me here but a skeleton in a shroud, Marl?'

'Leave him alone,' said John, and when they were alone in the nave, 'You know he's a bit retarded.'

'Big words you use, John. I call him cracked. D'you know what he said to me yesterday? All them graves are going to open up and the dead bodies come out. On some special day that's going to be. What day's that then? I said. But he only wobbled his head.'

'The dreadful Day of Judgement,' said John, 'when the secrets of all hearts shall be revealed.'

'Wouldn't suit me, that. Some of them old skulls'd blush a bit if I told them what I'd been getting up to last night. The secrets of all hearts? Open some of them up and I'd have a good many blokes on my track, not to mention that old git, you-know-who. Break his bloody roulette wheel, he would.'

'Over your head, no doubt,' said John.

'A short life and a randy one, that's what I say.' They came out into the cold, pale sunlight. 'Here, have a shufty at this. Angelina Clara Bowyer, 1816 to 1839. Same age as what you are, mate, and she'd had five kids! Must have worn her old man out.'

'It wore her out,' said John, and he seemed to see her with her piled plaited hair and her long straight dress and the consumption in her face. He saw the young husband mourning among those five bread-and-butter-fed children, the crepe on his hat, the black coat. Under a sky like this, the sun a white puddle in layered cloud, he came with the clergyman and the mourners and the coffin-bearers to lay her in the earth. The flowers withered in the biting wind—or did they bring flowers to funerals then? He didn't know, and not knowing broke the

vision and brought him back to the clink of spade against granite, the smell of
Marlon's cigarette, Gilly talking, talking, as boringly as an old woman of her
aches and pains only he was talking of sex.

They always stopped work at four now the dusk came early. 'Nights are
drawing in,' said the foreman, brewing tea, filling up with dog ends the can
Gilly had found in the grave.

'When'll we get it over with?' Marlon faltered, coming close to the stove,
coughing a little.

'Depends on what we've got to get over,' said the foreman. 'Digging a bit
here, clearing a bit there. My guess is that council fellow'll come round one of
these days and say, That's it, lads, now you can leave it to the squirrels.'

Gilly was looking at his calendar, turning over the November nightdress
girl to the December Santa Claus girl. 'If I had my way they'd level it all over,
the centre bit, and put grass down, make the whole place a park. That's healthy,
that is. Somewhere a young kid could take his girl. Lover's Lane Park, that'd be
a good name. I'd like to see real birds there, not them bloody crows.'

'You can't do that,' said Marlon. 'There's the dead people in there.'

'So what? There was dead people round the edges, but they took them up.
They done something—what they call it, John?'

'They deconsecrated the ground.'

'Hear what John says? He's educated, he knows.'

Marlon got up, the cigarette clinging to his lip. 'You mean they dug them
up? There was others and they dug them up?'

''Course they did. You didn't think they was under there, did you?'

'Then where'll they be when the Day comes? How'll they lift up the stones
and come out?'

'Here, for Christ's sake,' said the foreman, 'that's enough of that, young
Marlon. I don't reckon your mum'd better take you to church no more if that's
what you come out with.'

'They must come out, they must come and judge,' Marlon cried, and then
the foreman told him sharply to shut up, for even he could be shaken by this

sort of thing, with the darkness crowding in on the hut, and the heart of the cemetery a black mound horned by the spires of the chapel.

John wondered what church Marlon went to, that of some strange sect perhaps. Or was it only his incomplete brain that distorted the accepted meaning of the Day of Judgement into this version of his own? The resentful dead, the judging dead, lying censorious in the earth.

For his part, he had at first seen the cemetery as no more than a wooded knoll and the stones no more than granite outcroppings. It was not so now. The names in inscriptions, studied by him quietly or derisively read out by Gilly, evoked images of their bearers. James Calhoun Stokes, 1798–1862, Merchant of this City; 'Upright in all his dealings, he stood firm to meet his Maker'. Gilly had an obscene rendering of that, of course. Thomas Charles Macpherson, 1802–79, Master Builder; 'Blest are the Pure in Heart'. Lucy Matilda Osborne, 1823–96; 'Her submissive duty to her husband and devotion to her sons was exceeded only by her pious adoration of her God'. John saw them in cutaway coats, in bombazine gowns, or night-capped on their deathbeds.

But Marlon saw them as a magisterial procession. Listening, watching, waiting perhaps for the ultimate outrage.

'What a load of old cobblers! You'll be down there yourself soon, all the fags you get through in a day.' Gilly sat on a toppled stone, laughing. He had been telling John more about the casino man's wife, trying to find among the statues they had piled up one whose figure might be comparable to hers. Britannias, muses, embodiments of virtues or arts, they lay prostrate, their blank grey or bronze faces all staring upwards at the clouded sky.

'What are we going to do with them?' Marlon said in the voice that was as desperate when he asked about trivialities as when he gave his prophet-like cries.

'Ask the foreman,' said John.

'He won't bloody know.' And Gilly lifted on to his lap the bronze that was nearly nude, just veiled over her loins with metal drapery. 'Randy old devil, he must have been, that Sidney George Whatsit, having her sitting on top of him when he was dead.'

'He was a historian, the plaque says,' said John. 'She's supposed to be Clio, the Muse of History. That's why she's got a scroll in her hand.' And then, because he was bored with Gilly and afraid for Marlon, 'Let's stick them all in the chapel till the council guy comes.'

But Gilly refused to abandon the huge joke of caressing the bronze. Every reachable inch of her anatomy was examined until, suddenly, he jumped up, leaving her to roll into one of the muddy ruts the truck had made, and ran up to the pillared monument from whose dome she had toppled. He stood inside, a satyr, John thought, in a temple defiled by northern rains. He threw up his arms.

'I said you was a randy old goat, Sidney, and so you was! I had a bird called Clio once myself, real hot stuff.' His shouts punctured the thick greyness, the silence, the fog-textured air. He leapt down the steps, kicking a gravestone here, a marble urn there, and perched on a broken column. 'Come out, all the lot of you, if you want, only you can't because you're bloody dead!'

And then Marlon made a horrible sound, the moan a man makes in sleep, in a nightmare, when he thinks he is screaming. He got into the cab of the truck and hunched there.

'You stupid bastard.' John picked up Marlon's fallen cigarette packet, brushed the grit off it. 'D'you have to act like a kid of ten?'

'Got to get some sort of kick out of this dump,' Gilly said sulkily. 'Dead-end hole.'

'Well, that's what it is, isn't it? What d'you expect? A bar? Booze? Bring on the dancing girls?'

Gilly started to laugh again, picked up his muse again. 'I wouldn't mind this dancing girl. Don't reckon they'd miss her, do you? She'd look OK in my place. I could stand her on the table.'

'What for?'

'People have statues, don't they? They've got them in the town hall. It'd give my place a bit of class.'

'Come on,' said John, 'let's stick the lot of them in the chapel. The foreman'll do his nut if he sees you going off with that. She's too big to go under your jacket.'

So they piled the statues and the urns in the chapel, and Gilly amused himself by shouting insults and obscenities which the lofty walls echoed back at him, black pigeons, white doves flapping from the crannies in fear.

'What d'you do in that room of yours, John? Must be a real drag all on your own night after night. Fancy coming over to my bird's place? She's got a real dishy friend. We could have ourselves a ball, and I don't mean wining and dining.'

No, thanks, John said, and softened his refusal by saying he had to study which impressed Gilly. It wasn't that he was a prude so much as that the idea of association with Gilly's friends offended some snobbish delicacy in his nature, some fastidiousness. Better the speechless company of James Calhoun Stokes and Angelina Bowyer and the historian, better, in the evenings, the dreams of them and the wonderings about their lost lives. Though, in refusing, he thought it likely that brash insensitive Gilly might not take his no for an answer but turn up one night with his girl and that other girl to rout him out. He feared it a little, but not with Marlon's obsessional dread of threats from another world.

When at last Gilly did come, it was on a cold moonlit night, and he came alone.

'I'm going to split,' said Gilly, 'I'm getting the hell out. All good things come to an end. You can tell the foreman in the morning, OK? I'm going south. I've got a girl in London, worships the ground I tread on, poor cow. She'll take me in. But that's between you and I, right?'

'But why?'

'He's found out, her old man, and I reckon he'll have his heavies out gunning for me. He's beat her up—bunch of bloody gangsters that lot are. I'll miss her.' The tears stood in his eyes, and John stared, amazed, confounded. 'Poor cow,' said Gilly, the epithet an endearment, a caress.

'D'you want me to come to the station with you?'

'No need for that. I only come in to tell you to tell the foreman. Anyway, I got something to do first, get that statue, that Clio. The train don't go till eleven, and I want her.' He turned half away. 'For a souvenir like, she's the dead spitting image.'

'You'd go into the cemetery tonight, for *that*?'

'Like I said, I want her.' His eyes, glazed, held a pathetic hunger. Of love, in those bare words, he had expressed all he knew how to. On lechery only he was articulate. 'It's moonlight,' he said. 'I've got a torch. I'll climb the wall.'

'Goodbye, Gilly,' said John. 'Good luck.'

In the morning the sky was coppery, grey above, reddish on the horizon where the sun hung. The Winter Solstice had come.

'It's like the end of the world,' said Marlon.

The foreman came in, rubbing his hands. 'Going to have snow before the day's over. Gilly's late.' John told him Gilly wasn't coming in. He didn't tell him why not, and he expected an outburst. But the foreman only stuck out his lip and put the kettle on and helped himself to one of Marlon's cigarettes.

'No loss, that,' he said. 'We shan't miss him. And if I'm not much mistaken we'll all be laid off by tonight when this dump's snowed up. You'll be able to get yourselves dug in nice for Christmas, lads.'

Marlon showed no inclination to leave the stuffy warmth of the hut, where the foreman now had a brazier of coke, for the raw air and yellowed dimness of the cemetery. But the foreman wanted to be rid of them, to be on his own, to be idle and warm in peace. He took down Gilly's calendar and pushed it among the glowing coke, and the last John saw of it was the glossy tanned body of a naked girl gyrating in the fire. They moved out into the chill of the shortest day, the foreman hurrying them along by cleaning frost off the truck's windscreen himself.

John expected trouble from the boy, so forbidding was the cemetery in the gloom and under that strange sky. But Marlon, when John had repeated several times that Gilly was not coming, when this had at last sunk in, became more cheerful and more like a normal person than John had ever seen him. He even laughed. He pushed John about in the cab, and when this made the truck swerve, he hooted with laughter.

But when they had come to the centre and were working on clearing the main aisle, he fell silent, though he seemed tranquil enough. All those months John had longed for peace, for a respite from Gilly's ceaseless bragging and innuendo, but now he had it he felt only uneasy. Being alone up here with Marlon had something to do with it. He despised himself for being afraid of a poor retarded boy, yet he was afraid. The thickening atmosphere was part of it, and the windless cold, and the increasing darkness like an eclipse, and the way Marlon would stand for whole minutes on end, staring vacantly, swinging his spade. But what made him long for the snow to begin and drive them back to the hut was Marlon's new habit, now Gilly was not here to deride him, of touching the gravestones and seeming to whisper to them. That he did this reverently and cautiously did nothing to ease John's mind. It was as if he were placating the dead, assuring them that now all would be well. And John had an awareness, growing in intensity as the time slowly passed, that the cemetery had somehow undergone a change. For him it had been just a place to work in, later an abode of sadness and the lost past, never till now macabre. Perhaps much of this feeling was due to the strangeness of the day itself, the permanent twilight, the knowledge that in these hours the earth had turned to its ultimate distance away from the sun.

Yet it was more than that. That might account for the distortions he seemed to see, so that the tombs appeared more closely crowded and the chapel tower taller and darker, but not for his sensation that there had taken place in the cemetery since he had last seen it, some upheaval and some outrage. It was when these fancies grew so strong as to make him imagine some actual physical change, the positions of the slabs and stones altered, that he looked at his watch and told Marlon they could stop now for their midday meal.

The foreman said to bring down one truck-load of rubble from the chapel, and then they could knock off. The sky had lightened a little, becoming uniformly livid, but still they needed the headlights on. The pale misty shafts of light probed the undergrowth and died into blackness. They parked beside the tower.

'Can you make an effort and come in?' said John, 'Or do I have to do it on my own?'

Marlon managed a sheepish, crafty smile. 'You go first.'

The rubble was heaped against the furthest side of the octagon. He saw Gilly before he got there. Gilly was lying on his back among the muses and the virgins, his head, his face, a mass of black clotted blood to which fragments and crumbs of stone adhered. Clio, memento of love, had rolled from his grasp. His eyes still stared, as if they still saw those meters-out of vengeance.

'Gilly, Gilly!' John cried, and the eight walls called back, 'Gilly, Gilly!'— calling them to Marlon as he came through the tower and into the nave.

Marlon did not speak Gilly's name. He gave a great cry.

'The dead people came out! The dead people judged him! The day has come, the end of the world . . . the Day, the Day, the Day!'

From the eaves, out of the broken roof, the birds came, circling, cawing, a great rush of wings. And the echo roared like a knell. John stumbled out after Marlon, after the flying figure that cried like a prophet in the wilderness, into a whiteness that cleaned the world.

In great shaggy flakes, the snow had begun to fall.

A Spiritualist

★

JEAN RHYS

I ASSURE YOU,' SAID THE COMMANDANT, 'that I adore women—that
without a woman in my life I cannot exist.'

'But one must admit that one has deceptions. They are frankly disappointing, or else they exact so much that the day comes when, inevitably, one
asks oneself: Is it worthwhile?'

'In any case it cracks. It always cracks.'

He fixed his monocle more firmly into his eye to look at a passing lady, with
an expression like that of an amiable and cynical old fox.

'And it is my opinion, Madame, that that is the fault of the woman. All the
misunderstandings, all the quarrels! It is astonishing how gentle, how easily
fooled most men are. Even an old Parisian like myself, Madame. . . . I assure
you that of all men the Parisians are the most sentimental. And it is astonishing
how lacking in calm and balance is the most clever woman, how prone to weep
at a wrong moment—in a word, how exhausting!

'For instance: A few months ago I was obliged to break with a most charming little friend whom I passionately adored. Because she exaggerated her eccentricity. One must be in the movement, even though one may regret in one's
heart the more agreeable epoch that has vanished. A little eccentricity is per-
missible. It is indeed *chic*. Yes, it is now chic to be eccentric. But when it came
to taking me to a chemist and forcing me to buy her ether, which she took at
once in the restaurant where we dined: and then hanging her legs out of the taxi

window in the middle of the Boulevard: you will understand that I was *gêné:* that I found that she exaggerated. In the middle of the Boulevard!

'Most unfortunately one can count no longer on women, even French-women, to be dignified, to have a certain *tenue.* I remember the time when things were different. And more agreeable, I think.'

The Commandant gazed into the distance, and his expression became sentimental. His eyes were light blue. He even blushed.

'Once I was happy with a woman. Only once. I will tell you about it. Her name was Madeleine, and she was a little dancer whom some *sale individu* had deserted when she was without money and ill. She was the most sweet and gentle woman I have ever met. I knew her for two years, and we never quarrelled once or even argued. Never. For Madeleine gave way in everything. . . . And to think that my wife so often accused me of having a *sale caractère.* . . .'

He mused for a while.

'A *sale caractère.* . . . Perhaps I have. But Madeleine was of a sweetness . . . ah, well, she died suddenly after two years. She was only twenty-eight.

'When she died I was sad as never in my life before. The poor little one. . . . Only twenty-eight!

'Three days after the funeral her mother, who was a very good woman, wrote to me saying that she wished to have the clothes and the effects, you understand, of her daughter. So in the afternoon I went to her little flat, Place de L'Odéon, fourth floor. I took my housekeeper with me, for a woman can be useful with her advice on these occasions.'

'I went straight into the bedroom and I began to open the cupboards and arrange her dresses. I wished to do that myself. I had the tears in my eyes, I assure you, for it is sad to see and to touch the dresses of a dead woman that one has loved. My housekeeper, Gertrude, she went into the kitchen to arrange the household utensils.'

'Well, suddenly, there came from the closed sitting-room a very loud, a terrible crash. The floor shook.

'Gertrude and I both called out at the same time: What is that? And she ran to me from the kitchen saying that the noise had come from the salon. I said: Something has fallen down, and I opened quickly the sitting-room door.

'You must understand that it was a flat on the fourth floor; all the windows of the sitting-room were tightly shut, naturally, and the blinds were drawn as I had left them on the day of the funeral. The door into the hall was locked, the other led into the bedroom where I was.'

'And, there, lying right in the middle of the floor was a block of white marble, perhaps fifty centimeters square.

'Gertrude said: *Mon Dieu*, Monsieur, look at that. How did that get here?—Her face was pale as death.—It was not there, she said, when we came.

'As for me, I just looked at the thing, stupefied.'

'Gertrude crossed herself and said: I am going. Not for anything: for nothing in the world would I stay here longer. There is something strange about this flat.

'She ran. I—well, I did not run. I walked out, but very quickly. You understand, I have been a soldier for twenty-five years, and, God knows, I had nothing to reproach myself with with regard to the poor little one. But it shakes the nerves—something like that.'

The Commandant lowered his voice.

'The fact was, I understood. I knew what she meant.

'I had promised her a beautiful, white marble tombstone, and I had not yet ordered it. Not because I had not thought of it. Oh, no—but because I was too sad, too tired. But the little one doubtless thought that I had forgotten. It was her way of reminding me.'

I looked hard at the Commandant. His eyes were clear and as naïve as a child's: a little dim with emotion. . . . Silence. . . . He lit a cigarette.

'Well, to show how strange women are: I recounted this to a lady I knew, not long ago. And she laughed. Laughed! You understand. . . . *Un fou rire.* . . . And do you know what she said:

'She said: How furious that poor Madeleine must have been that she missed you!

'Now can you imagine the droll ideas that women can have!'

The Dummy

★

SUSAN SONTAG

SINCE MY SITUATION IS INTOLERABLE, I have decided to take steps
to resolve it. So I have constructed a lifelike dummy made of various
brands of Japanese plastic simulating flesh, hair, nails, and so forth. An
electronics engineer of my acquaintance, for a sizable fee, built the interior
mechanism of the dummy: it will be able to talk, eat, work, walk, and copulate.
I hired an important artist of the old realistic school to paint the features; it took
twelve sittings to make a face that perfectly resembles mine. My broad nose is
there, my brown hair, the lines on each side of my mouth. Even I could not tell
the dummy and myself apart, were it not that from my peculiar vantage point it
is quite obvious that he is he and that I am I.

What remains is to install the dummy in the center of my life. He will go
to work instead of me, and receive the approval and censure of my boss. He will
bow and scrape and be diligent. All I require of him is that he bring me the
check every other Wednesday; I will give him carfare and money for his
lunches, but no more. I'll make out the checks for the rent and the utilities, and
pocket the rest myself. The dummy will also be the one who is married to my
wife. He will make love to her on Tuesday and Saturday night, watch television
with her every evening, eat her wholesome dinners, quarrel with her about how
to bring up the children. (My wife, who also works, pays the grocery bills out of
her salary.) I will also assign the dummy Monday night bowling with the team
from the office, the visit to my mother on Friday night, reading the newspaper

each morning, and perhaps buying my clothes (two sets—one for him, one for me). Other tasks I will assign as they come up, as I wish to divest myself of them. I want to keep for myself only what gives me pleasure.

An ambitious enterprise, you say? But why not? The problems of this world are only truly solved in two ways: by extinction or by duplication. Former ages had only the first choice. But I see no reason not to take advantage of the marvels of modern technology for personal liberation. I have a choice. And, not being the suicidal type, I have decided to duplicate myself.

On a fine Monday morning I wind the dummy up and set him loose, after making sure he knows what to do—that is, he knows just how I would behave in any familiar situation. The alarm goes off. He rolls over and pokes my wife, who wearily gets out of the double bed and turns off the alarm. She puts on her slippers and robe, then limps, stiff-ankled, into the bathroom. When she comes out and heads for the kitchen, he gets up and takes her place in the bathroom. He urinates, gargles, shaves, comes back into the bedroom and takes his clothes out of the dresser and closet, returns to the bathroom, dresses, then joins my wife in the kitchen. My children are already at the table. The younger girl didn't finish her homework last night, and my wife is writing a note of excuse to the teacher. The older girl sits haughtily munching the cold toast. "Morning, Daddy," they say to the dummy. The dummy pecks them on the cheek in return. Breakfast passes without incident, I observe with relief. The children leave. They haven't noticed a thing. I begin to feel sure my plan is going to work and realize, by my excitement, that I had greatly feared it would not—that there would be some mechanical failure, that the dummy would not recognize his cues. But no, everything is going right, even the way he folds *The New York Times* is correct; he reproduces exactly the amount of time I spent on the foreign news, and it takes him just as long to read the sports pages as it took me.

The dummy kisses my wife, he steps out the door, he enters the elevator. (Do machines recognize each other, I wonder.) Into the lobby, out the door, on the street walking at a moderate pace—the dummy has left on time, he doesn't have to worry—into the subway he goes. Steady, calm, clean (I cleaned him myself Sunday night), untroubled, he goes about his appointed tasks. He will be happy as long as I am satisfied with him. And so I will be, whatever he does, as long as others are satisfied with him.

Nobody notices anything different in the office, either. The secretary says hello, he smiles back as I always do; then he walks to my cubicle, hangs up his coat, and sits at my desk. The secretary brings him my mail. After reading it, he calls for some dictation. Next, there is a pile of my unfinished business from last Friday to attend to. Phone calls are made, an appointment is set up for lunch with a client from out of town. There is only one irregularity that I notice: the dummy smokes seven cigarettes during the morning; I usually smoke between ten and fifteen. But I set this down to the fact that he is new at his work and has not had time to accumulate the tensions that I feel after working six years in this office. It occurs to me that he will probably not have two martinis—as I always do—during the lunch, but only one, and I am right. But these are mere details, and will be to the dummy's credit if anyone notices them, which I doubt. His behavior with the out-of-town client is correct—perhaps a shade too deferential, but this, too, I put down to inexperience. Thank God, no simple matter trips him up. His table manners are as they should be. He doesn't pick at his food, but eats with appetite. And he knows he should sign the check rather than pay with a credit card; the firm has an account at this restaurant.

In the afternoon there is a sales conference. The vice president explains a new promotional campaign for the Midwest. The dummy makes suggestions. The boss nods. The dummy taps his pencil on the long mahogany table and looks thoughtful. I notice he is chain-smoking. Could he be feeling the pressure so soon? What a hard life I led! After less than a day of it, even a dummy shows some wear and tear. The rest of the afternoon passes without incident. The dummy makes his way home to my wife and children, eats my dinner appreciatively, plays Monopoly with the children for an hour, watches a Western on TV with my wife, bathes, makes himself a ham sandwich, and then retires. I don't know what dreams he has, but I hope they are restful and pleasant. If my approval can give him an untroubled sleep, he has it. I am entirely pleased with my creation.

*   *   *

The dummy has been on the job for several months. What can I report? A greater degree of proficiency? But that's impossible. He was fine the first day. He couldn't be any more like me than he was at the very beginning. He does not have to get better at his job but only stick at it contentedly, unrebelliously, without mechanical failure. My wife is happy with him—at least, no more unhappy than she was with me. My children call him Daddy and ask him for their allowance. My fellow workers and my boss continue to entrust him with my job.

Lately, though—just the past week, really—I have noticed something that worries me. It is the attention that the dummy pays to the new secretary, Miss Love. (I hope it isn't her name that arouses him somewhere in the depths of that complex machinery; I imagine that machines can be literal-minded.) A slight lingering at her desk when he comes in in the morning, a second's pause, no more, when she says hello; whereas I—and he until recently—used to walk by that desk without breaking stride. And he does seem to be dictating more letters. Could it be from increased zeal on behalf of the firm? I remember how, the very first day, he spoke up at the sales conference. Or could it be the desire to detain Miss Love? Are those letters necessary? I could swear he thinks so. But then you never know what goes on behind that imperturbable dummy's face of his. I'm afraid to ask him. Is it because I don't want to know the worst? Or because I'm afraid he'll be angry at my violation of his privacy? In any case, I have decided to wait until he tells me.

Then one day it comes—the news I had dreaded. At eight in the morning the dummy corners me in the shower, where I have been spying on him while he shaves, marveling how he remembers to cut himself every once in a while, as I do. He unburdens himself to me. I am astonished at how much he is moved—astonished and a little envious. I never dreamed a dummy could have so much feeling, that I would see a dummy weep. I try to quiet him. I admonish him, then I reprimand him. It's no use. His tears become sobs. He, or rather his passion, whose mechanism I cannot fathom, begins to revolt me. I'm also terrified my wife and children will hear him, rush to the bathroom, and there find this berserk creature who would be incapable of normal responses. (Might they find both of us here in the bathroom? That, too, is possible.) I run the shower, open both the sink faucets, and flush the toilet to drown out the painful noises he is making. All this for love! All this for the love of Miss Love! He has barely spoken to her, except in the way of business. Certainly, he hasn't slept with her, of that I am sure. And yet he is madly, desperately in love. He wants to leave my wife. I explain to him how impossible that is. First of all, he has duties and responsibilities. He is the husband and father to my wife and children. They depend on him; their lives would be smashed by his selfish act. And second, what does he know about Miss Love? She's at least ten years younger than he is, has given no particular sign of noticing him at all, and probably has a nice boyfriend her own age whom she's planning to marry.

The dummy refuses to listen. He is inconsolable. He will have Miss Love or—here he makes a threatening gesture—he will destroy himself. He will bang his head against the wall, or jump out of a window, disassembling irrevocably his delicate machinery. I become really alarmed. I see my marvelous scheme, which has left me so beautifully at my leisure and in peace the last months, ruined. I see myself back at the job, making love again to my wife, fighting for space in the subway during the rush hour, watching television, spanking the children. If my life was intolerable to me before, you can imagine how unthinkable it has become. Why, if only you knew how I have spent these last months, while the dummy was administering my life. Without a care in the world, except for occasional curiosity as to the fate of my dummy. I have slid to the bottom of the world. I sleep anywhere now: in flophouses, on the subway (which I only board very late at night), in alleys and doorways. I don't bother to collect my paycheck from the dummy any more, because there is nothing I want to buy. Only rarely do I shave. My clothes are torn and stained.

Does this sound very dreary to you? It is not, it is not. Of course, when the dummy first relieved me of my own life, I had grandiose plans for living the lives of others. I wanted to be an Arctic explorer, a concert pianist, a great courtesan, a world statesman. I tried being Alexander the Great, then Mozart, then Bismarck, then Greta Garbo, then Elvis Presley—in my imagination, of course. I imagined that, being none of these people for long, I could have only their pleasure, none of their pain; for I could escape, transform myself, whenever I wanted. But the experiment failed, for lack of interest, from exhaustion, call it what you will. I discovered that I am tired of being a person. Not just tired of being the person I was, but any person at all. I like watching people, but I don't like talking to them, dealing with them, pleasing them, or offending them. I don't even like talking to the dummy. I am tired. I would like to be a mountain, a tree, a stone. If I am to continue as a person, the life of the solitary derelict is the only one tolerable. So you will see that it is quite out of the question that I should allow the dummy to destroy himself, and have to take his place and live my old life again.

I continue my efforts of persuasion. I get him to dry his tears and go out and face the family breakfast, promising him that we will continue our conversation in the office, after he dictates his morning batch of letters to Miss Love. He agrees to try, and makes his red-eyed, somewhat belated appearance at the table. "A cold, dear?" says my wife. The dummy blushes and mumbles something. I pray that he will hurry up. I am afraid he will break down again. I notice with alarm that he can hardly eat, and leaves his coffee cup two-thirds full.

The dummy makes his way sadly out of the apartment, leaving my wife perplexed and apprehensive. I see him hail a cab instead of heading for the subway. In the office, I eavesdrop as he dictates his letters, sighing between every sentence. Miss Love notices, too. "Why, what's the matter?" she asks cheerfully. There is a long pause. I peep out of the closet, and what do I see! The dummy and Miss Love in a hot embrace. He is stroking her breasts, her eyes are closed, with their mouths they wound each other. The dummy catches sight of me staring from behind the closet door. I signal wildly, trying to make him understand that we must talk, that I'm on his side, that I'll help him. "Tonight?" whispers the dummy, slowly releasing the ecstatic Miss Love. "I adore you," she whispers. "I adore you," says the dummy in a voice above a whisper. "and I must see you." "Tonight," she whispers back. "My place. Here's the address."

One more kiss and Miss Love goes out. I emerge from the closet and lock the door of the little office. "Well," says the dummy. "It's Love or death." "All right," I say sadly. "I won't try to talk you out of it any more. She seems like a nice girl. And quite attractive. Who knows, if she had been working here when I was here . . ." I see the dummy frowning angrily, and don't finish the sentence. "But you'll have to give me a little time," I say. "What are you going to do? As far as I can see, there's nothing you can do," says the dummy. "If you think I'm going home to your wife and kids any more, after I've found Love—" I plead with him for time.

What do I have in mind? Simply this. The dummy is now in my original position. His present arrangements for life are intolerable to him. But having more appetite for a real, individual life than I ever had, he doesn't want to vanish from the world. He just wants to replace my admittedly second-hand wife and two noisy daughters with the delightful, childless Miss Love. Well then, why shouldn't my solution—duplication—work for him as it did for me? Anything is better than suicide. The time I need is time to make another dummy, one to stay with my wife and children and go to my job while this dummy (the true dummy, I must now call him) elopes with Miss Love.

Later that morning, I borrow some money from him to go to a Turkish bath and get cleaned up, to get a haircut and shave at the barber's, and to buy myself a suit like the one he is wearing. On his suggestion, we meet for lunch at a small restaurant in Greenwich Village, where it is impossible that he meet anyone who might recognize him. I'm not sure what he is afraid of. Of having lunch alone, and being seen talking to himself? Of being seen with me? But I am perfectly presentable now. And if we are seen as two, what could be more normal than a pair of identical adult male twins, dressed alike, having lunch together and engaged in earnest conversation? We both order spaghetti *al burro* and baked clams. After three drinks, he comes around to my point of view. In consideration of my wife's feelings, he says—not mine, he insists several times in a rather harsh tone of voice—he will wait. But only a few months, no more. I point out that in this interim I will not ask that he not sleep with Miss Love but only that he be discreet in his adultery.

Making the second dummy is harder than making the first. My entire savings are wiped out. The prices of humanoid plastic and the other material, the fees of the engineer and the artist, have all gone up within just a year's time. The dummy's salary, I might add, hasn't gone up at all, despite the boss's increased appreciation of his value to the firm. The dummy is annoyed that I insist that he, rather than I, sit for the artist when the facial features are being molded and painted. But I point out to him that if the second dummy is modeled on me again, there is a chance that it would be a blurred or faded copy. Undoubtedly, some disparities have developed between the appearance of the first dummy and my own, even though I cannot detect them. I want the second dummy to be like him, wherever there is the slightest difference between him and me. I shall have to take the risk that in the second dummy might also be reproduced the unforeseen human passion that robbed the first dummy of his value to me.

Finally, the second dummy is ready. The first dummy, at my insistence (and reluctantly, since he wanted to spend his spare time with Miss Love), takes charge of his training and indoctrination period, lasting several weeks. Then the great day arrives. The second dummy is installed in the first dummy's life in the midst of a Saturday afternoon baseball game, during the seventh-inning stretch. It has been arranged that the first dummy will go out to buy hot dogs and Cokes for my wife and children. It is the first dummy who goes out, the second who returns laden with the food and drinks. The first dummy then leaps into a cab, off to the waiting arms of Miss Love.

That was nine years ago. The second dummy is living with my wife in no more exalted or depressed a fashion than I had managed. The older girl is in college, the second in high school; and there is a new child, a boy, now six years old. They have moved to a co-op apartment in Forest Hills; my wife has quit her job; and the second dummy is assistant vice president of the firm. The first dummy went back to college nights while working as a waiter during the day; Miss Love also went back to college and got her teacher's license. He is now an architect with a growing practice; she teaches English at Julia Richman High School. They have two children, a boy and a girl, and are remarkably happy. From time to time, I visit both my dummies—never without sprucing myself up first, you understand. I consider myself a relative and the godfather, sometimes the uncle, of all their children. They are not very happy to see me, perhaps because of my shabby appearance, but they haven't the courage to turn me out. I never stay long, but I wish them well, and congratulate myself for having solved in so equitable and responsible a manner the problems of this one poor short life that was allotted me.

The Girl I Left Behind Me

★

MURIEL SPARK

I T WAS JUST GONE QUARTER PAST SIX when I left the office. 'Teedle-um-tum-tum'—there was the tune again, going round my head. Mr Letter had been whistling it all throughout the day between his noisy telephone calls and his dreamy sessions. Sometimes he whistled 'Softly, Softly, Turn the Key', but usually it was 'The Girl I Left Behind Me' rendered at a brisk hornpipe tempo.

I stood in the bus queue, tired out, and wondering how long I would endure Mark Letter (Screws & Nails) Ltd. Of course, after my long illness, it was experience. But Mr Letter and his tune, and his sudden moods of bounce, and his sudden lapses into lassitude, his sandy hair and little bad teeth, roused my resentment, especially when his tune barrelled round my head long after I had left the office; it was like taking Mr Letter home.

No one at the bus stop took any notice of me. Well, of course, why should they? I was not acquainted with anyone there, but that evening I felt particularly anonymous among the homegoers. Everyone looked right through me and even, it seemed, walked through me. Late autumn always sets my fancy towards sad ideas. The starlings were crowding in to roost on all the high cornices of the great office buildings. And I located, amongst the misty unease of my feelings, a very strong conviction that I had left something important behind me or some job incompleted at the office. Perhaps I had left the safe unlocked, or perhaps it was something quite trivial which nagged at me. I had half a mind to turn back, tired as I was, and reassure myself. But my bus came along and I piled in with the rest.

As usual, I did not get a seat. I clung to the handrail and allowed myself to be lurched back and forth against the other passengers. I stood on a man's foot, and said, 'Oh, sorry.' But he looked away without response, which depressed me. And more and more, I felt that I had left something of tremendous import at the office. 'Teedle-um-tum-tum'—the tune was a background to my worry all the way home. I went over in my mind the day's business, for I thought, now, perhaps it was a letter which I should have written and posted on my way home.

That morning I had arrived at the office to find Mark Letter vigorously at work. By fits, he would occasionally turn up at eight in the morning, tear at the post and, by the time I arrived, he would have despatched perhaps half a dozen needless telegrams; and before I could get my coat off, would deliver a whole day's instructions to me, rapidly fluttering his freckled hands in time with his chattering mouth. This habit used to jar me, and I found only one thing amusing about it; that was when he would say, as he gave instructions for dealing with each item, 'Mark letter urgent.' I thought that rather funny coming from Mark Letter, and I often thought of him, as he was in those moods, as Mark Letter Urgent.

As I swayed in the bus I recalled that morning's access of energy on the part of Mark Letter Urgent. He had been more urgent than usual, so that I still felt put out by the urgency. I felt terribly old for my twenty-two years as I raked round my mind for some clue as to what I had left unfinished. Something had been left amiss; the further the bus carried me from the office, the more certain I became of it. Not that I took my job to heart very greatly, but Mr Letter's moods of bustle were infectious, and when they occurred I felt fussy for the rest of the day; and although I consoled myself that I would feel better when I got home, the worry would not leave me.

By noon, Mr Letter had calmed down a little, and for an hour before I went to lunch he strode round the office with his hands in his pockets, whistling between his seedy brown teeth that sailors' song 'The Girl I Left Behind Me.'

I lurched with the bus as it chugged out the rhythm, 'Teedle-um-tum-tum. Teedle-um . . .' Returning from lunch I had found silence, and wondered if Mr Letter was out, until I heard suddenly, from his tiny private office, his tune again, a low swift hum, trailing out towards the end. Then I knew that he had fallen into one of his afternoon daydreams.

I would sometimes come upon him in his little box of an office when these trances afflicted him. I would find him sitting in his swivel chair behind his desk. Usually he had taken off his coat and slung it across the back of his chair. His right elbow would be propped on the desk, supporting his chin, while from his left hand would dangle his tie. He would gaze at this tie; it was his main object of contemplation. That afternoon I had found him tie-gazing when I went into his room for some papers. He was gazing at it with parted lips so that I could see his small, separated discoloured teeth, no larger than a child's first teeth. Through them he whistled his tune. Yesterday, it had been 'Softly, Softly, Turn the Key', but today it was the other.

I got off the bus at my usual stop, with my fare still in my hand. I almost threw the coins away, absentmindedly thinking they were the ticket, and when I noticed them I thought how nearly no one at all I was, since even the conductor had, in his rush, passed me by.

Mark Letter had remained in his dream for two and a half hours. What was it I had left unfinished? I could not for the life of me recall what he had said when at last he emerged from his office-box. Perhaps it was then I had made tea. Mr Letter always liked a cup when he was neither in his frenzy nor in his abstraction, but ordinary and talkative. He would speak of his hobby, fretwork. I do not think Mr Letter had any home life. At forty-six he was still unmarried, living alone in a house at Roehampton. As I walked up the lane to my lodgings I recollected that Mr Letter had come in for his tea with his tie still dangling from his hand, his throat white under the open-neck shirt, and his 'Teedle-um-tum-tum' in his teeth.

At last I was home and my Yale in the lock. Softly, I said to myself, softly turn the key, and thank God I'm home. My landlady passed through the hall from kitchen to dining-room with a salt and pepper cruet in her crinkly hands. She had some new lodgers. 'My guests', she always called them. The new guests took precedence over the old with my landlady. I felt desolate. I simply could not climb the stairs to my room to wash, and then descend to take brown soup with the new guests while my landlady fussed over them, ignoring me. I sat for a moment in the chair in the hall to collect my strength. A year's illness drains one, however young. Suddenly the repulsion of the brown soup and the anxiety about the office made me decide. I would not go upstairs to my room. I must return to the office to see what it was that I had overlooked.

'Teedle-um-tum-tum'—I told myself that I was giving way to neurosis. Many times I had laughed at my sister who, after she had gone to bed at night, would send her husband downstairs to make sure all the gas taps were turned off, all the doors locked, back and front. Very well, I was as silly as my sister, but I understood her obsession, and simply opened the door and slipped out of the house, tired as I was, making my weary way back to the bus stop, back to the office.

'Why should I do this for Mark Letter?' I demanded of myself. But really, I was not returning for his sake, it was for my own. I was doing this to get rid of the feeling of incompletion, and that song in my brain swimming round like a damned goldfish.

I wondered, as the bus took me back along the familiar route, what I would say if Mark Letter should still be at the office. He often worked late, or at least, stayed there late, doing I don't know what, for his screw and nail business did not call for long hours. It seemed to me he had an affection for those dingy premises. I was rather apprehensive lest I should find Mr Letter at the office, standing, just as I had last seen him, swinging his tie in his hand, beside my desk. I resolved that if I should find him there, I should say straight out that I had left something behind me.

A clock struck quarter past seven as I got off the bus. I realized that again I had not paid my fare. I looked at the money in my hand for a stupid second. Then I felt reckless. 'Teedle-um-tum-tum'—I caught myself humming the tune as I walked quickly up the sad side street to our office. My heart knocked at my throat, for I was eager. Softly, softly, I said to myself as I turned the key of the outside door. Quickly, quickly, I ran up the stairs. Only outside the office door I halted, and while I found its key on my bunch it occurred to me how strangely my sister would think I was behaving.

I opened the door and my sadness left me at once. With a great joy I recognized what it was I had left behind me, my body lying strangled on the floor. I ran towards my body and embraced it like a lover.

Spirit of the House

★

FAY WELDON

SOME TIME AFTER THE TROUBLE WITH JENNY began, Christine wrote off to a professor of psychical research who lived in California. 'Whenever Jenny comes into the room,' Christine wrote, 'I feel cold. So I know there's *something* wrong with her. But what exactly it is?' She had an answer sooner than she expected. The professor wrote that the presence of evil was often registered, by sensitives, in this manner; and was there a bad smell as well?

Now Jenny did indeed quite often smell strongly of carbolic but Christine felt that this was not in itself significant. The soap provided for employees up at the Big House was a job-lot of hard, orange, carbolic tablets, bought cheap from an army surplus store, and Jenny washed herself with it, lavishly and often. Christine always took Mornay's Lavender to work with her, the more sweetly to wash her pretty hands. Christine liked to smell nice, and her husband Luke liked her to smell nice, and how he could put up with Jenny smelling of carbolic, Christine could not understand. And how he could love her, Christine could understand still less.

But carbolic was not, in itself, a bad smell, and nothing like the stench of sulphur and decomposition associated with the presence of the devil. Enough however, that the feeling of cold wafted around Jenny like an odour. She could be said to smell cold. Christine discontinued her correspondence with the Californian professor for fear of discovering worse. She prayed instead.

*   *   *

'Dear God, let him get over her. Dear God, let her not harm the baby. Dear God, let them believe me.'

But God seemed not to be listening. Luke went on loving Jenny, Jenny went on looking after Baby Emmy, and no one believed Christine when she said that Jenny was not to be trusted.

Christine had been married to Luke for nineteen years. She loved her husband with an energetic and consuming passion, well able to withstand his occasional adoration of passing girls. She would treat him, when he was thus enamoured, with a fond indulgence, saying, 'Well, men are like that, aren't they?' and waiting for common sense and reason to return, and uxorious content to shine once again from his gentle eyes. But Jenny was dangerous—Christine had suspected something unwholesome about her from the very first. In retrospect it was hard to tell, of course, quite when she had begun to think it—before Luke started mooning after Jenny, or after. But surely it was before—a sickly, chilly menace, a sudden shiver down the spine? Evil, the professor had written. Or perhaps he only wrote that, knowing what she wanted to hear? Americans were strange.

Even so, the damage was done. Now Christine feared for Luke, body and soul, and feared for Emmy, Lord Mader's baby daughter, even more. Jenny was Emmy's nanny. Little, pretty, safe words, adding up to something monstrous.

And of course if Christine murmured against Jenny, the other members of the staff assumed that Christine was jealous, and discredited what she said. Christine's husband, everyone knew, was in love with Jenny, trailing after her, gazing after her.

'But look,' Christine felt like saying, 'he's been in love a dozen times in as many years. It's just the way he is. I don't mind. He's a genius, you see. A mathematical genius, not one of your artistic geniuses, but a genius all the same. My feeling about Jenny is nothing to do with Luke's feeling for her.

But the rest of the staff were dull, if good-hearted, and had their preconceptions about the world, which nothing now would shake: it was almost as if the chilly presence of Jenny had cemented in these preconceptions. Their vision narrowed to what they already knew. Christine concluded that Jenny had a strange deadening power over everyone, excepting only, for some reason, herself.

Jenny had a white, dead face and large, pale eyes she magnified with round owl spectacles, and short plain hair and a child's body. The face was thirty, the body was thirteen. Perhaps that was her power—the desire of the grown man for the pre-pubertal girl? A sickly and insidious love! And did the women perhaps remember themselves at thirteen and set Jenny free now, to do what they would have liked then?

Christine herself, at forty, was plump and maternal and pretty and busy. There could be nothing unhealthy in anyone's desire for her, and many did desire her, but she seldom noticed. She loved Luke.

Christine, the Doris Day of Mader House! Wonderful Mader House, Stately Home, giving the lucky villagers of Maderley full employment! With its Elizabethan chimneys, and Jacobean mullions, Georgian casements and Victorian tiles, it still remained imposing, if hardly gracious. Its lands and gardens, its ancient oaks, its Disneyland and zoo, its Sunday lunches with Lord and Lady Mader (fifty pounds a place-setting), made it popular with the millions. Lord Mader was often indisposed at these luncheons and his young brother Martin sent in his place, but the third Lady Mader, Mara, was always there. She was young and did as she was told, as did the villagers.

The Maders, their disparagers murmured, once a powerful and wealthy family, were now a handful of publicity-seeking degenerates. Even Christine, who loved to be loyal, increasingly saw truth in this observation. Yves, the present Lord, was thrice married. His first wife had been barren, and for that reason divorced. Lucien, son by his second wife, was a junkie, and Lucien's little sister Deborah now played the lead in skin-flicks. Yet these seemed matters of mirth rather than shame to Yves. A further son, Piers, was in real estate, and considered too boring for discussion. Left a widower by his second wife's suicide, Yves had promptly married Mara, a twenty-year-old Greek heiress, and sired little Emmy.

Yves had selected Jenny from over two hundred applicants for the post of Nanny. He prided himself on being a good judge of character.

'Does he love the baby?' people would ask Christine. 'Oh yes,' she'd reply, adding in her heart, 'as much as he loves anything, which isn't very much.' The pressure of the words grew and grew and she was frightened that one day she would say them aloud.
'And the mother?'
'She's not very much at home, but I'm sure she does.' Christine was nice. She wanted to think well of everyone.

Mara loved treats and outings and hunting, and occasions on which she could wear a tiara, and the Mader family jewels—or, rather, their replicas. The originals had been sold in the thirties; and Maderley House itself would have followed in the fifties, had not Yves discovered that the people's fascination with their aristocracy could be turned to excellent financial account; whereupon he flung open the gates, and filled up the moat, and turned the stables into restaurants, and himself into a public show.

The show business side of Maderley was in Christine's charge—it was she who organised the guides, the cleaners, the caterers, even the vets for sick animals. She saw to brochures, catalogues and souvenirs. She took the takings to the bank. She had the status in the household of someone dedicated, who is despised for their dedication. She was underpaid, and mocked for being so by those who underpaid her, and did not notice.

Christine's husband Luke sat in the Great Library and worked out efficient mathematical formulae for the winning of the pools. Yves had once met, over dinner, a Nobel Prize winner, a mathematician, who had convinced him of the practicality of working out such formulae, computer-aided. Yves promptly had a computer-terminal installed in the Great Library, and Luke installed likewise. Visitors gawped at both between two and three on Wednesdays. Luke had a first-class honours degree in mathematics from Oxford. He had been a Maderley child with a peculiar gift for numbers and few social skills. He had returned to the village, married to Christine, a girl from far away, to write textbooks for graduates, which he did slowly, with difficulty, and for very little money.

The Great Library! There Christine fed the computer with data about visitors, gate takings, capital costs and so forth. And here Luke puzzled over his formulae, and here Jenny liked to sit in the winter sun beneath the mullioned windows, and rock the baby's pram, and watch Luke at work. The baby never cried. Sometimes it whimpered. The cover was pulled up well over its face.

Christine had tried to say something to Yves about Jenny and the baby.

'Yves'—his employees were instructed to call him by his Christian name—'can I talk to you about Jenny?'
'What do you want to say?' He was unfriendly. She knew he did not like trouble. It was her function, after all, to keep it away from him. She had once asked for a rise in her wages, and the same shuttered, cold look had fallen across his face, as it now did, when she wanted to talk about Jenny. 'I don't think she's very good with the baby,' said Christine, tentatively, and wanted to go on and say, 'My Lord, I have seen bruises on the baby's arm. I don't like the way the baby whimpers instead of crying. I don't like the thinness of the baby's wrists. A

baby's wrists should be chubby and creased, not bony.' But she didn't speak. She hesitated, looking at his cold face, and was lost.

'You mean she's too good with your husband, Christine,' was all Yves said. 'You sort out your own problems, don't come running to me.'

Christine, later that day, came across Yves with Jenny. They were together in the library. He had his hands on her thin shoulders: he, who seldom touched anyone. What were they saying?

Christine heard the baby make its little mewling cry, but Yves did not even glance into the pram.

Christine said to Mrs Scott the housekeeper. 'I'm worried about that baby. I don't think she gets enough to eat.'

Mrs Scott said, 'You don't know anything about babies. You've never had one. Jenny's a trained Norland nanny. She knows what she's doing.'

Jenny sat next to Mrs Scott at the staff lunch that day. They seemed very companionable.

Christine watched Luke watching Jenny being companionable with Mrs Scott, and the staff watched Christine watching Luke watching Jenny, and sniggered.

Christine telephoned the Norland nanny organisation, and they had no record of a Jenny Whitstone on their books.

Christine watched Jenny hold the baby's bottle an inch or so from the baby's mouth, so that the baby stopped whimpering and rooted with its mouth towards the warm, sweet smell and found it, and Christine watched Jenny tug out the bottle after the first few mouthfuls and put it back on the shelf. The baby moaned.

'What did you do that for?' asked Christine.

'I don't want the baby getting too fat,' said Jenny. 'It's a terrible thing to be fat.'

And Jenny eyed Christine's plump form with cold distaste.

Luke stopped making love to Christine altogether.

'It wouldn't be fair to you,' said Luke. 'How can I make love to you when I'm thinking of her? I wish I could, but I can't.'

'Why, why do you love her?' begged Christine.

But he didn't know, couldn't say.

It seemed to Christine that Luke felt cold in bed, as if his flesh was dying.

She spoke to the guides about Jenny, at their Monday morning meeting, where such things were discussed as meal breaks and the positioning of the silken ropes which guarded certain rooms and passages from the touch and view of ordinary people. 'Where did she come from?' Christine asked. 'Does anyone know?'

No one seemed to. It was as if she had always been there, along with the house itself, along with the family: the worm, or whatever it was, that nibbled away at the souls of the rich, so that born angels, they grew up devils.

For what could become of them but this? Generation succeeding generation: heartless mothers, distant fathers, and the distress of this made light of, by a surfeit of manners and money?

'The scale's all wrong,' Christine said in her heart. 'The house is just too big for people.'

*   *   *

Life's battles, life's events, triumphs and disasters—all were rendered puny by the lofty ceilings. Words of love and grief alike, hate and joy, all were muted beneath the arching vaults of the great hall, were sopped up and made one by ancient panelling. The stair was too high for the child to climb, or the old woman to descend. Marriages were lost in a bed so big it made passion trivial: the sexual act ridiculous under the cold eyes of ceiling cherubs. And animals! The love of dumb beasts put before the love of people; the death of a horse marking the year more than the death of a child; kennels always warmer than the nurseries. Manners replacing morals.

'They're born like anyone else,' Christine said in her heart, never aloud. 'And then I don't know what happens, but they end up monsters.'

So, now, it seemed to Christine, the damage which little Emmy could expect in the course of the next twenty years was being, at the hands of Jenny, inflicted upon her in as many months.

'I know why you love her,' she said presently to Luke, 'it's because she's the spirit of the House. And it's sickening and disgusting, and everyone loves it. Except me.'

'That isn't why I love her,' said Luke. 'And if you feel like that about the House, why go on working here?'
'What else could I do round here? There's no employment except at Maderley.'

But in spite of what she said, she stayed and she knew she stayed because she too, like Luke, was still under the spell of the Big House, and felt honoured by the company of Yves, whom she was privileged to call by his Christian name, and because she did not want to leave Emmy and Luke to the mercies of Jenny.

*   *   *

Lady Mara was due back from the Bahamas. The whole house gleamed with polish and glowed with flowers.

But Emmy was listless, and blinked a good deal, and flinched and grizzled the day Lady Mara came back.

'She isn't very pretty,' said Mara, disappointed, peering into the pram, and after that seldom asked to see the child at all. She rode to hounds a good deal, along with farmers and carpet manufacturers.

'I wish you wouldn't,' complained Yves. 'Only the bourgeoisie go hunting these days.' But Mara was regaining her spirit, and learning how to do not what she was told, and she persisted, slashing at grasses with her riding crop, as if she'd like to slash at life itself.

Presently, Christine came across Jenny in the Great Library. Jenny had taken Emmy, for once, out of her pram. Jenny stood there, among ten thousand books, which were beautifully bound but never read, turning her owl eyes up to where the sunlight glanced through the windows, so that her spectacles dazzled, and seemed to retain the blinding shine even when she turned her head out of the sunlight to face Christine. Jenny, with her child's thighs in their tight, faded jeans, and budding breasts beneath a white T-shirt, and a dazzle where her face should be.

Jenny, with her soft, flat, slightly nasal voice, which could turn sharp and cruel and hard. Christine had often heard it. 'Christ, you little monster!' And slap, slap, thump, and then the weary grizzle again from Emmy.

Christine had never managed to get pregnant.

'Well,' the doctor had said, 'I dare say you have a child already, in your husband.' Christine, cooking, nurturing, caring, worrying, had agreed with the doctor and not minded too much about their lack of children. Christine, after all, was the breadwinner. Perhaps what Luke saw in Jenny, suggested Christine, trying again, was his own unborn daughter? An incestuous love, given permission to live and thrive.

It was Yves who had given permission. Yes, he had.

'We all love Jenny,' Yves had said. 'Jenny saves us from our children.' Everyone except Christine, everyone's look said, watching Christine watching Luke watching Jenny, everyone loves Jenny.

Christine tried Yves' younger brother Martin, born by Caesarean while his mother lay dying from an overdose of sleeping pills and whisky, self-inflicted. Martin was the estate manager at Maderley. When Yves spoke to Martin it was in the same way he spoke to the upper servants—with a derisive politeness. Martin stuttered, so that Christine's conversation with him took a long time, and she was busy, needed at the toll-gate with new parking tickets.

'Sir, I don't think Jenny is what she says. She isn't a Norland nurse at all. I checked up.'

'No one round here is what they claim to be,' said Martin, sadly. 'And the baby is Lady Mara's business, not ours.'

'Couldn't you say something to Yves?'

'Not really,' said Martin. 'If you feel strongly about it, say something yourself.'

'I have, but he just got angry and wouldn't listen.'

'The baby looks like any other baby to me,' said Martin. 'Not that I know much about them, of course.' One of Martin's eyes turned inwards—a squint which had been left untreated in infancy, and so remained.

'Yves is a very good judge of character,' said Martin. 'If he employed Jenny she must be all right.'

The next day Christine saw Jenny wheeling the baby in the grounds, and Martin was with her. Even Martin! Martin, saying goodbye to Jenny, pecked her on the cheek, and she turned her face so that once again her glasses glinted and dazzled and the space beneath the pram hood seemed black, like the mouth of hell.

When Jenny wheeled the baby into the kitchen that day Christine bent to pick the baby up.

'Don't pick up the baby,' said Jenny sharply. 'She's sleeping quietly.' But to Christine the baby looked not so much asleep, as dead. And then an eyelash fluttered against the white cheek and Christine knew she was wrong. She went on counting sandwiches—two hundred ham, one hundred cheese—for the special Maderley tea, four pounds a head, served in the converted stable block.

'But *how* do you love her, *why* do you love her?'

She knew that she was nagging: she couldn't help it. She kept Luke awake at night now, working away at the truth. It was only while he slept that his body grew cold, and the pain of his answers was preferable to the chilly numbness of his sleep; she knew that, sleeping, he drifted off somewhere away from her, over the safe, surrounding walls of her love and, moth-like, floated towards the chilly, blinding light which used Jenny as its beacon.

It was at that time that she wrote to the professor of psychical research, and had confirmation of her fears. Jenny was evil.

'Lady Mara?'
'What is it, Christine?'

Lady Mara, broken arm in a sling—her horse had lurched and reared at nothing in particular, a sudden bright light in the grounds was all she could think of—was lately very much the grande dame. She would have bathed in asses' milk if she could.

'Lady, Mara, I'm worried about the baby.'

'The baby is nothing to do with you. You look after the visitors and let Jenny look after the baby.'

Lady Mara was only twenty-one. The same age as Yves' daughter, the one who presented her body at rude, amazing angles for the benefit of the camera, a publisher and a million wistful men. But a title and wealth, and the assumption of power, of the right to tell other people what to do and what to say, add up to more than years. Mara stared coldly. Christine fumbled. Christine was impertinent. If she didn't stop meddling she might have to go. There were more than enough only too ready to take her place. Mara said nothing. There was no need to. Christine fell silent.

Yves and Mara went away to attend a wedding. Five thousand pounds, they had heard, were to be spent on flowers for the marquees alone. Who would miss a wedding like that?

Christine found her husband Luke weeping in the conservatory. 'What's the matter, Luke?'

But he was frozen into silence. Presently, he thawed, as if warmed by Christine's presence, her arm round his shaking shoulders, and spoke.

'I asked her. I plucked up courage and asked her. I said I wanted to sleep with her more than anything in the world.'

'And?' How cold the pit of the stomach, where words strike their message home.

'She laughed at me. She told me I was old and flabby. She said I was weak. She said I was a failure. Am I these things, Christine?'

'Of course not.'

'I love her more than ever.'

Christine went to see Jenny in her bedroom. 'You leave my husband alone,' said Christine, 'or I'll kill you.'

'Get him to leave me alone,' said Jenny, laughing, a cold, dead laugh. How could you kill what was already dead?

The baby murmured in its cot. Christine looked at little Emmy. Her eyes were black, and swollen. Christine lifted the baby out of its cot.

'You leave that baby alone,' snapped Jenny. 'You poor jealous frustrated barren old bitch.'

It was the cry of the world, but it was not true. Christine's spirit was warm, loving and fecund.

Christine unwrapped little Emmy from her soft blankets and found that her back was bruised and her right leg hung oddly. Christine cradled the baby carefully in her arms and ran down long, long corridors, hung with family portraits, and down the great staircase, and into the reception area, where the tickets were taken, and rang all the bells she could, and Martin came, and Luke and three of the guides and Mrs Scott the housekeeper, and a cleaner; and Jenny followed after but stopped halfway down the stairs, in a little patch where the sun shone in, so she glowed all over, the source and not the reflection of light.

'Look,' said Christine, showing what was in her arms. 'Look! See what she's done to the baby?'

'It was an accident,' called Jenny, in her soft, nasal voice. 'You're all my friends. You know I wouldn't do it on purpose.'

But the sun had shone in upon the wrong stair. She was just too far away, her voice just a little too faint. Jenny's words meant nothing to the cluster of people gazing at the baby, Lord Mader's baby, with its swollen eyes and its blue-black back.

'I'll get an ambulance,' said Christine.

'Think of the publicity,' said Martin, but he spoke without much conviction. 'Yves won't like it.'

'Perhaps we'd better telephone him and get permission,' said Mrs Scott.

'Let me take the baby,' called Jenny. 'It's me Emmy loves. You're all strangers to her. She'll get better if I hold her.'

And what Jenny said was true, but she couldn't make up her mind to lose the sun and step another stair down into the hall, and she faltered and was lost.

Martin rang Yves. Christine had his number: flicked through her efficient files and found it at once.

'Yves,' said Martin, stuttering his message out. 'You'd better come back here. The baby's got a bruise on its back. Christine thinks we should call an ambulance.'

'Christine would,' said Yves, sourly. 'Well, stop her. We'll be right back.'

But Christine called the ambulance all the same. They took the baby away and just as well, because Yves and Mara didn't return for three days.

Emmy had a fractured skull, two broken ribs, a broken thigh and a damaged kidney, but they patched her up quite well, and returned her after eight weeks looking quite pretty, so that her mother picked her up and murmured endearments and nuzzled into her baby neck, and fortunately Emmy smiled at that moment and didn't cry, which would have spoiled everything.

Christine lost her job, and Yves abandoned his hopes of breaking the Great Proletariat Pools Swindle and fired Luke too.

'You'd think they'd be grateful for my saving their baby,' said Christine. 'But the upper classes are just plain twisted.'

'The Greeks used to kill the bearer of bad news,' said Luke, 'so think yourself lucky.'

The sight of the damaged baby had made him fall out of love with Jenny, and now he slept warm at night, and Christine beside him. Jenny did not lose her job, but at least she was no longer allowed to look after the baby. Instead, she did what Christine had been doing, for twice the money and with the help of an assistant.

'What a great judge of character Yves is!' said Christine sourly. Everyone she asked, and ask she did, everyone, agreed with her. The Maders were degenerate and decadent. She could say the words aloud now, not just in her heart.

Later she heard that Jenny had taken another post as nanny to two little girls whose mother had died, and that Yves had written her an excellent reference.

'Your employees reflect back on you,' said Luke. 'That's what it is.'

Christine wondered whether to telephone the father of the two little girls and warn him, but knew she would never be believed. And perhaps, who was to say, there was someone like her in every little pocket of the world? Someone to save while others destroyed, or looked away. Wherever Jenny went, there would be someone like Christine.

'I loved her because she was evil,' said Luke, at last, explaining. 'She anaesthetised my moral nerve endings and that at the time was wonderful. And you were right: she was the spirit of the house.'

Clytie

⭐

EUDORA WELTY

I T WAS LATE AFTERNOON, WITH HEAVY silver clouds which looked bigger and wider than cotton fields, and presently it began to rain. Big round drops fell, still in the sunlight, on the hot tin sheds, and stained the white false fronts of the row of stores in the little town of Farr's Gin. A hen and her string of yellow chickens ran in great alarm across the road, the dust turned river-brown, and the birds flew down into it immediately, sitting out little pockets in which to take baths. The bird dogs got up from the doorways of the stores, shook themselves down to the tail, and went to lie inside. The few people standing with long shadows on the level road moved over into the post office. A little boy kicked his bare heels into the sides of his mule, which proceeded slowly through the town toward the country.

After everyone else had gone under cover, Miss Clytie Farr stood still in the road, peering ahead in her nearsighted way, and as wet as the little birds.

She usually came out of the old big house about this time in the afternoon, and hurried through the town. It used to be that she ran about on some pretext or other, and for a while she made soft-voiced explanations that nobody could hear, and after that she began to charge up bills, which the postmistress declared would never be paid any more than anyone else's, even if the Farrs were too good to associate with other people. But now Clytie came for nothing. She came every day, and no one spoke to her any more: she would be in such a hurry, and couldn't see who it was. And every Saturday they expected her to be run over, the way she darted out into the road with all the horses and trucks.

It might be simply that Miss Clytie's wits were all leaving her, said the ladies standing in the door to feel the cool, the way her sister's had left her; and she would just wait there to be told to go home. She would have to wring out everything she had on—the waist and the jumper skirt, and the long black stockings. On her head was one of the straw hats from the furnishing store, with an old black satin ribbon pinned to it to make it a better hat, and tied under the chin. Now, under the force of the rain, while the ladies watched, the hat slowly began to sag down on each side until it looked even more absurd and done for, like an old bonnet on a horse. And indeed it was with the patience almost of a beast that Miss Clytie stood there in the rain and stuck her long empty arms out a little from her sides, as if she were waiting for something to come along the road and drive her to shelter.

In a little while there was a clap of thunder.

"Miss Clytie! Go in out of the rain, Miss Clytie!" someone called.

The old maid did not look around, but clenched her hands and drew them up under her armpits, and sticking out her elbows like hen wings, she ran out of the street, her poor hat creaking and beating about her ears.

"Well, there goes Miss Clytie," the ladies said, and one of them had a premonition about her.

Through the rushing water in the sunken path under the four wet black cedars, which smelled bitter as smoke, she ran to the house.

"Where the devil have you been?" called the older sister, Octavia from an upper window.

Clytie looked up in time to see the curtain fall back.

She went inside, into the hall, and waited, shivering. It was very dark and bare. The only light was falling on the white sheet which covered the solitary piece of furniture, an organ. The red curtains over the parlor door, held back by ivory hands, were still as tree trunks in the airless house. Every window was closed, and every shade was down, though behind them the rain could still be heard.

Clytie took a match and advanced to the stair post, where the bronze cast of Hermes was holding up a gas fixture; and at once above this, lighted up, but quite still, like one of the unmovable relics of the house, Octavia stood waiting on the stairs.

She stood solidly before the violet-and-lemon-colored glass of the window on the landing, and her wrinkled, unresting fingers took hold of the diamond cornucopia she always wore in the bosom of her long black dress. It was an un-withered grand gesture of hers, fondling the cornucopia.

"It is not enough that we are waiting here—hungry," Octavia was saying, while Clytie waited below. "But you must sneak away and not answer when I call you. Go off and wander about the streets. Common—common—!"

"Never mind, Sister," Clytie managed to say.

"But you always return."

"Of course. . . ."

"Gerald is awake now, and so is Papa," said Octavia, in the same vindictive voice—a loud voice, for she was usually calling.

Clytie went to the kitchen and lighted the kindling in the wood stove. As if she were freezing cold in June, she stood before its open door, and soon a look of interest and pleasure lighted her face, which had in the last years grown weather-beaten in spite of the straw hat. Now some dream was resumed. In the street she had been thinking about the face of a child she had just seen. The child, playing with another of the same age, chasing it with a toy pistol, had looked at her with such an open, serene, trusting expression as she passed by! With this small, peaceful face still in her mind, rosy like these flames, like an in-spiration which drives all other thoughts away, Clytie had forgotten herself and had been obliged to stand where she was in the middle of the road. But the rain had come down, and someone had shouted at her, and she had not been able to reach the end of her meditations.

It had been a long time now since Clytie had first begun to watch faces, and to think about them.

Anyone could have told you that there were not more than 150 people in Farr's Gin, counting Negroes. Yet the number of faces seemed to Clytie almost infinite. She knew now to look slowly and carefully at a face; she was convinced that it was impossible to see it all at once. The first thing she discovered about a face was always that she had never seen it before. When she began to look at people's actual countenances there was no more familiarity in the world for her. The most profound, the most moving sight in the whole world must be a face. Was it possible to comprehend the eyes and the mouths of other people, which concealed she knew not what, and secretly asked for still another unknown thing? The mysterious smile of the old man who sold peanuts by the church gate returned to her; his face seemed for a moment to rest upon the iron door of the stove, set into the lion's mane. Other people said Mr. Tom Bate's Boy, as he called himself, stared away with a face as clean-blank as a watermelon seed, but to Clytie, who observed grains of sand in his eyes and in his old yellow lashes, he might have come out of a desert, like an Egyptian.

But while she was thinking of Mr. Tom Bate's Boy, there was a terrible gust of wind which struck her back, and she turned around. The long green window shade billowed and plunged. The kitchen window was wide open—she had done it herself. She closed it gently. Octavia, who never came all the way down-stairs for any reason, would never have forgiven her for an open window, if she knew. Rain and sun signified ruin, in Octavia's mind. Going over the whole house, Clytie made sure that everything was safe. It was not that ruin in itself could distress Octavia. Ruin or encroachment, even upon priceless treasures and even in poverty, held no terror for her; it was simply some form of prying from without, and this she would not forgive. All of that was to be seen in her face.

Clytie cooked the three meals on the stove, for they all ate different things, and set the three trays. She had to carry them in proper order up the stairs. She frowned in concentration, for it was hard to keep all the dishes straight, to make them come out right in the end, as Old Lethy could have done. They had had to give up the cook long ago when their father suffered the first stroke. Their father had been fond of Old Lethy, she had been his nurse in childhood, and she had come back out of the country to see him when she heard he was dying. Old Lethy had come and knocked at the back door. And as usual, at the first disturbance, front or back, Octavia had peered down from behind the curtain and cried, "Go away! Go away! What the devil have you come *here* for?" And although Old Lethy and their father had both pleaded that they might be allowed to see each other, Octavia had shouted as she always did, and sent the intruder away. Clytie had stood as usual, speechless in the kitchen, until finally she had repeated after her sister, "Lethy, go away." But their father had not died. He was, instead, paralyzed, blind, and able only to call out in unintelligible sounds and to swallow liquids. Lethy still would come to the back door now and then, but they never let her in, and the old man no longer heard or knew enough to beg to see her. There was only one caller admitted to his room. Once a week the barber came by appointment to shave him. On this occasion not a word was spoken by anyone.

Clytie went up to her father's room first and set the tray down on a little marble table they kept by his bed.

"I want to feed Papa," said Octavia, taking the bowl from her hands.

"You fed him last time," said Clytie.

Relinquishing the bowl, she looked down at the pointed face on the pillow. Tomorrow was the barber's day, and the sharp black points, at their longest, stuck out like needles all over the wasted cheeks. The old man's eyes were half closed. It was impossible to know what he felt. He looked as though he were really far away, neglected, free. . . . Octavia began to feed him.

Without taking her eyes from her father's face, Clytie suddenly began to speak in rapid, bitter words to her sister, the wildest words that came to her head. But soon she began to cry and gasp, like a small child who has been pushed by the big boys into the water.

"That is enough," said Octavia.

But Clytie could not take her eyes from her father's unshaven face and his still-open mouth.

"And I'll feed him tomorrow if I want to," said Octavia. She stood up. The thick hair, growing back after an illness and dyed almost purple, fell over her forehead. Beginning at her throat, the long accordion pleats which fell the length of her gown opened and closed over her breasts as she breathed. "Have you forgotten Gerald?" she said. "And I am hungry too."

Clytie went back to the kitchen and brought her sister's supper.

Then she brought her brother's.

Gerald's room was dark, and she had to push through the usual barricade. The smell of whisky was everywhere; it even flew up in the striking of the match when she lighted the jet.

"It's night," said Clytie presently.

Gerald lay on his bed looking at her. In the bad light he resembled his father.

"There's some more coffee down in the kitchen," said Clytie.

"Would you bring it to me?" Gerald asked. He stared at her in an exhausted, serious way.

She stooped and held him up. He drank the coffee while she bent over him with her eyes closed, resting.

Presently he pushed her away and fell back on the bed, and began to describe how nice it was when he had a little house of his own down the street, all new, with all conveniences, gas stove, electric lights, when he was married to Rosemary. Rosemary—she had given up a job in the next town, just to marry him. How had it happened that she had left him so soon? It meant nothing that he had threatened time and again to shoot her, it was nothing at all that he had pointed the gun against her breast. She had not understood. It was only that he had relished his contentment. He had only wanted to play with her. In a way he had wanted to show her that he loved her above life and death.

"Above life and death," he repeated, closing his eyes.

Clytie did not make an answer, as Octavia always did during these scenes, which were bound to end in Gerald's tears.

Outside the closed window a mockingbird began to sing. Clytie held back the curtain and pressed her ear against the glass. The rain had stopped. The bird's song sounded in liquid drops down through the pitch-black trees and the night.

"Go to hell," Gerald said. His head was under the pillow.

She took up the tray, and left Gerald with his face hidden. It was not necessary for her to look at any of their faces. It was their faces which came between.

Hurrying, she went down to the kitchen and began to eat her own supper.

Their faces came between her face and another. It was their faces which had come pushing in between, long ago, to hide some face that had looked back at her. And now it was hard to remember the way it looked, or the time when she had seen it first. It must have been when she was young. Yes, in a sort of arbor, hadn't she laughed, leaned forward . . . and that vision of a face—which was a little like all the other faces, the trusting child's, the innocent old traveler's, even the greedy barber's and Lethy's and the wandering peddlers' who one by one knocked and went unanswered at the door—and yet different, yet far more—this face had been very close to hers, almost familiar, almost accessible. And then the face of Octavia was thrust between, and at other times the apoplectic face of her father, the face of her brother Gerald and the face of her brother Henry with the bullet hole through the forehead. . . . It was purely for a resemblance to a vision that she examined the secret, mysterious, unrepeated faces she met in the street of Farr's Gin.

But there was always an interruption. If anyone spoke to her, she fled. If she saw she was going to meet someone on the street, she had been known to dart behind a bush and hold a small branch in front of her face until the person had gone by. When anyone called her by name, she turned first red, then white, and looked somehow, as one of the ladies in the store remarked, *disappointed.*

She was becoming more frightened all the time, too. People could tell because she never dressed up any more. For years, every once in a while, she could come out in what was called an "outfit," all in hunter's green, a hat that came down around her face like a bucket, a green silk dress, even green shoes with pointed toes. She would wear the outfit all one day, if it was a pretty day, and then next morning she would be back in the faded jumper with her old hat tied under the chin, as if the outfit had been a dream. It had been a long time now since Clytie had dressed up so that you could see her coming.

Once in a while when a neighbor, trying to be kind or only being curious, would ask her opinion about anything—such as a pattern of crochet—she would not run away; but, giving a thin trapped smile, she would say in a childish voice, "It's nice." But, the ladies always added, nothing that came anywhere close to the Farrs' house was nice for long.

"It's nice," said Clytie when the old lady next door showed her the new rosebush she had planted, all in bloom.

But before an hour was gone, she came running out of her house screaming. "My sister Octavia says you take that rosebush up! My sister Octavia says you take that rosebush up and move it away from our fence! If you don't I'll kill you! You take it away."

And on the other side of the Farrs lived a family with a little boy who was always playing in his yard. Octavia's cat would go under the fence, and he would take it and hold it in his arms. He had a song he sang to the Farr's cat. Clytie would come running straight out of the house, flaming with her message from Octavia. "Don't you do that! Don't you do that!" she would cry in anguish. "If you do that again, I'll have to kill you!"

And she would run back to the vegetable patch and begin to curse.

The cursing was new, and she cursed softly, like a singer going over a song for the first time. But it was something she could not stop. Words which at first horrified Clytie poured in a full, light stream from her throat, which soon, nevertheless, felt strangely relaxed and rested. She cursed all alone in the peace of the vegetable garden. Everybody said, in something like deprecation, that she was only imitating her older sister, who used to go out to that same garden and curse in that same way, years ago, but in a remarkably loud, commanding voice that could be heard in the post office.

Sometimes in the middle of her words Clytie glanced up to where Octavia, at her window, looked down at her. When she let the curtain drop at last, Clytie would be left there speechless.

Finally, in a gentleness compounded of fright and exhaustion and love, an overwhelming love, she would wander through the gate and out through the town, gradually beginning to move faster, until her long legs gathered a ridiculous, rushing speed. No one in town could have kept up with Miss Clytie, they said, giving them an even start.

She always ate rapidly, too, all alone in the kitchen, as she was eating now. She bit the meat savagely from the heavy silver fork and gnawed the little chicken bone until it was naked and clean.

Halfway upstairs, she remembered Gerald's second pot of coffee, and went back for it. After she had carried the other trays down again and washed the dishes, she did not forget to try all the doors and windows to make sure that everything was locked up absolutely tight.

The next morning, Clytie bit into smiling lips as she cooked breakfast. Far out past the secretly opened window a freight train was crossing the bridge in the sunlight. Some Negroes filed down the road going fishing, and Mr. Tom Bate's Boy, who was going along, turned and looked at her through the window.

Gerald had appeared dressed and wearing his spectacles, and announced that he was going to the store today. The old Farr furnishing store did little business now, and people hardly missed Gerald when he did not come; in fact, they could hardly tell when he did because of the big boots strung on a wire, which almost hid the cagelike office. A little high-school girl could wait on anybody who came in.

Now Gerald entered the dining room.

"How are you this morning, Clytie?" he asked.

"Just fine, Gerald, how are you?"

"I'm going to the store," he said.

He sat down stiffly, and she laid a place on the table before him.

From above, Octavia screamed, "Where in the devil is my thimble, you stole my thimble, Clytie Farr, you carried it away, my little silver thimble!"

"It's started," said Gerald intensely. Clytie saw his fine, thin, almost black lips spread in a crooked line. "How can a man live in the house with women? How can he?"

He jumped up, and tore his napkin exactly in two. He walked out of the dining room without eating the first bite of his breakfast. She heard him going back upstairs into his room.

"My thimble!" screamed Octavia.

She waited one moment. Crouching eagerly, rather like a little squirrel, Clytie ate part of her breakfast over the stove before going up the stairs.

At nine Mr. Bobo, the barber, knocked at the front door.

Without waiting, for they never answered the knock, he let himself in and advanced like a small general down the hall. There was the old organ that was never uncovered or played except for funerals, and then nobody was invited. He went ahead, under the arm of the tip-toed male statue and up the dark stairway. There they were, lined up at the head of the stairs, and they all looked at him with repulsion. Mr. Bobo was convinced that they were every one mad. Gerald, even, had already been drinking, at nine o'clock in the morning.

Mr. Bobo was short and had never been anything but proud of it, until he had started coming to this house once a week. But he did not enjoy looking up from below at the soft, long throats, the cold, repelled, high-reliefed faces of those Farrs. He could only imagine what one of those sisters would do to him if he made one move. (As if he would!) As soon as he arrived upstairs, they all went off and left him. He pushed out his chin and stood with his round legs wide apart, just looking around. The upstairs hall was absolutely bare. There was not even a chair to sit down in.

"Either they sell away their furniture in the dead of night," said Mr. Bobo to the people of Farr's Gin, "or else they're just too plumb mean to use it."

Mr. Bobo stood and waited to be summoned, and wished he had never started coming to this house to shave old Mr. Farr. But he had been so surprised to get a letter in the mail. The letter was on such old, yellowed paper that at first he thought it must have been written a thousand years ago and never delivered. It was signed "Octavia Farr," and began without even calling him "Dear Mr. Bobo." What it said was: "Come to this residence at nine o'clock each Friday morning until further notice, where you will shave Mr. James Farr."

He thought he would go one time. And each time after that, he thought he would never go back—especially when he never knew when they would pay him anything. Of course, it was something to be the only person in Farr's Gin allowed inside the house (except for the undertaker, who had gone there when young Henry shot himself, but had never to that day spoken of it). It was not easy to shave a man as bad off as Mr. Farr, either—not anything like as easy as to shave a corpse or even a fighting-drunk field hand. Suppose you were like this, Mr. Bobo would say: you couldn't move your face; you couldn't hold up your chin, or tighten your jaw, or even bat your eyes when the razor came close. The trouble with Mr. Farr was his face made no resistance to the razor. His face didn't hold.

"I'll never go back," Mr. Bobo always ended to his customers. "Not even if they paid me. I've seen enough."

Yet here he was again, waiting before the sickroom door.

"This is the last time," he said. "By God!"

And he wondered why the old man did not die.

Just then Miss Clytie came out of the room. There she came in her funny, sideways walk, and the closer she got to him the more slowly she moved.

"Now?" asked Mr. Bobo nervously.

Clytie looked at his small, doubtful face. What fear raced through his little green eyes! His pitiful, greedy, small face—how very mournful it was, like a stray kitten's. What was it that this greedy little thing was so desperately needing?

Clytie came up to the barber and stopped. Instead of telling him that he might go in and shave her father, she put out her hand and with breath-taking gentleness touched the side of his face.

For an instant afterward, she stood looking at him inquiringly, and he stood like a statue, like the statue of Hermes.

Then both of them uttered a despairing cry. Mr. Bobo turned and fled, waving his razor around in a circle, down the stairs and out the front door; and Clytie, pale as a ghost, stumbled against the railing. The terrible scent of bay rum, of hair tonic, the horrible moist scratch of an invisible beard, the dense, popping green eyes—what had she got hold of with her hand! She could hardly bear it—the thought of that face.

From the closed door to the sickroom came Octavia's shouting voice.

"Clytie! Clytie! You haven't brought Papa the rain water. Where in the devil is the rain water to shave Papa?"

Clytie moved obediently down the stairs.

Her brother Gerald threw open the door of his room and called after her, "What now? This is a madhouse! Somebody was running past my room, I heard it. Where do you keep your men? Do you have to bring them home?" He slammed the door again, and she heard the barricade going up.

Clytie went through the lower hall and out the back door. She stood beside the old rain barrel and suddenly felt that this object, now, was her friend, just in time, and her arms almost circled it with impatient gratitude. The rain barrel was full. It bore a dark, heavy, penetrating fragrance, like ice and flowers and the dew of night.

Clytie swayed a little and looked into the slightly moving water. She thought she saw a face there.

Of course. It was the face she had been looking for, and from which she had been separated. As if to give a sign, the index finger of a hand lifted to touch the dark cheek.

Clytie leaned closer, as she had leaned down to touch the face of the barber.

It was a wavering, inscrutable face. The brows were drawn together as if in pain. The eyes were large, intent, almost avid, the nose ugly and discolored as if from weeping, the mouth old and closed from any speech. On either side of the head dark hair hung down in a disreputable and wild fashion. Everything about the face frightened and shocked her with its signs of waiting, of suffering.

For the second time that morning, Clytie recoiled, and as she did so, the other recoiled in the same way.

Too late, she recognized the face. She stood there completely sick at heart, as though the poor, half-remembered vision had finally betrayed her.

"Clytie! Clytie! The water! The water!" came Octavia's monumental voice.

Clytie did the only thing she could think of to do. She bent her angular body further, and thrust her head into the barrel, under the water, through its glittering surface into the kind, featureless depth, and held it there.

When Old Lethy found her, she had fallen forward into the barrel, with her poor ladylike black-stockinged legs up-ended and hung apart like a pair of tongs.

About the Authors

MARGARET ATWOOD

MARGARET ATWOOD is one of the most powerful voices in contemporary Canadian literature and a leading feminist writer. Her novels, which include *The Edible Woman* (1969), *Surfacing* (1972), and *Life before Man* (1979), have been praised for their compassionate explorations of male-female relationships and traditional gender roles. *The Handmaid's Tale* (1985), a grim dystopic parable about a future America where women have become a subjugated servile class, became a national best-seller. It received both Canada's prestigious Governor General Award and the Arthur C. Clarke Award for best science fiction novel of that year, and was filmed in 1990 by Volker Schlöndorff. Atwood's other novels include the satirical *The Robber Bride* (1993) and the historical murder mystery *Alias Grace* (1996). Her short fiction has been collected in *Dancing Girls and Other Stories* (1977), *Bluebeard's Egg and Other Stories* (1983), and *Wilderness Tips and Other Stories* (1991). *Murder in the Dark: Short Fiction and Prose Poems* (1983) and *Good Bones and Simple Murders* (1994) are filled with her witty tales of mystery and the macabre.

A. S. BYATT

A. S. BYATT's work as a scholar and critic often informs her fiction. She is the author of critical studies of the novelist Iris Murdoch and the poets William Wordsworth and Samuel Taylor Coleridge, as well as several novels that have been praised for their scrupulous recreation of past historical eras and their literary sensibilities. Of these, the best known is *Possession* (1990), the story of two contemporary literary scholars who fall in love while researching a secret romance between two Victorian poets. The novel won the prestigious Booker Prize for fiction. She is also a highly regarded writer of novellas, which have been collected in *Angels and Insects* (1992) and *The Matisse Stories* (1994). Her occasional forays into fantasy and the supernatural can be found among the stories collected in *Sugar and Other Stories* (1987) and *The Djinn in the Nightingale's Eye* (1995).

ANGELA CARTER

ANGELA CARTER's first novel, *Shadow Dance*, was published in 1966 but it was her second novel, *The Magic Toyshop* (1967), an eerie coming-of-age tale with undercurrents of eroticism, that established her as a leading writer of modern Gothic fiction. Much of her writing is steeped in fantasy, including the futuristic novel *The Passion of the New Eve* and the award-winning *Nights at the Circus* (1985), a picaresque chronicle of the lives and loves of a winged circus performer. In the United States, Carter is best known as the author of several collections of provocative short fiction, including *The Bloody Chamber and Other Stories* (1979), a volume of classic fairy tales retold as contemporary parables of gender roles. She is the author of the feminist study *The Sadeian Woman and the Ideology of Pornography* and has edited the anthologies *Don't Bet on the Prince: Contemporary Feminist Fairy Tales in North America and Europe* (1987) and *The Second Virago Book of Fairy Tales* (1992). She scripted the screenplay for the 1986 television adaptation of *The Magic Toyshop* and co-wrote the script for her tale "The Company of Wolves," which Neil Jordan filmed in 1985. Her work has been collected as *Expletives Deleted: Selected Writings* (1992) and *Burning Your Boats: The Complete Short Stories* (1996). Angela Carter died in 1992.

DAPHNE DU MAURIER

DAPHNE DU MAURIER refined the template for the contemporary Gothic romance with *Rebecca* (1938), her fifth published novel. Her suspense novel *Jamaica Inn* (1936) established her reputation for thrilling melodrama and inaugurated a fruitful relationship with renowned director Alfred Hitchcock, who adapted it for the screen in 1939. Hitchcock was also responsible for the Academy Award–winning adaptation of *Rebecca* in 1940, and "The Birds," based on her short story of the same name, in 1963. Many of du Maurier's novels are set in her native Cornwall, including (in addition to *Jamaica Inn* and *Rebecca*) *Frenchman's Creek* (1941), *My Cousin Rachel* (1951), and the time-travel tale *The House on the Strand* (1969). Her collections of short fiction include *Come Wind, Come Weather* (1940), *The Apple*

Tree (1952), and *The Breaking Point* (1959). *Echoes from the Macabre* (1976), a compilation of her best short weird fiction, includes "Don't Look Now," which Nicolas Roeg filmed in 1973. Her nonfiction includes a family history, *The du Mauriers* (1937), and her literary biography *The Infernal World of Branwell Brontë* (1960).

LOUISE ERDRICH

LOUISE ERDRICH's first novel, *Love Medicine* (1984), won the National Book Critics Circle Award, and laid the foundations for her ongoing fictional chronicle of Native American experience in twentieth-century America. With her novels *The Beet Queen* (1986), *Tracks* (1988), *The Bingo Palace* (1994), and *Tales of Burning Love* (1996), it forms a complex historical tapestry that interweaves the lives and heritages of several recurring Chippewa, white, and half-breed characters and their families. The novels have been praised for their colorful characters and vivid elaborations of Native American mythology and folk beliefs. Their episodic style of storytelling and their deft blending of historical fact and fiction have earned comparisons to the fiction of William Faulkner. For the Columbian quincentennial, Erdrich collaborated with her husband, the late Michael Dorris, on *The Crown of Columbus* (1992), a novel concerned with the contemporary cultural ramifications of Columbus's explorations. She has also written two collections of poetry, *Jacklight* (1984) and *Baptism of Desire* (1989), and the personal memoir *The Blue Jay's Dance: A Birth Year.* "Fleur," the story included in this volume, was incorporated into *Tracks.*

MAVIS GALLANT

Canadian-born MAVIS GALLANT is acknowledged as one of the preeminent writers of short fiction in the postwar era. Her stories, which have been praised for their treatment of the themes of spiritual isolation and emotional dislocation, have been collected in *The Other Paris* (1956), *My Heart Is Broken* (1964), *The End of the World and Other Stories* 1974), and *Home Truths* (1981). Although much of her shorter fiction is set in Canada, she has lived in France since 1950. She is also the author of the novels *Green Water, Green Sky* (1989) and *A Fairly Good Time* (1970). Her stories appear regularly in *The New Yorker,* and her reviews and essays, which have been published in the *New Republic, The New York Review of Books,* and other distinguished periodicals, have been collected as *Paris Notebooks* (1986).

NADINE GORDIMER

Nearly all of NADINE GORDIMER's novels and short stories have been shaped by the pressures of apartheid, of which she has been an outspoken critic since the publication of her first short-fiction collection, *Face to Face*, in 1949. Set primarily in her native South Africa, her fiction is renowned for its portrayals of both white and black characters whose lives are thrown into turmoil through the bewildering political and social strictures of their homeland. Her novels, which include *The Lying Days* (1953), *A World of Strangers* (1958), and *Burger's Daughter* (1979), have been praised for their sensitive treatment of both the outrage and the ambivalence of people attempting to grapple with complex issues of social intolerance and racial segregation. She was awarded the Booker Prize for her 1974 novel, *The Conservationist*. Her numerous short-fiction collections include *Six Feet of the Country* (1956), *Not for Publication and Other Stories* (1965), *Something Out There* (1984), and *Jump and Other Stories* (1991). Her story "City Lovers" was adapted for television in 1982, and several of her tales were adapted as part of *The Gordimer Stories* television series in 1985. She received the Nobel Prize for Literature in 1991.

PATRICIA HIGHSMITH

With the publication of her first novel, *Strangers on a Train*, in 1950, PATRICIA HIGHSMITH helped to break down the wall between the suspense genre and mainstream fiction. Her best-known works are complex studies of guilt and the ordinary individual's capacity for evil. In the introduction to her short-fiction collection, *The Snail Watcher and Other Stories* (1970), Graham Greene praised Highsmith as a "poet of apprehension" whose stories are set in "a world without moral endings" where "actions are sudden and impromptu and the motives sometimes so inexplicable that we simply have to accept them on trust." Five of her twenty-two novels feature Tom Ripley, an amoral murderer-hero: *The Talented Mr. Ripley* (1955), *Ripley under Ground* (1970), *Ripley's Game* (1974), *Ripley under Water* (1991), and *The Boy Who Followed Ripley* (1993). Her short fiction, much of which verges on the macabre, has been collected in *Little Tales of Misogyny* (1974), *Slowly, Slowly in the Wind* (1987), and *The Black House* (1979). Her stories have lent themselves to memorable film adaptations, including Alfred Hitchcock's treatment of *Strangers on a Train* in 1950 and Wim Wender's adaptation of *Ripley's Game* as *The American Friend* in 1978. Patricia Highsmith died in 1995.

A. M. HOMES

A. M. HOMES's first novel, *Jack* (1989), is an uncompromising coming-of-age tale in which a teenage boy must cope with his parents' divorce, the revelation of his father's latent homosexuality, and the subsequent cruelties of his peers. Praised for its realistic and unsentimental portrait of a troubled modern family, the novel mapped the coordinates of a literary terrain Homes has revisited many times since: one in which innocence and naïveté are regularly threatened by the corrupting potential of experience. Homes's tales of the spiritual ennui and denatured lives of ordinary people have been collected in *The Safety of Objects* (1990). Her novel *The End of Alice* (1995), which features a young woman who becomes infatuated with the life and crime of an imprisoned sexual psychopath, is one of the most controversial works of American fiction in the 1990s.

SHIRLEY JACKSON

Much of SHIRLEY JACKSON's fiction is concerned with the dark side of ordinary life. Her landmark short story "The Lottery," about a barbaric ritual that shaped society in a modern New England town, was among the most controversial ever to be published in *The New Yorker*. It served as the anchor of her first collection, *The Lottery; or, The Adventures of James Harris* (1949), and has since become a staple of literary anthologies. Her novels *The Road through the Wall* (1948), *Hangsaman* (1951), and *The Bird's Nest* (1954) all feature young women who find their personalities crumbling under the conforming pressures of everyday life. Families and their peculiar dynamics are the subject of both her Gothic novels *The Sundial* (1958) and *We Have Always Lived in the Castle* (1963), and her collections of comic domestic vignettes include *Life among the Savages* (1954) and *Raising Demons* (1957). *The Haunting of Hill House* (1959), her landmark tale of supernatural and psychological horror, was filmed by Robert Wise in 1963. At her death in 1965, Jackson left an incomplete novel, *Come Along with Me*, which eventually became the title story for her second short-fiction collection (1968). Many of her uncollected and unpublished stories were assembled in *Just an Ordinary Day* (1997).

JAMAICA KINCAID

JAMAICA KINCAID's writing includes short fiction, novels, and fictional biography, much of which is steeped in the color and details of life in her native Antigua. Her novels *Annie John* (1985), *Lucy* (1990), and *Autobiography of My Mother* (1995) have been cited for their sensitive treatment of themes that include the emotional trauma of separation from one's homeland, and the tensions that drive children and parents apart. The evocative and poetic stories in her collection *At the Bottom of the River* (1983) earned praise for their rich portraits of people and places in west India. Her essays, which have appeared in *The New Yorker* and other leading literary magazines, have been collected in *A Small Place* (1988). *My Brother,* her poignant biographical memoir, was published in 1997.

MADELEINE L'ENGLE

Generations of young readers know MADELEINE L'ENGLE through her Newbery Award–winning *Time Fantasy* series, which includes the novels *A Wrinkle in Time* (1962), *A Wind in the Door* (1973), *A Swiftly Tilting Planet* (1978), and *Many Waters* (1986). Her many books for children have been praised for their realistic depictions of boys and girls caught up in adventures that teach the lessons of adult responsibility. Her writing for adults includes the semiautobiographical novel *The Small Rain: A Novel* (1945) and its sequel, *A Severed Wasp* (1982). She has also written four highly regarded volumes of autobiographical reminiscences, beginning with *A Circle of Quiet* (1972). "Poor Little Saturday," reprinted in this volume, represents one of her rare excursions into short fiction.

URSULA K. LE GUIN

URSULA K. LE GUIN is one of the most respected authors in science fiction. Her first novel, *Rocannon's World* (1966), was the first of her Hainish tales, a series of novels and short stories concerned with the anthropological and cultural differences of human societies that develop under the varying conditions of different planets in the galaxy. It includes her Hugo and Nebula Award–winning *The Left Hand of Darkness* (1969), an award-winning exploration of gender roles set on a planet whose inhabitants regularly change their sexual identities. *The Lathe of Heaven* (1971), about a man whose dreams can alter reality, was adapted for television in 1980. Her novels *A Wizard of Earthsea* (1968), *The Tombs of Atuan* (1971), and *The Farthest Shore* (1972) comprise *The Earthsea Trilogy*, a coming-of-age saga for young adult readers that has also been praised for its social and cultural insights. *Always Coming Home* (1985) is a multimedia concept work that uses text, music, and art to describe a future matriarchal society on Earth. Le Guin's short fantasy and science fiction have been collected in *The Wind's Twelve Quarters* (1975), *The Compass Rose* (1982), and *Buffalo Gals and Other Animal Presences* (1987). Her illuminating essays on writing have been collected in *From Elfland to Poughkeepsie* (1973) and *Dancing at the Edge of the World: Thoughts on Words, Women, Places* (1989). "The Ones Who Walk Away from Omelas," reprinted in this volume, won the Hugo Award for best short science fiction story in 1973.

DORIS LESSING

DORIS LESSING's first novel, *The Grass Is Singing*, was published in 1950. Two years later, with the publication of *Martha Quest*, she embarked on her *Children of Violence* series, a multinovel bildungsroman that explores the growth and development of its heroine's sexual identity and political consciousness against the backdrop of the major historical events of the second half of the twentieth century. The series, which includes *A Proper Marriage* (1954), *A Ripple from the Storm* (1958), *Landlocked* (1966), and *The Four-Gated City* (1969), is universally acclaimed as one of the most important literary creations of the postwar years. Lessing has extended her reputation as a novelist of ideas through *The Golden Notebook* (1962), *Briefing for a Descent into Hell* (1971), *The Good Terrorist* (1985), and her *Canopus in Argos: Archives*, a series of science fiction novels that extrapolate the apocalyptic possibilities of current social and political trends in a futuristic interstellar setting. Lessing's short fiction is regarded as highly as her novels and has been collected in *Habit of Loving* (1958), *African Stories* (1964), and *The Real Thing: Stories and Sketches* (1992). *Under My Skin*, published in 1994, is the first book in her projected three-volume autobiography.

ALISON LURIE

ALISON LURIE's novels include *Love and Friendship* (1962), *The Nowhere City* (1965), *Imaginary Friends* (1967), *Real People* (1969), and *The War between the Tates* (1974). All are modern comedies of manners that use humor to explore such serious subjects as marital infidelity, midlife crisis, and the generation gap. Her fiction invariably features sophisticated but sympathetic academics and artists undone by their neuroses and all-too-human frailties. *Foreign Affairs* (1984), a culmination of her interest in class differences, the battle of the sexes, and the culture gap that separates England from America, won the Pulitzer Prize. The stories in her sole collection, *Women and Ghosts* (1994), are brilliantly crafted modern fantasies that use the supernatural to crystallize aspects of human behavior. Lurie is the author of several books for children, and of the critical study *Don't Tell the Grown-ups: Subversive Children's Literature* (1990). She has also edited *The Oxford Book of Modern Fairy Tales* (1993).

VALERIE MARTIN

VALERIE MARTIN's stories are memorable for their Gothic mood and relationships defined by psychological turmoil and physical violence. Her novels include *Set in Motion* (1978), *Alexandra* (1979), and *A Recent Martyr* (1987), the last a vivid account of a sadomasochistic love affair set against the backdrop of a plague-infested future New Orleans. Her best-known work, *Mary Reilly* (1990), a variation on the theme of *Dr. Jekyll and Mr. Hyde,* tells Robert Louis Stevenson's tale of a benevolent benefactor with a violent alter ego from the viewpoint of his housemaid, who has endured an abusive upbringing as a member of London's lower class. An indictment of social and domestic violence, it was filmed in 1996. Martin's collection *The Consolation of Nature and Other Stories* (1988) features short fiction that uses wild and ferocious natural imagery as a lens for examining human relationships.

JOYCE CAROL OATES

JOYCE CAROL OATES's prolific output as a fiction writer spans so many genres and embraces so many different styles that it is impossible to pigeonhole. Her novels and short stories are memorable for their depictions of average Americans whose lives are touched and often deformed by the inescapable circumstances of their environments and the greater historical and political forces that shape their world. Her more than two dozen novels, including *them* (1969), *Son of the Morning* (1978), *American Appetites* (1989), *Black Water* (1992), and *What I Lived For* (1994) fit together as a mosaic that chronicles the dark side of American experience in the twentieth century. Her many collections of short fiction include *Where Are You Going, Where Have You Been?* (1974), *Heat and Other Stories* (1992), and *Will You Always Love Me?* (1995). Several of her more ingenious creations are period genre tales informed by a twentieth-century sensibility: *Bellefleur* (1980), a Gothic family chronicle; *A Bloodsmoor Romance* (1982), which was inspired by the classic Gothic romance; and *Mysteries of Winterthurn* (1984), derived from the Victorian penny dreadful. Her macabre short fiction can be found in the collections *Night Side: Eighteen Tales* (1977), *Haunted: Tales of the Grotesque* (1994), and *Demon and Other Tales* (1995). She has also written *Zombie* (1996), the fictional diary of a serial killer, and six novels of psychological suspense under the pseudonym Rosamond Smith. Her nonfiction includes the critical study *New Heaven, New Earth: The Visionary Experience in Literature* (1974), the essay *On Boxing* (1987), and the collections *Contraries* (1981) and *The Profane Art* (1983). She is the editor of *American Gothic Tales* (1996) and a recipient of the National Book Award for fiction.

EDNA O'BRIEN

In her controversial *Country Girls Trilogy,* which includes her first three novels *Country Girls* (1960), *The Lonely Girls* (1962), and *Girls in Their Married Bliss* (1964), EDNA O'BRIEN turned her native Ireland into a dramatic landscape of loss and longing. She has returned to this landscape regularly in *Casualties of Peace* (1966), *Johnny I Hardly Knew You* (1978), and other novels that examine the complicated lives of contemporary Irish women. Her story collections include *A Fanatic Heart* (1984), a retrospective collection of her first three decades of writing, and *Lantern Slides* (1990). She has written the pictorial essays *Mother Ireland* (1976) and *Vanishing Ireland* (1986), the poetry volume *On the Bone* (1989), and several books for children. O'Brien has adapted several of her novels for the stage as well as Flaubert's *Madame Bovary* and is the author of numerous teleplays and screenplays.

FLANNERY O'CONNOR

FLANNERY O'CONNOR's tales of rural southern characters who inhabit a world shaped equally by divine grace and violent experience are an outgrowth of the southern Gothic tradition. She is the author of two novels: *Wise Blood* (1952), which John Huston adapted for film in 1980, and *The Violent Bear It Away* (1960). Her best-known works, however, are her short stories, which include "A Good Man Is Hard to Find"—one of the most reprinted stories in twentieth-century American fiction and the title selection of her first collection (1955)—and the tales assembled in *Everything That Rises Must Converge* (1965). O'Connor died in 1964 at the age of thirty-nine. Her *Complete Short Stories* (1971) was awarded the National Book Award. Posthumous collections of her nonfiction include *Mystery and Manners: Occasional Prose* (1969), *The Habit of Being: Letters* (1969), and *The Presence of Grace and Other Book Reviews* (1983).

RUTH RENDELL

As a writer of mystery stories and tales of psychological suspense, RUTH RENDELL has achieved a critical recognition that elevates her work above that of her peers in the genre. Her novels and short fiction have been praised for both their intricate, ingenious plots and their insightful explorations of the criminal mind. Her first novel, *From Doon with Death* (1964), introduced Chief Inspector Wexford, a series detective based in the Sussex town of Kingsmarkham. Wexford is the hero of the majority of her more than three dozen novels and his adventures have been adapted for television in both England and America. Rendell's stories, lauded by many critics as paragons of the short crime tale, have been collected in *The Fallen Curtain and Other Stories* (1976), *Means of Evil and Other Stories* (1979), *The Copper Peacock and Other Stories* (1991), and the omnibus *Collected Short Stories* (1987). She has also written under the pen name Barbara Vine, and is the recipient of multiple awards from the Mystery Writers of America and the Crime Writers of America.

JEAN RHYS

JEAN RHYS's candid stories of strong-willed women who weather the injustices of their social positions and the indignities inflicted on their sex are informed by her own experiences as a woman of Creole descent who moved from the Dominican Republic to England and eventually The Continent. She was born Ella Gwendolen Rhys Williams in 1890 and held a variety of clerical and modeling positions in her early years. Eventually she became part of Ford Madox Ford's literary circle and began writing short stories that were collected in 1927 as *The Left Bank and Other Stories*. Her first novel, *Postures* (retitled *Quartet* for American publication), appeared in 1928. It was followed by *After Leaving Mr. Mackenzie* (1930), *Voyage in the Dark* (1934), and *Good Morning, Midnight* (1939), novels that established her abilities to combine deeply reflective character sketches with scenes of terse, understated realism. *The Wide Sargasso Sea*, a prequel to Charlotte Brontë's *Jane Eyre*, was published to critical acclaim in 1966 and eventually adapted for film. Before her death in 1979, she was awarded the prestigious Commander of the British Empire for her contributions to literature. Her collected works include *Complete Novels* (1985) and *Complete Short Stories* (1987). Her autobiography *Smith Please*, left incomplete at her death, was published in 1980.

SUSAN SONTAG

Esteemed as a fiction writer, essayist, and filmmaker, SUSAN SONTAG is regarded as a leading American intellectual and cultural critic. Her stories and novels, like her nonfiction, are steeped in progressive philosophies of art, science, and social thinking. She is the author of three novels: *The Benefactor* (1963), *Death Kit* (1967), and *The Volcano Lover: A Romance* (1992). The last, a historical novel with contemporary overtones, was a national best-seller. Her sole collection of short fiction, *I, Etcetera*, was published in 1978. Her nonfiction books *Illness as Metaphor* (1978) and its follow-up, *AIDS and Its Metaphors* (1989), are groundbreaking studies of changing literary and social attitudes toward sickness. Her essays and reviews of art, literature, and society have been collected in *Against Interpretation and Other Essays* (1966), *Styles of Radical Will* (1969), and *Under the Sign of Saturn* (1980). *On Photography* (1977), her study of the aesthetics of photography, received the National Book Critics Circle Award for Criticism.

MURIEL SPARK

Dame MURIEL SPARK was a published poet and award-winning short story writer before the publication of her first novel, *The Comforters*, in 1957. Her distinguished body of work includes *The Ballad of Peckham Rye* (1960), *The Girls of Slender Means* (1963), *Symposium* (1990), and other novels that examine the religious and moral sensibilities of contemporary upper-class characters. Her best-known novel, *The Prime of Miss Jean Brodie* (1961), was adapted for both stage and screen. Her short stories, which are clever amalgams of social drama and biting humor, have been collected in *The Go-Away Bird and Other Stories* (1958), *Collected Stories I* (1967), and *The Stories of Muriel Spark* (1985). *Open to the Public* (1997) contains most of her short masterpieces of horror and suspense. She is also the author of the seminal critical study *Child of Light: A Reassessment of Mary Wollstonecraft Shelley* (1951) and the editor of *The Letters of the Brontës: A Selection* (1954).

FAY WELDON

Although identified frequently as a feminist writer, FAY WELDON writes fiction filled with sharply etched female characters who are memorable as individuals rather than representatives of a particular ideology. Her first published novel, *The Fat Woman's Joke* (1967), grew out of her experience as a writer of scripts for radio, television, and the stage. *Female Friends* (1974), *Praxis* (1978), *The Life and Loves of a She Devil* (1984), and other of her novel-length works are witty and subversive commentaries on the battle of the sexes. Weldon has used both science fiction and fantasy as vehicles for satirical treatment of domestic relationships in *The Cloning of Joanna May* (1989) and several of the stories collected in *Watching Me, Watching You* (1981). Her other short-fiction collections include *Polaris and Other Stories* (1985) and *Moon over Minneapolis, or Why She Couldn't Stay* (1991).

EUDORA WELTY

EUDORA WELTY's stories are exquisitely detailed portraits in miniature of ordinary people whose lives and actions resonate with the power of myth. Most of her fiction is set in her native South, a region she came to know intimately through her travels as a publicity agent for the WPA in the 1930s. Several years later she began publishing short stories drawn from her experiences. Her first collection, *A Curtain of Green*, was published in 1941, and was followed quickly by her novella *The Robber Bridegroom* (1942) and the collection *The Wide Net and Other Stories* (1943). Elements of the southern Gothic, the regional tall tale, and the comic pastoral that color her short fiction also inform her novels *Delta Wedding* (1946), *The Ponder Heart* (1954), *Losing Battles* (1970), and *The Optimist's Daughter* (1972). *One Writer's Beginnings* (1984), her best-selling compilation of autobiographical lectures, is a vivid documentary of the people and places that have shaped her creativity. She received the Pulitzer Prize for Fiction in 1973 and the American Book Award for *The Collected Stories of Eudora Welty* in 1984.

Acknowledgments

GRATEFUL ACKNOWLEDGMENT is made to the following for permission to reprint their copyrighted material:

"Death by Landscape" by Margaret Atwood. Copyright © 1991 by O. W. Toad Limited. First published in *Wilderness Tips* by Bloomsbury in 1991. Reprinted by permission of the author and Doubleday, a division of Bantam Doubleday Dell Publishing Group, Inc.

"The July Ghost" by A. S. Byatt. Copyright © 1982 by A. S. Byatt. Reprinted by permission of the author and her agents, Peters Fraser & Dunlop Group, Ltd.

"The Bloody Chamber" by Angela Carter. Copyright © 1979 by Angela Carter. Reprinted by permission of the Estate of Angela Carter c/o Rogers, Coleridge & White Ltd., 20 Powis Mewes, London W11 1JN.

"Don't Look Now" by Daphne du Maurier. Copyright © 1966, 1970, 1971 by Daphne du Maurier. Reprinted by permission of Doubleday, a division of Bantam Doubleday Dell Publishing Group, Inc.

"Fleur" by Louise Erdrich. Copyright © 1986 by Louise Erdrich. Reprinted by permission of the author and her agent, Rembar & Curtis. This story first appeared in *Esquire* magazine and was later adapted and made part of Ms. Erdrich's novel *Tracks* (Henry Holt & Company, 1988).

"Up North" by Mavis Gallant. Copyright © 1956, 1959, 1963, 1965, 1966, 1968, 1971, 1975, 1976, 1977, 1978, 1981. First published in *Home Truths: Sixteen Stories.* Reprinted by permission of Random House, Inc.